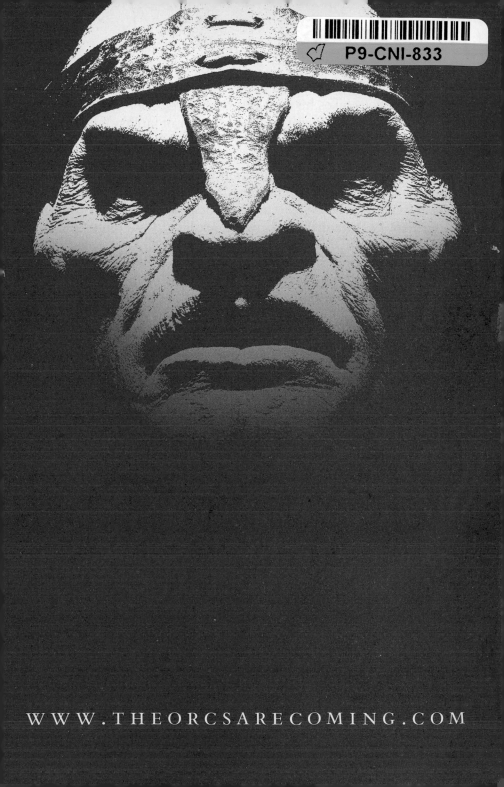

WWW.THEORCSARECOMING.COM

Praise for ORCS

"Stan Nicholls takes his well-deserved place beside Robert Jordan and George R. R. Martin as a modern star of fantasy."
— *The Independent*

"Incorporating wall-to-wall action with undercurrents of dark humor, *Bodyguard of Lightning* is a gritty, fast-paced novel with a neat twist. The heroes are orcs—though you wouldn't want to meet any of them on a dark night!" — David Gemmell

"Weirdly charming, fast-moving, and freaky, *Bodyguard of Lightning* is the most fun you're ever likely to have with a warband of orcs. Remember, buy now or beg for mercy later." — Tad Williams

"A neat idea and Stan Nicholls pulls it off with great panache . . . enough weird sex to keep the tabloids outraged for weeks. You'll never feel the same about *Lord of the Rings*."
— Jon Courtenay Grimwood, *SFX*

"A warning: if you don't wish to become addicted to the most impressive new fantasy sequence in many a moon, you should avoid *Bodyguard of Lightning*."
— Genre Hotline/LineOne Science Fiction Zone

"Stan Nicholls tries to correct the bad press authors such as Tolkien have given to orcs. Nicholls tells his tale briskly and entertainingly. . . . If you like lots of hacking and slashing, *Bodyguard of Lightning* is for you!" — *Starburst*

"*Bodyguard of Lightning* is naturally full of fighting, bloodletting, and double-crossing. Nicholls has created a fast-paced adventure." — *The Mentor*

"In the fantasy field, Stan Nicholls's *Legion of Thunder* demonstrates a truly coruscating imagination in its outrageous narrative." — *Publishing News* Books of the Year 1999

"Nicholls knows how to describe a battle in gritty detail, in such a way that it grabs your interest and yet still appears as unglamorous and unromantic as it should. A strange tale of magic, fantastic creatures, and mythical elder races that warps your expectations."   —The SF Site

"*Warriors of the Tempest* is, above all, a wonderful piece of story-telling; fast-paced with plenty of hairpin twists, crammed with loads of juicy battles and properly bad baddies, racing towards a carefully set up conclusion that's both exciting and genuinely moving. . . . Underlying all the fun and games are a core of skillfully drawn, fully realized characters who engage your sympathy from the start and never let go. . . . Sweet and sour orc, a feast for the most jaded fantasy-lover's palate."
                                    —Tom Holt, *SFX* magazine

"The prose flows smoothly and the story is exciting."
                                    —*Science Fiction Chronicle*

"Breathless and ruthless, menacing and fun. Easy to read and totally engaging."   —The Alien Online

"Stan Nicholls's excellent *Orcs* sequence . . . is a welcome counterblast to the anti-orc onslaught due with the film launch of *The Lord of the Rings*."   —*The Guardian*

"Now's your chance to catch up with one of the most unusual writers in the genre. And it's particularly wonderful not to have to put your brain to bed while reading Nicholls —unlike many of his writing peers, there's a real intelligence always at work here. Not that we don't get the requisite rip-roaring action and colorful world-building—along with some cutting humor."
                                    —Tiscali SF Zone

"It is an excellent adventure read. A good adventure story with plenty of action, humorous and well crafted. Thoroughly recommended."   —SF Crowsnest

By Stan Nicholls

"Gladiators" Game Book No. 1
Tom and Jerry: The Movie

Cool Zool
Strange Invaders
Spider-man: The Hobgoblin

The Nightshade Chronicles
The Book of Shadows
Shadow of the Sorcerer
A Gathering of Shadows

Fade to Black

Dark Skies: The Awakening

Orcs

The Dreamtime Trilogy
The Covenant Rising
The Righteous Blade
The Diamond Isle

Nonfiction
Wordsmiths of Wonder: Fifty Interviews with
Writers of the Fantastic

Ken and Me
Gerry Anderson: The Authorized Biography

Graphic novels (as adaptor)
David Gemmell's *Legend*
David Gemmell's *Wolf in Shadow*

O R C S

STAN NICHOLLS

www.orbitbooks.net

New York   London

Orbit
Hachette Book Group USA
237 Park Avenue, New York, NY 10017
Visit our Web site at www.HachetteBookGroupUSA.com

First Orbit edition: September 2008
Originally published in Great Britain in paperback by Gollancz, 2004

Orbit is an imprint of Hachette Book Group USA. The Orbit name and logo are trade-
marks of Little, Brown Book Group Limited.

The characters and events in this book are fictitious. Any similarity to real persons,
living or dead, is coincidental and not intended by the author.

ISBN 978-0-316-03370-1
LCCN 2008927108

10 9 8 7 6 5 4 3 2 1

RRD-IN

Printed in the United States of America

The *Orcs* omnibus is dedicated to
Marianne Gay and Nick Fifer, for being happy,
and for being a loving inspiration.

CONTENTS

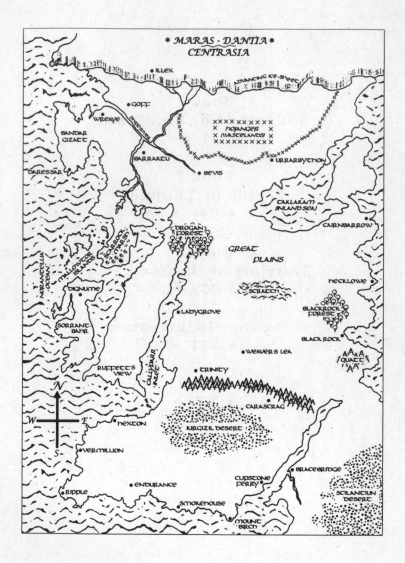

BOOK

1

BODYGUARD OF LIGHTNING

This is, of course, for Anne and Marianne.

Oh we'll rant and we'll roar like true orcish warriors
We'll rant and we'll roar for all that we be
We'll march back from yonder all laden with plunder
Oh what treasures, what pleasures, then you will see

Farewell and good-bye to you fair orcish ladies
Farewell and good-bye to you ladies of hame
We've taken a liking to mayhem and fighting
Our blades we will bring down and sharpen again

We'll burn and we'll plunder and then we will sunder
Their heads from their necks and their gold from their purse
We'll meet them in battle and kill them like cattle
We'll drink their beer dry while the poor bastards curse

The first land we sighted we saw a tall spire
We crept up in darkness and set it aflame
We took silver and chalice for we bore them such malice
And we hope that next year they won't be there again

We found a fat farmer, we found his fair daughter
We tickled him up with the point of a knife
He babbled and gabbled, gave us gold without haggle
The girl ran off screaming so we roasted his wife

Now let every orc warrior take up his full tankard
Now let every orc warrior drink deep of strong ale
Our Wolverines' spearpoints will skewer 'em like pork joints
Far richer and fatter the orcs will prevail!

Traditional warband marching song

1

Stryke couldn't see the ground for corpses.

He was deafened by screams and clashing steel. Despite the cold, sweat stung his eyes. His muscles burned and his body ached. Blood, mud and splashed brains flecked his jerkin. And now two more of the loathsome, soft pink creatures were moving in on him with murder in their eyes.

He savoured the joy.

His footing unsure, he stumbled and almost fell, pure instinct bringing up his sword to meet the first swinging blade. The impact jarred but checked the blow. He nimbly retreated a pace, dropped into a half crouch and lunged forward again, below his opponent's guard. The sword rammed into the enemy's stomach. Stryke quickly raked it upward, deep and hard, until it struck a rib, tumbling guts. The creature went down, a stupefied expression on its face.

There was no time to relish the kill. The second attacker was on him, clutching a two-handed broadsword, its glinting tip just beyond the limit of Stryke's reach. Mindful of its fellow's fate, this one was more cautious. Stryke went on the offensive, engaging his assailant's blade with a rain of aggressive swipes. They parried and thrusted, moving in a slow, cumbersome dance, their boots seeking purchase on bodies of friend and foe alike.

Stryke's weapon was better suited to fencing. The size and weight of the creature's broadsword made it awkward to use in close combat. Designed for hacking, it needed to be swung in a wider arc. After several passes the creature strained with effort, huffing clouds of icy breath. Stryke kept harrying from a distance, awaiting his chance.

In desperation, the creature lurched toward him, its sword

slashing at his face. It missed, but came close enough for him to feel the displaced air. Momentum carried the stroke on, lifting the creature's arms high and leaving its chest unprotected. Stryke's blade found its heart, triggering a scarlet eruption. The creature spiralled into the trampling mêlée.

Glancing down the hill, Stryke could make out the Wolverines, embroiled in the greater battle on the plain below.

He returned to the slaughter.

Coilla looked up and saw Stryke on the hill above, not far from the walls of the settlement, savagely laying into a group of defenders.

She cursed his damned impatience.

But for the moment their leader would have to look after himself. The warband had some serious resistance to overcome before they could get to him.

Here in the boiling cauldron of the main battlefield, bloody conflict stretched out on every side. A crushing mob of fighting troops and shying mounts churned to pulp what had been fields of crops just hours before. The cacophonous, roaring din was endless, the tart aroma of death soured the back of her throat.

A thirty-strong flying wedge bristling with steel, the Wolverines kept in tight formation, powering through the struggling mass like some giant multi-stinged insect. Near the wedge's spearhead, Coilla helped clear their path, lashing out with her sword at enemy flesh obstructing the way.

Too fast to properly digest, a succession of hellish tableaux vivants flashed past her. A defender with a hatchet buried in its shoulder; one of her own side, gore-encrusted hands covering his eyes; another silently shrieking, a red stump in lieu of an arm; one of theirs staring down at a hole the size of a fist in its chest; a headless body, gushing crimson as it staggered. A face cut to ribbons by the slashing of her blade.

An infinity later the Wolverines arrived at the foot of the hill and began to climb as they fought.

A brief hiatus in the butchery allowed Stryke to check again the progress of his band. They were cleaving through knots of defenders about halfway up the hill.

He turned back and surveyed the massive wooden-walled stronghold topping the rise. There was a way to go before they reached its gates, and several score more of the enemy to overcome. But it seemed to Stryke that their ranks were thinning.

Filling his lungs with frigid air, he felt again the intensity of life that came when death was this close.

Coilla arrived, panting, the rest of the troop close behind.

"Took your time," he commented drily. "Thought I'd have to storm the place alone."

She jabbed a thumb at the milling chaos below. "Weren't keen on letting us through."

They exchanged smiles that were almost crazed.

Bloodlust's on her too, he thought. *Good.*

Alfray, custodian of the Wolverines' banner, joined them and drove the flag's spar into the semi-frozen earth. The warband's two dozen common soldiers formed a defensive ring around the officers. Noticing one of the grunts had taken a pernicious-looking head wound, Alfray pulled a field dressing from his hip bag and went to staunch the blood.

Sergeants Haskeer and Jup pushed through the troopers. As usual, the former was sullen, the latter unreadable.

"Enjoy your stroll?" Stryke jibed, his tone sarcastic.

Jup ignored it. "What now, Captain?" he asked gruffly.

"What *think* you, shortarse? A break to pick flowers?" He glared at his diminutive joint second-in-command. "We get up there and do our job."

"How?"

Coilla was staring at the leaden sky, a hand cupped over her eyes.

"Frontal assault," Stryke replied. "You have a better plan?" It was a challenge.

"No. But it's open ground, uphill. We'll have casualties."

"Don't we always?" He spat copiously, narrowly missing his sergeant's feet. "But if it makes you feel better we'll ask our strategist. Coilla, what's your opinion?"

"Hmmm?" Her attention remained fixed on the heavy clouds.

"*Wake up*, Corporal! I said —"

"See that?" She pointed skyward.

A black dot was descending through the gloom. No details were obvious from this distance, but they all guessed what it was.

"Could be useful," Stryke said.

Coilla was doubtful. "Maybe. You know how wilful they can be. Best to take cover."

"Where?" Haskeer wanted to know, scanning the naked terrain.

The dot grew in size.

"It's moving faster than a cinder from Hades," Jup observed.

"And diving too tight," added Haskeer.

By this time the bulky body and massive serrated wings were clearly visible. There was no doubt now. Huge and ungainly, the beast swooped over the battle still raging on the plain. Combatants froze and stared upwards. Some scattered from its shadow. It carried on heedless in an ever-sharper descent, aimed squarely at the rise where Stryke's Wolverines were gathered.

He squinted at it. "Can anybody make out the handler?"

They shook their heads.

The living projectile came at them unerringly. Its vast, slavering jaws gaped, revealing rows of yellow teeth the size of war helms. Slitty green eyes flashed. A rider sat stiffly on its back, tiny compared to his charge.

Stryke estimated it to be no more than three flaps of its powerful wings away.

"Too low," Coilla whispered.

Haskeer bellowed, *"Kiss the ground!"*

The warband flattened.

Rolling on to his back, Stryke had a fleeting view of grey leathery skin and enormous clawed feet passing overhead. He almost believed he could stretch and touch the thing.

Then the dragon belched a mighty gout of dazzling orange flame.

For a fraction of a second Stryke was blinded by the intensity of light. Blinking through the haze, he expected to see the dragon smash into the ground. Instead he caught sight of it soaring aloft at what seemed an impossibly acute angle.

Further up the hillside, the scene was transformed. The defenders and some attackers, ignited by the blazing suspiration, had been turned into shrieking fireballs or were already dead in smouldering heaps. Here and there, the earth itself burned and bubbled.

A smell of roasting flesh filled the air. It made the juices in Stryke's mouth flow.

"Somebody should remind the dragonmasters whose side they're on," Haskeer grumbled.

"But this one eased our burden." Stryke nodded at the gates. They were well alight. Scrambling to his feet, he yelled, *"To me!"*

The Wolverines sent up a booming war cry and thundered after him. They met little resistance, easily cutting down the few enemy still left standing.

When Stryke reached the smoking gates he found them damaged enough to offer no real obstacle, and one was hanging crookedly, fit to fall.

Nearby, a pole held a charred sign bearing the crudely painted word *Homefield*.

Haskeer ran to Stryke's side. He noticed the sign and swiped contemptuously at it with his sword, severing it from the upright. It fell and broke in two.

"Even our language has been colonised," he growled.

Jup, Coilla and the remainder of the band caught up with them. Stryke and several troopers booted the weakened gate, downing it.

They poured through the opening and found themselves in a spacious compound. To their right, a corral held livestock. On the left stood a row of mature fruit trees. Ahead and set well back was a sizeable wooden farmhouse.

Lined up in front of it were at least twice as many defenders as Wolverines.

The warband charged and set about the creatures. In the intense hand-to-hand combat that followed, the Wolverines' discipline proved superior. With nowhere to run, the enemy was fuelled by desperation and they fought savagely, but in moments their numbers were drastically depleted. Wolverine casualties were much lighter, a handful sustaining minor wounds. Not enough to slow their advance or impede the zeal with which they plundered their foes' milky flesh.

At length, the few remaining defenders were driven back to bunch in front of the entrance. Stryke led the onslaught against them, shoulder to shoulder with Coilla, Haskeer and Jup.

Yanking his blade free of the final protector's innards, Stryke spun and gazed around the compound. He saw what he needed at the corral's fence. "Haskeer! Get one of those beams for a ram!"

The sergeant hurried away, barking orders. Seven or eight troopers peeled off to run after him, tugging hatchets from their belts.

Stryke beckoned a footsoldier. The private took two steps and collapsed, a slender shaft projecting from his throat.

"Archers!" Jup yelled, waving his blade at the building's upper storey.

The band dispersed as a hail of arrows peppered them from an open window above. One Wolverine went down, felled by a shot to the head. Another was hit in the shoulder and pulled to cover by his comrades.

Coilla and Stryke, nearest the house, ran forward to take shelter under the building's overhang, pressing themselves to the wall on either side of the door.

"How many bowmen have *we?*" she asked.

"We just lost one, so three."

He looked across the farmyard. Haskeer's crew seemed to be taking the brunt of the archers' fire. As arrows whistled around them, troopers gamely hacked at the uprights supporting one of the livestock pen's immense timbers.

Jup and most of the others sprawled on the ground nearby. Braving the volleys, Corporal Alfray knelt as he improvised a binding for the trooper's pierced shoulder. Stryke was about to call over when he saw the three archers were stringing their short bows.

Lying full-length was a less than ideal firing position. They had to turn the bows sideways and aim upwards while lifting their chests. Yet they quickly began unleashing shafts in a steady stream.

From their uncertain sanctuary Stryke and Coilla were powerless to do anything except watch as arrows winged up to the floor above and others came down in exchange. After a minute or two a ragged cheer broke out from the warband, obviously in response to a hit. But the two-way flow of bolts continued, confirming that at least one more archer was in the building.

"Why not tip the shafts with fire?" Coilla suggested.

"Don't want the place to burn till we get what we're after."

A weighty crash came from the corral. Haskeer's unit had freed the beam. Troopers set to lifting it, still wary of enemy fire, though it was now less frequent.

Another triumphant roar from the pinned-down grunts was followed by a commotion upstairs. An archer fell, smacking to the ground in front of Stryke and Coilla. The arrow jutting from its chest was snapped in half by the impact.

At the livestock pen, Jup was on his feet, signalling that the upper storey was clear.

Haskeer's crew ran over with the beam, muscles taut and faces strained with the effort of shifting its mass. All hands to the improvised ram, the warband began pounding the reinforced door, splintering shards of wood. After a dozen blows it gave with a loud report and exploded inwards.

A trio of defenders were waiting for them. One leapt forward, killing the lead rammer with a single stroke. Stryke felled the creature, clambered over the discarded timber and laid into the next. A brief, frenzied trading of blows pitched it lifeless to the floor. But the distraction left Stryke open to the third defender. It closed in, its blade pulling up and back, ready to deliver a decapitating swipe.

A throwing knife thudded hard into its chest. It gave a throaty rasp, dropped the sword and fell headlong.

Stryke's grunt was all Coilla could expect in the way of thanks.

She retrieved the knife from her victim and drew another to fill her empty hand, preferring a blade in both fists when close-quarter fighting seemed likely. The Wolverines flowed into the house behind her.

Before them was an open central staircase.

"Haskeer! Take half the company and clear this floor," Stryke ordered. "The rest with me!"

Haskeer's troopers spread right and left. Stryke led his party up the stairs.

They were near the top when a pair of creatures appeared. Stryke and the band cut them to pieces in combined fury. Coilla got to the upper level first and ran into another defender. It opened her arm with a saw-toothed blade. Hardly slowing, she dashed the weapon from its hand and sliced its chest. Howling, it blundered through the rail and plunged to oblivion.

Stryke glanced at Coilla's streaming wound. She made no complaint, so he turned his attention to this floor's layout. They were on a long landing with a number of doors. Most were open, revealing apparently empty rooms. He sent troopers to search them. They soon reappeared, shaking their heads.

At the furthest end of the landing was the only closed door. They approached stealthily and positioned themselves outside.

Sounds of combat from the ground floor were already dying down. Shortly, the only noise was the distant, muffled hubbub of the battle on the plain, and the stifled panting of the Wolverines catching their breath as they clustered on the landing.

Stryke glanced from Coilla to Jup, then nodded for the three burliest footsoldiers to act. They shouldered the door once, twice and again. It sprang open and they threw themselves in, weapons raised, Stryke and the other officers close behind.

A creature hefting a double-headed axe confronted them. It went down under manifold blows before doing any harm.

The room was large. At its far end stood two more figures, shielding something. One was of the defending creatures' race. The other was of Jup's kind, his short, squat build further emphasised by his companion's lanky stature.

He came forward, armed with sword and dagger. The Wolverines moved to engage him.

"No!" Jup yelled. "Mine!"

Stryke understood. "Leave them!" he barked.

His troopers lowered their weapons.

The stocky adversaries squared up. For the span of half a dozen heartbeats they stood silently, regarding each other with expressions of vehement loathing.

Then the air rang to the peal of their colliding blades.

Jup set to with a will, batting aside every stroke his opponent delivered, avoiding both weapons with a fluidity born of long experience. In seconds the dagger was sent flying and embedded itself in a floor plank. Soon after, the sword was dashed away.

The Wolverine sergeant finished his opponent with a thrust to the lungs. His foe sank to his knees, toppled forward, twitched convulsively and died.

No longer spellbound by the fight, the last defender brought up its sword and readied itself for a final stand. As it did so, they saw it had been shielding a female of its race. Crouching, strands of mousy hair plastered to its forehead, the female cradled one of their young. The infant, its plump flesh a dawn-tinted colour, was little more than a hatchling.

A shaft jutted from the female's upper chest. Arrows and a longbow were scattered on the floor. She had been one of the defending archers.

Stryke waved a hand at the Wolverines, motioning them to stay, and walked the length of the room. He saw nothing to fear and didn't hurry. Skirting the spreading pool of blood seeping from Jup's dead opponent, he reached the last defender and locked eyes with it.

For a moment it looked as though the creature might speak.

Instead it suddenly lunged, flailing its sword like a mad thing, and with as little accuracy.

Untroubled, Stryke deflected the blade and finished the matter by slashing the creature's throat, near severing its head.

The blood-soaked female let out a high-pitched wail, part squeak, part keening moan. Stryke had heard something like it once or twice before. He stared at her and saw a trace of defiance in her eyes. But hatred, fear and agony were strongest in her features. All the colour had drained from her face and her breath was laboured. She hugged the young one close in a last feeble attempt to protect it. Then the life force seeped away. She slowly pitched to one side and sprawled lifeless across the floor. The hatchling spilled from her arms and began to bleat.

Having no further interest in the matter, Stryke stepped over the corpse.

He was facing a Uni altar. In common with others he'd seen it was quite plain: a high table covered by a white cloth, gold-embroidered at the edges, with a lead candleholder at each end.

Standing in the centre and to the rear was a piece of ironwork he knew to be the symbol of their cult. It consisted of two rods of black metal mounted on a base, fused together at an angle to form a simple X.

But it was the object at the front of the table that interested him. A cylinder, perhaps as long as his forearm and the size of his fist in circumference, it was copper-coloured and inscribed with fading runic symbols. One end had a lid, neatly sealed with red wax.

Coilla and Jup came to him. She was dabbing at the wound on her arm with a handful of wadding. Jup wiped red stains from his blade with a soiled rag. They stared at the cylinder.

Coilla said, "Is that it, Stryke?"

"Yes. It fits her description."

"Hardly looks worth the cost of so many lives," Jup remarked.

Stryke reached for the cylinder and examined it briefly before slipping it into his belt. "I'm just a humble captain. Naturally our mistress didn't explain the details to one so lowly." His tone was cynical.

Coilla frowned. "I don't understand why that last creature should throw its life away protecting a female and her offspring."

"What sense is there in anything humans do?" Stryke replied. "They lack the balanced approach we orcs enjoy."

The cries of the baby rose to a more incessant pitch.

Stryke turned to look at it. His green, viperish tongue flicked over mottled lips. "Are the rest of you as hungry as I am?" he wondered.

His jest broke the tension. They laughed.

"It'd be exactly what they'd expect of us," Coilla said, reaching down and hoisting the infant by the scruff of its neck. Holding it aloft in one hand, level with her face, she stared at its streaming blue eyes and dimpled, plump cheeks. "My gods, but these things are *ugly*."

"You can say that again," Stryke agreed.

2

Stryke led his fellow orcs and Jup from the room. Coilla carried the baby, a look of distaste on her face.

Haskeer was waiting at the foot of the stairs. "Find it?" he said.

Nodding, Stryke slapped the cylinder in his belt. "Torch the place." He headed for the door.

Haskeer poked a finger at a couple of troopers. "You and you. Get on with it. The rest of you, *out!*"

Coilla blocked the path of a startled-looking grunt and dumped the baby in his arms. "Ride down to the plain and leave this where the humans will find it. And try to be . . . *gentle* with the thing." She hurried off, relieved. The trooper left, clutching the bundle as though it contained eggs, a bemused expression on his face.

There was a general exodus. The appointed arsonists found lanterns and began sloshing oil around. When they'd done, Haskeer dismissed them, then slipped a hand inside his boot for a flint. He ripped a length of shirt off the corpse of a defender and dipped it in oil. Igniting the sodden cloth with a spark, he threw it and ran.

A *whoomp* of yellow flame erupted. Sheets of fire spread over the floor.

Not bothering to look back, he jogged across the compound to catch up with the others.

They were with Alfray. As usual, the corporal was doubling as the warband's surgeon, and as Haskeer arrived he was tying the last stay on a trooper's makeshift splint.

Stryke wanted a casualty report.

Alfray pointed at the bodies of two dead comrades laid out on the ground nearby. "Slettal and Wrelbyd. Apart from them, three wounded. Though none so bad they won't heal. About a dozen caught the usual minor stuff."

"So five out of action, leaving us twenty-five strong, counting officers."

"What's an acceptable loss on a mission like this?" Coilla asked.

"Twenty-nine."

Even the trooper with the splint joined in the laughter. Although they knew that when it came down to it, their captain wasn't joking.

Only Coilla remained straight-faced, her nostrils flaring slightly, undecided whether they were making her the butt again because she was the newest recruit.

She has a lot to learn, Stryke reflected. *She'd best do it soon.*

"Things are quieter below," Alfray reported, referring to the battle on the plain. "It went our way."

"As expected," Stryke replied. He seemed uninterested.

Alfray noticed Coilla's wound. "Want me to look at that?"

"It's nothing. Later." To Stryke, she added stiffly, "Shouldn't we be moving?"

"Uhm. Alfray, find a wagon for the wounded. Leave the dead to the scavenging parties." He turned to the nine or ten troopers hanging around listening. "Get ready for a forced march back to Cairnbarrow."

They pulled long faces.

"It'll be nightfall soon," Jup remarked.

"What of it? We can still walk, can't we? Unless you're all frightened of the dark!"

"Poor bloody infantry," a private muttered as he passed.

Stryke delivered a savage kick to his backside. *"And don't forget it, you miserable little bastard!"*

The soldier yelped and limped hurriedly away.

This time, Coilla laughed with the others.

Over at the livestock pen a chorus of sound arose, a combination of roars and twittering screeches. Stryke set off in that direction. Haskeer and Jup trailed him. Coilla stayed with Alfray.

Two soldiers were leaning on the corral's fence, watching the milling animals.

"What's going on?" Stryke demanded.

"They're spooked," one of the troopers told him. "Shouldn't be cooped up like this. Ain't natural."

Stryke went to the rail to see for himself.

The nearest beast was no more than a sword's length away. Twice the height of an orc, it stood rampant, weight borne by powerful back legs, taloned feet half buried in the earth. The chest of its feline body swelled, the short, dusty yellow fur bristling. Its eagle-like head moved in a jerky, convulsive fashion and the curved beak clattered nervously. The enormous eyes, jet-black orbs against startlingly white surrounds, were never still. Its ears were pricked and quiveringly alert.

It was obviously agitated, yet its erect pose still maintained a curious nobility.

The herd beyond, numbering upwards of a hundred, was mostly on all fours, backs arched. But here and there pairs stood upright, boxing at each other with spindly arms, wickedly sharp claws extended. Their long curly tails swished rhythmically.

A gust of wind brought with it the fetid odour of the gryphons' dung.

"Gant's right," Haskeer remarked, indicating the trooper who had spoken, "their pen should be all of Maras-Dantia."

"Very poetic, Sergeant."

As intended, Stryke's derision cut Haskeer's pride. He looked as near embarrassed as an orc was capable of. "I just meant it was typical of humans to pen free-roaming beasts," he gushed defensively. "And we all know they'd do the same to us if we let 'em."

"All I know," Jup interjected, "is that yonder gryphons smell bad and taste good."

"Who asked *you*, you little tick's todger?" Haskeer flared.

Jup bridled and was about to retaliate.

"Shut up, both of you!" Stryke snapped. He addressed the troopers. "Slaughter a brace for rations and let the rest go before we leave."

He moved on. Jup and Haskeer followed, exchanging murderous glances.

Behind them, the fire in the house was taking hold. Flames

were visible at the upper windows and smoke billowed from the front door.

They reached the compound's ruined gates. On seeing their commander, the guards stationed there straightened themselves in a pretence of vigilance. Stryke didn't bawl them out. He was more interested in the scene on the plain. The fighting had stopped, the defenders either being dead or having run away.

"It's a bonus to win the battle," Haskeer observed, "seeing as it was only a diversion."

"They were outnumbered. We deserved to win. But no loose talk of diversions, not outside the band. Wouldn't do to let the arrow fodder know the fight was set up to cover our task." Automatically his hand went to the cylinder.

Down below, the scavengers were moving among the dead, stripping them of weapons, boots and anything else useful. Other parties had been detailed to finish off the enemy wounded, and those of their own side too far gone to help. Funeral pyres were already burning.

In the gathering twilight it was growing much colder. A stinging breeze whipped at Stryke's face. He looked out beyond the battlefield to the farther plains, and the more remote, undulating tree-topped hills. Softened by the lengthening shadows, it was a scene that would have been familiar to his forebears. Save for the distant horizon, where the faint outline of advancing glaciers showed as a thin strip of luminous white.

As he had a thousand times before, Stryke silently cursed the humans for eating Maras-Dantia's magic.

Then he cast off the thought and returned to practicalities. There was something he'd been meaning to ask Jup. "How did you feel about killing that fellow dwarf back in the house?"

"Feel?" The stocky sergeant looked puzzled. "No different to killing anyone else. Nor was he the first. Anyway, he wasn't a 'fellow dwarf.' He wasn't even from a tribe I knew."

Haskeer, who hadn't seen the incident, was intrigued. "You killed one of your own kind? The need to prove yourself must be strong indeed."

"He took the humans' part and that made him an enemy. I've no need to prove anything!"

"Really? With so many of your clans siding with the humans, and you the only dwarf in the Wolverines? I think you've much to prove."

The veins in Jup's neck were standing out like taut cords. "What's your meaning?"

"I just wonder why we need *your* sort in our ranks."

I should stop this, Stryke thought, *but it's been building too long. Maybe it's time they beat it out of each other.*

"I earned my sergeant's stripes in this band!" Jup pointed at the crescent-shaped tattoos on his rage-red cheeks. "I was good enough for that!"

"*Were* you?" Haskeer taunted.

Coilla, Alfray and several troopers arrived, drawn by the fuss. More than one of the soldiers wore a gleeful expression at the prospect of a fight between officers. Or in anticipation of Jup losing it.

Insults were now being openly traded, most of them concerning the sergeants' parentage. To rebut a particular point, Haskeer grasped a handful of Jup's beard and gave it a forceful tug.

"Say that again, you snivelling little fluffball!"

Jup pulled free. "At least I *can* raise hair! You orcs have heads like a human's arse!"

Words were about to give way to action. They squared up, fists bunched.

A trooper elbowed through the scrum. "Captain! *Captain!*"

The interruption wasn't appreciated by the onlookers. There were disappointed groans.

Stryke sighed. "What *is* it?"

"We've found something you should see, sir."

"Can't it wait?"

"Don't think so, Captain. Looks important."

"All right. Leave it, you two." Haskeer and Jup didn't move. "'That's *enough*," he growled menacingly. They lowered their fists and backed off, reluctant and still radiating hatred.

Stryke ordered the guards to admit no one and told the others to get back to work. "This better be good, Trooper."

He guided Stryke back into the compound. Coilla, Jup, Alfray and Haskeer, their curiosity whetted, tagged along behind.

The house was blazing furiously, with flames playing on the roof. They could feel the heat being thrown out as far away as the orchard, where the trooper took a sharp left. The higher branches of the trees were burning, each gust of wind liberating showers of drifting sparks.

Once through the orchard they came to a modest wooden barn, its double doors wide open. Inside were two more grunts, holding burning brands. One was inspecting the contents of a hessian sack. The second was on his knees and staring down through a lifted trapdoor.

Stryke crouched to look at the bag, the others gathering around him. It was filled with tiny translucent crystals. They had a faintly purple, pinkish hue.

"Pellucid," Coilla said in a hushed tone.

Alfray licked his finger and dabbed the crystals. He took a taste. "Prime quality."

"And look here, sir." The trooper pointed at the trapdoor.

Stryke snatched the torch from the kneeling soldier. Its flickering glow showed a small cellar, just deep enough for an orc to stand without bending. Two more sacks lay on its earthen floor.

Jup gave a low, appreciative whistle. "That's more than I've seen in all my days."

Haskeer, his dispute with the dwarf forgotten for the moment, nodded in agreement. "Think of its value!"

"What say we sample it?" Jup suggested hopefully.

Haskeer added his own petition. "It wouldn't hurt, Captain. Don't we deserve that much after pulling off this mission?"

"I don't know . . ."

Coilla looked pensive but held her tongue.

Alfray eyed the cylinder in Stryke's belt and injected a note of caution. "It wouldn't be wise to keep the Queen waiting *too* long."

Stryke didn't seem to hear. He scooped a palmful of the fine crystals and let them trickle slowly through his fingers. "This cache is worth a small fortune in coin and influence. Think how it would swell our mistress's coffers."

"*Exactly*," Jup eagerly concurred. "Look at it from her point of view. Our mission successfully accomplished, victory in the battle and a queen's ransom of crystal lightning to boot. She'll probably promote you!"

"Dwell on this, Captain," Haskeer said. "Once delivered into the Queen's hands, how much of it are *we* ever likely to see? There's enough human in her to make the answer to that question no mystery to me."

That did it.

Stryke dusted the last crystals from his hands. "What she doesn't know about won't hurt her," he decided, "and starting out an hour or two later won't make *that* much difference. And when she sees what we've brought, even Jennesta's going to be satisfied."

3

Some endure the frustration of their will with grace and forbearance. Others see obstacles to their gratification as intolerable burdens. The former embody admirable stoicism. The latter are dangerous.

Queen Jennesta belonged firmly in the second category. And she was growing impatient.

The warband she had entrusted with the sacred mission, the Wolverines, had yet to return. She knew the battle was over, and that it went in her favour, but they had not brought their monarch what she craved.

When they came she would have them skinned alive. If they had failed in their task she would inflict a much worse fate.

An entertainment had been arranged for her while she waited. It was necessary and practical as well as promising a certain pleasure. As usual, it would take place here in her *sanctum sanctorum*, the innermost of her private quarters.

The chamber, deep below her palace at Cairnbarrow, was constructed of stone. A dozen pillars supported the distant vaulted ceiling. Just enough light was provided by a scattering of candelabra and guttering brands, for Jennesta favoured shadows.

Wall hangings depicted complex cabalistic symbols. The floor's time-worn granite blocks were covered by woven rugs bearing equally arcane designs. A high-backed wooden chair, ornately carved but not quite a throne, stood next to an iron brazier of glowing coals.

Two features dominated the apartment. One was a solid chunk of black marble that served as an altar. The other was set in front of and below it, of the same material but white, and shaped like a long, low table or couch.

A silver chalice stood on the altar. By it lay a curved dagger, its hilt inlaid with gold, runic devices etched into the blade. Along-side was a small hammer with a weighty, rounded head. It was decorated and inscribed in a similar way.

The white slab had a pair of shackles at each end. She ran her fingertips, slowly and lightly, along its surface. The smooth cool-ness of the marble felt sensuous to her touch.

A rap at the studded oak door broke her reverie.

"Come."

Two Imperial Guards herded in a human prisoner at spear point. Chained hand and foot, the man wore only a loincloth. Around thirty seasons old, he was typical of his race in standing head and shoulders taller than the orcs prodding him forward. Bruises discoloured his face. Dried blood encrusted his blond hair and beard. He walked stiffly, partly due to the manacles but mostly because of a flogging he had been given after his capture during the battle. Vivid red weals criss-crossed his back.

"Ah, my guest has arrived. Greetings." The Queen's syrupy tone held pure mockery.

He said nothing.

As she languorously approached, one of the guards jerked the trailing chain at the captive's wrists. The man winced. Jennesta studied his robust, muscular frame, and decided he was suit-able for her purpose.

In turn, he inspected her, and it was obvious from his expres-sion that what he saw confounded him.

There was something wrong about the shape of her face. It was a little too flat, a mite wider than it should have been across the temples, and it tapered to a chin more pointed than seemed reasonable. Ebony hair tumbled to her waist, its sheen so pronounced it looked wet. Her dark fathomless eyes had an obliqueness that extraordinarily long lashes only served to stress. The nose was faintly aquiline and the mouth appeared overly broad.

None of this was exactly displeasing. It was rather as if her features had deviated from Nature's norm and pursued their own unique evolution. The result was startling.

Her skin, too, was not quite right. The impression, in the flicker-ing candleglow, was of an emerald hue one moment and a silvery lustre the next, as though she were covered in minute fish scales. She wore a long crimson gown that left her shoulders exposed and clung tightly to the outlines of her voluptuous body. Her feet were bare.

Without doubt she was comely. But her beauty had a distinctly alarming quality. Its effect on her prisoner was to both quicken his blood and excite vague feelings of disgust. In a world teeming with racial diversity, she was totally outside his experience.

"You do not show proper deference," she said. Her remarkable eyes were mesmeric. They made him feel that nothing could be kept concealed.

The captive dragged himself out of the depths of that devouring gaze. Despite his pain, he smiled, albeit cynically. He glanced down at the chains binding him, and for the first time spoke. "Even if I were so inclined, I could not."

Jennesta smiled too. It was genuinely disquieting. "My guards will be happy to assist," she replied brightly.

The soldiers forced him roughly to his knees.

"That's better." Her voice dripped synthetic sweetness.

Gasping from the added discomfort, he noticed her hands. The length of the slender fingers, extended by keen nails half as long again, bordered abnormal. She moved to his side, reaching to touch the welts covering his back. It was done softly, but he still flinched. She traced the angry red lines with the tips of her nails, releasing trickles of fresh blood. He groaned. She made no attempt to hide her relish.

"Damn you, you heathen bitch," he hissed weakly.

She laughed. "A typical Uni. Any rejecting your ways must be a heathen. Yet you're the upstarts, with your fantasies of a lone deity."

"While you follow the old, dead gods worshipped by the likes of these," he countered, glaring at the orc guards.

"How little you know. The Mani faith reveres gods even more ancient. *Living* gods, unlike the fiction you cleave to."

He coughed, misery racking his frame. "You call yourself a Mani?"

"What of it?"

"The Manis are wrong, but at least they're human."

"Whereas I'm not, and therefore cannot embrace the cause? Your ignorance would fill this place's moat, farmer. The Manifold path is for all. Even so, I am human in part."

He raised his eyebrows.

"You've never seen a hybrid before?" She didn't wait for an answer. "Obviously not. I'm of mixed nyadd and human parentage, and carry the best of both."

"The best? Such a union is . . . *an abomination!*"

The Queen found that even more amusing, throwing back her head to laugh again. "Enough of this. You're not here to engage in a debate." She nodded at the soldiers. "Make him ready."

He was yanked upright, then goaded to the marble slab, where they lifted him bodily by his arms and legs. The agony of being dumped unceremoniously on its surface made him cry out. He lay panting, his eyes watery. They removed the chains and fastened his wrists and ankles with the shackles.

Jennesta curtly dismissed the guards. They bowed and lumbered out.

She went to the brazier and sprinkled powdered incense on the coals. Heady perfume filled the air. Crossing to the altar, she took up the ceremonial dagger and the chalice.

With an effort, the man turned his head her way. "At least allow me the mercy of a quick death," he pleaded.

Now she loomed over him, the knife in her hand. He drew an audible breath and started to recite some prayer or incantation, his panic making the words an incomprehensible babble.

"You're spouting gibberish," she chided. "Still your tongue." Blade in hand, she stooped.

And cut through the loincloth.

She sliced away the material and tossed it aside. Placing the knife on the edge of the slab, she contemplated his nudity.

Slack-jawed, he stammered, "What—?" His face reddened with embarrassment. He gulped and squirmed.

"You Unis have a very unnatural attitude to your bodies," she told him, matter-of-factly. "You feel shame where none should exist."

She lifted his head with one hand and put the chalice to his lips with the other. "Drink," she commanded, sharply tilting the vessel.

Enough of the potion poured down his throat before he gagged and clamped his teeth on the rim. She removed the cup, leaving him coughing and spluttering. Some of the urine-coloured liquid dribbled from the sides of his mouth.

It was quick-acting but short-lived, so she wasted no time. Untying the straps of her gown, she let it fall to the floor.

He stared at her, wide-eyed with disbelief. His gaze took in her generous, jutting breasts. It moved down past her taut midriff to the pleasing camber of her hips, the long, curvaceous sweep of her legs and the luxuriant downy mound at her crotch.

Jennesta had a physical perfection which combined the sumptuous charms of a human woman with the alien heritage of her crossbred origins. He had never seen the like.

For her part, she recognised in him a struggle between the prudery of his Uni upbringing and the innate hunger of male lust. The aphrodisiac would help tilt the balance in the right direction, and deaden the pain of his ill-treatment. If need be she could add the persuasive powers of her sorcery. But she knew the best inducement required no magic.

She slid on to the side of the slab and brought her face close to his. The strange, sweet muskiness of her breath made the hairs on the back of his neck prickle. She blew gently in his ear, whispered shockingly explicit endearments. He blushed again, though this time perhaps not entirely because of abashment.

At last he found his voice. "Why do you torment me this way?"

"You torment yourself," she responded huskily, "by denying the joys of the flesh."

"Whore!"

Giggling, she leaned nearer, the tips of her swaying breasts tickling his chest. She made as if to kiss him, but drew back at the last. Wetting her fingers, she slowly trailed them around his nipples until they became erect. His breathing grew heavier. The potion was beginning to work.

Swallowing loudly, he summoned enough resolution to utter, "The thought of congress with you is repulsive to me."

"Really?" She eased on to him, straddling his body, her pubic hair pressed against his abdomen. He strained at the shackles, but feebly.

Jennesta was enjoying his humiliation, the destruction of his resolve. It heightened her own excitement. She parted her lips and disgorged a tongue that seemed overlong for the cavity of her mouth. It proved coarse-textured when she started licking his throat and shoulders.

Despite himself, he was becoming aroused. She squeezed her legs more firmly against the sides of his sweat-filmed body and caressed him with renewed ardour. A succession of emotions passed rapidly across his face: expectancy, repellence, fascination, eagerness. Fear.

He half cried, half sobbed, "No!"

"But you *want* this," she soothed. "Why else make yourself ready for me?" She lifted herself slightly. Reaching down, she took hold of his manhood and guided it.

Gradually she moved against him, her lithe form rising and falling in a deliberate, unhurried rhythm. His head rolled from side to side, eyes glazed, mouth gaping. Her tempo increased. He writhed and began moaning. The motion grew faster. He started to respond, tentatively at first, then thrusting deeper and harder. Jennesta tossed back her hair. The cloud of raven locks caught pinpoints of light that wreathed her in a nimbus of fire.

Aware he was on the verge of gushing his seed, she rode him mercilessly, building to a frenzy of wanton rapture. He twisted, flailed, shuddered his way to culmination.

Suddenly she had the dagger in both hands, lifting it high.

Orgasm and terror came simultaneously.

The blade plunged into his chest, again, again and again. He shrieked hideously, tearing the skin from his wrists as he fought the shackles. Unheeding, she stabbed and hacked, cleaving at flesh.

His screams gave way to a moist gurgle. Then his head fell back with a meaty thump and he was still.

She cast away the knife and scrabbled with her hands, delving into the gory hollow. Once the ribs were exposed she took up the hammer and pounded at them. They cracked, white shards flying. This obstruction removed, she dropped the hammer and clawed through viscera, arms blood-drenched, to grasp his still faintly beating heart. With an effort she ripped it free.

She lifted the dripping organ to her widening mouth and sank her teeth into its warm tenderness.

Great as her sexual gratification had been, it was as nothing compared to the fulfilment she now experienced. With each bite her victim's life force reinvigorated her own. She felt the flow replenishing her physically and feeding the spring from which she drew her vital magical energies.

Sitting cross-legged on the steaming corpse's chest, her face, breasts and hands smeared with blood, she happily feasted.

At length she was replete. For the time being.

As she sucked the last of the juices from her fingers, a young black and white cat slunk from a dark corner of the chamber. It mewed.

"Here, Sapphire," Jennesta crooned, patting her thigh.

The she-cat leapt effortlessly and joined her mistress to be petted. Then she sniffed at the mutilated body and began lapping at its open wound.

Smiling indulgently, the Queen got down from the slab and padded to a velvet bellcord.

The orc guards wasted no time in obeying her summons. If they had any feelings about the scene that greeted them, or her appearance, they gave no hint.

"Remove the carcass," she ordered.

The cat darted for the shadows on their approach. They set to work on the shackles.

"What news of the Wolverines?" Jennesta asked.

"None, my lady," one of the guards replied, avoiding her gaze.

It wasn't what she wanted to hear. The benefits of the refreshment were already fading. Regal displeasure returned.

She made a silent vow that the warband's deaths would surpass their worst nightmares.

Two Wolverine footsoldiers lay stretched out with their backs against a tree, enraptured by a swarm of tiny fairies fluttering and gambolling above their heads. Soft multicoloured light shimmered on the fairies' wings and their gentle singing tinkled melodiously in the late-evening air.

One of the orcs abruptly shot out a hand and snatched a fistful of the creatures. They squeaked pitifully. He stuffed their wriggling bodies into his mouth and crunched noisily.

"Irritating little bastards," his companion muttered.

The first trooper nodded sagely. "Yeah. But good to eat."

"And stupid," the second soldier added as the swarm formed again overhead.

He watched them for a while, then decided to grab a handful for himself.

They sat chewing, staring dumbly at the smoking embers of the farmhouse on the other side of the compound. The fairies finally got the message and flittered away.

A moment passed and the first orc said, "Did that really just happen?"

"What?"

"Those fairies."

"Fairies? Irritating little bastards."

"Yeah. But good to—" A light kick from a boot against his shin interrupted the discourse.

They hadn't noticed the approach of another trooper standing beside them. He stooped, grunted, "Here," and handed over a clay pipe. Swaying slightly, he stumbled off again.

The first soldier raised the pipe and inhaled deeply.

His comrade smacked his lips and pulled a face. He dug a grubby fingernail between his front teeth and picked out something that looked like a minute shiny wing. Shrugging, he flicked it into the grass. The other orc passed him the cob of pellucid.

Nearer the remains of the house, Stryke, Coilla, Jup and Alfray sat around a small campfire sharing their own pipe. Haskeer was using a stick to stir the contents of a black cooking pot hanging over the crackling flames.

"I'll say it one last time," Stryke told them, mildly exasperated. He pointed to the cylinder in his lap. "This thing was taken from a heavily armed caravan by Unis who killed the guards. That's the story." His voice was growing slurred. "Jennesta wants it back."

"But why?" Jug wondered, drawing from the pipe. "After all, it's only a cessage marrier . . . I mean, it's only a message carrier." Blinking, he handed the pipe to Coilla.

"We know *that*," Stryke replied. He waved a dismissive, lazy hand. "Must be an important message. Not our concern."

Dishing out steaming milky-white liquid from the pot and into tin cups, Haskeer commented, "I wager this pellucid was part of the caravan's cargo too."

Alfray, displaying characteristic correctness even in his present state, again tried reminding Stryke of his responsibilities. "We mustn't linger here too long, Captain. If the Queen—"

"Can't you chirrup a different song?" Stryke interrupted testily. "Mark me; our mistress will welcome us with open arms. You worry overmuch, sawbones."

Alfray lapsed into moody silence. Haskeer offered him a cup of the infused drug. He shook his head. Stryke accepted the brew and downed an ample draft.

Coilla had been vacant-eyed and half drowsing under the pellucid's influence. Now she spoke. "Alfray has a point. Incurring Jennesta's wrath is never a good scheme."

"Must you nag me too?" retorted Stryke, raising the cup once more. "We'll be on our way soon, never fear. Or would you deny them a little leisure?" He looked in the direction of the orchard, where most of the Wolverines were taking their ease.

The band's troopers sprawled before a larger fire. There was rude laughter, rough horseplay and raucous singing. A pair engaged in arm-wrestling. Several were slumped in ungainly postures.

Stryke turned back to Coilla. But the scene had changed completely.

She was curled on the ground with her eyes closed. All the others were also prone, one or two of them snoring. The fire was long dead. He returned his gaze to the main band. They too were sleeping, their fire also reduced to ashes.

It was the depth of night. A full panoply of stars dusted the sky.

What had seemed to him no more than an instant of time had proved an illusion.

He should rouse everyone, organise them, issue orders for the march to Cairnbarrow. And he would. Certainly he would. But he needed to rest his leaden limbs and clear the muzziness from his brain. Only a minute or two was all it would take. Just a minute.

His nodding head drooped, chin meeting neck.

A warm stupor crept into every fibre of his being. It was so hard to keep his eyes open.

He surrendered to the dark.

4

He opened his eyes.

The sun blazed directly overhead. He lifted a hand to shield himself from the light and, blinking, slowly rose to a standing position. The carpet of lush sward felt springy underfoot.

Before him stood a distant range of softly rolling hills. Above them, pure-white clouds drifted serenely across a sky of flawless blue. The landscape was verdant, uncorrupted.

Off to his right the view was dominated by the brim of an immense forest. On his left a shallow stream flowed down an incline before curving round a bend and out of sight.

It occurred to Stryke to wonder, in an abstract sort of way, what had happened to the night. And he had no idea where the other Wolverines might be. But these questions did no more than mildly stroke some small corner of his mind.

Then it seemed to him that he could hear other sounds beyond the tumbling water. Sounds resembling voices, and laughter, and the faint, rhythmic pounding of a drum. Their source was either in his head or at the brook's destination.

He followed the stream, walking in it, his boots crunching on the shingle washed smooth by its endless polishing. His sloshing descent inspired rustling in the undergrowth on either side as tiny furtive creatures darted from his path.

A pleasantly warm breeze caressed his face. The air was fresh and clean. It made him feel light-headed.

He reached the point where the rivulet turned. The voices were louder, more distinct, as he rounded the crook.

Before him was the mouth of a small valley. The stream ran on, snaking through a cluster of circular timber huts, roofed with straw. Set to one side was a longhouse, decorated with embellished shields of a clan Stryke didn't recognise. War trophies hung there, too; broadswords, spears, the bleached skulls of sabrewolves. The air was perfumed with the fragrance of smoky kindling and roasting game.

There were tethered horses, roaming livestock, strutting fowl.

And orcs.

Males, females, hatchlings. They carried out chores, tended fires, hewed wood, or simply lounged, watching, talking, bragging. In the clearing outside the longhouse a group of young tyros sparred with swords and staffs, the beating of a hide tambour harmonising their mock combat.

No one paid him any particular attention as he entered the settlement. All the orcs he saw bore weapons, as was only fitting for their kind, but despite this clan being unknown to him, Stryke didn't feel threatened. Just curious.

Someone came towards him. She strode with easy confidence, and made no move for the sword hanging in its scabbard at her belt. He judged her a head shorter than himself, though her flaming crimson headdress, shot through with streaks of gold, made up the height. Her back was straight, her build attractively muscular.

She showed no surprise at his presence. Indeed her expression was almost passive, or at least as passive as a face so strong and active could be. As she neared him, she smiled, openly and with warmth. He was aware of a faint stirring in his loins.

"Well met," she said.

Reflecting on her comeliness, he did not immediately respond. When he replied, it was hesitantly. "Well . . . met."

"I don't know you."

"Nor I you."

She asked, "What is your clan?"

He told her.

"It means nothing to me. But there are so many."

Stryke glanced at the unfamiliar shields on the longhouse. "Your clan isn't known to me either." He paused, captivated by her fetching eyes, before adding, "Aren't you wary of greeting a stranger?"

She looked puzzled. "Should I be? Is there a dispute between our clans?"

"Not that I know of."

She flashed her appealing, sharpened yellow teeth again. "Then there's no need for caution. Unless you come with evil intent."

"No, I come in peace. But would you be as welcoming if I were a troll? Or a goblin? Or a dwarf of unknown allegiance?"

Her mystified look returned. "Troll? Goblin? Dwarf? What are they?"

"You do not know of dwarves?"

She shook her head.

"Or gremlins, trolls, elves? Any of the elder races?"

"Elder races? No."

"Or . . . humans?"

"I don't know what they are, but I'm sure there aren't any."

"You mean there aren't any in these parts?"

"I mean that your words are lost on me. You're odd." It was said without malice.

"And you speak in riddles," he told her. "Where are we in Maras-Dantia that you do not know of the other elder races, or of humans?"

"You must have journeyed a long way, stranger, if your land has a name I've never heard of."

He was taken aback. "Are you telling me you don't even know what the world is called?"

"No. I'm telling you it isn't called Maras-Dantia. At least, not here. And I've never known another orc who spoke of us sharing it with these . . . elder races and . . . humans."

"Orcs decide their own fate here? They make war as they choose? There are no humans or—"

She laughed. "When was it otherwise?"

Stryke furrowed his craggy brow. "Since before my father's father was hatched," he muttered. "Or so I thought."

"Perhaps you've marched too long in the heat," she offered gently.

He gazed up at the sun, and a realisation came to him. "The heat . . . No chill wind blows."

"Why should it? This isn't the cold season."

"And the ice," Stryke continued, ignoring her answer. "I haven't seen the advancing ice."

"Where?"

"From the north, of course."

Unexpectedly, she reached out and grasped his hand. "Come."

Even in his confusion he was aware that her touch was agreeably cool and clammy. He allowed her to lead him.

They followed the downward path of the stream until they left the village behind. Eventually they came to a place where the land fell away, and Stryke and the female stood on the edge of a granite cliff. Here the stream became a pool, slipping from its far lip as a waterfall, a foamy cascade that plunged to rocks far below in a greater valley.

The silver thread of a river emerged from somewhere at the foot of the cliff, slicing across olive plains that stretched endlessly in all directions. Only the tremendous forest to their right curbed the ocean of grassland. Vast herds of grazing beasts, too numerous to count, ranged further than Stryke could see. An orc might spend a lifetime hunting here and never want for prey.

The female pointed, dead ahead. "North," she said.

There were no encroaching glaciers, no looming slate sky. All he saw in that direction was more of the same: luxuriant foliage, an infinity of green, a thriving abundance of life.

Stryke experienced a strange emotion. He could not explain why, but he had a nagging sensation that all this was somehow familiar, as though he had seen these wondrous sights and breathed deep of this unsullied air before.

"Is this . . . Vartania?" He all but whispered the sacred word.

"Paradise?" She smiled enigmatically. "Perhaps. If you choose to make it so."

The alchemy of sunlight and airborne spray birthed an arcing rainbow. They silently marvelled at its multicoloured splendour.

And the soothing rush of water was balm to Stryke's troubled spirit.

He opened his eyes.

A Wolverine grunt was pissing into the ashes of the fire.

Stryke snapped fully awake. *"What the fuck do you think you're doing, Private?"* he bellowed.

The grunt scooted off like a scalded whelp, head down, fumbling at his breeches.

Still muzzy from the dream, or vision, or whatever it was, Stryke took a moment to realise that the sun had risen. It was past dawn.

"Gods!" he cursed, scrambling to his feet.

He checked his belt for the cylinder, then quickly took in the scene. Two or three of the Wolverines were unsteadily exploring wakefulness, but the rest, including the lookouts he'd posted, lounged all over the compound.

Sprinting to the nearest huddle of sleeping figures, he laid about them with his boot. "Up, you *bastards!*" he roared. "Up! *Move yourselves!*"

Some rolled from the kicks. Several came alive with blades in their hands, ready for a fight, then cowered on recognising their tormentor. Haskeer was among them, but less inclined to quail at his commander's rage. He scowled, returning his knife to its sheath with deliberate, insolent slowness.

"What ails you, Stryke?" he rumbled sullenly.

"What ails me? The *new day* ails me, scumpouch!" He jabbed a thumb skyward. "The sun climbs and we're still here!"

"And whose fault is that?"

Stryke's eyes narrowed dangerously. He moved closer to Haskeer, near enough to feel the sergeant's fetid breath against his face. "*What?*" he hissed.

"You blame us. Yet you're in charge."

"You'd like to try changing that?"

The other Wolverines were gathering around them. At a distance.

Haskeer held Stryke's gaze. His hand edged to his scabbard. "*Stryke!*"

Coilla was elbowing the grunts aside, Alfray and Jup in tow. "We don't have time for this," she said sternly.

Captain and sergeant paid her no heed.

"The Queen, Stryke," Alfray put in. "We have to get back to Cairnbarrow. Jennesta—"

Mention of her name broke the spell. "I *know*, Alfray," Stryke barked. He gave Haskeer a last, contemptuous look and turned away from him.

Sullenly, Haskeer backed off, directing a venomous glare at Jup by way of compensation.

Stryke addressed the warband. "We'll not march this day, we'll ride. Darig, Liffin, Reafdaw, Kestix: round up horses for all. Seafe, and you, Noskaa: find a couple of mules. Finje, Bhose: gather provisions. Just enough to travel light, mind. Gant, take who you need and release those gryphons. The rest of you, collect up our gear. *Now!*"

The grunts dispersed to carry out their orders.

Scanning his officers, Stryke saw that Alfray, Jup, Haskeer and Coilla looked as bleary-eyed as he probably did himself. "You'll see they waste no time with those horses and mules, Haskeer," he said. "You too, Jup. And I want no trouble from either of you." He curtly jerked his head to dismiss them.

They ran off, keeping well apart.

"What do you want us to do?" Alfray asked.

"Pick one or two grunts to help divide the pellucid equally among the band. It'll be easier to transport that way. But make it clear they're carrying it, not being given it. And if any of 'em has other ideas, they'll get more than their arses tanned."

Alfray nodded and left.

Coilla lingered. "You look . . . strange," she said. "Is everything all right?"

"No, Corporal, it isn't." Stryke's words dripped venom. "If you hadn't noticed, we should have reported to Jennesta hours since. And that might mean getting our throats cut. *Now do as you're told!*"

She fled.

Wisps of the vision still clung to his mind as he damned the rising sun.

They left behind the ruins of the human settlement, and the trampled, deserted battlefield beneath it, and headed north-east.

An upgrade in their trail took them above the rolling plains. The liberated gryphons were spreading across the grasslands.

Riding beside Stryke at the head of the column, Coilla indicated the view and said, "Don't you envy them?"

"What, beasts?"

"They're freer than us."

The remark surprised him. It was the first time she'd made any comment, even indirectly, that referred to the situation their race had been reduced to. But he resisted the temptation to agree with her. These days an orc did well not to speak too freely. Opinions had a way of reaching unintended ears.

He kept his response to a noncommittal snort.

Coilla regarded him with an expression of curiosity, and dropped the subject. They rode on in grim silence, maintaining as rapid a pace as they could over the uneven terrain.

At mid-morning they came to a winding track that led through a narrow ravine. It was deep, with tall grassy walls rising at gentle gradients, making the pass wedge-shaped. The constricted path meant the band could ride no more than two abreast. Most took it single-file. Stony and cramped, the trail slowed them to a trot.

Frustrated at the delay, Stryke cursed. "We *have* to move faster than this!"

"Using the pass gains us half a day," Coilla reminded him, "and we'll make up for more on the other side."

"Every passing minute is going to sour Jennesta's mood."

"We've got what she wanted, and a cargo of pellucid as bonus. Doesn't that stand for something?"

"With *our* mistress? I think you know the answer to that, Coilla."

"We can say we ran into strong opposition, or had trouble finding the cylinder."

"No matter the story we tell, we aren't there. That's enough." He glanced over his shoulder. The others were far enough behind to be out of earshot. "I wouldn't admit this to everybody," he confided in a hushed tone, "but Haskeer was right, blast his eyes. I let this happen."

"Don't be too hard on yourself. We all—"

"*Wait!* Ahead!"

Something was coming towards them from the opposite end of the ravine.

Stryke held up a hand, halting the column. He squinted, trying to identify the low, broad shape moving their way. It was obviously a beast of burden of some sort, and it had a rider. As he watched, several more came into view beyond it.

Down the line, Jup passed the reins to a grunt and dismounted. He jogged to Stryke. "What is it, Captain?" he said.

"I'm not sure . . ." Then he recognised the animals. "*Damnation!* Kirgizil vipers!"

Though commonly referred to as such, kirgizils weren't vipers at all. They were desert lizards, much shorter than horses but of roughly the same mass, with wide backs and stumpy, muscular legs. Albino-white and pink-eyed, they had forked tongues the length of an orc's arm. Their dagger-sharp fangs held a lethal venom, their barbed tails were powerful enough to shatter a biped's spine. They were stalking creatures, capable of remarkable bursts of speed.

Only one race used them as war chargers.

The lizards were near enough now to leave no doubt. Sitting astride each was a kobold. Smaller than orcs, smaller than most dwarves, they were thin to the point of emaciation, totally hairless and grey-skinned. But appearances were deceptive. Despite the gangly arms and legs, and elongated, almost delicate faces, they were obstinate, ravening fighters.

Pointed ears swept back from heads disproportionately large in relation to their bodies. The mouth was a lipless slash, filled with tiny, sharp teeth. The nose resembled a feral cat's. The eyes were golden-orbed, glinting with spite and avarice.

Quilled leather collars wrapped their unusually extended necks. Their reed-slim wrists prickled with razor-spike bracelets. They brandished spears and wicked-looking miniature scimitars.

In the business of thievery and scavenging, kobolds had few equals in all Maras-Dantia. They had even fewer when it came to meanness of temperament.

"*Ambush!*" Jup yelled.

Other voices were raised along the column. Orcs pointed upward. More kirgizil-mounted raiders were sweeping down at them from both sides of the gully. Standing in his saddle, Stryke saw kobolds pouring in to block their exit.

"Classic trap," he snarled.

Coilla tugged free a pair of throwing knives. "And we walked right into it."

Alfray unfurled the war banner. Horses reared, scattering loose shingle. The orcs drew their weapons and turned to face the enemy on every side.

Half befuddled from the pellucid, looted wine and rougher

alcohol of the night before, the Wolverines were outnumbered with barely room to manoeuvre.

Blades flashing in the sun, the kobolds thundered in for the attack.

Stryke roared a battle cry and the warband took it up.

Then the first wave was on them.

5

Stryke didn't wait to be attacked.

Digging his heels into the flanks of his horse, he spurred it toward the leading raider, pulling to the left, as though to pass the kobold's charging lizard. The horse shied. Stryke kept it firmly on course, reins wrapped tightly around one hand. With the other he brought his sword up and back.

Caught out by the swiftness of the move, the rider tried to duck. Too late.

Stryke's blade cleaved the air. The kobold's head leapt from its shoulders, flew to the side and hit the trail bouncing. Sitting upright, a fountain of blood gushing from its stump, the corpse was carried past by the uncontrolled kirgizil. It ran on into the mêlée at Stryke's rear.

He laid into his next opponent.

Coilla lobbed a knife at the raider nearest to her. It buried itself in the kobold's cheek. The creature plunged screaming from its mount.

She singled out another target and threw again, underarm this time, as hard as she could. Her mark instinctively pulled back sharply on its reins, bringing up the viper's head. Her missile struck it squarely in the eye. Roaring with pain, the animal's body pitched to one side, crushing its rider. Both writhed in thrashing agony.

Coilla steadied her horse and reached for more knives.

On foot when the attackers swept in, Jup had armed himself with an axe and was swinging it two-handed. A kobold, unsaddled by a glancing blow from a Wolverine sword, lurched into range. Jup split its skull. Then a mounted attacker side-swiped the dwarf. He spun and chopped deep into the rider's twig-thin leg, completely severing it.

All around, orcs were engaged in bloody exchanges. About a third of them had been de-horsed. Several of the archers had managed to notch their bows and wing bolts at the raiders. But the fight was already too close-quartered to make this feasible for much longer.

Haskeer found himself boxed in. One opponent hacked at him from the trail side. The other delivered slashing downward blows from the gully's slope, its dextrous kirgizil gripping the treacherous incline with ease. Fearful of the lizards, Haskeer's panicking horse bucked and whinnied. He lashed out to the right, to the left and back again.

An orc arrow smacked into the chest of the kobold on the slope, knocking it clean off the viper's back. Haskeer turned full attention to the opponent on his other side. Their blades clashed, returned, clashed once more.

A pass sliced across Haskeer's chin. It wasn't a serious wound, though the steel was keen, but it caught him off balance and he fell from the horse. His sword was lost. As he rolled from pounding hooves and swishing reptilian tails, a spear was hurled at him. It narrowly missed. He struggled to his feet and wrenched it from the ground.

The kobold that had unseated him came in for the kill. Haskeer had no time to straighten the spear. He brought it up to fend off the creature's arcing sword. It sliced the shaft in two, showering slivers of wood. Discarding the shorter end, Haskeer swung the remainder like an elongated club, swiping the kobold full in the face. The impact sent it crashing to the ground.

Haskeer rushed in and began viciously booting the creature's head. For good measure he jumped on its chest, pounding up and down with all his might, knees bent, fists clenched. The kobold's ribcage snapped and crunched. Blood disgorged from its mouth and nose.

Alfray fought for possession of the Wolverines' banner. A kobold, standing in its stirrups, had hold of the pole. Grimly, Alfray maintained an iron grasp, his knuckles whitening as the rod went back and forth in a bizarre tug-of-war. For such an insubstantial-looking creature, the kobold was tenacious. Avaricious eyes narrowed, spiky teeth bared, it hissed horribly.

It was close to gaining its prize when Alfray delivered an orc's kiss.

Throwing himself forward, he head-butted the kobold solidly in its bony forehead. The creature flew backwards, letting go of the pole as though it were a hot poker. Alfray quickly levelled the shaft and rammed the sharpened end into his assailant's abdomen.

He turned, ready to inflict the same fate on any enemy near enough. What he saw was a Wolverine grunt trading blows with a raider and getting the worst of it. Exploiting an opening, the kobold lunged in, its scimitar swiftly carving a scathing X on the orc's chest. The trooper went down.

Urging on his horse, Alfray galloped full pelt at the kobold, holding the banner pole like a lance. It penetrated the creature's midriff and exited its back with an explosion of gore.

Working his way up the trail, Stryke was heading for his fourth or fifth opponent. He wasn't sure which. He rarely kept count. Two or three kills earlier he'd abandoned the reins, preferring his hands free for combat. Now he held on to and guided the horse solely by applying pressure with his thighs. It was an old orc trick he was adept at.

The kobold he was fast approaching held a large, ornate shield, the first he had seen any of them carrying. That probably made this particular individual a chieftain. Of more concern to Stryke was how the shield might hinder him in killing its owner. He decided to adopt a different strategy.

Just before drawing level with the striding reptile, he grabbed a handful of his horse's mane and jerked it, slowing their pace. Now parallel with the kirgizil, he stretched down and snatched the harness encasing its huffing snout. Careful to avoid the animal's snaking tongue, he heaved the yoke upwards, muscles straining. Half strangulated, the kirgizil lashed and struggled, its taloned feet pawing the ground. It twisted its head, snorting for breath.

Stryke pummelled his heels into his horse's sides, driving it on. The steed was labouring to move, bearing as it was both Stryke's weight and the mass of the viper. Unable to control its mount, the kobold rider leaned from the saddle, impotently swiping at Stryke with its blade.

Finally, its neck bent to an untenable angle, the kirgizil tilted to one side. The kobold let out a dismayed yelp and slid from its back, parting company with the shield. Stryke let go of the lizard's harness. Ignoring the beast as it fought to right itself, he wheeled round the horse to face the fallen kobold. A sharp tug on the mane made the steed rear.

The kobold was on its knees when the hooves came down and stove in its skull.

Stryke looked back. He caught a glimpse of Coilla. She'd lost her mount and was in the thick of the ferocious scrum. Several bandits, parted from their chargers, were moving in on her.

She couldn't hold them off with knife-throws any longer; it was down to close combat. Using her knives as daggers, she stabbed and slashed, spinning and dodging to avoid thrusts from spears and swords.

A leering kobold took a swipe from the edge of her blade across its throat and spiralled away. Another jumped in to take its place. As it raised its sword she darted under it, dealing two rapid stabs to the heart. It collapsed. A third raider appeared in front of her, holding a spear. It was too far away to engage with her daggers, too close for a throw. She stepped back, transfixed by the menacing, barbed spearhead.

From behind, a hatchet came down heavily on the creature's shoulder. With an eruption of blood and sinew, it severed the kobold's spear arm from its trunk. Wailing terribly, the raider fell.

Hefting his gore-spattered axe, Jup ran forward to join her.

"We can't take much more of this!" he yelled.

"Keep killing!"

They fought back to back.

Alfray kicked out at a kobold on foot, while simultaneously crossing swords with another, alongside on its kirgizil. The lizard was snapping at Alfray's spooked horse, and it was all he could do to keep it in check. Nearby, two orc grunts were cutting a lone raider to ribbons.

Haskeer's newly retrieved sword was dashed away by a passing kobold rider. Another raider immediately loomed up, sneering evilly at the Wolverine's empty hands. Its scimitar flashed. Haskeer ducked. The blade whistled overhead. Diving at his opponent, Haskeer drove his massive fist into its face. With his free hand he caught the wrist of the bandit's sword arm and squeezed until the bones popped. The kobold shrieked. Haskeer resumed pounding at its face until it let go of the sword. Scooping it up, he ran the creature through.

Far gone in bloodlust, he turned to an adjacent mounted enemy. The kobold had its back to him, preoccupied with a fight on its other side. Haskeer dragged it from the viper and set to battering it. Its slender arms and legs snapped like dry kindling under the onslaught.

A bellowing grunt tumbled past, swatted by a kirgizil's tail. He collided with a brawling mass of combatants. Orcs and kobolds went down in a tangle of thrashing limbs.

The last ambusher blocking Stryke's path proved skilful as well as obstinate. Instead of hacking and slashing, Stryke was embroiled in something like a fencing match.

As his foe's mount was lower than Stryke's, the Wolverine commander had to lean over to clash blades. That disadvantage, along with the kobold's adeptness at swordplay, made it difficult penetrating the creature's guard. Every blow was parried, each stroke countered.

After a full minute of stalemate, the kobold's blade was the one to break through. It gashed Stryke's upper arm, spraying blood.

Enraged, he renewed his attack with fresh energy. He showered blows on the raider, seeking to overcome its skill with sheer force. The ceaseless buffeting lacked finesse, and the strokes were scarcely aimed, but soon paid dividends. In the face of the lashing storm, the kobold's defences weakened, its reactions slowed.

Stryke's blade sliced through one of the creature's upswept ears. It shrieked. The next pass laid open its shoulder, bringing forth an anguished howl.

Then Stryke landed a vicious blow to the side of the bandit's head and ended it.

Panting, his limbs afire from exertion, he slumped in his saddle. There were no more kobolds on the trail ahead.

Something jolted his horse from behind. The steed bolted. Before he could turn, he felt an impact against his back. A clawed hand snaked around his body and dug painfully into his chest. Hot breath prickled the nape of his neck. The other hand appeared, clutching a curved dagger, and made for his throat. He grabbed the wrist and checked its upward transit.

The horse was running, unrestrained. From the corner of his eye, Stryke saw a riderless kirgizil passing them: the mount his attacker must have leapt from.

Stryke twisted the wrist he held, intent on breaking it. At the same time he repeatedly jabbed the elbow of his other arm into the kobold's solar plexus. He heard a guttural moan. The dagger slipped from its hand and fell away.

Another mounted bandit appeared at his side. It was waving a scimitar.

He kicked out, his boot thudding against the creature's wiry shoulder. The momentary loss of concentration loosened his grip on the kobold at his back. Its hands quickly withdrew. Stryke jabbed his elbow again, sinking it deep in flesh. Once more he aimed a kick at the mounted raider. This time he missed.

His horse thundered on. The kobold on the viper kept pace, and drew ahead a little.

Now the tiny, loathsome hands were eagerly scrabbling at Stryke's belt. He managed to half turn and lash out at the unwanted passenger. His knuckles struck its face, but ineffectually.

Avidly, the hands encircled his waist again, probing, searching. And he realised what the bandit was after.

The cylinder.

No sooner had the thought occurred than the kobold reached its goal. With a triumphant hiss, it seized the artifact and pulled it free.

As he felt the prize being tugged away, it seemed to Stryke that time slowed, became pliable, stretching the following instant to an eternity.

Laggard-paced, as though seen with a dreamer's eye, several things happened at once.

He caught the horse's flailing reins and yanked on them with all his might. The steed's head whiplashed back. A great shudder ran through its body.

The mounted kobold slowly rose in its saddle, arm outstretched, taloned hand open.

An object sailed leisurely over Stryke's right shoulder. It turned end over end, burnished surface briefly flashing reflected sunlight as it descended.

Time's frantic tempo returned.

The rider snatched the cylinder from the air.

Stryke's horse went down.

He hit the ground first, rolling the width of the trail. The kobold sitting behind fetched up a dozen paces away. Vision swimming, breath knocked out of him, Stryke watched as his horse struggled to its feet and galloped off. It headed for the far end of the gully, the same direction as the raider bearing the cylinder.

A groan came from the kobold that had fallen with him. Possessed of a berserk frenzy, Stryke stumbled over to the creature and vented his anger. Kneeling on its chest, he reduced its face to a bloody pulp with the hammering of his fists.

The air was rent by a keening, high-pitched blast of sound.

He looked up. Well clear by now, the escaping bandit held a slender, copper-coloured horn to its lips.

As the intonation reached the raiders engaging Coilla and Jup, they backed off and began to run.

Jup took a last, wide swing at his fleeing opponent and shouted, "Look!"

All the kobolds were withdrawing. Most retreated on foot; some dashed to mount loose kirgizils. They ran and rode in the direction of the gully's entrance, or up its steep sides. A handful of orcs harried the escaping creatures, but most were licking their wounds.

Coilla saw Stryke loping towards them. "Come on!" she said. They rushed to meet him.

"The cylinder!" he raged, half demented.

No further explanation was necessary. It was obvious what had happened.

Jup carried on along the trail, legs pumping, a hand shading his eyes as he peered into the distance. He made out the kirgizil and its rider, climbing the wall of the gully at its far end. As he watched, they reached the top. They were outlined against the sky for a second before disappearing.

He trotted back to Stryke and Coilla.

"Gone," he reported baldly.

Stryke's face was black with fury. Without a word to either of them, he turned and headed for the rest of the band. Corporal and sergeant exchanged barren glances and followed.

Where the fighting had been most intense the ground was littered with kobold dead and wounded, downed horses and kirgizils. At least half a dozen orcs had more than superficial injuries, but were still on their feet. One was stretched on the ground and being tended by comrades.

Sighting their commander, the Wolverines moved to him.

Stryke marched to Alfray, eyes blazing. "Casualties?" he barked.

"Give me a chance, I'm still checking."

"Well, *roughly*, then." The tone was menacing. "You're supposed to double as our combat physician; *report*."

Alfray glowered. But he wasn't about to challenge the Captain in his present mood. "Looks like no loss of life. Though Meklun yonder's in a bad way." He nodded at the downed trooper. "Others took deep wounds, but can stand."

Haskeer, wiping blood from his chin, said, "Lucky as devils, us."

Stryke glared at him. *"Lucky?* Those bastards took the cylinder!"

Palpable shock ran through the band.

"Thieving little *fuckers*," Haskeer responded indignantly. "Let's get after 'em!"

The Wolverines chorused approval.

"Think!" Stryke bellowed. "By the time we've cleared this shambles, rounded up the horses, tended our wounded—"

"Why not send a small party after them now, and the rest can follow?" Coilla suggested.

"They'd be well outnumbered, and those kirgizils can go where we can't. The trail's cold already!"

"But what good is it if we wait until we sort ourselves?" Alfray put in. "Who knows where they've gone?"

"There's plenty of their wounded lying about," Haskeer reminded them. "I say we make 'em tell us." He slipped out a knife and flicked his finger against its edge to underline the point.

"Can *you* speak their infernal language?" Stryke demanded. "Can *any* of you?" They shook their heads. "No, I thought not. So torture's hardly the answer, is it?"

"We should never have entered this valley without scouting it first," Haskeer grumbled lowly.

"I'm just in the mood for your griping," Stryke told him, his expression like flint. "If you've got something to say about how I'm leading this band, let's hear it now."

Haskeer held up his hands in a placating gesture. "No, chief." He turned on an empty grin. "Just . . . thinking aloud."

"Thinking's not your strong point, Sergeant. Leave it to me. And that goes for *all* of you!"

A tense silence descended. Alfray broke it. "What do you want us to do, Captain?" he asked.

"Find as many horses as we can, for a start. If Meklun can't ride, make a litter for him." He bobbed his head at the carnage. "Don't leave any kobolds alive. Cut their throats. Get on with it."

The Wolverines melted away.

Coilla remained, looking at him.

"Don't say it," he told her. "I know. If we don't get that damn thing back for Jennesta, we're as good as dead."

6

Jennesta stood on the highest balcony of her palace's tallest tower.

The eastern ocean was to her back. She looked north-west, where curling yellow mist rose over Taklakameer, the inland sea. Beyond that, she could just make out the city spires of Urrarbython, on the margin of the Hojanger wastelands. In turn, Hojanger eventually gave way to the ice field dominating the horizon, bathed by a crimson sun.

To Jennesta it resembled a frozen tidal wave of blood.

An icy breeze swept in, acute as a blade, stirring the heavy cerise drapes on the balcony's entrance. She wrapped the cloak of milky-hued sabrewolf pelts tighter around herself. Autumnal conditions belied the season, and each passing year was worse.

The advancing glaciers and frigid winds were harbingers of the encroaching humans, ever expanding their hold, tearing the heart from the land, interfering with the balance.

Eating Maras-Dantia's magic.

She heard that in the south, where they were most densely concentrated and sorcery worked poorly if at all, humans had even abandoned the hallowed name and taken to calling the world Centrasia. At least the Unis had, and they were still more numerous than the Manis.

Not for the first time, she fell to wondering what her mother, Vermegram, would have made of the schism. There was no doubt she would favour the Followers of the Manifold Path. After all, they adhered to pantheistic tenets remarkably similar to those of the elder races. Which was why Jennesta herself supported their cause, and would continue to do so for as long as it suited her. But whether her mother, a nyadd, would have approved of Jennesta actually siding with incomers was a moot point. Notwithstanding Vermegram's human consort.

And what of him? Would Jennesta's father have approved of Unity and its nonsensical monotheistic creed?

Whenever she dwelt on these matters she always came up against the ambiguity of her hybrid origins. Inevitably, that led to thoughts of Adpar and Sanara, and anger rose.

She brought her mind back to the artifact. It was the key to her ambitions, to victory, and it was slipping out of her grasp.

Turning, she entered the chamber.

An attendant stepped forward and took her cloak. Slimly built, almost petite, the servant was pallid-skinned and dainty of face. The sandy hair, powder-blue eyes with long golden lashes, button nose and sensuous lips were typically androgynous.

The servant was new, and Jennesta was still uncertain whether the creature was predominantly male or female. But everyone had that problem with elves.

"General Kysthan is here, Your Majesty," he or she announced in a piping, sing-song voice. "He, er, has been waiting for some time."

"Good. I'll see him now."

The elf ushered in the visitor, bowed discreetly and left.

Kysthan was probably in late middle-age, as far as she could tell, and in orc terms, distinguished-looking. He had ramrod-backed military bearing. An accumulation of criss-crossed tattoos on both cheeks recorded his rise through the ranks. His expression spoke of unease, and not a little apprehension.

There were no opening formalities.

"I can see from your face that they haven't come back," she said, regal displeasure barely in check.

"No, Your Majesty." He failed to meet her eyes. "Perhaps they ran into greater opposition than expected."

"Reports from the battle don't indicate that."

He made no reply.

"What do you propose doing about it?"

"A detachment will be sent with all speed to find out what's happened to them, my lady."

"Are we dealing with treachery here?"

The General was offended. "We've never had reason to doubt the loyalty of any of the Wolverines," he replied gravely. "Their service records are excellent, and —"

"I know *that*. Do you think I'd send them on so sensitive a mission if it were otherwise? Do you take me for such a fool?"

Kysthan's gaze fell to his feet. "No, my lady."

"'*No, my lady,*'" she mimicked sarcastically. After a tense pause she added, "Tell me about their leader, this Stryke."

He produced several sheets of parchment from inside his jerkin. She noticed that his hands were trembling slightly.

"I had few dealings with him personally, Your Majesty. But I know he's from a good clan. Been in military service since hatching, of course. And he's bright."

"For an orc."

"As you say," Kysthan muttered. He cleared his throat, awkwardly, and consulted the papers. "It seems that he decided early on to increase his chances of promotion by applying total dedication to every duty given to him. His superior officers report that he always obeyed orders instantly and took beatings without complaint."

"Intelligent *and* ambitious."

"Yes, my lady." The General shuffled his notes, a task soldier's hands were too gauche to achieve with grace. "In fact, it was during his very first detail that—"

"What was it?"

"Hmm?"

"His first detail. What was it?"

"He was assigned as a menial to the dragonmasters, working in the pens." Kysthan scrutinised the parchment. "Shovelling dragon dung."

A small gesture of her hand indicated he should continue.

"While on that detail he caught the eye of an officer who recommended his promotion from drone to footsoldier. He did well and was made a corporal, then sergeant. He was raised to his present rank shortly after. All within four seasons."

"Impressive."

"Yes, ma'am. Of course, up to then he'd served exclusively in the Expeditionary Force of the United Orc Clans—"

"Although in truth it does not represent all orc clans and is frequently far from united." She smiled at him with all the warmth of a Scilantium pit spider. "Is that not so, General?"

"It is so, my lady."

She relished his humiliation.

"As you know," he went on, "the Orc Supreme Council of War, short of coin to feed and supply the troops, was forced into certain economies. One of those economies involved several thousand warriors being . . ."

"The word is *sold*, General. To me. You were part of the purchase, as I recall."

"Yes, Majesty, as was Stryke. We both came into your gracious service at that time."

"Don't ooze. I despise crawlers."

He blushed, a light cerulean tint colouring his cheeks.

"How long before the detachment you'll send reports back?" she asked.

"About five days, assuming they don't run into problems."

"Then they must be careful not to. Very well. I expect this . . . *shit shoveller* to be brought here in five days at most. But be clear, General; what he holds is mine, and I will have it. I want the cylinder above all else. Bringing back the Wolverines for punishment is secondary. *Everything* is secondary to the cylinder. Including the lives of Stryke and his band."

"Yes, my lady."

"The lives of those sent after them are also expendable."

He hesitated before replying, "I understand, my lady."

"Be sure you do." She made a series of swift, mysterious movements with her hands. "And lest you forget . . ."

The General looked down. His uniform was smouldering. It caught fire. The blaze enveloped his jerkin, and instantly spread to his arms and legs. Intolerable heat scorched his limbs. Smoke billowed.

Nostrils smarting from the odour of singeing, he beat at the flames. His palms stung and blistered. Fire leapt to his shoulders, neck, face. It completely engulfed him. His flesh blackened. Excruciating agony seared his body.

He cried out.

Jennesta's hands moved again, in a perfunctory, almost dismissive motion.

There was no fire. His clothes were not charred. The smell of burning had vanished, and there were no blisters on his hands. He felt no pain.

Dumbly, he stared at her.

"If you or your subordinates fail me," she stated evenly, "that's just a taste of what you'll get."

Embarrassment, shame, and above all fear were stamped on his features. "Yes, Majesty," he whispered.

His reaction was gratifying. She enjoyed making a grown orc quake.

"You have your orders," she told him.

He bowed stiffly and turned to the door.

Once the General had left, Jennesta sighed. Making for a couch, she sank into its plump cushions. She was drained. With the natural energy sources so depleted, even casting a simple glamour took considerable effort. Though it was worth it to keep her underlings in line. But now she would have to replenish her powers. The other way.

She remembered the elf servant.

And decided that might be an agreeable way of doing it.

In the corridor outside, Kysthan's upright demeanour deserted him. His nerve was near doing the same. He slumped against a wall, eyes closed, slowly expelling the breath he'd been holding.

It wouldn't do for him to be seen this way. He fought to pull himself together.

After a moment he straightened his shoulders and ran the back of his hand across his sweat-sheened brow. Then with measured deliberateness he resumed his short journey.

The curving passageway took him to an adjacent anteroom. A young officer snapped to attention when he entered.

"As you were, Captain," the General told him.

The officer relaxed, marginally.

"You're to leave immediately," Kysthan said.

"How long do we have, sir?"

"Five days, maximum."

"That's tight, General."

"It's as long as she'll allow. And let me make myself plain, Delorran. You're to bring back that artifact. If you can return with the Wolverines too, that's fine. But should they prove . . . unco-operative, she'll settle for their heads. Given your past history with Stryke, I imagine you have no problem with that."

"None, sir. But . . ."

"But what? You'll outnumber them at least three to one. That seems like good odds to me. Or have I got the wrong orc for the job?"

"*No*, sir," Delorran quickly responded. "It's just that the Wolverines' kill tally is one of the highest of any of the warbands in the horde."

"I know that, Captain. It's why I've assigned the best troopers we have to this mission."

"I'm not saying it's going to be impossible, sir. Just difficult."

"Nobody promised you an easy ride." He stared hard at the officer's earnest face, and added, "Her Majesty's position is that, as with the Wolverines, the loss rate of the troopers under your command is . . . without limit."

"Sir?"

"Do I have to spell it out? You will spend as many lives on this mission as may be necessary."

"I see." His tone was doubtful, troubled.

"Look at it this way, Delorran. If you return without her prize, she'll have you all put to death anyway. Horribly, knowing her. Weigh that against losing only some of your troop, and your cer-tain promotion. Not to mention evening the score in the griev-ance you have with Stryke. Of course, if you'd prefer me to find someone else—"

"No, General. That won't be necessary."

"Anyway, such talk could be pointless. Your quarry may already be dead."

"The Wolverines? I doubt it, sir. I'd say they weren't that easy to kill."

"Then why no word from them? If they're not dead it's just as unlikely they've been captured. They might have fallen prey to one of the afflictions the humans spread, of course, but I think them too careful for that. Which only leaves betrayal. And there were no grounds to believe any of them might turn out traitors."

"I'm not so sure. Not all orcs are happy with our present situation, as you know, sir."

"Do you have reason to believe Stryke and his band harboured such thoughts?"

"I claim no knowledge of their thoughts, sir."

"Then keep your fancies to yourself, that kind of talk is dangerous. Think only of the cylinder. It has the highest priority. I'm relying on you, Delorran. If you fail, we both suffer Jennesta's wrath."

The Captain nodded grimly. "Stryke's death will prevent that fate. I won't let you down, sir."

They were ready to move. The only disagreement was where.

"I say we get ourselves back to Cairnbarrow and confess all to Jennesta," argued Haskeer. A handful of his supporters in the assembled warband murmured approval. "We have pellucid, and that should stand for *something*. Let's go back and throw ourselves on her mercy."

"We'd be in for a hard landing, comrade," Alfray said. "And the crystal wasn't what she sent us for."

"Alfray's right," Stryke agreed. "The only chance we have is to regain that cylinder."

"If we are going to look for it, why don't we send one or two of the band to Jennesta to explain what the rest of us are doing?" Alfray suggested.

Stryke shook his head. "To their deaths? No. All of us and the cylinder, or not at all."

"But where do we look?" Coilla wanted to know.

"It has to be the kobolds' homeland," Jup said.

"All the way to Black Rock?" Haskeer scoffed. "That's long odds, shortshanks."

"Can you think of a *better* idea?"

Haskeer's resentful silence indicated he couldn't.

"They could have gone anywhere," Coilla told the dwarf.

"True. But we don't know where anywhere is. Black Rock we know how to get to."

Stryke smiled thinly. "Jup's got a point. We might spend our lives combing this countryside for those bastards. Black Rock makes more sense, and if the group that robbed us aren't there now, they might turn up."

Haskeer spat. *"Might."*

"You want to head back to Cairnbarrow, Sergeant, go ahead." Stryke scanned the Wolverines' faces. "That goes for anybody here. You can tell Jennesta where we've gone before she skins you."

Nobody took him up on the offer.

"It's settled, then; Black Rock. What do you think, Alfray, a week?"

"About that. Maybe more 'cause of the horses we lost. Five or six of us are going to have to double up. And don't forget Meklun. It was bad luck not finding a wagon at Homefield. Dragging him's going to slow us."

Heads turned to the wounded trooper, strapped to his make-shift litter. His face was deathly pale.

"We'll look for more horses on the way," Stryke said, "maybe a wagon."

"We could always leave him," Haskeer put in.

"I'll remember that if you ever catch a bad wound yourself."

Haskeer frowned and shut up.

"What about splitting into two groups?" proposed Coilla. "One of the fit, going ahead to Black Rock; the other Meklun, the walking wounded and some able bodies, following on."

"No. Too easy pickings for more ambushes. I've lost the cylinder, I don't want to lose half the band as well. We stick together. Now let's get out of here."

Some of the Wolverines' less essential kit had to be discarded, and the pellucid redistributed, to make up for the shortage of horses. There were a few petty squabbles over who had to share mounts, but several well-aimed kicks from the officers restored order. Iron rations and water were shared out. Meklun's litter was harnessed.

It was late afternoon before they set off on a southerly bearing. This time Stryke didn't neglect to send scouts ahead of the main party.

He rode at the head of the column, Coilla beside him.

"What do we do when we get to Black Rock?" she said. "Would you have us take on the whole kobold nation?"

"The gods alone know, Coilla. I'm making this up as I go along, if you hadn't noticed." He glanced behind him and added in a conspiratorial tone, "But don't tell them that."

"This is all we can do, isn't it, Stryke? Make for Black Rock, I mean."

"Only thing *I* could think of. Because the way I see it, if we can't get the cylinder back, at least we can have the glory of dying while we try."

"I see it that way too. Though it seems a pity we have to do it for Jennesta, and a human cause."

There she goes again, he thought. *What does she expect me to say?*

He was tempted to speak frankly, but didn't have the chance.

"You've no idea what's in the cylinder?" she wondered. "You were given no hint as to why it's so important?"

"Like I said, Jennesta didn't take me into her confidence," he replied wryly.

"Yet the kobolds obviously thought it was worth facing a warband to gain it."

"You know kobolds, the thieving little swine. They'll go for anything they think they can get away with."

"Your reckoning is that they were just acting on a venture?"

"Yes."

"So with all sorts of travellers crossing these parts, including merchant caravans, who wouldn't give them half the fight we did, they pick on us, a heavily armed band of a race that lives for combat. All on the off-chance we'd have something worth stealing. Does that seem likely?"

"You're saying they were after the cylinder? But how would they know we had it? Our mission was secret."

"Perhaps our secret mission wasn't so secret after all, Stryke."

7

". . . and ram what's left up your butt!" Stryke concluded.

His captain's feelings having been made clear, in vivid detail, Haskeer glowered murderously and tugged on his horse's reins. He cantered back to his place in the column.

"Don't bite *my* head off," Coilla ventured, "but didn't he have a point about stopping to rest?"

"Yes," Stryke grunted, "and we will. If I give the order now, though, it'll look like his doing." He nodded at a rise further along the trail. "We'll wait till we get to the other side of that."

They hadn't stopped since setting out, travelling through the night and the new morning. Now the sun was at its highest point, its meagre warmth finally dispelling the lingering chill.

The bluff surmounted, Stryke called a halt. A couple of troopers were sent ahead to alert the forward scouts. Meklun's litter was disengaged from the horse dragging it, and the make-shift stretcher carefully laid flat. Alfray pronounced him little improved.

As fires were lit and horses watered, Stryke went into a huddle with the other officers.

"We're not making bad headway," he announced, "despite the handicaps. But it's time for a decision on our route." He drew a dagger and knelt. "The human settlement . . . what was it called?"

"Homefield," Jup offered.

Stryke made a cross in a patch of hardened mud. "Homefield was here, in the northern end of the Great Plains, and the nearest hostile human colony to Cairnbarrow."

"Not any more," Haskeer remarked with dark glee.

Disregarding him, Stryke slashed a downward line. "We've been moving south." He carved another cross at the line's end. "To here.

We need to turn south-east for Black Rock. But we've got a problem." To the right and down a little from the second cross, he gouged a circle.

"Scratch," Coilla said.

"Right. The trolls' homeland. It's smack in the path of the most direct route to Black Rock."

Haskeer shrugged his shoulders. "So?"

"Given how belligerent trolls can be," Jup told him, "we should avoid it."

"*You* might want to run from a fight; *I* don't."

"We've no need of one, Haskeer," Stryke intervened coolly. "Why make extra trouble for ourselves?"

" 'Cause going round Scratch will cost us time."

"We'll lose a lot more if we get caught up in a fight there, and a fully armed warband riding through their territory is just the thing to start one. No, we'll skirt the place. Question is, which way?"

Coilla jabbed her finger at the improvised map. "The next-shortest way would be to head due east now, toward Heck-lowe and the coast. Then we'd make our way south, through or around Black Rock Forest, to Black Rock itself."

"I'm not happy about going near Hecklowe either," Stryke said. "It's a free port, remember. That means plenty of other elder races. We're bound to tangle with at least one that has a grudge against orcs. And the forest's infested with bandits."

"Not to mention that turning east from here takes us a bit too close to Cairnbarrow for comfort," Alfray added.

"The advantage of approaching Black Rock from the forest side is that we'd have the cover of trees," Jup put in.

"That's scant return for all the risks we'd run." Stryke employed his knife again, extending the line down beyond the elliptical shape he'd drawn. "I think we have to carry on south, past Scratch, *then* turn east."

Coilla frowned. "In which case, don't forget this." She leaned over and used her finger to outline a small cross below Scratch. "Weaver's Lea. A Uni settlement, like Homefield, but much bigger. Word is that the humans there are more fanatical than most."

"Is that possible?" Jup asked drily of no one in particular.

"We'd have to pass between the two," Stryke granted. "But it's all flat plains in those parts, so at least we could see trouble coming."

Alfray studied the markings. "It's the longest route, Stryke."

"I know, but it's also the safest. Or the least dangerous, anyway."

"Whatever damned route we take," Haskeer rumbled, "nobody's said anything about Black Rock being a short piss away from *there*." He plunged his own knife into the ground, to the right of Coilla's crude addition.

Jup glared at him. "That's supposed to mean Quatt, is it?"

"Where your kind comes from, yes. Being so close should make you feel at home."

"When are you going to stop blaming me for the wrong done by all dwarves?"

"When your race stops doing the humans' dirty work."

"I answer for myself, not my whole race. Others do what they must."

Haskeer bridled. "There's no *must* about helping the incomers!"

"What do you think *we're* doing? Or are you too stupid to notice who Jennesta's allied with?"

As with most spats between the sergeants, this one escalated rapidly.

"Don't lecture *me* on loyalty, rat's prick!"

"Go shove your head up a horse's arse!"

Faces twisted with malice, they both began to rise.

"Enough!" Stryke barked. "If you two want to tear each other apart, that's fine by me. But let's try to get home alive first, shall we?"

They eyed him, weighed the odds for a second, then backed off.

"You've all got your duties," he reminded them. "Move yourselves."

Haskeer couldn't resist a parting shot. "If we're going anywhere near Quatt," he snarled, "better watch your backs." He shot the dwarf a malicious look. "The locals are treacherous in those parts."

He and his fellow officers scattered to their chores. But Stryke motioned for Jup to stay.

"I know it's hard," he said, "but you have to hold back when you're provoked."

"Tell Haskeer that, Captain."

"You think I haven't? I've made it clear he's heading for a flogging, and not for the first time since I've led this band."

"I can take the insults about my race. The gods know I'm used to that. But he never lets up."

"He's bitter for his own reasons, Jup. You're just a handy scapegoat."

"It's when he questions my allegiance that my blood really boils."

"Well, you have to admit your race is notorious for selling its loyalty to the highest bidder."

"Some have, not all. *My* loyalty isn't for sale."

Stryke nodded.

"And there are those among the dwarves who say similar things about orcs," Jup added.

"Orcs fight only to further the Mani cause, and indirectly at that. We've little choice in the matter. At least your race has free will enough to decide. We were born into military service and have known no other way."

"I know that, Stryke. But you *do* have a choice. You could determine your own fate, as I did when I chose which side to back."

Stryke didn't like the way the conversation was going. It made him uneasy.

He avoided a direct reply by steering Jup to the topic he'd wanted to raise in the first place. "Maybe we orcs have a choice, maybe we don't. What we haven't got is farsight. Dwarves have, and we could use it now. Has your skill improved?"

"No, Stryke, it hasn't, and I've been trying, believe me."

"You're sensing nothing?"

"Only vague . . . *traces* is the nearest word, I suppose. Sorry, Captain; explaining to somebody from a race with no magical abilities isn't easy."

"But you are getting traces. Of what? Kirgizil tracks? Or—"

"As I said, *traces* is an inexact word. Language isn't enough to describe the skill. The point is that what I'm picking up doesn't help us. It's weak, muddled."

"Damn."

"Perhaps it's because we're still too close to Homefield. I've often noticed that the power seems lower where humans are concentrated."

"It could come back the further away we get, you mean?"

"It *might*. Truth to tell, farsight was always pretty basic in dwarves anyway, and nobody really knows how we or the other elder races draw the power, except it comes from the earth. If humans are digging and tearing in one place they can sever a line of energy, and it bleeds, starving wherever else it goes. So in some areas magic works, in others it doesn't."

"Know what I've never understood? If they're eating the magic, why don't they use it against us?"

Jup shrugged. "Who can say?"

After a couple of hours' fitful sleep, the Wolverines resumed their journey.

Far to their right flowed the Calyparr Inlet, marked by a fringe of trees. To their left, the Great Plains rolled in seemingly endless profusion. But the scene was askew. What had once been fecund now lacked vitality, and it seemed that much of the colour had washed out of the landscape. In many places the grass was turning yellow and dying in patches. Low-growing shrubbery was stunted and brittle. Tree barks were patterned with sickly parasitic growths. A brief fall of light rain was tawny-hued and smelt unwholesome, as though sulphurous.

Dusk saw them arriving at a point roughly parallel with Scratch. If they continued at the same rate, Stryke reckoned, they could turn east at dawn.

Riding alone at the head of the file, he was preoccupied with weightier thoughts than navigation. He pondered the mystery of the dreams that were afflicting him, and his sense of futility in the face of the odds stacked against them was growing. But what would happen if they didn't find the kobold raiding party, and the cylinder, was something he tried not to think about.

Melancholy had as cold a grip on him as the chill night air by the time one of the advance scouts appeared. The grunt was approaching at speed, his mount's nostrils huffing steamy clouds.

Reaching the column, he reined in sharply and wheeled the sweating horse about.

Stryke put out a hand to catch the trooper's reins, steadying his ride. "What is it, Orbon?"

"Encampment ahead, sir."

"Do they have horses?"

"Yes."

"Good. Let's see if we can parley for some."

"But Captain, it's an orc camp, and it looks deserted."

"Are you sure?"

"Zoda and me have been watching the place, and there's no sign of anything stirring 'cept the horses."

"All right. Go back to him and wait for us. Don't do anything till we get there."

"Sir!" The scout goaded his steed and galloped off.

Stryke called forward his officers and explained the situation.

"Is an orc camp something you'd expect to come across in these parts?" Jup asked.

"They're more common in our native northern regions, it's true," Stryke explained, "but there are a few nomadic orc clans. I suppose it could be one of those. Or a military unit on a mission, like us."

"If the scouts are reporting no activity, we should approach with caution," Coilla suggested.

"That's my feeling," Stryke agreed. "It may be an orc encampment, but that doesn't mean it's orcs we'll find there. Until we know better, we treat it as hostile. Let's go."

Ten minutes later they found Orbon waiting for them by a large copse. Its trees shed brown leaves and the bushes were turning autumnal colours, though summer's mid point was still a phase of the moon away.

Stryke had the band quietly dismount. The healing wounded were left with Meklun and the horses. Orbon in the lead, the rest stealthily entered the grove.

Ten paces in, the ground began to slope, and it was soon clear that the copse sheltered a sizeable trench-shaped indentation. They descended on a pulpy carpet of leaves to a fallen tree where Zoda, stretched full-length, kept watch.

Enough dappled light from the setting sun penetrated the swaying canopy to show what lay below.

Two modest roundhouses, topped with thatch, and a third, smaller still, its roof incomplete. Five or six lean-tos built of angled, lashed saplings covered by irregular-shaped remnants of coarse cloth. Sluggish spring water trickling feebly through churned mud. A pair of tree stumps and a connecting bough forming a roughly constructed hitching rail. Seven or eight cowed, strangely silent horses tethered to it.

As Stryke took it all in, the memory of the dream or vision he'd had came back to him, but in diametric opposition to what he now saw. The orc settlement in his dream had had a feeling of permanence. This was itinerant and ramshackle. The dream was redolent with light and clean air. This was dark and stifling. The dream was life-affirming. This spoke of death.

He heard Coilla whisper, "Abandoned, you think?"

"Wouldn't be surprised," Alfray replied in hushed tones, "bearing in mind it's close to Scratch *and* not that far from a Uni colony."

"But why leave the horses?"

Stryke roused himself. "Let's find out. Haskeer, take a third of the band and work your way round to the other side. Jup, Alfray, move another third to the right flank. Coilla and the rest, stay with me. We go in on my signal."

It took a few minutes for the groups to position themselves. When he was sure all were in place, Stryke stood and made a swift chopping motion with his arm. The Wolverines drew their weapons and began moving down toward the camp in a pincer formation.

They reached level without incident, save the nervous shying of several of the horses.

Around the crude dwellings the ground was strewn with objects of various kinds. An upended cooking cauldron, broken pottery, a trampled saddlebag, the bones of fowl, a discarded bow. Ashes of long-dead fires were heaped in several places.

Stryke led his detachment to the nearest roundhouse.

He raised a finger to his lips, and pointed with his blade to deploy the group around the shanty. When they were in place, he and Coilla crept to the entrance. It had no door; a piece of tattered sacking served the purpose. Swords up, they positioned themselves.

He nodded. Coilla ripped aside the cloth.

An overpoweringly foul smell hit them like a physical blow. It was mouldy, sweet, sickly and unmistakable.

The odour of decaying flesh.

Covering his mouth with his free hand, Stryke stepped inside. The light was poor, but it only took a few seconds for his eyes to adjust.

The hut was filled with dead orcs. They lay three and four deep on makeshift cots. Others completely covered the floor. A pall of corruption hung heavy in the air. Only the scurrying of carrion eaters disturbed the stillness.

Coilla was at Stryke's side, palm pressed against her mouth. She tugged at his arm and they backed out. They retreated from the entrance and gulped air as the rest of their group craned for a look inside the hut.

Stryke moved to the second of the larger roundhouses, Coilla in tow, arriving as Jup emerged ashen-faced. The stench was just as strong. A glance at the interior revealed an identical scene of huddled corpses.

The dwarf breathed deeply. "All females and young ones. Dead for some time."

"The same over there," Stryke told him.

"No adult males?"

"None I could see."

"Why not? Where are they?"

"I can't be sure, Jup, but I think this is a dispossessed camp."

"I'm still learning your ways, remember. What does that mean?"

"When a male orc's killed in military service, and his commander says it's cowardice, the dead warrior's mate and orphans are cast out. Some of the dispossessed band together."

"The rule's being rigidly applied since we came under Jennesta," Coilla added.

"They're left to fend for themselves?" Jup asked.

Stryke nodded. "It's an orc's lot."

"What did you expect?" Coilla said, reading the dwarf's expression. "A stipend and a tithed farm?"

Jup ignored the sarcasm. "Any idea what killed them, Captain?"

"Not yet. Mass suicide's not impossible, though. It's been known. Or maybe they—"

"*Stryke!*"

Haskeer was standing by the smallest hut, waving him over. Stryke went to him. Coilla, Jup and some of the others followed.

"One of 'em's still alive in there." Haskeer jerked his thumb at the entrance.

Stryke peered into the gloom. "Get Alfray. And bring a torch!" He entered.

There was just one prone figure, lying on a bed of filthy straw. Stryke approached, and heard strained breathing. He stooped. In the poor light he could just make out the features of an old orc female. Her eyes were closed and her face glistened under a film of perspiration.

A murmur at Stryke's back heralded Alfray's arrival.

"Is she wounded?"

"Can't tell. Where's that torch?"

"Haskeer's bringing it."

The aged orc's eyes opened. Her lips trembled, as though she were trying to say something. Alfray bent to listen. There was a final outrush of breath, like a sigh, and the distinctive sound of the death rattle.

Haskeer came in with a burning brand.

"Give it here." Alfray took the torch and held it over the dead female. "*Gods!*"

He quickly pulled away from her, nearly colliding with Stryke.

"What is it?"

"Look." Alfray stretched the torch at arm's length, bathing the corpse in light.

Stryke saw.

"Get out," he said. "Both of you. *Now!*"

Haskeer and Alfray scrambled to exit, Stryke in their wake.

Outside, the rest of the band had gathered.

"Did you touch her?" Stryke demanded of Haskeer.

"Me? No . . . no, I didn't."

"Or any of the other dead?"

"*No.*"

Stryke turned to the Wolverines. "Did *any* of you touch the corpses?"

They shook their heads.

"What's going on, Stryke?" Coilla asked.

"Red spot."

Several of the band stepped back on reflex. Exclamations and curses ran through the ranks. Grunts began covering their mouths and noses with kerchiefs.

Jup hissed, "*Bastard* humans."

"The horses can't get it," Stryke said. "We'll take them. I want us out of here fast. And burn everything!"

He snatched the torch from Alfray and hurled it into the hut. The straw caught immediately. In seconds the interior was an inferno.

The band dispersed to spread the fire.

8

Delorran's boot crunched against something. Looking down, he found he'd trodden on a broken slab of wood displaying part of a neatly painted word.

It read: *Homef*

He kicked it aside and returned his attention to the burnt-out human settlement. His troopers were sifting through the ruins, rummaging in debris, upending charred planks, disturbing clouds of ash dust.

The search had begun before dawn. Now it was early afternoon and they were no nearer finding anything of importance, least of all the cylinder. Nor was there any sign of what had happened to the Wolverines. That much had been obvious from shortly after they arrived, and Delorran had sent out parties to scour the surrounding area for clues. None had yet returned.

He paced the compound. An unseasonable wind was gusting in from the north, picking up bite as it funnelled over the chalky line of far-off glaciers. The Captain puffed into his cupped hands.

One of his sergeants came away from the search and trotted toward him. He shook his head as he approached.

"Nothing?" Delorran said.

"No, sir. Neither the item nor any orc bones in the ashes. Only human."

"And we know none of the scavengers reported collecting Wolverine corpses for their pyres after the battle, except possibly a couple of grunts. Stryke and most of his officers are well enough known to be recognised, so we can take that as true."

"Then you reckon they're still alive, sir?"

"I never really doubted it. I couldn't see a quality band losing out to the kind of opposition they met here. The real mystery is what's happened to them."

The sergeant, a stolid veteran, his tattoos of rank fading, was better suited to combat than solving riddles. The best he could do was remind Delorran of another puzzle. "What about the empty cellar in the barn, Captain? You think that's anything to do with it?"

"I don't know. But a cleaned-out silo, not even a grain, at a time when you'd expect to find corn down there seems odd. I'd wager the humans were using it to store *something*."

"Loot?"

"Could be. What it comes to is that the Wolverines aren't dead, they're gone; and it looks like they've taken at least one valuable with them."

Delorran's rivalry with the Wolverines' leader and his belief that he, not Stryke, should have been given command of the band were widely known. As was the long-standing animosity between their respective clans. Aware of the possibility that Delorran might have his own reasons for questioning Stryke's honesty, and the shoals of inter-clan politics, the sergeant made no comment. He kept to a neutral "Permission to resume duties, sir."

The Captain waved him away.

Well beyond midpoint, the arching sun continued its inexorable journey across the sky. Half his allotted time used up, Delorran's apprehension was growing. He should be heading back for Cairnbarrow in the next couple of hours to meet the deadline. And quite possibly his death.

A rapid decision had to be made.

There were three options. Finding the cylinder here and returning home in triumph seemed less likely by the minute. That left going back without it and facing Jennesta's wrath, or disobeying orders and continuing to look for the Wolverines.

Cursing the Queen's impatience, he agonised about what to do.

His deliberations were interrupted by the appearance of two of the scouts he'd sent out earlier.

They reined in their lathering horses beside him. One rider was a lowly grunt, the other a corporal. The latter dismounted.

"Pack four reporting, sir!"

Delorran gave him a curt nod.

"I think our group's come up with something, sir. We've found signs of a fight south of here, in a small valley."

A fragile hope stirred in the Captain's breast. "Go on."

"The place is littered with dead kobolds, kirgizils and horses."

"Kobolds?"

"From the lizard tracks down the valley sides it looks like they ambushed somebody."

"Doesn't mean it was the Wolverines. Unless you found any of their bodies."

"No, sir. But we came across discarded rations, standard orc issue. And this." The corporal dug into his belt pouch and retrieved the find. He dropped it on to Delorran's outstretched palm.

It was a necklace of three snow-leopard fangs, its strand broken.

Delorran stared at it, absently fingering the five identical trophies looped around his own throat. Orcs were the only race that wore these particular emblems of their mettle, and they were a prerequisite of the officer class.

He made his decision.

"You've done well."

"Thank you, sir."

"Your group will lead us to this valley. Meanwhile, I want you to find yourself a fresh horse and carry out a special mission."

"Yes, sir."

"Congratulations, Corporal. You're going to get home earlier than the rest of us. I need you to carry a message to Cairnbarrow with all speed. For the Queen."

"Sir." This time there was a slight hesitancy in the corporal's response.

"You're to deliver the message to General Kysthan personally. No one else. Is that understood?"

"Sir."

"The General is to tell Jennesta that I have a lead on where the Wolverines have gone and am in hot pursuit. I'm sure I can catch them and return the item the Queen desires. I beg more time, and will send further messages. Repeat that."

The corporal paled a little as he recited it. He didn't doubt it wasn't what Jennesta would want to hear. But he was disciplined enough, or fearful enough, to obey orders without question.

"Good," Delorran said. He handed back the necklace. "Give this to the General and explain how it was found. Best pick a couple of troopers to go with you, and burn hell for leather. Dismissed."

Gloomy-faced, the corporal remounted and made off, the silent grunt in his wake.

Delorran was giving Jennesta no choice. It was a dangerous ploy, and his only chance of surviving it lay in recovering the artifact. But he couldn't see another way.

He consoled himself with the thought that she had to be amenable to reason, notwithstanding her dreadful reputation.

Jennesta finished eviscerating the sacrifice and laid down her tools.

Her work had left a sizeable opening in the cadaver's chest, and entrails dangled wetly from his excavated abdomen. But her skill was such that only one or two tiny crimson flecks stained her diaphanous white shift.

She went to the altar and used the flame of a black candle to light another bundle of incense sticks. The heady fug already perfuming the chamber grew thicker.

A pair of her orc bodyguards were moving back and forth clutching heavy buckets in both hands. One of them spilled a dribble of the contents, leaving a thin trail on the flagstones.

"Don't waste that!" she snapped irritably. "Unless you want to replace it yourselves!"

The guards exchanged furtive looks, but exercised more care as they lugged their pails to a large round tub and emptied them into it. The tub was built like a barrel, with seasoned wooden uprights sealed at the joins and embraced by metal hasps. It differed from a barrel in having much lower sides, and in being big enough to comfortably hold a reclining dray horse, should Jennesta choose to use it for such a purpose. Which as far as her orc attendants were concerned was not beyond the bounds of possibility.

She walked over to the vessel and contemplated its interior. The orcs returned, the muscles on their arms standing out as they hauled four more buckets. Jennesta watched as they tipped in the load.

"That'll do," she said. "Leave me."

They bowed, demonstrating a peculiarly orcish form of inelegance. The echoing thump of the weighty door marked their departure.

Jennesta turned back to the tub of fresh blood.

She knelt and breathed deep of its unique aroma. Then she swished her fingertips through the viscous liquid. It was warm, not far short of body temperature, which made it a better medium. As an agent of the ritual it would intensify the power that had once come naturally but these days had to be nourished.

Her cat sashayed into range, meowing.

Jennesta stroked her between the ears, light fingers softly massaging the animal's furry crown. "Not now, my love, I have to concentrate."

Sapphire purred and slunk away.

Jennesta focused on her meditations. Brow furrowed, she began reciting an incantation in the old tongue. The strange concatenation of guttural and singsong phrases rose from a near whisper to something resembling a shriek. Then it fell and climbed again.

The candles and torches scattered around the chamber billowed in an unseen wind. Somehow the very atmosphere seemed to compress, to converge and bear down on the tub's scarlet cargo. The blood rippled and churned. It sloshed about disgustingly. Bubbles appeared and burst, sluggishly, releasing wisps of foul-smelling rust-coloured vapour.

Then the surface settled and rapidly coagulated. A crust formed. It took on a different aspect, a rainbow effect, like oil on water.

Beads of perspiration dotted Jennesta's forehead and lank strands of hair were plastered to it. As she looked on, the clotted gore gently shimmered as though lit by an inner radiance. A wavering image started to form slowly on the lustre.

A face.

The eyes were its most striking feature. Dark, flinty, cruel. Not unlike Jennesta's own. But overall the face was much less human than hers.

In a voice that might have been coming from the depths of a fathomless ocean, the phantasm spoke.

"What do you want, Jennesta?" There was no element of surprise in the imperious, disdainful tone.

"I thought it was time we talked."

"Ah, the great champion of the incomers' cause deigns to speak to me."

"I do *not* champion humans, Adpar. I simply support certain elements for my own benefit. And for the benefit of others."

That was greeted by a mocking laugh. *"Self-deceiving as ever. You could at least be honest about your motives."*

"And follow *your* example?" Jennesta retorted. "Pull your head from the sand and join with me. Then perhaps we'd stand a better chance of preserving the old ways."

"We live the old ways here, without stooping to consort with humans, or asking their permission. You'll come to regret allying yourself with them."

"Mother might have taken a different view on that."

"The blessed Vermegram was great in many ways, but her judgement was not perfect in all respects," the apparition replied frostily. *"But we cover old ground. I don't suppose it was your intention to engage in small talk. Why are you troubling me?"*

"I want to ask you about something I've lost."

"And what might that be? A hoard of gems, perhaps? A prized grimoire? Your virginity?"

Jennesta clenched her fists and held her building irritation in check. "The object is an artifact."

"Very mysterious, Jennesta. Why are you telling me this?"

"The thought occurred that you might have . . . heard word of its whereabouts."

"You still haven't said what it is."

"It's an item of no value to anyone but me."

"That's not very helpful."

"Look, Adpar, either you know what I'm talking about or you don't."

"I can see your difficulty. If I know nothing of this artifact, *you don't want to run the risk of giving details lest it whet my interest. If I do know, it must be because I had a hand in taking it from you. Is that what I'm accused of?"*

"I'm not accusing you of anything."

"That's just as well, because I have no idea what you're talking about."

Jennesta wasn't sure if this was the truth, or whether Adpar was playing a familiar game. It aggravated her that she still couldn't tell after all these years. "All right," she said. "Leave it be."

"Of course, if this . . . whatever it is is something you want so badly, perhaps I should take an interest in it . . ."

"You'd be well advised to stay out of my affairs, Adpar. And if I find you had anything to do with what I've lost—"

"You know, you look peaky, dear. Are you suffering from a morbidity?"

"No I am not!"

"I expect it's the drain of energy in your part of the country. There isn't anything like as much of a problem here. I wonder if there could be a connection? Between the thing you've lost and your need to make up for the missing energy, I mean. Could it be a magical totem of some kind? Or—"

"Don't play the innocent, Adpar, it's so bloody infuriating!"

"No more than being suspected of theft!"

"Oh, for the gods' sake go and—"

A little undulation started up the side of the conjured face. From a pinpoint epicentre, tiny waves moved indolently across the surface, distorting the face and lapping against the tub's wall.

"Now look what you've done!" Adpar complained.

"Me? *You,* more like it!"

A miniature sparkling whirlpool curled into existence, turning lethargically. The eddies calmed down and an oval silhouette appeared. Gradually it became more distinct.

Another face appeared on the soupy crimson surface.

It, too, had eyes that were striking, but for the opposite reason that Jennesta's and Adpar's were. Of the three, it had features most resembling a human's.

Jennesta adopted an expression of distaste. *"You,"* she said, making the word sound like a profanity.

"I should have known," Adpar sighed.

"You're disturbing the ether with your bickering," the new arrival told them.

"And you're disturbing us with your presence," Jennesta retorted.

"Why can't we ever communicate without you butting in, Sanara?" Adpar asked.

"You know why; the link is too strong. I can't avoid being drawn in. Our heritage binds us together."

"One of the gods' crueller tricks," Jennesta muttered.

Adpar piped up with, *"Why don't you ask Sanara about your precious bauble?"*

"Very funny."

"What are you talking about?" Sanara wanted to know.

"Jennesta's lost something she's desperate to get back."

"Leave it, Adpar."

"But surely, of us all Sanara is in a location where a boost to magic is most needed."

"Stop trying to stir trouble!" Jennesta snapped. "And I never said the artifact had to do with magic."

"I'm not sure I'd want to be involved with something you've lost, Jennesta," Sanara remarked. *"It's likely to be troublesome, or dangerous."*

"Oh, shut up, you self-righteous prig!"

"That's very unkind," Adpar said with transparently false sympathy. *"Sanara has some terrible problems at the moment."*

"Good!"

Relishing Jennesta's exasperation, Adpar burst into derisive laughter. And Sanara looked on the point of mouthing some piece of wholesome advice Jennesta was bound to find nauseating.

"You can both go to hell!" she raged, bringing her fists down hard on the pair of smug faces.

Their images fragmented and dissolved. Her pummelling split the gory crust. The blood was cool now, almost cold, and it splashed as she rained wrathful blows, showering her face and clothing.

Fury vented, Jennesta slumped, panting, by the side of the tub.

She berated herself. When would she learn that contact with Adpar, and inevitably Sanara, never did anything to improve her temper? The day was fast approaching, she decided for the hundredth time, when the link between them all would have to be severed. Permanently.

Sensing a titbit, in the way of cats, Sapphire arrived and rubbed sensuously against her mistress's leg. A scab of congealed blood had stuck to Jennesta's forearm. She peeled it off and dangled it in front of the animal. Sapphire sniffed it, whiskers quivering, then sank her teeth into the scummy treat. She made wet, mushy sounds as she chewed.

Jennesta thought of the cylinder, and of the wretched warband she had been foolish enough to send for it. More than half the time she had granted for the item's return was used up. She would have to make contingency plans in the event of Kysthan's emissary failing to recover her prize. Though even the gods wouldn't be able to help him if he hadn't.

But she would have what was hers. The warband would be hunted down like dogs and delivered to her justice, whatever it took.

She idly licked the blood from her hands and dreamed of torments to inflict on the Wolverines.

9

"You must feel bad," Stryke said.

Alfray touched his bare neck and nodded. "I took my first tooth at thirteen seasons. Haven't been parted from the necklace since. Till now."

"Lost in the ambush?"

"Had to be. So used to wearing it, I didn't even notice. Coilla pointed it out today."

"But you won the trophies, Alfray. Nobody can take that away. You'll replace them, given time."

"Time I haven't got. Not enough to gain another three, anyway. Oldest in the band, Stryke. Besting snow leopards unarmed is a sport for young orcs."

Alfray fell into a brooding silence. Stryke let him be. He knew what a blow to his pride it was to lose the emblems of courage, the symbols that testified to full orchood.

They rode on at the head of the convoy.

None spoke of it, but what they had seen at the orc encampment, and their perilous situation, hung heavy on the entire band. Alfray's melancholy chimed with the Wolverines' generally gloomy mood.

With horses for all, they made better progress, though Meklun, unable to ride and still on his litter, continued to slow them. Several hours earlier they had veered south-east, cutting across the Great Plains toward Black Rock. Before the day was out they should have reached a point midway between Scratch and Weaver's Lea.

Stryke's hope was that they'd pass through the corridor without meeting trouble from either disputatious trolls to the north or zealous humans in the south.

The terrain had begun to change. Plains were giving way to

hilly country, with shallow valleys and winding trails. Scrub was more prevalent. Pastures shaded into heathlands. They were nearing an area dotted with human settlements. Stryke decided it was safer to treat them all as hostile, whether Uni or Mani.

A commotion down the line broke his train of thought. He looked back. Haskeer and Jup were squabbling loudly.

Stryke sighed. "Keep our heading," he told Alfray, and swung his horse out.

In the moment it took to gallop to them, the sergeants had come close to blows. They quietened on seeing him.

"You two my joint seconds or spoilt hatchlings?"

"It's his fault," Haskeer complained. "He—"

"*My* fault?" Jup snapped. "You bastard! I should—"

"*Shut it!*" Stryke ordered. "You're supposed to be our chief scout, Jup; earn your keep. Prooq and Gleadeg need relieving. Take Calthmon, and leave your shares of crystal with Alfray."

Jup shot his antagonist a parting scowl and spurred off.

Stryke turned his attention to Haskeer. "You're pushing me," he said. "Much more and I'll have the skin off your back."

"Shouldn't have his kind in the band," Haskeer muttered.

"This isn't a debate, Sergeant. Work with him or make your own way home. Your choice." He headed back to the column's prow.

Haskeer noticed that the grunts within hearing distance of the dressing-down were staring at him. "We wouldn't be in this mess if we were properly led," he grumbled sourly.

The troopers looked away.

When Stryke reached Alfray, Coilla came forward to join them.

"On this bearing we'll be passing nearer Weaver's Lea than Scratch. What's our plan if we meet trouble?" she asked.

"Weaver's Lea's one of the older Uni settlements, and one of the most fanatical," Stryke said. "That makes them unpredictable. Just bear that in mind."

"Uni, Mani, who cares?" Alfray put in. "They're all *humans*, aren't they?"

"We're supposed to be helping the Manis," Coilla reminded him.

"Only because we've no choice. What choice did we *ever* have?"

"All we wanted, once," Stryke told him. "Anyway, it makes sense to support the Manis. They're less hostile to the elder races. More important, it helps us to have the humans divided. Think how much worse it'd be if they were united."

"Or if one side won," Coilla added.

Ahead of the column, and out of its sight, Jup and Calthmon took over as pathfinders. Jup watched as the pair of troopers they had relieved, Prooq and Gleadeg, rode back towards the main party.

Only now was he beginning to calm down from his latest tangle with Haskeer. He goaded his mount, a mite harder than necessary, and concentrated on trail-blazing.

The landscape grew more cluttered. Hillocks and clumps of trees were increasingly common, taller grass made the track less certain.

"Know these parts, Sergeant?" Calthmon asked. He spoke quietly, as though a raised voice might betray their presence, despite the wilderness in all directions.

"A little. From here on we can expect the terrain to alter quite a bit."

As though on cue, the track they followed dipped and started to curve. The undergrowth on either side thickened. They began to round a blind bend.

"But if the band keeps to its present path," Jup continued, "we shouldn't have anything . . ."

A roadblock stretched across the trail.

". . . to worry about."

The barricade was made up of a side-on farm wagon and a wall of sturdy tree trunks. It was guarded by humans dressed uniformly in black. They numbered at least a score and were heavily armed.

Jup and Calthmon pulled back on their reins just as the humans spotted them.

"Oh *shit*," Jup groaned.

A great yell went up from the roadblock. Waving swords,

axes and clubs, all but a handful of the humans rushed to mount their horses. Dwarf and orc fought to turn their own steeds.

Then they were racing away, pursued by a howling posse baying for blood.

"One day a member of the United Expeditionary Force, the next bartered into Jennesta's service," Stryke recalled. "You know how it was."

"I do," Coilla replied, "and I expect you felt the same way I did."

"How so?"

"Weren't *you* angry at having no say in the matter?"

Again, he was confounded by her frankness. And by her accurate reading of his feelings. "Perhaps," he conceded.

"You're at war with your upbringing, Stryke. You can't bring yourself to admit it was an injustice."

The way she had of gauging his innermost thoughts was discomforting for Stryke. He answered in a roundabout fashion. "It was hardest on the likes of Alfray." A jab of his thumb indicated their field surgeon, down the line, riding next to Meklun's litter. "Change isn't easy at his age."

"It's you we were talking about."

His response was deferred by the sight of Prooq and Gleadeg appearing on the trail ahead. They galloped to him.

"Advance scouts reporting, sir," Prooq recited crisply. "Sergeant Jup's taken over."

"Anything we should look out for?"

"No, sir. The way forward seemed clear."

"All right. Join the column."

The troopers left.

"You were saying," Coilla prompted. "About the change."

Are you just naturally single-minded, Stryke thought, *or is there a reason for all these questions?* "Well, things didn't change that much for me under our new mistress," he said. "Not at first. I kept my rank, and I could still fight the real enemy, if only one faction of them."

"And you were given command of the Wolverines."

"Eventually. Though not everybody liked it."

"What did you think about finding yourself serving a part-human ruler?"

"It was . . . unusual," he responded cautiously.

"You resented it, you mean. Like the rest of us."

"I wasn't happy," he admitted. "As you said yourself, we're in a tough spot. Victory for either Manis or Unis can only strengthen the human side." He shrugged. "But it's an orc's lot to obey orders."

She looked at him long and hard. "Yes. That's what it's come to." There was no misreading her bitterness.

He felt an affinity, and wanted to take the conversation further.

A nearby grunt shouted something. Stryke couldn't make it out. The rest of the band started yelling.

Jup and Calthmon were returning, riding all-out.

Stryke raised himself in his stirrups. "What the—?"

Then he saw the mob of humans chasing them. They were black-garbed, in long frock coats and breeches of coarsely woven cloth, with high leather boots. He reckoned their number matched the Wolverines'. There was no time to charge.

"*Close ranks!*" he roared. "*To me! Close up!*"

The band surged forward, rallying to their commander. Swiftly the horses were formed into a defensive semi-circle facing the enemy, with Meklun's litter behind them. The company drew their weapons.

Jup and Calthmon's pursuers slowed on seeing the band, allowing the pair to increase their lead. But they still kept coming, spreading out from a bunch to a line.

"Hold fast!" Stryke ordered. "No quarter and no retreat!"

"As if we would," Coilla remarked in a gallows-humour tone. She swiped the air with her blade, limbering for a fight.

Cheered on by their comrades, Jup and Calthmon reached the Wolverines, their steeds lathering.

Two heartbeats later the humans came in like a storm tide.

Many of the horses of both groups wheeled round at the last moment, their riders engaging side-on.

Stryke faced a heavily bearded, weather-beaten attacker, eyes flaming with bloodlust. He brandished a hatchet and was swinging it wildly, but the weapon was being used with more energy than precision.

Blocking a pass, Stryke delivered a thrust of his own. His opponent's horse bucked and the sword plunged harmlessly over the human's shoulder. Stryke quickly returned the blade and parried another swing. They exchanged half a dozen ringing blows. The human overreached himself. Stryke chopped down hard on his exposed arm, severing hand from wrist. It fell away, still clutching the axe.

Gushing blood and bellowing, the human took a death stroke to the chest and went down.

Stryke turned to a second assailant as Coilla despatched her first. She wrenched free her blade just in time to throw up a guard. It stopped a swipe from a dumpy, muscular individual armed with a broadsword. Batting off several more lunges, she sent a whistling slash at the human's head. He ducked and avoided it.

Without pause, Coilla went in again, ramming her sword low. Unexpectedly dextrous, the human twisted in his saddle and the blade pierced only air. He went on the offensive again. While she held him at bay with the sword, Coilla's other hand found her belt and plucked a knife. She flung it underarm and punctured his heart.

Off to the left, Haskeer held his sword two-handed, flapping reins forgotten, as he laid about the enemy. He split skulls, caved chests, hacked deep into limbs. Pink flesh was lacerated, bones cracked, ruby showers soaked all in range. Far gone in berserk frenzy, Haskeer took no account of human or animal, his blade carving horses and riders alike.

In the screaming, trampling chaos, a handful of the attackers flowed around the defensive barrier to strike at the Wolverines' vulnerable rear. Alfray and a couple of grunts turned to deal with the threat. Battle raged about Meklun's litter, crashing hooves and plummeting bodies failing to stir the insensible form.

Almost toppled from his mount by a club's glancing blow, in righting himself Alfray slashed his foe's saddle straps. The human pitched to one side and hit the ground. As he struggled to his feet, a riderless horse flattened him.

Joining the defence of the band's rump, Jup sideswiped one of two raiders who had Alfray boxed in. Dwarf and human crossed swords. Jup laid open the man's arm and followed through by planting cold steel in his ribcage.

A human's sword connected with Stryke's and bounced off. Stryke's response was a grievous blow to the other's neck, hewing flesh to the bone. The next to take the victim's place got equally short shrift. He managed to conjoin with Stryke's blade twice before a raking sword tip ribboned his face and sent him howling.

Fighting with sword and dagger, Coilla held off a pair of aggressors employing a crude pincer movement. One caught the long blade's edge across his throat. A second later the other halted the short blade's flight with his chest.

There being no other opponent to deal with, she turned her attention to Stryke. He was locked in combat with a scrawny, long-limbed antagonist, sandy-haired and blotchy-skinned. She judged it an adolescent of the species, and its artless movements betrayed a life unsullied by warfare. The youth's fear was palpable.

Stryke put an end to it with a swinging blow to the thorax. A smartly administered follow-through to the neck brought clean decapitation. Coilla's face was speckled with red drizzle from the spray.

She wiped the back of a hand across her eyes and spat to clear her mouth. It was a purely reflex action, undertaken with no more distaste than if the liquid had been rainwater. "They're finished, Stryke," she stated flatly.

He didn't need her confirmation. Human corpses littered the area. Only two or three remained alive to engage the band, and all were getting the worst of it. Haskeer was beating one over the head repeatedly with what looked like a cudgel. Closer examination showed it to be a human arm, white bone protruding from its sticky end.

A handful of the enemy were fleeing on horseback. About a third of the Wolverine grunts, whooping triumphantly, started after them. Stryke bawled and they abandoned the chase, though

returning reluctantly. The human survivors disappeared from
view.

Alfray knelt by Meklun's litter. The band began gathering
discarded weapons and binding their wounds. Haskeer and Jup
made their separate ways to Stryke and Coilla's side.

"Seems the injuries we took weren't too serious," Jup related.

"No wonder," Haskeer sneered. "They fought like pixies."

"They were farmers, not fighters. Uni zealots, by the look
of them, probably out of Weaver's Lea. Hardly a true warrior
among 'em."

"But you didn't know that," Haskeer growled accusingly.

"What you getting at?" Jup demanded.

"You brought them straight to us. What kind of idiot does
something like that? You put the whole band in danger."

"What did you expect me to do, meathead?"

"You should have led them away from here, taken them somewhere else."

"Then what? Were Calthmon and me supposed to have lost
ourselves out there?" He swept a hand at the wilderness. "Or let
'em take us to protect *you?*"

Haskeer glared at him. "That would've been no great loss."

"Well, fuck you, pisspot! This is a warband, remember? We
stick together!"

"They're gonna have to stick *you* together when I'm finished,
you little snot!"

"*Hey!*" Coilla snapped. "How about you two shutting your
mouths long enough for us to get out of here?"

"She's right," Stryke said. "We don't know how many more
humans might be heading for us. And farmers or not, if there's
enough of them, we've got a problem. Where did you run into
them, Jup?"

"Roadblock," he replied sullenly. "Up the trail."

"So we have to find another way forward."

"More time wasted," Haskeer grumbled.

The shadows were lengthening. Another couple of hours and
they'd be travelling in the dark, a prospect Stryke didn't welcome if there were rampaging mobs of humans on the loose.

"I'm doubling the number of scouts riding ahead," he decided, "and I want four covering our rear. You're in charge of that, Haskeer. I'll organise the advance scouts myself. Get on and pick your detail."

Glowering, the sergeant moved away.

"I'm going to check on Meklun," Stryke told Coilla and Jup. "You two get the column moving, but keep it slow until the outriders have left."

He trotted off.

The dwarf gave Coilla a rueful look.

"Spit it out," she told him.

"This all seemed so simple when it started; now things are getting complicated," he complained. "*And* more dangerous than I counted on."

"What's the matter, you want to live forever?"

Jup thought about it.

"Yes," he said.

10

Jennesta had made the woman's end swift compared to her normal practice. Not through any sense of mercy, but rather a mixture of boredom and the need to attend to more pressing matters.

She climbed down from the altar and unstrapped the bloodied unicorn horn she used as a dildo. With the deft skill of experience she quickly disembowelled the human's corpse, so speedily that the heart was still throbbing as she raised it to her mouth.

The repast was no more than adequate. Her tastes were growing either more refined or more jaded.

Physically and magically refreshed, but hardly better tempered, she sucked the juices from her fingers and brooded about the cylinder. The deadline she'd imposed on the hunting party was nearly up. Whether they'd succeeded or not, the time had come to hedge her bets and increase pressure in the search for the Wolverines.

It felt cold. The chill penetrated even here, in her inner sanctum. A log fire had been laid in the huge hearth but remained unlit. Jennesta stretched a hand. A pulsing bolt of luminescence, straight as a die, stabbed the air silently. The fire ignited with a roar. Basking in its warmth, she remonstrated with herself for needlessly wasting the energy just obtained. But, as ever, her delight at manipulating physicality was the stronger emotion.

Reaching out, she tugged a bell pull. Two orc guards entered. One had a bolt of sacking under his arm.

"You know what to do," she told them. Her tone was offhand and she didn't bother looking their way.

They set about cleaning up the mess. The sacking was shaken

out and placed on the floor. Taking the body by its wrists and ankles, the guards lowered and covered it.

Uninterested, Jennesta pulled the cord again, twice this time.

As they left, the orcs passed another attendant coming in. Momentarily wide-eyed at the sight of their blood-soaked bundle, the elf hastily adopted a bland, impassive expression.

The menial was new, and Jennesta found it as hard to guess its sex as she had its recent predecessor. Although she'd found out in the end, of course. She made a mental note, again, to slow down the rate at which she was getting through the servants. None of them was around long enough to learn the job.

Curtly instructed, the elf assisted the Queen in dressing. Jennesta chose black, as was her custom for excursions outside the castle; skin-tight leather top and riding breeches, the latter tucked into thigh-high, tall-heeled boots of the same material. Over this she donned an ankle-length sable cloak, fashioned from the pelts of forest bears. Her hair was pinned up under a matching fur cap.

She discharged the servant brusquely. The elf retreated, bowing low and ignored.

Jennesta went to a table by the altar and inspected a collection of coiled whips. She selected one of her favourites to complete her ensemble. Slipping a slender hand through its wrist thong, she walked to the door, pausing for a second to check herself in an adjacent mirror.

The orc bodyguards outside snapped to attention as she exited, then made to accompany her. She dismissed them with a careless wave and they resumed their positions. Following the corridor, she came to a staircase, lit by burning torches in iron brackets every ten or twelve steps. As she climbed, she lifted the hem of her cloak, almost daintily, to stop the trim getting dirty.

She reached a door. An orc sentry opened it for her. Jennesta stepped out into a large courtyard surrounded by high walls, the castle towers looming far above. It was dusk and the air was frigid.

A dragon was tethered in the centre of the quadrant, one foreleg ringed by an iron fetter the size of a barrel. An equally colossal chain ran from the shackle and encircled the stump of a mature oak.

The dragon's snout was buried in a small mountain of fodder that blended hay, brimstone, the carcasses of several whole sheep and other, less identifiable titbits. Ample quantities of steaming droppings, containing white slithers of bone and shiny clinker, had already been deposited at the beast's rear end.

Jennesta pressed a delicate lace handkerchief to her nose.

The dragon's handler walked towards her. She was dressed in tan-coloured garb of various shades. Her jerkin and trews were chestnut and soft as chamois, her sturdy knee boots mahogany-hued brushed suede. The only variations were a white and grey feather in her narrow-brimmed hat, and discreet cords of gold about her neck and wrists. Unusually tall even by the standards of her rangy species, she wore a proud, near-haughty expression.

The Dragon Dam's race always intrigued Jennesta. She had never had a brownie. But she harboured a small, grudging respect for them, too. Or at least as much as she was capable of feeling for any other than herself. Perhaps because, like her, brownies were hybrids, the offspring of unions between elves and goblins.

"Glozellan," Jennesta said.

"Majesty." The Mistress of Dragons gave a minimal bow of her head.

"You've had your briefing?"

"Yes."

"And my orders are understood?"

"You wish dragon patrols sent out to search for a warband." Her voice was high-pitched, reedy.

"The Wolverines, yes. I sent for you in person to emphasise how vital your mission is."

Should Glozellan have thought it strange that the Queen wanted her own followers hunted down, she didn't betray the fact. "What would you have us do if we find them, my lady?"

Jennesta didn't like the *if*, but let it pass. "That's where you and your fellow handlers must take the initiative." She selected her words with care. "In the case of sighting the band in a place where they can be captured, our land forces are to be alerted. But if there's the slightest possibility of the Wolverines escaping, they are to be destroyed."

Glozellan's pencil-thin eyebrows rose. She knew better than to comment more explicitly, let alone protest.

"If you have to kill them you'll send word immediately," Jennesta continued, "and guard their remains, with your lives if necessary, until reinforcements arrive." She was confident that the cylinder was capable of withstanding the heat of a dragon's breath. Fairly confident, anyway. There was an element of unavoidable risk.

The dragon chewed noisily on the spine of a sheep.

After mulling over what had been said for a moment, Glozellan replied, "We'd be looking for a small group. We don't know exactly where they are. It won't be easy, unless we fly low. That leaves us vulnerable."

Jennesta's composure was strained. "Why does everyone bring me problems?" she snapped. "I want solutions! *Do as I say!*"

"Your Majesty."

"Well, don't just stand there! Get on with it!"

The Dragon Dam nodded, turned and loped to her mount. Having clambered up the rigging to the saddle, she signalled an orc guard waiting by a far wall. He approached bearing a mallet. Several heavy blows to the shackle clasps released the chain. The guard retired to a safe distance.

Glozellan stretched forward, a lean hand on either side of the dragon's neck. It twisted its head, bringing a cavernous ear to her face. She whispered into it. Sinewy wings spread and billowed with a leathery crackling sound. The dragon let out a thunderous roar.

Gigantic muscles in its legs and flanks stood out like smooth scaly boulders. The wings flapped, sluggishly at first, then with gathering speed, displacing great gusts of air that lashed the courtyard with the strength of a minor storm.

Jennesta held on to her cap, and her cloak swirled as the dragon rose. The feat seemed impossible for such a behemoth, but the miracle was achieved, marrying the absurdly cumbersome with the surprisingly graceful.

For a few seconds the creature hung motionless, save for the laboured strokes of its mighty wings, about halfway up the side of the castle's edifice. The newly visible moon and stars were part obscured by its bulky, ragged-edged silhouette. Then the shape continued its ascent, took a heading towards Taklakameer and soared away.

The door Jennesta had passed through opened. General Kysthan emerged, escorted by a small contingent of her personal guard. He looked pale.

"You have word of our quarry?" she asked.

"Yes and . . . no, Majesty."

"I'm in no mood for riddles, General. Just tell me straight." She patted the side of her leg impatiently with the coiled whip.

"I've had a message from Captain Delorran."

Her eyes narrowed. "Go on."

The General fished a square of folded parchment from his tunic pocket. Despite the cold, he was sweating. "What Delorran has to say may not immediately seem like news Your Majesty would wish to hear."

With a deft flick of her hand, Jennesta unwound the whip.

The night was moonlit and starry. A gentle breeze pleasantly tempered its warmth.

He stood at the door of a grand lodge. There were sounds inside.

Stryke looked around. Nothing troubled the genial countryside and it did not feel threatening. In itself that was almost beyond his comprehension. The normality seemed disturbing.

Hesitantly, he reached out to try the door.

Before he could, it opened.

Light and noise blasted him. A figure was outlined by brightness. He couldn't see its features, only an inky contour. It came toward him. His hand went to his sword.

The shape became the female orc he had met before. Or imagined. Or dreamt. She was just as handsome, just as proud, and her eyes held the same tender steel.

Stryke was taken aback. She was, too, but less so.

"You've returned," she said.

He stammered some banal reply.

She smiled. "Come, the festivities are well under way."

He let her usher him into the great hall.

It was crowded with orcs, and only orcs. Orcs feasting at long tables laden with food and drink. Orcs engrossed in good-natured conversation. Orcs laughing, singing, enjoying raucous horseplay and rough games.

Females made their way through the company bearing tankards of ale and horns of ruby wine, baskets of fruit and platters of tender meats. A fire burned in the middle of the floor on slate blocks, with joints of game and hunks of fowl roasting over it on spits. Smoke suffused with dancing sparks drifted up to a hole in the roof. Perfumed woods released their aromas to mingle with the myriad other smells scenting the air. Among them, Stryke thought he detected the sweetly pungent odour of crystal.

At one end of the hall, adult males lounged on skins of fur, drinking and roaring at ribald jokes. At the other, boisterous adolescents engaged in sham combat with wooden swords and muffle-ended staves. Drummers beat jaunty rhythms. Squealing youngsters chased each other through the throng.

Many revellers greeted Stryke warm-heartedly, despite him being a stranger.

"Are you celebrating?" She snatched a flagon from a tray held high by a passing server, and drank from it. Then she passed it to him.

Stryke took a deep draught. It was mulled ale, flavoured with honey and spices, and it tasted wonderful. He drained the cup.

The female moved closer to him. "Where have you been?" she asked.

"That's not an easy question." He put his flagon down on a table. "I don't know if I'm sure of the answer myself."

"Again you shroud yourself in mystery."

"I see you as a mystery, and this place."

"There's nothing mysterious about me, or this place."

"I know it not."

She shook her head in good-natured pique. "But you're here."

"That means nothing to me. Where is here?"

"I see you're no less eccentric than when we first met. Come with me."

She led him across the hall to another, smaller door. It opened to the back of the lodge. The cooler air outside had a sobering effect, and closing the door deadened most of the clamour.

"See?" She indicated the calm night-time landscape. "All is as you'd expect."

"As I would have expected once, perhaps," he replied. "Long ago. But now . . ."

"You're talking giddiness again," she cautioned.

"What I mean is, is it like this . . . everywhere?"

"Of course it is!" A second passed as she made a decision. "I'll show you."

They walked to the end of the lodge. When they turned its corner they came to a stand of horses. Most were war chargers, magnificent, immaculately groomed animals with elaborate, gleaming tackle. The female selected two of the finest, a pure white and a pure black stallion.

She told him to mount. He hesitated. She climbed onto the white, her movements fluid, dextrous, as though she were born to the saddle. He took the black.

They rode off. At first she led, then he caught up and they galloped through the velvety countryside together.

Silver moonlight dusted the boughs of trees and painted the meadows with spurious frost. It bathed the upper slopes of rolling hills, as though snow had fallen, despite the temperate climate.

Burnished rivers and shimmering lakes were fleetingly sighted. Flocks of birds took wing at the approach of pounding hooves. Swarming insects lit the heart of brooding forests with their mottled fireglow. All was fresh, vibrant, teeming.

Above hung a glorious array of stars, crystalline in the virgin night sky.

"Don't you see?" she called. "Don't you see that all is as it should be?"

He was too intoxicated by the undefiled air, by the sense of innate rightness, to reply.

"Come on!" she cried, and urged her horse to greater effort.

Her mount surged ahead of him. He spurred his own ride to match the pace.

They raced, exhilarated, the wind buffeting their faces. She laughed *at the sheer joy of it, and so did he. It was a long time since he had felt quite so alive.*

"Your land is wondrous!" he shouted.

"Our land!" she returned.

He looked to the way ahead.

The way ahead was barren.

It was cold. The trail was rocky. Nothing stirred. The moon and stars were visible, but dingy in the clouded sky. Stryke was riding alone at the head of the column.

The chill hand of fear caressed his spine.

What in the name of the gods is happening to me? he thought. *Am I going insane?*

He tried to be rational. He was exhausted and under pressure. They all were. All that had happened was that he'd fallen asleep in the saddle. Fatigue had conjured the pictures in his mind. They were vivid and realistic, but only pictures. Like a story the wordsmiths told around winter fires.

It would be comforting if he believed that.

He unclipped his canteen and took a gulp of water. As he replaced the stopper, he caught a familiar bouquet on the breeze. A whiff of pellucid. He shook his head, half convinced the smell had carried over as a sort of olfactory memory from his dream. Then it came again. He looked around.

Coilla and Alfray were riding behind him. Their faces were tired and passive. His gaze travelled beyond them, down the lines of sleepy grunts. He saw Jup, slumped with weariness. A place or two further back, near the column's end and riding alone, was Haskeer. He seemed furtive, turning his head in an obvious attempt to avoid scrutiny.

Stryke swung his horse out. "Take the lead!" he barked at Alfray and Coilla.

They reacted and at least one said something. He didn't hear it, and ignored them anyway. His attention was focused on Haskeer. He galloped his way.

When he reached him, the rich odour of burning crystal was unmistakable, and the sergeant was making a ham-fisted job of trying to conceal something.

"Give it up," Stryke said, icy menace in his voice.

With lazy insolence, Haskeer opened his hand to reveal the tiny clay pipe he'd been hiding. Stryke snatched it.

"You took this without permission," he growled.

"You didn't say we couldn't."

"I didn't say you could either. You're on your last warning, Haskeer. And think on this." Lightning fast, Stryke leaned in and swung his fist at the sergeant's head. It landed on his temple with a meaty smack. The blow knocked Haskeer clean off his horse. He hit the ground heavily.

The column stopped. Everybody was watching.

Haskeer groaned and got unsteadily to his feet. For a moment it looked as though he might retaliate, but he thought better of it.

"You'll walk till you learn some discipline," Stryke told him, gesturing for a trooper to take the reins of Haskeer's mount.

"I haven't slept," Haskeer complained.

"Never leave off bellyaching, do you, Sergeant? *None* of us have slept, Wolverine, and none of us are going to till I say. Got it?" Stryke turned to the rest of the band. "Anybody else feel like defying me?"

They let silence answer for them.

"Nobody touches the crystal until, and if, I say so!" he told them. "I don't care how much there is, that's not the point. It might be all we've got to bargain for our lives with *her*. Jennesta. Particularly if we don't get that fucking cylinder back, which right now looks pretty unlikely. Understood?"

Another eloquent silence spoke for them.

Coilla eventually broke it.

"Looks like we'll get to find out about the cylinder any time now," she said, nodding at what was coming into sight as they rounded a bend.

A vast outcrop of granite sat by the trail, squat and contorted, as though melted by inconceivable heat. It was an unmistakable landmark even to those who had never set eyes on it before. Whether by chance or some design of the gods, the likeness it bore was true enough to have been carved by a titanic sculptor.

"Demon's Claw," Stryke declared, though none of them needed telling. "We'll be in Black Rock in less than an hour."

11

Stryke knew that if the Wolverines were to function properly, if they were to survive, he had to put the disturbing dreams out of his mind. Fortunately, the prospect of a raid into enemy territory was more than enough to keep him occupied.

He ordered a temporary camp to be struck while they prepared for their assault on Black Rock. Several troopers were sent to rendezvous with the forward scouts spying the land. The rest of the Wolverines set about checking their kit and honing their weapons.

Stryke decided that no fires were to be lit, in order not to betray their position. On this, Alfray asked him to think again.

"Why?" Stryke said.

"We've got a problem with Darig. He took a leg wound when we fought the Unis. Fact is, it's in a worse state than I thought. Gangrenous. I need a fire to heat my blades."

"It's got to come off?"

Alfray nodded. "He loses the leg or he loses his life."

"*Shit*. Another wounded trooper to move. We don't need it, Alfray." He nodded at Meklun. "How's he?"

"No improvement, and there are signs of fever now."

"At this rate we won't need to worry about Jennesta. All right, a fire. But small, and covered. Have you told Darig?"

"He's guessed, I think, but I'm about to spell it out to him. It's a damn shame. He's one of the youngest in the band, Stryke."

"I know. Anything you need?"

"I've got herbs that might dull the pain a bit, and a little alcohol. Probably not enough. Can I try some crystal?"

"Have it. But it won't block the pain that much, you know."

"At least it should take his mind off it. I'll get to work on an infusion."

Alfray went back to his patient.

Coilla took the field surgeon's place. "Got a minute?"

Stryke grunted that he had.

"You all right?" she said.

"Why ask?"

"Because you've not been yourself lately. Kind of distant. And then piling into Haskeer back there—"

"He's been asking for it."

"You can say that again. But it's you I'm talking about."

"We're in a mess. What do you expect, a song and a dance?"

"I just thought that if you're—"

"Why the touching concern for my state of health, Corporal?"

"You're our commander, it's in my interests. All our interests."

"I'm not going to crack, if that's what you think. I'll get us through this."

She didn't reply.

He took a different tack. "Heard about Darig?"

"Yes. It stinks. What are we going to do about the kobolds?"

Stryke was grateful that she wanted to talk about tactics. It made him feel more comfortable. "Hit them when they least expect it, of course. That might be in what's left of the night, it might be at daybreak."

"Then I want to get up there with the scouts and check the layout for myself."

"Right. We'll go together."

"Black Rock's big, Stryke. Suppose the kobolds we're after are right in the middle of it?"

"From what I've heard, the raiding parties camp around the main settlement. They keep the females and young at the core. The raiders can come and go more easily like that, as well as guard the place."

"That sounds a dangerous set-up. If we're walking into some kind of defensive ring—"

"We just have to be careful how we do it."

She regarded him with troubled eyes. "You know this is insane, don't you?"

"Can you think of another way?"

For the briefest instant, he hoped she was going to say yes.

*   *   *

An hour flew by while the Wolverines busied themselves
with the countless tasks needed to make a fighting unit
combat-ready.

With everything in hand, Stryke went to the makeshift bender
used as a medical tent. He found Alfray tending an oblivious
Meklun, stretched at the far end of the shelter, a damp cloth
resting on his forehead. Most of the remaining space was taken
up by Darig, also lying but somewhat more animated. A vacant
grin on his face, eyes glazed, he rolled his head from side to side,
mumbling incessantly. In the flickering candlelight, Stryke saw
that the blanket covering him was twisted and blotched with
sweat.

"Just in time," Alfray said. "I need some help."

"He's ready?"

Alfray looked down at Darig. He was giggling.

"I've given him enough crystal to poleaxe a regiment. If he's
not ready now he never will be."

"Mahogany elbows bushels of songbirds tied with string,"
Darig announced.

"Take your point," Stryke said. "What do you want me to do?"

"Get somebody else in here. It'll take two to hold him down."

"Pretty string," Darig added. *"Pretty . . . smitty . . . pring."*

Alfray crouched next to the patient. "Take it easy," he
soothed.

Stryke peered out of the tent and saw Jup nearby. He beckoned him. The dwarf jogged over and sidled in.

"You're in luck," Stryke told him drily. "You get to hold one of
the bits that's coming off." He nodded at the grunt's legs.

The tent was about as crowded as it could get. Jup edged gingerly to the end of the trooper's bed. "Wouldn't do to step on
him," he explained.

"Don't think he'd notice," Alfray said.

"There's a weasel in the river," Darig confided knowingly.

"He's been given some crystal as a painkiller," Stryke
explained.

Jup raised an eyebrow. *"Some?* To use an old dwarf expression, I'd say he's ripped out of his crust."

"And it won't last forever," Alfray reminded them, a mite testily. "Let's get on with it, shall we?"

"The river, the river," Darig chanted, saucer-eyed.

"Take hold of his ankles, Jup," Alfray instructed. "Stryke, bear down on his arms. I don't want him moving when I start."

They did as they were told. Alfray pulled aside the blanket, revealing the infected leg. The angry wound was drenched in pus.

"Gods," Jup muttered.

Alfray dabbed gently with a cloth. "Not too pretty, is it?"

Stryke wrinkled his nose. "Or very sweet-smelling. Where are you going to cut?"

"Here, across the thigh, well above the knee. And the trick is to do it fast." He finished cleaning the affected area and wrung the cloth in a wooden bowl. "Hang on and I'll get what I need."

He ducked out of the tent. A small fire was burning in a pit a couple of paces away. "You!" he snapped at a passing grunt. "Stand here and hand me what I want when I tell you." The trooper nodded and padded over.

Alfray tore the damp cloth into two pieces and gave him one. He used the other to grasp the hilt of a long-bladed knife protruding from the fire. Its blade glowed cherry-red. A hatchet he left in the flames. With his foot, he nudged the business end of a shovel in beside it.

Back in the tent, he knelt again, pulling from his jerkin pocket a scrap of thick, sturdy rope, about equal to a hand's span.

Darig smiled beatifically. "Pig's riding the horse, pig's ridin-*mumph.*"

"*Bite!*" Alfray ordered, jamming the chunk of rope into the trooper's open mouth.

"Now?" Stryke said.

"Now. Hold him tight!"

He brought the scalding blade into play. Darig's eyes widened and he began struggling. Jup and Stryke strained against his writhing limbs.

With several rapid, skilful strokes, Alfray excavated the wound. He folded aside flaps of skin and began digging through the flesh beneath. Darig struggled the harder, and spat out the rope. His agonised yelling had Meklun stirring restlessly, but was short-lived; Alfray rammed the restraint back in. Holding it in place with the heel of his palm, he carried on working one-handed. In short order he had the bone exposed.

Darig groaned and passed out.

Tossing the knife aside, Alfray bellowed, "*Hatchet!*"

It was passed in over Stryke's head, stock wrapped against the blistering, near-white heat of its cleaving end.

Alfray grasped it two-handed and raised it high. He aimed, took a breath and brought it down with all his might. The blow landed with a muffled *thunk*, dead on target. Stryke and Jup felt the grunt's body buck under the impact. But the leg was only half severed.

Darig snapped back into consciousness, a wild expression on his face, and resumed thrashing. He spat out the gag again and commenced shrieking. No one had a hand free to stop him.

"Hurry!" Stryke urged.

"Hold him still!" Alfray demanded. He disengaged the axe and lined up another swing.

The second blow also struck true, and if anything had greater force behind it. This almost finished the job, save the last remaining threads of sinew and skin. A third weighty chop parted them, carrying the cleaver through the horse blanket Darig lay on and into the hardened earth below.

The screaming continued. Stryke ended it by landing a smart punch to the side of Darig's head, knocking him cold.

"We've got to stem the flow of blood," Alfray told them, pulling away the amputated leg. "Get me that shovel."

The spade was carefully delivered. Its flat was crimson-coloured, and when Alfray blew on it, a patch shone sparkly yellow-white for an instant. "Should be hot enough," he decided. "Keep holding him. This is going to be another rude awakening."

He laid the shovel against the stump. The tangy odour of burnt flesh filled the air as the heat did its work and cauterised. Darig was dragged into wakefulness once more, and emptied his lungs in protest, but the shock and blood loss had taken their toll. The clamour he sent up was faint compared to the noise he'd made moments before.

Jup and Stryke kept pressing down as Alfray sprinkled alcohol over his handiwork, then applied dressings smeared with healing balms.

Darig fell to low, repetitive muttering, and his breath took on a regular, if shallow, rhythm.

"His breathing's even," Alfray pronounced. "That's something."

"Will he pull through?" Jup wondered.

"I'd give him a fifty-fifty chance." He bent to the amputated leg and rolled it in a square of fabric. "What he needs now," he said, lifting his load, "is rest and good nourishment to help rebuild his strength." He tucked the bloody bundle under his arm.

"That's a tall order," Stryke told him. "We're only carrying iron rations, remember, and I can't spare anybody to hunt."

"Leave that to me," Alfray said. "I'll take care of it. Now get out, the pair of you. You're disturbing my patients." He shoved at them.

Stryke and Jup found themselves outside the tent, staring at the lowered flap.

The last of the night would soon give way to dawn.

Stryke had mustered a group of twenty for the raid, including the scouts already positioned on the outskirts of Black Rock. A skeleton crew would be left to guard the camp and the wounded. Needing to talk to Alfray about this, he made his way to the medical tent.

Meklun was as far gone as ever. Darig was sitting up. His eyes were bleary and his skin was pale; otherwise he seemed to be doing well after such a short time. And the effects of the pellucid had all but worn off. Alfray was serving him a platter of stew from a black iron cauldron.

"Got to keep your strength up," he ordered, handing over the steaming dish.

Darig spooned a tentative mouthful. His uncertain expression vanished at the first bite and he tucked in with relish. "Hmmm, meat. Tasty. What is it?"

"Er, don't worry about that now," Alfray told him. "Just eat your fill."

Stryke caught his eye. "Needs must," Alfray mouthed, then looked away, uncharacteristically sheepish. They sat in slightly awkward silence as Darig cleared his plate.

Then Haskeer stuck his head into the tent and provided a distraction. "Something smells good," he said, staring hopefully at the cauldron.

"It's for Darig," Alfray replied hurriedly. "It's . . . special."

Haskeer looked disappointed. "Pity."

"What do you want?" Stryke asked pointedly.

"We're waiting for the order to move, chief."

"Then wait a bit longer. I'll be out soon."

The sergeant shrugged, gave the cooking pot a last, hankering glance and left.

"If the stew's special in the way I think it is," Stryke remarked, "you should have given him some."

Alfray smiled.

Darig looked from one to the other, baffled.

"Rest now," Alfray said, taking his shoulders and easing him back to a recumbent position.

"It might be a good idea if you stayed to look after him and Meklun," Stryke suggested.

"There are grunts who can do that. Vobe or Jad, for instance. Or Hystykk. They're capable."

"Just thought you'd prefer to be here with them."

"I'd rather be in on the action." Alfray's furrowed chin jutted stubbornly. "Unless you think I'm getting too *old* for that kind of—"

"*Whoa!* Age is nothing to do with it. Only giving you the choice, that's all. Come. Glad to have you."

"All right. I will."

Stryke made a note to tread carefully with Alfray when it came to the question of age. He was getting damn prickly about it.

"I'll finish here and follow on," Alfray added.

As Stryke went out, Darig stirred. "Sir?" he ventured. "Is there any more of that stew?"

The band had gathered fifty paces distant. By the time Stryke reached them, Alfray had caught up with him.

"Report, Coilla," Stryke ordered briskly.

"According to our scouts, the group we're after seem to be at the western edge of Black Rock. Direct heading from here, in other words."

"How can we be sure it's them?"

"We can't. But it looks that way. I've been up there, and I saw a bunch of kobolds corralling war lizards. Seemed to me they were a raiding party, not long back."

Stryke frowned. "Doesn't prove it's the same one."

"No," she agreed. "But unless you can come up with a better way of knowing, that's all we've got."

"Even if it ain't them, I say we get in there and kick arse anyway," Haskeer offered.

Some of the band muttered agreement.

"If they *are* the ones we're looking for," Jup said, "it's a bit of luck to find 'em camped outside Black Rock proper."

"Though we'll still have the whole population down on our necks if we put a foot wrong," Alfray cautioned. He turned to their commander. "Well? Do we go in?"

"We go in," Stryke decided.

12

They left the horses behind and set out for the forward observation point on foot.

The blades of their weapons had been blackened with damp charcoal lest they catch a glint from the waning moon. Senses alert for sight or sound of trouble, the band moved stealthily.

A change took place in the terrain. It became pulpy underfoot as the margins of the plains gave way to marshland.

Dawn was breaking as they arrived, the sun a bloody-red harbinger of another overcast, rain-sodden day.

The silent rendezvous with the scouts took place on the crest of a small hill, crowned with a modest copse, from which they could see but not be seen. As the sun climbed they watched Black Rock emerge from the clinging mist.

A jumble of single-storey buildings, crude wooden huts of various shapes and sizes, stretched as far as they could see in the unclear air. The scouts indicated a pair of huts almost directly below their viewing point, set some way apart from the settlement proper. One was small, the other much larger and similar in dimensions, if not in ornamentation, to an orc longhouse. Between and beyond them was a corral in which a herd of kirgizils was penned, recumbent and motionless in the way of lizards. They looked sluggish, no doubt suffering from the relentless drop in temperature that all parts of the land were enduring. Stryke wondered how much longer the kobolds could continue using them.

He leaned to one of the scouts and whispered, "What's been happening, Orbon?"

"There were a few bandits around until about an hour ago. Most went into the big hut. One went into the smaller building. We've seen no movement since."

Stryke motioned Coilla and Haskeer over. "Take four grunts and get down there. Orbon, you're one of them. I want to know the lie of the land and the kobolds' deployment. If there are guards, deal with 'em."

"What if we're spotted?" Coilla asked.

"Be damn sure you're not! Otherwise, it's every orc for himself."

She nodded, attention half on selecting a pair of knives from her arm sheath.

"And you behave yourself," Stryke warned Haskeer darkly.

The sergeant's face was a picture of offended innocence.

Coilla quickly picked the other troopers to go with them and the group made its way down the incline.

They progressed from tree to tree. When there were no more to shelter behind they headed for a line of bushes, the last hiding place before the level clearing. Crouching low, they scrutinised the way ahead.

From this angle they could see four kobold guards. They wore furs against the night's chill. Two of the wiry creatures were at the side of the big hut, two beside the smaller. None was moving.

Swiftly deciding a strategy, Coilla conveyed it to the others via sign language. Her plan was that she would go to the right with two grunts, toward the small hut, Haskeer and his grunts to the large hut on the left. The gesticulations ended with her drawing a finger across her throat.

Tensely, they awaited their opportunity, and the open ground to be crossed meant that when it came they would have to move fast. Several minutes went by. Then in conjunction both sets of guards were vulnerable. One pair engaged in conversation, half turned away from the hill. Their fellows at the large hut began a patrol, backs to the orcs.

Haskeer and Coilla broke cover and ran. The grunts fanned out behind them.

A knife gripped between her teeth, the other in her hand, Coilla moved as lightly and swiftly as she could. She was little more than halfway across the clearing when the guards finished talking and parted.

Coilla froze, signalling the others to do the same.

Without looking their way, one guard went to the end of the hut and turned its corner. The other still faced away from Coilla, but was slowly turning as he scanned his turf.

She glanced at the larger hut. The guards there were oblivious to what was happening. Haskeer's group must have been further back; she didn't see them.

A fraction of a second had gone by. There were perhaps thirty paces between her and the turning guard. It was now or never. She drew back her arm and hurled the knife with all her force. The momentum bent her forward at the waist and expelled the breath she held.

The throw was true, catching her target squarely between its shoulder blades. A muffled *thock* marked the impact. The kobold went down without a sound.

Coilla dashed forward, the grunts at her side. They arrived just as the second guard came back round the corner. The grunts piled into the startled creature, denying it time to draw a weapon. It was dealt with quietly and brutally.

The bodies were dragged out of sight. Coilla and the others hid themselves as best they could and looked to the big hut. They saw Haskeer's group creeping up on their prey.

Around the larger building the ground had been more thoroughly trampled by kirgizils and the going was muddier. Never the most graceful of orcs, but often the most overconfident, Haskeer managed to get one of his boots stuck in the slime. In pulling it free, with a loud sucking sound, he lost balance and pitched headlong. His sword went flying.

The kobold he was sneaking toward spun around. Its jaws gaped. Haskeer scrabbled for his sword. It was out of reach, so he grabbed a rock and pitched it. The missile struck the creature's mouth, bringing a spray of blood and broken fangs. Then the grunts rushed in and finished the job with daggers.

Haskeer snatched his sword, tumbling forward. He skidded as much as sprinted at the remaining sentry. The kobold had its own weapon drawn, and fended off the first blow. Knocking the scimitar aside with his second, Haskeer drove his blade deep into the guard's chest.

Again, bodies were hauled away and concealed.

Panting, Haskeer looked to Coilla, and exchanged a triumphant thumbs-up with her. A few further signs established that their next move would be checking the huts.

The one Haskeer's group had reached was without windows. Its door was not a door as such, but rather an open entrance covered by a rush hanging. He led the way to it and they positioned themselves, ready for trouble. Very carefully, Haskeer edged the curtain aside a little, vigilant for the tiniest sound. The frail dawn allowed in enough light for him to see.

What he saw was kobolds. Their sleeping forms covered the floor, and each cot in a line against the far wall was shared by heaps of them. Weapons were scattered everywhere.

Haskeer held his breath, fearful of waking the overwhelming force. He began to withdraw slowly. A kobold stretched out near the door stirred fitfully in its sleep. Haskeer went rigid, and stayed that way until he was absolutely sure it was safe to move again. Then he gently replaced the curtain and silently expelled a relieved breath.

He backed off three paces. The curtain stirred. Haskeer and the grunts flattened themselves to the wall on either side of the door.

A dishevelled kobold came out of the hut, too drowsy to pay much attention to its surroundings. It staggered a couple of steps and pawed at its groin. A vacantly blissful expression on its face, and swaying gently, the creature let loose a hissing stream of urine. Haskeer pounced, locking his arm around the creature's neck. There was a brief struggle. The kobold's gush of water splashed uncontrollably. A muscular jerk of Haskeer's forearm snapped the bandit's neck.

The orc sergeant remained stock still, holding up the limp body, listening for any further movement. Satisfied, he dragged the corpse to the spot where their other victims were dumped, cursing soundlessly all the while at the piss soaking his boots. After dropping the body he continued grumbling as he rubbed them on the back of his breeches.

Apart from size, the hut Coilla's group were investigating differed from the larger building in two respects. It had a door, and at the side, a window. Coilla ordered the grunts to keep a look-out while she tiptoed to it. Stooped beneath the opening, which had neither shutter nor blind, she tried to gauge any noises from inside. Once attuned, she heard a rhythmic, wheezy sound that took a moment to identify as snoring.

She slowly raised her head and looked in.

The single room had three occupants. Two of them were kobold guards, sitting on the floor with their backs against the wall and legs outstretched. Both seemed to be asleep, and one was the source of the snoring.

But it was the third occupant that drew her attention.

Tied to the room's only chair was a being at least as short as the kobolds, though of much chunkier build. Its rough hide had a green tinge. The large pumpkin-shaped head appeared out of proportion with the rest of the body, and the ears jutted outward slightly at an angle. There was something of the vulture about its neck. The elongated eyes had excessively fleshy lids, with black elliptical orbs against white surrounds shot through with yellow veining. Its pate and face were hairless, save for whiskery sideburns of reddish-brown tufts of fur, turning flaxen.

It wore a simple grey robe, the worse for being obviously long unwashed. Its feet were shod in suede ankle boots, with tarnished buckles, that had also seen better days. Where skin showed, on the face and hands, which were not unlike an orc's, it was wrinkly like a serpent's. Coilla reckoned the creature was very old.

As the thought occurred, the gremlin looked up and saw her.

His eyes widened. But he made no sound, as she feared he might. They stared at each other for a few seconds, then Coilla dropped out of sight.

With signs and whispers she conveyed her discovery to the grunts, and ordered them to stay while she reported. As they hid, she signalled Haskeer. He left his own troopers behind and joined her for the jog back to the hill.

By the time they rejoined the rest of the band, Stryke was growing anxious.

"We took care of all the guards we came across," Haskeer blurted. "And that big hut's full of the whole fucking raiding party by the looks of it. The little bastards."

"Any sign of the cylinder?"

Haskeer shook his head.

"No," Coilla concurred. "But what I saw in the smaller hut was interesting. They've got a prisoner in there, Stryke. A gremlin. He looked pretty old, too."

"A gremlin? What the hell's that about?"

Coilla shrugged.

Haskeer was getting impatient. "What are we waiting for? Let's whomp 'em while they're sleeping!"

"We're going to," Stryke told him. "But we're doing it right. The cylinder's the reason we're here, remember. This is our only chance of finding it. And I don't want that prisoner hurt."

"Why not?"

"Because our enemy's enemy is our friend."

The concept seemed alien to Haskeer. "We have no friends."

"Ally, then. But I want him alive, if possible. If the cylinder *isn't* here, he might be able to tell us where to look. Unless any of you have worked out how to understand that kobold gibberish."

"We should be moving," Jup urged, "before the bodies are found."

"Right," Stryke agreed. "This is how we're doing it. Two groups. Me, Coilla and Alfray will join the grunts already at the small hut. I want to be sure of the prisoner. Haskeer and Jup, you take everybody else and surround the big hut. But don't do anything till I get there. Got that?"

The sergeants nodded, but avoided looking at each other.

"Good. Let's go."

The Wolverines divided into their assigned groups and flowed down to the settlement. They met no resistance and saw no movement.

Once Stryke's party had joined with the grunts left on guard, they positioned themselves outside the smaller hut. They could see Jup and Haskeer's group doing the same.

"Stand ready for my order," Stryke instructed in a hushed tone. "Coilla, let's see that window."

She went ahead, staying low, and he followed. After peeking through the opening she beckoned him to look. The scene was as before; two lounging kobold guards, spark out, and their bound prisoner. This time the gremlin was unaware of being watched and didn't look up. Coilla and Stryke crept back to the others.

"Time to take a gamble," Stryke whispered. "Let's do this fast and quiet."

He rapped on the door and ducked to the side, out of sight. A long half-minute passed as they waited tensely. Stryke wondered if things had gone sour, and wouldn't have been surprised if the entire kobold nation had appeared and fallen on their necks. He scanned the terrain, saw nothing, then knocked again, a little louder. After a few more seconds crawled by they heard the scrape of a bolt.

The door opened and one of the kobolds stuck its head out. It was done casually enough to indicate it wasn't expecting trouble. Stryke seized the creature by its neck and savagely tugged it aside. The other Wolverines poured into the hut.

Stryke killed the squirming kobold with a single dagger-thrust to its heart. Dragging the body behind him, he quickly entered the building. The second sentry was already dead. It hadn't even had a chance to rise, and the rigour of violent death was frozen on its face. Stryke dropped the first guard's corpse next to it.

Coilla had her hand over the mouth of the trembling prisoner. With the other she held a knife to his throat.

"Make a sound and you follow them in death," she promised. "If I take my hand away, will you keep quiet?"

The gremlin nodded, eyes wide with fear. Coilla removed her hand, but kept the knife near enough to underline her threat.

"We've no time for a polite chat," Stryke told the captive. "Do you know about the artifact?"

The gremlin seemed confused.

"The *cylinder?*"

Looking from one grim orc face to another, then down to the slaughtered kobolds, the gremlin returned his gaze to Stryke. Again, he nodded.

"Where is it?"

The gremlin swallowed. When he spoke, his voice had a gravelly, bass quality. But it was tempered by the higher notes of age-stretched vocal cords, and terror. "It is in the longhouse with those who sleep."

Coilla gave him a hard look. "You'd better not be lying, ancient one."

Stryke pointed at a grunt. "Stay with him. The rest of you come with me."

He led them across to the longhouse.

The band armed themselves with their preferred weaponry for close-quarter fighting. Most chose knives. Stryke favoured a sword and knife combination. Haskeer settled on a hatchet.

As they'd already discovered, there was only one door. They clustered around it, Stryke, Coilla, Haskeer, Jup and Alfray to the fore.

Despite being on the edge of a township housing unknown numbers of a hostile race, certainly hundreds, Stryke was aware of a strange quietness that amounted to a kind of serenity. He put it down to the sense of calm he often felt before combat, the unique feeling of being centred, of being whole, that only the nearness of death engendered. The air, for all its impurities, had never smelt quite so sweet.

"Let's do it," he growled.

Haskeer ripped aside the cloth.

The Wolverines piled into the hut, laying about them with unstoppable ferocity, hacking, slashing, stabbing everything in their path. They trampled the kobolds, kicked them, bayoneted them with swords, slashed their throats, pummelled their bodies with axes. A deafening cacophony of screams, squeals and foreign-tongued curses rose from their victims to add to the chaos.

Many of the creatures died without rising. Others got to their feet only to be instantly cut down. But some, further into the packed room, did manage to stand and mount a defence. The slaughter became vicious hand-to-hand combat.

Facing a wildly slashing scimitar, Stryke ran through its owner with such force that his sword tip penetrated the wall beyond. He had to apply his boot to the kobold's chest to prise the blade free. Without pause, he sought fresh meat.

Belying his advancing years, Alfray deftly felled a bandit to his right, switched tack and skewered another to his left.

Coilla dodged a spear-wielding assailant, slashed bare its knuckles and buried both her daggers in its chest.

Haskeer slammed his ham-like fist on top of a kobold's head, shattering its skull, then turned and swiped his hatchet into the next foe's stomach.

Fencing with a hissing bandit clutching a rapier, Jup knocked the weapon aside and sent his blade into the kobold's brain via its eye.

The frenzy continued unabated. Then, as suddenly as the carnage had begun, it ended. None of the enemy was left standing.

Stryke ran a hand across his face, clearing it of sweat and blood. "Hurry!" he barked. "If that doesn't bring more of 'em, nothing will. *Find that cylinder!*"

The band began a frantic search of what had become a charnel house. They rummaged through the bodies' clothing, rooted in straw on the floor, tossed aside the possessions of the vanquished.

As Stryke reached for a corpse it proved less dead than he thought, lashing out at him with a wickedly jagged-edged cleaver. He planted his sword on its chest and fell on it with all his weight. The kobold convulsed, gurgled, died. Stryke resumed his ransacking.

He was starting to think it had all been in vain when Alfray cried out.

Everybody stopped and stared. Stryke pushed his way through them. Alfray pointed at a mutilated kobold. The cylinder was looped into the creature's belt.

Stryke knelt and eagerly disengaged it. He held it up to the light. It looked complete. Unopened.

Haskeer was smirking, gleefully triumphant. "Nobody takes from orcs!"

"Come on!" Stryke hissed.

They poured out of the place and ran to the other hut.

If anything, the gremlin looked in even more of an agitated state. But he couldn't take his eyes off the cylinder.

"We have to get out of here!" Jup urged.

"What do we do with him?" Haskeer asked, pointing at the quailing gremlin with his sword.

"Yes, Stryke," Coilla said, "what about him?"

Haskeer had a typically straightforward solution. "I say we kill him and get it over with."

Alarmed, the gremlin cowered.

For the moment, Stryke was undecided.

"This cylinder is of great significance!" the gremlin suddenly exclaimed. "For orcs! With my knowledge, I can explain it to you."

"He's bluffing!" Haskeer reckoned, brandishing his sword menacingly. "Finish it, I say!"

"After all," the gremlin added tremulously, "that's why the kobolds kidnapped me."

"What?" Stryke said.

"To make sense of it for them. That's why they brought me here."

Stryke studied the captive's face, trying to decide whether he was telling the truth. And if it made any difference to them if he was.

"What do we *do*, Stryke?" Coilla demanded impatiently.

He made up his mind. "Bring him. Now let's get the hell out of here."

13

The Wolverines wasted no time getting away from Black Rock settlement. They dragged the gremlin after them, still bound and at the end of a rope. By the time their rapid route march was over, the aged creature was panting from the effort of keeping pace.

Stryke issued orders to break camp and prepare for a quick exit.

Haskeer was jubilant. "Back to Cairnbarrow, at last. I tell you, Stryke, I didn't think we were going to do it."

"Thanks for trusting me," his commander replied coolly.

The sarcasm was lost on Haskeer. "We'll be heroes when we turn up with that thing." He nodded at the cylinder in Stryke's belt.

"It isn't over yet," Alfray warned him. "We have to get there first, and that means crossing a lot of hostile territory."

"And there's no telling how Jennesta's going to react to the delay," Jup added. "The cylinder and pellucid's no guarantee we'll come out of this with our heads."

"Gloom merchants," Haskeer sneered.

Stryke thought that was rich coming from him, but decided against pointing it out. After all, this was supposed to be a joyful occasion. He wondered why he didn't feel that way.

"Shouldn't we hear what this one has to say?" Coilla said, indicating the gremlin. He sat on a tree stump, exhausted and frightened.

"Yes," Haskeer agreed, "let's get it over with or we'll have another free-loader to drag around with us."

"Is that what you think of our wounded comrades?" Alfray flared.

Stryke held up his hands to silence them. "That's enough. I

don't want us standing here bickering when a couple of hundred kobolds come looking for revenge." He addressed their involuntary guest. "What's your name?"

"Mmm . . . Mmoo . . ." The elderly gremlin cleared his throat nervously and tried again. "M-M-M . . . *Mobbs*."

"All right, Mobbs, what was that about the kobolds kidnapping you? And what do you know of this?" He tapped the cylinder.

"You have your life in your hands, gremlin," Alfray cautioned. "Choose your words with care."

"I'm just a humble scholar," Mobbs said, and it sounded like a plea. "I was going about my business north of here, in Hecklowe, when those wretched bandits seized me." An edge of indignation crept into his voice.

"Why?" Coilla asked. "What did they want from you?"

"I have made languages my life's work, particularly dead languages. They needed my skills to decipher the contents of the artifact. I believe it to be a message carrier, you see, and—"

"We know that," Stryke interjected.

"Therefore it is not the cylinder itself that is of interest but rather the knowledge it may contain."

"Kobolds are stupid," Alfray stated bluntly. "What use would they have of knowledge?"

"Perhaps they were acting for others. I know not."

Haskeer scoffed.

But Stryke was intrigued enough that he wanted to hear more. "I've a feeling your story isn't one to be told in a hurry, Mobbs. We'll get ourselves into the forest and hear the rest. And it better be good."

"Oh, *come on*, Stryke!" Haskeer protested. "Why waste time when we could be heading for home?"

"Getting ourselves hidden from another kobold attack isn't wasting time. Do as you're told."

Haskeer went off in a sulk.

The camp was cleared, the wounded were made ready to travel, and Mobbs was placed on the horse pulling Meklun's litter. All traces of their presence erased, the Wolverines made haste for the shelter of Black Rock Forest.

*   *   *

They reached their goal three hours later.

The forest was fully mature. Its towering trees spread a leafy ceiling far overhead, filtering the already weak sunlight, making ground-level shadowy and moist. Crunching on a brittle carpet of brown mulch, they set up a temporary camp. Grunts were assigned to keep their eyes peeled for signs of trouble.

For security, no fires were lit. So their first meal of the day was another austere ration: wedges of dense black bread, solid plugs of cured meat, and water.

Stryke, Coilla, Jup and Haskeer sat with Mobbs. Everybody else gathered around and looked on. Alfray came back from checking the wounded and pushed through the lounging troopers.

"Darig's not too bad," he reported, "but Meklun's fever's got worse."

"Do what you can for him," Stryke said. Then he, and the whole band, turned their attention to Mobbs.

The gremlin had refused food and taken only a little water. Stryke reckoned fear had dulled his appetite. Now their scrutiny was making him even more uncomfortable.

"You've nothing to fear from us," Stryke assured him, "as long as you're honest. So no more puzzles." He held up the cylinder. "I want to hear exactly what you know about this thing, and why it's worth your life."

"It could be worth *yours*," Mobbs replied.

Coilla frowned. "How so?"

"That depends on how much you value your heritage, and the destiny denied you."

"These are empty words, meant to postpone his death," Haskeer thundered. "Stick 'im, I say."

"Give him his due," Jup said.

Haskeer glared at the dwarf. "Trust *you* to take his side."

"*I'll* decide if there's meaning in his words," Stryke stated. "Make yourself plain, Mobbs."

"To do that, you need to know something of our land's history, and I fear history is something we are all losing."

"Oh yes, tell us a story," Haskeer mouthed acerbically. "We've all the time in the world, after all."

"*Shut up*," Stryke intoned menacingly.

"I for one know something of Maras-Dantia's past," Alfray put in. "What are you trying to say, gremlin?"

"With respect, most of what you think you know, what many of us believe to be so, is only a mishmash of legends and myths. I have devoted myself to understanding the true course of events that led us to the present sorry situation."

"Humans have brought us to our present state," Stryke declared.

"Yes. But that was a fairly recent development in historical terms. Before then, life in Maras-Dantia had remained unchanged since time out of mind. Of course there was always enmity between the native races, and ever-shifting alliances often led to conflict. But the land was big enough for all to live in harmony, more or less."

"Then the humans came," Coilla said.

"Aye. But how many of you know that there were *two* influxes of that wretched race? And that at first relations between them and the elder races were not hostile?"

Jup looked sceptical. "You jest."

"It is a fact. The first immigrants to arrive through the Scilantium Desert were individuals and small groups. They were pioneers looking for a new frontier, or fleeing persecution, or simply wanting to make a fresh beginning."

"*They* were persecuted?" Haskeer exclaimed. "Your tale beggars belief, wrinkled one."

"I tell you only the truth as I have found it, unpalatable as it may be." The gremlin sounded as though his pride had been hurt.

"Go on," Stryke urged.

"Although their ways seemed mysterious to the native population, and still do to most of us, those early incomers were left in peace. A few gained some respect. Hard to believe now, is it not?"

"You can say that again," Coilla agreed.

"Tiny numbers of the outsiders even bred with members of elder races, producing strange hybrid offspring. But this you know, as I believe you are followers of the fruit of one such union."

Coilla nodded. "Jennesta. *Followers* isn't quite the right word."

Stryke noted the spleen in her voice.

"That comes later in the story," Mobbs told them, "if you will allow me to return to it." A vague expression clouded his features. "Now, where was I . . . ?"

"The early incomers," Alfray prompted.

"Oh yes. As I said, the first wave actually got on with the elder races quite well. At least, they gave more cause for curiosity than concern. The second wave was different. They were more a flood, you might say." He gave a snorting little laugh at his own witticism. The orcs remained granite-faced. "Er, yes. This second and larger inflow of humans was different. They were land grabbers and despoilers, and at best they saw us as a nuisance. It wasn't long before they began to fear and hate us."

"They showed contempt," Coilla murmured.

"Yes, and no more so than in renaming our land."

"*Centrasia*," Haskeer spat. He voiced it like an obscenity.

"They treated us like beasts of burden, and set to exploiting Maras-Dantia's resources. You know about that; it continues to this day, and grows more fevered. The rounding-up of free-roaming animals for their meat and hides, the overgrazing . . ."

"The fouling of rivers," Coilla added, "the levelling of forests."

"Putting villages to the torch," Jup contributed.

"Spreading their foul diseases," Alfray said.

Haskeer looked particularly aggrieved at the last point.

"Worse," Mobbs went on, "they ate the magic."

A stir went through the band, a murmur of agreement at the outrage.

"To we elder races, our powers diminishing, that was a final insult. It sowed the seeds of the wars we have endured ever since."

"I've always been puzzled why the humans don't use the magic they've taken against us," Jup commented. "Are they too stupid to employ it?"

"I think it possible that they are simply ignorant. Perhaps they are not taking our magic for themselves but wasting it."

"That's my feeling."

"The bleeding of the earth's magic is bad," Stryke said, "but their overturning of the natural order of the seasons is much worse."

"Without doubt," Mobbs agreed. "In tearing the heart out of the land, the humans interfered with the flow of energies sustaining nature's balance. Now the ice advances from the north as surely as humans pour in from the south. And all this has happened since your father's father's time, Stryke."

"I never knew my father."

"No, I know you orcs are raised communally. That isn't my point. I'm saying all of this has happened to Maras-Dantia in fairly recent times. The coming of the ice has only really begun in my lifetime, for example, and despite what you may think, I am not *that* old."

Stryke couldn't help noticing Alfray giving Mobbs a fleeting, sympathetic glance.

"In my time I have seen the purity of the land ravished," the gremlin recalled. "I have seen the treaties races built smashed and realigned by the Manis and Unis."

"And the likes of us forced to fight for one of those factions," Coilla remarked, her depth of resentment apparent.

Mobbs sighed ruefully. "Yes, many noble races, the orcs included, have been reduced to little more than serfdom by the outsiders."

Coilla's eyes were blazing. "And suffered their intolerance."

"The two factions are indeed intolerant of us. But perhaps no more so than they are of each other. I am told that the more zealous of them, particularly among the Unis, regularly burn their own kind at the stake for something they call *heresy*." He saw their curious expressions. "It is to do with breaking the rules about how their god or gods are to be served, I believe," he explained. "Elder races have been known to behave in similar ways, mind. The history of the pixie clans, to take one example, is not without persecution and bloodshed."

"And there's a race that can't afford to lose anybody," Haskeer pronounced, "seeing as how they're such notorious butt bandits."

"What with that and their fire-starting abilities," Jup pitched in, "I don't know how they've survived this long. All that friction . . ."

The band roared with bawdy laughter. Even Haskeer cracked a grin.

Mobbs's green hide took on a pink hue of embarrassment. He cleared his throat in an attempt at delicacy. "Er, quite."

Coilla seemed less amused than the rest, and impatient. "All right, we've had a history lesson. What about the cylinder?"

"Yes, get to the point, Mobbs," Stryke said.

"The point, Commander, is that I believe this artifact has its origins long, long before the events we have just discussed. Back to the earliest days of Maras-Dantia, in fact."

"Explain."

"We spoke of symbiotes, those rare hybrids produced from unions between elder races and humans."

"Like Jennesta."

"Indeed. And her sisters, Adpar and Sanara."

"They're mythical, aren't they?" remarked Jup.

"They are thought to exist. Though where they are, I have no idea. It is said that while Jennesta is a balance of the two races, Adpar is more purely nyadd. No one knows much about Sanara."

"Real or not, what have they to do with the cylinder, beyond Jennesta laying claim to it?" Stryke asked.

"Directly, nothing that I know of. It is their mother, Vermegram, of whom I am thinking. You know the stories of how mighty a sorceress she was, of course."

"But not as great as the one said to have slain her," Stryke commented.

"The legendary Tentarr Arngrim, yes. Though little is known of him either. Why, even his race is in doubt."

Haskeer sighed theatrically. "You repeat stories made up to frighten hatchlings, gremlin."

"Perhaps. I think not. But what I am saying is that I believe this artifact dates from ancient times, the golden age when

Vermegram and Tentarr Arngrim were at the height of their powers."

Jup was puzzled. "I never understood how Vermegram, if she did exist, could possibly have been the mother of Jennesta and her sisters. Having lived so long ago, I mean."

"It is said that Vermegram's life was of incredible longevity."

"What?" Haskeer said.

"She was *long-lived*, blockhead," Coilla informed him. "So Jennesta and her sisters are also incredibly old. Is that it, Mobbs?"

"Not necessarily. In fact, I think Jennesta is probably no older than she appears to be. Remember, Vermegram's death and whatever fate befell Arngrim occurred not that long ago."

"That must mean Vermegram was an ancient crone when she birthed her brood. Are you saying she stayed fertile into her dotage? That's insane!"

"I don't know. All I *would* say is that scholars are agreed she possessed magic of remarkable potency. Given that, anything is possible."

Stryke slipped the cylinder free of his belt and laid it at his feet. "What had she to do with this thing?"

"The earliest annals that mention Tentarr Arngrim and Vermegram contain hints about what I believe to be this cylinder. Or rather, what it contained: knowledge. And knowledge means power. A power many have given their lives to possess."

"What kind of power?"

"The stories are vague. As best as I can grasp it, it is a . . . key, let us call it. A key to understanding. If I am right, it will throw light on many things, not least the origin of the elder races, including orcs. All of us."

Jup stared at the cylinder. "Whatever's inside this little thing would tell us all that?"

"No. It would *begin* to tell you. If my reasoning is correct, it would set you on that path. Such knowledge does not come easy."

"This is horse shit," Haskeer complained. "Why don't he talk in plain language?"

"All right," Stryke intervened. "What you're saying, Mobbs, is that the cylinder contains something important. Given how

much Jennesta wants it, that hardly comes as a surprise. What
are you getting at?"

"Knowledge is neutral. It is generally neither good nor bad.
It becomes a force for enlightenment or evil depending on who
controls it."

"So?"

"If Jennesta has command of this knowledge it's likely no good
will come of it, you must know that. It could be better used."

"You're saying we shouldn't return the cylinder to her?"
Coilla asked.

Mobbs didn't answer.

"You *are*, aren't you?" she persisted.

"I have lived for many seasons and seen many things. I would
die content if I thought my one cherished wish might come
true."

"Which is?"

"You do not know, even in your heart? My dearest wish is
that our land be returned to us. That we could go back to the
way things were. The power of this artifact is the nearest we
may ever get to a chance of that. But just a *chance*. It would be the
first step in a long journey."

The passion of his words quietened them all for a moment.

"Let's open it," Coilla said.

"*What?*" Haskeer exclaimed, leaping to his feet.

"Aren't you curious about what we might find inside? Don't
you wish, too, for a power that might free our land?"

"Like fuck I do, you crazy bitch. Do you want to get us all
killed?"

"Face it, Haskeer; we're as good as dead anyway. If we go back
to Cairnbarrow, that cylinder and the pellucid will count for
nothing as far as Jennesta's concerned. Any of you think otherwise and you're fooling yourselves."

Haskeer turned to the other officers. "You've more sense than
she has. Tell her she's wrong."

"I'm not sure she is," Alfray replied. "I think the minute we
screwed up our mission we signed our own death warrants."

"What have we got to lose?" Jup added. "We have no home
now."

"I'd expect that of *you*," Haskeer gibed. "Your place was never with orcs anyway. What do you care if we live or die?" He looked to Stryke. "That's right, isn't it, Captain? We know better than a female, a has-been and a dwarf, don't we? Tell them."

Every eye was on Stryke. He said nothing.

"*Tell* them," Haskeer repeated.

"I agree with Coilla," Stryke said.

"You . . . you can't be *serious!*"

Stryke ignored him. What he saw was Coilla smiling, and few faces in the band showing disapproval.

"Have you all gone fucking *mad?*" Haskeer demanded. "You, Stryke, of all orcs; I didn't expect this of you. You're asking us to throw everything away!"

"I'm asking that we open this cylinder. Everything else we've thrown away already."

"Stryke's just saying we should look," Jup said. "We can reseal it, can't we?"

"And if the Queen discovers we've tampered with it? Can you imagine her wrath?"

"I've no need to imagine it," Stryke told him. "That's one reason we should seize any chance to change things for ourselves. Or perhaps you're happy with the way they are?"

"I *accept* the way things are, because I know we *can't* change anything. At least we've got our lives, and now you want to waste them."

"We want to *find* them," Coilla said.

Stryke addressed the whole band. "For something this important, something that touches all of us, we're going to do what we've never done before. We're going to have a show of hands. All right?"

Nobody objected.

He held up the cylinder. "Those who think we should leave this be and return to Cairnbarrow, raise your hand."

Haskeer did. Three grunts joined him.

"Those who say we should open it?"

Every other hand went up.

"You're outvoted," Stryke declared.

"You're making a big mistake," Haskeer muttered grimly.

"You're doing the right thing, Stryke," Coilla assured him.

Right or not, the relief he felt was almost physical. It was as though he was doing something honest for the first time in as long as he could remember.

But that didn't stop the icy tingle of fear that caressed his spine as he looked at the cylinder.

14

As the band looked on in silence, Stryke took a knife to the cylinder's seal. Having cut through it, he prised off the cap. There was a faint whiff of mustiness.

He pushed his fingers inside. Their clumsiness made for a moment of awkward fumbling before he slipped out a rolled parchment. It was fragile and yellowing with age. This he handed to Mobbs. The gremlin accepted it with a mixture of eagerness and reverence.

Stryke shook the cylinder. It rattled. He held it up and looked into it.

"There's something else in here," he said, half to himself.

He patted the tube's open end on his palm. An object slid out.

It consisted of a small central sphere with seven tiny radiating spikes of variable lengths. It was sandy-coloured, similar to a light, polished wood. It was heavier than it looked.

Stryke held it up and examined it.

"It's like a star," Coilla decided. "Or a hatchling's toy of one."

He thought she was right. The object did resemble a crude representation of a star.

Mobbs had the parchment unrolled on his lap, but was ignoring it. He stared awestruck at the object.

"What's it made of?" Alfray wondered.

Stryke passed it to him.

"It's no material I know," the field surgeon pronounced. "It's not wood, nor bone."

Jup took it. "Could it be fashioned from some kind of stone?" he asked.

"Something precious?" Haskeer ventured, interest overtaking his resentment. "Carved from a gem, maybe?"

Stryke reached for it. "I don't think so." He squeezed it in his fist, gently at first, then applying all his strength. "Whatever it is, it's tough."

"How tough can it be?" Haskeer grunted. "Give it here."

He raised the object to his mouth and bit it. There was a crack. A spasm of pain creased his face and he spat out a bloody tooth. *"Vuckk!"* he cursed.

Stryke snatched the star and wiped it on his breeches. He inspected it. There wasn't a mark. *"Very* tough then, if your fangs can't make an impression."

Several band members sniggered. Haskeer glared at them.

Mobbs's attention was torn between the object and the parchment. His expression was intense, excited, as his gaze went from one to the other.

"What do you make of it, scholar?" Stryke asked.

"I think . . . I think this is . . . it." The gremlin's hands were shaking. "What I hoped for . . ."

"Don't keep us in the dark," Coilla demanded impatiently. "Tell us!"

Mobbs indicated the parchment. "This is written in a language so old, so . . . obscure, that even I have difficulty understanding it."

"What *can* you make out?" she persisted.

"At this stage, merely fragments. But I believe they confirm my suspicions." He was jubilant, in a Mobbs kind of way. "That object . . ." he pointed to the star in Stryke's hand, ". . . is an instrumentality."

"A *what?*" Haskeer said, dabbing at his mouth with a grubby sleeve.

Stryke gave the thing to Mobbs. He accepted it gingerly. "An instrumentality, in the old tongue. This is tangible proof of an ancient story hitherto thought a myth. If the legends are true, it could have been handled by Vermegram herself. It may even have been created by her."

"For what purpose?" Jup asked.

"As a totem of great magical power, and of great truth, in that it hints at a mystery concerning the elder races."

"How so?" Stryke demanded.

"All I really know is that each instrumentality is part of a larger whole. One fifth, to be precise. When this is united with its four fellows, the truth will be revealed. I have no idea what that means, to be honest. But I would stake my life on this being the most significant object any of us has ever seen."

He spoke with such conviction that all were held by his words.

Jup pricked the bubble. "How could it be united with the others? What happens if they are? *Where* are they?"

"Mysteries within mysteries and unanswered questions. It has always been so for any student of these matters." Mobbs sniffed, matter-of-factly. "I have no answers to your first two questions, but something I overheard from my captors might be a clue to the location of another instrumentality. *Might*, I say."

"What was it?" Stryke asked.

"The kobolds were not aware that I have a rudimentary grasp of their language. I thought it useful not to reveal the fact. Consequently they spoke freely in my presence, and several times referred to the Uni stronghold called Trinity. They were convinced that the sect holding sway there had incorporated the legend of the instrumentalities into their religion."

"Trinity? That's Kimball Hobrow's redoubt, isn't it?" Coilla remarked.

"Yes," Alfray confirmed, "and he's notorious for being a fanatic. Rules his followers with a rod of iron. Hates elder races, by all accounts."

"You think they might have one of these . . . stars at Trinity, Mobbs?" Stryke said.

"I do not know. But the odds are fair. Why else would the kobolds be interested in the place? If they are gathering the instrumentalities, either for themselves or somebody else, it would be logical."

"Just a minute," Jup interrupted. "If these instrumentalities are so powerful—"

"*Potentially* powerful," Mobbs corrected him.

"All right, they promise power. That being the case, why isn't Hobrow searching for them? Why aren't others?"

"Quite likely they don't know the legends of their power. Or perhaps they know enough of the legends to realise an instrumentality is a revered object, but don't know that it's necessary to unite them. Then again, who is to say that Hobrow or others are *not* looking? Such an aim is best served by secrecy."

"What about Jennesta?" Coilla said. "Is she likely to know about the legend of the five stars, Mobbs?"

"I cannot say. But if she is so anxious to get this one, quite possibly she does."

"So she could have searches under way too?"

"It is what I would do in her position. But remember, orcs, that I told you the power the instrumentalities offer would not be easily gained. That does not mean you should give up."

"Give up?" Haskeer blustered. "Give up *what?* You're not going on this insane quest, are you, Stryke?"

"I'm thinking about several ways we could jump."

"You know what chasing another of these star things means, don't you? Desertion!"

"We must be listed as deserters already, Haskeer. It's been over a week since we should have returned to Cairnbarrow."

"And whose fault was *that?*"

For a brace of heartbeats, those looking on didn't know how Stryke would take the accusation. He surprised them.

"All right, blame me. I can't argue with that."

Haskeer pressed a little further. "I wonder how much you *wanted* to put us in this position. Particularly as now you're trying to push us into making things worse."

"I didn't set out to make life harder for us. But now it's happened, it's happened. We should make the best of it."

"By swallowing these stories of myths and legends? They're tales for the hatcheries, Stryke. You can't believe this gryphon shit."

"Whether I do or not isn't the point. What matters is that Jennesta does. That gives us a powerful bargaining counter. This star could mean the difference between us living or dying. I'm not sure it's enough, knowing Jennesta. But if we had more than one, even all five . . ."

"So you think it's better to set off on this brainless quest than go back and throw ourselves on the Queen's mercy?"

"She *has* no mercy, Haskeer. Can't you get that through your head? Or does it take my fists to do it?"

"But you want to make this move on the word of an old gremlin." He jabbed his finger at Mobbs, who flinched. "How do you know he's telling the truth? Or that he isn't just plain crazy?"

"I believe him. Even if I didn't, we can't go back. Look, if you and the ones who voted with you, Jad, Finje, Breggin, if you want to go, then do it. But there's safety in numbers."

"You want to break up the band?"

"No, I don't."

"You only got us to vote on the cylinder, Stryke, not turning renegade."

"Fair point. Though I reckon we're renegades already. You just haven't realised it." He faced the assembled Wolverines. "You've heard what's been said. I want to go after another star, and Trinity looks the best bet. I won't pretend it'll be anything but rough. But then we're orcs, and that's what we do best. If any of you don't want to come, if you'd prefer to go back to Cairnbarrow or anywhere else, you'll be given rations and a horse. Make yourselves known now."

No one, not even those who had voted with Haskeer, came forward.

"So, are you coming?" Stryke asked him.

After a pause, he replied moodily, "Don't have much choice, do I?"

"Yes, you do."

"I'm coming. But if things go against my liking, I'll leave."

"All right. But mark this. We might not be part of Jennesta's horde any more, but that doesn't mean discipline isn't going to hold in this band. It's what makes everything work. If you've got a problem with that, we'll take another vote. On who's going to be leader."

"Keep your leadership, Stryke. I just want to get out of this mess with my head."

"You have taken the first step of a long and perilous journey," Mobbs told them all. "You cannot go back. You are outlaws now."

The sobering atmosphere that brought down was cut into by Stryke. "Let's get ready to move."

"To Trinity?" Coilla said.

"To Trinity."

She smiled and went off.

Alfray left to check his patients. The rest of the band dispersed.

Mobbs looked up at Stryke and asked hesitantly, "What about . . . me?"

Stryke regarded him for a few seconds, an unreadable expression on his face. "I don't know whether we should thank you for helping us break away or kill you for turning our lives upside down."

"I think you had already started to do that before you met me, Stryke."

"I think perhaps we had."

"What *are* you going to do with me?"

"Let you go."

The gremlin gave a little bow of gratitude.

"Where will you go?" Stryke said.

"Hecklowe. I still have business to finish." His eyes took on a shine. "A trunk full of writing tablets was found in a cellar there. Tax records, apparently, from the . . . You don't find this quite as fascinating as I do, do you, Stryke?"

"Each to his own, Mobbs. Can we escort you part of the way?"

"I am for Hecklowe, you for Trinity. They are in opposite directions."

"We'll let you have a horse and some victuals for the journey."

"That is generous."

"You may have given us back our freedom, it's little enough in exchange. Anyway, we have spares, not least Darig's. He won't be needing one for a while. Oh, and you might as well keep that." He nodded at the parchment in Mobbs's hand.

"Truly?"

"Why not? We have no need of it. Do we?"

"Er, no, indeed not. It has no bearing on the function of the instrumentalities. I thank you for it, Stryke. And for freeing me from the kobolds." He sighed. "I would love to accompany you, you know. But at my age . . ."

"Of course."

"But I wish you and your Wolverines all good luck, Stryke. And if you'll take the counsel of an old gremlin . . . beware. Not only because you have made many enemies on all sides by your recent actions, but also because your search for the instrumentalities may well lead you into conflict with others on the same mission. With so much at stake, your rivals will stop at nothing to gain the prize."

"We can look after ourselves."

Mobbs regarded the orc's massive chest, imposing shoulders, muscular arms and proudly thrusting jaw. He read the determination in the craggy face, the flint in the eyes. "I have no doubt you can."

Haskeer returned, hefting a saddle one-handed. He dropped it nearby and began arranging his kit.

"What route will you take to Hecklowe?" Stryke wanted to know.

Mobbs cracked a thin smile. "Not through this forest, that is for certain. I will go west, in order to leave it as quickly as possible, then turn north to skirt it. It's a longer way—"

"But much safer. I understand. We'll ride to the forest's edge with you."

"Thank you. I shall make ready."

He walked off clutching the parchment.

"That could be a mistake too," Haskeer commented. "He knows too much. What if he talks?"

"He won't."

Before Haskeer could offer any more unwanted advice, Alfray arrived, his face troubled.

Without preamble he announced, "Meklun's dead. The fever took him."

"Shit," Stryke said. "But it's not a surprise."

"No. At least his suffering's over. I hate losing them, Stryke. But I did my best."

"I know."

"Question now is, what do we do with him? Given the fix we're in."

"A funeral pyre's going to be like a beacon for kobolds and any other race looking for trouble. We can't risk it. This once, forget tradition. Bury him."

"I'll get it done."

As Alfray made to leave, he glanced at Haskeer and stopped. "You all right?" he enquired. "You look a bit off-colour."

"I'm *fine*," Haskeer replied sharply. "I'm just sick of what's happening to this band! Now leave me alone!"

He turned his back on them and stormed off.

Jennesta stared at the necklace of snow leopard's teeth.

It had arrived with an impertinent message from the captain that Kysthan had sent after the Wolverines. Despite his orders, Delorran had taken it upon himself to extend the deadline she had decreed. The necklace was a reminder of how minions would resort to insubordination the moment they were out of sight. And of the punishment she would inflict for the transgression.

She slipped the necklace into the pouch in her cloak and gazed at the sky. The flock of dragons was no more than a distant speckle of black dots now. They were off on yet another patrol, searching for her quarry.

The wind changed and brought the odour of something unpleasant her way. She looked at the gibbet set in the middle of the courtyard.

General Kysthan's body hung from it, swaying gently.

Decomposition was setting in. Soon birds of prey as well as dragons would be circling above her castle. But she would leave the carcass there for a while yet. It served as an example to others who might fail her. In particular it would be a warning to the one she was about to receive.

She watched as the dragons were completely swallowed by the overcast sky.

Then several of her orc bodyguards approached, escorting another of their kind. He was young, or at least youngish, being perhaps thirty seasons old. His physique spoke of a warrior, rather than the general his abnormally clean and tidy uniform indicated.

Naturally he couldn't resist a sidelong glance at the suspended corpse.

He clicked his heels smartly and gave a bobbing head bow. "My lady."

She waved away the guards. "At ease, Mersadion."

If he relaxed at all, it was imperceptible.

"I'm told you're ambitious, energetic, and more politically adept than Kysthan was," she said. "You've also risen well in the ranks. Having been a soldier in the field until recently could prove to both our advantages. That you are not still there is due entirely to me. Be sure that, having made you, I can break you."

"Ma'am."

"What did you think of Kysthan?"

"He was . . . of an older generation, my lady. One with which I have not a great deal of sympathy."

"I do hope you're not going to begin our working relationship with mealy words, General, or it won't last long. Now try the truth."

"He was a fool, Your Majesty."

She smiled. An act which, had Mersadion known her better, would not have reassured him even to the limited extent it did. "I picked you for preferment because I understand foolishness is *not* one of your weaknesses. Do you know the situation concerning the Wolverines?"

"The warband? All I know is that they've gone missing, presumed dead or captured."

"Presumed nothing. They're absent without leave, and they have an item of great value that belongs to me."

"Isn't Captain Delorran searching for them already?"

"Yes, and he's overdue. You know this Delorran?"

"A little, my lady, yes."

"What's your opinion of him?"

"Young, headstrong, and driven by his hatred of the Wolverines' commander, Stryke. Delorran has long harboured resentments about Stryke. But he's an orc you'd expect to obey orders."

"He's gone beyond the time limit I set for his return. This displeases me greatly."

"If Delorran's late returning it must be for a good reason, ma'am. A warm trail left by the Wolverines, for example."

"He sent a message to that effect. Very well. For the moment I won't add him and *his* band to those regarded as outlaws. But every day the Wolverines are absent the more it looks as though they've gone renegade. Your first assignment, and it's by far the most important, is to take command of the search for them. It's vital to get back the artifact they've stolen."

"What is this artifact, ma'am?"

"That you don't need to know, beyond its description. I have other assignments for you, related to the recovery of this item, but my orders about those will be passed to you in due course."

"Yes, Your Majesty."

"Serve me well, Mersadion, and I'll reward you. Further advancement will be yours. Now take a good look at your predecessor." A note of menace crept into her voice. "Be clear that if you fail me you will share his fate. Understood?"

"Understood, my lady."

She thought he took that well. He looked respectful of the threat but not overawed by it. Perhaps she could work with this one, and not have to submit him to the kind of death she had in mind for Stryke. And when he finally returned, Delorran.

Delorran surveyed the charred remains of the tiny makeshift village.

Most of the foliage that had hidden the depression where the settlement was located had been destroyed by fire. Only skeletal trees and the stumps of burnt bushes were left.

He sat astride his horse, his sergeant mounted beside him, as the grunts investigated the ruins.

"It seems the Wolverines leave destruction everywhere they go," Delorran commented.

"That's their job, isn't it, sir?" the sergeant replied.

Delorran gave him a disdainful look. "This wasn't a military target. It looks like a civilian camp."

"But how do we know the Wolverines had anything to do with it, sir?"

"It would be too great a coincidence if they hadn't, given that their trail led straight here."

A trooper ran to them. The sergeant leaned over and heard his report, then dismissed him.

"The bodies in the burnt-out huts, sir," the sergeant related. "They're orcs. All women and young ones, apparently."

"Any signs of what killed them?"

"The bodies are too far gone for that, sir."

"So, Stryke and his gang have sunk low enough to slay their own kind now, and defenceless ones at that."

"With respect, sir . . . ," the sergeant ventured carefully.

"Yes, Sergeant?"

"Well, these deaths could have been due to any number of things. It could have been the fire. We have no proof that the Wolverines—"

"I have the proof of my own eyes. And knowing what Stryke's capable of, it doesn't surprise me at all. They're renegades now. Maybe they've even gone over to the Unis."

"Yes, sir." It was a muted, less than enthusiastic response.

"Get the company together, Sergeant, we've no time to waste. What we've seen here gives us even more reason to catch these bandits, and put a stop to them. We're pushing on."

They could do no more for Meklun than commend his spirit to the gods of war and bury him too deep for scavenging animals.

Having escorted Mobbs from Black Rock Forest, the Wolverines headed south-west on the first leg of their journey to Trinity. This time, their course would take them between Weaver's Lea and Quatt, the dwarves' homeland. The most direct route put Weaver's Lea directly in their path, but bearing in mind the trouble they'd had with the roadblock near there earlier, Stryke was determined to approach the human settlement with caution. His plan was to bypass it and make for the foothills of the Carascrag Mountains. Then they'd turn due west in the direction of Trinity. That would greatly lengthen the journey, but he thought it a price worth paying.

As the day wore on they sighted a sizeable herd of gryphons. The animals were heading north, travelling at speed with the loping, jerky movement peculiar to their species. An hour or two later a far-off group of dragons was spotted, soaring high above the western horizon. That the beasts enjoyed a freedom threatened by the turmoil engulfing the land somehow made it seem sweeter. The parallel with the Wolverines' liberation was not lost on Stryke.

Typically, Haskeer failed to appreciate any similarity, and continued to complain as they rode.

"We don't even know what this star thing is, or what it does," he moaned, repeating a point already made numerous times before.

Stryke's patience was wearing thin, but he took another shot at explaining. "We know Jennesta wants it, that it's important to her, which in itself gives it power. That's all you need to hold on to."

Haskeer effectively ignored that and kept the questions coming. "What do we do even if we find the second star? What about the other three? Suppose we never find them? Where do we go? Who do we ally ourselves with when all hands are turned against us? How can—"

"For the gods' sake!" Stryke flared. "Stop telling me what we *can't* do. Concentrate on what's possible."

"What's possible is that we'll all lose our heads!" Haskeer yanked on his horse's reins and rode back down the column.

"I don't know why you wanted him to stay, Stryke," Coilla remarked.

"I'm not sure myself," he sighed. "Except I don't like the idea of breaking up the band, and whatever else you can say about the bastard, at least he's a good fighter."

"We might be needing that particular skill," Jup said. "Look!"

A column of thick black smoke was rising from the direction of Weaver's Lea.

15

Mobbs was happy.

He had been liberated from the kobolds. The orcs that had rescued him had spared his life, despite their fearsome reputation. Given the choice, he could think of more suitable guardians of an instrumentality, but at least it looked as though they weren't going to hand it to Jennesta. To Mobbs' way of thinking, that seemed the lesser of two evils. And he hoped he had been able to impress on the orcs that their future course of action should be designed to help all the elder races. He even had a fascinating historical document as a souvenir of his adventure. Perhaps some good would come from his ordeal after all.

But the last couple of days had seen more than enough excitement for a humble scholar, particularly one of his age, and he was glad to be out of it.

It was more than six hours since the orcs had taken him to the edge of Black Rock Forest and pointed him north. All he had to do was keep the forest on his right and, when it came to an end, veer east for the coast and then along to Hecklowe. What he hadn't bargained on was the forest being so large and the journey so long. Or perhaps it just seemed that way to an old academic unused to travelling. The first time he had made this journey, going the other way, he was the kobolds' captive, and they had brought him blindfolded in a covered wagon.

He was a little worried that he might run into the kobolds again, or some other group of brigands, particularly as he was far from being a good rider and unlikely to outrun them. In fact, as a member of such a small race, his feet did not reach the horse's stirrups. All he could do was trust in the gods and make as fast a pace as he was able.

But the world had a way of imposing its troubles on him. An

hour or two before, he had noticed a column of black smoke behind him, in the south. If he had his bearings correctly, it was coming from the area of Weaver's Lea. Every so often he glanced over his shoulder. The pillar of smoke seemed no more distant and ever higher.

He was thinking about what its cause might be when he became aware of movement to his left.

The land in that direction was hilly, and dotted with patches of trees seeded from the main forest by birds and the wind. So he couldn't make out what was approaching other than that it appeared to be a party of horse riders. He assumed it wasn't kobolds because they rode not horses but kirgizils. His fading eyesight wouldn't let him make out more and he grew apprehensive. All he could do was stay on his trail and hope they passed without seeing him.

It was a forlorn hope.

The riders turned from their parallel heading, put on a spurt of speed and made for the path he was travelling. He clung to the belief that he had not been spotted until they climbed the slight rise leading to his track, emerging ahead of and behind him.

Then he saw that they were orcs. He felt relief. This must be the band that had freed him, Stryke's band, probably back to ask more about the instrumentality. Or perhaps to escort him through this troubled region.

Mobbs pulled back on the reins and halted. The orcs trotted to him.

"Greetings," he hailed. "Why have you returned?"

"Returned?" one of them said. He bore the facial tattoos of a sergeant.

Mobbs blinked. He didn't recognise the one who had spoken. None of the others looked familiar either. "Where's Stryke?" he asked jauntily. "I can't see him."

The looks on their faces showed it was the wrong thing to say. He was confused. An orc with captain's tattoos steered his horse through the troopers. Again, Mobbs didn't remember seeing him before.

"He mistook us for the Wolverines," the sergeant reported, nodding at Mobbs. "He mentioned Stryke."

Delorran drew level with the gremlin and studied him, hard-eyed. "Perhaps all orcs look the same to him," he said. There was no trace of humour in his voice, and certainly no warmth.

"I can assure you, Captain, that—"

"If you know Stryke's name," the Captain cut in, "you must have encountered the Wolverines."

Mobbs sensed danger. Somehow he knew that admitting to it put him in a difficult position. But he couldn't see how to deny it.

While he dithered, the Captain's patience visibly stretched. "You've had contact with them, yes?"

"It's true I did run into a band of orc warriors," Mobbs finally replied, choosing his words prudently.

"And what?" Delorran pressed. "Passed the time of day? Chatted about their exploits? Aided them in some way, perhaps?"

"I cannot see what aid an old gremlin like myself, and a lowly scholar at that, could possibly offer such as yourselves."

"They're not like ourselves," the Captain snapped. "They're renegades."

"*Really?*" Mobbs put on what he hoped was a convincing show of surprise. "I had no idea of their . . . status."

"Perhaps you were more successful in learning where they were going?"

"Going? You don't know, Captain?"

Delorran drew his sword. Its menacing tip hovered at Mobbs's chest. "I've not time to waste, and you're a bad liar. Where are they?"

"I . . . I don't . . ."

The blade pricked the gremlin's matted robe. "Talk now or never again."

"They . . . they mentioned that they might be going . . . going to . . . Trinity," Mobbs imparted reluctantly.

"Trinity? That hotbed of Unis? I *knew* it! What did I tell you, Sergeant? They've not only deserted, they've turned traitors, the bastards."

The sergeant looked Mobbs over. "Suppose he's lying, sir?"

"He's telling the truth. Look at him. It's all he can do not to piss himself."

Mobbs rose in the saddle to his full, modest height, ready to deliver a dignified rebuttal of the insult.

Without warning, Delorran drove his sword into the gremlin's chest.

Mobbs gasped and looked down at the blade. Delorran tugged it free. Blood flowed freely. Mobbs looked at the orc officer, incomprehension written all over his face. Then he toppled from the saddle.

The alarmed horse bucked. Reaching out for its reins, the sergeant steadied it.

Delorran noticed a saddlebag that had been concealed by the gremlin's robe. He flipped it open and began rifling. It held little more than the rolled parchment. Delorran realised that it was very old, but could otherwise make no sense of it.

"This might have some bearing on the object we're looking for," he admitted lamely. "Perhaps we could have questioned him more closely."

The sergeant thought his superior looked faintly embarrassed. Naturally he didn't draw attention to it. Instead he glanced at the gremlin's body and contented himself with, "Bit late to put that right now, sir."

The irony was lost on Delorran. He was staring at the column of smoke.

By evening, the Wolverines were much nearer the pillar of smoke, which now showed white against the darkness. They were close to Weaver's Lea, and expected to reach it at any time. As they rode, they spoke in hushed tones.

"Something big's going on around here, Stryke," Jup said. "Shouldn't we try avoiding Weaver's Lea altogether?"

"There's no way of reaching Trinity without going *somewhere* near the place."

"We could turn back and not go to Trinity at all," Alfray suggested. "Regroup and think again."

"We're committed," Stryke told him, "and wherever we go, we'd have to expect trouble."

The exchange was cut short by the return of an advance scout.

"The settlement's just on the other side of a rise about half a mile further along, sir," he reported. "There's trouble there. It'd be best to dismount when you reach the hill and approach on foot."

Stryke nodded and sent him back.

"The gods know what we're walking into," Haskeer grumbled.

But the complaint wasn't delivered in his usual acerbic style and Stryke ignored it. He passed on an order for silence in the ranks and the band resumed its journey.

They got to the rise without hindrance, dismounted and climbed to join the waiting scouts.

Weaver's Lea stretched out below them. It was a sizeable human community, and typical in consisting mainly of cottages, most built of part stone, part wood. There were some larger buildings: barns, grain stores, meeting halls and at least one place of worship, bearing a spire.

But the most striking thing about the town was that much of it was on fire.

A few figures could be seen, outlined by the blaze, running to and fro. Here and there they were trying to douse the flames, but their efforts looked futile.

"There should be many more humans about than this," Coilla reckoned. "Where are they?"

The scouts shrugged their shoulders.

"There's no point in hanging around here waiting to be spotted," Stryke decided. "We'll circle this and push on."

An hour later, having topped a higher range of hills, they found out what had happened to all the humans.

In a valley below, two armies faced each other.

An engagement was near, and had probably only been delayed by nightfall. The number of torches and braziers twinkling like a swath of stars on either side indicated that the conflict was major.

"A Uni and Mani battle," Jup sighed. "Just what we needed."

"How many would you say there were?" Coilla said. "Five or six thousand a side?"

Stryke squinted. "Hard to tell in this light. Looks like at least that many to me."

"Now we know why Weaver's Lea was burning," Alfray concluded. "It must have been the opening shot."

"So what do we do, Stryke?" Coilla wanted to know.

"I'm not keen on backtracking and risking another clash with the kobolds, and trying to get round a field of battle in the dark's too chancy unless we want to run into raiding parties. We'll stay put here tonight and look at the situation tomorrow."

Unable to move on, unwilling to go back, they watched the unfolding scene below.

When dawn broke, most of the band were sleeping. A roar from the battlefield roused them.

In the cold light of morning, the size of the armies could be clearly seen, and they were easily as large as Coilla had estimated.

"Not long before they meet now," Stryke judged.

Jup rubbed sleep from his eyes. "Human against human. No bad thing from our point of view."

"Maybe not. I just wish they weren't doing it now, and here. We've enough problems."

Somebody pointed to the sky. Several dragons were approaching at a distance.

"So the Manis have help," Alfray said. "From Jennesta, you think, Stryke?"

"Could be. Though she's not the only one with command of them."

Haskeer came out with, "Well, wouldn't you know it. Both armies have dwarves in their ranks."

"So?" Jup responded.

"Says it all, doesn't it? Your kind will fight for anybody with enough coin."

"I've told you before: I'm not responsible for every dwarf in the land."

"Makes me wonder how much their loyalty's to be valued when it goes to the highest bidder. For all we know, you . . ." A coughing fit broke the invective. Red-faced, he barked and hawked.

"You all right, Haskeer?" Alfray asked. "That doesn't sound too good to me."

Haskeer caught his breath and responded angrily. "Get off my back, sawbones! I'm fine!" He resumed coughing, though less violently.

Stryke was about to put in a word when a grunt's yell distracted him.

The band turned and looked down the hill behind them. A group of mounted orcs were approaching the foot of the rise. They outnumbered the Wolverines by about three to one.

"A search party?" Coilla wondered.

"For us? Could be," Stryke said.

"Maybe they've been sent to reinforce the Mani side in the battle," Jup suggested.

The newcomers were nearer. Stryke cupped his eyes and concentrated on them. "Shit!"

Coilla looked at him. "What's the matter?"

"The officer leading them. I know him. He's no friend."

"He's an orc, isn't he?" Alfray reasoned. "We're on the same side, after all."

"Not when it comes to Delorran."

"*Delorran?*" Alfray exclaimed.

"You know him too?" Coilla said.

"Yes. He and Stryke have a lot of . . . history."

"That's one way of putting it," Stryke granted. "But what the hell's he doing here?"

It was no mystery to Alfray. "It's obvious, isn't it? Who better to hunt you down than somebody who hates you enough not to give up?"

The search party halted. Delorran and another orc rode forward a little further and stopped too. The second orc raised a war banner and moved it slowly from side to side.

They all understood the signal. Coilla articulated it. "They want to parley."

Stryke nodded. "Right. You'll come with me. Get our horses."

She ran off to obey the order.

Stryke leaned over to Alfray and slipped him the star. "Guard this." Alfray put it in his jerkin. "Now signal that we're going down to talk."

The Wolverines' own standard was lying in the grass nearby. Alfray unfurled it and sent the message.

"Get Darig to a horse," Stryke added.

"What?"

"I want him ready, I want you *all* ready, in case we need to move fast."

"I don't know if he's in a fit state to ride."

"It's that or we leave him, Alfray."

"Leave him?"

"Just do as you're told."

"I'll double with him on my horse."

Stryke thought about that for a moment. "All right. But if he slows you, dump him."

"I'll pretend you didn't say that."

"Remember it. It could be the difference between us losing one life or two."

Alfray looked far from happy, but nodded agreement. Not that Stryke believed he'd do it.

"If this Delorran is such an enemy," Jup said, "are you sure it's wise for you to go?"

"It has to be me, Jup, you know that. And it's under truce. Stand ready, all of you."

He went to Coilla. They mounted and began riding down the hill.

"Leave the talking to me," he told her. "If we have to get out fast, don't hesitate, just do it."

She gave an almost imperceptible nod.

They reached Delorran and what they could now tell was his sergeant.

Stryke spoke first. He kept it even and cool. "Well met, Delorran."

"Stryke," he responded through clenched teeth. Even a basic civility seemed an effort for him.

"You're a long way from home."

"Let's cut the niceties, shall we, Stryke? We both know why I'm here."

"Do we?"

"If you want to play out this farce to its bitter end, I'll tell you. You and your band are absent without leave."

"I hope you're going to let me explain why."

"The reason's obvious. You've deserted."

"Is that a fact?"

"And you have something belonging to the Queen. I've been sent to get it back. By any means necessary."

"*Any* means? You'd take up arms against fellow orcs? I know we've had our differences, Delorran, but I'd have thought even you—"

"I've no scruples when it comes to traitors."

Stryke bridled. "So we've gone from deserters to traitors, have we? That's quite a jump." There was steel in his tone.

"Don't play the innocent with me. What else would you call it when you fail to return from a mission, steal Jennesta's property and side with the Unis?"

"That's some set of charges, Delorran. But no way have we gone over to the Unis or anybody else. Use your head. We couldn't approach them without being cut down, even if we wanted to."

"I should think they'd welcome an orc fighting unit with open arms. Probably be good for recruiting others as treacherous as you. But I'm not here to bandy words. I judge you by your actions, and slaughtering a camp of orc females and hatchlings tells me all I need to know."

"*What?* Delorran, if you're talking about what I think you are, the orcs in that camp died from disease. We just torched it to—"

"Don't insult me with your lies! My orders are clear. You'll hand over the artifact, and your band will lay down their weapons and surrender."

"Like hell we will," Coilla said.

Delorran shot her a look of fury. "You exercise little discipline over your subordinates, Stryke. Not that it surprises me."

"If she hadn't said it, I would. If we've got something you want, come and get it."

Delorran reached for his sword.

"And if you want to violate a flag of truce, go ahead," Stryke added, raising a hand to his own blade.

They glared at each other.

Delorran didn't draw his sword. "You've got two minutes to think about it. Then give up or put up."

Stryke turned his horse without a word. Coilla, after a parting scowl at Delorran, joined him. They galloped back up to the band.

Swinging from his saddle, Stryke outlined the exchange. "They've got us marked as traitors, and they think we massacred those orcs in the camp we torched."

Alfray was shocked. "How could they think we'd do *that*?"

"Delorran's ready to believe anything about me, as long as it's bad, and in about a minute and a half they'll be coming up here to take us. Dead or alive." He looked to the gathered Wolverines. "It's crunch time. Surrender and we face certain death, either at Delorran's hands or when he takes us back to Cairnbarrow. If I'm to meet my death it's going to be here and now, with a sword in my hand." He scanned their faces. "How say you? Are you with me?"

The band let him know they were. Even Haskeer and the trio who supported him were game for a fight, although their assent was a little less enthusiastic than the others'.

"All right, we're prepared to make a stand," Jup said. "But look at the situation we're in: a battle about to start behind us and a determined force of hardened warriors ahead. What the fuck do we do?"

A few other voices were raised, wanting to know the same thing.

"We strengthen our position if we hold off their first attack," Stryke told them. "And it's coming any second."

At the bottom of the hill, Delorran's force was massing for a charge.

"Mount up!" Stryke shouted. He waved his sword at a couple of grunts. "Help Darig on to Alfray's horse. Alfray, I want you to the back of our defences. Move! All of you!"

The band scrambled for their horses and filled their hands with weapons. Stryke retrieved the star from Alfray and remounted.

Delorran's band was galloping up to them, with perhaps a third of the group holding back as reserves.

Stryke voiced a final thought. "It goes against the grain to meet our own kind in battle. But remember they believe we're renegades and they'll kill us if they get the chance."

The time for talk was over. Stryke raised his arm, brought it down hard and yelled, "Now . . . *charge!*"

The Wolverines turned their horses and swept down to meet the first wave.

They might have been outnumbered, despite the reserve left behind, but they had the advantage of defending higher ground.

Blades clashed, horses milled and shied, blows were delivered and returned. The air was filled with the sound of steel impacting steel as swords met shields.

For Stryke and the others, fighting their own race was a unique and disturbing experience. He hoped it didn't curb their determination. He wasn't sure if it affected Delorran's troop.

But it could have been significant that after five minutes of intense swordplay the attackers began to fall back without major injuries on either side.

As they retreated down the hill, Stryke shouted, "Their hearts weren't in it! If I know Delorran, he'll be giving them hell for that effort. We can't expect it so easy when they come back."

Sure enough, they watched as Delorran addressed his band, and it didn't look like a gentle lecture.

"We can't hold them off forever," Coilla stated grimly.

Jup glanced down at the battlefield behind them. The two sides were slowly advancing towards each other. "Nor do we have anywhere to run."

Delorran's group prepared to attack again, this time with the entire force.

Stryke made a decision. It bordered insanity, but he saw no other way.

"Listen to me!" he bellowed at the Wolverines. "Trust the order I'm going to give, and follow me!"

"We're going to charge them again?" Coilla asked.

Delorran's troop was thundering up the rise.

"Trust me!" Stryke repeated. "Do as I do!"

The enemy was nearer and gathering speed. There was no doubt of their greater resolve. They advanced to a point no more than a short spear throw away.

Stryke's gaze flicked to the battlefield. *"Now!"* he yelled.

Then he turned his horse and spurred it to the top of the rise.

In seconds he had reached the crest and was down the other side.

"Oh no . . ." Jup moaned.

Haskeer was slack-jawed, unable to take in what was happening. He wasn't alone. None of the rest of the band moved.

Delorran was almost on them.

It was Coilla who seized the initiative. "Come on!" she roared. "It's our only chance!"

She brought her horse around and followed Stryke.

"Shit!" Haskeer cursed. But he did the same, along with the other Wolverines.

Alfray, with Darig hanging on, even managed to raise their banner.

As they reached the hill's summit, Stryke was already well down the other side.

In the valley below, the two armies were approaching each other with increasing speed. Humans ran with pikes and spears. Cavalry charged.

The gap between them was closing fast. Like bats out of hell, the Wolverines headed for it.

Delorran and his troops arrived at the top of the hill.

The fact that there was a battle going on in the valley below came as a shock to them. Horses were suddenly reined in, and would have been even if Delorran hadn't thrown up a hand to halt them.

They gazed down, astonished, as the charging orcs made straight for the point where the front lines of the two opposing armies were about to meet.

"What do we do, sir?" the sergeant said.

"Unless you've got a better idea," Delorran replied, "we watch them commit suicide."

16

The angle the Wolverines were racing down was so acute they slid as much as rode.

Coilla turned in her saddle and looked back up the hill. She saw the rest of the band close behind. Above, their pursuers had stopped and were watching them. She goaded her horse and drew parallel with Stryke.

"What the hell are we doing?" she bellowed.

"We just go through!" he mouthed over the wind whipping at their faces. "They won't be expecting it!"

"They're not the only ones!"

The opposite armies were moving closer by the moment.

Stryke pointed downward. "But we have to keep going! And we don't stop even when we reach the other side!"

"*If* we reach the other side!" she yelled at him.

With a jarring thud they bumped on to the flat, the other Wolverines close behind. Stryke glanced over his shoulder. The band were still together. Alfray, with Darig hanging on grimly, was at the rear, but holding his own.

Now that they were on the level the going was faster. The drawback was losing the vantage point they had had on higher ground. From this angle the armies looked a lot closer together, and the increasingly narrow space between them was harder to gauge. Stryke spurred his already lathering horse and called out for the others to keep pace.

Onward, onward, into the valley of death they rode.

They hurtled towards the killing field, the roar of thousands of battle-crazed combatants filling their ears.

Then they were between the advancing lines. Enemies to the left of them, enemies to the right.

A blur of bodies and indistinct faces flashed by. Stryke was dimly aware of heads turning, arms pointing, inaudible shouts aimed in their direction. He prayed that the element of surprise and the confusion of imminent battle would give the Wolverines some kind of edge. And he hoped that the band could benefit from neither army being sure whose side these unexpected intruders were on. Though once they were identified as orcs, he knew the Unis would assume they were here to support the Manis.

They were less than a quarter of the way across the battlefield when arrows and spears began winging their way. Fortunately the two hordes were still far enough apart that the missiles fell harmlessly short. But the soldiers were covering ground at even greater speed. If they flagged for a moment, the Wolverines would be dashed by lethal tides on either side. Here and there, knots of warriors faster on their feet, or mounted on horses with a clear path, were already rushing to block the band's progress.

A group of footsoldiers, armed with pikes and broadswords, ran forward just ahead of Stryke. He rode through them, knocking them aside. Coilla and the band trampled the rest. The orcs were lucky. Had the ground troops been less taken by surprise, and more organised, they could have put a stop to the Wolverines' flight there and then.

Arrows were landing nearer. A spear cut the air between the rump of Stryke's horse and the snout of the one behind. Individual soldiers dashed in right and left to harry the galloping orcs. They lashed out in their turn, cutting down Unis and Manis indiscriminately.

A black-garbed human ran forward and leapt at Coilla's horse, grabbing its reins. He hung on, pulling down with all his weight. Her horse faltered and wheeled, bunching up the Wolverines behind her. More humans were running from all directions to join the fray.

She plucked free a knife and slashed at the face of the man slowing her. He screamed and fell. The following orcs rode over him. Coilla dug in her heels. The band put on a burst of speed and outpaced the running soldiers.

On the flank of the column and more vulnerable, Haskeer swung his axe, to one side then the other, cracking the skulls of pikemen trying to unseat him. Roaring, he made his getaway.

The Wolverines rode on, the view to either side choked with endless twin seas of charging human warriors.

Stryke knew the band was losing momentum. He feared they'd be overwhelmed at any second.

Seen from atop the hill, the band's progress across the valley resembled a handful of tiny black pearls rolled by a giant. Delorran and his troopers watched as the vice closed in to crush them.

"The *lunatics*," Delorran exclaimed. "They'd rather throw their lives away than face my justice."

"They're finished right enough, sir," his sergeant agreed.

"We can't linger here and risk being seen. Make ready to leave."

"What about the artifact, sir?"

"Do *you* want to go and get it?"

The Wolverines' way across the battlefield was about to be blocked. Hundreds of humans, Uni and Mani, were converging ahead of them, from left and right.

"Come!" Delorran barked.

He turned his horse and led his troopers down their side of the hill.

In the valley, Stryke saw humans running forward to obstruct the band's path. He kept going, barrelling into them, lashing out with his sword. A brace of heartbeats later the rest of the Wolverines smacked into the human wall and began carving through it. More chaos ensued as the two sides also started fighting each other.

The scene tipped from confusion into bloody anarchy.

Jup came close to being pulled from his horse by a small mob of Unis with spears. His wild slashing held them off, but he would have been dragged down if a knot of other Wolverines hadn't joined in beating off the attackers. He and they resumed the dash.

Alfray kept pace with the others, but because of his passenger inevitably fell back. They too were targeted for an attack, this time by Manis who had by now abandoned any idea that the orcs were there to aid them. He gave as good an account of himself as he could. But carrying a wounded comrade hampered him, as did bearing the Wolverines' banner, which proved less effective a weapon than a broadsword would have done in the circumstances. And no other Wolverines were near enough to help.

Alfray and Darig were almost out of the mob's grasp when Darig caught the full force of a spear thrust.

He cried out.

Alfray slashed down at the spear carrier, gouging a chunk out of his shoulder. But as far as Darig was concerned, the damage was done.

He swayed in the saddle, head lolling.

Alfray was too busy fending off other attackers to pay Darig much heed. Then another mounted warrior confronted him and Alfray's horse reared. Darig toppled. As soon as he hit the ground, a mass of humans rushed in. Their swords, axes, spears and knives rose and fell.

Alfray cried out in rage and despair. With a single blow he struck down the cavalryman blocking his way. A quick glance at the mob around Darig confirmed that there was nothing he could do. Spurring on his horse, he escaped another onslaught by the skin of his teeth. He joined the tail end of the Wolverines, fighting their way through the bottleneck at the edge of the battlefield. By now he was convinced they wouldn't make it.

Behind them, the armies met and melded in savage conflict.

The start of the battle full-blown proved a boon. The two sides' preoccupation with killing each other, and preserving their own lives, meant the Wolverines were a lesser priority.

Two more minutes of furious slaughter, stretched to infinity, saw the band off the battlefield. They galloped at high speed across the sward and up the opposite bank.

As they climbed, Coilla looked back. A group of humans, twenty or thirty strong, was riding after them. From their appearance, she took them for Unis.

"We've got company!" she yelled.

Stryke already knew as much. "Keep going!" he shouted.

When they got to the top of the valley side they found beyond a sweeping slope leading to grassy flatlands dotted with woods. They kept moving. Their pursuers bobbed over the hill behind them, riding just as swiftly.

The going was softer on this side of the valley. Clods of earth were kicked up by the hooves of hunters and hunted.

A grunt yelled. Everybody looked skyward.

Three dragons were gliding in from the direction of the battlefield.

Stryke had to assume they were after his band. He led the Wolverines in the direction of trees, gambling on cover.

"Heads down!" Jup cried.

A dragon swooped. They felt a blast of heat at their backs. The dragon soared low over their heads and climbed to rejoin its fellows.

The band looked to their rear and saw the pursuing humans had been decimated. Charred corpses of men and horses littered the ground. Some still burned. Several humans, blazing head to foot, tottered and fell. A few hadn't been hit, but they'd had the heart knocked out of them as far as the chase was concerned. Their horses halted, they simply stared at the fallen, or watched dumbly as the orcs slipped from their grasp.

Stryke wondered if the carnage was intentional or not. You never knew with dragons. They were an imprecise weapon at the best of times.

As if in answer, they came in for another attack. The band strained their mounts to reach the fringes of the wood.

A great jagged shadow covered them. The dragon's scalding breath flamed a vast swath of grass a couple of yards to their right. They goaded their shying horses harder still.

Another dragon dived, its mighty wings flapping. A downrush of air battering them, they raced to the wood.

They reached it, with stragglers, including Alfray, barely making the shelter in time. The dragon unleashed its scalding breath, igniting the trees overhead with a roar. Burning branches fell, smouldering leaves and sparks showered down.

Maintaining their pace, the Wolverines drove deep into the wood. Through gaps in the curtain above their heads they caught glimpses of their flying antagonists keeping pace.

At length the sightings grew rarer. Eventually the dragons were apparently eluded. The band slowed but kept moving. They stopped when they reached the wood's far limit.

Concealed within the treeline, they spotted the dragons again, passing overhead in a circling reconnaissance. Not daring to break cover, the band dismounted and guards were posted to watch for any humans that might be following. As far as they could tell, none were. They settled, weapons to hand, waiting for a chance to break cover.

Gulping a long draught from his water sack, Haskeer hammered back the stopper and commenced complaining. "That was one hell of a risk we took back there."

"What else could we have done?" Coilla said. "Anyway, it worked, didn't it?"

Haskeer couldn't argue with that and contented himself with some moody scowling.

His temper wasn't shared by most of the others. The grunts in particular were jubilant about getting away with it, and Stryke had to bark at them to keep the racket down.

Alfray was less joyful. His thoughts lay with Darig. "If I'd just hung on to him, perhaps he'd still be here now."

"There was nothing you could do," Stryke told him. "Don't scourge yourself with what might have been."

"Stryke's right," Coilla agreed. "The wonder is there weren't more lost."

"Even so," Stryke murmured, half to himself, "if anyone's to be blamed for the waste of lives, perhaps it's me."

"Don't start getting sappy," Coilla warned him. "We need you clear-headed, not wallowing in guilt."

Stryke took the point and dropped the subject. He reached into his pocket and brought out the star.

"That odd-looking thing's caused us so much trouble," Alfray said. "It's turned our lives upside down. I hope it's worth it, Stryke."

"It could be our furlough from serfdom."

"Perhaps. Perhaps not. I think you've been looking for any excuse to break away for some time."

"In truth, haven't we all?"

"That could be so. But I'm more wary of change at my age."

"This is a time of change. Everything's changing. Why not us?"

"Huh, change," Haskeer sneered. "There's too much . . . talk of . . ." He appeared breathless and swayed unsteadily. Then he went down like a felled ox.

"What the *hell?*" Coilla exclaimed.

They gathered around him.

"What's the matter?" Stryke asked. "Has he taken a wound?"

After a quick examination, Alfray replied, "No, he hasn't." He laid a hand on Haskeer's forehead, then checked his pulse.

"So what's wrong with him?"

"He's got a fever. Know what I think, Stryke? I reckon he's got the same thing Meklun had."

Several of the grunts backed away.

"He's been hiding this, the fool," Alfray added.

"He's not been himself for the last couple of days, has he?" Coilla remarked.

"No. All the signs were there. And here's another thought, and it's not a pleasant one."

"Go on," Stryke urged.

"I was suspicious of what it was that killed Meklun," Alfray admitted. "Because although his wounds were bad, he could have recovered. I think he picked up something at that encampment we torched."

"He didn't go near the place," Jup reminded him. "He *couldn't.*"

"No. But Haskeer did."

"Gods," Stryke whispered. "He said he didn't touch any of the bodies. He must have lied."

Coilla said, "If Haskeer got the disease there, and passed it on to Meklun, couldn't he have given it to the rest of us too?"

There was a murmur of unease from the band.

"Not necessarily," Alfray told her. "Meklun was already weakened by his wounds, and open to the infection. As for the rest of us, if we were infected, you'd expect to see the signs by now. Does anybody feel unwell?"

The band chorused no or shook their heads.

"From what little we know about these human diseases," Alfray went on, "the greatest risk of infection seems to be in the first forty-eight hours or so."

"Let's hope you're right," Stryke said. He looked down at Haskeer. "Think he'll pull through?"

"He's young and strong. That helps."

"What can we do for him?"

"Not much beyond trying to keep his fever down and waiting for it to break."

"Another problem," Coilla sighed.

"Yes," Stryke agreed, "and we don't need it."

"It's a good thing for him we don't follow his own suggestion about what to do with the wounded. Remember his idea about Meklun?"

"Yeah. Ironic, isn't it?"

"What now, chief?" Jup wondered.

"We stick to the plan." He indicated the dragons circling above. "As soon as they've gone, assuming they *do* go, we push on to Trinity."

It was several hours before the coast was clear.

The dragons, having flown over the wood numerous times, finally headed north and disappeared. Stryke ordered Haskeer to be put over a horse and tied in place. A grunt was assigned to lead it. Cautiously, the band set out in the direction of Trinity. Stryke estimated the journey would take about a day and a half, assuming no obstacles.

With Weaver's Lea behind them, they were free to take a more or less direct route. But now that they were in the south, that part of Maras-Dantia where humans had established themselves in greatest numbers, they had to be even more cautious. Wherever possible they sought the shelter of timberland, blind valleys and other naturally protective areas. Though the further south they travelled, the more evidence they saw of human habitation, and of despoliation.

On the morning of the second day, they came to what had been a small forest, now almost completely felled. Much of the wood had been removed, but large amounts had simply been left to rot. The severed stumps were overgrown with mosses or brown with fungi. Which meant the felling was at least several months old.

They marvelled at the destruction, and the amount of effort needed to achieve it. And they grew more wary, knowing that such devastation required many hands to accomplish.

Several hours later they discovered the use the wood had been put to.

They reached a river, its course running south-west toward the Carascrag mountain range. As rivers were the most reliable navigational aids, they followed it. Soon they noticed that the water flowed deep and was turning sluggish.

Rounding a bend, they found out why.

The river became an enormous, shimmering lake, covering many acres of previously open country. It had been created by a massive wooden dam, constructed they felt sure with trunks taken from the denuded forest. The dam both appalled and impressed them. Standing higher than the tallest pine, it consisted of a barrier six trunks in depth, running a distance a good archer would be sore put to match with an arrow's flight. The timbers had been fitted with a high standard of precision, then lashed with what must have been miles of cable-thick twine. Mortar sealed the joins. On either bank, and emerging from several places in the river itself, were vast angled props, adding to the dam's stability.

Despite the great structure, scouting parties found no sign that humans were present. There having been no let-up in their journey since the previous day, Stryke ordered a halt and posted lookouts.

Once Alfray attended Haskeer's fever, which had grown worse, he joined the other officers to discuss their next move.

"This capturing of the water means we must be near Trinity," Stryke reasoned. "They'd need that much to serve a large population."

"It represents power, too," Alfray suggested. "The power that controlling the water supply brings."

"Not to mention the power it represents in terms of the number of hands needed to build such a thing," Stryke said. "The humans of Trinity must be highly organised as well as numerous."

"Yet they ignore the *magical* power they damaged by perverting the river's course," Jup told them. "Even I can sense the negative energy here."

"And *I* sense a major problem," Coilla said, bringing the conversation to more immediate matters. "Trinity's a fanatical Uni stronghold. Word is they aren't exactly crazy about elder races there. How the hell are we going to get in to try for the star? Or are you planning a suicide mission, Stryke?"

"I don't know what we're going to do. But we'll follow basic military strategy: get as near as we can, try to find ourselves a hiding place and assess the situation. There has to be a way, we just don't know what it is yet."

"What if there isn't?" Alfray asked. "What if we can't get near the place?"

"Then we'll have to rethink everything. Maybe we'll negotiate with Jennesta for the one star we have, in exchange for some kind of amnesty."

"Oh yes, of course," Coilla remarked cynically.

"Or it could be that this is the beginning of a new life for us, as outlaws. Which, let's face it, is what we are anyway."

Jup looked troubled. "That doesn't sound an appetising prospect, chief."

"Then we'll have to do our best to avoid it, won't we? Now get some rest, all of you. I want us back on the road to Trinity in no more than an hour."

17

They spotted Trinity in late afternoon.

Hidden by the cover of vegetation, eyes peeled for patrols, the Wolverines took in the distant settlement. The town was an enclave, completely surrounded by a high timber wall, with lookout towers.

The Carascrag Mountains loomed above and beyond it, steely blue with saw-jagged peaks. Shimmering air played over the mountains, heated by thermals rising from the Kirgizil Desert on the far side of the range.

A well-used road led to a pair of huge gates that served as Trinity's main entrance. They were closed. The township was surrounded by fields of crops so extensive they almost reached the band's hiding place. But the yield looked frail and stunted.

"Now we know what they need all that water for," Coilla said.

"For all the good it does them," Jup replied. "Look at how mean the crops are. These humans are stupid. They can't see that messing with the earth magic affects them as well as us."

"How in damnation are we going to approach the place, Stryke?" Alfray wanted to know. "Let alone get in?"

"We might have one piece of luck on our side. We haven't seen any humans yet. Most of them were probably drawn to the battle at Weaver's Lea."

"But they wouldn't have left the settlement undefended, would they?" Coilla reminded him. "And if most of the population *is* there, they'll be back at some point."

"I meant it might help, not that it solved our problem."

"So what to do?" Jup wondered.

"We scout for somewhere to hide and make a base camp. Coilla, take three grunts and work your way on foot around the township left to right. Jup, pick your three and do the same the other way. Note anything that'll do as a hiding place, and remember it has to be suitable for the horses as well as us. Got that?"

They nodded and moved off to obey their orders.

Stryke looked to Alfray. "How's Haskeer?"

"About the same."

"Trust the bastard to make a nuisance of himself even when he's unconscious. Do what you can for him." He turned to the remainder of the band. "The rest of you keep yourselves alert and combat-ready."

They settled down to watch and wait.

"I'm not sure about this," Jup whispered.

Concealed by bushes, they stared over at the yawning tunnel mouth cut into the bluff.

"What worries me is that there's only the one entrance," Alfray said, "and I don't know how spooked the horses might be in there."

"It's all we could come up with," Coilla repeated, a little exasperated.

"Coilla's right," Stryke decided. "We'll have to make the best of it. Are you *sure* it's disused?"

She nodded. "A couple of the grunts went quite a way in. It's been abandoned."

"We'd be rats in a trap if the humans knew we were hiding there," Jup opined.

"That's a risk we'll have to take," Stryke told him. He checked that the way was clear. "Right, get in there fast. Horses first."

The band swept over to the mine-shaft entrance. Not all the horses went into the black maw willingly and had to be forced the last few yards.

Inside it was dank and much cooler than the open air.

The daylight let them see dimly perhaps thirty paces along the tunnel, at which point it became lower and narrower. After that, all was pitch darkness.

"We stay away from the mouth," Stryke decreed, "and I want no lights used unless absolutely necessary."

Coilla shivered. "I won't be going far enough in to need one. Give me open skies any time."

Jup touched the rough-hewn wall. "What do you think they dug this for?"

Bent over applying a damp cloth to Haskeer's forehead, Alfray ventured, "Gold, probably. Or some other of the earth's booty they think precious."

"I've seen this kind of thing before," Jup said, tapping some stones with the tip of his boot. "I reckon they were going for the black rocks they burn as fuel. Wonder how long it took them to exhaust the seam?"

"Not very, knowing humans," Coilla suggested. "And I think you're right, Jup. I'd heard that Trinity was founded here because there's so much of the black rock to be dug in these parts."

"Again the land is raped," Jup muttered. "We should have breached that dam and given them something to think about."

"We would have had a job doing it," Stryke told him. "An army would be hard put to bring it down. But that's not our concern at the moment. What we need to do is find Trinity's weak point."

"If it has one."

"We won't find out sitting here, Jup."

"So what's your plan?" Coilla asked.

"One thing we need to avoid is having too big a group of us out there, particularly in daylight. So I want to take a look around myself, along with you and Jup."

Coilla nodded. "Suits me fine. I'm not keen on living like a troglodyte."

"The rest will stay here, out of sight," Stryke ordered. "Post a couple of guards, Alfray, and one or two more out there in the undergrowth, to warn of anyone approaching. And try to keep those horses quiet. Come on, you two."

Coilla and Jup followed him from the shaft.

They darted for the first available cover and headed in the direction of the township. Moving cautiously for perhaps half a mile, keeping low, they were going through one of the cultivated fields when Coilla grabbed Stryke's arm. *"Down!"* she hissed, tugging him groundward.

The trio burrowed into the corn. Twenty yards away stood the first humans they'd seen at Trinity. A small group of women, dressed simply and mostly in black, were working in an adjacent field. They were picking a crop of some kind, loading the harvest into baskets borne by mules. Two armed men, bearded and also black-garbed, stood guard as the women worked.

A finger to his lips, Stryke motioned Coilla and Jup to follow him. Their route took them quietly around the toilers. Several more detours then proved necessary to avoid other heads they spotted bobbing above the crops.

Crawling on their hands and knees, they came unexpectedly to a track of compacted earth with a shingle surface. Peeping out from the shelter of the corn, they realised it was the road leading to Trinity's gates. As there were no humans in sight in the fields opposite, they prepared to cross. Coilla was about to lead off when they heard the rumble of approaching wagons. They ducked back and watched.

A procession of vehicles came into view. The first was an open carriage, drawn by a pair of fine white mares. In the front sat the driver and another human, both heavily armed, both dressed in black. There were two other people in the back. Again, both wore black. One was obviously another guard, this time armed with a bow. But the man sitting next to him, on a higher seat, was the most arresting.

He was the only one wearing a hat, a tall, black piece of headgear that Stryke thought was called a stovepipe. Even seated it was obvious that the man was tall, and his build was thin and wiry. He had a weathered face ending in a pointed chin adorned with greying whiskers. The mouth was a thin, featureless slit, the eyes dark and intense. It was a forceful face, unaccustomed to smiling.

The carriage passed.

It was followed by three wagons drawn by teams of oxen. Each wagon was steered by a black-garbed human, with an accompanying guard. The wagons carried passengers, so crammed there was standing room only. All were dwarves.

Stryke noticed Jup's preoccupied reaction to this as the wagons trundled on toward the township's gates.

Jup let out a breath. "Imagine what Haskeer would have made of *that*."

"They weren't prisoners, were they?" Coilla said.

Stryke shook his head. "I'd say they were working parties. What interests me more is that human in the back of the carriage."

"Hobrow?"

"He certainly had the bearing of a leader, Coilla."

"And dead-fish eyes," Jup added.

They watched the convoy's procession to the gates. Guards appeared at the top of the township's wall. The gates swung slowly open, affording a brief glimpse of the scene within as the carriage and wagons entered. Then the gates were pushed shut again. They heard the sound of a weighty crossbar being dropped into place.

"That's it, isn't it?" Jup announced. "Our way in."

Stryke missed his point. "What do you mean?"

"Do I have to spell it out? They're using dwarves in there. I'm a dwarf."

"That's a risky plan, Jup," Coilla responded.

"Can you think of a better one?"

"Even if we could get you in," Stryke said, "what would you expect to achieve?"

"I'd gather information. Check the layout and defences. Maybe even get some idea where they keep the star."

"Assuming Mobbs was right about them having one," Coilla reminded him.

"We'll never find out unless we get somebody in there."

"We don't know what kind of security they have," Stryke pointed out. "Suppose all the dwarf workers are known to them?"

"Or known to each other," Coilla put in. "How would they react to a stranger in their ranks?"

"I didn't say it wouldn't be dangerous," Jup stated. "But I think it's fair to assume that the humans are unlikely to know the dwarves by name. Everything I've heard about this place, and everything we know about humans, tells me they've nothing but contempt for the elder races. I can't see them bothering to learn names."

Coilla frowned. "That's a big assumption."

"It's a chance to be taken. The other thing, about the dwarves themselves noticing a stranger, might not be such a problem. You see, those dwarves were from at least four different tribes."

"How do you know?" Stryke wondered.

"The way they dress, mostly. Neckerchiefs of certain colours, a particular cut of jerkin, and so on. They all indicate a tribal origin."

"What are the signs you wear to indicate your tribe?" Coilla said.

"I don't. You have to get rid of them when you go into Jennesta's service. That's so there's no problem identifying our allegiance. But I can easily put that right."

Stryke was still doubtful. "It's an awful lot of if's and maybe's, Jup."

"Sure, and I haven't mentioned the toughest problem yet. They must have *some* kind of security here as far as workers coming and going is concerned. Probably a simple head-count."

"Which means we couldn't just mix you in with the other dwarves. Assuming we could find a way of doing it."

"Right. I'd have to be *swapped* for one of them."

Coilla gave him a quizzical look. "How the hell are we going to do that?"

"Offhand, I don't know. But if we can, there are a couple of things in our favour. First, I don't think a new face would arouse too much suspicion as far as the other dwarves are concerned, because they're being drawn from different tribes. Second, the humans can't tell us apart anyway. They usually can't when it comes to elder races, you know that."

"And?" Coilla prompted.

"The humans wouldn't be expecting a hostile dwarf to want to get in there."

Stryke shook his head slowly. "Don't take this the wrong way, Jup, but your race does have a reputation for . . . blowing with the wind, let's say. Humans know that dwarves fight for all sides."

"No offence taken, Stryke. You know I've long stopped apologising for the ways of my kind. But let's say they wouldn't expect a *lone* dwarf to be insane enough to infiltrate the place. And remember that in some ways humans are like elder races in seeing what they expect to see. They're using dwarves. I'm a dwarf. Hopefully they wouldn't think much further than that."

"Hopefully," Coilla echoed in a slightly mocking tone. "Humans are bastards but that doesn't make them half-wits, you know."

"I'm aware of that."

"So what are you going to do about your rank markings?" She pointed at the tattoos on his face.

"Garva root. You grind it up with water and add just a little clay for colouring. That'll cover 'em, and it's good enough to match my skin."

"Unless anybody takes a *close* look," Stryke said. "You'd be taking a hell of a lot of chances."

"I know. But will you agree to the plan in principle?"

Stryke pondered it for a moment. "I can't see another way of doing it. So . . . yes."

Jup smiled.

Combat instinct had the three of them craning to check their surroundings. There were no humans in sight.

Coilla sounded a note of caution. "Don't get too excited. We still have to work out the practicalities. Like how we'll swap you for one of the workers."

"Any ideas?" Stryke asked.

"Well, assuming the dwarves are brought in and out every day, and that's a big if in itself, maybe we could ambush one of those wagons. Then we'd take out a passenger and Jup could mingle with the workers in the confusion."

"No. Too much to go wrong, and it'd alert the humans to some kind of trickery."

"You're right," she conceded, "it wouldn't work. What about you, Jup?"

"All I can think of would be to go to the source of the dwarf workers. I mean, they have to come from somewhere, and I'd bet it isn't too far away. It wouldn't make sense bringing them great distances. Somewhere around here there must be a village or pick-up point."

"That makes sense," Stryke agreed. "So to find it, we'd just have to trail those wagons the next time they leave."

"Exactly. We'd have to do it on foot, of course, but those wagons move pretty slow."

"Then let's hope you're right about the pick-up point being near." He turned the notion over in his mind for a second. "We'll do it. Coilla, get back to the others and tell them what's happening. Then come back here with a couple of grunts and we'll wait for the wagons to come out."

"You do realise this is insane, don't you?" she said.

"Insanity's something we're getting quite good at. Now go."

She smiled thinly and snaked into the field.

The wagons carrying the dwarves left Trinity at dusk. There was no sign of the carriage this time.

Stryke, Coilla, Jup and two troopers waited for the carts to pass and get a head start, then followed, keeping low and under cover. When the fields of crops petered away they had to be more inventive in staying out of sight, but they had enough experience to manage that. Fortunately the trio of laden wagons moved ponderously enough to make trailing them no problem.

Eventually the wagons left the path and struck out across open countryside. The orcs tracked the little convoy for about two miles in the direction of the Calyparr Inlet. Just as Stryke was beginning to worry that they'd be led all the way to the inlet itself, the wagons turned into a glade and halted.

The orcs watched as the wagon tailgates were lowered and the dwarves dismounted. They began leaving, in groups and singly, in different directions.

"So it's a meeting point, not a village," Stryke said.

"They must be drawing labour from the whole area," Jup suggested. "That's better for us. One of them is much less likely to be missed in this situation."

Circling round, the wagons started their journey back to Trinity. The orcs kept their heads down as the transports passed, moving faster now they'd rid themselves of their load. Several dwarves, too, passed nearby without seeing them.

"So far, so good," Stryke judged. "Now we wait until morning and hope there's another pick-up."

He allotted turns as lookouts and they settled down to their vigil.

The night passed uneventfully.

Shortly after daybreak, dwarves began drifting in to the meeting place. Jup tied a rusty-red bandanna around his neck, the emblem of an obscure and distant tribe. Then he smeared the garva-root paste over his cheeks, covering the tattoos. Stryke had feared that it wouldn't look convincing, but it worked remarkably well.

"What we need now is a worker on his own," he said, "and we need him at a distance from the glade."

They all looked out for a likely candidate. One of the grunts nudged Stryke and pointed. A lone dwarf was wading through long grass over to their right.

Jup began to move. "I'll do it."

Stryke laid a hand on his arm. "But—"

"It has to be me, Stryke. You can see that, can't you?"

"All right. Take Coilla with you, to cover your back."

They set off, creeping low through the cover.

The others watched the dwarf they'd targeted moving towards the glade. At the same time they kept an eye on the other workers converging on the pick-up.

Suddenly the lone dwarf went down and there was a brief rustling in the grass. A moment later Jup popped up in his victim's stead and began walking in the direction of the waiting wagons.

The orcs watched intently, ready to break cover and rush to his aid if anything went wrong. Jup moved with a relaxed, unhurried stride.

"He's doing a good job of looking casual, I'll give him that," Stryke commented.

There was a movement in the grass nearby and Coilla reappeared. "Is he there yet?"

"Nearly," Stryke reported.

Jup reached the glade, which now had several dozen other dwarves milling around in it. It was a moment of tenseness, the first test of many. But neither the dwarves nor the wagon drivers paid him any particular attention. A few minutes later they began to mount the wagons. Having stood apart from the others, Jup now had to come into close contact with them. This was when his disguise proved either passable or worthless.

The orcs looked on with bated breath.

Mingling with the crowd, Jup climbed aboard a wagon. There was no uproar, no hue and cry. The wagons' tailgates were secured. Whips cracked over the oxen and the convoy moved off.

Keeping very still, the orcs watched the convoy pass. A moment later, the coast clear, they followed. There was no deviation in the route back to Trinity.

But as the wagons rolled on to the road leading to the township's gates, the orcs saw more humans working in the fields than there had been yesterday. Again, they were mostly women, and there were a larger number of guards protecting them.

The Wolverines had to be even more careful to avoid being seen, and there was a limit to how near the wall they could get. But they found a vantage point, crouching in a field of wheat, from where they could follow the wagons' progression.

As before, guards appeared on the walls above and scanned the arrivals. A moment later the vast gates began creaking open. Again, there was a tantalising glimpse of the interior. The wagons moved forward and entered. Black-clad men rushed to shut the gates.

They closed with a booming crash.

Stryke hoped it didn't mark a death knell for Jup.

18

The great gates slammed behind Jup with a terrible finality.

Without obviously appearing to do so, he looked around. The first thing he saw was several dozen guards, dressed uniformly in black and all bearing arms.

What he could make out of Trinity was formal to the point of severity. The place seemed to be arranged in a way that would have satisfied the most pedantic military commander. All the buildings were neatly positioned in rows. Some were cottages, made of stone with thatched roofs, of a size to house a family. Others were larger, barracks-like buildings, fashioned from timber. Without exception they were pristine in appearance. Further on, towers and spires of equal correctness poked above the rooftops. Arrow-straight roads and lanes cut through the concise landscape. Even the trees, of which there were a few, had been marshalled into regimented lines.

There were humans, men, women and children, going about their business in the stifling orderliness. Like the guards, the men were dressed in uncompromised black. Those of the women and children who weren't wore clothes of bland plainness.

No sooner had he taken in the scene than Jup and his fellow dwarves, none of whom had spoken to him, or to each other in most cases, were herded off the wagons.

It was another moment of truth. Now he'd find out if the humans kept a list of their guest workers' names. If they did, what followed was likely to be unpleasant, and almost certainly terminal.

As seemed fitting in a place obsessed by symmetry, the dwarves were mustered into tidy columns beside the wagons that had brought them. Then to Jup's relief men went along the lines, finger-jabbing each dwarf in turn as they counted them.

The human on Jup's line moved his lips in the process, but passed him by without a second look.

Jup was wondering what happened next when there was a flurry of activity at the door of one of the buildings that resembled a barracks. The man he, Stryke and Coilla had seen the day before in his carriage, and whom they assumed to be Kimball Hobrow, appeared at the entrance.

His eyes were just as chill, his expression no less unsmiling. Jup wondered, as he had the previous day, how old the man might be. This closer look was hardly more telling than his first fleeting glimpse, but Jup reckoned him to be about middle-aged in human terms, though he always found it hard to tell when it came to that race. It was rumoured there was some kind of formula for working it out, similar to the one used for dogs and cats, but he was damned if he could remember it.

One thing of which there was no doubt, however, was Kimball's charismatic presence. He radiated an aura of authority, of power, and not a little menace.

The settlers fell silent and parted to let him through. He made his way to a wagon and climbed on to the seat. It added to his already commanding height, making him an even more imposing figure. He scrutinised the dwarves. Despite himself, Jup shrank a little under that penetrating gaze.

Hobrow raised his hands in a gesture that called for quiet, though as there had barely been a sound since he appeared, this was hardly necessary.

"I am Kimball Hobrow!" he boomed. It came across as a profound statement rather than mere information. His voice was bass and silken, belying the slender frame it came from.

"Some of you are new here," Hobrow continued.

Jup was glad to hear that. It made his position a bit more tenable.

"Those of you who have been here before will have heard what I'm about to say," Hobrow went on, "but it bears repeating. You'll do as you're told and remember at all times that you're guests, allowed here so my people can devote themselves to more important tasks."

We're going to be shovelling shit for them, Jup thought. *What a surprise.*

Hobrow scanned his audience with those beguiling eyes, in a pause obviously intended to hammer home his point.

"There are certain things we permit here and certain things we don't," he said. "We allow you to work hard at the labours for which you're being well rewarded. We allow you to show deference to your betters. We allow you to express respect for our belief in the one true Supreme Creator."

So much for the stick, Jup reflected. *What about the carrot?*

"We don't allow laziness, insolence, insubordination, lax morals or profane language."

Gods, Jup realised, *that* was *the carrot.*

"We don't tolerate alcohol, pellucid or any other intoxicant. You'll not speak to any citizen without first being spoken to, and you'll obey without question any order given to you by a custodian or a citizen. You will at all times abide by the laws of this place, which are the laws of our Lord. Transgress and you'll be punished. Like the Supreme Being, what I've given I can take away."

He ran his steely eyes over them again. Jup noticed that few if any of his fellow dwarves met that disturbing gaze. He tried to avoid it himself, if only so he wouldn't attract attention.

Hobrow plucked off his hat, revealing a shock of ebony hair touched with silvery grey. "We'll now offer up a prayer for our endeavours," he announced.

Jup looked to the others. Such dwarves as had hats were doffing them too. Following their example, and Hobrow's, he bowed his head, feeling foolish and conspicuous. Why this was necessary, he didn't know. He didn't go through such a performance when he needed to speak to his gods. Whether they listened surely had nothing to do with whether you wore a hat or not.

"O Lord, who created all things," Hobrow began, "we humbly beseech You to heed our prayer. Bless the labours of these lowly creatures, O Lord, and help us raise them from their ignorance and savagery. Bless too the efforts of we, Your chosen, that we might best serve and honour You. Strengthen our arm in pursuit of our mission as instruments of Your wrath, O Lord. Let us be Your sword and You our shield against the unrighteous and the blasphemers. Keep pure our race and smite without mercy our enemies and Yours. Make us truly thankful for the infinite bounty You bestow upon us, Lord."

Without another word, Hobrow replaced his hat, climbed down from the wagon and headed back for the building he had come from. A knot of followers walked respectfully in his wake.

"Bit keen, isn't he?" Jup remarked to the dwarf next in line.

This unsmiling individual ignored the comment. He did look Jup up and down, but without too much curiosity.

I'm going to love it here, Jup thought.

A guard, or custodian, as Jup supposed he had to call him, took Hobrow's place on the wagon's seat. Several of his fellows hovered in the background.

"You new ones, stay here to be given your duties," the man said. "Those of you who know your duties, go to your places of work."

Most of the dwarves streamed off in different directions.

"Be back here at dusk for your transport away!" he shouted after them.

Jup and four others were left. Now that he was no longer part of a crowd he felt more vulnerable. The other four moved in nearer to the custodian. Not wanting to stand out, he did the same.

"You heard the master's words," the custodian told them. "Make sure you heed them. We have ways of punishing those who don't," he added menacingly. He consulted a sheet of parchment. "We need three more on the rebuilding in Central Square. You, you and you." He pointed to a trio of dwarves. "Follow him."

One of the other custodians beckoned and they went off with him.

The man went on to the next item on his list. "One needed to help dig the new cesspit on the south side."

Jup decided it would be just his luck to pull that job.

"You."

The custodian indicated the other remaining dwarf. He didn't look like a beam of sunshine as a guard took him off.

As the last one left, Jup began to feel uncomfortable. It crossed his mind that they *had* realised his true intentions, and that this was a trap, designed to get him alone. The custodian stared at him.

"You look strong," he said.

"Er, yes, I suppose I am."

"You'll call me *sir*," the custodian informed him cuttingly. "All humans are *sir* to your kind."

"Yes . . . sir," Jup corrected, doing his best to suppress the resentment he felt at having to kow-tow to an incomer.

The custodian consulted his parchment again. "Another pair of hands are wanted at the arboretum kilns."

"The what?" Jup quickly added, "Sir."

"The hothouse. We're growing plants there that need warmth. Your job's helping to feed the fires that heat—" He dismissed him with a careless wave. "It'll all be explained."

Jup followed the custodian he'd been assigned to. The man was silent, and the dwarf didn't try to start a conversation.

What Jup had hoped for was a job that gave him enough freedom to slip off and spy out this place. He didn't know if that was what he'd got. But judging by the way they took security so seriously here, he doubted it. There might not be anything to show for this day other than callused hands. And maybe a lost head.

With Jup a couple of paces to the human's rear, they walked along one of the precise avenues, passing buildings in all major respects identical. At the road's end they turned right into another, which exactly resembled the one they'd just left. Jup was finding all the uniformity a bit disturbing.

They turned again. This time, the walkway was distinguished by something different: the largest building Jup had seen in Trinity so far. It stood a good four or five times higher than the surrounding houses, and was built of granite slabs.

What distinguished it apart from its size was a great oval above the double oak doors. The oval, a window, was equivalent in size to two or three humans laid head to foot. More remarkable, it was filled with glass. Jup had only ever seen glass once before, at Jennesta's palace, and knew it to be a rare and expensive material whose creation was difficult. This glass was blue-tinted, and bore at its centre a representation, uncoloured, of the Uni X motif. He assumed it was a place of worship. His escort was watching him looking at it, so he dropped his gaze and pretended indifference.

Jup pondered the fact that what he had to do must be done within the day. Because although the body of the dwarf he'd replaced would be well hidden by the band, there was a distinct risk of him being reported missing and questions asked.

They passed the temple, turned again and came to another large and extraordinary structure. It was smaller than the temple, but much more eccentric in appearance. The outer walls, of brick-sized stone slabs, were no taller than Jup. Or at least their brick part was no taller. Above the low walls extended a curtain of plain glass, in wood-frame squares, that met a flat roof. The building was box-shaped, at least two-thirds fashioned from glass, and the glass was misty with condensation. All Jup could make out through it was a jumble of jagged shapes and a faint hint of greenness.

Tacked to one end of the building was an extension of stone and wood, containing no glass at all. It was this that the custodian made for.

When they entered, a blast of heat hit them.

Jup registered the fact that there was no wall between this structure and the house of glass, what they called the arboretum presumably, that abutted it. A humid atmosphere pervaded the whole interior. The hothouse was stocked with plants large and small. They stood in containers on the floor and were stacked on shelves. Some were in flower, many weren't. There were tall, slender-stalked varieties, short bushy ones and others that looked like climbers. He didn't recognise any of them.

In the building Jup had entered, which was whitewashed, there were three large kilns, like oversized open grates, set against the far wall. All had fires roaring in them. Heaps of wooden logs and a copious pile of the black fuel stones were being used to feed the flames. Jup could see how at least some of the fruits of the mining and tree-felling were being used.

Across the top of the grates ran a wide clay gully, from which steam rose. The gully, an open pipe, entered the building through a hole in the wall. It channelled water that the grates heated and passed into enclosed pipes which snaked around the hothouse.

It was a clever arrangement. Jup admired its ingenuity, but had no idea why it should be necessary.

There were two dwarves in the room, one shovelling the black rocks into the grates, the other tossing in logs. They were sweating and grimy. A human was present too, sitting in a chair near the door, as far from the heat of the kilns as possible. When Jup and his human came in, he stood up.

"Sterling," he greeted Jup's custodian.

"Istuan," the custodian returned. "New one for you," he added, jabbing a thumb at Jup but not bothering to look at him.

Istuan didn't take much of a look either. "About time," he grumbled. "We're finding it hard keeping up the temperature with only two."

Jup liked the *we*.

Sterling bade his farewells and left.

"There are water tanks out the back," Istuan explained without preamble. "They feed the channel above the kilns in here." He pointed. "The water has to be kept hot at all times so the plants are happy."

He ran through the set-up mechanistically, as though addressing a stupid pet.

"What kind of plants are they, sir?" Jup asked.

Istuan looked startled that the pet could talk. That expression was quickly overtaken by suspicion. "None of your concern. All you need to know is that the temperature can't be allowed to drop. If it does, you get a whipping."

"Yes, sir," Jup responded, acting suitably cowed.

"Your job's to keep the fuel stockpiles up, check the water levels in the tanks and to take over banking these kilns when the others need relieving. Understand?"

Jup nodded.

"Now take a spade and start bringing in some fuel from out there," the custodian ordered, indicating a door in the side wall.

The door led outside to an enclosed yard. There were small

mountains of wood and burning-stones, and a pair of round wooden tanks, similar to very large barrels, mounted on legs, that supplied the water. He set to replenishing the fuel supply.

It was back-breaking work, and as neither his fellow dwarves or the custodian went in for much in the way of conversation, Jup undertook it in silence.

About an hour into the job, the custodian stood up and stretched. "I've got a report to make," he informed them. "Don't slack, and keep those fires steeped."

Once he'd gone, Jup tried getting the other dwarves to talk.

"Strange plants," he said.

One shrugged indifferently. The other didn't even bother doing that. Neither spoke.

"Never seen anything quite like them," Jup persisted. "They're obviously not vegetables."

"They're herbs or something," one of them finally revealed. "For medicines . . ."

"Is that so?" He approached the plants for a closer look.

"You can't go in there," the other dwarf piped up sharply. "It's forbidden."

Jup spread his hands out submissively. "All right. Just curious."

"Don't be. Just do the work and earn your coin."

Jup returned to his chores and no further words were exchanged until the custodian came back. He sent Jup to check the water levels in the tanks with a measuring stick.

As it happened, they were low enough to need refilling, which proved a stroke of luck. It meant the custodian and the dwarves had to go for fresh supplies. Warning Jup to keep the fires banked, the man and the dwarves set off in a wagon.

As soon as they had left, Jup investigated the plants. He still couldn't identify any, which wasn't surprising as it was a subject he had little interest in, but decided it might be useful to take some samples to show the band. Selecting three plants at random, he carefully stripped off some leaves. It occurred to him that anybody leaving Trinity could well be searched, so he took off one of his boots and lined it with the leaves.

Knowing this could be his only chance, he made up his mind

to take a bigger risk. He fed a plentiful supply of fuel into the kilns, hoping it would keep them going for the amount of time he thought he needed. Then he went to the door, opened it carefully and peered into the street. There was no one around. He slipped out.

When he was being escorted in he'd seen other dwarves on the streets, presumably carrying messages or running errands. So he walked with purpose, hoping any humans he encountered would think he was acting under orders.

He'd already made up his mind where to go, though it was a long shot. His reasoning was that if the instrumentality had been included in the Unis' religious practices, the logical place to keep it was the temple. He headed that way.

Jup didn't need to be told that dwarves wouldn't be welcome in such a human holy place. Nor that the penalty for being caught there would be dire. But he saw no point in taking the risk of getting into Trinity if he didn't try to do the job he had come for.

As before, the doors of the temple were closed. There could be humans in there. The place could be filled with them for all he knew.

He took a deep breath, strode to the entrance and turned the handle. The door opened. He looked in. The place was empty. Quickly, he slipped inside.

The interior of the temple was simple to the point of plainness, but its austerity had a kind of elegance. Its effect derived from the use of a number of different kinds of wood, rather than more obvious adornments. Rows of benches faced an elementary altar. The ceiling was high and vaulted.

Most striking was the blue oval window over the doors, which now that he was inside Jup could see had a twin above the altar. This second window was tinted ruby and also had the Uni emblem set at its heart. The light from outside struck the design, throwing an elongated X across the polished pine floor.

He crept along the aisle to the altar. This too was basic: a modest white cloth covering, a metal Uni symbol, a pair of wooden candlesticks, a silver goblet. And a cube of the precious clear glass.

It held the star.

Jup had assumed that if they ever found another instrumentality it would be identical to the one they already held. This turned out to be only partly true. The object he gazed at was of the same size and spiky appearance. But whereas the other was sandy-coloured, this was green, and the arms extending from the central core numbered five, not seven, and were differently arranged.

He hesitated. His instinct was to smash the glass and take the star, in the hope that he could smuggle it out of the township. His good sense told him this was a bad, quite possibly suicidal idea.

His decision was postponed when he heard voices outside. More than one human was approaching the doors. Jup had seen no other exit. Near panic, he looked for a hiding place: There was nowhere except the back of the altar. He all but fell behind it as the doors opened.

Stretched full-length on the floor, he dared to peek around the side.

Kimball Hobrow entered, removing his hat as he strode in. Two equally grave-looking humans followed him. They walked up the aisle, and for a moment Jup thought they knew he was there and were coming for him. He bunched his fists, determined to make a fight of it.

But they stopped short of the altar and sat themselves on the first row of benches. Jup's next thought was that they were going to perform an act of worship. He was wrong about that too.

"How does the matter of the water progress, Thaddeus?" Hobrow asked one of the duo.

"All done. We could begin drawing from our own protected supplies today, if necessary."

"And the essences? They'll take to the waters without betraying themselves?"

"Once introduced they're not obvious. Until they have their effect, of course. We run the final test in two days."

"See that you do. I'll have no delays."

"Yes, master."

"Take heart, Thaddeus. The Lord's scheme proceeds well, and

once we've triumphed here we'll spread the scourge much farther afield. The day of our race's deliverance is at hand, brethren. As is ridding ourselves of the Mani pestilence."

Jup had no idea what they were talking about, but it didn't sound good.

Then Hobrow suddenly stood and made his way to the altar. Jup tensed. He couldn't see Hobrow properly, but had the impression that he was looking at the star, or possibly even handling its container. The dwarf was relieved when the zealot turned to face his cohorts.

"We mustn't lose sight of the fact that the crusade to Scratch is of equal importance. Are we up to strength on that front, Calvert?"

At mention of the trolls' homeland, Jup's ears pricked.

"The battle at Weaver's Lea was ill-timed," the second man answered, a little nervously, Jup thought. "It drew too many away from the plan. It'll be a couple of weeks before we have enough men."

Hobrow wasn't pleased. "That won't do. The ungodly have what must be ours. The Lord will not be frustrated."

"We can't open hostilities there with less than a full complement, master. It invites disaster."

"Then bring in more of the non-humans to free our own for this work. Let nothing stand in the way of the plan, brethren. We'll speak again on the morrow. Now go about your duties and trust in the Lord. We do His work and will prevail."

Hobrow's men departed. But Hobrow himself stayed. He returned to the bench, clasped his hands and lowered his head.

"Give me the strength I need, Lord," he intoned. "We're eager to carry out Your plan, but You must give us what we need to do it. Bless our efforts to cleanse this land, that Your chosen may harvest it unmolested."

Jup was worried about the time passing. If Hobrow took much longer he was in trouble.

"Shower Your divine blessings, too, on our mission to the heathen non-human nest at Scratch. Let us gain that which they have and which we need to do Your bidding. Keep firm my resolve, O Lord, and let me not waver in your service."

Hobrow stood, turned away and left the temple.

Jup forced himself to wait a moment before leaving his hiding place. With trepidation, he opened the doors a crack. There was no sign of anyone nearby and he left the building, making as much haste getting back to the hothouse as he could without actually running. All the way he puzzled over what he'd just heard.

There was a moment of suspense when he arrived, as he couldn't be certain if the others had returned. Or whether another custodian had visited in his absence.

In the event, the building was empty. But the fires had burnt dangerously low. He shovelled fuel on to them like a maniac. The task was barely complete when he heard the sound of a wagon outside.

Istuan came in and cast a critical eye about the room. Jup steeled himself against the accusation he more than half expected.

"You've worked up a fine sweat there," the custodian said. It was as near a compliment as he'd yet paid him.

Jup smiled thinly and nodded, too breathless to speak.

He was assigned the back-breaking work of transferring the water from the wagon to the tanks. After that, there were other strenuous chores. He didn't mind. It gave him time to think. One conclusion he came to was that what needed to be achieved wouldn't be done today after all. But at least he knew where the star was kept, and he had some other information, although it made little sense to him.

The work continued in virtual silence until dusk. Then Istuan told them to make their way to the main gate to be picked up. They were allowed to go unaccompanied.

On the way, Jup's fellow workers were no less taciturn. In the main avenue leading to the gates they were passed by Hobrow in his carriage. Sitting next to him was a human female. No longer a child but not yet a woman, she was dressed a little more flamboyantly than any other human Jup had seen in Trinity. In build she was chubby, almost fat. Her hair was honey blonde and her eyes china blue. But it seemed to Jup that her scowling face spoke of greed and bad temper. She had an unpleasant mouth.

When proud Hobrow and the haughty child-woman had gone by, Jup asked his companions who she was.

"Hobrow's daughter," the more voluble one replied, then cracked the first smile he had favoured Jup with. Not that it contained much humour.

"What's funny?" Jup said.

"Her name. It's Mercy."

They arrived at the main gates. The other dwarves were there and the wagons were waiting. All were counted and, as Jup feared, they were searched. But it consisted of no more than the patting of clothes and a quick delve into pockets. Nobody, thank the gods, wanted to look in his boots. At least it confirmed his hunch that smuggling out the star wasn't a very smart idea.

Some coins were dropped into his hand and he climbed aboard a wagon.

The opening of the gates was the most comforting thing he'd seen all day.

19

Safely installed in their mine-shaft hideaway, Jup related the day's events to the Wolverines. Alfray was busy examining the plant samples.

"You've done well, Jup," Stryke praised, "but I'm not keen on you going back in there. Apart from anything else, there's too high a chance that the dwarf you killed might be reported missing."

"I know that. Believe me, I'm not happy about it myself, chief. But if we want that star, I can't see how else to do it."

"Finding it's one thing, getting it out is another," Coilla said. "What's the plan?"

"I was wondering if I could get it over the wall to you somehow," Jup suggested.

Stryke was unimpressed. "Not practical."

"What about making a copy of the star and swapping it for the real one?" Coilla pitched in.

"Nice idea. But that wouldn't work either. We haven't got the skill to make even a half-convincing copy. Nor do we have anything that comes anywhere near the kind of material we'd need."

"The one I saw in Trinity's different to ours, too," Jup reminded them. "We'd have to do it from what I could remember. Even if we could copy it, that doesn't solve the problem of getting the original out."

"No, it doesn't," Stryke agreed. "I think the only way is a more direct approach. Of the kind we do best."

"You don't mean we should storm the place?" Coilla said. "A handful against an entire township?"

"Not exactly. But what I have in mind would put a lot on you, Jup. It's much more dangerous than anything you've done so far."

"What are you getting at, Stryke?"

"I'm thinking of you getting hold of the star then us getting hold of you."

"What?"

"It's simple really. All being well, tomorrow you and the star will be together behind the walls at Trinity and we'll be outside. Is there any way you could let us in?"

"Shit, Stryke, I don't know . . ."

"Did you notice any way in or out apart from the main gates? Anything we missed on our reconnaissance?"

"Not that I saw."

"It'd have to be the main gates then."

"How?"

"We'll agree a time. You'll have to get away from the hot-house, grab the star—"

"And get to the gates and open them for you. That's asking a hell of a lot, Stryke. Those gates are massive, and they're guarded."

"I didn't say it'd be easy. You'd have to deal with the guards and get those gates unbarred. We'd be waiting close by to help open them. Then it's a quick getaway. If you think it's too risky, we'll try to come up with something else."

"Well, there were only two guards by the gates when I left tonight, so I suppose it wouldn't be impossible overcoming them. All right, let's go for that."

Alfray joined them, frowning, the plant samples in his hand. "Well, what you've brought us adds another twist to things, Jup."

"Why? What are they?"

"I know two of the three types, although they're quite rare." He held up a leaf. "This is wentyx, which you can find in a few places down here in the south." He indicated another. "This one, the vale lily, tends to grow more in the west, though you could spend years looking for it." He showed them the third sample. "This is new to me, and I suspect it's something the humans brought with them to Maras-Dantia. But I'd guess it does the same thing these others do."

"Which is what?" Stryke asked.

"Kills. The two I know are among the most lethal plants in existence. The vale lily yields berries that always prove fatal even in tiny amounts. With the wentyx you have to boil the stalk for a residue that's even more potent, if anything. The gods know how dangerous the one I can't identify is. And the first two have something else in common. They're so potent that large quantities of water hardly dilutes them. Does what Hobrow has in mind seem clearer now?"

Jup was stunned. "Hell, yes. They're growing these things for poisons to kill elder races with."

Alfray nodded. "Massacre, more like. This explains the dam. Hobrow's protecting Trinity's own water supply so they'll be safe when they poison the other sources."

"I saw wells in Trinity."

"Then the reservoir's a further guarantee for them."

"Or else it's the reservoir they'll poison," Stryke said. "If you control the major water supply for a whole area, then let it be known that any of the races can use it—"

"Or just leave it unguarded," Coilla added, "knowing they'll come and draw from it. Particularly if there's a drought, which isn't impossible, seeing how the weather's been so unpredictable in recent seasons."

"Either way, the result's likely to be the slaughter of every race but humans in these parts," Alfray said.

Jup recalled something. "Hobrow said that if it works here, they'll try it on a wider scale. They go in for a lot of purity-of-the-race stuff in Trinity, certainly if the way they treat dwarves is anything to go by. How much purer can you get if there *are* no other races?"

"It's an insane plan," Alfray judged. "Think about it. The first to drink the water would die, and that would warn off others. How can these Unis believe it would work?"

"Maybe they're too blinded by hatred to see things straight," Stryke said. "Or it could be they think enough would be killed to make it worthwhile."

"The *bastards*," Coilla seethed. "We can't let them get away with it, Stryke."

"What can we do? Things are going to be hard enough for Jup tomorrow without another near-impossible task."

"We're just going to walk away from this?"

"From what Jup says, that plant house is a fair distance inside Trinity. There's no way we're going to get to it, particularly if the alarm's gone out about the missing star. All we can do is spread the word among local elder races and hope they can act on the warning."

She wasn't happy. "It doesn't seem much."

"What if I can do anything while I'm in there, Stryke?" Jup asked. "Without putting the star in peril, that is?"

"Then good luck. But the star's your first priority. The power the stars promise could do a lot more good for Maras-Dantia than us throwing away our lives to stop this scheme."

"Have any of you wondered where Hobrow got his star?" Alfray wanted to know.

Stryke had. "Yes. But I remember what Mobbs said. It's possible that the humans came upon it by chance, the gods know how, and just haven't an idea of what it's for."

"Any more than we have," Coilla put in.

"Hobrow's enough of a tyrant to go after the other stars if he knew their power, and to use it," Jup informed them.

"Wiping out whole races seems to back that," Coilla agreed, more than a little cynically.

"All right, there's not much else we can do tonight," Stryke decided.

Jup turned to Alfray. "How's Haskeer?"

If Alfray was surprised at Jup asking after the health of his antagonist, he didn't show it. "Fair. I'm hoping his fever's going to break soon."

"Pity he's out of it. Irritating fucker he may be, but we could use him tomorrow."

They talked a while longer about tomorrow's plans, and the expedition Hobrow planned to Scratch particularly intrigued them. But in the end they settled down to catch what sleep they could with more questions than answers.

Getting into Trinity the next day proved no harder than before.

Jup presented himself at the pick-up point, boarded a wagon and was delivered to the township. This time he took especial notice of the number of guards manning the gates. There were five. His heart sank. But he consoled himself with the thought that perhaps more were assigned at busy times like this.

One thing Jup did differently for his second visit was to conceal a knife in his boot. His reasoning was that as they hadn't searched him coming in yesterday, they wouldn't today. In the event, his gamble paid off.

This time, there was no lecture from Hobrow. And when the dwarves were told to report to their places of work, Jup didn't check with the custodians. He simply went with the two other dwarves assigned to the hothouse. Istuan told Jup what to do, which was a rerun of his previous day's duties, and Jup got on with it.

The time agreed for Jup to be at the gates was midday, which he reckoned was in about four hours. Which meant he needed to be out of the arboretum well before that. As he worked, his mind and eye kept returning to the small jungle of plants in the adjacent glassed area. He didn't favour leaving Trinity without at least trying to do something about them. As Stryke had said, that was all right as long as it didn't endanger gaining the star. He thought it worth the additional risk.

The plan he had for getting away from the hothouse and to the temple was basic, direct and by necessity brutal. He pondered it as he lugged the wood and black burning-stones to the piles that fed the kilns. Time dragged, as it often did when a particular moment was anticipated, but he knew that when it came to it things would move fast enough. He carried on shovelling the fuel, working up a sweat and casting shifty glances at the toxic nursery.

When he judged the moment near, he left the furnace room by way of the back door, ostensibly to check the tank's water levels.

Jup didn't want to use his knife against fellow dwarves unless he had to, no matter how treacherous they might seem. So he selected a sturdy timber bough, concealed himself behind the door and waited.

Several long minutes passed before a voice was raised inside. The words were unclear, but he was obviously being called for. He ignored it.

The door opened and one of the dwarves came out.

Jup waited for the door to close again, then stepped forward and rapped the dwarf smartly across the back of the head with his improvised bludgeon. His victim went down. Jup dragged him out of sight.

He returned to his hiding place and renewed the vigil. There were no warning shouts before the door opened a second time. Then not one but two figures exited.

Jup found himself facing Istuan and the other dwarf. He laid into them. The dwarf went down first, and without too much effort, if only because he had no weapon to defend himself with.

But the custodian put up a fight.

"You filthy little freak!" he bellowed, swinging his own club, which unlike Jup's improvised version was designed for the purpose.

They stood toe to toe and exchanged grunting blows. Jup's concern was that the human would cry out loudly enough to bring help. He had to finish this quickly.

The custodian proved no easy prey, however, and one of his swings caught Jup's arm. It was a painful but not crippling strike, and it spurred him to greater effort. He powered into Istuan, battering at him in search of an opening. Another swing by the human gave him his chance. Jup ducked and brought his club up to connect heavily with the custodian's chin.

Istuan gasped and the weapon fell from his loosened fingers. Jup quickly followed through with a swinging blow to his head, knocking him cold.

Tossing aside the piece of timber, he took up a two-handed axe used to chop the logs. A single swipe severed the pipe carrying water from the tanks into the furnace room.

He rushed through the door. The water in the open gully above the kilns was already drying up. Snatching one of the stoking shovels, he loaded it with glowing coals. He turned, ran the few paces to the hothouse and tossed the coals into the jumble of plants. This he repeated several times, with both hot coals and flaming logs, until the plants in the hothouse began to burn and the wooden shelving caught.

His hope was to kill two birds with one arrow. The fire should create a diversion, and destroying the plants might scupper Hobrow's plan, or at least delay it.

Satisfied the blaze had taken, he checked the street and left, firmly slamming the door behind him. As he hurried past the glass end of the structure he saw smoke inside, and pinpoints of yellow flame. He set off for the temple, careful not to break into a run no matter how much he wanted to.

He wondered how long he had before the alarm was raised.

Glancing at the sky showed the sun was near its highest point. The Wolverines would now be in position. He hoped he wasn't going to disappoint them.

Moving as fast as he dared, he tried not to dwell on the enormity of the task he'd agreed to.

Jup turned into the avenue of the temple. Almost as soon as he did, the doors opened and a crowd of humans flooded out, presumably from attending a service. He froze, shocked at this sudden profusion of the species.

Conscious that standing in the road and staring was likely to attract attention, he snapped out of his paralysis and resumed walking. Very slowly, with his head down. He went past the place of worship, staying on the other side of the road, careful not to obstruct any of the departing worshippers scattering in all directions. Very few took much notice of him. For the first time he appreciated how being regarded as a member of a lowly race had its advantages.

He rounded a corner, making out that he was heading somewhere else. As the worshippers thinned he turned back and walked towards the temple again.

The street outside was clear now, except for a few humans moving off with their backs to him. He decided on a direct approach and damn the consequences. Marching straight to the temple doors, he shoved them open.

Much to his relief, the building was deserted.

He ran to the small glass case, grabbed it and dashed it against the altar, shattering it. Snatching up the star, he stuffed it into his pocket and fled.

Outside, he noticed smoke rising from the next street where the hothouse was located. Behind him, somebody shouted. He looked over his shoulder.

Four or five custodians were running his way.

He ran too. There was no point in trying to avoid attention now.

They chased him through the streets, yelling and waving their fists. Others joined in. By the time he turned the last corner and saw the gates, a howling mob was at his heels.

That wasn't all he saw. For a start there were more guards than he had anticipated. He counted eight. There was no way he was going to overpower that number single-handed. Two, certainly; three, possibly; four, maybe. Twice that number, never.

The other thing he saw was Hobrow's carriage. His daughter, Mercy, was sitting in it alone. Hobrow was standing some way off, talking to a custodian.

It gave him an idea. A desperate one, admittedly, but he could see no other choice.

Hobrow and the guards, alerted by the cries of the pursuing mob, turned and looked his way. Several of the custodians were already drawing weapons and starting to move in Jup's direction.

Jup put on a spurt of speed and ran for all he was worth. He made a beeline for the carriage. The guards raced forward to cut him off. Hobrow himself, seeing Jup's intention, also began to run.

Heart pounding, Jup reached the carriage just a few paces ahead of Hobrow and the custodians. He leapt on to it. Mercy Hobrow squealed. Jup grabbed her, ripped the knife from his boot and held the blade to her throat.

Hobrow and the guards were clambering on to the carriage.

"*Hold it!*" Jup yelled, pressing the knife closer to the trembling girl's pinky-white flesh.

"Let her go!" Hobrow demanded.

"Another step and she dies," Jup said.

The holy man and the dwarf locked gazes. Jup inwardly prayed for him not to call his bluff. The girl might have been a pretty unpleasant example of humanity, and the offspring of a ruthless dictator, but she was little more than a child for all that. Given the choice, he would rather not harm her.

"My daddy will *kill* you for this," Mercy promised. It was all the more chilling a threat coming from the lips of one so young.

"Button it," Jup sneered.

"You monster!" she wailed. "You stunted ogre! You . . . *eyesore!* You—"

He let her feel the keenness of his blade. She gulped and shut up.

"Open the gates!" he said.

The mob had halted and were watching in silence. Their weapons half raised, the custodians stared. Hobrow pinned Jup with his searing gaze.

"Open them," Jup repeated.

"There's no need for this," Hobrow told him.

"Open the gates and I'll let her go."

"How do I know you will?"

"You'll just have to take my word for it."

Hobrow's expression turned meaner, his tone took on a harsher edge. "How far do you think you're going to get out there?"

"That's my problem. Now are you going to open those gates or do I spill her blood?"

The preacher's fury was building. "You harm one hair on that child's head—"

"Then open the gates."

Hobrow fumed silently for a moment and Jup wondered what his daughter's life was worth to him. Then the holy man turned and gave the custodians a curt order. They ran to lift the crossbar. Others pulled open the gates.

For Jup it was another moment of truth. If the Wolverines weren't out there his chances of escaping were down to near zero.

The reins of the horses in one hand and the knife at Mercy's neck in the other, he edged the carriage through the gates and out into the road.

There was no sign of the Wolverines. That didn't worry him unduly. He hadn't expected to be able to see them.

Then, as he moved into the open, the band appeared from the cover of the long grass.

"Get off," he told the girl.

She stared at him, wide-eyed.

"Get off!" he barked.

She winced and jumped down from the carriage, then started running back toward her father's outstretched arms.

Now she was free, the humans had no constraint. Yelling and screaming, they charged. Jup cracked the reins and started to move.

As they spilled through the gates, the wave of humans got their first sight of the Wolverines. They thought they were going to lynch a dwarf, not engage in a minor battle. The suddenness of the orcs' appearance, and the ferocity of their onslaught, threw the humans into disarray. Further discord was sown by Coilla picking off the guards in their towers with her bow. Three grunts peppered the crowd with arrows.

Led by Stryke, the remainder of the band beat back the mob, which broke ranks and fled for the safety of the enclave. Hobrow could be heard shrieking orders and vowing revenge.

Stryke jumped up beside Jup. "They'll be getting horses! Let's move!"

Coilla and several other band members leapt aboard; the rest jogged along beside the speeding carriage.

"Did you get it?" Stryke said.

Jup grinned. "I got it!"

The Wolverines raced from Trinity with their prize.

20

Amid the chaos, Kimball Hobrow was beside himself with rage.

Custodians were scrambling for horses and climbing to re-man the walls. Citizens armed themselves for the chase. The wounded were being tended, the dead dragged clear of the gates. A team of fire fighters carted water to the blazing arboretum.

Mercy Hobrow, tearful and petulantly angry, tugged at her father's frock coat and wailed. "Kill them, Daddy! Kill them, *kill them!*"

Hobrow raised his arms, fists clenched, and bellowed over the confusion. "Track them down, brethren! As the Almighty is your guide and your sword, find them and smite them!"

Heavily armed riders galloped out of the gates. Wagonloads of citizenry, bristling with weapons, careered through to join the hunt.

A dishevelled custodian, ashen-faced, ran to Hobrow. "The temple!" he cried. "It's been desecrated!"

"Desecrated? How?"

"They've taken a relic!"

A deeper fury creased the preacher's face. He reached out and grasped the man's coat, pulling him close with maniacal strength. His eyes blazed.

"*What* have they taken?"

The Wolverines had left their horses with Alfray and a trooper in a copse several fields distant. Haskeer, semi-conscious and groggy with fever, was there too, lashed to his steed.

Abandoning the carriage, the band wasted no time mounting. As they rode off, a massive posse appeared on the road from Trinity.

Stryke had earlier decided that they'd head due west toward the Calyparr Inlet. This gave them the advantage of an open run, and once they reached it, a terrain varied enough to hide them.

The pursuers were disorganised and still recovering from the shock of the unexpected. But they were also tenacious. For several hours they hunted the band doggedly, rarely losing sight of them. Then the less able or less energetic began to fall back, with the overladen wagons the first to be lost.

By the end of the day only a comparative handful of diehards were still on the Wolverines' trail. Some high-speed, devious riding on the band's part eventually shook them off, too.

Having reached the vicinity of the inlet, riders and horses near exhaustion, Stryke allowed the pace to drop to a canter.

Coilla was the first to speak since the chase began. "Well, that's one more enemy we've made."

"And a powerful one," Alfray agreed. "I wouldn't count on Hobrow letting the star go as easily as that."

"Which reminds me," Stryke said. "Let me see it, Jup."

The dwarf dug out the instrumentality and handed it over. Stryke compared it to the one he already had, then slipped both into his pouch.

"I had my doubts about pulling that off," Alfray admitted.

"It was as much luck as anything," Jup remarked. He produced a cloth and began wiping the paste off his face. It was the first chance he'd had to do it.

"Don't undervalue yourself," Stryke told him. "You did well back there."

"The big question now," Alfray went on, "is what do we do next."

"I figured we might have had similar thoughts on that," Stryke said.

Alfray sighed. "That's what I was afraid you were going to say. Scratch?"

"There could be another star there."

"*Could* be. We have no proof of it. All we know for sure is that Hobrow intends going there. Which might not make it the most ideal destination for us."

"After the blow we've dealt him, I reckon he's not going just yet."

"Supposing Hobrow's expedition to Scratch doesn't have anything to do with the stars?" Jup suggested. "What if he's going there as part of his crazy plan to wipe out the elder races?"

"What, to force-feed the trolls poison? I don't think so. There has to be another reason."

"Slaughtering other races is what humans do, isn't it?"

"When they can let tainted water do it for them? It's too much of a risk. I mean, would you willingly go into that labyrinth unless you had to?"

"But that's exactly what you're asking *us* to do!"

"Like I said, Jup, unless you had to. Let's find a place to camp and at least think about it."

A little later, when Stryke and Coilla found themselves riding alone at the column's head, he asked her opinion on going to Scratch.

"It's no more mad than most other things we've done lately, though I think we'd face a much more fearsome enemy in the trolls than even Hobrow's fanatics. I'm not keen on the idea of entering that underground hellhole."

"So you're against it?"

"I didn't say that. Having some kind of mission certainly beats wandering aimlessly. But I'd want to see a well-thought-out strategy before we went near the place. Another thing you shouldn't forget, Stryke, is that we've managed to upset just about everybody in the last couple of weeks. We'll have to expect enemies on every side."

"Which can be a good thing."

"How do you figure that?"

"It'll keep us on our toes, spur us on."

"It's going to do *that*, all right. Tell me true, how much would going to Scratch be based on logic and how much on clutching at straws?"

"About half and half."

She smiled. "At least you're honest about it."

"Well, I am to you. Don't think I'd be quite so straight with them about it." He nodded at the band riding behind.

"They have a right to a say, don't they? Particularly as we're now outlaws, and maybe the command structure isn't as strong."

"Yes, they have a say, and I wouldn't try getting them to do anything they really didn't want to. As for command: like I said before, we have to keep discipline to stand a chance. So unless anybody else puts themselves up for it, I'm staying in charge."

"I'll go along with that. I'm sure the others do, too. But there's one decision you're going to have to make soon, and it affects all of us. The crystal."

"Whether it should be divided up or kept as collective band property, you mean? I've been thinking about that. Maybe it's something else we'll have to have a vote on. Not that I'm happy with the idea of voting on every move, mind."

"No, that could undermine your authority."

They rode in silence for a few minutes, then she said, "Course, there is an alternative to going to Scratch."

"What?"

"Returning to Cairnbarrow and bargaining the two stars for our lives."

"We know from Delorran what they think of us there. Whatever the rest of you decide, it's not something I'll be doing."

"Gods, I'm pleased to hear you say that, Stryke." She beamed at him. "I'd rather face anything than the reception Jennesta would have waiting for us."

There was something like a banquet in the grand hall of Jennesta's palace.

But only something like. Although the long, highly polished dining table was set out for a meal, there was no food. There were five guests present, apart from the Queen herself, not to mention twice that number of servants, flunkies and bodyguards. But there was little evidence of gaiety.

Two of Jennesta's guests were orcs: the newly elevated General Mersadion, and Captain Delorran, fresh back from his unsuccessful pursuit of the Wolverines. There was no mistaking their nervousness. But they were not the source of the tension. That had its axis in the three other guests.

They were humans.

Jennesta dealt with humans because of her support for the Mani cause, so seeing members of the race about her palace wasn't in itself that unusual. What was troubling was the nature of these particular humans.

Noticing Mersadion and Delorran's discomfort, Jennesta spoke. "General, Captain, allow me to introduce Micah Lekmann." She indicated the tallest of the trio.

A beard would have disguised an old scar that ran from the centre of his stubbled right cheek to the corner of his mouth. Instead he favoured an unkempt black moustache. His hair was a greasy mop and his skin weather-beaten where it wasn't pock-marked. Lekmann's muscularity and the cut of his clothes spoke of a life of combat. He looked like a man untroubled by notions of gallantry.

"And these are his . . . associates," Jennesta added. She left hanging an unspoken invitation for him to make the introductions.

Lekmann flashed an unctuous smile and jabbed a lazy thumb at the human on his right. "Greever Aulay," he announced.

Where Lekmann was tall, Aulay was the shortest of the three. In contrast to his leader's well-bulked physique, he was lean and slight. He had the face of a baby rat. His hair was sandy blond and his visible eye, the left one, hazel. A black leather patch concealed the other. His wispy goatee beard clung tenuously to a weak chin. Thin lips stretched to reveal bad teeth.

"And this is Jabeez Blaan," Lekmann grated.

The man on his left was the biggest by far in terms of mass. He probably weighed as much as the other two put together, but it was all brawn, not fat. His totally shaved, spherical head seemed to meet his body without the necessity of an intervening neck. The nose had been broken at least once and now impersonated a doorknob. His eyes looked uncannily like twin piss-holes in snow. The pair of ham fists he rested on the table could have been called upon to demolish a stout oak.

Neither spoke nor smiled, contenting themselves with small and perfunctory tilts of the head.

Delorran and Mersadion eyed the trio uneasily.

"They have very special talents to employ on my behalf," Jennesta explained. "But more of that later." The parchment Delorran had brought back lay in front of her. She tapped it with one of her unfeasibly long fingernails. "Thanks to Captain Delorran, who has just returned from a vitally important mission, we know that my property has been violated. Regrettably, the Captain's efforts did not extend to returning the object itself, or to bringing the thieves to justice."

Apprehensively, Delorran made a tiny throat-clearing sound. "Begging your pardon, ma'am, but on that score at least the Wolverines received their just deserts. They were all lost, as I reported."

"You saw them die?"

"Not . . . as such, Your Majesty. But when I last saw them they had no hope of escape. Their deaths were certain."

"Not as certain as you think, Captain."

Delorran gaped at her. "Ma'am?"

"Reports of their deaths were somewhat exaggerated, shall we say."

"They survived the battlefield?"

"They did."

"But—"

"How do I know? Because they were pursued by a dragon patrol after crossing the battlefield, and lived through their attack, too."

"Your Majesty, I—"

"You would have been well advised to stay a little longer and confirm the Wolverines' destruction, rather than assuming it, would you not, Captain?" Her tone was more chiding than angry, as though she addressed an errant child.

"Yes, Majesty," he replied meekly.

"You've heard of General Kysthan's . . . demise." Delorran looked uncomfortable. "He has paid the price of your failure."

The Captain had no time to reply before Jennesta snapped her fingers. Elf servants began moving among them, dispensing goblets of wine from silver trays. One was handed to Jennesta with a bow.

"A toast," she said, raising her glass. "To the return of that which is mine, and the confounding of my enemies."

She drank and they all followed suit.

"Which does not mean that there's no price for you to pay as well, Captain," she added.

Delorran did not immediately get Jennesta's meaning and stared at her in puzzlement. Then the import of her words began to soak in. He looked to the goblet he held, the colour draining from his face.

The glass slipped from his fingers and broke. His jaw dropped and he brought a hand to his throat. "You . . . *bitch*," he croaked. He rose clumsily, knocking over his chair.

Jennesta sat impassively, watching him.

Delorran staggered a step or two in her direction, and his shaking hand went to his sword.

She didn't move.

He couldn't co-ordinate himself sufficiently to draw the blade, and was sweating freely now, his face contorted with building agony. A rasping, rattling sound came from his throat and he began choking. Then he buckled and went down. He fell into a jolting, foaming-mouthed fit, spasms running through his body. A trickle of blood seeped from his mouth. His back arched, his legs kicked convulsively. He was still.

Death stamped a dreadful expression on his face.

"Why waste precious magic?" Jennesta asked the silent company. "Anyway, I wanted to test that particular potion."

Sapphire the cat appeared and slunk over to the pool of spilt wine. She would have lapped at it if Jennesta hadn't laughingly shooed her away.

The Queen looked up. The three humans were regarding their own half-finished drinks with concern. It rekindled her laughter.

"Don't worry," she reassured them. "I've no need to bring in people specially in order to poison them. And you can stop looking at me that way, Mersadion. I would hardly have gone to the trouble of promoting you only to consign you to your grave. Not so soon, anyway."

It could have been a joke.

She stepped over the corpse and went to sit nearer them. "Enough of pleasure, now to business. I said that Lekmann and his company have special skills, General. Their particular ability is finding outlaws."

"They're bounty hunters, you mean?"

Lekmann answered. "It's what some call us. We prefer to think of ourselves as freelance law enforcers."

Jennesta laughed again. "As good a description as any. But don't be modest, Lekmann. Tell the General your speciality."

Lekmann nodded at Greever Aulay. Aulay produced a sack and dumped it on the table.

"Our business is hunting orcs," Lekmann said.

Aulay upended the sack. Five or six round yellowy-brown objects bounced across the surface. Mersadion stared at them. Then what they were slowly dawned on him. Shrunken orc heads. An appalled expression crossed his face.

Lekmann gave one of his oily grins. "We only deal in renegades, you understand."

"I do hope you're not going to allow any kind of prejudice to colour our dealings with these agents, General," Jennesta remarked. "I expect you to give them the fullest co-operation in their work."

Ambition battled with disgust in Mersadion's features. He began to pull himself together. "What exactly *is* this work, Your Majesty?" he asked.

"The hunting of the Wolverines, of course, and the recovery of my property. Not instead of the efforts you're making, but in addition to them. I judged the time right to bring in professionals seasoned in this kind of task."

Mersadion turned to Lekmann. "There are just the three of you? Or do you have . . . helpers?"

"We can call on others if need be, but usually we work alone. We find it best that way."

"Where does your allegiance lie?"

"With ourselves." He glanced at Jennesta. "And whoever's paying us."

"They follow neither the Mani nor Uni path," Jennesta said. "They're irreligious, and simple opportunists. Is that not so, Lekmann?"

The bounty hunter smirked and nodded. Although whether

he had any idea what *opportunists* meant, let alone *irreligious*, was a moot point.

"Which makes them ideal for my purposes," the Queen continued, "unlikely as they are to be swayed by anything other than the reward. Which would be substantial enough to ensure their loyalty."

Mersadion had put aside any scruples. "How are we to proceed, ma'am?"

"We know that the last sightings of the Wolverines had them moving in the direction of Trinity. You'll agree that's an odd destination. Unless, as Delorran believed, they've turned traitor and joined the Unis. I find that hard to credit. But if they really are in Trinity, for whatever reason, our friends here are obviously best suited to following them there."

"What are your orders?" Lekmann enquired.

"The cylinder has absolute priority. If you can slay the band that stole it, their leader in particular, all the better. But not at the expense of gaining that artifact. Employ any methods you see fit."

"You can rely on us. Er, Your Majesty," he tacked on, remembering the protocol.

"I hope so. For your sakes." Her face and voice took on a distinctly chilly aspect. "For should you think of double-dealing, know that my wrath is limitless." They all glanced at the body on the floor. "You'll also learn that no other will pay you as handsomely for the return of what I seek." Her smile returned. It was possible to mistake it for warm. "I would leave no stone unturned in the search for this renegade band, so I intend following tradition."

She beckoned a pair of her orc bodyguards. They moved forward and dragged Delorran's body to a small side door.

Jennesta turned to a servant. "Let them in."

The servant went to the dining room's large twin doors and opened them. Two elf elders entered and bowed low.

"I have a proclamation for you," Jennesta told them. "Spread these words throughout the realm, and send runners to all parts where such information will be of value." She waved a hand at the servant by the door. "Proceed."

The servant unrolled a parchment and began reading in the characteristically piping elfin lilt. " 'Be it known that by order of Her Imperial Highness Queen Jennesta of Cairnbarrow that the orc warband attached to Her Majesty's horde, and known as the Wolverines, are henceforth to be regarded as renegades and outlaws, and are no longer afforded the protection of this realm. Be it further known that a bounty of such precious coin, pellucid or land as may be appropriate will be paid upon production of the heads of the band's officers. To wit, Captain Stryke, sergeants Haskeer and the dwarf Jup, corporals Alfray and Coilla. Furthermore, a reward proportionate to their rank shall be paid for the return, dead or alive, of the band's common troopers, answering to the names Bhose, Breggin, Calthmon, Darig, Eldo, Finje, Gant, Gleadeg, Hystykk, Jad, Kestix, Liffin, Meklun, Nep, Noskaa, Orbon, Prooq, Reafdaw, Seafe, Slettal, Talag, Toche, Vobe, Wrelbyd and Zoda. Be it known that any harbouring said outlaws will be subject to full penalties as laid down by law. By order of Her Majesty Queen Jennesta. All hail the highborn monarch.' "

The servant rolled the parchment and handed it to one of the elders.

"Now go and issue it," Jennesta ordered.

The elders backed out, bowing.

The Queen rose, causing the others to scramble to their feet. She fixed the bounty hunters with a searching gaze. "You'd best be on your way if you want to beat the opposition," she said. With a smile, she added, "Let's see the Wolverines find sanctuary now."

Then she turned her back on them and swept from the chamber.

21

Jup gently mopped Haskeer's brow with a damp cloth.

From outside the field tent, Stryke, Alfray and a handful of grunts watched the scene with something like amazement.

Incredulous, Alfray slowly shook his head. "Now I've seen everything."

"Just goes to show there's nothing as queer as species," Stryke said.

They went about their business, shooing the troopers away in the process.

Haskeer started to come round. Blinking as though the light was painful for his eyes, he mumbled something incomprehensible. Whether he realised it was Jup tending him, the dwarf wasn't sure. He rinsed the cloth and reapplied it.

"What . . . the . . . fu—" Haskeer slurred.

"That's right," Jup told him cheerfully. "You'll soon be back to your old self."

"Er?"

The befuddlement on Haskeer's face could have been due to his groggy state or finding the dwarf looming over him. Either way, Jup took no notice of it.

"A lot's happened while you've been out of your head," Jup stated, "so I thought I'd fill you in."

"Wha—?"

"I don't care whether you understand me or not, you bastard, I'm going to go through it anyway."

He proceeded to bring the semi-comatose orc up to date on developments, heedless of the patient's apparent lack of comprehension. But about two-thirds of the way through his story Haskeer's eyes drifted shut again and he immediately began snoring loudly.

Jup got to his feet. "Don't think you're getting off that easy," he promised. "I'll be back."

He crept out of the tent.

There was dilute sunshine outside. The tinkling drone of fairy swarms could be heard in the distance. He surveyed the landscape. The tracts of land abutting Calyparr Inlet were marshy and inhospitable. They had set up camp on as dry a patch as they could find, but it was still sodden underfoot and pretty miserable.

The band were spread around gathering firewood, grubbing for food and carrying out other mundane but necessary tasks.

Alfray and Coilla wandered over.

"How is he?" Alfray asked.

"Came round for a minute or two." Jup smiled. "I think my telling of what's been going on put him out again. He seemed kind of muddled."

"That's not unusual with some of these human maladies. He should be all right in a while. What surprises me is why you're being so nice to him."

"Never had anything against him, the way he thinks he does against me. And when all's said and done, he's a comrade."

"Anybody can look pathetic when they're that ill," Coilla reminded him. "Don't go too soft on the awkward bugger."

"Not much danger of that."

Alfray took a deep breath. "You know, it's colder than it should be, and I've been in drier places, but it's not so bad here. This little bit of land in this tiny slice of time is just about the way things must have been in Maras-Dantia before the troubles. If you kind of squint your eyes and use your imagination, that is."

Coilla was about to have her say on that when they were interrupted by shouts from a nearby glade. They were more raucous than alarming but the officers set off to investigate anyway. As they walked, Stryke joined them.

They were met by a running grunt.

"What's up, Prooq?" Stryke said.

"Bit of bother, sir."

"What kind?"

"Well . . . best come and see, sir."

They went a little further and found the rest of the grunts hanging around near the mouth of the glade. A small group of figures were parading themselves in front of them.

"Oh no," Alfray sighed. "Bloody pests!"

"What is it?" Jup wanted to know.

"Wood nymphs."

"And a succubus or two by the looks of it," Stryke added.

The voluptuous females were dressed in gowns of rustic colours, provocatively low-cut to display maximum cleavage and slashed to the waist, revealing shapely limbs. They cavorted, swung about their autumnal-coloured hair and struck exaggeratedly seductive poses. A keening, wailing, unmelodious screech filled the air.

"What the *hell* is that racket?" Jup said.

"Their siren song," Alfray explained. "It's supposed to be alluring and impossible to resist."

"Not all it's cracked up to be, is it?"

"They're said to be mistresses of deception."

"They're only deceiving themselves," Coilla put in grumpily. "They look like well-worn strumpets to me."

The nymphs continued adopting crude postures, and were now adding even cruder language to their wailing. Some of the grunts were obviously tempted.

"Look at them!" Coilla seethed. "I expected better of this band than it should be controlled by a swelling of their fertilising sacs!"

"They're young, they probably haven't come across the like before," Alfray said. "They don't know it's an illusion, and that it's likely to kill them."

"Literally?" Jup asked.

"Given half a chance those whores will suck the life essences from any stupid enough to fall under their spell."

Jup eyed the fleshy pageant. "I can think of worse ways to go . . ."

"*Jup!*" Coilla scolded.

He blushed.

"What are they doing in a place like this anyway?" Stryke wondered. "It's hardly an ideal spot for luring the unwary."

"Either they've been driven away from more pleasant parts because they're such a nuisance," Alfray speculated, "or they're getting too ravaged for their usual haunts."

"The latter by the looks of them," Coilla sniffed.

"They're not particularly dangerous in themselves," Alfray added. "They rely on their victims going to them willingly. They have no fighting skills that I'm aware of."

The grunts were shouting ribald comments back at the nymphs, and several were edging closer to them.

"It's a good thing Haskeer isn't here," Jup remarked.

Alfray pulled a face. "Perish the thought."

"We don't have time for this nonsense," Stryke decided.

"Just what I was thinking," Coilla declared, drawing her sword. She strode in the direction of the glade.

"As I said," Alfray called after her, "there's no need to fight them!"

She ignored him and kept going. But her target was the grunts. She laid about them with the flat of her sword, singling out their backsides for special attention. Half a dozen whacks and a chorus of yelps later and they were running for the camp.

The would-be nymph seducers jeered in a distinctly unlady-like fashion and slunk away.

Coilla marched back to the others. "There's nothing like a tanned arse to dampen passion," she proclaimed, re-sheathing her sword. "Though I'm disgusted that any of our troopers should have been interested in the first place."

"We've wasted enough time," Stryke complained. "We can't kick our heels around here for the rest of our lives. I want a decision on Scratch, and I want us to reach it now."

They argued the pros and cons, and in the end decided to set out for the trolls' homeland. Once there, they'd reassess the position.

The route they chose followed an ancient trading trail, north towards the Mani settlement of Ladygrove. Before reaching it they would turn north-east to Scratch. It was a journey not without peril, but any movement in the human-infested south had its dangers. All they could do was proceed with caution and stay alert for trouble.

Haskeer had taken no part in the discussion about travelling to Scratch. On his past record, that was unprecedented. They put his taciturn state down to the illness. But he had recovered enough physically to ride unaided. Certainly his stubbornness was sufficiently restored for him to insist he would.

Stryke made a point of riding with him. After an hour or so of virtual silence, he said, "How you feeling?"

Haskeer stared at him, as though surprised to be asked. Finally he came out with, "I've never felt better."

Stryke couldn't fail to pick up the strangely subdued edge to Haskeer's reply, and begged to differ. But he didn't do it aloud, just responded with a neutral "Good."

Another wordless moment or two passed before Haskeer said, "Can I see the stars?"

Stryke was a little taken aback at the request, and hesitated. But then he thought, *Why shouldn't he want to see them? Doesn't he have a right?* It wasn't as if he couldn't handle any problems Haskeer might cause.

Stryke dug into his belt pouch and held the stars out for him to look at.

From the expression on Haskeer's face he was much more interested in them than he had ever appeared to be before. He stretched out his own hand and waited for Stryke to place them in it. Again Stryke hesitated. Then he laid them on the open palm.

Haskeer stared at the objects, fascinated.

The silence went on long enough, as they rode, for Stryke to start feeling a little restive. Something strange, a look Stryke hadn't seen there before, burned in Haskeer's eyes.

At last the sergeant looked up and said, "They're beautiful."

It was such an uncharacteristic thing for him to say that Stryke didn't know how to respond. In the event, he didn't have to. A forward scout appeared, galloping hard towards him.

"Tidings from the advance," Stryke said, holding out his hand. "Give 'em back."

Haskeer continued gazing at the artifacts.

"*Haskeer!* The stars."

"Eh? Oh, yes. Here."

He passed them over and Stryke returned them to his pouch. The scout arrived.

"What is it, Talag?"

"Party of humans coming this way, sir. Twenty or thirty of them, about a mile further along."

"Hostile?"

"I don't think they're a threat, unless it's a trick. They're females, children and babes mostly, with some old of both sexes. Look like they're refugees."

"Did they see you?"

"Don't think so. They're not a fighting unit, Captain. Most of them can hardly walk."

"Hold on here, I'll come forward with you."

Stryke looked at Haskeer. He would have expected him to have something to say about the possibility of an encounter with humans, but he seemed unperturbed. So he ignored him and pulled back to the next rank, where Coilla and Jup were riding abreast.

"Did you hear that?"

They had.

"I'm going ahead. Bring along the column. And, er, keep an eye on things, yes?" He nodded at Haskeer. They got his meaning and nodded back.

"Alfray!" Stryke called. "Follow me!"

Coilla and Jup assumed the lead as he set off with Talag and Alfray. Spurring their horses, they sped ahead of the column. Rounding a curve or two in the track, they came to the group of humans.

They were as Talag had described: mostly women, some with babes in arms, and children. There was a smattering of hobbling ancient ones. The orcs' arrival sent a ripple of alarm through the ragged company. Children hugged their mothers' legs, old men did their best to stand defensively.

Stryke saw no threat, nor any reason to alarm them further. He drew up his horse and, in order to seem less intimidating, dismounted. Alfray and Talag did likewise.

A lone woman stepped forward. She seemed quite young under the grime. Her unwashed waist-length blonde hair was plaited down her back, and her clothing was bedraggled. She was obviously frightened, but faced Stryke with a straight back and proud demeanour.

"We're only women and children," she said, her voice wavering nervously, "and a few old ones. We've no ill-intent, nor could we offer you violence if we did. We only want to pass."

Stryke thought her little speech was delivered bravely. "We don't make war on females and young ones," he replied. "Or on any offering us no threat."

"I've your word none will be harmed?"

"You have." He scanned their exhausted, worried faces. "Where are you from?"

"Ladygrove."

"So you're Manis?"

"Yes. And you orcs have fought on our side, haven't you?" It was probably said as much to reassure herself as ask a question.

"We have." Stryke didn't like to tell her that they had had little choice in the matter.

"That's as it should be. You elder races, like us, believe in the pantheon of gods."

Stryke nodded but said nothing on the subject. There were greater differences between orcs and humans than there were similarities. He saw no point in raising them now. Instead he asked, "What's happened at Ladygrove that's made you leave it?"

"An onslaught by a Uni army. Most of our menfolk were killed, and we only narrowly escaped."

"The settlement's fallen?"

"It hadn't when we left. A few were holding out, but in truth they stand next to no chance of avoiding being overrun." Her glum face brightened a little. "Are you on your way to help defend it?"

Stryke had been hoping she wouldn't ask that. "No. We're on . . . another mission. To Scratch. I'm sorry."

The shadow recast itself over her features. "I was hoping you

were the answer to our prayers." She put on a bold and unconvincing smile. "Oh well, the gods will provide."

"Where are you heading?" Alfray wanted to know.

"Just . . . away. We were hoping to make contact with another
of the Mani settlements."

"Take our advice and don't stray on to the plains. The area
around Weaver's Lea is especially perilous at the moment."

"We'd heard as much."

"Stick to the inlet," Stryke added. "You won't need to be told to
avoid Trinity." He agonised about whether to mention Hobrow's
posse. In the event he didn't.

"Our thought was to make for the west-coast settlements,"
she explained. "Hexton, perhaps, or Vermillion. We should have
a favourable reception there."

Stryke took in their pathetic state. "It's a long march." *A murderously long march if the truth be known*, he thought.

"With the gods' help we'll prevail."

He had no reason to be well disposed towards humans, but
he wanted to believe she was right.

At that moment the rest of the Wolverines came into view and
galloped up to join them. There was another stirring of unease
among the refugees.

"Don't be concerned," Stryke assured them. "Our band won't
hurt you."

The orcs dismounted and gazed at the raggle-taggle collection of humans facing them.

Most came forward, Coilla and Jup at their head. The sight of
a female orc, and a dwarf in orcs' company, drew many curious
looks and whispered comments. Haskeer hung back, but Stryke
had no time to think about his eccentricities at the moment.

"We left with little more than the clothes on our back," the
woman told them. "Could you spare us some water?"

"Yes," Stryke agreed, "and perhaps some rations. Though not
a lot; we're short ourselves."

"You're kind. Thank you."

Stryke set a couple of troopers to the task.

A small child, a female of the species, moved hesitantly

forward, eyes wide, a thumb planted firmly in her mouth. She clutched the woman's skirt and stared at the orcs. The woman looked down at her and smiled.

"You must forgive her. Forgive us all. Few of us have been in the company of orcs before, for all that your race has fought on our behalf."

The child, blonde like the woman and sharing her features, let go of the skirt and walked the last few steps to the orcs. Her gaze went from Coilla to Stryke to Alfray to Jup and back again.

She removed her thumb and said, "What's that?" She pointed at Coilla's face.

Coilla didn't take her meaning. She was puzzled.

The child added, "Those marks. On your face."

"Oh, the tattoos. They're emblems of our rank."

The girl looked blank.

"They let everyone know who's in charge." Coilla saw a stick by the trail and bent to pick it up. Then she crouched next to a patch of denuded earth. "Look, I'll show you. Our . . . chief is Stryke here." She indicated him with the stick, then began drawing a crude picture. "You see, he has two stripes like this on each cheek." She scraped ((. "That means he's a captain. The boss, if you like." She pointed at Jup. "He's a sergeant, so the marks make his face look like this." She drew -(- -)-. "Sergeants are second in command to captains. I'm the next one down, a corporal, and my marks go this way." She scratched ( ). "Understand?"

Entranced, the child nodded. She smiled at Coilla and reached for the stick, then began scraping her own meaningless designs.

The grunts returned with the water and some rations.

"They're meagre," Stryke apologised, "but you're welcome to them."

"It's still more than we had before meeting you," the woman replied. "May the gods bless you."

Stryke felt uncomfortable. After all, most of his contacts with humans had been to do with trying to kill as many as he could. At his word, the grunts began moving among the humans and distributing the sparse supplies.

Stryke, Alfray and Jup watched as the troopers were thanked profusely, and Coilla on her hands and knees with the child.

"The twists fate keeps in store are odd, aren't they?" Jup whispered.

But the woman overheard. "You find this strange? So do we. But in truth we're not so different to you, or to any of the elder races. At heart, all want peace and despise war."

"Orcs are born to war," Stryke replied, a little indignantly. He softened slightly at the look she gave him. "But it must be just. Destruction for its own sake holds no appeal for us."

"My race has done you many wrongs."

He was surprised to hear such an admission from a human, but again held his tongue.

A trooper was passing by the child kneeling with Coilla. He held a water sack. The child reached for it. Removing the stopper, the grunt handed it to her. She was raising it to her lips when her face distorted in a peculiar way. Then a terrible sound issued from her.

"Atishoo!"

Coilla scrambled to her feet. She and the trooper quickly backed off.

To Stryke's horror, the woman smiled. "Poor little thing. She has a chill."

"Chill?"

"Just a mild one. She'll be over it in a day or two." She laid her hand on the child's brow. "As if she didn't have enough to put up with. I guess we'll all have it before long."

"This . . . chill," Coilla said. "Is it a disease?"

"Disease? Well, yes; I suppose it is. But it's just—"

"Back to the horses, all of you!" Stryke barked.

The band rushed for their mounts, abandoning the water sacks and rations.

The woman was baffled. All the humans were.

"I don't understand. What's wrong? The child has no more than a cold."

Stryke's fear was that the band would lay into the humans and slay them. He saw no benefit in delay. "We have to leave. I'm sorry. I wish you . . . well."

He turned and made for his own horse.

"Wait!" she called. "Wait! I don't—"

He ignored her, yelled an order and led the band away.

They galloped off at speed, leaving the humans standing in the road looking totally baffled.

As they rode, Jup said, "That was a near thing."

"It just goes to show that you can't trust humans," Alfray remarked. "Mani *or* Uni."

As far as Jennesta was concerned, the only good Uni was a dead Uni.

Certainly the Uni corpses half submerged in the bloody water-filled ditch she gazed into had proved useful in providing what she needed. Now, though, she saw it as a mixed blessing.

Jennesta's intention had been to use the pool's gory contents as a medium for farsight. It was a particularly beneficial tool when in the middle of a conflict. Knowing the enemy's deployment gave an obvious advantage. The trouble was that no sooner had she begun scrying than Adpar's smug face appeared in the pool.

At least Sanara's priggish features were absent for once.

Jennesta suffered a moment's barrage of insincere and empty greetings before interrupting. "This is not the most convenient time for chit-chat," she snarled.

"*Oh dear,*" Adpar's likeness replied. "*And there was I thinking you'd be interested in news of those outlaws you've been getting so fussed about.*"

Alarm drums pounded in Jennesta's head. She adopted an air of sham indifference. "Outlaws? What outlaws?"

"*You may come over as a good liar to your underlings, dear, but you could never fool me. So stop the little-girl-lost act, it's sickening. We both know what I'm talking about.*"

"Supposing I did. What could you possibly have to say on the matter?"

"*Only that those you seek have another of the relics.*"

"What?"

"*Or perhaps you have no idea what I'm talking about. Again.*"

"How did you come by this news?"

"*I have my sources.*"

"If you had anything to do with this—"

"Me? *And to do with what, exactly?*"

"It would be just like you to try to scupper my plans, Adpar."

"*So you have plans, do you? Perhaps I will take an interest after all.*"

"Stay out of this, Adpar! If you so much as—"

"Ma'am!" someone called from nearby.

Jennesta looked up, glaring. General Mersadion was standing several paces away, looking like a child who'd come to announce he'd fouled himself.

"What is it?" she snapped.

"You told me to let you know when we reached the point of—"

"Yes, yes! I'll be there!"

He backed off, humbly.

Jennesta turned back to Adpar's grimacing visage. "You've not heard the last of this!" Then she slashed her hand through the icy, bloodied water, banishing the image.

She got to her feet and strode to the bowing general.

They were on a hill overlooking a battlefield. The battle about to start was not particularly large, having perhaps a thousand combatants on either side, but it was to be fought over a point of strategic importance.

The Queen's side consisted of Manis, dwarves and orcs, the latter, as ever, forming the backbone. The other side was almost entirely composed of Unis, with a smattering of dwarves.

"I'm ready," she told Mersadion. "Prepare the protection."

He swiped down his hand and a row of orc buglers further along the hill turned their backs on the battlefield and sounded a shrill blast. Mersadion covered his eyes.

Down below, Jennesta's army, hearing the signal, did the same thing. Much to the mystification of the Unis.

She raised her hands and wove a magical conjuration. Next she reached inside her cloak and produced an object resembling an extraordinarily large gem. The multi-faceted fist-sized jewel shimmered, its interior swirling with a myriad of colours.

She tossed it into the air.

Jennesta exerted no more than casual force, yet the bizarrely sized gem travelled up and up as though it were a feather caught by the wind. Many of the opposing army below saw it, glinting in the weak sunlight, and followed its climb with fascination. She noticed that a few of the enemy warriors aped her force and covered their eyes. There were always one or two smarter than the rest. But never enough.

The jewel rose lazily, turning slowly end on end, a glittering pinpoint of concentrated illumination.

Then it detonated with a silent flash of light that would have shamed a hundred thunderbolts.

The intense explosion of radiance lasted barely a second. It had hardly faded when the screaming started down below. The enemy were staggering in panic, pawing at their eyes, dropping their weapons, colliding with each other.

There was another blast from the bugles. Her army uncovered their eyes and rushed in for the slaughter.

Mersadion was at the Queen's side.

"A useful addition to our armoury," she said, "optical munitions."

The screams of the helplessly blind were drifting up to them.

"We can't use it too often, though," she added. "They'll be wise to it. And it is dreadfully draining." She patted at her forehead with a lace handkerchief. "Bring me my horse."

The General ran off to obey her order.

On the battlefield, the butchery reached a pitch. It was gratifying, but not her immediate concern.

Her mind was on the Wolverines.

22

The following days passed more or less uneventfully for the Wolverines.

Only Haskeer's mood caused them concern. He swung between periods of elation and depression, and often said things they found difficult to understand. Alfray assured the band that their comrade was still recovering from an illness most elder-race members were lucky to survive, and that he should soon be on the mend. Stryke wasn't alone in wondering when that would happen.

But this was put to the back of everyone's mind when they arrived at Scratch on the evening of the third day.

The trolls' homeland was in the centre of the Great Plains, as near as damn, but the terrain couldn't have been more different to its lush surroundings. Rolling grassland gave way to shrub. In short order the shrub itself blended into shale, and the shale gave way to a landscape more rock than soil.

Scratch proper was heralded by a collection of what seemed to be ragged hills. Closer inspection revealed them to be rock. It was as though mountains had somehow been covered by earth to ninety per cent of their height, leaving only their rugged peaks exposed.

What the orcs knew, as everybody did, was that the action of water, aided by troll mining, had honeycombed the porous ground beneath with a labyrinth of tunnels and chambers. What they held was a mystery. Few if any of those bold enough to enter had ever returned to tell their tale.

"How long has it been since anybody mounted an armed attack on this place?" Stryke wondered.

"I don't know," Coilla admitted. "Though it's a good bet they were of greater strength than a depleted warband."

"Kimball Hobrow seems to think he can do it."

"He's unlikely to go in with anything less than a small army. We're not much more than a score."

"We're small in number, yes, but experienced, well armed, determined—"

"You don't have to sell it to me, Stryke." She smiled. "Not that I'm overly keen on anything that takes me away from the open air." She glanced around the rocky terrain they were creeping through. "But none of this means a thing unless we can find a way in."

"There're said to be secret ways. We don't have much hope of stumbling on any of those. But a main entrance is spoken of as well. That'd be a start."

"Wouldn't they hide a main entrance too?"

"They might not need to. They'd probably have it well guarded, and perhaps more importantly, the reputation Scratch has is enough to keep most away."

"Right on cue. Look."

She pointed at a massive outcropping of rock. The face it turned to them was a pool of blackness, much darker than any of the other jutting slabs around it. Staring hard, Stryke realised it was an opening.

They approached it warily.

It was a cave-like aperture, but not very big; the size perhaps of a modestly proportioned farmhouse. The interior seemed empty, though they couldn't be entirely sure as it was so dark inside.

"Just a minute," Coilla said. "This should help."

She took a flint from her belt, and one of the cloths she used to polish her knives. Making fire, she ignited the twisted rag, producing just enough light for them to see a few steps ahead. They edged in.

"I'm beginning to think this is just a hollowed rock," Stryke commented.

Coilla happened to glance down. "*Stop!*" she hissed, grabbing his arm. Her voice echoed. "Look."

No more than three paces ahead of them was a cavernous hole in the ground. They crept to it and peered over, but couldn't make out anything in its inky depths. Coilla dropped the burning cloth. They watched as it became a minute pinpoint of light, then vanished.

"Could be bottomless," Coilla speculated.

"I doubt it. Anyway, unless the other search parties come up with anything better, this might be our only way in. Let's get back."

Greever Aulay fingered his eye-patch.

"It always hurts when those bastards are around," he complained.

Lekmann gave a derisive laugh.

Aulay scowled. "You can mock. But it was paining like hell when we were in Jennesta's palace with all those damn orcs about the place."

"What do you think, Jabeez?" Lekmann said. "Reckon the boy's got an orc sniffer in that empty socket of his?"

"Nah," Blaan replied. "Reckon *he* does though, ever since one of 'em took his eye."

"You don't know what you're talking about, the pair of you," Aulay grumbled. "And don't call me *boy*, Micah."

Trinity was well behind them now. Their search hadn't taken them into the Uni settlement. They wouldn't be so foolhardy. But they knew from speaking to women working in the fields, to whom they presented themselves as good, upright Uni gentlemen, that the Wolverines had been there.

There had apparently been some kind of a fuss. But when Lekmann tried to find out exactly what, the women clammed up. All they could find out was that the orcs had done something bad enough that it warranted half the township chasing them clear over to Calyparr Inlet. Which seemed to point to the warband not being in league with the Unis. The bounty hunters didn't care about that. All that concerned them was getting the relic, and as many renegade heads as they could carry back for the reward.

So they headed for Calyparr too, in the hope of picking up the trail. But they had wandered along the water's edge for nearly a day now without seeing hide nor hair of the outlaws.

"I think we ain't going to find them in these parts," Blaan declared.

"You leave the thinking to me, big man," Lekmann advised him. "It never was your strong point."

"Maybe he's right, Micah," Aulay said. "If they were ever here, they've long gone."

"Oh, so your eye ain't that reliable after all," Lekmann mocked.

Their exchange was cut short as they rounded a knot of trees. Lekmann's eyes widened. "Now what we got here?"

By the side of the trail was a pitiable makeshift camp. It was populated by a motley crew of human women, children and oldsters. They looked all but done in.

"Don't see no men," Aulay remarked. "None likely to trouble us at any rate."

The humans, seeing the approaching riders, began to stir.

A woman detached herself from the rest and came forward. Her garb was grubby and her lengthy blonde hair was bound in a single strand. Lekmann thought there was a certain haughtiness about her.

She looked at the oddly matched trio. The tall, skinny one with the eye-patch. The short, hard-faced one with the scar. The one with no hair and built like a brick shit-house.

Lekmann gave her a leering smile. "Good day."

"Who are you?" she asked suspiciously. "What do you want?"

"You got nothing to worry about, ma'am. We're just going about our business." He looked the crowd over. "In fact we got a lot in common."

"You're Manis too?"

That was what he wanted. "Yes, ma'am. We're just good gods-fearing folk like yourselves."

She seemed relieved at that, but not much.

Lekmann slipped a foot from its stirrup. "Mind if we dismount?"

"I can't stop you."

He climbed off his horse, keeping his movements slow and deliberate so as not to spook them. Aulay and Blaan did the same.

Lekmann stretched. "Been riding a long time. It's good to take a break."

"Don't think we're being unneighbourly," the woman told him, "but we've no food or water to share."

"No matter. I can see you're down on your luck. Been on the road long?"

"Feels like forever."

"Where you from?"

"Ladygrove. There's trouble in those parts."

"There's trouble in all parts, ma'am. These are tormented times and that's a fact."

She eyed Blaan and Aulay. "Your friends don't say much."

"Men of few words. More doers than talkers, you might say. But let's not waste words ourselves. We stopped because we were hoping you could help us."

"Like I said, we don't have any—"

"No, not that way. It's just that we're looking for . . . certain parties, and as you've been travelling a while we thought you might have seen 'em."

"We've seen precious few people on our journey."

"I'm not talking people. I'm referring to a bunch of elder racers."

What could have been a cloud of renewed suspicion passed across her face. "What race might that be?"

"Orcs."

He thought the word hit some kind of target. The shutters seemed to come down behind her eyes. "Well, I don't—"

"Yes we did, Mummy!"

The bounty hunters turned and saw a girl child skipping forward. "Those funny men with the marks on their faces," she said. Her voice was nasal, as though she had a cold. "You remember!"

Lekmann knew they'd struck gold.

"Oh yes." The woman strained to sound casual. "We did run into a group of them, couple of days back. Did no more than pass the time, really. They seemed in a hurry."

Lekmann was about to put another question when the child came up to him.

"Are you their friends?" she asked, sniffily.

"Not now!" he snapped, irritated at the interruption.

The girl backed off, frightened, and ran for her mother's protection. Lekmann's reaction made the woman even warier. A look of defiance came to her face. The other Manis were stiffening with tension too, but he saw little to worry about there and paid them no heed.

He dropped the friendly manner. "You know where these orcs went?"

"How should I?"

Now she'd got her back up. That was a shame.

"Anyway, why do you want to find them?" she added.

"It's to do with some unfinished business."

"You sure you aren't Unis?"

He grinned like a latrine rat. "We're not Unis, that's for sure."

Aulay and Blaan laughed. Unpleasantly.

The woman was growing alarmed. "Who *are* you?"

"Just travellers who want to be on our way once we've got some information." He looked around slyly. "Maybe your menfolk would know where the orcs went?"

"They're . . . they're out hunting for food."

"Don't think they are, ma'am. I don't think you've got any menfolk." He glanced at her companions. "At least none young and fit. One or two would have stayed with you if you had."

"They're nearby, and they'll be back any time now." A note of desperation crept into her voice. "If you don't want trouble—"

"You're a bad liar, ma'am." He stared pointedly at the child. "Now let's keep this nice and friendly, shall we? Where did those orcs go?"

She saw what was in his eyes and visibly gave up. "All right. They did mention something about heading for Scratch."

"The trolls' place? Now why would they be doing that?"

"How should I know?"

"It don't add up. You sure they didn't tell you anything else?"

"No, they didn't." The child tugged at her skirt and started to cry. "It's all right, darling," the woman soothed. "Everything's fine."

"Don't believe you're telling me all you know," Lekmann said menacingly. "Maybe they ain't even heading for Scratch at all."

"I've told you all I know. There's no more."

"Well, ma'am, you'll appreciate I have to be sure of that."

He nodded at Blaan and Aulay. The three of them moved forward, fanning out.

By the time they left, he knew she had been telling the truth.

The way Stryke saw it, circumstances dictated a straightforward plan.

"We've got just one chance, and I say we have no choice but a direct assault. We go in, do the job, get out."

"That sounds fair enough," Coilla said. "But think about the difficulties. First, going in. The only possible way we've found is that shaft in the cave. It might not lead into the trolls' labyrinth. Or even if it does, it could be incredibly deep."

"We've got plenty of rope. If we need more we can find some vines and make it."

"All right. Then you say we'll do the job. A lot easier said than done, Stryke. We don't know how many miles of tunnels there are down there. If they have a star, which is only a maybe at best, we have to find the thing. Don't forget that for all we know, it's going to be pitch black down there. The trolls have eyesight that copes with the dark. We don't."

"We'll take torches."

"And really make ourselves obvious. We'll be on their ground and at a disadvantage."

"Not as far as our blades go, we won't."

"Finally, getting out," she ploughed on. "Well, that speaks for itself, doesn't it? You're assuming we could."

"We've taken on long odds before, Coilla. I'm not going to let that stand in my way."

She gave a resigned sigh. "You're not, are you? You're determined to go through with this."

"You know I am. But I'll not take any with me who don't want to go."

"That's not the point. It's *how* we do it that concerns me. Just charging in isn't always the solution, you know."

"Sometimes it is. Unless you can see a better way."

"That's just it, damn you, I can't."

"I know you're worried there's so much that could go wrong. So am I. So we'll take a little time getting this right."

"Not too much," Alfray interjected. "What about Hobrow?"

"We bloodied his nose. I don't think he'll be here for a while yet, if at all."

"It isn't only Hobrow. For all we know, everybody's out for us. And moving targets are the hardest to hit."

"Granted. But targets that hit back tend to get left alone too."

"Not when the whole damn country's after their heads."

"What did you mean about taking time, Stryke?" Coilla asked. "How much?"

He glanced up at the gathering twilight. "The light's nearly gone. We could spend tomorrow searching for another way in. A really thorough search, with the area sectioned out. If we find a better way in, we'll use it. Otherwise we'll go for the entrance we know."

"Or what we think is an entrance," Coilla corrected him.

"Stryke, I don't want to put a damper on things," Jup said, "but *if* there's a star here and *if* we can get it . . . what then?"

"I was hoping nobody would ask that question."

Alfray backed Jup. "It has to be asked, Stryke. Else why go on here?"

"We go on because . . . well, because what else is there for us to do? We're orcs. We need a purpose. You know that."

"If we carry on as we have, if we're being logical, and assuming we get out of Scratch in one piece, then we need a plan to find out where the other stars are," Coilla reckoned.

"We've been lucky so far," Jup said. "It won't hold forever."

"We make our own luck," Stryke maintained.

Coilla had an idea. "I was thinking that if trading the star, or stars, with Jennesta is out—"

"Which it is," Stryke interrupted, "as far as I'm concerned."

"If that's not an option, perhaps we could trade them with somebody else."

"Who?"

"I don't know! I'm clutching at straws here, Stryke, like the rest of you. I'm just thinking that if we can't find all five stars then the others aren't of any use to us. Whereas a good hoard of coin might make our lives easier."

"The stars mean power. A power that could maybe do a lot of good for orcs and all the other elder races. I won't let that go easily. As for coin, you're forgetting the pellucid. Even a small amount would bring a good price."

"What about the crystal, by the way?" Alfray asked. "Have you thought of how it should be distributed?"

"I reckon that for now we keep it as communal property, for the benefit of the band in general. Any of you object?"

None did.

Haskeer, who had been standing at a distance and taking no part in the conversation, wandered over to them. He wore the vacant expression they'd almost got used to.

"What's happening?" he said.

"We're talking about how to get into Scratch," Coilla told him.

Haskeer's face lit up as a notion hit him. "Why don't we talk to the trolls?"

They laughed. Then it dawned on them that he wasn't trying to be funny.

"What do you mean, talk?" Alfray said.

"Think how much better things would be if the trolls were our friends."

Alfray's jaw dropped. "What?"

"Well, they could be, couldn't they? All our enemies could if we talked rather than fought them all the time."

"I can't believe you're saying this, Haskeer," Coilla confessed.

"Does it seem wrong?"

"Er, it just seems not . . . *you*."

He considered the proposition. "Oh. All right. Let's kill them then."

"That's kind of what we thought we'd do, if we have to."

Haskeer beamed. "Good. Let me know when you need me. I'll be feeding my horse."

He turned and walked away.

Jup said, "What the *hell*?"

Coilla shook her head. "He's seriously dippy these days."

"Do you still say it's something he'll get over, Alfray?" Stryke asked.

"He's taking his time about it, I'll admit. But I've seen something similar to this before when troopers were recovering from heavy fevers. Or when they get ague of the lungs; you know, water in 'em. Quite often they spend days afterwards in a sort of daze, and it's not unknown for them to behave out of character."

"Out of character!" Coilla exclaimed. "He's about as far from his character as he can get."

"I don't know whether to be worried or to thank the gods for the mood he's in," Jup confessed.

"At least it's giving you a break from his bullying, and all of us a rest from his constant grumbling."

"You're assuming he's this way because of the illness, Alfray," Stryke said. "Is it possible there's another reason? Could he have taken a blow to the head we don't know about?"

"There's no sign of that. He might have, I suppose, but you'd expect to see some marks of it. I'm no great expert on head injuries, Stryke, I just know, like you, that they can cause an orc to do and say odd things."

"Well, he seems harmless enough, but keep an eye on him, all of you."

"You can't let him take part in the mission, can you?" Coilla wanted to know.

"No, he'd be a burden. He'll stay behind, along with a grunt or two to guard the camp and horses. Not to mention the crystal. I thought you might like to stay with them, Coilla."

She flared her nostrils. "You're not saying I'd be a burden?"

"Course not. But you're not keen on enclosed places, you've made that clear more than once, and I need to leave somebody I can rely on. Because I'm not taking the stars with me. That's too much of a risk. You could look after them until we get back." He noticed her expression. "All right, it had crossed my mind that if we don't get back you could carry on the work, so to speak."

"All by myself?"

Jup grinned. "You'd have Haskeer."

She glared at him. "Very funny."

They all looked in Haskeer's direction.

He was patting his horse's head and feeding it from the palm of his hand.

23

It was the Lord's wrath in action. Kimball Hobrow had no doubt of it.

His search for the ungodly, the thieving non-humans that had taken what was his, had led him to range the shores of Calyparr, a group of followers ten score and more at his back. Now, as night fell, they had come upon a charnel scene. The bodies of some two dozen humans, mostly women and children, littered a stretch of land beside the merchants' trail.

Hobrow recognised their dress. It was immodest and self-indulgent, its bright colours pandering to vanity. He knew their kind: blasphemers, deviators from the path of righteousness. Wretched adherents of the Manifold spoor.

He walked among the slaughtered, a clutch of custodians in his wake. If the signs of butchery, of mangled limbs and rendered flesh, had any effect on the preacher he didn't show it.

"Take heed," he intoned. "These souls digressed from the true and only way. They embraced the obscene paganism of the impure races, and the Lord punished them for it. And the irony, brethren, was that He used non-humans as His tool, the instrument of His revenge. They lay down with the serpent and the serpent devoured them. It is fitting."

He continued his inspection, studying the faces of the dead, the severity of their wounds.

"The arm of the Almighty is long and His ire knows no limit," he thundered. "He strikes down the unrighteous as surely as He rewards His chosen."

A custodian called out to him from the other side of the killing ground. He strode to the man.

"What is it, Calvert?"

"This one's still alive, master." He pointed to a woman.

She had a braid of long blonde hair. Her breast was bloody, her breathing shallow. She was near her end.

Hobrow knelt beside her. She seemed dimly aware of him and tried to say something, but no words came from her quivering lips.

He leaned closer. "Speak, child. Confess your sins and unburden yourself."

"They . . . they . . ."

"Who?"

"They came . . . and . . ."

"They? The orcs, you mean?"

"Orcs." Her glazed eyes focused for a second. "Yes . . . orcs."

"They did this to you?"

"Orcs . . . came . . ."

The custodians had gathered around. Hobrow addressed them. "You see? No humans are safe from the accursed inhuman races, even those foolish enough to take their part." He turned back to the dying woman. "Where did they go?"

"Orcs . . ."

"Yes, the orcs." He spoke slowly and deliberately. "Do you know where they went?"

She made no reply. He grasped her hand and squeezed it. "Where did they go?" he repeated.

"Scr . . . Scratch . . ."

"My God." He let go of her and stood. Her hand reached for his and, unnoticed, feebly dropped back.

"To your horses!" he boomed, messianic passion burning in his eyes. "The vermin we seek are in league with others of their kind. We embark upon a crusade, brethren!"

They dashed for their mounts, infected with his fervour.

"We'll have our revenge!" he vowed. "The Lord will guide us and protect us!"

The Wolverines spent the entire day searching for another way into Scratch. If such existed, it was too well hidden for them to find. But they didn't encounter any trolls either, as they had feared they might, and that at least was a stroke of luck.

Stryke decided they would enter the labyrinth by the main

entrance, as they'd come to call it, first thing in the morning. Now that night had fallen, all they could do was wait for the dawn. As some held that trolls came to the surface in the dark, double guards were posted, and all kept their arms near to hand.

Alfray suggested that a little pellucid be shared out. Stryke had no objection, providing they kept to a small quantity and none was allowed the guards. He didn't use any himself, but instead laid out a blanket at the edge of the camp and settled down to think and plan.

The last thing he was aware of as he drifted into sleep was the crystal's pungent odour.

Stars were beginning to show through in the gathering twilight. They were as sharp and clear as he had ever seen them.

He stood on a cliff's edge.

A good spear throw away a corresponding wall of sheer rock faced him. He saw trees on the other side, tall and straight. The space between was a deep canyon. Far below roared a white-foamed river, throwing up clouds of vaporous mist as it pounded at boulders in its path. The channel of rock extended for as far as he could see on either side.

The cliffs were spanned by a gently swaying suspension bridge built from stout rope and woven twine, with wooden slats to walk on.

For no other reason than that it was there, he set his foot upon it and began to cross.

Away from the shelter of the rock face, a stiff breeze tempered the pleasant warmth of the maturing evening. It carried a fine spray of droplets from the torrent beneath, cooling his skin. He walked slowly, savouring the magnificence of the scenery and breathing deep of the crystal air.

He was perhaps a third of the way across when he became aware of someone walking towards him from the other side. He couldn't make out their features, but saw that they moved with a purposeful step and easy confidence. He kept on and didn't slow his pace. Soon the other traveller was near enough to be properly seen.

It was the orc female he had met here before. Wherever here *might be.*

She wore her head-dress of flaming scarlet war feathers, and her sword was strapped to her back, its hilt visible above the left shoulder. One of her hands lightly touched the guide rope at her side.

They recognised each other at the same time, and she smiled. He smiled too.

They came together midway.

"Our paths cross again," she said. "Well met."

He felt the same strange tug at his feelings that he had in his previous encounters with her.

"Well met," he returned.

"You're truly an orc of passing strangeness," she told him.

"How so?"

"Your comings and goings are veiled in mystery."

"I might say the same of you."

"Not so. I'm always here. You appear and disappear like the haze bred by the river. Where are you going?"

"Nowhere. That is, I . . . explore, I suppose. And you?"

"I move as my life dictates."

"Yet you carry your sword where it can't be quickly drawn."

She glanced at his blade, hanging in its belt sheath. "And you don't. My way is better."

"Your way used to be the custom in my land, at least when travelling in safe parts. But that was long ago."

"I offer none a threat and travel as I please without danger. It's not so where you come from?"

"No."

"Then your land must be grim indeed. I offer it no offence in saying that."

"I take none. You speak the truth."

"Perhaps you should come here and make your camp."

He wasn't sure if it was some kind of invitation. "That would be pleasant," he replied. "I wish I could."

"Something stops you?"

"I don't know how to reach this land."

She laughed. "You can always be counted on for riddles. How can you say that when you're here now?"

"It makes no more sense to me than it does to you." He turned from her and looked down at the thundering water. "I understand my coming here no more than the river understands where it flows. Less so, for the river has always flowed to the ocean, and is timeless."

The female moved closer to him. "We are timeless too. We flow with the river of life." She reached into her pouch and took out two small pebbles, round and smooth. "I took these from the river's bank." She let them slip from her hand and they fell away. "Now they're one with the river again, as you and I are one with the river of time. Don't you see how apt it is that we should meet on a bridge?"

"I don't know if I understand your meaning."

"Don't you?"

"I mean, I feel there's truth in what you say, but it's just beyond my grasp."

"Then reach further and you'll understand."

"How would I do that?"

"By not trying."

"Now who's talking in riddles?"

"The truth is simple, it's we who choose to see it as a riddle. Understanding will come to you."

"When?"

"It begins by asking that question. Be patient, stranger." She smiled. "I still call you 'stranger.' I don't know your name."

"Nor I yours."

"What are you called?"

"Stryke."

"Stryke. It's a strong name. It serves you well. Yes . . . Stryke," she repeated, as though relishing it. "Stryke."

"Stryke. Stryke! *Stryke!*"

He was being shaken.

"Uh? Uhm . . . Wha . . . what's *your* name?"

"It's me, Coilla. Who did you think it was? Snap out of it, Stryke!"

He blinked and took in his surroundings. Realisation returned. It was daybreak. They were at Scratch.

"You look strange, Stryke. You all right?"

"Yes . . . yes. Just a . . . a dream."

"Seems to me you've been having a lot of those lately. Nightmare, was it?"

"No. It was far from being a nightmare. It was only a dream."

*   *   *

Jennesta dreamt of blood and burning, of death and destruction, suffering and despair. She dreamt of the principles of lust, and the enlightenment to be gained thereof.

As was her wont.

She woke up in her inner sanctum. The mangled body of a human male, barely into manhood, lay on the crimson altar amid the detritus of the previous night's ritual. She ignored it, rose and wrapped her nakedness in a cloak of furs. A pair of high leather boots completed her wardrobe.

It was first light and she had business to attend to.

As she left the chamber the orc guards outside stiffened to attention. "Come," she ordered briskly.

They fell in behind her. She led them through a maze of corridors, up flights of stone-slab stairs and finally into the open air, emerging on to a parade ground in front of the palace.

Several hundred members of her orc army were there, standing in well-ordered ranks. The audience, for that was what it amounted to, had been made up of representatives from each regiment. It was an efficient way of ensuring that word of what they were about to witness would spread quickly through the whole of Jennesta's horde.

The troops faced a stout wooden stake the height of a small tree. An orc soldier was lashed to it. There were bundles of faggots and kindling stacked almost to his waist.

General Mersadion met Jennesta with a bow. "We're ready to proceed, Your Majesty."

"Let the verdict be known."

Mersadion nodded at an orc captain. He stepped forward and raised a parchment. In a booming voice, the attribute that had landed him his unpopular task, he began to read.

"'By order of Her Imperial Majesty Queen Jennesta, let all note the findings of a military tribunal in the case of Krekner, sergeant ordinary of the Imperial Horde.'"

All eyes were on the soldier at the stake.

"'The charges laid against said Krekner were, one, that he knowingly disobeyed an order issued by a superior officer and, two, that in disobeying that order he did show cowardice in the face of the enemy. The tribunal's findings were that he be judged guilty on both counts and should be condemned to suffer such penalty as the above charges carry.'"

The Captain lowered the parchment. It was deathly silent in the square.

Mersadion addressed the prisoner. "You have the right of final appeal to the Queen. Will you exercise it?"

"I will," Krekner replied. His voice was even and loud. He was bearing the ordeal with dignity.

"Proceed," Mersadion said.

The sergeant turned his head to Jennesta. "I meant no disrespect as far as my orders went, ma'am. Only we were told to re-engage when there were comrades lying wounded that we could have helped. I held back just long enough to stem a fellow orc's flow of blood, and believe I saved his life by doing it. Then I obeyed the order to advance. It was a delay, not disobedience, and I plead compassion as the cause. I feel that my sentence is unjust on that count."

It was probably the longest, and certainly the most important, speech he had ever made. He looked to the Queen expectantly.

She kept him, and all of them, waiting for a full half-minute before speaking. It pleased her that they might think she was considering mercy.

"Orders are given to be obeyed," she announced. "There are no exceptions, and certainly not in the name of . . . *compassion*." She mouthed the word as though it were distasteful to her. "Appeal denied. The sentence will be carried out. Let your fate be an example to all."

She lifted a hand, muttering the while an incantation. The condemned orc braced himself.

A slither of concentrated light spurted from her fingertips, arced through the air and bathed the kindling at his feet. The fuel ignited immediately. Orange-yellow flames erupted and instantly began to climb.

The orc sergeant faced his death courageously, but in the end he could not hold back the screams. Jennesta looked on impassively as he writhed in the blaze.

In her mind's eye, the victim was Stryke of the Wolverines.

*   *   *

The Wolverines were ready to set out.

Stryke thought that Haskeer would object to not being included in the mission. He was wrong. His sergeant accepted the news without complaint. In a way, that was more troubling than one of the rants they'd become accustomed to.

Taking aside Coilla, Alfray and Jup, Stryke outlined his plan.

"As agreed, Coilla, you'll stay here at base camp with Haskeer," he said. "I've assigned Reafdaw to stay too."

"What about the pellucid?" she asked.

"Rather than leave it divided up in individual saddlebags, I've ordered it to be pooled." He pointed at a bundle of sacks stacked near the tethered horses. "You might like to load it on to a couple of mounts. That way, if you need to make a quick getaway, without the rest of us, you'll save time."

"I understand. What about the stars?"

Stryke reached into his pouch. "Here. What you do with them if we don't get out is up to you."

She studied the strange objects for a second, then slipped them into her own belt bag. "In the event, I hope it'll be something you'd approve of." They exchanged smiles. "But what *are* the contingency plans if you don't come back?"

"None that involves you coming in after us. Is that understood?"

"Yes." It was a reluctant reply.

"It's an order. I'd say that if we're not out by this time tomorrow, we won't be out at all. In which case get yourselves away from here. You might use the time to think about where to go."

"The gods know where that'll be. But we'll think of something if we must. Just don't give us cause to, right?"

"We'll do our best. And it goes without saying that if any trolls turn up above ground before the deadline's reached, that's likely to mean only one thing. In which case get out of here anyway."

She nodded.

"What's the plan for us once we get down there, Stryke?" Alfray said.

"Flexible. Has to be. We don't know what we'll find, or even if what we think is an entrance will turn out to be one."

"A blind mission. Not ideal."

"No, but we've been on them before."

"What worries me is that we'll be literally blind down there if anything goes wrong," Jup confessed.

"The trolls have the advantage in terms of the darkness, it's true. But we're taking plenty of torches. As long as we have them, we should be a match for any opposition. And don't under-estimate the element of surprise."

"It's still a hell of a risk."

"Taking risks is what we're trained for, and I'd wager we have more experience in it than the cave dwellers below."

"Let's hope so. Shouldn't we be going?"

"Yes. Muster the grunts. Gather the ropes and torches."

Jup and Alfray went off to do it.

"I want to come as far as the entrance with you," Coilla stated. "All right?"

"Come. But don't linger there. I want you back here helping to guard base camp and that pellucid."

The band left Haskeer with Reafdaw and marched to the entrance.

Daylight made the interior of the cave look even darker, and they entered with caution. At the edge of the shaft they ignited torches.

"Toss over some light," Stryke ordered in a hushed tone.

A pair of grunts dropped two brands each. They watched them plummet. This time, unlike the burning rag Coilla had dropped, they didn't disappear from sight. They landed on something solid, but it was a long way down.

"At least it doesn't look too deep for the amount of rope we have," Alfray judged.

The guttering torches threw out a circle of light, though not enough for the band to make out any details of what lay below. At least nothing seemed to be moving down there.

Several grunts were given the job of firmly securing the ends of three ropes around rocks and trees outside the cave.

"Just in case there's some kind of trap waiting to be sprung below," Stryke told them all, "we go down quickly and in force."

The band formed three lines by the ropes. More torches were lit and passed out to them. Some band members clutched knives in their teeth.

Coilla wished them luck and backed off.

Stryke nodded. "Let's go," he said, clasping a rope.

He went over the edge first. The rest of the band quickly spilled into the pit after him.

24

Stryke let go of the rope and dropped the last ten feet or so.

He quickly drew his sword. Jup landed beside him and likewise plucked free his blade. The rest of the band landed in short order and looked around.

They were in a roughly circular chamber that opened out to about three times the diameter of the shaft they had just climbed down. Two tunnels ran from it, the larger directly ahead, a smaller one to their left.

The place was as quiet as the grave and there was no sign of inhabitants. It smelt unpleasantly earthy.

"What now?" Jup whispered.

"First we secure our bridgehead." Stryke motioned over a couple of grunts. "Liffin, Bhose. You'll stay here and guard the exit. Don't move from this spot until we come back or the deadline expires."

They nodded and took up position.

"The question now is which way to go," Alfray said, eyeing the tunnels.

"Do you think we should split into two groups, Captain?" Jup asked.

"No, that's something I definitely want to avoid. Our force is small enough as it is."

"What, then? Toss a coin?"

"My feeling is that a large tunnel leads to something important. I'm drawn that way. But we should check the smaller one first, just in case it holds any unpleasant surprises."

He sent Kestix and Jad to stand guard at the larger tunnel's mouth. Then he called over Hystykk, Noskaa, Calthmon and Breggin. He hefted a coil of rope and tossed it into the latter's hand. "I want you four to walk that tunnel to the extent of this rope. If it looks as though it leads anywhere interesting, one of you can come back and let us know. But take no risks. At the first sign of trouble, head home."

Jup took hold of one end of their rope. Breggin looped the other about his wrist, lifted his torch and led the others into the tunnel.

The band waited tensely as the rope played out. After a few minutes it went taut.

"What if they run into something they can't handle?" Alfray wondered. "Do we go in after them?"

"That's a headache we could do without," Stryke said. "Let's see what happens."

They didn't have long to wait. The troopers soon returned.

"Well?"

"Nothing to tell really, sir," Breggin reported. "The tunnel just went on and on, much further than the rope. There weren't any side passages or anything."

"All right, we'll concentrate on the other tunnel. And we'll lay a rope trail along that one too, though I doubt the rope's going to go very far."

"Won't that be a giveaway to any troll coming across it?" Jup put in.

"I think a warband tramping around with flaming torches is enough of a giveaway by itself, don't you?" He addressed them all. "If we meet any defenders, strike first, ask questions later. We can't afford to give quarter. Stay together and keep noise to a minimum."

With a final reminder to Liffin and Bhose to remain alert, he led the band into the main tunnel. Alfray walked beside him, holding a torch.

The tunnel ran arrow-straight, although it sloped downward at a gentle gradient. As they walked, Stryke became aware of a drop in temperature, and his nostrils were assailed by a disagreeably stale odour. They kept up an even pace for what Stryke judged to be around five minutes, but he suspected his time sense was distorted in this dark, silent world. Then they came to a side tunnel.

It was narrow, not much more than the width of an average doorway, and the entrance was low. The walls were damp and slimy. When they threw light into it they saw that the floor inclined to almost vertical. A rope around his waist and clutching a torch, one of the grunts edged down for a look.

When they tugged him back up, he said, "It ends in a narrow shaft, like a well."

"I reckon it's a storm channel," Alfray speculated. "To siphon off water if there's a flood."

Stryke was impressed. "Clever."

"They've had a long time to build in such touches, Stryke. The trolls may be savage but they're not necessarily ignorant barbarians. We'd do well to remember that."

They resumed their exploration of the main tunnel, which now dipped a little more sharply. Twenty or thirty paces later, the guide rope ran out. They left it and carried on. Another five minutes passed, in Stryke's quite possibly skewed estimation, and the tunnel began to widen. A little further on it opened out into another chamber. They paused.

As it seemed empty, and there were no sounds to be heard, they went in.

Barely had they entered when shapes suddenly disgorged from the shadows and rushed at them.

Their antagonists only half visible in the light of the flickering torches, the band laid into them. Fights broke out all around, near silently save for the clashing of blades, grunts of effort as weapons were swung, and occasional yells.

A fast-moving, dimly perceived figure came at Stryke and he lashed out at it. The blow was countered. He slashed again and missed. By sheer chance he caught sight of the glint off a blade aimed at his neck. He ducked and heard steel whistle above his head.

Stryke lunged forward, sword at arm's length. It impacted soft flesh and his foe went down. He turned to engage another shadowy attacker.

Beside him, Alfray and Jup were slugging it out with their own opponents. The dwarf battered open a skull. Alfray thrust his burning brand into a troll's face, inspiring a horrible screech. He cut it short with a follow-on from his blade.

Then there were no more of the enemy to fight. The skirmish had been brief and brutal, with the Wolverines prevailing despite the trolls' vision advantage.

Stryke looked around. He saw there was another passageway set in the far wall of the chamber.

"Guard that tunnel!" he barked.

Several grunts ran to stand by it, peering into its mouth, their swords at the ready.

"Anybody down?" he said. "Any hurt?"

None had taken more than minor wounds.

"We were lucky," Alfray panted.

"Yes, but only because we outnumbered them, I think. It could easily have gone the other way. Let's see what we've got here." Stryke took Alfray's torch and held it over one of the bodies littering the ground.

The troll was short, very muscular and covered in shaggy grey fur. It had the kind of physique, and wan complexion, to be expected of a subterranean race. The barrel chest had developed from living in rarefied air at lower depths. There were disproportionately long arms and legs. The hands were powerful, with long, thick taloned fingers, due to burrowing.

Though dead, its eyes were still open. They'd adapted to a lack of light by evolving to a much larger size than most races', with enormous black orbs. There was something pig-like about them. The nose was bulbous and soft like a dog's. In contrast to the washed-out appearance of the fur and beard, the creature's head was topped by a shock of almost primary-coloured hair. As far as they could tell in the uncertain light, it was a rusty orange.

"Not the sort of thing you'd like to bump into in the dark, is it?" Jup remarked wryly.

"Let's keep moving," Stryke said.

They went into the new tunnel with renewed caution.

This passageway soon curved sharply to the right before straightening again. They passed a couple of side chambers, which proved small and empty. Then the tunnel narrowed to such an extent that they had to walk single-file. Perhaps a hundred feet further along they came to a stretch where the walls and ceiling were shored up with tree trunks and propped with wooden joists.

Stryke and Alfray were walking a little way ahead of the others. They reached a thick, jutting beam, and Alfray was first to start edging past, holding his torch aloft.

He was through before he realised the strut hid a blind tunnel.

By then it was too late.

A troll leapt at him from the shadows. The impact of its loathsomely hairy body sent Alfray flying and the torch was knocked from his hand.

Stryke moved in fast, slashing at the attacker, which danced back a step or two to avoid his blade. Springing forward again, it unleashed a torrent of blows that Stryke was hard put to hold at bay.

The space was so confined that the rest of the band couldn't get near enough to aid him. They were forced to watch helplessly as orc and troll exchanged hefty blows.

Stryke aimed a swing at the creature's chest. It jumped aside with amazing speed and his sword thudded deep into a wooden upright. A drizzle of dust descended.

The precious second it took Stryke to dislodge the blade almost cost him his life. Growling ferociously, the troll came at him, swiping the air madly.

But the creature hadn't counted on Alfray. On his hands and knees now, recovering from the initial clash, he reached out and grabbed the troll's legs. It wasn't sufficient to bring down the attacker but it distracted it long enough for Stryke to land a hit. His stroke cleaved into the troll's side. It wailed and fell back, smashing with force into the already half-severed upright.

The joist cracked with an echoing report.

An ominous rumbling came from above. Earth and stones began showering down. The troll let out a hideous, despairing scream.

Stryke snatched Alfray's jerkin and dragged him clear. He caught a fleeting glimpse of Jup and the rest of the band, behind them on the other side of the propped section.

There was a sound like a thunderclap. Then the ceiling

crashed down on the blundering troll, crushing it instantly under masses of rocks and rubble. A shockwave like a mini-earthquake threw Alfray and Stryke to the ground. Clouds of choking dust swept over them.

They lay there with their hands over their heads, not daring to move, for what seemed like an eternity as the after-shocks reverberated.

Finally the cacophony died away, the avalanche subsided, the dust started to settle. Coughing and gasping for breath, they climbed to their feet.

At their rear the tunnel was completely blocked from floor to ceiling. Several huge boulders were among the debris. Alfray snatched up the still burning torch, their only source of light, and they scrambled to investigate.

It was instantly obvious that they couldn't hope to shift the downfall.

"Not a chance," Alfray said, pushing uselessly at the immovable barrier. "It must weigh tons."

"You're right, we're not going to get through it."

"You don't think it caught any of the band, do you?"

"No, I'm sure they were clear. But I can't see them being able to shift any of this from their side either. *Fuck it!*"

Alfray expelled a long breath. "Well, if there was any doubt the trolls didn't know about us, that settles it. Unless they're all deaf."

"We can't go back, and we can't stay here in case there's another fall. That only leaves one choice."

"Let's hope the rest of the band find a way round this mess."

"Or we find a way to them. But I wouldn't count on it, Alfray."

"Two against the troll kingdom. Not very good odds, is it?"

"Let's hope we don't have to find out."

They took a last look at the blocked tunnel, then turned and headed into the unknown.

Coilla reflected that while it had never exactly been fun to be in Haskeer's presence, at least it used to be a lot livelier when he was his old self.

She glanced at him, sitting opposite. He was using a saddle

for a seat, hands hanging to either side, staring vacantly at nothing in particular.

Reafdaw was carrying out her orders and loading the sacks of pellucid on to a pair of the stronger horses. Just in case. Apart from that, there wasn't a lot they could do except wait. Certainly conversation with Haskeer was a dismal prospect. She'd already asked him how he felt half a dozen times and received the same unconvincing assurances of good health. That left few other topics of discussion, and the silence was uncomfortable.

So she experienced a mixture of relief and some apprehension when Haskeer looked up, seemed to see her properly for the first time, and said, "Do you have the stars?"

"Yes, I do."

"Can I look at them?"

Innocence seemed a wildly inappropriate word to apply to Haskeer at the best of times, but the way he made the request brought it to mind.

"Why not?" she replied.

She was aware of him watching her closely as she dug into her belt pouch. When the instrumentalities were produced, he held out his hand to take them. She thought that was where to draw the line.

"I think it'd be best if you looked but didn't touch," she told him. "No offence," she added hurriedly, "but Stryke ordered me not to let anybody else handle them. Nobody, not even you."

It was a lie, but she knew Stryke would have intended that. She waited for Haskeer's blustery protest. It didn't come. This new Haskeer seemed infuriatingly reasonable. She wondered how long it would last.

Coilla sat there facing him with the stars sitting in her outstretched palm, and he stared. He seemed transfixed by the strange relics in the way a hatchling might be enchanted by a particularly shiny toy.

After a couple of minutes of Haskeer regarding their booty with an unbroken gaze, Coilla started to feel uncomfortable again. She could easily imagine this going on for hours, and she had better things to do. Actually, she didn't. But she was damned if she was going to sit there pretending to be a pedestal for the rest of the day.

"I reckon that's enough for now," she announced, closing her fist on the stars. She returned them to her pouch.

Again, she was conscious of him watching her every move, the expression on his face mingling fascination and disappointment.

Another pall of silence descended. It was getting too oppressive for her.

"I'm just going over to the lookout point," she said. "They might be on their way back." She didn't really think they would be; it was far too soon for that. But it gave her something to do.

Haskeer said nothing, just watched her walk away.

Coilla passed Reafdaw at the horses and called out to tell him what she was doing. He nodded and carried on working.

Their observation point wasn't far. It was an elevated slab of rock in sight of the camp, and from which the entrance to Scratch could just be seen. She walked to it unhurriedly, more intent on killing time than expecting to see her returning comrades.

Having climbed to the rock's flat plateau, she looked back. There was no sign of Reafdaw. She assumed he'd finished the chore and was with Haskeer. Good. Let somebody else share the boredom.

She turned around and concentrated on the distant cave-like entrance to the troll underworld. It wasn't a particularly sunny day, as was usual of late, but she still had to shield her eyes to make out any details.

There was no movement. That wasn't a surprise. She didn't expect any results yet.

Anything was better than going back to the tedium below, so she decided to kill a few more minutes up there. She got to wondering whether Stryke hadn't bitten off more than he could chew this time. With a shudder, her mind went to that pit of darkness her fellow warriors had climbed into.

Then something heavy smashed into the back of her head and she fell into a black pit of her own.

Coilla returned to consciousness and a sea of pain.

There was the most gods-awful ache running from the back of her head and down her neck. She gingerly reached for the source of agony and her fingers came away bloody.

Realisation hit. She quickly sat up. Too quickly. She gasped, her head throbbed and spun.

There must have been an attack. The trolls! She got unsteadily to her feet and surveyed the surroundings. There was no sign of anybody in any direction, and their base camp looked deserted.

Groaning with the effort, she scrambled down from the rock and headed back as fast as she could. It crossed her mind to wonder how long she'd been lying on the rock. It could have been hours, though a glance at the sky indicated that was unlikely. She dabbed at the back of her head again. It was still bleeding but not profusely. She'd been lucky.

At that point it occurred to her that if her attacker had been a troll she wouldn't be alive now. That led to a second, far more dreadful thought. Her hand went to her belt pouch.

It was open. The stars were gone.

She cursed aloud and started running, the pain be damned.

When she reached camp there was no sign of Haskeer or Reafdaw. She called out their names. Nothing.

She called again. This time she was answered by groans coming from the direction of the horses. She sped that way.

Reafdaw was spread out on the ground, dangerously near the tethered mounts. Which explained why she hadn't seen him earlier. She knelt at his side. He too had a bloodied head. His complexion was chalky white.

"Reafdaw!" she said, shaking him violently.

He groaned again.

"*Reafdaw!*" Her shaking grew even more insistent. "What happened?"

"I . . . he . . ."

"Where's Haskeer? What's going on?"

The grunt seemed to gather a little strength. "*Haskeer. Bastard . . .*"

"What do you mean?" She was afraid she already knew the answer to that.

"Just . . . just after you left he came . . . over to . . . me. Didn't say . . . much. Then he went . . . berserk. Near . . . near stove my head . . . in."

"He did the same to me, the swine." She looked at the trooper's wound. "It could be a lot worse," she told him. "Reafdaw, I know you feel like shit, but this is important. What happened then? Where did he go?"

The grunt swallowed, the pain clear in his eyes. "He went . . . off. I was out . . . for a . . . while. Came round. He was back. Thought . . . thought he was going to finish . . . me. But no. Took . . . a horse."

"*Damn!* He got the stars."

"Gods," Reafdaw responded weakly.

"Which way? Did you see which way he went?"

"North. I think . . . it was . . . north."

She had to make a decision, and fast.

"I've got to go after him. You'll have to look to yourself until the others get back. Can you do that?"

"Yes . . . Go."

"You'll be all right." She got up, her head blazing, and snatched a water sack from the nearest horse. She laid it in his hands. "Here. I'm sorry, Reafdaw, I have to do this."

She staggered to the fastest-looking horse and unhitched it. Clambering on to its back, she spurred it hard.

And headed north.

25

Jup and the remainder of the band hadn't been able to dig through to Stryke and Alfray. They weren't even sure if they'd escaped the collapse of the tunnel roof.

The only thing they could do was turn around and head back the way they'd come.

Having rendezvoused with Liffin and Bhose, standing guard beneath the shaft, they had their first disappointment. The slim hope that Stryke and Alfray might have found a way round the blocked tunnel and back to the entrance was dashed.

Jup's next thought was to try to reach them another way. The only possibility was the smaller of the two tunnels. He led the band into it. But after a long and uneventful walk, during which they found only empty side chambers and cul-de-sacs, they reached its end.

With heavy hearts they returned to the starting point.

There seemed little point in waiting. The only remaining hope was that the pair might have discovered another way out of the labyrinth and to the surface. Jup ordered a retreat. They all climbed back up the shaft and headed for camp at speed.

On arrival, the further crushing disappointment of not finding their comrades had returned was overlaid with disaster when they came across Reafdaw.

He'd managed to rise to a sitting position, and nursed his head as they stood around him, horrified at the tale he had to tell.

"So that was it," the grunt concluded. "Haskeer attacked me and Coilla like a madman and he got the stars. She went haring after him. That's all I can tell you."

Jup ordered that his injuries be dressed.

The band set up a clamour about what they should do.

"*Shut up!*" the dwarf yelled, and they quietened. "Trying to get Stryke and Alfray out of that labyrinth should be the priority. We know they're living on borrowed time down there. On the other hand, we can't let Haskeer get away with the stars, and it sounds as though Coilla might not be in a fit state to stop him."

"Why not split the band and try both?" somebody shouted.

"We'd be slicing our forces too finely. A rescue bid down below needs all we've got, and more. Scouring the countryside for Haskeer could easily take all of us."

Another voice was raised. "So what *are* we going to do?" it demanded. Then added "Sergeant" as a far from respectful after-thought.

There was an unmistakable edge of hostility in the question, and on more than one of the anxious faces surrounding him. The simmering resentment some felt about his race and rank was in danger of breaking surface.

But he didn't know what to say. He had to make a choice and make it now, and it would be so easy to get it wrong.

He stared at them, saw the expectation in their eyes, and in a few, something more menacing.

Jup had always been ambitious for command. But not this way.

Coilla had a stroke of luck about half an hour after setting out on her search.

She was beginning to think she'd never find him, and have to return in shame, when she caught a glimpse of a distant rider, galloping across the skyline along a ridge of hills further north.

She wasn't certain, but it looked like Haskeer.

Digging in her heels, she urged her mount to greater effort.

The horse was foaming by the time she made the hills, and she allowed it no rest in climbing. Once at the top she paused, raising herself in the saddle to scan the land in the direction of distant Taklakameer. She couldn't see the rider. But it was a mixed terrain and there were endless places that might conceal him. Having no other option, she galloped onward.

The route she followed took her into a shallow, verdant valley, with clumps of trees on either side and others scattered in her path. She didn't allow that to slow her speed, though now she began to fear that the horse wouldn't be able to sustain the pace much longer.

Then she caught another glimpse of the rider, far off at the valley's end. She bore down and rode like fury.

Suddenly she wasn't alone.

Two riders came in from the trees at her right, another appeared on her left. They seemed to be humans.

She was so taken by surprise that when the one on her left quickly moved in and sideswiped her mount with a leather whip, she lost control. The reins flew from her hands. Her horse stumbled and went down. The world tilted at a crazy angle.

Coilla thudded into the ground, rolled several times and came to a stop, the wind knocked out of her.

Head swimming, she tried to rise, but only got as far as her knees.

The trio of humans had pulled up and dismounted. She looked at them, her vision clearing.

One was tall and guileful-eyed. He had a mean, pinched face disfigured by a scar. The second was short and lithe. He worried at a black eye-patch and grimaced at her through rotten teeth. The last had the build of a mountain bear and it was all muscle. He was completely hairless and had an oft-broken nose.

The tall one grinned and it wasn't friendly. "Now what do we have here?" he said, his voice oily and laden with menace.

Coilla shook her head, trying to clear the pain away. She wanted to stand but couldn't manage it.

The three humans moved forward, reaching for their weapons.

For something like an hour, Stryke and Alfray walked the tunnel they had no choice but to follow. They were no side-shoots or chambers leading off from it, and it altered only in descending at an ever-increasing rate.

Finally they came to another chamber, by far the biggest they'd seen so far. They knew it to be untenanted because, unlike the others, it was brightly lit by scores of flaming brands. Its jagged ceiling was far overhead, prickling with stalactites, and at least six tunnels ran off from it in different directions.

The chamber housed just one object, a vast block of fashioned stone resembling a lidded sarcophagus. Mysterious symbols were carved on its sides and top.

They walked to it, their footsteps echoing in the great hollow space.

"What do you suppose this might be?" Alfray wondered.

"Who can say?" Stryke replied. "It's said these denizens of the lower world worship dark and terrible gods. This has the look of ritual about it." He laid his hand on the time-smoothed surface. "We'll probably never know."

"You are wrong!"

They spun to the source of the voice.

A troll, clothed in robes of spun gold and with a silver crown upon his head, had entered the chamber unseen behind them. He was of mightier build than any they had slain, and he held an ornate crook almost equal to his height.

Stryke and Alfray brought up their swords, ready to take on the unexpected visitation. But as they did so, a multitude of trolls poured into the chamber from all the other tunnels. They numbered scores, and all were armed, many with spears bearing barbed tips.

The orcs glanced at each other.

"I'm for taking as many as we can," Stryke hissed.

"Well said," Alfray agreed.

"That would be foolish indeed," the troll boomed, sending forward his troops with a flick of his hand.

A forest of spears was aimed at the orcs, and now they saw that the second ranks bore notched bows with arrows aimed at them. They couldn't reach their foes, let alone set about killing them.

"Lay down your arms," the troll demanded.

"That's not something an orc's used to doing," Stryke told him contemptuously.

"The choice is yours," the creature returned. "Surrender them or die."

The mass of spears edged closer. The archers' strings were made more taut.

Alfray and Stryke exchanged a look. An unspoken agreement passed between them.

They threw down their swords.

The trolls rushed forward and seized them. But if the orcs expected instant death, they were wrong.

"I am Tannar," the troll headman informed them, "king of the inner realm. Monarch and high priest in one, servant of the gods that protect our domain from such as you."

Neither orc replied, but showed him a proud demeanour.

"You'll pay for your intrusion," Tannar went on, "and pay for it in a way most beneficial to our gods."

The troll soldiers forced Stryke and Alfray back to the stone slab. And then they knew beyond a doubt what function it served.

It was a sacrificial altar.

Rough hands bound them. The troll army parted to allow their king through.

As he slowly approached, he produced something from the folds of his cloak. The vile keenness of its curved steel caught glints of light. Deep and sinister, the assembled trolls began to chant in an outlandish tongue.

Moving towards the orcs at a funereal pace, Tannar raised the sacrificial blade.

"The knife," Alfray whispered. "Stryke, *the knife!*"

Stryke looked at it and understood.

To have tasted freedom and then have it snatched away like this was as cruel a jest as any the darkest gods could devise. That all had come to nought was bad enough. But what Stryke saw was the bitterest blow imaginable.

The richly ornamented knife the troll king held aloft was further decorated with a very particular addition. Attached to its hilt was an instantly recognisable object.

They had found the star they sought.

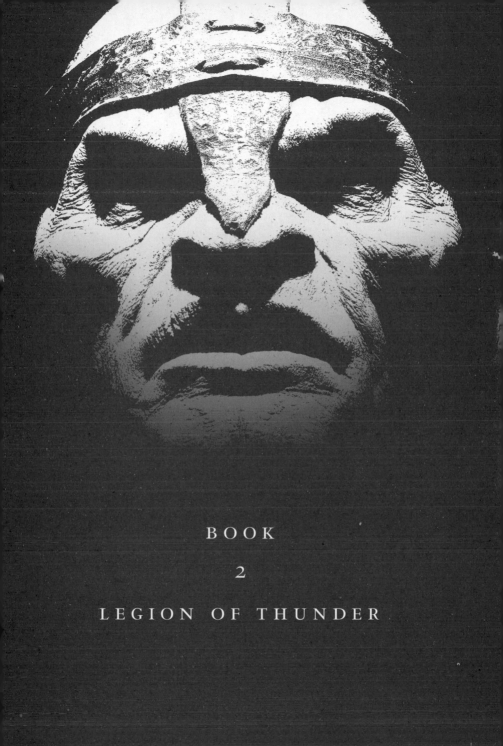

BOOK

2

LEGION OF THUNDER

1

Death moved sinuously through the water.

Grim purpose set her face like stone. She dived deep, impelling herself with powerful strokes from splayed, webbed hands. Her ebony hair flowed free, an inky squid cloud billowing in her wake. Tiny threads of bubbles streamed from her palpitating gills.

She looked back. Her nyadd raiding swarm, massed ranks swimming in formation, was wreathed in an eerie green glow from the phosphorescent brands they carried to light their way. They held jagged-edged coral pikes. Bowed adamantine daggers were sheathed in reed halters criss-crossing their scaly chests.

The murk started to clear, allowing glimpses of the sandy ocean floor, peppered with jutting rocks and swaying foliage. Soon the beginnings of a reef came into view, white and craggy, smothered with purple-tinged fungus. She swept over it, her warriors in tow. They followed the reef's outline, moving fast just above its surface, and this close the corruption was plain to see. Diseased vegetation, and the scarcity of fish, bore witness to the creeping taint. Scraps of dead things floated past, and the unseasonable cold, near freezing the water, was greater at such a depth.

She lifted a hand as they sighted their goal. The troopers let go of the radiant brands, showering the seabed with an emerald cascade. Then they glided in to gather around her.

Ahead of them, where the reef's spine widened, was a stony bluff, riddled with hollows and caves, both natural and artificial. From this distance there was no sign of occupants. She signalled her orders. A dozen warriors separated and made for the enemy cluster, low and stealthy. The rest, with her leading, slowly brought up the rear.

As they neared the redoubt they spotted their first merz, a scattered handful of sentries, ignorant of the approaching advance party. She regarded them with loathing. Their resemblance to humans was only partial, yet she was disgusted by it. To her mind, this, as much as any dispute over territory or food supplies, justified making war. Halting the column, she watched as her scouts moved in.

Two or three warriors targeted each guard. The one closest was male. His bearing was careless, and it seemed he was mindful only of the odd predator rather than the threat of a sneak attack. He drifted, half turning, and confirmed her repugnance.

The merzmale's upper body and head were much like a human's, except for razor thin gills on either side of its torso. Compared to a human's, its nose was more broad and flattened, and the eyes were covered with a filmy membrane. There was no hair on the creature's chest or arms. But it did sport a head of rust-coloured locks and a short curly beard.

Below the waist it differed radically from the human form and was closer in appearance to the nyadds. Here the milky flesh gave way to shiny overlapping scales covering a long, slender tail that ended in a large, fan-shaped fin.

The merz was armed with its race's traditional weapon, a spear-length three-pronged trident with arrowhead points.

Two warriors closed in on him. They advanced from the back and side, exploiting the sentry's blind spots, swimming at speed. The merzmale stood little chance. Levelling its barbed pike, the nyadd from the right struck hard, piercing the merz just above his waistline. The shallow blow wasn't fatal, but it served as a painful distraction. As the astonished merz turned to face his attacker, the second nyadd arrived at his back. He held a saw-toothed dagger. Snaking his hand around the enemy's neck, he slashed the merz's throat.

The sentry thrashed wildly for a moment, a crimson cloud billowing from the gaping wound. Then his lifeless body began sinking toward the seabed, trailing red streamers like scarlet ribbons.

Holding back with the main force, she looked on as her forward scouts tackled the rest of the guards.

Similarly taken unawares, a merz was being held by one nyadd as another used a dagger to puncture his chest. A female of the species, a merzmaid, spiralled to the bottom with a spear jutting from between her bare breasts. She fell silently mouthing her pain. Lashing out in panic, a merzmale swiped at a nyadd with his knife, forgetting that jabbing is more effective than slashing movements underwater. He paid for the lapse with a pike thrust to his innards.

Swiftly, brutally, the sentinels were efficiently murdered. When the last was overcome, the killers signed word to her through water tinted with a pink haze.

It was time to deploy the entire swarm. At her direction they advanced, filling their hands with weapons and spreading out. The silence was total. All that moved apart from the nyadd warriors was the guards' floating corpses.

The force had almost reached its goal when there was a flurry of activity at the honeycombed stronghold. Suddenly the edifice disgorged a horde of heavily armed merz. They made a strange sound as they poured out, a high-pitched oscillating wail that served as their language, a noise made more bizarre as it was distorted by travelling through water.

That was something else she hated about them. Now her loathing found a purpose.

At the prow, she led her corps to meet the unorganised defenders. In seconds, invaders and protectors were flowing into each other, the two sides instantly fragmenting into a myriad of lethal skirmishes.

Merz magic, like the nyadds' own, was of the descry variety, and most often employed to hunt food or navigate the deep. It had little martial importance. This was a battle to be fought with brawn and skill, blade and spear.

Giving off its keening song, a merzmale swooped in from above bearing a trident. The triple spikes drove deep into the chest of the warrior beside her. Mortally wounded, the nyadd writhed and twisted so much that he tore the trident from the merz's grasp. He sank from view clutching the spear and leaving a red trail.

His main weapon lost, the merzmale drew a knife, a miniature version of the trident, and turned his attention to her. He lashed out. She avoided the blow. The force of the merz's action had its reaction, propelling him to one side and putting him into a half-spin. But he recovered quickly and returned to face her.

She swiftly seized the wrist of his knife hand. Then he saw that her knuckles were wrapped in leather thongs dotted with sharpened metal dowels. He made a desperate grab for her free wrist. Too late. Still holding on to him with one hand, she made a fist of the other and set to pummelling his midriff. At the precise instant she delivered the third punch, she released her grip. The power of the blow impelled him away from her. He looked down at his flowing lacerations, face wreathed in agony, and was swallowed by the chaos.

There were shreds of fishy tissue on her knuckle studs.

A movement at the corner of her vision made her turn. A merzmaid was swimming at her, pointing a trident. With a powerful surge of her muscular tail the nyadd shot upwards, narrowly escaping the charge. Unstoppable, the merzmaid sailed into a knot of the nyadd's followers. They speared and slashed the life from her.

All around, fights raged; one on one, group against group. Everywhere, pairs of antagonists were locked in the outlandish spiral dance, hands clamped to wrists, arms straining to plunge home a dagger. Grievously wounded dyed the water; the dead were elbowed aside.

The nyadd vanguard was fighting on the redoubt itself. Some were battling their way into its entrances. She made to join them.

A merzmale with blazing eyes darted in to block her. He held a toothed blade the length of a broadsword, with a two-handed hilt. To counter the weapon's reach, she produced her own blade, shorter but acute as a scalpel. They circled each other, oblivious to the mêlée on every side.

He lunged forward, intent on running her through. She dodged, batting his blade with her own, hoping to knock it free. He held on to the weapon, quickly rallied and plunged it at her again. A pirouette movement turned her from the blade's path. His outstretched arm was exposed. She struck out at it with a studded knuckle, managing only a glancing blow but still slicing deep into flesh. Her foe was preoccupied enough to let her follow through with the blade. It found his heart. There was an eruption of gore. Pulling loose the blade, she released a gush of ruby-coloured globs. Open-mouthed, the merz died.

She kicked away the corpse and returned her attention to the storming of the redoubt.

By now her swarm was all over it. Many had entered to complete the slaughter. In obedience to her orders, the remaining merz were being brutally despatched and the enemy nest was being cleared. She swam past one of her warriors strangling a thrashing merzmale with a chain while another nyadd stabbed at the victim with a spear.

Few merz remained alive. One or two survivors had fled and were swimming away, but she was content with that. They would spread the word that colonising anywhere near her domain was a bad idea. As she looked on, the young of the merz race were dragged from the redoubt and put to death, according to her instructions. She saw no point in letting trouble brew for the future.

When the deed was done, and she was satisfied that the mission had been accomplished successfully, she ordered the swarm to withdraw.

While heading away, accompanied by her minions, a warrior beside her pointed back to the redoubt. A pack of shony were moving in to feast. These were long and sleek, with skins that glistened silvery blue. Their mouths were impossibly long gashes which in side view parodied a smile. When opened, endless rows of sharp white teeth were exposed. Their eyes were dead.

The creatures didn't unduly bother her. Why should they attack the swarm when they had an abundant supply of ready-butchered meat available?

Maddened with greed, the shony set to downing chunks of bloody flesh in great gulps. They stirred up fusty clouds on the seabed as they thrashed and snapped at each other. Several fought for the same morsel, teeth fastened, tugging at it from opposite sides. More scavengers swept in.

The swarm left the feeding frenzy behind, and in due course began to travel upward, towards a distant ring of light. As they ascended she allowed herself a moment's gratification at the fate of the merz. A little more decisive action and any threat they posed to her sovereignty would be nipped in the bud.

If only the same could be said of other races, especially the human pestilence.

They reached the mouth of a spacious underwater cave, its interior lit by nuggets of the phosphorescent rock. She entered at the head of the swarm. Ignoring the obeisance of the detachment of guards inside, she rose to a large vertical shaft in the cave's ceiling, which was also illuminated. The shaft came to a junction and branched into twin channels, like vast flues. Accompanied by two lieutenants, she swam up into the right-hand passage. The rest of the swarm took the left, to their billet.

Minutes later her party emerged from the water. They surfaced in an immense space flooded almost waist deep, permanently and deliberately so, to meet the needs of an amphibious race requiring constant access to water. The half-submerged structure was part coral, part crumbling rock. Overhead, stalactites had formed. To an untutored eye it might appear a ruin, with a portion of one wall absent and the others covered in slime and patterned with lichen. The smell of rotting vegetation hung in the air. But in nyadd terms it was an antechamber to a palace.

The missing section of wall afforded a view of marshlands, and beyond that the grey ocean, dotted with sinister, craggy islands. An angry sky met the horizon.

Nyadds were perfectly suited to their environment. If a slug had grown to the size of a small horse, developed a carapace like armour and learned to stand upright on a brawny, muscle-lined tail; if it had sprouted back-fins and arms with wickedly clawed hands; if its yellow-green hide dripped with tendrils and it had a head like a reptile's, with thrusting jaw, mandible mouth, needle teeth and sunken beady eyes, it would have been something like a nyadd.

But it wouldn't have been like her.

Contrary to the nyadds she ruled, she was not pure bred. Her mixed-race origins had given her a unique physiognomy. She was a symbiote, in her case a blend of nyadd and human, though the nyadd strain was primary. Or at least she chose to think it so. Her human ancestry was abhorrent to her, and none who valued their lives would dare remind her of it.

In common with her subjects, she possessed a sturdy tail, and back-fins, though the latter more closely resembled flaps of skin than the hardier, toughened membranes of her subjects. Her upper body and mammary glands, which were bare, combined skin with scales, the scales being much smaller than the nyadd norm and faintly rainbow-hued. Gill slashes patterned both sides of her trunk.

Her head, while unmistakably reptilian in aspect, was where her human heritage was most obvious. As distinct from the pure bred, she had hair. Her face had a faintly bluish tint, but her ears and nose were nearer human than nyadd shape, and her mouth could pass for a woman's.

She had eyes that were much rounder, and lashed, though their vivid green orbs had no comparison.

Only in her nature was she typical nyadd. Of all the sea-dwelling races, theirs was the most obstinate, vindictive and warlike. If anything, she had these traits to a greater degree than her subjects, and perhaps owed that to her human legacy too.

Wading to the breach in the wall, she surveyed the bleak land-scape. Aware of her lieutenants hovering nearby, anticipating any need she might express, she sensed how tense they were. She liked tense.

"Our losses were meagre, Queen Adpar," one of her lieuten-ants ventured to report. His voice was deep, and had a gritty quality.

"Whatever the number it's a small price to pay," she replied, pulling off her studded knuckle straps. "Are our forces ready to occupy the liberated sector?"

"They should be on their way now, ma'am," the other lackey told her.

"They'd better be," Adpar retorted, casually tossing the knuckle straps his way. He caught them awkwardly. It wouldn't have gone well with him if he hadn't. "Not that they'll get much trouble from the merz," she went on. "It'd take more than peace-loving vermin to prevail against an enemy like the nyadd."

"Yes, Majesty," said the first lieutenant.

"I don't look kindly on those who take what is mine," she added darkly, and unnecessarily as far as her minions were concerned.

She glanced at a niche carved in one of the coral walls. It housed a fluted stone pedestal obviously intended to display something. But whatever it was had gone.

"Your leadership assures our victory," the second lieutenant fawned.

Unlike one of her siblings, who cared nothing about what others thought but expected absolute obedience, Adpar demanded both submission *and* praise. "Of course," she agreed. "Merciless supremacy, backed with violence; it runs in my side of the family."

Her attendants wore looks of incomprehension.

"It's a female thing," she said.

2

Coilla was in pain.

Her entire body ached. She was on her knees in muddy grass, dazed and winded. Shaking her throbbing head to clear it, she tried to make sense of what had happened.

One minute she was chasing that fool Haskeer. The next, she was thrown from her horse when three humans came out of nowhere.

Humans.

She blinked and focused on the trio standing in front of her. The nearest had a scar running from the middle of his cheek to the corner of his mouth. His pockmarked face wasn't improved by an untidy moustache and a mass of greasy black hair. He looked fit in an unfit sort of way. The one next to him appeared even more dissolute. He was shorter, leaner, slighter. His hair was tawny and a near-transparent goatee clung to his chin. A leather patch covered his right eye, and his leering grin revealed bad teeth. But the last of them was the most striking. He was the biggest by far, easily outweighing the other two combined, but it seemed like all muscle, not flab. His head was shaved, he had a squashed, abused nose and deep-sunk piglet eyes. He was the only one not holding a weapon, and probably didn't need to. All of them gave off the distinctive, faintly unpleasant odour peculiar to their race.

They stared back at her. There was no mistaking their hostility.

The one with the bad skin and oily hair had said something, but she hadn't taken it in. Now he spoke again, addressing his companions, not her.

"I reckon she's one of them Wolverines," he said. "Matches the description."

"Looks like we struck lucky," the one with the eyepatch decided.

"Don't put a wager on it," Coilla rumbled.

"Oooh, she's *feisty*," One-Eye jeered in mock dread.

The big, stupid-looking individual appeared less smug. "What do we do, Micah?"

"She's but one, and a female at that," Pox Face told him. "You ain't afeared of a little lone orc, are you? We've dealt with enough of 'em in the past."

"Yeah, but the others could be about," Big and Stupid replied.

Coilla wondered who the hell these characters were. Humans were bad enough at the best of times, but *these* . . . Then she noticed the small, rough, blackened objects hanging from Pox Face's and One-Eye's belts. They were shrunken orcs' heads. That left no doubt about what kind of humans she'd fallen among.

One-Eye was glancing warily into the surrounding trees.

Pox Face scanned the terrain too. "Reckon we would have seen 'em if they was." He pinned Coilla with a hard gaze. "Where's the rest of your band?"

She adopted an air of sham innocence. "Band? What band?"

"Are they in these parts?" he persisted. "Or did you leave 'em back in Scratch?"

She kept silent and hoped her face didn't betray anything.

"We know that's where you were heading," Pox Face said. "Are the others still there?"

"Fuck off and die," she suggested sweetly.

He gave her an unpleasant, thin-lipped smile. "There's hard ways and easy ways of making you talk. Don't much matter to me which you want."

"Should I start breaking her bones, Micah?" Big and Stupid offered, lumbering closer.

Coilla had been putting an effort into re-gathering her wits and strength. She centred herself, getting ready to act.

"I say we kill her and be done with it," One-Eye offered impatiently.

"Ain't no use to us dead, Greever," Pox Face retorted.

"We get the bounty on her head, don't we?"

"*Think*, stupid. We want all her band, and so far she's our best chance of finding 'em." He turned back to her. "So what you got to tell me?"

"How about eat dung, scum sucker?"

"Wha—?"

She kicked out at him with all her force, the heels of her boots cracking hard against his shins. He yelled and went down.

The other two humans were slow to react. Big and Stupid literally gaped at the speed of her movement. Coilla leapt to her feet, despite the pain in her legs and back, and snatched up her sword.

Before she could use it, One-Eye recovered and piled into her.

The impact knocked the air from her lungs and slammed her to the ground again, but she held on to the blade. They fought for possession, rolling, kicking, punching. Then Big and Stupid and an enraged Pox Face joined in. Coilla took a whack to the jaw. Her sword was dashed from her hand and bounced away. Delivering a roundhouse punch to One-Eye's mouth, she twisted from his grasp. She scrambled away from the scrum.

"Get her!" One-Eye yelled.

"Take her alive!" Pox Face bellowed.

"Like *fuck* you will!" Coilla promised.

Big and Stupid charged in and grabbed one of her thrashing legs. She turned and swung at him, battering his head with her fists, putting all she had into the blows. It did about as much good as spitting to put out Hades. So she slammed the boot of her other foot into his face and pushed. He grunted with the effort of hanging on, her boot sinking deeper into his reddening, fleshy cheek. The boot won. His hold on her leg broken, he staggered backwards and fell awkwardly.

Coilla started to get up. An arm came round her neck and tightened. Gasping for breath, she drove her elbow into Pox Face's stomach, hard. She heard him gasp and did it again. He let go. This time she got as far as standing, and was trying to draw one of the knives holstered in her sleeve when One-Eye, mouth bloodied, crashed into her again. As she went down, the other two returned to the fray.

Still suffering the after-effects of her fall, she knew she was no match for them. But it wasn't in her nature, or that of any orc, to surrender meekly. They fought to pin down her arms. Twisting about to escape this, she found herself in close proximity to the side of One-Eye's head. Specifically, his ear.

Coilla sank her teeth into it. He shrieked. She bit down harder. One-Eye thrashed wildly, but couldn't free himself from the tangle of limbs. She tore at the ear savagely, provoking ever louder agonised howls. Flesh stretched and began parting. There was a salty taste in her mouth. With a final jerk of her head, a chunk of ear ripped off. She spat it out.

One-Eye struggled free and rolled on the ground, clutching the side of his head and wailing.

"Bitch . . . whore . . . freak . . . !"

Suddenly Pox Face was looming over Coilla. His fist came down several times on her craggy temple, knocking her senseless. Big and Stupid clamped her shoulders and finished the job.

"Tie her," Pox Face ordered.

The big man hauled her to a sitting position and took a length of cord from the pocket of his squalid jerkin. Roughly, her wrists were bound.

Stretched in the dirt, One-Eye was still shouting and cursing.

Pox Face lifted Coilla's sleeve and took away her knives. He commenced patting the rest of her for more weapons.

Behind them, One-Eye moaned loudly and thrashed about some more. "I'll . . . fucking kill . . . her," he bleated.

"Shut up!" Pox Face snapped. He dug into his belt pouch and found a piece of grubby cloth. "Here."

The balled cloth landed beside One-Eye. He took it and tried to staunch the blood. "My ear, Micah," he grumbled. "The fucking little monster . . . My ear!"

"Ah, stow it," Pox Face said. "You never did listen anyway, Greever."

Big and Stupid boomed with laughter. Pox Face took it up.

"It ain't funny!" One-Eye protested indignantly.

"One eye, one ear," the vast human cackled, jowls undulating. "He's got . . . the set!"

The pair of them roared.

"Bastards!" One-Eye exclaimed.

Pox Face looked down at Coilla. His mood changed instantly

and completely. "I reckon that wasn't too friendly, orc." The tone was pure menace.

"I can be a lot more unfriendly than that," she promised him.

Big and Stupid sobered. Muttering, One-Eye climbed to his feet and tottered over to them.

Crouching beside her, reeking fetid breath, Pox Face said, "I'm asking again: are the other Wolverines still in Scratch?"

Coilla just stared at him.

One-Eye kicked her in the side. "Talk, bitch!"

She took the blow and repaid it with another show of silent defiance.

"Cut it out," Pox Face told him. But he didn't sound overly concerned about her welfare.

Glowering, One-Eye pressed the cloth to his ear and looked murderous.

"Is it Scratch?" Pox Face repeated to her. "Well?"

"You really think the three of you could go against the Wolverines and live?"

"*I'm* asking the questions, bitch, and I'm not good at patience." He pulled a knife from his belt and held it in front of her face. "Tell me where they are or I start with your eyes."

A slow pause and some quick thinking occurred. Finally she said, "Hecklowe."

"What?"

"She's lying!" One-Eye interjected.

Pox Face looked sceptical too. "Why Hecklowe? What are they doing there?"

"It's a freeport, isn't it?"

"So?"

"If you have something to sell, it's where you'll get the highest price." She made it seem that she was giving this out with reluctance.

"Hecklowe's that kind of place, Micah," Big and Stupid offered.

"I know *that*," Pox Face retorted testily. He returned his attention to Coilla. "What have your kind got to sell?"

She baited the hook with a strategic silence.

"It's what you stole from the Queen, ain't it?"

Coilla slowly nodded, desperately hoping they'd buy the lie. "Seems to me it must be something real precious to go renegade and upset the likes of Jennesta. What is it?"

She realised they didn't know about the instrumentalities, the artifacts she and the band called stars. No way was she going to enlighten them. "It's a . . . trophy. A relic. Very old."

"Relic? A valuable of some kind? Treasure?"

"Yes, a treasure." She meant the word in a way he'd never understand.

"I *knew* it!" There was avarice in his eyes. "It had to be something big."

Coilla realised these bounty hunters, which was obviously what they were, could accept that the Wolverines had gone rogue in pursuit of gain. They would never have bought the notion of them acting for an ideal. It fitted their jaundiced view of the world.

"So why ain't you with 'em?" One-Eye butted in, glaring at her suspiciously.

It was the question she was dreading. Whatever she came out with had to be convincing. "We had some trouble on the trail. Ran into a bunch of Unis and I got parted from the band. I was trying to catch them up when—"

"When you ran into us," Pox Face interrupted. "Your bad luck, our good fortune."

She dared to hope that he at least believed her. But Coilla knew she was taking a risk if they did. They might decide she'd served her purpose, kill her and be on their way. Taking her head with them.

Pox Face stared at her. She braced herself.

"We're going to Hecklowe," he announced.

"What about her?" asked One-Eye.

"She's coming with us."

"Why? What do we need her for now?"

"A profit. Hecklowe's just about the best place to strike a deal with slavers. Some pay plenty for an orc bodyguard in times like this. Particularly for an orc from a crack fighting unit." He jerked his head at the big man. "Get her horse, Jabeez."

Jabeez trudged toward her mount, which was grazing a little way off, unconcerned.

One-Eye, still fussing with what was left of his ear, didn't look happy. But he kept his peace.

To Coilla it seemed like a good time for token objections. "Slavery." She almost spat the word. "Another sign of Maras-Dantia's decline. That's something else we owe you humans for."

"Shut your noise!" Pox Face snapped. "Get this straight, orc. All you mean to me is the amount you're worth. And you don't need a tongue to ply your trade. Understand?"

Coilla breathed an inward sigh of relief. Greed had rescued her. But all she'd done was buy a little time, both for her and, she hoped, the band.

The band. Shit, what a mess. Where were they? Where was Haskeer? What would become of the stars?

Who was there to help?

For a long, long time he had done nothing but watch. He had contented himself with observing events from afar and trusting fate. But fate couldn't be trusted. Things just got more involved, more unpredictable, and chaos loomed ever larger.

The draining of the magic brought about by the destructive ways of the incomers meant that when he finally decided to act even his powers were too unreliable, too weakened. He had to involve others in the search and that proved a mistake.

Now the instrumentalities were back in the world, back in history, and it was just a matter of time before somebody harnessed their power. Whether it would be used for good or ill was the only question that mattered a damn now.

He couldn't argue to himself any longer that none of it affected this place. Even his own extraordinary domain was threatened. With his abilities diminishing it was all he could do to maintain its existence, notwithstanding that his small elite of acolytes called him Mage and believed he was capable of anything.

It was time to take a more direct hand in what was happening. He had made mistakes and he had to try rectifying them. Some things he could do to help. Others he couldn't.

But he saw what had been, and something of what was to come, and knew he might already be too late.

3

The large, spherical chamber, deep in the underground labyrinth of Scratch, was poorly lit. Such light as there was came from innumerable, faintly glowing crystals embedded in the walls and roof, and from a few discarded torches scattered about the floor. Half a dozen ovals of pitch blackness marked tunnels running off from the cavern. The air was unwholesome.

Above, two score trolls were gathered. Theirs was a squat, beefy race, covered in coarse grey fur and of waxen complexion. Incongruously, their heads were crowned with a mass of vivid, rusty orange hair. Their chests were expansive, their limbs overly long, and their eyes had evolved into vast black orbs to cope with subterranean darkness.

For all Stryke and Alfray knew, the chamber was only a small part of the troll kingdom, and these warriors were only a fraction of its population. But separated from the rest of their band by a rock fall, the Wolverine captain and corporal were destined never to find out. Their hands were bound and they stood with their backs pressed against a sacrificial altar. The trolls arrayed against them were armed with spears, and some had bows.

At their head was Tannar, the troll monarch. He stood taller than any other present. His build was brawnier than all save the orcs'. Robes of gold, a silver crown and the long, ornate crook he bore marked his status. But it was what he held aloft in his other hand that mesmerised the captives. He brandished a curved-bladed sacrificial knife, and fixed to its hilt was the very thing the Wolverines had braved Scratch to find.

One of the ancient instrumentalities. A relic the orcs referred to as a star.

The trolls were chanting a guttural dirge. Tannar slowly advanced, intent on murder in the name of his fearful Cimmerian gods. Hardly crediting the bitter irony of their situation, Stryke and Alfray readied themselves for death as the chanting reached a mesmeric pitch.

Eyeing the dagger, Alfray said, "Some joke fate's played on us, eh?"

"Shame I don't feel like laughing." Stryke strained at his bonds. They held firm.

Alfray glanced his way. "It's been good, Stryke. Despite everything."

"Don't give in, old friend. Even to death. Die like an orc."

A mildly indignant look passed across Alfray's face. "There's another way?"

The dagger was close.

There was a flash of light at the mouth of one of the tunnels. What followed seemed to Stryke like an hallucinogenic experience brought on by pellucid. Something shot across the cavern. For a fragment of a second whatever it was left an intensely bright yellow and red trail line.

Then a burning arrow struck the head of one of the trolls standing next to them. Sparks flew as the arrow hit, and the impact knocked the troll to one side. His bushy mane burst into flames as he went down.

Tannar froze. The chanting stopped. A ripple of gasps ran through the chamber. The trolls turned *en masse* to face the tunnel. There was a commotion there. Yells and shrieks rang out.

The rest of the Wolverines were fighting their way in. They were led by Jup, the band's dwarf sergeant, laying into the startled enemy with a broadsword. Orc archers began picking off more targets with fire-tipped arrows. Light was anathema to trolls and the flaming shafts sowed utter confusion in their ranks.

As best he could with hands tied, Stryke took advantage of the distraction. He rushed at the nearest troll and delivered an orc's kiss, a vicious head-butt that buckled the creature's knees and dropped him like a dead weight. Alfray charged an off-guard troll and rapidly kicked him twice in the crotch. The anguished victim collapsed with rolling eyes and twisted mouth.

Tannar had lost interest in his captives and was bellowing

orders. His subjects needed directing; their response to the attack was shambolic. The entire chamber housed a furious battle, lit by bursts of illumination from winging arrows and torches the orcs employed as clubs. Screams, wails and the clash of steel echoed from all sides.

A pair of orc grunts, Calthmon and Eldo, battled their way through the tumult to Alfray and Stryke. The prisoners' bonds were slashed and weapons pressed into their eager hands. They immediately turned the blades on anything that moved and wasn't a Wolverine.

Stryke wanted Tannar. To get to him he had to pass through a wall of defenders. He set about the task with a will. The first troll blocking his path thrust a spear at him. Stryke side-stepped, avoiding the lunge by a whisker, and brought his sword down hard on the spear. The blow sliced it in two. A stab to the bewildered spear-carrier's guts put him out of the picture.

The next defender came at Stryke swinging an axe. He ducked and the cleaver whistled in an arc inches above his head. As the troll pulled back to try again, Stryke bought a second's grace by lashing out at his shin with a boot. The kick connected heavily. Unbalanced, the troll's next swing was wild, and well off its mark. Stryke exploited an opening and slashed at his chest. The blade cut deep. Staggering a few steps and spraying blood, the troll went down.

Stryke moved in on another foe.

Jup was employed carving his way towards Stryke and Alfray. Behind him, grunts were igniting more brands, and the light from them was increasingly affecting the trolls. As they covered their eyes, roaring, the band felled them. But many were still fighting back.

Alfray faced a pair of trolls trying to corral him with levelled spears. He sparred with them, his sword bouncing off the javelins' sharpened metal points. After a moment's to-ing and fro-ing, one opponent overreached himself, his leading arm exposed, and Alfray hacked into it. The troll screamed, let go of his spear and caught the full might of a follow-up slash to the chest.

His maddened companion attacked. Alfray found himself being pushed back as he batted at the menacing spear tip, trying to turn it aside. The troll was too determined for that and pushed on relentlessly. Alfray was close to being pinned to the wall. With the tip jabbing uncomfortably close to his face, he fell into a stoop, then pitched to one side, fetching up next to the troll. He instantly aimed a blow at its legs. The blade sliced flesh, not badly but usefully. It sent the troll into a limping retreat, his spear slackly held.

Alfray leapt to his feet and swung his blade at the creature's head. The troll dodged to the left. Twisting to compensate, Alfray's blade turned in flight, so it was the flat, not the edge, that smacked against the troll's cheek. It yelled its pain and came in with crazy eyes and thrashing spear. The reckless move suited Alfray. He evaded the weapon with ease, spun himself parallel to the troll and sent in a blow. The blade chopped halfway through its neck. A shower of crimson drenched the area.

Alfray expelled a breath from puffed cheeks and thought he was getting too old for this.

Slipping on blood underfoot, Stryke all but collided with the last of Tannar's defenders. This glowering troll had a scimitar. He proceeded to slash with it ferociously, trying to drive the orc away from his monarch. Stryke stood his ground and returned blow for blow. It was a stalemate for a moment or two as each fighter parried the other's attacks.

The breakthrough came when Stryke's blade rapped across the troll's knuckles and laid them open. Mouthing a curse, the troll aimed a downward stroke that would have parted Stryke's sword arm from his trunk had it connected. Some deft footwork on Stryke's part made sure it didn't. After that he swerved and took a chance on a swipe to the troll's throat. It paid off.

At last he faced Tannar.

Racked with fury, the king tried braining Stryke with his ornamental crook. The orc was agile enough to avoid that. Tannar threw the unwieldy crook aside and drew a sword, its silvered blade inscribed with swirling runic patterns. He still had the ceremonial dagger, and prepared to work the weapons in unison. Troll and orc squared off.

"What are you waiting for?" Tannar rumbled. "Taste my steel and wake in Hades, overlander."

Stryke laughed derisively. "You talk a good fight, windbag. Now put your blade where your mouth is."

They circled, each seeking a flaw in the other's guard.

Tannar eyed the combat going on all around. "You'll pay for this with your life," he vowed.

"So you said." Stryke kept his tone insolent.

The goading had its effect. Tannar roared in with a swingeing blow. Stryke checked it, the jarring impact he absorbed bearing witness to the strength of his opponent. He sent in a quick counterblow. The king blocked it. Now that their blades had met, the pair flowed into a regular exchange, attacking and defending by turn.

Tannar's style was all power and little subtlety, though that made him no less dangerous a foe. Stryke's technique was not dissimilar, but he had the advantage of much more experience, and was certainly nimbler. He also lacked Tannar's bluster, which showed itself in excessive feinting. Stryke laid on some extra provocation.

"You're soft," he taunted, swatting aside a pass. "Lording it over this rabble's spoilt you, Tannar. It's made you mushy as tallow."

Bellowing, the troll charged at him, knife slashing the air, sword raking. Stryke braced himself and swiped, targeting the point where hilt met blade. He struck true. The sword flew from Tannar's hand, clattering beyond reach. He hung on to the dagger with its precious ornament and brought it to bear. But the shock of losing his sword had turned him leaden-footed. He hadn't a hope of besting Stryke with the knife and every move now was defensive.

The orc crowded him. Tannar began to back off. What he didn't know, but Stryke could see, was that Jup and a couple of grunts had got themselves behind him. Stryke hurried the pace of Tannar's retreat with a torrent of blows.

Jup seized his opportunity. He leapt on to the monarch's back and threw an arm around his neck. With his other hand he pressed a knife to Tannar's jugular. The dwarf's legs were clear of the ground and kicking. One of the grunts moved in and pointed his sword at the king's heart. Tannar thundered his impotent anger. Stryke stepped forward and prised the sacrificial dagger from his hand.

One or two trolls saw what was happening. Most were unaware and continued fighting.

"Tell them to stop," Stryke demanded, "on pain of your life."

Tannar said nothing, eyes blazing defiance.

"Stop them or die," Stryke repeated.

Jup applied pressure with his knife.

Reluctantly, Tannar shouted, "Throw down your arms!"

Some of the trolls disengaged. Others kept on.

"*Drop your weapons!*" Tannar barked.

This time, all obeyed. Jup withdrew, but they kept the king well covered.

Stryke placed the ceremonial dagger at Tannar's throat. "We're leaving. You're coming with us. If anybody gets in our way, you're dead. Tell them."

The king nodded slowly. "Do as they say!" he yelled.

"You won't need this stuff," Stryke said, "it'll slow us." He snatched Tannar's crown and threw it to one side.

The impiety brought intakes of breath from many of the watching trolls. Stryke inspired more when he ripped off the king's elaborate robe and abandoned that in the dirt too.

He returned the dagger to Tannar's throat. "Let's go."

They began to move across the cavern, a knot of orcs and a dwarf surrounding the towering figure of their hostage. Dazed trolls stood by and let them pass. As the procession made its way to the main tunnel, stepping over enemy corpses, the rest of the band joined it. Several were lightly wounded. It seemed to Stryke that all the fallen were trolls.

At the tunnel mouth he yelled, "Follow and he dies!"

Hurriedly they backed out of the chamber.

They made as good a pace as they could through the maze of unlit tunnels, their torches throwing huge, grotesque shadows on the walls.

"Nice timing," Stryke told Jup. "*Tight*, but nice."

The dwarf smiled.

"How the hell did you get through the roof fall?" Alfray asked.

"We found another way," Jup said. "You'll see."

They became aware of soft sounds behind them. Turning his head to squint into the darkness, Stryke could make out dim, grey shapes in the distance.

"They'll hunt you down," Tannar promised. "You'll die before reaching the overland."

"Then you'll be joining us." Stryke realised he was practically whispering. To the rest of the band, he ordered, "Stay together, keep alert. Particularly the rearguard."

"Don't think they need telling, chief," Jup said.

A minute or two later they entered the tunnel where the fall took place. Twenty paces ahead it was shut off by weighty boulders and rubble. Before they got to the blockage they came to a crudely cut hole in the wall on their right. The wall was thin, of shale-like material, and another tunnel ran behind it. They began to clamber through. Tannar needed prodding.

"How did this come about, Jup?" Stryke asked.

"Funny what you can do when needs must. This is that dead-end tunnel running from the entrance. Had the band sound the walls with hatchets. We got lucky."

The new passageway took them to another chamber, not unlike a pit, that lay below the shaft to the surface. There was weak light above. A couple of tense grunts were waiting by a brace of dangling ropes. Peering up the shaft, Stryke saw the heads of two more.

"Move it!" he ordered.

The first band members started to climb. Tannar was stubborn. They lashed a rope around him and hauled him up hand over hand. He cursed all the way. Stryke was the last to leave, the blade of the ceremonial dagger clamped in his teeth.

A small cave housed the shaft. Morning light flooded through its entrance. Stryke and the others came out of it blinking.

Tannar covered his eyes with a hand. "This is pain to me!" he complained loudly.

"Put this on him," Alfray suggested, passing over a cloth.

As the king was blindfolded and led off stumbling, Stryke held back and examined the sacrificial dagger. The star was attached to its hilt with a tight winding of twine. He took his own knife, cut through this and discarded the dagger.

The star was recognisable as such but differed from the other two, as they differed from each other. In the light he could see that it was dark blue in colour, whereas the first one they found was yellow, the second green. Like the others it consisted of a round central ball with spikes radiating from it, apparently randomly. It had four spikes; they had seven and five respectively. The same incredibly tough but unknown material had been used to make it.

"Come *on*, Stryke!" Alfray called.

He crammed the star into his belt pouch and jogged after them.

The band headed for their base camp at speed, or at least as fast as they could with Tannar slowing them. They were greeted by Bhose and Nep, and neither grunt tried to disguise his relief.

"We have to get out of here, fast," Stryke told them all. "It might be day but I wouldn't put it past them to venture out for him." He nodded at Tannar.

"Wait, Stryke," Jup said.

"Wait? What do you mean, wait?"

"I've got to tell you something about Coilla and Haskeer."

Stryke looked around. "Where are they?"

"This isn't easy, Captain."

"Whatever it is, just make it quick!"

"All right, short version. Haskeer went berserk, battered Reafdaw here and made off with the stars."

"*What?*" Stryke felt as though he'd been poleaxed.

"Coilla went after him," Jup continued. "We haven't seen either since."

"Went . . . went where?"

"North, far as we know."

"As far as you know?"

"I had to make a decision, Stryke. It was either search for Coilla and Haskeer or try to get you and Alfray out of that warren. We couldn't do both. Rescuing you seemed the best use of resources."

Stryke was absorbing the news. "No . . . no, you're right." His face darkened. "Haskeer! That stupid, crazy *bastard!*"

"That illness, fever, whatever it was," Alfray said, "it had him acting oddly for days."

"I never should have left him," Stryke decided. "That or taken the stars with me."

"You're being too hard on yourself," Jup ventured. "Nobody knew he'd do something so lunatic."

"I ought to have seen it coming. The way he behaved when I let him look at the stars, it was . . . deranged."

"There's no point in breast-beating," Alfray told him. "What do we *do* about it?"

"We go after them, of course. I want us ready to leave here in two minutes."

"What about him?" Jup asked, indicating Tannar.

"He stays with us for now. Collateral."

The grunts broke camp at speed and the horses were readied. Tannar was manhandled on to one and his hands were lashed to the pommel on its saddle. The cache of pellucid was divided up among the band members, as it had been before the underground sortie. Alfray found the Wolverines' banner and reclaimed it.

As Stryke moved off at the head of the band his head buzzed with possibilities. All of them bad.

4

Everything seemed so clear to Haskeer now, so obvious. The fog that clouded his mind had lifted and he knew exactly what needed to be done.

Spurring his horse, he entered another valley that would take him further north-east. Or at least he hoped it would. In truth his new clarity didn't extend to all his senses, and he was a little hazy about the precise direction in which Cairnbarrow lay. But he pushed on none the less.

For the hundredth time his hand went instinctively to his belt pouch, where he had the strange objects the warband called stars. Mobbs, the gremlin scholar who had told the Wolverines something about them, said their proper name was *instrumentalities*. Haskeer preferred *stars*. It was easier to remember.

He didn't know what the objects were or what they were supposed to do, any more than Stryke and the others did. But although he couldn't understand the stars' purpose, something had happened. Something that made him feel he had a kind of union with them.

They sang to him.

Sang wasn't the right word. It was the nearest he could come up with for what he heard in his head. He might have thought of it as whispering or chanting or the faint sound of an unknown musical instrument, and would have been just as inaccurate. So he settled for *singing*.

He could hear them doing it now, even while they were in his pouch and out of sight. The things that looked like a hatchling's idea of stars were vocalising at him. Their language, if that's what it was, meant nothing to Haskeer, yet he caught its gist. It told him everything would be all right once he got them to where they belonged. The balance would be restored. Things would go back to being the way they were before the Wolverines went renegade.

All he had to do was take the stars to Jennesta. He expected her to be so grateful she'd pardon the band. Perhaps even reward them. Then Stryke and the other Wolverines would appreciate what he'd had to do, and be grateful.

Leaving the valley, he came to a trail. It seemed to run the way he wanted to go, so he joined it. The track climbed to a rise and he urged his already lathering horse upward to the crest.

When he reached the top he saw a group of riders coming the other way. They were four in number. And they were humans.

They were all dressed in black, and each was more than adequately armed. One of them had the disgusting facial growth their kind called a beard.

Haskeer was too close to avoid being seen, or to turn back without them easily catching him. But in his present mood he didn't care about being seen. His only thought was that it was bad enough them being humans, worse that they were in his path. He wasn't going to tolerate anything that delayed him.

The humans looked taken aback at running into a lone orc in the middle of nowhere. They glanced around suspiciously for sign of others as they galloped towards him. Haskeer kept to the trail and didn't slacken pace. He only stopped when they blocked him, their mounts in a semicircle not much more than a sword's length away.

They took in his weather-beaten, craggy features, the crescent-shaped sergeant's tattoos on his cheeks, the string of snow leopard teeth at his throat.

He stared back, evenly, hard-faced.

The bearded human seemed to be their leader. He said, "He's one of them all right." His companions nodded.

"Ugly bastard, ain't he?" a clean-shaven one opined.

They laughed.

Haskeer heard them over the stars' beguiling song. Its urgency couldn't be denied.

"Are there more of your band around, orc?" the bearded one demanded.

"Just me. Now move."

That set them laughing again.

Another clean-shaven had his say. "It's you that's moving, back to our master. Dead or alive."

"Don't think so."

The bearded rider leaned in to Haskeer. "You sub-humans are lower than swine when it comes to head work. Try and understand this, stupid. In that saddle or over it, you're coming with us."

"Stand aside. I'm in a hurry."

The leader's expression turned flint-like. "I'm not telling you again." His hand went to his sword.

"Your horse is better than mine," Haskeer decided. "I'll be taking it."

This time there was a pause before they laughed, and it sounded less assured.

Haskeer gently tugged the reins of his mount, turning it slightly. He slipped his feet from the stirrups. A warm feeling began radiating from the pit of his stomach. He recognised the sign of an imminent frenzy and welcomed it like an old friend.

The bearded human glared. "I'm going to cut your tongue out, you freak." He started to draw his sword.

Haskeer leapt at him. He struck square, slamming into the human's chest. Locked together, they plunged from the horse's other side and hit the ground, Haskeer on top. Taking the brunt of the fall, the human was knocked senseless. Haskeer rained punches on him, quickly rendering his face a bloody, pulpy mess.

The other riders were yelling. One jumped down from his mount and rushed in with sword drawn. Haskeer rolled aside from his lifeless victim, scrambling to his feet just as the swordsman launched an attack. Backing off fast from the slashing blade, Haskeer wrenched free his own sword, levelling it to deflect the blows.

As they duelled, the two mounted riders jockeyed to take swipes at him. Dodging their blows, and the careening horses, Haskeer concentrated on the nearest threat. He drove forward, bombarding the human with a relentless series of hefty strikes. Soon he had his opponent in defensive mode, all his energy directed to fending off Haskeer's onslaught.

Ten seconds later Haskeer went into a feint, skirted an ill-judged swing and brought his blade down on the human's forearm. Still gripping the sword, the severed limb portion fell away. His stump pumping blood, the screaming human pitched headlong beneath the hooves of a rearing horse.

While its rider fought to disentangle his mount, Haskeer went for the other horseman. His method was straightforward. Snatching the reins he pulled down with all his strength, as though tugging a bell rope to warn of invasion. The rider was hurled from his saddle and smashed into the earth. Delivering a hearty kick to his head, Haskeer vaulted on to the animal's back. Bringing the horse about, he faced the last opponent.

Spurs biting into his mount's flanks to impel it forward, the black-garbed human met him. Haskeer engaged his whipping sword. They hacked at each other savagely, chopping, bludgeoning, trying to find a way through to flesh, all the while fighting to control their wheeling horses.

At length, Haskeer's stamina proved the greater. His continuous battering found less and less resistance. Then his strikes began to evade the human's guard. One scored, raking the man's arm and bringing a pained cry. Haskeer kept on with new-found vigour, dealing unstoppable passes, hacking like a crazed thing. The human's guard vanished. A well-aimed slash hewed inches deep into chest tissue. He toppled.

Haskeer steadied his new horse and surveyed the corpses. He felt no particular triumph at overcoming the odds; he was more irritated at having been held up. Wiping the gory blade on his sleeve, he returned it to its sheath. Yet again his hand unconsciously went to the belt pouch.

He was reorienting himself, figuring which way to go now, when his attention was caught by movement at the corner of his eye. Looking west, he saw another party of humans, also dressed in black, galloping in his direction. He reckoned there were thirty or forty of them.

Even in his battle-crazed state he knew he couldn't fight a mob of that size single-handed. He urged the horse forward and fled.

The stars filled his mind with their singing.

*   *   *

On a hilltop a quarter of a mile away, another group of humans watched the tiny figure riding across the plains, and a band of their fellows pursuing it.

Foremost of the watchers was a lofty, slender individual, dressed like his Uni companions in head-to-toe black. Unlike them, he wore a tall, round, black hat. The garment was a sign of his authority, though none present would have questioned his leadership whether he wore it or not.

His face was best described as resolute, and showed no hint of ever having been burdened with a smile. Greying whiskers adorned an acute chin, the mouth was a bloodless slit, his eyes were dark and brooding.

Kimball Hobrow's mood, not unusually, was apocalyptic.

"Why do You forsake me, Lord?" he ranted skyward. "Why let the ungodly, inhuman vermin go unpunished for defying Your servant?"

He turned to his followers, his inner elite known as custodians, and berated them. "Even the simple task of hunting down the heathen monsters is beyond you! You have the Creator's blessing through me, His worldly disciple, yet still you fail!"

They avoided his gaze, sheepishly.

"Be certain that I can take back what I have bestowed in His exalted name!" he threatened. "Return what is rightfully the Lord's, and mine! Go forth now and smite the depraved subhumans! Let them feel the wrath!"

His followers ran for their horses.

Down on the plain, the orc renegade and the humans chasing him were almost lost from sight.

Hobrow sank to his knees. "Lord, why am I cursed with such fools?" he implored.

Mersadion, recently elevated to commander of Queen Jennesta's army, approached a sturdy oak door in the lower depths of the palace at Cairnbarrow. The orc Imperial Guards standing on either side of it stiffened to attention. He acknowledged them with a curt nod.

Reflecting on the fate of his predecessor, and on his own comparative youth, the orc General applied an effort of will to control his nerves as he rapped on the door. He took a morsel of comfort from knowing that obeying a summons from *her* affected everyone this way.

From within, faintly through the solid door, came a response. It sounded melodious and unmistakably feminine. Mersadion entered.

The chamber was of stone with a high vaulted ceiling. There were no windows. Drapes and tapestries decorated the walls, some of the latter depicting scenes and practices he preferred not to dwell upon. At one end of the room stood a small altar, and before it a coffin-shaped marble slab. The purpose of these items of furnishing was something else he elected not to think about.

Jennesta sat at a large table. Scattered about its surface were candles that provided most of the chamber's light. The dim illumination gave her already outré appearance an even more bizarre aspect. There was something almost spectral about her.

Her half-nyadd, half-human origins meant Jennesta's skin had a shimmery green and silver glitter, as though she was covered in tiny scales. A face a mite too flat and broad was framed by ebony hair with a sheen that made it appear wet. She had an overly sharp chin, a somewhat aquiline nose and an ample mouth. Her striking, uncommonly long-lashed eyes were oblique, and seemed fathomless.

She was beautiful. But it was a kind of beauty observers were unlikely to have known existed until seeing her.

Mersadion stood rigidly just inside the door, not daring to speak. She was preoccupied, poring over ancient-looking tomes and yellowing charts. A massive book with metal clasps lay open beside her. He noticed, as he had more than once before, that her fingers were peculiarly long, an impression added to by lengthy nails.

Without lifting her eyes, she said, "Be at ease."

That was something no one managed in her presence. He relaxed a little, but knew better than to overdo it.

An awkward silence stretched as she continued studying. He leaned forward slightly to sneak a look. She noticed and her glance flicked up to him. To his surprise, instead of reacting furiously, as he feared, she smiled indulgently. Naturally that made him feel even warier.

"You are curious, General," she said. It wasn't a question.

"Ma'am," he replied hesitantly, mindful of her unpredictability.

"As you have many different weapons in your armoury, so do I. This is one."

He took in the untidily piled desk. "Majesty?"

"I grant it doesn't cut or pierce or slash, but its power is as keen as any blade."

She noticed his blank expression, and added with brittle patience, "As above, so below, Mersadion. The influence of heavenly bodies on our daily occasions."

He grasped her meaning. "Ah, the stars."

"The stars," she confirmed. "More accurately, the Sun, the Moon and other worlds in their relationship to ours."

He was losing her meaning already, but it was unwise to say so. He remained silent and hoped he looked suitably attentive.

"These," she went on, tapping one of the charts, "are a tool in our hunt for the Wolverines."

"How so, my lady?"

"It isn't easy explaining to . . . lowly intelligences."

He felt almost relieved at the casual insult. It was more in keeping with her style.

"The position of the celestial spheres resolves both character and coming events," she explained. "Character is moulded at the instant of birth according to which spheres are in the sky. The cosmic wheels turn slow and exceeding fine." She reached for a scroll. "I had the birth records of the Wolverines' commanders sought out. Naturally the lower ranks are of no consequence. Now I know the natal marks of the five officers, and thus something of their essential natures."

"Natal marks, Majesty?"

She sighed, and he feared having gone too far. "You *know* what natal marks are, Mersadion, even if you've never heard them called that before. Or are you going to tell me that the Viper, the Seagoat or the Archer are unknown to you?"

"No. No, of course not, ma'am. Sol signs."

"As the rabble would have it, yes. But at its heart this discipline is far more profound than the rubbish mouthed by soothsayers in the marketplace. They degrade the art."

He nodded, judging it wisest to say nothing.

"The . . . *sol signs* of the Wolverine officers give an insight into their personalities," Jennesta continued, "and how they might act in certain circumstances." She weighted the scroll with a couple of candlesticks. "Pay attention, General. Perhaps you'll learn something."

"Ma'am."

"The sergeant Haskeer is ruled by the natal mark Longhorn. That makes him bull-headed, stubborn, impetuous, in extreme situations inclined to savagery. The dwarf sergeant, Jup, is a Balladier. The warrior with a soul. He tends to see the mythic element in events. But he is equally blessed with practicality. The corporal Alfray is ruled by the Spanglefish. That means he can be a dreamer. He has a tendency to live in the past, and is probably conservative. He may possess healing powers. The female orc, Corporal Coilla, is a Basilisk. A spitfire, headstrong, given to reckless bravery. But also a loyal comrade."

Jennesta paused long enough for Mersadion to venture a prompt. "And their Captain, Majesty? Stryke?"

"He is in some ways the most interesting of this ragtag band. A Scarab. It rules the divine, the revelation of things hidden, change and the mystical. It also has strong martial properties." She removed the candlesticks and let the scroll re-roll itself. "Of course, these are just thumbnail sketches, and all are tempered, strengthened or weakened, depending on many factors."

"You mentioned coming events, Your Highness."

"Our future paths are mapped out for us. For every action there is a reaction, and this too is pre-ordained."

"So all is written beforehand?"

"No, not all. The gods have given us the wild card of free will. Though I could wish it were not so in every case," she added darkly.

Emboldened by her apparent openness, he asked, "What have your studies revealed of the future, ma'am?"

"Not enough. And to know more I would need the *exact*

moment and location of their births in order to cast more accurate charts. Such details are not recorded for mere orcs."

Mersadion kept to himself his reaction to yet another casually thrown slight.

"The precision of divination," she said, "is only found if your aim is on time."

He looked baffled.

"Don't bother trying to understand. I can't say how the present situation will resolve itself. Not with assurance. But in the matter of the Wolverines I see no let-up in blood and burning, death and war. Their path is fraught with peril. Whatever it is they are trying to achieve, their chances are slim."

"Will this help us to find them, Your Majesty?"

"Perhaps." She slammed shut the huge book. Dust motes swirled in the candlelight. "To matters at hand. Has there been any word from the bounty hunters?"

"Not yet, Majesty."

"I suppose that was too much to hope for. I trust you have more positive news concerning the divisions I ordered made ready for tomorrow's action."

"Three thousand light infantry, fully armed and provisioned, ma'am. They await your word."

"Muster them at dawn. I can at least take pleasure in bloodying some Uni noses."

"Yes, Majesty."

"All right. Dismissed."

He bowed and left.

As he walked away from her chamber he began breathing properly again. In his short time serving as the general of Jennesta's army Mersadion had suffered many insults and humiliations at her hands. He had feared for his life on several occasions. But none of that matched the relief he felt at having survived an exhibition of her reasonableness.

5

Stryke got the band away from Scratch as fast as possible. He took them north, reasoning that Haskeer would most likely head in the direction of Cairnbarrow.

At mid-morning they slowed their flight, sufficient distance having been put between them and any trolls that might be in pursuit, even though Stryke was of the opinion that they were very unlikely to follow in daylight. Tannar was no help in verifying this. He refused to do anything but curse.

The Wolverines continued at a more measured pace throughout the day. All the while they searched for sign of Haskeer or Coilla, with scouts sent out ahead and from the left and right flanks. The lengthening shadows brought by dusk made their task near impossible, and there was a palpable atmosphere of despondency in the band.

More than an hour of grim silence was broken when Alfray turned in his saddle and said, "This is hopeless, Stryke. All we're doing is drifting. We need a plan."

"And rest," Jup added. "None of us has slept for two days now."

"We've got a plan; we're looking for Coilla and Haskeer," Stryke told them, his manner surly. "This is no time to rest."

Jup and Alfray exchanged mournful looks.

"It's not like you to act without a scheme, Captain," Alfray responded. "In a crisis we need a strategy more than ever. You've said that yourself often enough."

"Then there's him," Jup reminded them, jerking a thumb at Tannar, riding further back in the column with a grunt on either side. He remained bound and blindfolded.

Alfray nodded. "Yes, are we going to drag that gargoyle around with us everywhere?"

Stryke glanced back himself and gave a resigned sigh. "All right, we'll make camp at the first likely place. But we're not stopping long."

Jup studied the terrain. "Why not right here?"

Stryke checked for himself. "It'll do." He pointed to a dip in the landscape, where an easily defendable knoll had formed. "There. I want double sentries posted. Tell the grunts to keep down the prattle. No fires."

Jup relayed the order, minus Stryke's frosty delivery.

They dismounted. Swearing and cursing, the troll king was taken from his horse and lashed to the trunk of a nearby tree, its greenery turning to autumn colours, months prematurely. The guards fanned out, but stayed close. Stryke, Alfray and Jup came together, and the remainder of the band gathered around them. With a wave of Stryke's hand they sat, many stretching exhausted on the mean sward.

Alfray wasted no time getting to the point. "What the hell we going to do, Stryke?"

"What *can* we do that we're not doing already? All we have to go on is that Haskeer headed north. Chances are he's making for Cairnbarrow."

"If he thinks Jennesta's going to show him any mercy, he really is crazy," Jup said.

"We know *that*," Alfray retorted. "But as to him travelling north, I reckon he's too demented to be that predictable. We can't rely on it. He could be riding around in circles out there somewhere."

"When we find him," Stryke said, "*if* we find him, I'm going to be in two minds about killing the swine."

"One mad orc's put us back to square one," Alfray stated gloomily.

"And Coilla," Stryke went on. "Her not coming back's starting to look bad."

"You're still blaming yourself," Jup told him. "You can't keep—"

"Of course I am!" Stryke flared. "That's what leadership's about, taking responsibility, weighing the odds, foreseeing things."

Jup snapped his fingers. "Foreseeing things. *Farsight*, chief. I haven't tried it for a while. It might be worth a go now, yes?"

Stryke shrugged. "Why not? We've nothing to lose."

"No promises, mind. You know how low the energy was just about everywhere we've been."

"Do your best."

The dwarf moved away from the group, found a piece of ground a little more lush than the average and sat cross-legged. He bowed his head, laid his palms flat on the earth and closed his eyes. The rest of them ignored him. Stryke and Alfray carried on discussing their options.

A few minutes later he was back. They couldn't tell from his neutral expression if he had anything worth telling them.

"Well?" Stryke asked.

"Mixed. The power's definitely waning. But I picked up something. I got a very faint energy pattern I reckon is Haskeer's. Much stronger than that, I felt a female presence, and I figure it's Coilla. Both north of here, her nearer than him."

"So maybe they aren't together. That's something we didn't know, I suppose."

Jup's face clouded. "Might not be good, though. Varying distance isn't the only reason you get one pattern stronger than another. Other things can affect it."

"Such as?"

"Such as high emotions."

"You're saying that's why Coilla's coming through stronger? 'Cause her feelings are more fierce?"

"It's a possibility, chief."

"Good feelings or bad? Can you tell?"

"Could be either. But given what she's doing, I think it's less likely to be good, don't you? If the energy lines weren't so fucked up I might be a bit more certain."

"Bastard humans, bleeding the magic," Alfray muttered.

"This just confirms what we thought," Stryke decided. "It doesn't change my mind about pushing on northwards." He turned it over for a moment, then addressed the grunts. "We're all in this together. I'm for the north and seeking our comrades. Anybody got any better ideas? I mean it. I'll listen."

Apart from some shuffling and blank faces, there was no response.

"All right," he said, "I'll take that as a yes vote. We'll rest a short while before moving. From now on our only priority is finding our comrades, and the stars."

"Then all you'll find is your deaths!"

They all looked to Tannar, who had been more or less forgotten while they talked.

"That sounds like wishful thinking," Jup answered.

"It is a prophecy," the troll king assured him.

"Based on what?" Alfray wanted to know.

"My knowledge of the objects you call stars, which is obviously greater than yours."

Stryke went to the tree and crouched beside him. Evening was setting in, so he took off the blindfold. Tannar blinked and scowled.

"Let's hear it," Stryke said.

"Not until I am untied," the troll demanded with regal arrogance. "My limbs ache. I'm not used to being treated this way."

"I'll bet you're not. But maybe we can manage it."

"Have a care, Stryke," Alfray cautioned.

"If this warband can't deal with one unarmed tunnel dweller we're in the wrong business." He drew a knife to cut Tannar's bonds, then stayed his hand. "Anybody know what kind of magic trolls have?"

Jup did. "It's two-fold, chief. One part's to do with night vision. Darker it gets, better they see. The other's a sharpened ability to forage food. Rats, fungus, whatever it is they eat. Can't think either would be a threat. Unless he tries snuffling us to death."

A ripple of laughter went through the band.

"That's what I thought," Stryke said. He slashed the rope.

Tannar massaged his furry wrists and glared at his captors. "I'm parched. Give me water."

"Demands, demands," Jup mocked, tossing over a canteen.

The troll king downed half the contents, and would have drained it all if Stryke hadn't snatched the bottle away. Tannar coughed, dribbling water.

"So what is it you know?" Stryke asked.

"My race has stories and legends concerning these objects. It seems your kind does not. Perhaps because orcs are rare among the elder races in having no magic. I do not know."

"What do the legends say?"

"That these . . . stars are very old, and may have been created at the same time Maras-Dantia itself was fashioned from chaos by the gods."

"Is there proof for this?" Alfray wondered.

"Yours is such a down-to-earth race. How could there be *proof*? It is a matter of faith."

"Go on," Stryke prompted. "What else?"

"Members of many elder races have died and killed for the power the stars represent, as you are now. All that was long ago. Of late, they have disappeared from the ken of most Maras-Dantians. But they remain a part of this land's secret history, as tales handed down within sects and hidden orders."

"So it's all yarns and moonfluff."

"You must think it more than that or you wouldn't risk so much to find them."

"We seek them because they're important to others with sway over us. That makes them useful in our situation."

"They are so much more than bargaining counters. To see them in so lowly a way is to play with fire when blind."

"We don't know anything about the stars' power, beyond the hold it has over the beliefs of others."

"From what I've heard you say, they've changed your lives," Tannar replied. "Isn't that power?"

"You mentioned a secret history," Alfray broke in. "What did you mean by that?"

"Down through the ages these things you call stars are supposed to have influenced many great Maras-Dantians. They are said to have inspired the making of Azazrel's mighty golden bow, the sublime poetry of Elphame, the fabled Book of Shadows, Kimmen-Ber's celestial harp and much more. You've heard of *those*, no doubt?"

"Yes, even we've heard of those," Stryke came back gruffly. "Though in truth we're not much given to poetry, books and fancy music. Ours is more of a . . . practical profession."

"*How* did the stars bring about these things?" Alfray persisted.

"Revelations, visions, prophetic dreams," Tannar returned. "The yielding of a small part of their mystery to those with the knowledge to extract it."

While Stryke and Alfray were mulling that over, Jup had his own question. "No one's been able to tell us what the stars *are*, what they do, what they're for. Can you?"

"They're a pathway to the gods."

"A fine phrase. What does it mean?"

"The schemes of the deities are beyond the grasp of us mortals."

"Another way of saying you don't know."

"How did your star come to Scratch?" Stryke wondered.

"A legacy from one of my predecessors, Rasatenan, who gained it for my race long ago."

"Never heard of him," Jup commented dismissively.

Tannar scowled. "He was a mighty hero of trollkind. His exploits are still celebrated by the songsmiths. They tell of how he once caught an arrow in flight, of how he downed fifty enemy single-handed and—"

"You'd do well in an orcs' boasting tourney," Jup ribbed.

". . . and of how he took the star from a tribe of dwarfs after defeating them in combat," Tannar finished deliberately.

Jup coloured. "I find that hard to believe," he countered with wounded dignity.

"However you got it," Stryke intervened, "what are you trying to say about the stars, Tannar?"

"That they have only ever brought death and destruction unless properly handled."

"By which you mean fed the blood of sacrifices."

"You kill too!"

"In warfare. And we lift our swords against other warriors, not the innocent."

"Sacrifice brings my race prosperity. The gods favour it and protect us."

"Until now," Alfray reminded him.

The king didn't try to conceal his displeasure at the gibe. "And your hands are unsullied by the blood of sacrifice, are they?"

"Never higher lifeforms, Tannar. And mostly we sacrifice to

our gods by going into battle. The spirits of those we slay are our offerings."

"Maybe the fact that you've found more than one star in a short time means the gods favour you too. Or perhaps they're just making you the butt of a jest."

"Perhaps," Stryke conceded. "But why are you telling us all this?"

"So that you'll see how important this artifact is to my race. Return it and release me."

"Why should we abet you in more slaughter? Forget it, Tannar."

"I demand that you return it!"

"Demand be damned. We didn't gamble our lives in that hole you call a homeland just to hand the star back. We need it."

The troll adopted a conspiratorial manner. "Then consider a trade."

"What have you got to bargain with that we could possibly want?"

"Another star?"

Stryke, Jup and Alfray traded sceptical glances.

"You expect us to believe you have such a thing?" Stryke said.

"I didn't say I had it. But I might know where one could be found."

"Where?"

"There's a price."

"Your freedom and the star back."

"Of course."

"How would you expect such a trade to be carried out?"

"I reveal the location and you let me go."

Stryke pondered that for a moment. "All right."

Jup and Alfray made to object. He silenced them with a slash of his hand.

"I have heard that a centaur armourer called Keppatawn possesses a star," Tannar explained, "and that it's guarded by his clan in Drogan Forest."

"Why haven't you trolls tried for it yourselves?"

"We have no insane ambitions to collect them like you. We are content with one."

"How did this Keppatawn get a star?"

"I don't know. What does it matter?"

"Drogan's a centaur stronghold," Jup put in, "and they can be mean about their territory."

"That isn't my problem," the king announced loftily. "Now give me the star and set me free."

Stryke shook his head. "We keep the star. And we won't be letting you go just yet."

The king was infuriated. *"What?* I kept my half of the bargain! You agreed!"

"No. You just thought I did. You're coming with us, at least until we know you're telling the truth."

"You doubt my word? You stinking overlanders, you mercenaries, you . . . *scum! You* question *my* word?"

"Yeah, life's unfair, isn't it?"

Tannar began raging incoherently.

"You've had your say," Stryke told him. He beckoned a grunt. "Nep. Secure him to that tree again."

The trooper grabbed the king's arm and started to guide him away. Tannar complained loudly of betrayal, of the indignity of being held captive, of having an inferior lay hands on him. He cast vivid aspersions on the entire band's parentage. Stryke turned his back on the scene to speak further with his officers.

A chorus of yells and expletives burst from the grunts. Tannar bellowed, *"No!"*

Stryke spun around.

Tannar and Nep were facing him, a couple of yards away. The troll had the orc in a neck-lock. He held a knife to the grunt's throat.

"Shit!" Jup exclaimed. "Nobody searched him!"

"No!" the troll repeated. "I'll not submit to this violation! I am a *king!"*

Nep stood stiffly, ashen-faced, eyes wide. "Sorry, Captain," he mouthed.

"Easy," Stryke called. "Be calm, Tannar, and nobody gets hurt."

The troll tightened his grip and pressed the knife closer to the trooper's jugular. "To hell with calm! I'm taking the star and my freedom."

"Let him go. This serves no sane purpose."

"Do as I say or he dies!"

Nep flinched.

Jup slowly drew his sword. Alfray took up a bow and shaft. All around, the band armed themselves.

"Drop your weapons!" Tannar demanded.

"No way," Stryke replied. "Kill our comrade and what do you think happens next?"

"Don't try bluffing, Stryke. You'll not throw away this one's life."

"We look out for each other, you're right. But that's just part of the orcs' creed. The rest of it is one on one, all on one. If we can't protect, we avenge."

Alfray notched an arrow and levelled his bow. Several grunts did the same. Nep contorted, trying to make himself less of a target. Tannar grimly hung on to him.

"You can come out of this alive," Stryke said, "and see Scratch again. Just throw down the knife."

"And the star?"

"You've had my answer on that."

"Then damn your eyes, all of you!"

He made to drag the knife's edge across the grunt's neck. Nep twisted violently, his head instinctively moving forward and down. Alfray loosed his shaft. The arrow skimmed the troll's cheek, gouging flesh, and soared onward. Tannar roared and let go of Nep. The grunt dropped and half ran, half scrambled away, hand to streaming neck.

Two more arrows slammed into Tannar's chest. He staggered under the impact but didn't go down. Slashing the air with his knife and yelling incomprehensibly, he managed to take a few steps in the band's direction.

Tearing his sword from his scabbard, Stryke rushed in and finished the job with a heavy backhand swipe to the king's vitals. Open-mouthed, the troll monarch collapsed.

Stryke nudged him with a boot. There was no doubt.

Alfray was examining Nep's wound. "You were lucky," he pronounced, applying a cloth to sop the blood, "it's superficial. Keep this tight against it."

He and Jup went over to Stryke. They regarded the body.

"How could he be so *stupid* as to think you'd go for a deal like that?" Jup wondered.

"I don't know. Arrogance? He was used to absolute rule, having everything he said taken as perfect truth. That's bad for any elder racer. Softens the brain."

"You mean he's talked shit all his life with nobody to gainsay him. Maybe he just couldn't get out of the habit with us."

"Total power seems to be a kind of insanity in itself."

"The more I see of rulers, the more I agree with you. Aren't there any *benevolent* dictators left?"

"So now we've added regicide to the list," Alfray said.

Stryke glanced at him. "What?"

"Murder of a monarch."

"It's hardly murder," Jup suggested. "More tyrannicide, I'd say. That means—"

"I figured what it means," Stryke informed him.

"Now we've made another set of enemies in the trolls," the dwarf added.

Stryke sheathed his blade. "We've made so many another bunch won't make much difference. Get a hole dug for him, will you?"

Jup nodded. "Then north?"

"North."

It was unusual to find a dry spot anywhere in Adpar's realm. Given nyadd physiology, a dearth of water made no more sense than an absence of air. For creatures even more liquid-dependent, like merz, a lack of water inevitably led to a lack of life. Albeit slowly.

The one place in Adpar's citadel where waterless conditions held sway was the holding area for prisoners, which due to the nature of her rule was rarely occupied for long. Not that she saw that fact as a reason to make it any less unpleasant. Particularly when information was required from the occupants.

Liking to take a hand in such things, she accompanied warders to the cell of two merzmale captives taken after a recent raid. They were spread, chained, upon dusty rock slabs in their arid cells, and had already been given a beating. For the best part of a day moisture had been denied them.

Adpar dismissed the guards and let herself be seen by the prisoners. Their rheumy eyes widened at sight of her, their flaking lips quivered.

"You know what it is we want," she intoned, her voice soft and bordering the seductive. "Just tell me where the remaining redoubts are to be found and you can put an end to your suffering."

Their refusal, croaked from parched throats, was no less than she expected, or in truth hoped for. There had to be a sense of achievement or these visits weren't worth making.

"Bravery can sometimes be misplaced," she argued reasonably. "We'll find what we need to know sooner or later whether you help us or not. Why undergo the torment?"

One cursed her, rasping; the other shook his head, painfully slow, dehydrated skin flaking.

Adpar produced the water bottle and turned uncorking it into something like an erotic display. "Are you sure?" she taunted. She drank, deep and long, allowing the liquid to dribble and gush from either side of her mouth as she did so.

Again they refused to treat with her, though the longing in their eyes grew ever more rapacious.

She took up a fluffy sponge, saturated it and squeezed its contents over her head and body, luxuriating sensuously in the drenching. Silver droplets glistened on her scaly skin.

They ran blackened tongues around barren lips and still refused her.

Adpar soaked the sponge again.

It turned out to be two hours well spent, both in terms of the information they gave up and the pleasure she derived from extracting it.

She made a show of taking the bottle and sponge with her when she left. The despairing expressions they wore added a final *frisson* to her enjoyment.

The guards were waiting outside the cell. "Let them desiccate," she said.

6

The band resumed their journey before first light. They veered north-east, still working on the assumption that Haskeer was making for Cairnbarrow. And they clung to the hope that Coilla was somewhere between him and them.

They were on the upper Great Plains now, an area where cover was less plentiful, so even more care had to be taken. But occasionally they encountered copses and other clusters of trees, and the trail they currently followed wound into a wood. Alive to the possibility of danger, Stryke ordered two advance scouts to be sent forward, and a pair were sent out on either side.

As they entered the trees, Jup said, "Shouldn't we be thinking about what happens if we haven't found Coilla and Haskeer? By the time we're in sight of Cairnbarrow, I mean. We're hardly going to get a warm reception there, Stryke."

"I think it'd be *very* warm. But I don't know the answer to your question, Jup. To be honest, I've been starting to fear they might have veered off in a totally different direction."

Alfray nodded. "That's in my mind, too. If they have, we could spend our lives looking for them just in these parts. And if they've moved on to somewhere else completely . . ."

"That doesn't bear dwelling on," Stryke told him.

"Well, we'd better. Unless you plan on us chasing our own tails for ever."

"Look, Alfray, I don't know any more than you do what we're—"

There was a disturbance at their right. The greenery shook, branches cracked, leaves fell. Smaller trees were pitched aside. Something bulky began crashing its way out of the wood.

Stryke pulled back on his reins. The column halted. Swords were drawn.

A creature emerged. Its grey body resembled that of a horse, but it was bigger even than a war charger, and it walked on clawed feet, not hooves. Powerful muscles rippled beneath its hide. Its neck was elongated like a serpent's, and a woolly black mane ran along the back of it. The head was almost pure gryphon, with a feline nose, a yellow, horny beak and upswept fur-trimmed ears.

They saw too that it was young, nowhere near full-grown, and that one of its sinewy wings was broken and hung limp at its side. Which was why, despite its obvious panic, the animal wasn't flying. Notwithstanding its mass it moved with surprising speed.

Crossing their path, the hippogryph whipped its head round to look at them. They caught a glimpse of enormous green eyes. Then it plunged into the trees on the opposite side and was gone.

Several of the orcs' mounts reared and snorted.

"Look at it go!" Jup exclaimed.

"Yes, but *why?*" Alfray cautioned.

A heartbeat later the two right-flank scouts tore out of the woods. They were yelling but the words were unclear. One of them pointed back the way they'd come.

Alfray peered into the trees. "Stryke, I think—"

Dozens of figures exploded on to the trail. The foremost were mounted, the second rank on foot. They were humans, every one of them dressed in black and heavily armed.

"Shit," Jup gasped.

For an eternal second the two sides gaped at each other.

Then the spell was broken. Mutual shock evaporated.

Wheeling about, the humans started yelling and moved in to attack.

"We're outnumbered two to one!" Alfray cried.

Stryke raised his sword. "So let's cut down the odds! *No quarter!*"

The black-garbed horsemen charged. Stryke dug his mount's flanks and led the band to meet them. Orcs and humans clashed with a roar and the sound of ringing steel.

Stryke barrelled into the foremost rider. The man flourished a broadsword, slicing the air as he leaned out to engage the orc's blade. Their swords impacted twice before Stryke got under the other's guard and hewed him at the waist. The human pitched to the ground. His empty horse ploughed into the enemy at its rear, adding to the confusion.

The human who took the fallen man's place confirmed Stryke's suspicion of easy victories. This was a much more formidable opponent. He was armed with a double-headed axe, and handled it with practised skill. They exchanged one or two blows. After that, Stryke tried to avoid his blade coming into contact with the axe, lest the heavier weapon snap it.

As they manoeuvred for advantage, Stryke's sword collided with the axe's wooden shank, splintering a notch. It didn't noticeably slow the wielder. But soon the effort of swinging the cumbersome axe did. The man's movements grew leaden, his reactions more prolonged. Not greatly, just enough to give Stryke a precious edge.

The marginal speed advantage allowed Stryke to send in a low pass. It ripped open the human's thigh. He stayed in the saddle, but the pain served to throw him off his balance mentally. His defence went to pieces. Stryke targeted a stroke at his upper chest and it landed true. The human dropped his axe. His hands went to the gushing wound and he doubled over. Bolting, his horse carried him out of range.

A third antagonist instantly filled the void. Stryke commenced fencing again.

Alfray found himself having to deal with a rider on one side and a footsoldier on the other. The human on foot was the greater danger. Alfray took care of him by driving the pointed spar of the Wolverines' banner into his chest. He went down, taking the lance and banner with him. Alfray turned his attention to the horseman. Their swords crossed. On the third strike the human's blade was dashed from his grasp. A length of cold steel to the stomach put an end to him.

Clutching a short spear, another footsoldier tackled Alfray, who rained blows down on him. The spear was sliced in two, and before he could dodge, his skull was cleaved.

Individual fights boiled across and along the trail. A number of humans were trying to get round either side of the band and outflank them. Battling ferociously, the grunts held them back.

Finishing off a mounted human with a sword thrust, Jup didn't notice a footsoldier arriving at his side. The man reached up, seized the dwarf's leg and pulled him from his horse. Jup hit the ground heavily. Looming over him, the human raised his sword to deliver a death blow. Jup gathered his wits just in time to roll from it. Surprised in his dazed state to find he was still clutching his sword, he used it to chop at the human's legs. Hamstrung and screaming, the man collapsed. Jup buried the sword in his ribcage.

Being on foot in such a tumult was unwise. Jup looked around frantically for a horse to mount. That ambition was delayed by a rider singling him out as easy prey. Stretching down from his saddle, the man hacked at him. Jup lifted his sword and began parrying blows. As much by chance as design, he hit lucky and knocked away his foe's blade. Leaping to his feet, Jup slashed upwards with all the force he could muster, inflicting a wound in the human's side. The man fell. Jup took his horse and rejoined the fray.

An arrow whistled past Stryke's shoulder. Its source was one of two human archers further along the trail. Between batting off opponents' advances, he saw the pair of Wolverine forward scouts returning. They galloped up behind the human bowmen and laid about them. Taken unawares, the archers succumbed. Stryke renewed his onslaught.

With a footsoldier attacking from each side of his mount, Alfray had his work cut out. Fending off one then turning to fight the other was exhausting. But they had hold of his horse's trailing reins and left him no option.

Jup hastened in to even the odds. He tackled the human on Alfray's left, chopping his blade deep into the man's shoulder. Alfray himself concentrated on the remaining attacker. He was on the point of besting him when the two left flank scouts, alerted by the uproar, rode in to help. They made short work of the chore.

Stryke parted a human's head from his shoulders with a powerful two-handed swipe. As the lifeless corpse dropped, he looked for his next opponent. But those still alive were retreating. Five or six, on foot and horseback, fled into the woods. Stryke yelled an order and a bunch of grunts rode off after them.

He went to Alfray, who was pulling the banner lance from the dead human's chest.

"How do you figure our casualties?" Stryke asked.

"No fatalities, far as I can tell." He was panting. "We were lucky."

"They weren't fighters. Not full-time anyway."

Jup joined them. "Think they were after us, Captain?"

"No. A hunting party, I reckon."

"I've heard humans hunt for pleasure, not just food."

"That's *barbaric*," Alfray said, wiping blood from his face with the back of a sleeve.

"But typical of the race," Stryke judged.

Grunts were already searching the enemy corpses, taking weapons and anything else useful.

"What do you think they were?" Alfray wondered. "Unis? Manis?"

Jup went to the nearest body and examined it. "Unis. Don't the black outfits jog your memory? Kimball Hobrow's guardians. From Trinity."

"You sure?" Stryke said.

"I saw more of them than you did, and up close. I'm sure."

Alfray stared at the body. "I thought we'd shaken off those maniacs."

"We shouldn't be surprised we haven't," Stryke replied. "They're fanatics, and we took their star. Seems nobody's too keen on letting us get away with that." The grunts despatched after the fleeing humans came back, holding up their bloodied swords in triumph. "At least there's fewer of them now," he added.

Jup came away from the body. "Could they have taken Coilla and Haskeer?"

Stryke shrugged. "Who knows?"

A grunt ran to them holding a piece of rolled parchment. He handed it to Stryke. "Found this, sir. Thought it might be important."

Stryke unrolled it and showed it to Alfray and Jup. Unlike the grunts, they could read, to varying levels of proficiency. Their task was made easier by it being in universal script.

"It's about us!" Jup blurted.

"I think the whole band should hear this," Stryke decided.

He called them all over, then asked Alfray to read it out.

"This seems to be a copy of a proclamation," Alfray explained, "and it bears a likeness of Jennesta's seal. The heart of it reads: 'Be it known that by order of . . . ,' well, by order of Jennesta, that, er, '. . . the orc warband attached to Her Majesty's horde, and known as the Wolverines, are henceforth to be regarded as renegades and outlaws, and are no longer afforded the protection of this realm. Be it further known that a bounty of such precious coin, pellucid or land as may be appropriate will be paid upon production of the heads of the band's officers. To wit . . .' The names of the five officers follow that bit. Let's see. It goes on, 'Furthermore, a reward proportionate to their rank shall be paid for the return, dead or alive, of the band's common troopers, answering to the names . . .' Then it lists all the grunts. Even the comrades we've lost. It ends, 'Be it known that any harbouring said outlaws . . .' The usual sort of thing."

He gave the scroll back to Stryke.

A pall of silence had descended over everyone present. Stryke broke it. "Well, this only bears out what most of us suspected, doesn't it?"

"It's kind of a shock to have it confirmed," Jup commented dismally.

Alfray indicated the slain guardians. "Doesn't this mean they were looking for us, Stryke?"

"Yes and no. I think we just blundered into each other this time. Though they must be in these parts because of their master, Hobrow, and the star we took. But plenty *will* be seeking us for the reward." He sighed. "So. A moving target is hardest to hit. Let's get on."

As they rode out of the wood, Jup said, "Still, look on the bright side. For the first time in my life I'm worth something. Pity it's only if I'm dead."

Stryke smiled. "Look." He pointed. To the west, far off, the hippogryph was making its way across the plain. "At least he escaped."

Alfray nodded sagely. "Yes. Shame he won't live much longer."

"Thank you very much for that thought," Jup told him.

They rode for another three or four hours, moving in a great circular sweep as they continued the fruitless search for their fellow band members. To make things worse, they hit a pocket of inclement weather. It was colder. Showers of icy rain and biting squalls came and went unpredictably. The damp, miserable atmosphere did little to lift the Wolverines' morale.

For Stryke it was a time of reflection, and at length he made a decision, though what he settled on went against the grain. He halted the column by a grassy hillock. The advance and out-flank guards were called in.

He urged his horse to the crest of the rise, the better to address them all. "I've decided on a different course of action," he began without preamble, "and I reckon we're best starting on it now."

There was a low-key rumble of anticipation from the ranks.

"We've been running around like headless rocs looking for Haskeer and Coilla," he went on. "There's a bounty on us, and there might even be others after the stars. All hands are turned against us now. We have no friends, no allies. It's time to take another tack."

He scanned their rapt faces. Whatever they expected, it wasn't what he said next. "We're going to split the band."

That brought a general outcry.

"*Why*, Stryke?" Jup shouted.

"You said we'd never do that," Alfray added.

Stryke's raised hands, and the expression on his face, killed their racket. *"Hear me!"* he bellowed. "I don't mean splitting us permanently, just until we do what has to be done."

"Which is what, chief?" Jup asked.

"Both finding Coilla and Haskeer, and at least checking on the possibility of a star at Drogan."

Alfray looked far from happy. "You were against the band splitting before. What's changed?"

"We didn't know about the chance of another star before. Nor did we have proof that we were officially renegades, and all that follows from it. Finding our comrades isn't our only priority now. I can't see another way we can search for our friends *and* a further star without dividing."

"You're supposing Tannar was telling the truth about there being a star at Drogan. He could have been lying to save his skin."

More than a few of the band murmured agreement on that point.

Stryke shook his head. "I think he was telling the truth."

"You can't know that for sure."

"You're right, Alfray, I can't. But what have we got to lose in believing him?"

"Everything!"

"If you hadn't noticed, that's what we're already gambling. There's something else. Putting all our eggs in one basket might not be good at this time. With two groups, our enemies have less chance of getting us all. And if each group has one or more stars—"

"*If!*" Jup retorted. "Remember, we still don't know what the hell the stars do, what they're *for*. It's a gamble on a blind throw."

"You're right; we're no nearer understanding their purpose than when we started, unless you count the stories Tannar told us. But we *do* know they have a value, if only because Jennesta's after at least one of them. The power we can be certain they have is the power of possession. I still think that if we have them we've got something to bargain with, and that might just get us out of this mess. As I said, what have we got to lose?"

"Isn't what you're saying an argument for *keeping* the band split?" Alfray suggested.

"No, it's not. These are unusual circumstances. We're missing two band members and we have to do our best to find them. Wolverines stick together."

"You still think of Haskeer as a member of this band? After what he's done?"

"Yes, Stryke," Jup agreed. "It looks like treachery. If we do find him, what are we going to do about him?"

"I don't know. Let's find him first, shall we? But even if he has betrayed us, is that any reason not to look for Coilla?"

Alfray sighed. "You're not going to be moved on this, are you?"

Stryke shook his head.

"So what's your plan?"

"I'll lead half the band in continuing to search for Coilla and Haskeer. You, Alfray, will take the other half to Drogan and make contact with this Keppatawn."

"What about me?" Jup said. "Which party do I go with?"

"Mine. Your farsight could be useful in the search."

The dwarf looked a little rancorous. "The power's fading, you know that."

"Even so. We need every bit of help we can get."

"What kind of welcome can I expect from centaurs?" Alfray wondered.

"We have no argument with them," Stryke told him.

"We started out having no argument with *most* Maras-Dantians. Look how *that* turned out!"

"Just don't do anything to offend them. You know how proud they can be."

"They're a warlike race."

"So are we. That should give some mutual respect."

"What do you expect me to do once I get there?" Alfray persisted. "Ask nicely if they've got a star and whether they'd give it to us?"

"Assuming they do have a star, maybe we could parley for it."

"What with?"

"I should think the pellucid's a good enough trade, wouldn't you?"

"And if it isn't? Or they just decide to take it off us? I'll be leading just half of an already depleted band. The whole band would have a job coping with who knows how many centaurs, and on their home ground."

"Alfray, I'm not asking you to take them on. All I want is for you to get yourself to Drogan and judge the lie of the land. You don't even have to make contact with them if you think it's too risky. Just wait for the rest of us to get there."

"When's that going to be?"

"I want to give at least another couple of days to searching. Then there's travelling time. Say five days, maybe six."

"Where would we rendezvous?"

Stryke thought about it. "East bank of the Calyparr Inlet, where it enters the forest."

"All right, Stryke, if you really think this is the only way," Alfray conceded resignedly. "How do we allot the groups?"

"A straight split of the troopers, which gives each party an even number." He looked them over. "Alfray, your group will be made up of Gleadeg, Kestix, Liffin, Nep, Eldo, Zoda, Orbon, Prooq, Noskaa, Vobe and Bhose. Jup and I will take Talag, Reafdaw, Seafe, Toche, Hystykk, Gant, Calthmon, Breggin, Finje and Jad."

He made a point of including the last three in his group because they voted with Haskeer not to open the cylinder containing the first star. He had no reason to doubt their loyalty, but thought it best not to have them on Alfray's mission, just in case.

Alfray didn't object to his allocation, and when Stryke gave the grunts themselves an opportunity to protest, none did.

He looked to the sky. "I want as little delay as possible, but I reckon a couple of hours' rest's in order. Get yourselves ready. There'll be two turns of guards, an hour each. The rest of you get your heads down. Dismissed."

"I'm going to share out my healing herbs and balms between both groups," Alfray announced. "Chances are they'll be needed." He went off, less than cheerfully.

Jup lingered with Stryke.

Reading his expression, Stryke anticipated his sergeant's thoughts. "Purely in terms of rank you should be leading the Drogan mission, Jup. But to be blunt, you know there's prejudice against dwarves, maybe even in our ranks. Anything that erodes your authority, inside or outside the band, imperils the mission."

"Leading the rescue of you and Alfray doesn't count for anything?"

"It counts for a hell of a lot with me and Alfray. That's not the point, and you know it. Anyway, I'd like you with me. We work well together."

Jup smiled thinly. "Thanks, chief. Matter of fact, I don't feel that bad about it. When you're one of my kind, you get used to attitudes. Can't argue, either; my race mostly brought it on themselves."

"All right. Now get yourself some rest."

"One thing, Stryke: what about the crystal? Should Alfray's group take more of it, given they might have to use it for barter?"

"No, I think we'll keep things as they are. Each band member carrying a ration's the best way of handling it. Still gives Alfray enough should he need to trade. But we make it clear again that nobody dips in without permission."

"Right, I'll get on that."

He left Stryke to bed down for a while.

Wrapping himself in a blanket and laying his head on a saddle, Stryke realised how bone tired he was.

As he drifted into sleep he fancied he caught a whiff of pellucid in the air. He put it down to imagination and let the darkness take him.

7

Something large and indistinct loomed over him.

His vision was blurred and he couldn't make out what it was. He blinked several times, focused, and realised it was a tree, lofty and of ample girth. Looking around, he saw that he was in a forest where all the trees were tall and robust, with abundant greenery. Beams of sunlight knifed through the emerald ceiling high above.

There was an almost palpable sense of peace here. Yet it wasn't entirely silent. He was aware of gentle birdsong, and behind that a sound he couldn't identify, like continuous, muted thunder. It wasn't threatening, just totally unfamiliar.

In one direction, where the woodland thinned, brighter light entered. He walked that way. Passing over a bed of crisp fallen leaves, he came to the forest's edge. The roaring, crashing noise was louder. Still he had no notion of what it might be.

Away from the shade of the trees, he was briefly ankle deep in succulent blades of grass. As the ground swept into a mild incline, the grass gave way to an expanse of fine white sand.

Beyond the sand lay a mighty ocean.

It stretched as far ahead as he could see, and to the left and right. It sent white-flecked waves rumbling lazily to the shore. Its opulent blue near matched the perfectly cerulean sky, where chalky, sculptured clouds majestically drifted.

Stryke was awed by it. He had never seen the like.

He went out across the sand. A pleasantly warm sea breeze caressed his face. The air was perfumed with the quickening bouquet of ozone. Looking back to the treeline, he saw the trail his footprints had left in the sand. He could not say why he found the sight so strangely affecting.

It was then that his eye was caught by something reflecting the sun, perched atop a rocky rise perhaps half a mile along the beach and set a hundred yards back from the shoreline. They were structures of some kind, sharply white. He moved in that direction.

The bluff proved further away than it looked, but was no great hardship to reach. Trudging the hot sand, he passed dunes massed by the industrious wind. Here and there, brilliantly green shoots of tiny plants stabbed through the powdery layer.

As he approached, it was obvious more than one construction sat on top of the black rock. Reaching the seaward face of the cliff, he discovered it was tiered. So he began to climb.

Soon he arrived at what turned out to be a modest plateau. What it housed was ruins: tumbled fluted columns, the remains of buildings, scattered blocks of fashioned stone, a cracked, truncated staircase. It was all surrounded by a crenellated wall, now breached and crumbling. The material used to construct the place had the bleached look of old marble. Mosses and ivy colonised much of its soft dilapidation.

The architecture was unfamiliar to him, its detail and decoration resembling nothing he had seen before. But there were elements that told him what he was looking at was obviously a fortification. Its positioning too, overlooking the ocean and on a high point, confirmed this. It was exactly where he would have put it himself. Anybody with a military slant would have done the same.

Palm shading his brow, he surveyed the view. The wind whipped at his face and clothes.

He stood that way for some time before he noticed movement. A group of riders was coming along the beach from the opposite direction to the way he had. As they got nearer, he could see there were seven of them. Nearer still, it was apparent they were heading for the fortification. A small voice in the back of his mind warned of the possibility of conflict.

Then he saw that they were orcs, and the voice was stilled.

The riders stopped at the foot of the rock pile. As they dismounted, he recognised one of them. It was the female he had encountered here before. Assuming it was here, and wherever "here" might be.

He let that thought pass over him like a night zephyr.

She led her party in climbing the bluff. Her movements were agile and confident. Reaching the top before the others, she stretched a hand to him. He took it and hoisted her the remaining couple of feet. As with the last time he had her hand in his, he noticed how firm and pleasantly cool it was.

Nimbly springing to him, she smiled. It warmed her strong, open face. She was a mite shorter than Stryke, but the difference was made up by the ornamental headdress she wore, this time a shock of lustrous green and blue feathers. Her physique was fetchingly muscular, her back straight. There was no denying she was a handsome orc indeed.

"Greetings," she said.

"Well met."

The other orcs scrambled on to the plateau. Two of them were female. They nodded as they passed him, seemingly friendly and unconcerned with who he might be or why he was there.

"Some of my clansfolk," she explained.

He watched as they went to stand on another part of the level. They looked out to sea and talked amongst themselves.

Stryke turned back to her. She was staring at him. "It seems we are drawn together again."

"Why is that so, do you think?"

Her expression indicated she found the question eccentric. "Fate, the gods. Who knows? Would you have it otherwise?"

"No! Er, no, I wouldn't."

She smiled again, a little knowingly, he thought, then grew more serious. "You always look so troubled."

"Do I?"

"What is it that ails you?"

"It's . . . hard to explain."

"Try."

"My land is tormented. Greatly so."

"Then leave it. Come here."

"There is too much of importance to hold me in my own place. And how I get here is something over which I seem to have no say."

"That's hard to understand. You visit with such facility. Can you explain?"

"No. I'm puzzled too, and I have no explanation."

"Perhaps in time you will. No matter. What can be done to ease your burden?"

"I'm on what could be called a mission which might do that."

"There is hope then?"

"Might, I say."

"All that should concern you is doing that which is right and just. Do you think you are?"

He answered without hesitation. "Yes."

"And you believe you are being true to yourself in undertaking this mission?"

"I do."

"Then you have made yourself a promise, and since when did orcs go back on their word?"

"Too often, where I come from."

She was shocked by that. "Why?"

"We are forced to."

"That is sad, and all the more reason not to bend this time."

"I can't afford to. The lives of comrades are at stake."

"You'll stand by them. It's the orc way."

"You make it all seem so simple. But events are not always easy to master."

"It takes courage, I know, but I can tell that's not something you lack. Whatever this task you have set yourself, you must undertake it to the best of your ability. Else why are we alive?"

It was his turn to smile. "There is wisdom in your words. I'll reflect on them."

They felt no discomfort in letting a moment pass in silence.

At length he said, "What is this place?" He indicated the ruins.

"Nobody knows, except it's very old and orcs lay no claim to it."

"How can that be? You've already told me that this country of yours is home to no other race but ours."

"And you've told me that your land is shared with many races. I find that at least as great a mystery."

"Nothing I see around me accords with my experience," he confessed.

"I thought I hadn't seen you waiting here before. Is this the first time you've come to greet them?"

"Waiting? And who am I supposed to greet?"

She laughed. It was good-natured. "You really don't know?"

"I've no idea what you're talking about," he told her.

Turning, she scanned the ocean. Then she pointed. "Them."

He looked and saw the billowing white sails of several ships on the horizon.

"You're so strange," she added kindly. *"You never cease to make me wonder, Stryke."*

Of course, she knew his name. But he still didn't know hers.

He was about to ask when a black maw opened and swallowed him.

He woke up haunted by her face, and sweating despite the cold.

After the brightness he had experienced, it took a few seconds for him to adjust to the watery daylight that was becoming the norm in this world. He checked himself. What was he doing thinking in terms of "this world"? What other world was there, apart from the one he'd created for himself in his dreams? If dreams they were. Whatever he called them, they were becoming more vivid. They made him doubt his sanity. And at a time like this the last thing he needed was his mind playing tricks on him.

Nevertheless, though he didn't understand the dream, it had somehow stiffened his resolve. He felt absurdly optimistic about the decision he'd made, never mind the many fresh obstacles it threw in their path.

His reverie was broken by a shadow falling across him. It was Jup's.

"Chief, you don't look too good. You all right?"

Stryke gathered his wits. "I'm fine, Sergeant." He got up. "Is everything ready?"

"More or less."

Alfray had mustered his half of the band and was supervising the loading of their horses. Stryke and Jup went towards him.

As they walked, Stryke asked, "Did anybody use crystal last night?"

"Not that I know of. And nobody would without permission. Why?"

"Oh . . . no reason."

Jup gave him an odd look, but before he could say anything they were with Alfray.

He was tightening his horse's saddle straps. Giving the leather stay a final jerk, he said, "Well, that's it. We're all set."

"Remember what I said," Stryke reminded him. "Don't make contact with the centaurs unless you're sure there's no danger."

"I'll remember."

"Got everything you need?"

"I reckon so. We'll be looking out for you at Calyparr."

"Six days at most."

Stryke stretched his arm and they shook warrior-fashion, clasping each other's wrist. "Fare well, Alfray."

"And you, Stryke." He nodded at the dwarf. "Jup."

"Good luck, Alfray."

The band's standard jutted from the ground next to Alfray's horse. "I'm used to having this in my charge," he said. "Do you mind, Stryke?"

"Course not. Take it."

Alfray mounted and pulled free the banner's spar. He raised it and his troopers took to their horses.

Stryke, Jup and the remaining grunts watched in silence as the small column headed west.

"So where to?" Jup wanted to know.

"We'll cover the ground eastward of here," Stryke decided. "Get 'em mounted."

Jup organised things while Stryke got on to his own horse. He was still disoriented by the lucidity of his dream, and took several deep breaths to centre himself.

He looked to his reduced band and dwelt again on the resolve the dream had given him. Still sure he was taking the right course, he nevertheless couldn't shake off the feeling that they might never see Alfray and the others again.

Jup brought his horse to Stryke's side. "All ready."

"Very good, Sergeant. Let's see what we can do about finding Haskeer and Coilla, shall we?"

They made Coilla walk, tied to the end of a rope attached to the pommel on Aulay's saddle. Her own mount was led by Blaan. Lekmann rode in front, setting a brisk pace.

She had learned their names by listening to their conversations. Something else she'd come to understand was that none of them had any regard for her wellbeing, beyond an occasional drink of water, grudgingly offered. Even this was only to protect what they saw as an investment they intended realising in Hecklowe.

The trio occasionally exchanged words, sometimes as whispers so she couldn't hear. They gave her sidelong glances. Aulay shot her murderous looks.

Coilla was fit and used to marching, but the speed they maintained was a punishment. So when they came across a stream and Lekmann, the pock-faced, greasy-haired leader, ordered camp struck, it was all she could do to contain her relief. She slumped to the ground, breath short, limbs aching.

The weaselly Aulay, whose ear she'd taken a chunk out of, secured her horse. What she didn't see was him giving Lekmann a conspiratorial wink from his one good eye. Then he tied her, in a sitting position, to a tree trunk. That done, the trio settled down.

"How much longer to Hecklowe?" Aulay asked Lekmann.

"Couple of days, I reckon."

"Can't be too soon for me."

"Yeah, I'm bored, Micah," piped up the big, stupid one called Blaan.

Aulay, fingering his grubbily bandaged ear, pointed a thumb at Coilla. "Maybe we should have some fun with her." Drawing a knife, he brought it back in a throwing position. "A little target practice would pass the time." He got a bead on her.

Blaan laughed inanely.

"Leave it be," Lekmann growled.

Aulay ignored him. "Catch this, bitch!" he yelled, and threw the knife. Coilla stiffened. The blade buried itself in the earth just beyond her feet.

"*Cut it out!*" Lekmann bellowed. "We won't get a good price for damaged goods." He tossed his canteen at Aulay. "Fetch us some water."

Grumbling, Aulay added his own canteen, collected Blaan's and went to the stream.

Lekmann stretched out, his hat over his eyes. Blaan laid his head on a rolled blanket, facing away from Coilla.

She watched them. Her eyes flicked to the knife, which they seemed to have forgotten. It looked to be just within reach. She carefully eased a foot in its direction.

Aulay returned with the canteens. She froze and lowered her head, pretending slumber.

The one-eyed human stared at her. "Just our luck to be stuck out here with a female and she ain't human," he complained.

Lekmann sniggered. "Surprised you don't try her anyway. Or are you fussy these days?"

Aulay pulled a disgusted face. "I'd rather do it with a pig."

Coilla opened her eyes. "That makes two of us," she assured him.

"Well, fuck you," he retorted.

"I'm not a pig, remember?"

"Valuable or not, I've got a mind to come over there and give you a kicking."

"Untie me first and we'll make a match of it. I'd enjoy doing some damage to whatever you've got between those scrawny legs."

"Big talk! With *what*, bitch?"

"With these." She flashed her teeth at him. "You know how sharp they are."

Aulay boiled, a hand to the remains of his ear.

Lekmann grinned.

"How do we know she ain't lying about her band going to Hecklowe?" Aulay said.

"Don't start that again, Greever," Lekmann replied wearily. He turned to Coilla. "You aren't lying, are you, sweetheart? You wouldn't dare."

She held her peace, contenting herself with an acid look.

Digging into a jerkin pocket, Lekmann brought out a pair of bone dice. "Let's all calm down and kill an hour with these, shall we?" He rattled the dice in his fist.

Aulay drifted over. Blaan joined them. Soon they were engrossed in a noisy game and lost interest in Coilla.

She concentrated on the knife. Slowly, with one eye always on the boisterous trio, she stretched her foot towards it. Eventually her toe touched the blade. Further straining and wriggling got her foot around the knife. She pulled back. It fell, fortunately her way. With some ungainly, stealthy acrobatics, she managed to get it near enough to reach.

A rope had been run around her, fastening her arms to her sides, but there was just enough give to allow her fingers to reach the weapon. Very carefully, she got the knife into her palm and, her hand at an awkward, painful angle, finally placed its cutting edge against the rope.

The bounty hunters were still playing, their backs to her.

She moved the knife on the rope, working it up and down as quickly as she dared. Shreds of hemp frayed. Applying pressure by flexing her muscles against the bond helped speed the process.

Then the last threads parted and she was free.

With imperceptible, almost glacial deliberation, she unwound the rope. The humans carried on throwing dice and yelling at each other, completely oblivious of her. She moved, ever so cautiously, towards her horse, which was also on their blind side.

Crouching low and clutching the knife, she reached the mount. Her worry now was that the animal might snort or make some other sound to alert them. She patted it gingerly and whispered softly to keep it docile. Slipping a foot into the stirrup, she reached for the saddle to pull herself up.

The saddle came away, sending her sprawling. Her knife flew out of her hand. Shying, the horse bucked.

Roars of laughter broke out. She looked over and saw the bounty hunters doubled up with barbarous mirth. Lekmann, sword drawn, came to her and kicked the knife out of reach.

It was then that she noticed the saddle straps had been undone.

"You've gotta make your own entertainment out here on the plains," Lekmann hooted.

"Her *face!*" Aulay mocked.

Blaan was holding his massive belly and rocking. Tears ran down his ample cheeks.

Suddenly something caught his attention and he stopped. He stared and said, "Hey, look."

A rider was approaching on a pure white stallion.

8

As the rider drew nearer they saw he was human.

"Who the hell's *that?*" Lekmann said. The other two shrugged, blank-faced. Lekmann knelt and bound Coilla's hands behind her back.

The bounty hunters armed themselves and watched as the horseman approached at a steady pace. Soon he was close enough for them to make out clearly.

Even seated it was obvious he was tall and straight-backed, but wiry rather than muscular. His auburn hair reached his shoulders, and he had a neatly trimmed beard. He wore a chestnut jerkin, lightly embroidered with silver thread. Below that were brown leather breeches tucked into high black boots. A swept-back dark blue cloak completed the outfit. Apparently he wasn't carrying a weapon.

He pulled on the reins of his white stallion and stopped in front of them. Without asking, he dismounted. His movements were easy and assured, and he was smiling.

"Who are you?" Lekmann demanded. "What do you want?"

The stranger's eyes flicked to Coilla, then back to Lekmann. The smile didn't waver. "My name's Serapheim," he replied in a sonorous, unhurried tone, "and all I want is water." He nodded at the spring.

His age was indeterminate. Blue-eyed, with a slightly hawk nose and a well-shaped mouth, his face was handsome in a nondescript sort of way. Yet there was something about him that had presence, and a command transcending looks.

Lekmann glanced at Blaan and Aulay. "Keep your eyes peeled for more."

"I'm alone," he told them.

"These are troubled times, Serapheim, or whatever you call

yourself," Lekmann said. "Wandering about with less than a small army's asking for trouble."

"You are."

"There's three of us, and that's enough. We know how to look after ourselves."

"I don't doubt it. But I offer none a threat and no one threatens me. Anyway, aren't you four?" He looked to Coilla.

"She's just with us," Aulay explained. "She ain't one *of* us."

The man made no reply. His expression stayed non-committal.

"Seen any more of her kind in these parts?" Lekmann asked.

"No."

Coilla studied the newly arrived human and reckoned his eyes spoke of more shrewdness than he was letting on. But she saw no realistic chance of him helping her in any way.

The stranger's horse walked to the stream, dipped its head and began drinking. They let it be.

"Like I said, in these dark days a lone man takes a risk approaching strangers," Lekmann repeated pointedly.

"I didn't see you until the last minute," Serapheim admitted.

"Going round with your eyes shut ain't wise either."

"I'm often in a dream. Living in my head."

"That's a good way of losing it," Aulay commented.

"You with the Unis or the Manis?" Blaan put in bluntly.

"Neither," Serapheim replied. "You?"

"Same," Lekmann said.

"That's a relief. I'm tired of walking on eggs. A stray word in the wrong company can be a problem these days."

Coilla wondered what he thought he was in now.

"You're godless, then?" Aulay asked.

"I didn't say that."

"Figured you had to have faith in some higher power not to carry a blade." It was a comment designed to mock.

"I don't need one in my trade."

"Which is what?" Lekmann said.

Serapheim gave a little flourish of his cloak and bowed his head theatrically. "I'm a roving bard. A storyteller. A wordsmith."

Aulay's groan summed up the low opinion they all had of that particular occupation.

Coilla was even more convinced this wasn't someone likely to aid her.

"And how do you gallants make *your* way in the world?"

"We supply freelance martial services," Lekmann replied grandly.

"With a little vermin control on the side," Aulay added. He gave Coilla a cold glance.

Serapheim nodded, the smile fixed, but said nothing.

Lekmann grinned. "With wars and strife and all it has to be a bad time in your line."

"On the contrary, uncertain times suit me." He noted their doubtful expressions. "When things look black, folk want to forget their everyday worries."

"If business is good, you must be doing well," Aulay suggested slyly.

Coilla thought this stranger was either a fool or too trusting for his own good.

"The riches I have can't be weighed or counted like gold."

That puzzled Blaan. "How so?"

"Can you put a value on the sun, the moon, the stars? On the wind in your face, the sound of birdsong? This water?"

"The honeyed words of a . . . *poet*," Lekmann responded disdainfully. "If Maras-Dantia makes up your riches you're hoarding shoddy goods."

"There's some truth in that," Serapheim allowed. "Things are not as they were, and getting worse."

Aulay applied some sarcasm. "You saying you eat the sun and stars? Dine on the wind? Sounds a poor return for your wares."

Blaan smirked inanely.

"In exchange for my yarns folk give me food, drink, shelter. The occasional coin. Maybe even a story of their own. Perhaps you have a story to pass on?"

"Of course not," Lekmann snorted derisively. "The sort of stories we have would be of little interest to you, word-forger."

"I wouldn't be so sure. All men's stories have a value."

"You ain't heard ours. Where you heading?"

"Nowhere in particular."

"And you've come from nowhere in particular too, have you?"

"Hecklowe."

"That's where we're going!" Blaan exclaimed.

"Shut your mouth!" Lekmann snapped. He directed a bogus smile at Serapheim. "How, er, how are things in Hecklowe these days?"

"Like the rest of the land—chaotic, less tolerant than it was. It's turning into a haven for felons. Place was crawling with footpads, slavers and the like."

It seemed to Coilla that the stranger placed more than a little emphasis on the word *slavers,* but she couldn't be sure.

"You don't say," Lekmann returned, feigning disinterest.

"The Council and the Watchers try to keep things under control, but the magic's as unpredictable there as anywhere else. That makes it hard for them."

"Guess it must."

Serapheim turned to Coilla. "What does your elder-race friend here think about visiting such a notorious place?"

"Having a choice would be a good start," she told him.

"She ain't got nothing to say on the subject!" Lekmann quickly interrupted. "Anyway, she's an orc and she can take care of herself."

"Believe it," Coilla muttered.

The storyteller took in the trio's harsh expressions. "I'll just get some of that water and be on my way."

"You'll have to pay for it," Lekmann decided.

"I didn't know anyone owned the stream."

"Today we do. Possession's nine-tenths and all that."

"As I said, I've nothing to give."

"You're a teller of tales, tell us one. If we like it, you get to join your horse and drink."

"And if you don't?"

Lekmann shrugged.

"Well, stories are my currency. Why not?"

"Suppose you'll give us something meant to frighten idiots," Aulay grumbled. "Like some tale sung by fairies about trolls eating babies, or the doings of the fearsome Sluagh. You word weavers are all the same."

"No, that's not what I had in mind."

"What then?"

"You mentioned the Unis earlier. Thought I might give you one of their little fables."

"Oh, no, not some religious trash."

"Yes and no. Want to hear it or not?"

"Go ahead," Lekmann sighed. "I hope you're not too thirsty, though."

"Like most people you probably think of the Unis as narrow-minded, unbending fanatics."

"Sure as hell we do."

"And you'd be right about most of them. They do have a woeful number of zealots in their ranks. But not every one of them is like that. A few can bend a bit. Even see the funny side of their creed."

"That I find hard to believe."

"It's true. They're just plain folk, like you and me, apart from the hold their faith has on them. And it comes out in stories they sometimes tell. Stories they're careful to tell in secret, mind. These stories pass around and some of them come to me."

"You gonna get on with it?"

"Do you know what the Unis believe? Roughly, I mean?"

"Some."

"Then maybe you know that their holy books say their lone God started the human race by creating one man, Ademnius, and one woman, Evelaine."

Aulay sneered suggestively. "One wouldn't be enough for me."

"We know this stuff," said Lekmann impatiently. "We ain't ignorant."

Serapheim ignored them. "The Unis believe that in those first days God spoke directly to Ademnius, to explain what He was doing and what His hopes were for the life He'd made. So one day God came to Ademnius and said, 'I have two pieces of good news and one piece of bad news for you. Which would you like to hear first?' 'I'll have the good news first, please, Lord,' Ademnius replied. 'Well,' God told him, 'the first piece of good news is that I've created a wonderful organ for you called the brain. It will enable you to learn and reason and do all sorts of clever things.' 'Thank you, Lord,' said Ademnius. 'The second piece of good news,' God told him, 'is that I've created another organ for you called the penis.' "

The bounty hunters smirked. Aulay nudged Blaan's well-padded ribs with his elbow.

" 'This will give you pleasure, and give Evelaine pleasure,'" Serapheim continued, "'and it will let you make children to live in this glorious world I've fashioned for you.' 'That sounds wonderful,' Ademnius said. 'And what's the bad news?' 'You can't use them both at the same time,' God replied."

There was a moment's silence while the payoff soaked in, then the bounty hunters roared with crude laughter. Though Coilla thought it quite possible that Blaan didn't get it.

"Not so much a story as a short jest, I grant you," Serapheim said. "But I'm glad it met with your approval."

"It was all right," Lekmann agreed. "And kind of true, I guess."

"Of course, as I said, it is customary to offer a coin or some other small token of appreciation."

The trio sobered instantly.

Lekmann's face contorted with anger. "Now you've gone and spoilt it."

"We was thinking more in terms of *you* paying *us*," Aulay said.

"As I told you, I have nothing."

Blaan grinned nastily. "You'll have less than that when we've done with you."

Aulay did some stocktaking. "You got a horse, a fine pair of boots, that fancy cloak. Maybe a purse, despite what you say."

" 'Sides, you know too much about our business," Lekmann finished.

Notwithstanding the menacing atmosphere, Coilla was convinced that the storyteller wasn't fazed. Though it must have been as obvious to him as it was to her that these men were capable of murder just for the hell of it.

Her attention was drawn by something moving on the plain. For a moment, hope kindled. But then she identified what she was looking at and realised it wasn't deliverance. Far from it.

Serapheim hadn't noticed. Neither had the bounty hunters. They were set on enacting a violent scene. Lekmann had his sword raised and was moving in on the storyteller. The other two were following his lead.

"We've got company," she said.

They stopped, looked at her, followed her gaze.

A large group of riders had come into sight, well ahead of them. They were moving slowly from east to south-west, on a course that would bring them close, if not actually to the stream.

Aulay cupped a hand to his forehead. "What are they, Micah?"

"Humans. Dressed in black, far as I can see. Know what I reckon? They're those Hobrow's men. Them . . . whatever they call themselves."

"Custodians."

"Right, right. Fuck this, we're out of here. Get the orc, Greever. Jabeez, the horses."

Blaan didn't move. He stood open-mouthed, staring at the riders. "You reckon they ain't got no sense of humour, Micah?"

"No, I don't! Get the horses!"

"Hey! The stranger."

Serapheim was riding away, due west.

"Forget him. We got more pressing business."

"Good thing we didn't do for him, Micah," Blaan opined. "It's bad luck to kill crazy people."

"Superstitious *dolt!* Move your fucking self!"

They bundled Coilla on to her horse and took off at speed.

9

"Look at it!" Jennesta shrieked. "Look at the scale of your *failure!"*

Mersadion stared at the parchment wall map and trembled. It was littered with markers: red for the queen's forces, blue for the Uni opposition. They were roughly equal in number. That wasn't good enough.

"We've suffered no *losses* as such," he offered timorously.

"If we had I would have fed you your own liver by now! Where are the *gains?"*

"The war is complex, ma'am. We're fighting on so many fronts—"

"I need no lectures on our situation, General! What I want is results!"

"I can assure—"

"This is bad enough," she sailed on, "but it's as nothing compared to the lack of progress in finding that wretched warband! Do you have news of them?"

"Well, I—"

"You do not. Have we heard from Lekmann's bounty hunters?"

"They—"

"No, you haven't."

Mersadion didn't dare remind her that bringing in the human bounty hunters had been her idea. He had quickly learned that Jennesta took credit for victories but saddled others with the blame for defeats.

"I had hopes of you doing better than Kysthan, your *late* predecessor," she added pointedly. "I trust you're not going to disappoint me."

"Majesty—"

"Be warned that as of now your performance is under even closer scrutiny."

"I—"

This time he was interrupted by a light rap at the door.

"Enter!" Jennesta commanded.

One of her elf servants came in and bowed. The androgynous creature had a build so delicate its limbs looked fit to snap. Its complexion was almost translucent, and the fragility of its face was emphasised by golden hair and lashes. The eyes were fairest blue, the nose was winsome.

The elf pouted and lisped, "Your Mistress of Dragons, my lady."

"Another incompetent," Jennesta seethed. "Send her in."

As a brownie, the hybrid progeny of a goblin and elf union, the Dragon Dam bore some resemblance to the servant. But she was more robust, and tall even by the norm of her lanky race. In keeping with tradition, she was dressed entirely in the reddish-brown colours of an autumnal woodland. Her only concessions to adornment were narrow gold bands at her wrists and neck.

She acknowledged Jennesta's superior station with the tiniest bow of her head.

As usual in her dealings with underlings, the queen squandered no breath on niceties. "I confess to being less than happy with your efforts of late, Glozellan," she informed her.

"Ma'am?" There was a piping quality to the brownie's voice, and a calm remoteness characteristic of her kind. Jennesta had been known to find it irritating.

"In the matter of the Wolverines," she emphasised with menacing deliberateness.

"My handlers have followed your orders to the letter, Majesty," Glozellan replied, an expression of self-esteem on her face that many would have equated with haughtiness. It was another trait of her proud race, and even more infuriating to the queen.

"But you have not found them," she said.

"Your pardon, ma'am, but we did engage with the band on the battlefield near Weaver's Lea," the dragon mistress reminded her.

"And let them escape! Hardly an engagement! Unless you think merely spotting the renegades counts as such."

"No, Majesty. In fact they were pursued and narrowly avoided our attack."

"There's a difference?"

"The uncertain nature of dragons means they are always unpredictable to some extent, ma'am."

"A bad artisan always blames her tools."

"I accept responsibility for my actions and those of my subordinates."

"That's as well. For in my service a responsibility shirked leads directly to consequences. And they aren't of an especially pleasant nature."

"I only make the point that dragons can be an erratic weapon, Majesty. They have notoriously obstinate wills."

"Then perhaps I should find a dam more capable of bending them."

Glozellan said nothing.

"I thought I'd made my wishes clear," Jennesta went on, "but it seems I need to repeat myself. This is for your ears too, General." Mersadion stiffened. "Do not delude yourselves that there is any cause more vital than locating and returning to me the artifact stolen by the Wolverines."

"It might help, Majesty," Glozellan said, "if we knew what this artifact was, and why—"

The sound of a weighty slap echoed off the stone walls. Glozellan's head whipped to one side under the impact. She staggered and raised a hand to her reddening cheek. A thin dribble of blood snaked from the corner of her mouth.

"Mark *that* on account," Jennesta told her, eyes blazing. "You've asked before about the item I seek, and I repeat what I said then: it is none of your concern. There'll be more and worse if you persist with insubordination."

Glozellan returned her gaze with a silent, lofty stare.

"*All* available resources will be devoted to the search," the queen declared. "And if you two don't give me what I want, I'll be looking for a new General and a new Mistress of Dragons. You might dwell on the form your . . . *retirement* would take. Now get out."

When they'd gone, Jennesta vowed to herself that she would

be having a much more direct hand in things from now on. But she put that aside for the time being. There was something else on her mind. Something that greatly displeased her.

Using another, less obvious door, she left the strategy room and descended a narrow, winding staircase. Footfalls reverberating, she trod subterranean passages to her private quarters in the bowels of the palace. Orc guards came to attention by the door as she swept in.

Others were busy inside the spacious chamber, lugging buckets to a large, shallow wooden tub reinforced with metal hasps. They finished the chore while she stood impatiently watching. Once they were dismissed she settled by the tub and rippled her fingers through its tepid contents.

The blood seemed adequate for her needs, but she was vexed to discover that a few small pieces of flesh had been left in it. When advocating this particular fluid as a medium, the ancients had been quite clear on it being as pure as possible. She made a mental note to remind the guards about the need for filtering, and to have a thrashing administered to underline the point.

As the blood's surface was already thickening, she undertook the necessary incantations and entreaties. The glutinous ruby broth hardened further and took on a burnished look. At length a small area palpitated, swirled sluggishly and formed the semblance of a face.

"You choose the damnedest moments, Jennesta," the likeness complained. *"This is not a good time."*

"You lied to me, Adpar."

"About what?"

"About that which was taken from me."

"Oh, no, not that doleful subject again."

"Did you or did you not tell me that you knew nothing about the artifact I've been seeking?"

"What you've been looking for I have no knowledge of. End of conversation."

"No, hold. I have ways, Adpar. Ways, and eyes looking out for me. And what I now know fits only with my artifact." She grew thoughtful. "Either that or . . ."

"I feel one of your bizarre fancies coming on, dear."

"It's another, isn't it? You have *another!*"

"*I'm sure I don't know what —*"

"You deceitful bitch! You've been hoarding one in secret!"

"*I'm not saying I did or I didn't.*"

"That's as good as an admission coming from you."

"*Look, Jennesta, it is possible that I had something not dissimilar to what you're looking for, but that's history now. It was stolen.*"

"Just like mine. How convenient. You don't expect me to believe that?"

"*I don't give a damn whether you believe it or not! Instead of persecuting me about your obsessions you should be concentrating on finding the thieves. If anybody's playing with fire, they are!*"

"Then you *do* know the object's significance! The significance of all of them!"

"*I just know it has to be something extreme for you to get so worked up about it.*"

A small eruption disturbed the dark red, coagulated skin. Another face formed and a new voice was added. "*She's right, Jennesta.*"

Adpar and Jennesta groaned simultaneously.

"*Stay out of this, prodnose!*" Adpar snapped.

"Why can we never have a conversation without you butting in, Sanara?" Jennesta grumbled.

"*You know why, sister; the bond is too close.*"

"*More's the pity,*" muttered Adpar.

"*This is no time for the usual petty squabbling,*" Sanara cautioned. "*The reality is that a group of orcs have at least one of the instrumentalities. How can they possibly understand their awesome power?*"

"What do you mean, at least one?" Jennesta said.

"*Do you know for certain they haven't? Events are moving apace. We are entering a period when all things are possible.*"

"I've got it under control."

"*Really?*" Sanara commented sceptically.

"*Don't mind me,*" Adpar sniffed, "*I've only got my own war to fight. I've plenty of time to sit here listening to you two swapping riddles.*"

"*Perhaps you don't know what I'm talking about, Adpar, but Jennesta does. What she needs to understand is that the power should be harnessed for good, not evil, lest complete destruction be brought down on all of us."*

"Oh, *please*," Jennesta hissed sarcastically, "not Sanara the martyr again."

"Think of me what you will, I'm used to it. Just don't underestimate what's about to be unleashed now the game's afoot."

"To hell with the pair of you!" Jennesta exclaimed, petulantly slashing her hand through the layer of crusty blood. The images disintegrated.

She sat there for some time going over everything in her mind, and it was indicative of her character that she gave no credence to Sanara having a valid point and did not give Adpar the benefit of the doubt. Rather she resolved that the time was near to do something about at least one of her troublesome siblings.

Mostly she burned at the thought of all the trouble the Wolverines had brought down on her. And of the punishment she would exact for it.

Haskeer was still not sure if he was travelling in the right direction. He wasn't even entirely aware of his surroundings, and he was indifferent to the worsening northern climate.

All that was real to him was the singing in his head. It drove him mercilessly, impelling him further and faster on a bearing which, if he thought about it at all, he trusted would take him to Cairnbarrow.

The trail he followed dipped into a wooded valley. He galloped on without hesitation, gaze fixed straight ahead.

About halfway through, at the valley's lowest point, water had settled and formed an expanse of mud. The path was narrower too, bringing the growth on either side nearer, which despite the wintry conditions was still quite dense. He had to slow to a canter, much to his irritation.

As he picked his way through the bog, he heard a soughing noise on the right. Then a creaking swish. He turned and caught a glimpse of something speeding towards him. There was no time to react. The object struck him with a tremendous crack and he toppled from the horse.

Lying dazed in the mud, he looked up and saw what had hit

him. It was a length of tree trunk, still swinging, suspended by stout ropes to a strong overhead branch. Someone in cover had launched it at him like a ram.

Aching, badly winded, he was only thinking of getting up when rough hands were laid on him. He had an impression of black-garbed humans. They set to punching and kicking him. Unable to fight back, the best he could do was cover his face with his hands.

They hauled him to his feet and took his weapons. The pouch was ripped from his belt. His hands were bound behind his back.

Through the agony, Haskeer focused on a figure that had appeared in front of him.

"Are you sure he's secure?" Kimball Hobrow asked.

"He's secure," a custodian confirmed.

Another henchman passed Haskeer's pouch to the preacher. He looked inside and his face lit with joy. Or it might have been avarice.

Thrusting in his hand he brought out the stars and gleefully held them aloft. "The relic, and another to match! It is more than I dared hope. The Lord is with us this day." He threw up his arms. "Thank You, Lord, for returning what is ours! And for delivering this creature to us, the instruments of Your justice!"

Hobrow scowled at the orc. "You will be punished for your wrongs, savage, in the name of the Supreme Being."

Haskeer's head was clearing a little. The singing had faded and been replaced by this ranting human lunatic. He couldn't move or get his hands free. But there was one thing he could do.

He spat in Hobrow's face.

The preacher leapt back as though scalded, his expression horrified. He began rubbing at his face with the back of his sleeve and muttering, "Unclean, unclean."

When he was through, he asked again, "Are you sure he's well bound?"

His followers assured him. Hobrow came forward, balled his fist and delivered several blows to Haskeer's stomach, yelling, "You will pay for your disrespect to a servant of the Lord!"

Haskeer had taken worse. A lot worse. The punches were quite feeble, in fact. But the custodians, probably realising how ineffective their leader's efforts were, also started laying into him.

Over the beating he heard Hobrow shout, "Remember the lost hunting party! There could be more of his kind around! We must leave here!"

Barely conscious, Haskeer was dragged away.

Alfray and his half of the Wolverines journeyed in the direction of Calyparr Inlet for most of the day without incident.

He had used his authority to confer a temporary field promotion on Kestix, one of the band's more able grunts. In effect, this meant Kestix acted as a kind of honorary second-in-command. It also meant Alfray had somebody to pass the time with on a nearly equal basis.

As they rode westward, through the yellowing grasslands of the plains, he sounded out Kestix about the mood in the ranks.

"Concerned, of course, sir," the trooper replied. "Or perhaps *worried* would be a better word."

"You're not alone in that."

"Things have changed so much and so fast, Corporal. It's like we've been swept along with no time to think."

"Everything's changing," Alfray agreed. "Maras-Dantia's changing. Maybe it's finished. Because of the humans."

"Since the humans came, yes. They've upset it all, the bastards."

"But take heart. We could make a difference yet, if we carry out our captain's plan successfully."

"Begging your pardon, Corporal, but what does that mean?"

"Eh?"

"Well, we all know it's important for us to find these star things, only . . . *why?*"

Alfray was nonplussed. "What are you getting at, trooper?"

"We still don't know what they do, what they're for. Do we, Corporal?"

"That's true. But apart from any . . . let's say any magical power they might command, we do know they have another

kind of power. Others want them. In the case of our late mistress, Jennesta, powerful others. Maybe that gives us an edge."

Alfray turned to check the column while Kestix digested that.
When he righted himself, there was another question.

"If you don't mind me asking, how do you see our mission
to Drogan, Corporal? Do we go straight in and try to grab the
star?"

"No. We get as near to this Keppatawn's village as possible
and observe. If things don't look too hostile, we might see about
parleying. But basically we watch and wait for the rest of the
band to turn up."

Hesitantly, Kestix asked, "You think they will?"

Alfray found that mildly shocking. "Don't be defeatist,
trooper," he replied, a bit sternly. "We have to believe we'll
rejoin with Stryke's party."

"I meant no disrespect to the captain," the grunt quickly
affirmed. "It's just that things don't seem in our control any
more."

"I know. But trust Stryke." He fleetingly wondered if that was
good advice. Not that he didn't think Stryke was to be trusted. It
was just that he couldn't shake off the nagging feeling that their
commander might have bitten off more than he could chew.

His reverie was cut through by shouts from the column, and
Kestix yelling, "Corporal! Look, sir!"

Alfray gazed ahead and saw a convoy of four wagons, drawn
by oxen, coming round a bend ahead. The trail the orcs and the
wagons were on ran through a low gully with sloping sides. One
party or the other would have to give way. It wasn't yet possible
to make out the wagons' occupants.

Several thoughts ran through Alfray's mind. The first was that
if his band turned around it was bound to attract attention. Not
to mention that it wasn't in the nature of orcs to run. His other
thought was that if whatever was in the wagons proved hostile,
they were unlikely to number many more than his company. He
didn't see that as insuperable odds.

"Chances are these are just beings going peacefully about
their business," he told Kestix.

"What if they're Unis?"

"If they're any kind of humans, we'll kill 'em," Alfray informed him matter-of-factly.

As the two groups drew nearer, the orcs identified the race in the wagons.

"Gnomes," Alfray said.

"Could be worse, sir. They fight like baby rabbits."

"Yes, and they tend to keep themselves to themselves."

"They're only ever a problem if anybody takes an interest in their hoards. And I seem to remember their magic has to do with finding underground gold seams, so that shouldn't be a problem."

"If there's any talking to be done, leave it to me." Alfray turned and barked an order to the column. "Maintain order in ranks. No weapons to be drawn unless necessary. Let's just take this easy, shall we?"

"Do you think they'd know about the band having a price on its head?" Kestix wondered.

"Maybe. But as you said, they're not usually fighters. Unless bad manners and foul breath count as weapons."

The lead wagon was now a short stone's lob from the head of Alfray's column. There were two gnomes on the riding board. A couple more stood behind them, in the wagon proper. Whatever load the wagon carried was covered by a white tarpaulin.

Alfray threw up a hand and halted the column. The wagons stopped. For a moment, the two groups stared at each other.

Some held that gnomes looked like dwarves with deformities. They were small in stature and disproportionately muscular. They had big hands, big feet and big noses. They sported white beards and bushy white eyebrows. Their clothing was no-nonsense coarse jerkins and trews in uninspiring colours. Some had cowls, others soft caps with hanging bobs.

All gnomes appeared incredibly old, even when new-born. All had made an art of scowling.

After a moment's silence, the driver of the lead wagon announced testily, "Well, *I* ain't moving!"

Further back, stony-faced wagoneers stood to watch.

"Why should we clear the road?" Alfray said.

"Hoard? *Hoard?*" the driver fog-horned. "We ain't got no hoard!"

"Just our luck to get one hard of hearing," Alfray grumbled. "Not *hoard*," he enunciated slow, loud and clear, "*road!*"

"What about it?"

"Are you going to shift?" Alfray shouted.

The gnome thought about it. "Nope."

Alfray decided to take a more conversational, less disputatious tack. "Where you from?" he asked.

"Ain't saying," the gnome replied sourly.

"Where you heading?"

"None of your business."

"Then can you say if the way to Drogan is clear? Of any humans, that is."

"Might be. Might not. What's it worth?"

Alfray remembered that gnomes were notorious for knowing the price of everything but the value of nothing. Good road courtesy, for instance.

He gave in. At his order, the column urged their horses up the sides of the gully and let the gnomes through.

As the lead wagon passed, its poker-faced driver mumbled, "This place is getting too damn crowded for my liking."

Watching them rumble away, Alfray tried jesting about the incident. "Well, we made short shrift of them," he stated ironically.

"That we did," Kestix said. "Er . . . Corporal?"

"Yes, Private?"

"Where exactly do shrifts come from?"

Alfray sighed. "Let's get on, shall we?"

10

Coilla had never spent so much time in the company of humans before. In fact most of her previous experience had to do with killing them.

But being with the bounty hunters for several days made her more aware than ever of their otherworldliness. She had always viewed them as strange, alien creatures, as rapacious interlopers with insatiable appetites for destruction. Now she saw the nuances that underlined the differences between them and the elder races. The way they looked, the way their minds worked, the way they smelt: in so many ways humans were *weird*.

She put the thought aside as they reached the crest of a hill overlooking Hecklowe.

It was dusk, and lights were beginning to dot the freeport. Distance and elevation made it possible to see that the place hadn't so much been planned as simply had happened. As befitted a town where all races met on an equal footing, Hecklowe consisted of a jumble of structures in every conceivable architectural style. Tall buildings, squat buildings, towers, domes, arches and spires cut the skyline. They were made from wood and stone, brick and wattle, thatch and slate. Beyond the town's far edge the grey sea could just be made out in the fading light. Masts of taller ships poked up over the rooftops.

Even from so far away a faint din could be heard.

Lekmann stared down at the port. "It's a while since I been here, but nothing's changed, I reckon. Hecklowe's permanent neutral ground. Don't matter how much you hate a race, in there it's a truce. No brawling, no fights. No settling of scores in a lethal way."

"They kill you for that, don't they?" Blaan said.

"If they catch you."

"Don't they search for weapons on the way in?" Aulay asked.

"Nah. They leave it to you to give 'em up. Searching ain't practical no more since Hecklowe became such a popular place. But if you're fighting in there, it's summary execution by the Watchers. Not that they're as lively as they used to be. They can still do for you, though, so be careful of 'em."

Coilla spoke out. "The Watchers don't work properly because your kind's bleeding the magic."

"Magic," Lekmann sneered. "You sub-humans and your fucking magic. Know what I think? I think it's all horse shit."

"You're surrounded by it. You just can't see it."

"That's enough!"

"If we find them orcs there's gonna be fighting, ain't there?" Blaan said.

"I'm thinking we're just going to stay on their tails until they come out, then move. If we have to face 'em inside, well, we're used to slipping a blade into somebody's ribs on the quiet."

"That sounds like your style," Coilla remarked.

"I told you to shut your face."

Aulay was unconvinced. "This ain't much of a plan, Micah."

"We work with what we got, Greever. Can you think of another way?"

"No."

"No, you can't. Be like Jabeez here, and leave the thinking chores to me. All right?"

"Right, Micah."

Lekmann turned to Coilla. "As for you, you'll behave down there and hold your tongue. "'Les' you want to lose it. Got that?"

She gave him an icy stare.

"Micah," Blaan said.

Lekmann sighed. *"Yes?"*

"Hecklowe's where all the races can go, right?"

"That's right."

"So there could be orcs there."

"I'm banking on it, Jabeez. That's why we're here, remember?" His synthetic patience was wearing thin.

"So if we see orcs, how do we know if they're the ones we're looking for?"

Aulay grinned, displaying rotting teeth. "He's got a point, Micah."

Lekmann obviously hadn't thought that aspect through. Finally he jabbed a thumb at Coilla. "She'll point them out for us."

"Like hell I will."

He leered menacingly at her. "We'll see about that."

"So what do we do about weapons?" Aulay said.

"We'll hand in our swords at the gates, but keep a little something in reserve."

He took a knife from his belt and slipped it into his boot. Blaan and Aulay did the same, only Aulay hid two knives — a dagger in one boot, a thrower in the other.

"When we get down there you'll say nothing," Lekmann repeated to Coilla. "You ain't our prisoner, you're just with us. Got it?"

"You know I'm going to kill you for this, don't you?" she replied evenly.

He tried to laugh that off. But he'd looked into her eyes and his performance was unconvincing. "Let's go," he said, spurring his horse.

They rode down to Hecklowe.

Near the gates, Aulay cut Coilla's bonds and whispered to her, "Try to run and you get a blade in your arse."

There was a small multiracial crowd at the gates, on foot and mounted, and a queue moving past a checkpoint where weapons were being handed in. The bounty hunters and Coilla got in line, and reached the checkpoint before they saw their first Watchers.

They were bipedal, but that was about as much resemblance as they had to flesh-and-blood creatures. Their bodies were solidly built and seemed to consist of a variety of metals. The arms, legs and barrel chests looked something like iron. Bands of burnished copper ran around their wrists and ankles. Another, wider band girdled their waists, and it could have been beaten gold. Where there were joints, at elbows, knees and fingers, silver rivets glistened.

Their heads were fashioned from a substance akin to steel

and were almost completely round. They had large red gems for some kind of eyes, punched-hole "noses" and a slot of a mouth with sharpened metal teeth. On either side of their heads depressed openings acted as ears.

They were of uniform height, standing taller than any of the bounty hunters, and despite the nature of their bodies they moved with surprising suppleness. Yet they did not entirely mimic the motions of an organic lifeform, being given to occasional ungainliness and a tendency to lumber.

Their appearance could only be described as startling.

The humans placed their weapons in a Watcher's outstretched arms and it moved off with them to a fortified gatehouse.

"Homunculi," Coilla mouthed. "Created by sorcery."

Aulay and Blaan exchanged awed glances. Lekmann tried to look casual.

Another Watcher arrived and dropped three wooden tags into Lekmann's palm by way of receipts. Then it waved them into the town.

Lekmann passed out the tags as they walked. "See, told you it was no problem getting a few blades in."

Stuffing his tag into a pocket, Aulay commented, "I thought they might have been a bit more thorough."

"I reckon the so-called Council of Magicians running this place is losing its grip. But if they ain't competent that's good news for us."

They made their way into the bustling streets, leading their horses and carefully keeping Coilla boxed in. Aulay saw to it that he covered her back, the better to deliver his threat.

Hecklowe swarmed with elder races. Gremlins, pixies and dwarves talked, argued, bargained and occasionally laughed together. Little groups of kobolds weaved through the crowd, chattering among themselves in their own unintelligible language. A line of stern-faced gnomes, pickaxes over shoulders, went purposefully about their business. Trolls wearing hoods as protection against the light were led by hired elf guides. Centaurs clopped along the cobbled roads, proudly aloof in the throng. There were even a few humans, though it was noticeable that they were less often to be seen mixing with other races.

"What now, Micah?" Aulay asked.

"We find an inn and work out our strategy."

Blaan beamed. "Ale, good!"

"This ain't no time to be getting all unnecessary, Jabeez," Lekmann warned him. "We need clear heads for what has to be done. Got it?"

The man mountain sulked.

"But let's get these horses stabled first," Lekmann suggested. To Coilla he added, "Don't get no smart ideas."

They worked their way further into the port's teeming thoroughfares. They passed stalls and handcarts brimming with sweetmeats, fish, breads, cheeses, fruit and vegetables. Costermongers sang out the quality of their trays of wares. Merchants pulled stubborn asses laden with bolts of cloth and sacks of spices. Wandering musicians, street performers and vociferous beggars added to the cacophony.

On corners, brazen succubus and incubus whores touted for customers with appetites jaded enough to brave the dangers of going with them. The smell of pellucid sweetened the air. It mingled with incense wafting from the open doors of a myriad of temples dedicated to every known pantheon of gods. Through it all Watchers patrolled, paths miraculously clearing for them in the chaos.

The bounty hunters found a stable run by a gremlin, and for a few coins housed their mounts. They continued on foot, Aulay still close to Coilla.

At one point she thought she glimpsed a couple of orcs, crossing a distant intersection. But a kirgizil dragon and its mean-faced kobold rider blocked her view and she couldn't be sure.

Aulay, she noticed, was fidgeting with his eye-patch. He obviously hadn't seen what she had, but for a moment she wondered if there might not be something in his "orc sense" after all.

She knew there was no reason orcs shouldn't be here, although they were less likely because most of the orc nation was under arms, fighting others' causes. As was their lot. If there were any they could be deserters, which wasn't unknown, or on official business. That might mean they were searching for the renegade Wolverines. The other possibility, of course, was that the two she glimpsed *were* Wolverines. It was too fleeting for her to tell. She decided to be positive and allow herself some small hope.

"This'll do," Lekmann decided.

He pointed to an inn. A coarsely painted wooden sign hung over the door. It read: *The Werebeast and Broadsword.*

The place was jammed with boisterous drinkers.

"Get in there and find us somewhere to sit, Jabeez," Lekmann instructed.

Blaan scanned the interior, then used his mass to barge through the press, the other three in his wake. With the innate instinct of a bully, he zeroed in on a group of pixies and turfed them out.

As soon as the bounty hunters and Coilla sat, an elf serving wench arrived. Lekmann opened his mouth to order. She plonked four pewter tankards of mead down on the table, reciting, "Take it or leave it."

Blaan contemptuously tossed her some coins. She scooped them up and left.

The three humans' heads came together for a hushed, conspiratorial discourse. Coilla leaned back in her chair with folded arms.

"The way I see it, we've got a small problem," Lekmann whispered. "The ideal thing would be to get rid of this bitch first and be done with watching her. But if she's sold we won't have her to pick out the other orcs."

"I told you," Coilla said, "I'm not doing that."

Lekmann bared his teeth and hissed, "We'll *make* you."

"How?"

"Leave it to me, Micah," Aulay offered. "I'll get her to do it."

"Eat shit, one-eye," she responded.

Aulay seethed.

"Look, let's assume this crazy freak *ain't* gonna help us," Lekmann argued. "Which case it might be best if we split up. Me and Jabeez will look for somebody to buy her. You, Greever, can start searching for orcs."

"Then what?"

"We meet back here in a couple of hours and pool stories."

"Fine by me," Aulay said, glaring at Coilla. "I'll be glad to see the back of it."

She took a deep draught of her ale and wiped the back of a hand across her mouth. "Couldn't put it better myself." She slammed her tankard down on Aulay's hand. Hard. There was a loud crack. His face convulsed and he let out an agonised yell.

He stared at his little finger. His face was ashen, his eyes watered. "*She . . . broke . . . it . . .*," he whined through trembling lips. Fury twisting his face, he reached for a boot with his other hand. "*I'm gonna . . . kill you . . .*," he promised.

"Shut up, Greever!" Lekmann snapped. "There's beings watching! You ain't doing nothing to her, she's valuable."

"*But she broke my little . . .*"

"Stop being such a baby. Here." He tossed over a rag. "Wrap this round it and close your trap."

Coilla treated them all to a warm smile. "Well, let's get me sold, shall we?" she purred sweetly.

"It's more of them, isn't it?" Stryke said.

"No doubt of it," Jup confirmed. "Same as at Trinity, and that hunting party."

They were concealed in a thicket, stretched flat and looking down at a camp in a hollow. It was occupied by a party of humans. The rest of the band had been ordered to stay back, out of sight, and from their position Stryke and Jup couldn't see them.

The black-garbed humans undertaking various chores below were all males and numbered around twenty. They were conspicuously and heavily armed. A makeshift corral had been built for their horses, and near the centre of the camp a covered wagon was parked.

"*Shit*, that's all we need," Stryke sighed. "Hobrow's custodians."

"Well, we knew they were likely to be somewhere in the area. We couldn't expect them to give up trying to get back the star we took."

"We could do without it, though. There's enough to worry about."

"Do you reckon they might have Coilla or Haskeer?"

"Who knows? Do you think your farsight might help?"

"It hasn't aided us much so far. But I'll give it a try."

He gouged a hole in the earth with his fingers and wormed a hand into it. Then he concentrated, eyes closed. Stryke held his peace and continued studying the camp.

Eventually Jup opened his eyes and let out a long breath.

"Well?"

"I picked up a faint orc presence, but I'd say it wasn't as close as down there. It's not too far away, though."

"Is that all?"

"Just about. Couldn't tell if it was male or female. Nor the direction. If those bastard humans weren't so keen on eating our magic—"

"Look."

Down in the camp, a figure was climbing from the back of the covered wagon. It was a human female. She was of an age where childhood had been left behind but womanhood had yet to blossom. The lingering puppy fat of youth, along with honey-coloured hair and china blue eyes, should have made her comely. But she wore a sullen, ill-tempered scowl and her mouth was mean.

"Oh, no," Jup groaned.

"What?"

"Mercy Hobrow. The preacher's daughter I told you about."

She moved around the camp with a cavalier gait, yelling at the custodians. They jumped to obey her.

"She's not much more than a hatchling," Stryke said. "Yet she's obviously issuing orders."

"Tyrants are often distrustful. They'd prefer to use a member of their family rather than rely on outsiders. And it looks like he's groomed his spawn well."

"Yes, but leaving a . . . *child* in command?"

"Humans are all fucking mad, Stryke, you know that."

Now the girl was laying about the custodians with a swish.

"Have those men no pride?" Stryke wondered.

"No doubt fear of her father is the stronger emotion. But you're right about the error of giving her authority; they haven't even put out any guards."

Stryke whispered, "Don't speak too soon."

Jup made to say something. Stryke clamped a hand over his mouth and moved the dwarf's head to face to their right. Two custodians were walking slowly toward their hiding place, swords drawn. Stryke removed his hand.

"They haven't seen us," Jup said.

"No. But if they carry on this way they will, or they'll see the band."

"We've got to take them out."

"Right, and without alerting the others. Feel like being bait?"

Jup smiled wryly. "Do I have a choice?"

Stryke glanced at the approaching sentries. "Just give me enough time to get in position." He snaked into the bushes, moving in the direction of the nearing sentries.

Jup counted to fifty in his head. Then he stood up and stepped out into the path of the sentries.

They froze, surprise on their faces.

He moved their way, hands well out from his sides, clear of his weapons. He added to their confusion by smiling.

One of the custodians barked, "Stay where you are!"

Jup kept coming and kept smiling.

The sentries raised their swords. Behind them, Stryke quietly emerged from the undergrowth, a dagger in his hand.

The custodian bellowed again. "Identify yourself!"

"I'm a *dwarf*," Jup replied.

Stryke piled into them from the rear. Jup ran forward, drawing his own knife.

The four of them went down in a scrum of twisting limbs and flying fists. A few seconds of struggling sorted them into two separate fights. But the custodian's swords were second-best at close quarters. Armed with knives, Jup and Stryke had the advantage.

Jup's kill was quick. He saw the way clear to his opponent's heart and took it. One blow was enough.

Stryke had more of a task. In the clash he lost his knife. Then his rival managed to get himself on top. He clutched his sword two-handed and made to bring it down like a dagger to Stryke's chest. Stryke had hold of his forearms and pushed back. The stalemate was broken when he somehow found the strength to topple the human. A brief tussle for the sword was won by Stryke. He planted it in the custodian's guts.

"Quick, let's get their bodies out of sight," Stryke ordered.

They were pulling the corpses into the undergrowth when three more sentries appeared from the opposite direction.

Jup swiftly whipped up his knife and lobbed it at one of them. The human took it in the midriff and hit the ground. His companions charged.

Orc and dwarf met them with drawn swords and they paired off to fence.

Aware of drawing attention from the camp, Stryke tried to end his foe as fast as possible. He went at the human furiously, pouring blows on him, and ducked and weaved to find an opening. The sheer force of his assault reduced the man's defence to tatters. With a hefty swing, Stryke cleaved his neck.

Adopting similar tactics, Jup's style was unsubtle frenzy. The custodian he faced parried the first half dozen blows, then flagged. Backing off, he started shouting. Jup moved in quickly and whacked him in the mouth with the flat of his blade. That put a stop to both the yelling and the human's guard. A follow-through to his stomach settled the issue.

Stryke padded to the bushes and peered down at the camp. His fear that the shouts might have been heard proved unfounded. With Jup's help, the bodies were concealed.

"What happens when they don't report back?" the dwarf panted.

"Let's not be here to find out."

"So where to?"

"The only direction we haven't tried—due east."

"That takes us dangerously near to Cairnbarrow."

"I know. Got a better plan?"

Jup slowly shook his head.

"Then let's do it."

It was half a day of hard riding before Jup said it. "Stryke, this is useless. There's just too much land to cover."

"We don't give up on our comrades. We're orcs."

"Well, not *all* of us," the dwarf reminded him, "but I'll take being included as a compliment."

His captain gave a tired smile. "You're a Wolverine. I tend to forget your race."

"It might be better for Maras-Dantia if more of us had such a poor memory in that respect."

"Perhaps. But like I said, one thing we can't forget is members of our band, whoever they are, whatever they've done."

"I'm not saying we should abandon them, for the gods' sake. It just seems so futile going about it this way."

"You've come up with another plan?"

"You know I haven't."

"Then whinging serves little purpose." It was said harshly. Stryke moderated his tone when adding, "We'll keep looking."

"What about Cairnbarrow? We're getting nearer all the time."

"And we'll get closer yet before I think of giving up."

A pall of silence fell over them as they continued their eastward trek.

Eventually they saw a rider galloping toward them from the direction they were heading.

Jup identified him. "It's Seafe."

Stryke halted the column.

Seafe arrived, pulling hard on the reins of his lathering horse. "Forward scout reporting, sir!"

Stryke nodded.

"We've found him, Captain! Sergeant Haskeer!"

"*What?* Where?"

"Mile or two north. But he's not alone."

"Don't tell me. Hobrow's men."

"Yes, sir."

"How many of them?" Jup said.

"Hard to tell, Sergeant. Twenty, thirty."

"And Hobrow himself?" Stryke asked.

"He's there."

"Any sign of Coilla?"

"Not that we could see. I left Talag keeping an eye on them."

"All right. Well done, Seafe." He turned and waved in the

band. "Seems we've found Sergeant Haskeer," he relayed. "But he's being held by Hobrow's Unis. Seafe's going to lead us there. Be ready, and approach with stealth. Let's go, Seafe."

In due course they came to a ridge beyond which, Seafe explained, the terrain swept into a dip.

"I reckon it'd be better to dismount here and lead the horses, sir," he suggested.

Stryke agreed and issued the order. They climbed quietly to an arrow's shot away from the top of the rise.

"Guards?" Stryke said.

"A few," Seafe confirmed.

"That's our first priority, then." What went through Stryke's mind was how much harder it was operating with half a band. He summoned Hystykk, Calthmon, Gant and Finje. "Find the sentries and deal with them," he ordered. "Then get yourselves back here."

As they moved off, Jup said, "Think four's enough?"

"I hope so. It's all we can spare." He collared a trooper. "Stay here with the horses, Reafdaw. When the others have finished with the guards, send them up."

"We'll be at the foot of that," Seafe told Reafdaw, pointing to a particularly tall, gaunt tree that could just be seen above the rise. Reafdaw nodded.

Seafe led Stryke, Jup, Breggin, Toche and Jad up the rise. A pitiably small crew, Stryke reflected.

They reached the crest and found themselves looking down into a lightly wooded area. Keeping low they got to Talag, stretched out beneath the tall tree. He signed for them to focus on a gap in the greenery.

Through it, they saw a clearing where trees were dotted much more sparsely. A temporary camp had been set up, with two dozen or more custodians moving about it. To one side stood a horseless buggy. Its shafts rested on a couple of downed tree trunks.

"Where's Haskeer?" Stryke whispered.

"Yonder," Talag replied, indicating an area to the left where trees blinded the view.

They stayed in position for a good ten minutes, waiting for

something significant to happen below. Then the other orcs returned. Gant gave the thumbs-up sign.

"Sure you got them all?" Stryke said.

"We covered the whole circuit, sir. If there were others, they were well hidden."

"Well, they won't be missed for long. Anything we do has to be soon. Are you sure you saw Haskeer down there, Seafe?"

"I'm sure, chief. Couldn't mistake his ugly puss." Hurriedly he added, "No offence, sir."

Stryke smiled thinly. "That's all right, trooper. I think we know what you mean."

More empty time passed. They were starting to get jumpy when there was a commotion below. Some kind of movement could be seen through the trees. The orcs tensed.

Kimball Hobrow appeared, straight-backed, striding purposefully. He was shouting, but they couldn't make out the words. Following him was a jeering mob of his black-costumed custodians.

They were frog-marching Haskeer.

His hands were tied behind his back and he staggered more than walked. Even from a distance it was obvious he'd been ill treated.

They took him to the middle of the clearing, by a high tree. A horse was brought over. The crowd hoisted him on to it.

Jup was puzzled. "They're not going to let him go, surely?"

Stryke shook his head. "No way."

One of the humans produced a noosed rope and slipped it over Haskeer's head. The rope was secured around his neck and the other end tossed over a projecting bough. Eager hands pulled it taut.

"If we leave it another minute," Jup whispered, "we'll be watching a lynching."

11

Stryke watched as the braying mob prepared for Haskeer's hanging.

"I wouldn't have your job at a time like this, chief," Jup told him.

Down below, Hobrow climbed on to his buggy and stood on the seat. He raised his arms. The mob fell silent. "The Supreme Creator has seen fit to return our holy relic!" he boomed. "More than that, He has gifted us another!"

"They've got the stars," Stryke said.

"And in His boundless wisdom, the Lord has also delivered to our justice one of the ungodly creatures who stole our birth-right!" Hobrow pointed an accusing finger at Haskeer. "And today we have the sacred task of putting the sub-human to death!"

"Fuck that!" Stryke exclaimed. "If anybody's going to kill Haskeer, it's me." As Hobrow ranted on, he beckoned over one of the grunts. "You're the best archer we've got, Breggin. Could you hit that rope from here?"

Breggin squinted and studied the target. He sucked a finger and held it up. His tongue poked from the corner of his mouth as he concentrated. Frowning, he considered the wind speed, angle of trajectory and force required to loose the shaft.

"No," he said.

". . . as we shall smite all our enemies with the aid of the Lord God Almighty, and . . ."

Stryke took another tack. "All right, Breggin. Take Seafe, Gant and Calthmon and get Reafdaw up here with the horses. *On the double!*"

The grunt scurried off.

"We're going in?" Jup asked.

"We've no choice." He nodded toward the clearing. "Assuming they don't kill Haskeer first."

"If they're waiting for that windbag to stop talking we might have time yet."

". . . to His everlasting glory! Behold the Lord's bounty!" Hobrow produced a small hessian sack and brought the stars out of it. He held them aloft and his followers roared.

Jup and Stryke looked at each other.

". . . He moves in mysterious ways, brethren, His wonders to perform! Praise Him, and send this creature's soul straight to perdition!"

Haskeer seemed only vaguely aware of what was going on.

Stryke glanced around. "They'd better hurry with those horses."

Hobrow sliced his arm downward. Haskeer's horse was struck on the flank with a whip. It bolted.

The grunts returned at a run, leading the horses.

Haskeer was suspended, feet kicking.

"Mount up!" Stryke barked. "I'm going for Haskeer. Jup, you'll back me. The rest of you, kill some Unis!"

He rode full pelt through the trees with the band following.

They ducked forks and swishing branches as they rushed down the incline. They weaved around tree trunks. They goaded their mounts to greater speed.

Then exploded into the clearing.

The custodians outnumbered them perhaps three to one. But the orcs were mounted and had the element of surprise. They charged into the mob and laid about them. Shocked by the unexpected attack, the humans' response was a shambles.

Haskeer squirmed and twisted on the end of the rope. Stryke fought desperately to get to him, Jup lashing out wildly at his side.

A howling wedge of humans came between their horses and separated them. Jup's spooked mount turned in the flow and fetched up at a right angle in a sea of hostile blades. Cutting at them like a scythe against wheat, he fought desperately to right himself.

Stryke stayed on course but met just as much resistance. He ploughed into them with the horse, kicked out with his boots, pummelled their swords with his blade. A custodian leapt up and grabbed his belt, and tried pulling him from the saddle. Stryke cracked his skull and sent him flying back into the throng.

Above the clamour, Hobrow could be heard screaming curses and loudly invoking the name of his god.

Battling on, Stryke caught sight of two of the grunts ploughing into the back of the mob surrounding him. The diversion drew away enough custodians to give him a fighting chance of reaching Haskeer. Only a pair of humans barred his way. He despatched the first with a downward swipe that hewed his throat. The second he hacked in the face. He fell, hands to the flowing gash.

Finally getting to Haskeer, Stryke found he'd stopped struggling and was hanging limply. It looked as if it was too late.

Suddenly Jup arrived. He manoeuvred his horse beneath Haskeer's dangling feet and seized his legs. "Hurry, Stryke!" he yelled.

Stryke stood in his stirrups and slashed through the rope. Jup gasped as he took the orc's apparently dead weight. Between them, awkwardly and very nearly unsuccessfully, Jup and Stryke got Haskeer over the dwarf's horse.

"Get him clear!" Stryke hollered.

Jup nodded and started to move off. A custodian blocked his way, waving his arms in an attempt to panic the horse. Jup rode him down. Then he headed for the treeline, taking a serpentine route in the hope of avoiding scattered humans.

Members of the band were embroiled in actions all over the clearing. Stryke looked towards the buggy. A couple of custodians stood there, trying to protect Hobrow. He was still shouting orders and hurling oaths. The sack was clutched in his hand.

Stryke decided to go for it.

He spurred his horse, but got only a short way before three custodians blocked his path. Stryke had enough speed up that he simply galloped by the first, who slashed at him ineffectually as he passed. The other two, further along, were more artful. They rushed in at him from either side. One directed an axe blow at Stryke's leg. It narrowly missed. The other leapt, intending to unhorse him. He was still in the air when Stryke's thrusting elbow met him on the bridge of his nose. The man spiralled away. Stryke resumed the dash.

In the greater mêlée, Seafe was pulled from his horse. He stood his ground against three or four encroaching custodians. Then Calthmon bowled into them and managed to haul Seafe on to his own mount.

Hobrow saw Stryke approaching and cowered, shouting for his pair of defenders to protect him. Almost immediately one of them was cut down by a passing orc. Stryke thundered in and buried his blade in the other's skull. But the victim went down with the embedded sword and it was lost.

Stryke wheeled about to face Hobrow. By now the preacher was gibbering. Stryke whipped his reins around one of the buggy's shafts and jumped, rocking the carriage as he landed. Unable to escape, Hobrow pressed himself into the seat and squirmed. Stryke grabbed a handful of his coat, pulled him to his feet and commenced battering him. His hat flew off, his face bloodied, but he held on to the sack.

A gang of custodians was running their way. Stryke increased the lathering and prised free the sack. Hobrow went down. He was still alive, much to Stryke's regret. But there was no time to rectify that now. He hastily remounted and pulled away as the first wave of would-be rescuers swept in.

Breggin and Gant had managed to loose the humans' horses and stampeded them. Several custodians tried to stem the bolting animals and were horribly trampled. The horses ran on to spread further chaos.

Stuffing the sack into his jerkin, Stryke bawled the order to retreat.

The Wolverines disengaged and began to move out. Where they could, they struck down the enemy as they left.

Into the trees and climbing the slope, Stryke spotted Jup ahead. He caught up with him. Haskeer was semi-conscious, his head rolling from side to side, and breathing shallowly. They came out of the trees and made the crest of the rise, the remainder of the band close behind. Stryke quickly checked. All were present.

Several loose custodians' horses also emerged from the dip and ran off in different directions.

"That should keep 'em busy!" Jup shouted.

"Look!" a grunt yelled.

From the south, another group of black-garbed humans was riding hard their way. At the rear was a covered wagon.

"Mercy's group," Stryke said.

Some of them made for the rise. Others started after the Wolverines.

Stryke spurred his mount and led the band across the plain.

Evening wasn't far off. A chill wind blew in from the great northern ice field. It grew even colder.

Alfray's half of the Wolverines was making good progress in its journey to Drogan. Good enough that when they came to a tributary that flowed inland from the Calyparr Inlet before taking a great loop back, he decided to make early camp on its bank. He reasoned they could start out again before first light.

When the band petitioned for a ration of pellucid, he reasoned further that it would do no harm. They deserved it. But just a little; they were still a fighting unit and, after all, the crystal was meant for bartering.

A cob or two of the drug was imbibed. Then Alfray and Kestix fell into what passed, in orc terms, for a philosophical discussion.

"I'm just a simple soldier, Corporal," the grunt said, "but it seems to me that no one could ask for better gods than ours. What need is there for others?"

"Ah, how much easier things would be if everybody agreed with us," Alfray replied, not entirely seriously.

Kestix saw no irony. Voice a little slurred and eyes glassy from the crystal, he pressed the issue. "I mean, when you've got the Square, what more could you want?"

"It's always seemed enough for me," Alfray agreed. "Which one of the Tetrad do you favour most?"

"Favour most?" Kestix looked as though no one had ever asked him the question before. "Well, the way I look at it, there's not much to choose between them." He thought for a moment. "Maybe Aik. Everybody likes the god of wine, don't they?"

"What about Zeenoth?"

"The goddess of fornication?" Kestix smirked like a hatchling. "She's worthy of glorifying, know what I mean?" He gave Alfray a lewd wink.

"And Neaphetar?"

"He'd have to be the one, wouldn't he? God of war and all that. He's the name on *my* lips when we go in for a fight. Boss orc, Neaphetar."

"You don't think him cruel?"

"Oh, he's cruel, yeah. But just." He stared vacantly at Alfray for a second, then asked, "Who's your favourite, Corp?"

"Wystendel, I think. The god of comradeship. I enjoy combat. *Course* I do, I'm an orc. But sometimes I think the camaraderie of a good band's the best of our lot."

"Anyway, I reckon the Square's got it right. Fighting, fucking, feasting. Rude and rowdy. That's how gods *should* be."

A grunt passed him a pipe. He sucked on it, his cheeks hollowing as the smoke went down. Pungent vapour billowed from the bowl. Kestix handed the cob to Alfray.

"What I don't understand," the grunt went on, "is this gassion, er, passion . . . this passion for a single pod. Shit! *God*. For a single god."

"It does seem a strange notion," Alfray allowed. "But then humans aren't short of crazed ideas."

"Yeah, I mean, how can *one* god handle everything all by himself? That's a team effort, surely?"

The pipe had Alfray comfort conscious. It set him ruminating. "You know, before the humans came, races used to be a damn sight more tolerant of each other's beliefs," he slurred. "Now everybody's trying to ram their religion down your throat."

Kestix nodded sagely. "The incomers have a lot to answer for. They've caused such ructions."

"Still, you've made me think that we haven't paid enough attention to our gods lately. Reckon I'll sacrifice to 'em soon as I get the chance."

They slipped into silence, each lost in his own kaleidoscopic mind theatre. The rest of the band slumped too, though there was a measure of horseplay and chuckling.

An indefinite amount of time passed. Then Kestix sat up. "Corporal."

"Hmmm?"

"What do you think that is?"

Creamy mist was rising from the rivulet. Through it, from the direction of the inlet, a vessel approached.

Alfray roused the band. Somewhat unsteadily, and grumbling, they lurched to their feet and armed themselves.

The tendrils of smog parted.

A barge glided majestically towards them. Low in the water, it was wide, its sides almost touching the banks. There was a spacious deck cabin astern. A carved figurehead in the likeness of a dove stood at the prow. The craft's single canvas sail rippled and crackled in the evening breeze.

When the barge was near enough for its crew to be seen, a groan went up from the band.

"Oh, no," Kestix sighed. "Just what we need."

"At least they're not life-threatening," Alfray reminded him.

"Bloody aggravating, though, sir."

"No need to kill unless you have to," Alfray told the grunts. "The only magic they've got is for moving themselves about, so that's no real threat. Hang on to anything of value."

He thought of simply ordering a speedy retreat. But that meant leaving behind possessions to be looted, and chances were that those on the barge would only follow them until their notorious curiosity was satisfied. Which could amount to being dogged for days. Better to get it over with and weather the squall.

"Perhaps they'll just go by," Kestix said, more in hope than expectation.

"I don't think that's in their nature, trooper."

"But we're *orcs.* Don't they know it's *dangerous* tangling with us?"

"Probably not; they aren't very bright. But remember it won't go on for ever. We can wait it out."

The barge's sail dropped. An anchor splashed.

Then a couple of dozen diminutive figures rose from the deck like balloons and headed for the orcs. It wasn't so much flying as directional floating. They pointed themselves the way they wanted to go, languidly flapped their stumpy little arms, and slowly glided.

They looked a bit like human or dwarf babies. Alfray knew they weren't. Some of them were probably older than he was, and all of them were well versed in thieving ways. But he reckoned it was their resemblance to young helpless lifeforms that prevented many more of them being slaughtered by irate travellers.

The imps had large heads and big, round eyes that would have been appealing but for their wicked glints. They were pink-skinned and hairless, save for short, wispy down on their heads. Their sex was undefined. They wore tanned hide loincloths not unlike shiny black diapers, ringed with cloth pouches. Imps did not bear arms.

As they floated, they babbled. High-pitched, unintelligible, annoying.

A cluster of the creatures arrived overhead. Then they swooped, and suddenly they weren't so indolent.

They descended on the band's heads, shoulders and arms. Tenaciously clinging to the orcs' clothes, their prying fingers scrabbled to filch anything they could find in pockets and pouches. They tried prising away weapons and trophy neck-laces. Petite hands snatched grunts' helmets.

Alfray grabbed and shook one of the miniature pilferers to disengage it from his jerkin. It was surprisingly hard work. When he got it loose he shoved it away forcefully. The imp sailed off, spinning on its axis.

More and more of them disgorged from the barge and col-lected over the band like winsome vultures. As an orc disentan-gled himself from one imp another dropped and took its place.

Swatting at an assailant with the back of his hand, Alfray yelled, "How do they get this many on a damn little boat like that?"

Kestix would have answered, except one of the creatures was tweaking his nose in its tiny fist. Its other hand was delving into the grunt's belt pouch. With an effort, Kestix pulled the imp off and flung it from him. It coasted into a hovering knot of its fel-lows, scattering them like slow-motion skittles.

As Alfray peeled away an imp hugging his chest, a grunt hopped past with one clutching his leg. He was kicking furi-ously in an attempt to shake it free.

But every so often evidence of Maras-Dantia's failing magic was apparent when an imp plummeted and landed hard on the ground. Bouts of frantic arm-waving were needed to get them unsteadily aloft again. Alfray figured this happened because the imps passed over weakened lines of energy that broke the spell. Unfortunately it didn't down enough of them.

Still they rained down, anchoring themselves on any unoccupied parts of their victims. Orcs booted them aside, elbowed them, ripped them from clothes and threw them clear. Alfray saw a grunt holding an imp by an arm and a leg. He spun around several times and let go. Thumb planted in its mouth, the imp shot towards the barge in a great arc.

Alfray started to worry that the grunts would lose patience and start killing the pests. "Get rope!" he bellowed, batting an imp from his face. "*Rope!*"

It was an order easier issued than obeyed. Bent double, a couple of grunts made for the horses, hands over their heads to fend off dive-bombing imps. With difficulty, they managed to retrieve a length of rope.

"Take ends and spread out with it!" Alfray shouted. As they battled to do that he drew his sword. "Present weapons! Use the flats to round them up!"

An awkward struggle ensued, with grunts doing their best to shed imps and corral them together. It took a lot of bottom-whacking and bullying, but after about ten frustrating minutes most of the bleating creatures were bunched. Some rose above the cluster, but there was nothing to be done about them.

Alfray barked an order. The grunts with the rope encircled the mass of imps with it. A couple of tugs and a hastily tied knot secured the bond.

Under Alfray's direction the band hauled the living load back to the barge. The rope was tied to the mast and the anchor brought up. They raised the sail. It caught the wind and billowed. With a helping push from all hands, the craft moved off, gathering speed.

Struggling ineffectually, the restrained imps squealed as the barge was swallowed by mist. A handful of stragglers flew after it.

Alfray expelled a breath as he watched it go. He ran the back of a hand across his forehead. "I hope Stryke's having a better time of it," he said.

Hobrow's men didn't pursue Stryke's group for long, so at the earliest opportunity he halted the band.

Haskeer was helped down from Jup's horse and his bonds were cut. He was conscious but largely insensible. They sat him down and gave him water, which he had trouble swallowing. His neck bore vivid rope burns.

"I wish Alfray was here," Stryke said as he examined Haskeer's injuries. "He's taken quite a battering, but I'd say there's no major damage."

"Except maybe to his brain," Jup returned. "Don't forget why he's in this state in the first place."

"I haven't." He slapped Haskeer's cheeks several times. "Haskeer!"

That brought him round a bit, but not enough. Stryke took the water canteen and poured its contents over Haskeer's head. The liquid streamed down his face. His eyes opened. He mumbled something they couldn't understand.

Stryke slapped him some more. "Haskeer! *Haskeer!*"

"Hmm? Wha—?"

"It's me. Stryke. Can you hear me?"

Haskeer responded weakly. "Stryke?"

"What the hell you been playing at, Sergeant?"

"Playing . . . ?"

Stryke shook him, not far short of violently. "Come on! Snap out of it!"

Haskeer succeeded in focusing. "Captain . . . what . . . what's happening?" He seemed totally bewildered.

"What's happening is that you're a fairy's breath away from a charge of desertion. Not to mention trying to kill other band members."

"*Kill* . . . ? Stryke, I swear—"

"Forget swearing, just explain yourself."

"Who am I supposed to have tried killing?"

"Coilla and Reafdaw."

Angrily, Haskeer snapped, "What do you think I am, a . . . a . . . *human?*"

"You did it, Haskeer. I want to know why."

"I . . . I can't . . . I don't *remember.*" He looked around, still dazed. Jup and the grunts were staring at him. "Where are we?"

"Never mind. Are you saying you don't know what's been going on? That you're not responsible?"

Haskeer slowly shook his head.

"All right. What *do* you remember?" Stryke persisted. "What was the last thing?"

Haskeer set to thinking. It was obviously an effort. Eventually he said, "The battlefield. We went through it. Then . . . dragons. Dragons chasing us. Fire."

"That's all?"

"The singing . . ."

"Singing? What do you mean?"

"There was . . . not singing exactly. A sort of music and words, but not singing."

Stryke and Jup exchanged glances. Jup raised his eyebrows meaningfully.

"This sound, whatever it was . . ." He gave up. "I don't know. Only other thing I remember was being sick. I felt bad."

"That's something you never let on about," Jup said, his tone accusing.

At one time Haskeer would have lashed out at the dwarf for a comment like that, for less, but now he just stared at him.

"Alfray thought you'd picked up a human disease from that orc encampment we torched," Stryke told him. "But I don't think that was enough in itself to explain your behaviour."

"*What* behaviour, Stryke? You still haven't told me what I'm supposed to have done."

"We were at Scratch. You attacked Reafdaw and Coilla, and made off with these." He reached into the sack taken from Hobrow and showed him the pair of stars.

Haskeer glazed over at the sight of them. He whispered, "Take them away, Stryke." Then yelled, "*Take 'em away!*"

Puzzled, Stryke put them in his belt pouch, where he already had the star from Scratch.

"Take it easy," Jup told Haskeer, near gently.

There was a sheen of sweat on Haskeer's forehead. He was breathing heavily.

"Coilla took off after you," Stryke continued. "We don't know where she is. Do you know what happened to her?"

"I told you, I don't know anything." He put his face in his hands. Just before he did, Stryke thought he looked frightened.

He and Jup moved away from him. Stryke nodded to a couple of the grunts. They went to keep an eye on Haskeer.

"What do you think, chief?"

"I don't know. He seems to be saying he had some kind of blackout. Maybe he's telling the truth, maybe not."

"I reckon he is."

"Why?"

"Nobody knows better than me what a bastard Haskeer is. But he isn't a deserter and, I don't know, call it my sixth sense, but something tells me that what happened was . . . beyond his control."

"Given the history you two have, I'm surprised to hear you say that."

"It's what I think. Not giving him the benefit of the doubt's answering injustice with injustice far as I can see."

"Even if what you say is true, and he was under the influence of the fever or whatever, how do we know it won't happen again? How can we trust him?"

"Think on this, Stryke. If you decide he can't be trusted, where does that leave us? What do we do? Abandon him? Cut his throat? Is that the way you want to run this band?"

"I need to think on it. And I have to decide what to do about Coilla."

"Don't delay, Captain. You know how short time is." He pulled his jerkin closer against a wind that had grown piercing. "The weather doesn't seem of a mind to be helpful either."

As he spoke, a scattering of snowflakes mixed with the wind.

"Snow," Stryke said. "In this season. The world's broken, Jup."

"Ah, and it might be beyond fixing, Captain."

12

Jennesta spelt it out. "I'm offering you an alliance, Adpar. Help me find the artifacts and I'll share their power with you."

The face on the surface of the congealed blood was impassive.

"It's only a matter of time before Sanara butts in on this," Jennesta added impatiently. "So will you *say* something?"

"She doesn't always. Or doesn't choose to take part. Anyway, to hell with Sanara; I don't mind saying this in front of her. No."

"Why?"

"I have more than enough to deal with here. And unlike you, my dear, I have no ambitions to build a bigger empire."

"The *biggest*, Adpar! Big enough for both of us! Power enough for both!"

"I have a feeling that sharing, even with your beloved sister, would prove something you couldn't manage for long."

"Then what about the gods?"

"What about them?"

"Plumbing the mysteries of the instrumentalities could restore our gods, the true gods, and see off this absurd lone deity the humans have brought."

"The gods are real enough here; they need no restoring."

"Fool! The taint will reach even you sooner or later, if it hasn't already."

"Frankly, Jennesta, the notion just doesn't appeal. I don't trust you. Anyway, are you capable of . . . 'plumbing the mysteries'?" It was meant insultingly.

"So you're going for them yourself, is that it?"

"Don't judge everybody by your own standards."

"You don't know what you're turning your snooty nose up at!"

"At least it's my nose, and not indentured to anybody else."

Jennesta fought to keep her temper in check. "All right. If you're not interested in joining me and you say you make no claim on the instrumentalities for yourself, why not trade me the one you have? I'd pay substantially for it."

"I don't have one! How many more times? It's gone!"

"You let somebody take something from you? I find that hard to believe."

"The thief was punished. He was lucky to escape with his life."

"You didn't even kill this convenient robber?" Jennesta mocked. "You're going soft, sister."

"Your stupidity I'm used to, Jennesta. What I can't stand is how boring you can be."

"If you ignore my offer you'll regret it."

"Will I? And who's going to make me? You? You could never best me when we were youngsters, Jennesta, and you can't do it now."

Jennesta seethed. "This is your last chance, Adpar. I won't ask again."

"If you want me so much you must need me. I take pleasure from that. But I don't take kindly to ultimatums, whoever issues them. I'll do nothing to hinder you, and nothing to help either. Now leave me alone."

This time it was Adpar who terminated the conversation.

Jennesta sat in deep thought for several minutes. She came out of it with resolve.

Dragging aside a heavy, ornate chair and pulling back several rugs, she revealed the flagstone floor. From a cabinet in a darkened corner she selected a particular grimoire, and on her way back to the cleared space plucked a curved dagger from the altar. These she deposited on the chair.

Having lit more candles, Jennesta skimmed handfuls of clotted gore from the tub. On hands and knees, she used it to mark out a large mullet on the floor, carefully ensuring that there were no breaks in the circle or its five-pointed star. That done, she took up the book and knife, and moved to the circle's centre.

She peeled back the sleeve of her gown and with a swift, deep slash of the blade cut into her arm. Her lighter blood dripped and mingled with the darker red of the pentagram. It intensified the link with her sibling.

Then she turned to the book and began something she should have done long ago.

Adpar enjoyed thwarting her sister. It was one of life's more sublime pleasures. But now she had a routine chore to attend to, though in its way it was no less gratifying.

She left the slime-encrusted viewing pool and waded from her private retreat to the larger chamber beyond. A lieutenant awaited her, along with a guard detail and two disgraced members of her swarm.

"The prisoners, Majesty," the lieutenant hissed in peculiarly nyadd fashion.

She looked over the accused. They hung their scaly heads.

Without preamble, Adpar outlined the charge. "You two have brought shame on the imperial swarm. That means shame on *me*. You were lax in carrying out your orders in the recent raid, and were seen by a superior officer to let several merz escape with their lives. Do you have anything to say in your defence?"

They didn't.

"Very well," she went on, "I take your silence as admission of dereliction. It should be well known that I'll not have weaklings in the ranks. We are fighting to keep our place in this world, and that leaves no room for idlers or cowards. Therefore the only possible verdict is guilty." A believer in the power of theatrics, she paused for effect. "And the penalty is death."

She beckoned the lieutenant. He came forward holding a basin-sized brown and white shell containing two coral daggers. A pair of guards followed him carrying deep, wide-mouthed earthenware pots.

"In accordance with tradition, and as a courtesy to your martial status, you are allowed a choice," Adpar told the condemned. She pointed to the knives. "Carry out the sentence with your own hand and you will die with a measure of honour." Her gaze flicked to the containers. "Or you have the right to place your fate in the hands of the gods. If they will it, you could keep your life."

Turning to the first prisoner, she commanded, "Choose."

The nyadd tensely weighed his options. Finally he uttered, "The gods, Majesty."

"So be it."

At her signal, several more guards moved in and held him firm. One of the pots was brought to her. She stared into it, one hand poised completely still above the opening. She stood that way for what seemed an eternity. Then suddenly her hand darted into the jar and she pulled something from the water.

It was a fish. She held it by the tail between two fingers and her thumb as it writhed and struggled in the air. The fish was about as long as a nyadd's hand and its girth equal to three arrows bound together. Its scales and stubby fins were silvery blue. Whiskers grew from either side of its mouth.

Handling it with care, Adpar tapped the fish's side and quickly withdrew her finger. Dozens of tiny quivering spikes shot out from its body.

"I envy the dowelfish," she stated. "It has no predators. Its spikes are not only sharp, they pump a lethal venom that kills with excruciating pain. The fish gives its own life but always takes its enemy's." She dipped the animal back into the pot, immersing it in water but keeping hold of it. "Prepare him," she ordered.

The guards forced the prisoner to his knees. A length of thread was passed to Adpar and she looped it around the dowelfish's back fin. Using the thread, she slowly pulled the fish from its pot again. Calmed by the water, it had retracted its spikes.

"Offer yourself to the gods' mercy," Adpar told the prisoner. "If they favour you three times, you'll be spared."

The accused's head was roughly pushed upwards and his mouth prised open to its fullest extent. He was held in position. Adpar approached, holding out the dangling fish. Very slowly, she lowered it into the nyadd's gaping mouth. He stayed absolutely motionless. The scene was not unlike the displays put on by sword-swallowers in marketplaces all over Maras-Dantia. Except that was a trick.

Everybody watched in silence as the fish disappeared from sight. Adpar paused for a second before continuing to play out the thread, guiding its load down the nyadd's gullet. At length she stopped. Then the process was reversed and she began winding the thread around a finger as she reeled the fish up. It emerged from the nyadd's mouth wriggling feebly.

The prisoner let out a shuddering breath.

"It seems the gods have smiled on you once," Adpar declared.

The fish was immersed in its jar once more and brought back for the second time. Again it was lowered at a leisurely pace, again she paused before its journey down the throat, again she wound the thread. In due course the dowelfish came out of the mouth without causing harm.

Shaking and gasping, the accused looked near collapse.

"Our gods are benign today," Adpar said. "So far."

A last return to the water and the apparently pacified fish was ready for the third trial. Adpar went through exactly the same routine. The point was reached where she stayed her hand before lowering the fish into the nyadd's craw. She began unwinding the twine.

The thread trembled. A shudder ran through the prisoner. Eyes wide, he took to retching, and struggled against the guards. The thread snapped. Adpar stood back and motioned for the guards to release him. They let go and involuntarily his mouth snapped shut.

Then he started screaming.

Hands clawing at his throat and chest, he rolled and contorted. Spasms racked his body, green bile erupted from his mouth. He shrieked and contorted.

The death throes lasted an unconscionable amount of time. They were terrible to witness.

When silence returned and the prisoner was still, Adpar spoke. "The gods' will has been done. They have called him to them. It is fitting."

She turned to the second quaking prisoner. The other pot and the knives were offered. Without a word he took a knife. The carapace at his throat meant the jagged blade had to be forcefully applied several times. At length a crimson spray marked his success.

At a wave of Adpar's hand the guard detail set to removing the bodies.

"We are fortunate that our culture is ruled by divine justice and compassion," she proclaimed. "Other realms are less benevolently governed. Why, I myself have a sister who would have *gloated* over a scene like this."

The snowfall was heavier, the sky black.

Much as he wanted to push on, Stryke had to concede that travel was impossible. He ordered the column to halt. There being no natural shelter, the band built a fire, which fought the snow and wind to burn. They huddled round it miserably, swathed in horse blankets.

Jup had used some of Alfray's salves to treat Haskeer's wounds. Now Haskeer sat in silence, staring at the meagre flames. Nobody else felt much like talking either.

The hours passed and the blizzard was constant. Despite the weather, some of the band managed to drowse.

Then something loomed out of the snow.

It was a tall figure mounted on a handsome white horse. As it drew closer they saw the figure was human.

The band leapt up and went for their weapons.

Now they could make out that the human male was wrapped in a dark blue cloak. He had shoulder-length hair and was bearded. His age was hard to reckon.

"There might be more of them!" Stryke yelled. "Stand ready!"

"I'm alone and unarmed," the human called out, his voice calm. "And with your leave I'll dismount."

Stryke glanced about, but saw nothing else moving in the snow. "All right," he agreed. "Do it slowly."

The stranger dismounted. He held out his hands to show he had no blade. Stryke ordered Talag and Finje to search him. That done, they brought him forward. Reafdaw took charge of his horse, winding its reins around a withered tree stump. The eyes of the band flicked in turn from the surrounding whited-out terrain to this tall, unruffled human who had arrived in their midst.

"Who are you, human?" Stryke demanded. "What do you want?"

"I am Serapheim. I saw your fire. All I want is warmth."

"It's dangerous riding into a camp uninvited these days. How do you know we won't kill you?"

"I trust in the chivalry of orcs." He glanced at Jup. "And of those they ally with."

"What are you, Mani or Uni?" the dwarf said.

"Not all humans are either."

"Huh!" Jup exclaimed sceptically.

"It's true. I carry no baggage of gods. May I?" He stretched his hands to the fire. But Stryke noticed that despite the bitter cold this stranger did not look discomforted; his teeth didn't chatter, his disgustingly pale skin showed no tinge of blue.

"How do we know you're not part of some trap?" Stryke asked.

"I can't blame you for thinking that. The perceptions my race have of yours are just as distrustful. But then, many humans are like mushrooms."

They gave him puzzled looks. Stryke thought he might be a simpleton. Or mad.

"Mushrooms?" he said.

"Yes. They live in the dark and are force-fed shit."

A ripple of laughter came from the band.

"Well put," Jup told the stranger in guarded good humour. "But who are you that you should be travelling a war-torn land alone and unarmed?"

"I'm a storyteller."

"A story's all we need right now," Stryke commented cynically.

"Then I'll tell you one. Though I fear it's short on plot and could end as a tragedy." There was something about the way he said it that held them. "Could it be that you're seeking one of your own kind?" the human added.

"What if we are?"

"A female member of your band?"

"What do you know of that?" Stryke rumbled darkly.

"A little. Enough to aid you perhaps."

"Go on."

"Your comrade's been captured by bounty hunters of my race."

"How do you know this? Are you one of them?"

"Do I *look* like a mercenary? No, my friend, I'm not one of them. I've just seen them with her."

"Where? And how many of them?"

"Three. Not far from here. But they would have moved on by now."

"How does this help us?"

"I know where they've gone. Hecklowe."

Stryke eyed him suspiciously. "Why should we believe you?"

"That's your choice. But why would I lie?"

"For a dark purpose of your own, maybe. We've learnt the hard way to doubt anything a human says."

"As I said, you can't be blamed for that. On this occasion a human is telling you the truth."

Stryke stared at him. He couldn't read his face. "I need to think," he said. He detailed a couple of grunts to keep an eye on the human and wandered away from the fire.

The snow might have been a little lighter. He didn't really notice. His mind was on weighing the stranger's words.

"Am I intruding?"

Stryke turned. "No, Jup. I was just trying to make sense of what we heard. Starting with why we should believe this Serapheim."

"Because there's a certain kind of logic to it?"

"Maybe."

"Because we're desperate?"

"That's more like it."

"Let's think this through, chief. *If* this human's speaking true, we assume the bounty hunters have Coilla because of the price on her head, yes?"

"If not, wouldn't they have killed her already?"

"That's what I figured. But why take her to Hecklowe?"

Stryke shrugged. "Could be one of the places where the bounty's doled out. Let's work on believing him. That leaves us with a decision. Should we go after Coilla or keep the rendezvous with the rest of the band first?"

"We're nearer Hecklowe than Drogan."

"True. But if Coilla has a value she's unlikely to be harmed."

"You're not taking her nature into account. She'll be no passive hostage."

"Let's trust to her good sense. In which case things are going to be hard for her but not life-threatening."

"So that's an argument for meeting with Alfray first and going into Hecklowe with the whole band."

"Yeah, better odds. The downside is that delay might mean Coilla being sent back to Jennesta. Then we really would have lost her."

They glanced in the direction of the stranger. He was still by the fire. The grunts by him seemed a little more relaxed, and several were engaged in conversations.

"On the other hand," Jup went on, "there *is* an agreed time for rendezvousing with Alfray. Suppose he thinks the worst's happened to us and goes into Drogan to tangle with the centaurs?"

"I wouldn't put it past him." Stryke sighed. "It's on a blade's edge, Jup, and we need to be absolutely sure that—"

A chorus of shouts interrupted. Stryke and Jup spun around.

The stranger had gone. So had his horse. They ran to the fire.

Grunts were stumbling and yelling in the swirling whiteness.

Stryke collared Gant. "What the hell happened, trooper?"

"The human, Captain, he just . . . went."

"Went? What do you mean, *went?*"

Talag intervened. "That's right, sir. I took my eyes off him for a second and he was gone."

"Who saw him go?" Stryke shouted.

None of the grunts owned to it.

"This is crazy," Jup said, squinting into the snow. "He couldn't have just disappeared."

Sword in hand, Stryke stared too, and wondered.

13

Voices and laughter were all around him.

He was walking in a crowd of orcs. Orcs of both sexes and all ages. Orcs he had never seen before.

They sported tiny adornments of dress that told him they were from many different clans. Yet there was no obvious animosity. They seemed happy and he didn't feel in any way threatened. In fact there was an air of anticipation, a holiday mood.

He was on the sandy beach. The sun was at its highest point and beating down intensely. Shrieking white birds circled far overhead. The crowd was heading for the ocean.

Then he saw that a ship was anchored a little way offshore. It had three sails, now resting, and from the foremost mast a flag flew, decorated with a red emblem he didn't recognise. The carved effigy of a female orc, resplendent with raised sword, stood out from the prow. Battle shields lined the ship's side, each bearing a different design. It was the biggest vessel Stryke had ever seen, and certainly the most magnificent.

The leaders of the crowd were already wading out to it. They didn't need to swim, so the ship was either flat-bottomed or stood in a deeper strait edging the beach. He was taken along by the flow of orcs. None of them spoke to him, but in a strange way that made him feel accepted.

Over the hubbub he heard his name, or at least he thought he did. He looked around, taking in the torrent of faces. Then he saw her, moving against the crowd, coming his way.

"There you are!" she greeted him.

Despite his confusion, despite not knowing where he was or what was going on, he smiled.

She returned the smile and said, "I knew you'd come."

"You did?"

"Well, hoped," she confessed. Her eyes sparkled.

Emotions welled up in him that he didn't understand, and certainly couldn't articulate. So he didn't try. He simply smiled again.

"Are you here to help?" she asked.

His reply was a baffled look.

She adopted the expression of good-natured pique that he was grow-ing used to. "Come on," she said.

Stryke went with her to the ocean. They walked into the mild, chalky-flecked waves lapping the beach and waded, thigh-deep, to the ship. Orcs were using ropes and ladders to reach the deck. He watched admiringly as the female, moving with athletic suppleness, joined the climbers and scaled the side. Then he hauled himself aboard the gently swaying vessel.

A hold was open mid-deck. Crates, barrels and chests were being passed up. The orcs began carrying them to the rail and over the side, where another chain was forming back to the beach. Stryke and the female took places in the line, passing along the cargo. He admired the rippling of her arm and leg muscles as she hefted boxes and swung them to him.

"What are these things?" he asked.

She laughed. "How do you make your way in the world knowing so little?"

He shrugged, abashed.

"Do they not import needed things where you come from?" she said.

"Orcs don't."

"Oh, yes; you say your land is home to more than orcs. Those dwarves and gremlins and . . . what was it? Humans."

His face darkened. "Humans are not of my land. Though they would make it so."

She handed him another piece of cargo. "My point is that even where you come from, needful things must be brought in."

"Where do these things come from?"

"From other orcs in other places that have things we don't."

"I haven't heard of other such places."

"You gall me." Smiling, she waved a hand at the ocean. "I mean those lands across the ocean."

"I didn't know there was anything across the ocean. Isn't the water all there is?"

"*Obviously not. Where do you think all this came from?*"

Suitably chided, he caught the next box she sent his way. Thrown with a little more force than before, he thought. He tossed it to the next orc in line, turned back to her and said, "*These are riches, then?*"

"*You could say that.*" She moved out of the line, taking the crate she had with her. "*I'll show you.*" He stepped aside too. The line closed up; there were more than enough orcs to help.

She put the crate on the deck. He knelt beside her. Producing a knife from her belt sheath, she used it to lever open the box. It was full of a reddish, powdery material that looked like dried leaves. He obviously didn't know what it was.

"*Turm,*" she explained. "*A spice. It makes food better.*"

"*This has value?*"

"*If we want our food to taste good, yes! That's its value. Not all riches come as coins or gems. Your sword, for example.*"

"*My sword?*" His hand went to it. "*It's a good blade, but nothing special.*"

"*In itself, perhaps not. But in skilful hands, in the hands of a warrior born, it becomes so much more.*"

"*I see. I really do see.*"

"*And so it is with orcs. With all living things.*"

His craggy face creased. "*Now I'm not so—*"

"*They're like blades. As sharp or as dull.*"

Now it was his turn to laugh.

"*Yet all have value,*" she emphasised.

"*Even my enemies?*"

"*It is right that orcs have enemies. Even if they change, and today's enemy becomes tomorrow's friend.*"

"*That's not my situation,*" he replied coolly. "*It won't happen.*"

"*Whether it comes to pass or not, even mortal enemies have their value.*"

"*How can they?*"

"*Because it's possible to respect, which is to say value, their fighting skills, their determination. Their courage, if they have it. Not least, they're precious in just being there for an orc to face. We need a foe. It's what we do. It's in our blood.*"

"*I'd never thought of it that way.*"

"*But although we fight that doesn't necessarily mean we have to hate.*"

Stryke couldn't entirely accept that. Though it did set him thinking.

"But what we must value most of all," she added, "are those closest to us."

"You make things seem so . . . straightforward."

"That's because they are, my friend."

"Here, perhaps. Where I come from, all hands are against us and there is much to be overcome."

Her expression grew sombre. "Then be a blade, Stryke. Be a blade."

He woke with a racing pulse. His breathing was so rapid he almost panted.

Light, fetid rain was falling from a dismal sky, and most of the snow had been washed away. It was miserable and cold. The couple of hours' sleep hadn't refreshed him at all. There was a bad taste in his parched mouth and his head pounded.

He lay there, letting the rain bathe his face, and dwelt on what, for want of a better word, he termed the dream. Dreams, visions, messages from the gods; whatever they were, they had grown more vivid, more intense. The smell of ozone, the motes in his eyes from the glaring sun, the warm breeze that caressed his skin: all were slow to fade.

Again the thought that he was being betrayed by his own mind and going insane clutched his heart like an icy claw. Yet another, contrary notion ran almost as strongly: the feeling that he'd come to expect the dreams, even welcome them.

That was something he didn't want to pursue, not now.

He sat up and looked around. All the others were awake and going about their chores. The horses were being tended, bedrolls shaken out, weapons sharpened.

The events of the night came back to him. Not those of his dream but what had occurred before that. They had kept their eyes peeled for the mysterious human for a long time, and even ventured out into the snow in small parties to search for him. There had been no sign and eventually they gave up. At some point Stryke must have drifted into sleep, although he couldn't remember doing it.

Serapheim, if that was the stranger's real name, was another mystery to add to the list. But it wasn't one Stryke was going to waste time pondering, mostly because he didn't want to consider the distinct possibility that the man was crazy. That would throw into doubt the only clue they had to Coilla's whereabouts. And at a time like this they needed something hopeful. Badly.

Stryke pushed all that from his mind. He had something more important to occupy his thoughts.

Jup stood by the horses, talking with a couple of the grunts. He strode over to them.

Without preamble he told the dwarf, "I've decided."

"We're going for Coilla, right?"

"Right."

"It must have occurred to you that this Serapheim character was lying. Or just plain mad."

"I've given some thought to both. If he was lying, why?"

"As bait for a trap?"

"Too fancy a way of doing it."

"Not if it works."

"Perhaps. I still don't think it's likely, though."

"What about him being insane?"

"I grant that's more possible. Maybe he is. But . . . I don't know, I just didn't feel that. Course, human madness isn't something I've had too much experience with."

"Really? Take a look around some time."

Stryke smiled, thinly. "You know what I mean. But what Serapheim said is the only clue we've had about Coilla." He saw Jup's face and qualified that. "All right, *possible* clue. I reckon Hecklowe's worth a try."

"What about that delaying us meeting up with Alfray?"

"We'll have to let him know."

"And what's your decision on him?" Jup nodded toward Haskeer, sitting to one side by himself.

"He's still part of this band. Only he's on probation. Object?"

"No. Just a little wary, that's all."

"Don't think I'm not. But we'll keep an eye on him."

"We've got time for that?"

"Believe me, Jup, if he causes any more trouble he's out. Or dead."

The dwarf didn't doubt his captain meant it. "We should tell him what's happening. He's an officer, after all. Isn't he?"

"For now. I hadn't planned on breaking him unless he gets out of hand again. Come on."

They walked over to Haskeer. He looked up at them and nodded.

"How're you feeling?" Stryke asked.

"Better." His tone and general demeanour indicated there was some truth in that. "I just want the chance to prove I'm still worthy of being a Wolverine."

"That's what I wanted to hear, Sergeant. But after what you did I'm going to have to put you on probation for a while."

"But I don't *know* what I did!" Haskeer protested. "That is, I know what you told me but I don't remember doing any of it."

"That's why we're going to keep an eye on you until we find out what caused it, or until your behaviour's good enough for long enough."

Jup put it less diplomatically. "We don't want you going gaga on us again."

Haskeer flared, *"Why don't you —,"* then checked himself.

Stryke reflected that this might be a good sign, a flash of the old Haskeer. "The point is that we don't need passengers and we certainly don't need a liability," he said. "Got it?"

"Got it," Haskeer confirmed, more subdued again.

"See that you have. Now listen. That human who came here last night, Serapheim, said that Coilla was being taken to Hecklowe. We're going there. What I want from *you* is to obey orders and act like a member of this band again."

"Right. Let's get on with it."

Reasonably satisfied, Stryke gathered the others and explained the new plan. He gave them an opportunity to comment or protest. That drew a minor question or two, but nothing significant. He got the impression they were relieved to be doing something positive at last.

He finished by saying, "I need two volunteers to take the message to Alfray. But be warned; it could be a dangerous mission."

Every grunt stepped forward. He picked Jad and Hystykk, mindful that he was about to deplete numbers even more perilously.

"The message is simple," he told them. "Let Alfray know

where we've gone, and that we'll get to Drogan as soon as we can." He thought for a moment and added a rider: "If from the time this message is delivered a week passes without sight of us, assume we're not coming. In which case Alfray and his band are free to act as they think best."

He broke the sober mood that brought down by ordering them all to get ready to move.

As they hastened to obey, he reached into his belt pouch and brought out the three stars. He examined them thoughtfully, then looked up and saw Haskeer staring at him.

"That means you too, Wolverine," he said.

Haskeer waved and jogged toward his horse. Stryke slipped the stars back into the pouch and climbed on to his own mount.

Then they were on the move again.

They called Hecklowe the city that never slept.

Certainly the normal rhythms of day and night meant little there, but it was not quite a city. Not in the way of great northern settlements like Urrarbython or Wreaye. Or even the human centres of the south like Bracebridge or Ripple, which were still growing at an alarming rate. But it was big enough to accommodate a constantly shifting population made up of all Maras-Dantia's elder races.

Some lived there permanently. They were mostly purveyors of vice, excess and usury. Not least among these were slavers and their agents, who found it convenient to be located in a place where a river of life constantly flowed. Although unrest was forbidden, all other kinds of crime had become common in Hecklowe. Many held this was another baleful effect of the incomers' influence, and there was truth in it.

These thoughts passed through Coilla's mind as the trio of bounty hunters hustled her out of the inn at dawn. They found the streets as crowded as they had been when they arrived the evening before.

After Lekmann warned her, again, about not trying to escape, Aulay had a question for him.

"You sure we're going to get more for her from a slaver than Jennesta?"

"Like I said, they pay good for orcs as bodyguards and such."

"Crossing Jennesta's not a good plan," Coilla put in.

"You shut up and leave the thinking to your betters."

Coilla glanced at Blaan, vacant-eyed and slack-jawed. She looked at Aulay, with his patched eye, bandaged ear and splinted finger. "Yeah," she said.

"Suppose she's lying about the Wolverines being here," Aulay said.

"Will you give that a rest?" Lekmann retorted. "This is the logical place for them to be. If they're not, we'll still make a profit selling this bitch, then we can carry on searching somewhere else."

"Where, Micah?" Blaan asked.

"Don't *you* start, Jabeez!" Lekmann snapped. "I'll figure something out if it comes to that."

They fell silent as a pair of Watchers lumbered by.

"Let's get on with it, Micah," Aulay pleaded impatiently.

"Right. Like we agreed, you're going to search for orcs. They're trying to sell something, remember. So look in the bazaar, the gem traders' quarter, the information barterers' neighbourhood — anywhere they might find a buyer."

Aulay nodded.

"Meanwhile, me and Jabeez are going to look for a new owner for her," Lekmann went on, jabbing a thumb at Coilla. "We'll see you back here no later than noon."

"Where you going?"

"To the east side, to look up a name I heard. Now move your arse, we ain't got time to burn."

They went their separate ways.

"What do you want me to do, Micah?" Blaan asked.

"Just keep an eye on the orc. If she gets smart, crack her."

They made Coilla walk between them, even though that irritated pedestrians in narrower streets. Coilla drew glances from passersby, many of them wary. She was, after all, an orc, and it was well known that orcs were best dealt with respectfully.

"Question," she said.

"Better be worth my breath answering," Lekmann replied.

"Who's this slave buyer we're going to?"

"He's called Razatt-Kheage."

"That's a goblin name."

"Yeah, that's what he is."

She sighed. "A damn goblin . . ."

"Not much love between orcs and goblins, eh?"

"Not much between orcs and just about anybody, shit face."

Blaan sniggered. Lekmann shot him a look that put a stop to it.

Lekmann transferred his glare to Coilla. "You've got any more questions, just fucking forget 'em, all right?"

They turned a corner. A small crowd had gathered around a pair of fays having a loud argument.

Fays were said to be the offspring of unions between elves and fairies, and were generally regarded as cousins to those races. They were insubstantially built, with spiky, slightly upturned noses and black button eyes. Their small, delicate mouths had tiny rounded teeth. They weren't a naturally belligerent race and certainly weren't designed for combat.

These two were reeling drunkenly. They shouted at each other and aimed feeble blows. It was unlikely either was going to be hurt unless they fell over.

The bounty hunters laughed. "Can't hold their liquor," Lekmann mocked.

"It was *your* kind that brought this sort of behaviour to Maras-Dantia," Coilla told him with withering scorn. "You're destroying my world."

"Ain't yours no more, savage. And it's called Centrasia now."

"Like fuck it is."

"You should be grateful. We're bringing you the benefits of civilisation."

"Like slavery? That was almost unknown until your race came. Maras-Dantians didn't *own* each other."

"What about you orcs? You're born into somebody or other's service, aren't you? That's serfdom, ain't it? We didn't start *that*."

"It's *become* slavery. You tainted it with your ideas. It used to be a good arrangement; it let orcs do what they were born for. Fighting."

"Talking of fighting . . ." He nodded to the other side of the

cobbled street. The fays were brawling, sending ineffective
punches at each other's heads.

Blaan laughed idiotically.

"See?" Lekmann taunted. "You barbarians don't need lessons
in violence from us. It's already there, just below the surface."

Coilla had never been so in need of a sword.

One fay produced a hidden knife and began swinging it,
though both combatants were obviously far too drunk to offer a
really serious threat.

Then a pair of Watchers suddenly appeared, perhaps the ones
they'd seen earlier; it was impossible to tell. Coilla was surprised
at how fast they moved. It belied their cumbersome mien. Three
or four more homunculi arrived, and all of them converged on
the fighting fays. They were so drunk, so busy with each other
and so taken by surprise by the Watchers' speed that they had
no time to try running.

The fragile creatures were overwhelmed and held by powerful arms. They were lifted bodily, their tiny legs kicking in
impotent anger. Little effort was required to disarm the one
with the knife.

As the crowd looked on in silence, two Watchers stepped
forward and took hold of the squealing fays' heads in their
massive hands. Then, in a matter-of-fact, almost casual manner,
the fays' slender necks were snapped. Even from where they
were standing the bounty hunters and Coilla heard the crack of
bones.

The Watchers trudged off, bearing the corpses of their victims
like slack rag dolls. Wiser about Hecklowe's level of tolerance,
the crowd began melting away.

Lekmann gave a low whistle. "They take law 'n' order serious
round here, don't they?"

"I don't like it," Blaan complained. "I've got a hidden weapon
too, like that dead fay."

"So keep it out of sight, then."

Blaan continued grumbling and Lekmann carried on
haranguing him. It diverted their attention from Coilla. She
seized her chance.

Lekmann was blocking her path. She rammed her boot into

his groin. He groaned loudly and doubled up. Coilla took the first step of a run.

An arm like an iron barrel band clamped around her neck. Blaan dragged her struggling into the mouth of an adjacent alley. Watery-eyed and white-faced, Lekmann limped in after them.

"You bitch," he whispered.

He looked back towards the street. Nobody seemed to have noticed what was going on. Turning to Coilla he delivered a swingeing whack across her face. Then another.

The briny taste of blood filled her mouth.

"Pull something like that again and to hell with the money," he snarled, "I'll kill you."

When he was satisfied she'd calmed, he told Blaan to let go of her. Coilla dabbed at trickles of blood from her mouth and nose. She said nothing.

"Now *move*," he ordered.

They resumed their journey, the bounty hunters keeping close to her.

Nine or ten twists and turns later and they entered the eastern quarter. If anything the streets there were narrower and even more jammed. It was a maze, and difficult for outsiders to navigate.

As they stood on a corner waiting for Lekmann to get his bearings, Coilla's eye was caught by a tall figure moving through the crowd two or three blocks away. As on the day before, when she'd thought she'd seen a couple of orcs, it was a fleeting glimpse. But it looked like Serapheim, the human wordsmith they'd encountered on the plains. He'd told them he had just left Hecklowe, so why return? Coilla decided she was probably mistaken. Which was quite likely as all humans looked the same to her anyway.

Then they were off again. Lekmann took them to the heart of the quarter and an area of winding high-walled passageways. After a tortuous journey through these shadowy lanes, where crowds were very much thinner, they came to the mouth of an alley. At its end and to the side stood a building that had once been white and handsome. Now it was grimy and dilapidated.

The few windows were shuttered, the sole door had been reinforced.

Lekmann got Blaan to rap on it, then nudged him aside. Having waited a full minute they were about to knock again when a viewing panel was slid aside. A pair of yellowy eyes scrutinised them, but nothing was said.

"We're here to see Razatt-Kheage," Lekmann announced.

There was no response.

"The name's Micah Lekmann," he added.

The disembodied eyes continued staring at them.

"A mutual friend cleared my path," Lekmann went on, patience thinning. "Said I'd be welcome."

The silent inspection lasted another few seconds, then the panel was slammed shut.

"Don't seem too friendly," Blaan commented.

"They ain't exactly in a friendly line of business," Lekmann reminded him.

There was the scrape of bolts being drawn inside and the door creaked open. Pushing Coilla in first, Lekmann and Blaan entered.

A goblin faced them. Another closed and re-bolted the door.

Their frames were skeletal, with knobbly green flesh stretched tight and resembling parchment. They had prominent shoulder-blades that gave the impression they were slightly hunchbacked. But what they lacked in excess fat was made up with sinew; these were strong, agile creatures.

Their heads were oval-shaped and hairless. Their ears were small and flapped, their mouths rubbery-lipped gashes. They had squashed noses with punch-hole nostrils and large tear-drop-shaped eyes with black orbs and jaundice-yellow surrounds. Both were armed with long, thick clubs topped with studded maces.

In the spacious room that spread out beyond them there were seven or eight more of their granite-faced comrades.

A wooden platform, level with a human's chest, ran the length of the room's far wall. It was scattered with rugs and cushions. At its centre stood an ornately carved, high-backed chair like a throne. A guard was positioned on either side.

Seated in it was another goblin. But where the rest wore martial leathers and chain mail, he was dressed more grandly in silk, and he was bedecked with jewellery. One of his languid talons held the mouthpiece of a tube that ran to a hookah, from which thin tendrils of white smoke drifted.

"I am Razatt-Kheage," the slaver said. His voice was sibilant. "Your name has been made known to me." He gave Coilla an appraising look. "I understand you have merchandise to offer."

"That we do," Lekmann replied in a tone seeping false bonhomie. "This is it."

Razatt-Kheage made an imperious gesture with his hand. "Come."

Lekmann shoved Coilla and the trio walked to a small staircase at one end of the dais. A pair of henchlins accompanied them. When they approached the throne, Lekmann nodded at Blaan and he put an armlock on Coilla. She was kept a safe distance from the slaver.

Razatt-Kheage offered Lekmann the hookah pipe.

"What is it, crystal?"

"No, my friend. I prefer more intense pleasures. This is pure lassh."

Lekmann blanched. "Er, no, I won't, thanks. I try to keep away from the more violent narcotics. And what with it being, uhm, habit forming and all . . ."

"Of course. It's a little indulgence I can afford, however." He inhaled deeply from the pipe. His eyes took on a more glazed sheen as he expelled the heady cloud. "To business. Let us examine the goods." He waved lazily at one of his minions.

This goblin left his place by the throne and scuttled to Coilla. As Blaan held her firm, the goblin proceeded to paw her. He squeezed the muscles on her arms, patted her legs, stared into her eyes.

"You'll find she's fit as a flea," Lekmann remarked, ladling the geniality some more.

The goblin roughly forced open Coilla's mouth and inspected her teeth.

"I'm not a damn horse!" she spat.

"She's a spunky one," Lekmann said.

"Then she will be broken," Razatt-Kheage replied. "It has been done before."

His henchlin finished with Coilla and nodded to him.

"It seems your wares are acceptable, Micah Lekmann," the slaver hissed. "Let us talk of payment."

While they negotiated, Coilla took a good look around the chamber. Its sole door, barred windows and profusion of guards, not to mention Blaan's hold on her, all quickly confirmed that she had no choice but to bide her time.

Lekmann and the slaver finally agreed a price. The amount was substantial. Coilla didn't know whether to be flattered by it.

"It is agreed, then," Razatt-Kheage said. "When will it be convenient for you to return for your money?"

That took Lekmann by surprise. "Return? What do you mean, return?"

"Do you think I would keep such a sum here?"

"Well, how quickly can you get it?"

"Shall we say four hours?"

"*Four hours?* That's a hell of a —"

"Perhaps you would prefer dealing with another agent?"

The bounty hunter sighed. "All right, Razatt-Kheage, four hours. Not a minute longer."

"You have my word. Do you wish to wait or return?"

"I have to meet somebody. We'll come back."

"It would make sense if you left the orc here in the meantime. She will be secure and you will not have the inconvenience of guarding her."

Lekmann eyed him suspiciously. "How do I know she's still going to be here when we get back?"

"Among my kind, Micah Lekmann, when a goblin gives his word it is a grievous insult to doubt it."

"Yeah, you slavers are such an honourable bunch," Coilla remarked sarcastically.

Blaan applied painful pressure to her arm. She gritted her teeth and didn't give them the satisfaction of crying out.

"As you say . . . *spunky*," Razatt-Kheage muttered unpleasantly. "What is your decision, human?"

"All right, she can stay. But my partner Blaan here stays with her. And if it ain't considered an insult to you and your race, I'm telling him that if there's any . . . problems, he's to kill her. Got that, Jabeez?"

"Got it, Micah." He tightened his hold on Coilla.

"I understand," Razatt-Kheage said. "In four hours, then."

"Right." He headed for the door accompanied by a henchlin.

"Don't hurry back," Coilla called after him.

14

"It's just not *natural*, Stryke. Giving up their weapons isn't something orcs should be asked to do."

It was the first definite thing Haskeer had said since being reunited with the band. He sounded almost like his old self.

"We don't get into Hecklowe otherwise," Stryke explained again. "Stop making a fuss."

"Why don't we conceal a few blades?" Jup suggested.

"Bet *everybody* does that," Haskeer said.

Stryke noted how Haskeer even seemed to be making an effort to be reasonable with Jup. Maybe he really had changed. "They probably do. But stopping weapons going in isn't the point. It's using them in there that brings the death penalty. The Council knows that, everybody going in knows it. Even Unis and Manis know it, for the gods' sake. It's just that they don't search all visitors thoroughly. Otherwise the place would grind to a halt."

Jup interjected, "But get caught in a fight with weapons—"

"And they kill you, yes."

"So we *don't* hide some weapons?"

"Are you mad? An orc without a blade? Of course we smuggle some in. What we don't do, *any* of us . . ." he gave Haskeer a pointed look ". . . is use them without my direct order. Any orc should be able to improvise. We've got fists, feet and heads. Right?"

The band nodded and began slipping knives into boots, sleeves and helmets. Stryke chose a favourite two-edged blade. Jup did the same. Haskeer went one better. Having concealed a knife, he also wrapped a length of chain around his waist and covered it with his jerkin.

Hecklowe by day was as impressive and strange a sight as Hecklowe by night. This day, rain had given its incredibly varied architecture an oily sheen. The tops of towers, the roofs of buildings, the sloping sides of mini pyramids glistened wetly and gave off a rainbow sheen.

The band made its way to the freeport's main entrance. As usual, a multi-racial crowd was massed at the gates. Dismounting, the orcs got in line, leading their horses.

They had an interminable wait, during which Haskeer scowled menacingly at kobolds, dwarves, elves and any other species he had real or imagined grudges against. But eventually they reached the checkpoint and found themselves dealing with the silent Watchers.

Jup was first. An homunculus sentinel stood with arms outstretched waiting for his weapons. The dwarf handed over his sword, an axe, a hatchet, two daggers, a knife, a slingshot and ammo, a spiked knuckle-duster and four sharpened throwing stars.

"I'm travelling light," he told the expressionless Watcher.

By the time the rest of the band had divested themselves of similar quantities of weapons the queue was much longer and shorter on patience.

Finally the band pocketed their wooden receipt tags and were waved in.

"The Watchers seem a lot more sluggish since I was last here," Stryke observed.

Jup nodded. "The bleeding of the magic is affecting everything. Though it probably isn't as bad here as further inland. I've noticed that the power's always stronger near water. But if humans keep carrying on the way they have been, even places like this are going to be in trouble."

"You're right. Even so, I'd rather we didn't have to tackle the Watchers. They might be less powerful than they were but they're still designed to be killing machines."

"I don't reckon they're so tough," Haskeer boasted.

"Haskeer, *please*. Don't get into any fights unless there's no other way."

"Right. You can rely on me, boss."

Stryke wished he could believe that. "Come on," he said, "let's get these horses stabled."

They managed that without too much bother, and Stryke made sure the caches of pellucid weren't left in the saddlebags. Each member carried their portion about his person.

Then they walked the crowded streets, attracting a certain amount of attention and turned heads, which was no mean feat in a place like Hecklowe. Though it was noticeable that nobody lingered in their path. At length they found a small plaza where it was a little easier to talk without being jostled. There were trees in the square, but even here, with strong flows of magic, they looked frail and mean-leafed.

Stryke's troops bunched around him. "Ten orcs and a dwarf hanging around together isn't tactful," he told them. "We're best splitting into two groups."

"Makes sense," Jup said.

"My group will be Haskeer, Toche, Reafdaw and Seafe. Jup, you'll take Talag, Gant, Calthmon, Breggin and Finje."

"Why ain't I leading a group?" Haskeer complained.

"There are six in Jup's group, only five in mine," Stryke explained. "So of course I want you with me."

It worked. Haskeer's chest swelled. Jup caught Stryke's eye, grinned and gave him an exaggerated wink. Stryke smiled thinly in return.

"We'll meet back here in . . . let's say three hours," he decided. "If either group comes across Coilla in a situation it can handle, we'll go for it. If that means not making the rendezvous here, we'll meet one mile west of Hecklowe's gates. If you find Coilla and the odds are too long, leave somebody watching and we'll go in with both groups."

"Any ideas about where we should look in particular?" Jup asked.

"Anywhere buying and selling takes place."

"That's the whole of Hecklowe, isn't it?"

"Right."

"Should be a piece of piss, then."

"Look, you cover the north and west sectors, we'll do south and east." He addressed all of them. "We know, or think we know, that Coilla's with three humans, probably bounty hunters. Don't undervalue them. Take no chances. And go steady on those concealed weapons. Like I said, we don't want the Watchers down on our necks. Now get going."

Jup gave a thumbs-up and led off his group.

Watching them go, Haskeer said, "We get smaller and smaller . . ."

Stryke's party searched fruitlessly for over two hours.

As they moved from the south to the east of the city, Stryke said, "The trouble is we don't know *how* to look."

"What?" Haskeer responded.

"We don't know anybody in Hecklowe, we've no contacts to help us, and slavers don't do business on the streets. The gods alone know what could be going on inside any of these buildings."

"So what we going to do?"

"Just keep looking and hope we catch a glimpse of Coilla, I suppose. It's not as though we can ask the Watchers where the local slavers live."

"Well, what's the point, then? I mean, what the hell are we doing here if we haven't got a hope of finding her?"

"*Just a minute*," Stryke seethed, barely containing his anger. "We're here because of *you!* If you hadn't gone AWOL with the stars in the first place we wouldn't *be* here. And Coilla wouldn't be in the mess she's in."

"That's not fair!" Haskeer protested. "I didn't know what I was doing. You can't blame me for—"

"Captain!"

"What is it, Toche?" Stryke replied irritably.

The grunt pointed to the intersection they were approaching. "There, sir!"

They all looked the way he indicated. A mass of beings swarmed where four streets met.

"What is it?" Stryke demanded. "What are we supposed to be seeing?"

"That human!" Toche exclaimed. "The one we saw in the snow. *There!*"

This time Stryke spotted him. Serapheim, the wordsmith who sent them to Hecklowe, and who disappeared so completely.

Taller than most around him, he was an unmistakable figure with his flowing locks and long, blue cloak. He was walking away from them.

"Reckon he's one of the bounty hunters?" Haskeer wondered, the argument forgotten.

"No more than I did when we first saw him," Stryke said. "And why send us here if he was? Come to that, what's he doing here?"

"He's moving off."

"It's too much of a coincidence that he should be here. Come on, we're going to follow. But take it easy, we don't want him seeing us."

They pushed through the crowd, careful to keep a safe distance. Serapheim didn't appear to know he was being trailed and acted naturally, though he walked purposefully. The orcs followed him to the core of the eastern quarter, where the streets became winding alleys and every cloak seemed to hide a dagger.

In due course he turned a corner, and when they got to it and peered round they found themselves looking into an empty cul-de-sac. At the far end and to the side was a decaying, once white building. It had a single door. Indeed it was the only door in the street.

They made the obvious assumption that he must have gone through it and crept that way. The door was slightly ajar. The orcs flattened themselves against the wall on either side.

"We go in?" Haskeer whispered.

"What else?" Stryke said.

"Remember what you told Jup. If in doubt get help."

Stryke thought that remarkably sensible coming from Haskeer. "I don't know if this situation warrants it." He glanced at the sky. "Then again, the time we set for the rendezvous isn't that far off. Seafe, get back to that square and bring Jup's group here. If we're not waiting at the mouth of the alley we'll be inside. On the double."

The grunt jogged away.

For the moment that left just Haskeer, Toche, Reafdaw and

Stryke himself. But he reckoned that was enough to deal with a crazy human storyteller.

"We're going in," he decided, discreetly slipping the knife from his boot. "Draw weapons."

He pushed the door and entered, the others close behind.

They were in a sizeable room with a long dais at one end supporting a massive chair. Other small items of furniture were scattered about the apartment. The place was deserted.

"What the hell happened to that Serapheim character?" Haskeer asked.

"There have to be other rooms, or another way out," Stryke said. "Let's—"

A sudden flurry of sound and movement cut him short. Wall hangings were torn aside. At the back of the dais a concealed door flew open. Ten or more armed goblins emerged and rushed to surround them. They held club maces, swords and short spears, weapons that outreached the Wolverines' knives. A goblin slammed and bolted the door to the street.

Spear tips and sword points were held to the orcs' throats and chests. Goblins snatched away the band's knives and searched their clothes for more. But they only seemed interested in weapons; the pellucid and stars were ignored. The blades, and Haskeer's chain, were tossed clanging into a pile on the floor.

Another goblin appeared on the platform. He was dressed in finery and gems. "I am Razatt-Kheage," he announced with more than a dash of melodrama.

"Slaver scum," Haskeer rumbled.

One of the goblins delivered a hefty blow to his stomach with the shaft end of his mace. Haskeer doubled over and wheezed.

"Have a care with the new merchandise," Razatt-Kheage cautioned.

"Bastard," Stryke spat. "Face me without these dolts and we'll settle this, orc to goblin."

Razatt-Kheage gave a snorting laugh. "How charmingly primitive. Put aside thoughts of violence, my friend, I have somebody for you to meet. Come!" he called.

Coilla appeared at the concealed door, Blaan holding her

arms from behind. She reacted with surprise at seeing Stryke, Haskeer and the others.

"Corporal," Stryke said.

"Captain," she responded with admirable cool. "Sorry you got involved."

"We're a band, we stick together."

She looked at Haskeer. "We have a few things to work out, Sergeant."

"This is all very touching," Razatt-Kheage interrupted, "but make the most of it. You'll be saying your goodbyes soon enough."

"This one's cohorts are due back!" Coilla yelled, indicating Blaan.

"Is Serapheim one of them?" Stryke said.

"Serapheim? The storyteller?"

"*Be silent!*" the slaver hissed. "Be still," he said in a calmer voice, "and we will wait for them together." Then he snapped something to his guards in goblin language.

The henchlins moved forward to corral Stryke, Haskeer and the grunts in a corner. Almost as soon as it was done, there was a rap on the door. A goblin went to it, checked through the viewing hatch and opened up.

Lekmann and Aulay swaggered in.

"The rest of the rats," Coilla said.

Blaan jerked her arm, hard. "Stow it!" he growled. She winced.

Lekmann surveyed the scene. "Now what have we got here? I heard you were a fixer, Razatt-Kheage, but this is something again. The rest of the bitch's band, yeah? Or some of them anyway."

"Yes," the slaver confirmed, "and worth a tidy amount to me."

"*To you?*" Aulay blurted. "What is this, Micah?"

"Sharp practice, I reckon."

"I hope you humans are not laying claim to my property," Razatt-Kheage told them. "That could be unfortunate."

Lekmann's face darkened. "Now look, these orcs are the ones my partners and me had a deal to bring in."

"So what? Any agreement you have doesn't hold in Hecklowe. You didn't bring them here."

"I brought *her*, and that brought them. Don't that stand for something?"

"Oi!" Haskeer roared. "You're talking about us like we weren't here! We're not pieces of meat to be squabbled over!"

The goblin who hit him before did it again. Once more, Haskeer doubled up.

"Meat's just what you are, orc," Lekmann sneered.

When Haskeer straightened he aimed a cold, level stare at the goblin that struck him. "That's twice, scumpouch. I'll be paying you back with interest."

The impassive-faced creature pulled back his club for another blow. Razatt-Kheage barked a curt order and the minion stayed his hand. In words all understood, he added, "I'm sure we can come to a mutually profitable arrangement, human."

"That's more like it," Lekmann replied, brightening a little. "Though from what I've heard of these renegades, you ain't gonna have an easy time turning them into something fancy like bodyguards."

The slaver looked at the orcs. He studied their muscular, combat-hardened physiques, saw the scars they bore, regarded their murderous, steely-eyed expressions.

"Perhaps they would be somewhat more of a challenge than the female," he conceded.

Stryke glanced at Coilla and thought how little the slaver knew.

"We're promised gold for their heads," Aulay interjected. "From Queen Jennesta."

Razatt-Kheage thought about it. "That may prove a less bothersome option."

Jup's group spent its time in a futile search. When his allotted three hours were almost spent, he took the grunts back to the square.

They found Seafe waiting for them. He conveyed Stryke's message.

"Let's hope it's not fool's gold," the dwarf said. "Come on."

If the passersby thought there was anything odd in a dwarf leading half a dozen orcs at double time through the streets of Hecklowe, they knew better than to show it. Fortunately no Watchers were encountered.

There was a sticky moment when they reached the eastern quarter and Seafe was unsure of which passage to take. But he chose right and five minutes later they got to the alley with the white house. Nobody was about.

Jup didn't like the look of it. "Stryke said they'd be waiting for us here, right?"

"Yes," Seafe confirmed. "If there was no trouble."

"Then we assume there has been." To the whole group he added, "We'll have to expect hostility in there. I reckon this is a time when weapons can be used, and to hell with Hecklowe law."

Keeping an eye on the street behind them, they pulled out their knives.

Jup stretched a hand to the door and pushed. It didn't shift. He signalled for the others to join him. At his word they shouldered the door *en masse* three times with all the force they could muster. It cracked, splintered and gave. They tumbled in.

And froze.

Ahead of them were two humans armed with knives. To their right, Stryke, Haskeer and the other orcs lined a wall. Seven or eight goblins with maces, swords and short pikes guarded them. On a raised platform at the far end of the room stood a goblin in silken robes. To his left a mountainous human had Coilla in a neck lock.

A goblin stepped from a corner and stood among the broken shards of the doorway, barring it with a spear, its barbed tip glinting.

"Ah," Jup said.

Lekmann grinned. "This just gets better and better."

Leering, Aulay chimed in with, "A regular little reunion."

"Drop your weapons," Razatt-Kheage hissed.

Nobody moved.

"Give it up," Lekmann said. "You're outnumbered and under-armed."

"I don't take orders from goblins, and certainly not from a stinking human."

"Do as you're told, freak!" Lekmann snarled.

Jup looked to Stryke. "Well, Captain?"

"Do what you have to, Sergeant."

There was no mistaking Stryke's meaning.

Jup swallowed. Sounding as casual as he could manage, he said, "Fuck it, what's life without a bit of excitement?"

15

Jup flung his knife at the nearest guard, striking him hard just above the collarbone. It broke the stand-off, and the goblin's neck.

Then all hell was let loose.

One of the grunts quickly snatched up the fallen guard's spear and turned it on another goblin. Simultaneously, Stryke and Haskeer leapt forward and grappled with their captors. A desperate struggle for the weapons began.

Jup's group rushed towards Lekmann and Aulay. They drew their blades and launched into a knife fight.

The dwarf himself was blocked from joining it. Waving a sword, a henchlin barred his way. Dropping to avoid the swinging blade, Jup drove himself at the creature's legs and brought him down. They rolled on the floor, fighting for possession.

Clutching the wrist of the goblin's sword arm, Jup repeatedly hammered it against the flagstones. But he wouldn't let go. Then a screaming guard collapsed beside them, its face ribboned by an orc dagger. Jup reached out and grabbed its sword. Still holding his opponent's wrist, he plunged the blade into its chest.

He leapt to his feet, tossed one sword to a comrade and used the other to rejoin the fray.

On the dais, Coilla was fighting like a wildcat to free herself of Blaan's hold. Nearby, Razatt-Kheage was yelling orders, interspersed with curses.

Stryke had managed to get his foe in a bear hug with the goblin's arms pinned to his sides. Wriggling, unable to lift his sword, he was trying to rake the orc's legs with it. Stryke cooled him with a couple of head butts to the brow. Eyes rolling, he went down. Prising the sword from his hand, Stryke slashed his throat.

He turned and saw Haskeer vying for a spear. It belonged to the guard who had hit him. As he passed, Stryke swiped at the goblin, slicing him in the side. The minor wound was distraction enough to throw the henchlin's poise. Stryke bowled off through the mêlée, making for the bounty hunters.

Haskeer wasn't slow exploiting the upset. He managed to seize the spear's shaft. They tussled for it. Using all his strength, he twisted the spear and got its lethally barbed point under the goblin's chin. Then he pushed upward with all his might. The howling creature was skewered. Haskeer ripped loose the spear in a burst of gore and looked for a fresh victim.

Still struggling in Blaan's arms, Coilla shouted something. The words were lost, but she seemed to be indicating a large chest on the dais.

Lekmann and Aulay slashed wildly with their knives, trying to keep the orcs clear. The arrival of Jup and Breggin with swords had them backing off.

Coilla's attempts to break loose of Blaan went on. She called out again. He began applying pressure to her neck and looked set to snap it.

Haskeer rushed at the platform. A henchlin stepped out to stop him. The orc levelled his spear and impaled the goblin, the shaft piercing his stomach, and tossed him back into the scrum. Abandoning the spear, Haskeer hurtled on and leapt up to the dais. He landed a couple of feet away from Coilla and Blaan. Razatt-Kheage was near the other end of the platform, shrieking at his bodyguards. Haskeer ignored him.

At a run, he landed a massive roundhouse blow to the side of Blaan's meaty head. The hulking human cried out in rage. Haskeer hit him again on the same spot, just as heavily. Bellowing, Blaan let go of Coilla and turned on the orc. They commenced swinging at each other in earnest.

Coilla dived across the platform and collided with the wooden chest. She wrenched open its lid. It was filled with cutlasses, rapiers and scimitars. She seized a broadsword, then overturned the chest, toppling it from the dais. It crashed to the floor, its weaponry spilling out.

She hadn't noticed in her haste that it would land at Aulay's and Lekmann's backs. They spun and fell upon the weapons, scrabbling for swords. They weren't alone. Four or five orcs piled in too, anxious to swap daggers for lengthier blades. Twenty seconds of kicking and punching saw all of them re-armed.

What had been a series of hand-to-hand brawls transformed into swordplay.

"*Bounty hunter!*" Stryke yelled, skidding to a halt in front of Lekmann. "Defend yourself!"

"Come and get it, freak!"

Jup and the grunts disengaged and quickly found other foes. Stryke and Lekmann squared off.

The human went for a quick kill. He powered in, his sword a blur as he carved air with shocking rapidity. Stryke stood his ground and parried everything coming at him. Deflecting a half-dozen passes cleared the way for advancing a step or two. He went into offensive mode. Lekmann countered with equal fluidity, reclaiming the gained space.

They fenced with total focus, oblivious to everything else, beating a steel rhythm with their blades.

Jup had Aulay to himself. The human was a lesser swordsman than his partner, which was to say he was merely good. But he was fuelled with anger and desperation. That fed him fury while clouding his skill.

The dwarf got off a weighty swing aimed at decapitation. Aulay ducked and returned a scything horizontal sweep meant for disembowelment. Jup sprang back and avoided it. Then he was in again and battering.

All across the room orcs and goblins went at the business of murder with a will. Blades hacked spears, knives slashed at mail, swords met in a ringing din. A grunt hefted a table and smashed it across the back of a henchlin, allowing another trooper to dart in and deliver a stabbing. An orc slammed against a wall, impelled by a flesh wound to the arm from a goblin mace. He dodged the follow-up and brought his sword into play.

On the platform, Haskeer and Blaan slugged it out in a furious bare-knuckle contest. Each sponged up the other's blows and dealt their own. Neither would give.

Blaan landed a piledriver punch to Haskeer's chin. "Go down!" he hollered.

The impact rocked Haskeer but didn't fell him. He responded with a crazed howl and a counterblow that sank his fist in the human's belly. Blaan staggered back a bit but otherwise seemed unaffected. Both of them were unused to anybody staying upright once they hit them. It stoked their wrath.

Arms outstretched, moving surprisingly fast for his bulk, Blaan shot forward and encircled Haskeer with his powerful arms. They set to wrestling, faces strained, muscles bulging.

Coilla thought about going for the slaver, but had a more longed-for target. She jumped down from the platform. A goblin came out of the mêlée and engaged her. They crossed swords, the goblin making up for subtlety by powering in with savage swipes. She countered every swing, batting aside the blade with ease. Then she wrong-footed him, shifted her centre of balance and sent her blade point into his eye. The shrieking henchlin dropped.

She headed for the humans.

Lekmann and Stryke were still matching knock for knock. That didn't interest Coilla. She wanted Aulay.

He and Jup battled on, toe to toe, sweat flecking their brows.

"*Mine!*" she yelled.

Jup understood. He pulled back, spun, and connected with a goblin sword. That duel moved him clear.

Coilla took his place and glared at Aulay. "I've dreamed of this, you *fucker!*" she spat.

"And I owe *you*, bitch!" He absently touched bandaged ear with wrapped finger.

The jarring impact of their clashing blades rang out. Coilla dodged and weaved, looking for any chance to plant cold steel in his flesh. Aulay fought back with a bravado bordering on panic. The homicidal expression she wore was enough to sustain the energy of his defence. It made his passes wild and not entirely accurate; it also added an element of unpredictability to his style.

For her part, Coilla poured all her resentment and hatred

of the bounty hunters into her onslaught. Only blood would assuage the injury they'd done her. She pounded at the one-eyed human's sword with such frenzy it was a wonder it didn't snap. He was hard put to fend off the assault. His attacking stance began dissolving into pure self-preservation.

Stryke had found that despite looking dissolute, Lekmann fenced like a demon. Theirs was a duel that demanded every ounce of concentration and strength.

It was an old orc adage that the way an enemy fought betrayed the way they thought. So it befitted his nature that the bounty hunter used feints and deceitful moves as key techniques. Stryke was equally adept at duplicity and replied in kind. Though he would have far preferred the honesty of straight-forward homicide.

They circled, alert for any flaw in each other's guard, ready to kill. Lekmann vaulted in, whipping his blade at Stryke's head. Stryke swatted it aside and paid him back with a swipe to the chest. It was short. They kept up their lethal dance.

Razatt-Kheage's outpourings of rage, frustration and orders continued, spouted in both his native tongue and universal. It stopped when a grunt on the floor below lashed out at his legs. The slaver jumped clear. In lieu of a weapon, he snatched up a bulky cloth sack and swung it down at the orc's head. He missed and nearly lost his balance. The grunt slashed the sack. A torrent of silver coins, the bounty hunters' payment, gushed out and bounced in all directions. Orcs and goblins slipped on them as they scattered.

Dozens of coins rolled the way of Stryke and Lekmann. Crunching underfoot, they slowed but didn't stop their combat. Both were tiring now and the fight was near the point where stamina could be the deciding element. Not that either allowed it to lessen the blows they dealt.

For all their strength, Haskeer and Blaan were hitting the same barrier. Haskeer knew he had to finish their bout quickly while he still had enough in reserve. He and the human were locked in a wrestling hold, Blaan's clasped hands in the small of Haskeer's back, one of Haskeer's arms trapped immovably. Drawing deep from his depleted well of energy, the orc slowly raised his free arm and repeatedly fisted the bounty hunter's head. Simultaneously he applied outward pressure with his snared arm.

The strain showed on Blaan's contorted face. He was struggling to contain his foe. Haskeer needed just one more bit of leverage. He found it. With all his might he stamped his boot down on Blaan's foot, heel first. The human cried out. Haskeer stomped repeatedly. With a great out-rush of breath, Blaan lost control and the hold was shattered.

He half staggered, half limped backwards. Haskeer lurched the few paces separating them and delivered a solid kick to Blaan's crotch. The human gave an anguished high-pitched scream. Without pause, and giving it all he'd got, Haskeer landed a swift combination of punches—to the chin, to the stomach, then to the chin again. Blaan went down like a felled oak. The wooden platform trembled.

Haskeer moved in and conferred a kicking on him, right foot, left foot, targeting any vulnerable spot that presented itself. Blaan's hand flashed out, grabbed one of Haskeer's legs, tugged and downed him. There was a scramble to be the first one up. They made it at the same time. Blaan closed the gap, his enormous face demonic with frenzy, and raised his ham fists. Bloodied and bruised, they were back to sparring.

Coilla was making headway with Aulay. She sent in blows high and low, forcing him to skip and swerve to avoid them. But his movements were leaden-footed, his vigour ebbing. She sensed a kill was close.

Jup and the grunts, working shoulder to shoulder, had thinned out the ranks of goblins. Just three or four were left, and they were retreating to the dais end of the room. When their backs were to the platform they put up a frenzied last stand. Two tried to break through the semicircle of approaching orcs. One swung his studded mace in a wide arc. A pair of orcs ducked under the flying weapon and shredded the henchlin's chest. Jup took care of the other. He dashed the sword from its grip and hacked into the creature's neck.

But that had given the two remaining goblins their chance. They sprang on to the dais and rained blows down on the

Wolverines' heads, preventing them from following. Razatt-Kheage sheltered behind them, raving encouragement.

Lekmann and Aulay, likewise being forced back by their implacable orc opponents, knew the game was up.

"Get out!" Lekmann bawled.

His partner needed no further encouragement. He swiftly backed off from Coilla, turned and ran. With a last flash of his blade in Stryke's direction, Lekmann did the same. The orc captain and corporal went after them.

Aulay tripped and fell. As he got up, Lekmann raced past him. He made the dais, arriving at a point between Haskeer and Blaan's fight to the left and the battling orcs and goblins to the right. Unimpeded, he scrambled up.

Swerving to evade a lone orc trying to stop him, Aulay got there too. Lekmann stretched a hand and hoisted him up. They turned to fend off Stryke and Coilla, who swept in a second later. All the humans and remaining goblins were on the platform. All the Wolverines battled to climb it.

All save Haskeer. Trading punches with Blaan at their end of the platform, he was oblivious. The human was more conscious of the need to withdraw. Still sparring, he began edging towards his comrades.

Alone among the Wolverines, Coilla managed to ascend the dais. She fetched up nearest Aulay and went for him.

"What does it take to stop you, bitch?" he snarled.

"Just die," she said.

He attacked. Coilla deflected the blows. Aulay turned his sword and started to advance again.

She held fast. Giving way to rage, he came at her recklessly with wild, ill-judged slashes. His guard was careless. A thrust missed her head by a good three inches. Seeing a chance, Coilla quickly spun to one side and chopped downward with all her strength.

Her blade sliced cleanly through the flesh and bone of his left wrist. The hand fell away and slapped wetly on the boards. A fountain of blood gushed from the stump. Agony and disbelief stamped on his face, Aulay began screaming.

Coilla drew back her sword to finish him.

From behind, a pair of massive arms encircled her waist. As though she weighed nothing, Blaan tossed her from the dais. She landed heavily on the floor below.

Lekmann pulled Aulay away. He was wailing. Copious quantities of his blood drenched the platform.

Haskeer caught up with Blaan. The human elbowed him in the stomach. Gasping, Haskeer doubled over. Blaan thundered in the direction of his fellow bounty hunters and the goblins. He stopped short of them and took hold of Razatt-Kheage's ponderous wooden throne. Haskeer was on his feet again and charging. Hoisting the chair like a toy, Blaan swung round and struck Haskeer with it. The force knocked the orc across the platform and slammed him into the wall.

Then Blaan hefted his load to the edge and hurled it down on the orcs. They scattered as it smashed to the floor.

Taking advantage of the confusion, the slaver led his henchlins and the bounty hunters to the door at the back of the dais. They were going through it before Stryke shouted out and everybody rushed the platform.

Too late. The door slammed in their faces. They heard bolts being thrown on the other side. Stryke and a couple of grunts shouldered it several times. Haskeer joined them and added his strength. But it wouldn't give.

"Forget it," Stryke panted.

Haskeer pounded his fist against the door in frustration. *"Damn!"*

Recovering from her fall, stretching her aching limbs, Coilla walked across the platform towards them. "I'm going to kill those bastards if it's the last thing I do," she vowed.

"Look out!" Jup yelled, pushing her aside.

A spear winged past and embedded itself in the wall.

It had been thrown by a goblin in the body of the room, wounded and bleeding but on his feet. Now he had a sword in his hand.

That was too much for Haskeer. He leapt from the platform and ran at the creature. The goblin took one ineffective swipe at him. Then Haskeer dashed away the sword with his bare hands and battered the henchlin senseless. Not content with that, he took the goblin by the scruff of its neck and hammered its head against the wall, again and again and again.

The others came over and watched the limp and lifeless body being reduced to pulp.

Jup said, "I think he's dead."

"I know that, short arse!" Haskeer snapped. He unceremoniously dumped the goblin's body.

Stryke smiled. "Good to have you back, Sergeant."

From their rear came the splintering crash of wood. They turned.

A Watcher, grim-faced and unstoppable, was beating its way through what was left of the door to the street. There were others beyond it.

Coilla sighed. "Fuck, what a day."

16

"Don't try taking on the things," Stryke warned. "Let's just get away from them."

"Easier said than done," Jup reckoned, staring at the lumbering homunculus.

They backed off as the Watcher moved into the room. The vast head slowly turned, its gem eyes, animated by synthetic life, surveying the scene. Two of its fellows filed through the door behind it.

The foremost Watcher lifted its hands, palms up. There was a loud click. Shiny metallic blades sprang from slots in the heels of the hands. They were half a foot long and wickedly keen. As though on signal, the other Watchers snapped out similar weapons.

"Uh-oh," Jup said.

"Minimum engagement, then," Stryke amended. "Just what it takes to get out of here."

"That could turn out to be *whatever* it takes to get out of here," Coilla remarked, eyeing the Watchers. "I've seen them in action. They're faster than they look, and mercy's not their strong point."

"You do realise they've seen the weapons and that means they're in execution mode?" Jup asked.

"Yes," Stryke replied. "But remember the bleeding of the magic's made them less effective."

"There's a comfort."

The Watchers were on the move again. Their way.

"Can we *do* something?" Haskeer growled impatiently.

"All right," Stryke said. "Simple mission. All of us through that door."

"Now?" Coilla prompted.

He studied the advancing Watchers. "Now."

The band rushed forward, flowing to either side of the lead Watcher, intending to go around it. Dazzlingly fast, its arms shot out horizontally, barring the way. The other two did the same. Light glinted from their extended blades. Everybody stopped.

"Any more bright ideas?" Haskeer wondered, flirting with insubordination.

The homunculi kept coming, arms outstretched as though shepherding cattle. The band backtracked.

"Maybe we shouldn't go at this as a group," Stryke suggested. "They might find individual action harder to deal with."

"If you mean every Wolverine for themselves," Haskeer grumbled, "I wish you'd say so."

"You and me are going to have to have a little talk, Sergeant."

"Let's try getting out of here alive first," Coilla reminded them.

Jup had a notion. "Why don't we attack this one all at once? I mean, how invulnerable can they be?"

"I'm game," Haskeer rumbled, hefting a goblin's mace.

"We'll go for it," Stryke decided. "But if it doesn't work, don't linger. Ready? *Now!*"

They charged again, and set about the first Watcher. They slashed at it with swords, stabbed at it with daggers, pounded it with maces, crashed spears against it. Haskeer tried kicking it.

The Watcher stood impassive, stock still and completely unaffected.

The band moved back and regrouped. The Watchers resumed their inexorable advance.

"We're running out of room," Jup said, glancing behind them. "One more time?"

Stryke nodded. "And give it all you've got."

They thoroughly assaulted the creature. To the extent that spears snapped, blades broke and knives were blunted. None of it had any greater effect than before.

"Retreat!" Stryke yelled.

Coilla jerked her head at the dais. "Up there, Stryke. It's all we've got left."

Haskeer grinned. "Yeah, I bet they can't climb!"

They made for the platform and swarmed on to it. The Watchers turned and followed.

"Now what?" Coilla wanted to know.

"Let's try that door again."

Battering it with maces made no difference.

"Inlaid with steel, I'd say," Stryke judged.

"We have to get out of this building fast," Coilla said, "before more of those damn things get here."

The three already in the room reached the platform and stopped.

"See?" Haskeer announced smugly. "Can't climb."

As one, the trio of Watchers retracted their blades. Their hands curled into fists. They lifted them above their heads. Then they brought them down on the dais with the force of a small earthquake. The platform shook mightily. They did it again. Wood cracked and splintered. The platform lurched at an angle. Wolverines fought to keep their footing. A final triple blow did it.

The dais collapsed with a roar.

Planks, struts and Wolverines crashed to the ground in a cloud of dust and chaos.

"They don't *need* to climb, bonehead!" Jup yelled.

"I think it's back to every orc for themselves," Coilla spluttered, extricating herself from a tangle of timber.

"I've had enough of these fucking pests!" Haskeer bellowed. He seized a large joist and made for a Watcher.

"*No!* Get back here!" Stryke ordered.

Haskeer ignored him. Muttering, he strode to the nearest Watcher and smashed the beam across its chest. The joist snapped in two. Nothing changed for the Watcher.

Suddenly it brought up an arm and delivered a weighty backhander that sent Haskeer flying. He collided with the remains of the platform. A couple of grunts ran to help him up. Haskeer cursed and waved them away.

Stryke spotted something that gave him an idea. "Calthmon, Breggin, Finje. Come with me, I want to try something."

As the rest of the band played cat and mouse with the

Watchers, he led them to the other side of the room. The chain Haskeer had brought with him was lying on the floor. Stryke explained the plan.

"The chain's a little short for our purposes," he added, "but let's give it a go."

Finje and Calthmon took hold of one end, Breggin and Stryke the other. He decided there weren't enough of them, and beckoned over Toche and Gant.

Three orcs at each end of the chain, they positioned themselves behind a Watcher. It was busy having chunks of wood thrown at it by the others. The missiles bounced off uselessly. At Stryke's word his group got a good grip on the chain, then they ran.

The taut chain hit the back of the Watcher's legs. The orcs kept going, pulling on the chain like two tug-of-war teams. At first nothing happened. They strained on the chain. The Watcher swayed a little. It took a step forward. They kept tugging, muscles standing out, breath laboured. The homunculus started swaying again, more pronounced this time. They pulled harder.

Suddenly the Watcher toppled. It hit the floor with a deafening crash.

Almost immediately its arms and legs began working frenziedly. It thrashed and wriggled in an attempt to right itself, making a metallic scraping noise on the flagstones.

"That'll give the bastard something to think about," Stryke said.

They were targeting another Watcher when the sound of Haskeer whooping distracted them.

Launching himself from the platform debris, he landed on the back of a Watcher. The creature twisted and shook, in a stiff kind of way, trying to dislodge him. Its arms were too rigid to reach the orc, so it snapped out its blades to poke at its unseen assailant. That made it even more dangerous for Haskeer, who had to dodge the probing steel.

He got his arms around the Watcher's neck and his feet in the small of its back. Pulling with the former and pushing with the latter, he rocked back and forth. The Watcher was soon rocking with him. Its efforts to skewer the tormentor on its back grew more urgent. Haskeer was hard put to avoid a hit, but he kept on pushing and pulling with all his strength. The fact that the Watcher was already moving and had its arms up helped Haskeer's scheme. It reeled like a drunk. Then its balance deserted it.

As it fell backwards, Haskeer swiftly disentangled himself and leapt clear. The Watcher smacked on to the floor with a resonant clang.

Stryke and the others, watching this, ran in and showered the downed creature with blows from their weapons. They needed a little fancy footwork to evade its flailing blades, but its accuracy was out of whack. Haskeer joined them, snatched a mace from a grunt and set to on the Watcher's face. He struck one of the gemlike eyes and it cracked. Encouraged, he hammered at it again. It smashed.

A high-pressure plume of green smoke spurted from the fissure. Almost reaching the ceiling, it formed a small cloud that shed verdant-coloured droplets. The smell it gave off was foul and some of the orcs clamped hands over their noses and mouths.

Following Haskeer's example, Stryke leaned in and hacked at the other eye with his sword. That shattered too, releasing another gassy spout. The Watcher shuddered, its legs and arms hammering the floor. Gagging at the odour, the band backed off.

"I don't think we could have done that in the old days," Stryke told them.

The remaining Watcher was nowhere near the door now and engaged with the rest of the band.

"*Get out!*" Stryke shouted at them.

"Orcs don't retreat!" Haskeer exclaimed.

Jup and Coilla arrived in time to hear that.

"We do this time, dummy!" Jup said.

"The way your kind does, eh?"

"For fuck's sake, *move*, you two!" Coilla urged. "Argue later!"

Everybody ran for the door.

Four more Watchers were coming along the alley from its

open end. Enough to block that as an escape route. The Watcher in the house was moving to the doorway.

"Don't give up, do they?" Jup remarked.

Stryke realised the only chance was to try getting over the wall that blocked their end of the alley. It was tall and plaster smooth. He got two of the band's beefier members, Haskeer and Breggin, to give leg-ups.

Two grunts went straight up and balanced on the wall's narrow top. They reported another alley on the other side, then started reaching down to help the next in line. Troopers began scrambling up and dropping down the other side. Because of his shortness, Jup needed an extra boost from a grumbling Haskeer, and the grunts above had to stretch lower for his hand.

Only Coilla, Stryke, Breggin and Haskeer were still to go when the Watcher came out of the house. Stryke and Coilla got to the top of the wall.

"Hurry!" Haskeer called out.

He and Breggin stood, arms above their heads. Eager hands clasped theirs and began pulling. The Watcher made a grab for Haskeer's foot. He shook free and scrambled frantically. The four other Watchers were near now.

Haskeer and Breggin made the top. Everybody lowered themselves into the next thoroughfare.

Jup made a face. "Phew, that was close!"

A section of the wall they'd just climbed exploded. Masonry fell, powdery dust billowed. Tearing aside the obstruction like paper, a Watcher appeared, white plaster coating its metal body. A little further along, the fist of another blasted through.

"Get out of here!" Stryke ordered. "And conceal your weapons! We don't want to attract even more attention."

Swords were awkwardly hidden. Larger weapons like spears and maces were reluctantly discarded. The Wolverines ran.

They got themselves into the main thoroughfares of the quarter and slowed down a bit. Stryke had them break up into three groups rather than attract attention as a mob. He led with Coilla, Jup, Haskeer and a couple of grunts.

"I don't know if the Watchers have a way of communicating

with each other," he told them in an undertone. "But sooner or later they're all going to know and be after us."

"So it's the horses, the weapons and out of here, right?" Jup said.

"Right, only we forget the weapons. It'd be too risky hanging around at the entrance checkpoint. Anyway, we've got some weapons."

"Getting the horses is a risk too," Coilla said.

"It's one we've got to take."

"I need one myself," she remembered. "We'll be short."

"We'll buy another."

"With what?"

"Pellucid's all we've got. Fortunately it's as good as any currency. I'll dig out a little before we go into the stables. Don't want to flaunt the stuff."

"Pity about those weapons," Haskeer complained. "I had a couple of favourites there."

"Me too," Jup agreed. "But it's worth it to get you and Coilla back."

Haskeer couldn't work out if the dwarf was being sarcastic, so he didn't reply.

All the way to the stables, near the main entrance, they were nervous of what might happen. At one point a pair of Watchers appeared ahead of them. Stryke signalled everybody to be calm and they walked past them without incident. It seemed the homunculi didn't have any way of communicating over distances. Stryke speculated that perhaps that was another consequence of the fading magic.

They got to the stables. Their horses were collected, and another was bought, without too much delay or attracting suspicion.

Back on the street, Jup said, "Why don't we stay in three groups while we make our way out? Less attention."

"Hang on," Coilla put in. "Won't it look suspicious when the first group leaves without collecting any weapons? Could go bad on groups two and three."

"Perhaps they'll just assume we didn't bring any."

"Orcs without weapons? Who's going to believe that?"

"Coilla's right," Stryke decided. "What we're going to do is stay together. We get as near the main entrance as we can on foot, then mount up and make a run for it."

"You're the boss," Jup conceded.

They were in sight of Hecklowe's main gate when a number of Watchers, perhaps a dozen or more, appeared a way behind them. They were marching purposefully in the same direction. A crowd was gathering and walking with them, aware that such a large number of the homunculi meant some kind of drama was about to unfold.

"For us, you think, Stryke?" Jup asked.

"I don't think they're out for a ramble, Sergeant." The band was further from the exit than he would have liked. But there was no choice now. "Right, let's go for it! Mount up!"

They hurriedly obeyed as passersby stared and pointed.

"Now move out!"

They spurred their horses and galloped for the open gates. Elves, gremlins and dwarves scattered, shaking fists and bawling insults.

The gallop became a charge. Up ahead, Stryke saw a Watcher starting to close the gate. It was heavy work, even for a creature of such prodigious strength, and went slowly.

Jup and Stryke got there first. Stryke took a chance and pulled up his horse. He sidled as close to the Watcher as he dared and booted it in the head. Coming in high, and with the added strength of a horse behind it, the blow toppled the creature. The Watchers tending the queue turned and made for Stryke. One came out of the guardhouse. Blades zinged from their palms.

Jup had stopped too. "Get going!" Stryke told him.

The dwarf rode off, dispersing the crowd waiting to get in. There were outraged shouts.

Then the rest of the band tore through the gates. Stryke prodded his mount and went after them.

They left Hecklowe behind.

They didn't slow until they'd put a good five miles between themselves and the freeport. Getting a bearing on the trail to Drogan, they fell to exchanging stories of what had befallen them since they were parted. Only Haskeer had nothing to contribute.

Recounting her experiences with the bounty hunters, Coilla still burned with resentment at the way she'd been treated.

"I'm not going to forget it, Stryke. I vow I'll make them pay, the human scum. The worst thing was the feeling of . . . well, helplessness. I'd rather kill myself than let that happen again. And you know what kept going through my head?"

"No, tell me?"

"I kept thinking how it was just like our lives. Like the lives of all orcs. Born into somebody else's service, having to be loyal to a cause you haven't chosen, risking your life."

They all saw her point.

"We're changing that," Stryke said. "Or at least trying to."

"Even if it means dying I'll never go back to it," she promised.

He wasn't alone in nodding agreement.

Coilla turned her attention to Haskeer. "You haven't explained your behaviour yet." Her tone was curt.

"It's not easy . . . ," he began, and trailed off.

Stryke spoke for him. "Haskeer's not entirely sure what did happen. None of us is. I'll fill you in as we ride."

"It's true," Haskeer told her. "And I'm . . . sorry."

It wasn't a word he was accustomed to using, and Coilla was a little taken aback. But as she couldn't decide to accept his apology until she knew more, she didn't answer.

Stryke changed the subject. He told her about their encounter with Serapheim. She recounted hers.

"Something didn't ring true about that human," she reckoned.

"I know what you mean."

"Do we count him as an enemy or a friend? Not that I'm used to thinking of humans in friendly terms."

"Well, we can't deny that he helped us find you by sending us to Hecklowe."

"But what about the trap at the house?"

"Might not have been his fault. After all, he got us to the right place, didn't he?"

"The biggest mystery," Jup said, "is how he seemed to

disappear each time. Particularly back there at the slaver's house. I don't understand it."

"He didn't come in," Coilla supplied.

"It's obvious," Stryke volunteered. "He went over the wall, same as us." He didn't entirely convince himself, let alone any of the others.

"And how does he *survive?*" Coilla added. "If he really does wander the country unarmed, that is. These are times when even an armed orc does that at their peril."

"Maybe he *is* mad," Jup offered. "Many of the insane seem to have the luck of the gods."

Stryke sighed. "Probably no sense in worrying about it. Whoever he is, chances are we'll never see him again."

The strategy meeting was held in the usual cavernous chamber. It was a place that looked more organic than fashioned, and water freely flowed through it.

Adpar's military commanders and her Council of Elders were present. She was contemptuous of both, particularly the latter, whom she regarded as senile fools. But she had to concede to herself that even an absolute ruler needed help administering her subjects. She saw no reason to hide her disdain, however.

They fell silent as she addressed them. "We are close to defeating the merz entirely," she announced. "Only two or three nests of the vermin remain to be cleared. It is my command . . ." She paused and corrected herself for the sake of tiresome nyadd politics. "It is my wish that this be achieved before summer is out. Or what passes for the season these days. I don't have to tell you that the *real* cold of winter will mean another year's delay. That isn't tolerable. It gives the enemy a chance to regroup, to . . . *breed.*" An expression of disgust passed across her face. "Do any of you see a problem with that?" Her tone didn't exactly invite dissent.

She scanned their sombre, and in most cases compliant, faces. Then a bolder-than-normal swarm commander raised a webbed hand.

"Yes?" she asked imperiously.

"If it pleases Your Majesty," the officer replied, his voice edged with timorousness, "there are logistic difficulties. The remain-

ing merz colonies are the hardest to get to, and they're bound to
be better defended now that our intentions are clear."

"Your point?"

"There are bound to be casualties, Majesty."

"I repeat: your point?"

"Majesty, we—"

"You think I'm concerned with the fact that a few lives may
be lost? Even *many* lives? The realm is more important than any
individual, as the swarm is more important than a single member. You, Commander, would do well to—"

Adpar stopped abruptly. A hand went to her head. She swayed.

"Majesty?" a nearby minion inquired.

Pain was coursing through her. It felt as though her heart was
pumping fire and searing her veins.

"Majesty, are you all right?" the official asked again.

Agony clasped her chest. She thought she might faint. The
thought of such a display of weakness gave her a little strength.

Her eyes had been closed. She hadn't realised. Several offi-
cials and a clutch of commanders were hovering around her.

"Would you like us to summon the healers, Majesty?" one of
them asked anxiously.

"Healers? Healers? What need have *I* of their kind? You think
me in need of their attentions?"

"Er, no, Majesty," the awed speaker replied. "Not if you say
so, Majesty."

"I *say* so! Your impertinence in bringing up the subject means
this meeting is at an end." She had to get away from them, and
could only hope they didn't see through her flimsy excuses and
haste. "I'm retiring to my private chambers. We'll discuss military matters again later."

All bowed as she left. None dared offer to help her. They
exchanged alarmed looks as she slithered into the tunnel leading to her quarters.

Once she was out of sight, Adpar began gulping air. She
leaned over, cupped her hands in water and splashed her face
with it. The pain was worse. It rushed from her stomach to her
throat. She retched blood.

For the first time in her life she felt afraid.

17

Alfray and his group were near enough to Drogan that they could see the trees fringing Calyparr Inlet. They were no more than a couple of hours away.

The weather grew ever more unpredictable. As opposed to yesterday, for instance, today had been sunny and noticeably warmer. Many suspected that the varying strength of magic created pockets of good and bad weather. Alfray was sure this was true. But one drawback of more clement weather was that it brought the fairies out. They mostly irritated the band, and led to much slapping of flesh, though some preferred snacking on them.

Alfray and Kestix were discussing the relative merits of other warbands and their place in the league table every orc kept in his head. The conversation was interrupted by the sighting of two riders coming in from the east. They were dots at first, but riding all-out. Soon they were near enough to be seen properly.

"They're orcs, Corporal," Kestix said.

Nearer still, they were identified as Jad and Hystykk.

By the time they drew up, Alfray was alarmed. "What's happened?" he asked. "Where are the others?"

"Take it easy, Corporal, everything's OK," Hystykk assured him. "The others are following. We've got news."

As it was an agreeable day, Jennesta decided to intimidate her general in the open air.

They were in a palace courtyard, with one of the citadel's massive walls towering over them. There was nothing as frivolous as a seat. All that broke the drab aspect was a large open-topped water butt. Its prosaic function was to feed horse troughs.

Mersadion stood in the wall's shadow. The queen faced him ten paces away. All things considered, he thought it incongruous that she should be the one in sunlight.

Jennesta was in full flow, berating him for his perceived shortcomings.

". . . and still no word from those wretched bounty hunters or any of the many other agents you've sent out at the expense of my coffers."

"No, ma'am. I'm sorry, ma'am."

"And now, when I tell you I want to take a hand in events myself and ask you to muster a modest army, what do you do? You give me excuses."

"Not so much excuses, my lady, with all due respect. But ten thousand is hardly *modest*, and—"

"Are you telling me I don't have even that trifling number of followers and bonded orcs?" She fixed him with a withering stare. "Are you saying that my popularity among the lower orders is insufficient to raise a meagre ten thousand willing to die for my cause?"

"Of *course* not, Majesty! It isn't a question of loyalty but logistics. We can build the army you need, only not as quickly as you've decreed. We are, after all, stretched on several fronts at the moment and . . ."

His defence trailed off when he saw what she was doing.

Jennesta was silently mouthing something, and weaving an intricate conjuration with her hands. Eventually she cupped them, three or four inches apart. As he watched, spellbound, a small swirling cloud formed between her palms. It looked like a miniature cyclone. She stared at it intently. Tiny streaks of yellow and white began rippling through the darkening mist, like diminutive lightning bolts. The little cloud, still twisting and flashing, slowly moulded itself into a perfectly round form, about the size of an apple.

It started to glow. Soon it shined brighter than any lamp, giving off a brilliance it was difficult to look at. Yet it was so beautiful that Mersadion couldn't tear his eyes away. Then he remembered the spell she had cast on a battlefield not long ago.

It began in a similar way to this and ended with countless numbers of the enemy rendered sightless for the slaughter. A cold chill tickled his spine. He sent a silent prayer to the gods, begging their grace.

She removed one hand and laid flat the palm of the other, so that the radiant ball balanced on it just above the skin. Mersadion's fear didn't lessen, but he remained transfixed.

Jennesta slowly raised her hand until the radiant sphere was level with her face. Then, looking almost coquettish, she puffed her cheeks and blew at it. Very gently, like a maiden with a dandelion clock.

The little ball, dazzling as a minute sun, sailed from her palm. It drifted in Mersadion's direction. His muscles tensed. When the sphere had almost reached him, and apparently following the Queen's hand movements, it veered to one side and headed for the wall. Mersadion's gaze followed as it floated into the brickwork.

There was a blinding flash of light and a detonation like a thunderclap. The force of displaced air buffeted Mersadion and breezed Jennesta's gown.

He cried out.

A black scorch mark scarred the wall. A sulphurous odour hung in the air.

Mersadion looked at her, slack-jawed. She held another glowing ball.

"You were saying?" she asked, as though she really expected a recap. "Something about not being willing to carry out a straightforward order, wasn't it?"

"I am more than *willing* to carry out your orders, ma'am," he babbled. "This is simply a case of numbers, of—"

This time she seemed to flick the ball, and it moved with greater speed.

It struck the wall a couple of feet above his head with another deafening bang. He flinched. Small bits of stone and flakes of masonry showered his quivering head.

"You're offering me excuses again, General," she chided, "when what I want are solutions."

As though having started the process made it easier for her,

yet another ball appeared on her palm, fully formed and pulsing. With a girlish laugh she tossed it like a child's toy.

It flew his way, looking as though it would hit him this time.
But the trajectory was finely judged, and as he pressed his back
to the wall the sphere went past.

The ball collided with the water butt. Though it wasn't really
a collision. The orb touched the wood of the barrel and was
absorbed by it. Instantly, the water bubbled and boiled. Steam
rose from the butt's open top and sprayed from between its
higher metal hasps.

Badly shaken, Mersadion looked back at Jennesta. She hadn't
produced another sphere so he started talking, fast. "Of course,
Majesty, anything you will is possible and can be undertaken
immediately. I'm sure we can overcome any minor obstacles in
the path of gathering an army."

"Good, General. I knew you'd see sense." Her point made, she
dusted her hands by slapping them lightly together, as though
giving him a round of slow applause. "One other thing," she
added.

All the tension seeped back into Mersadion's body. "Ma'am?"

"A question of discipline. You must be aware that this Stryke
and his warband are taking on the mantle of heroes for certain
sections of the army."

"Unfortunately that's true, Majesty. Though it's by no means
widespread."

"Be sure it doesn't become so. If a thing like that takes hold it
can fester. What are you doing to counter it?"

"We're making widely known your version . . . er, the *truth*,
that is, of how the Wolverines went renegade. Members of the
lower ranks heard defending the actions of the outlaws are subject to a flogging."

"Make that all ranks, and punish them for *any* mention of
Stryke and his band. I want their names stamped out. As to
flogging, it's too lenient. Execution should be the price. Burn a
few troublemakers as an example and you'll soon see an end to
sedition."

"Yes, ma'am." Whatever doubts he might have had about the
effectiveness of a strategy like that he kept to himself.

"Attention to detail, Mersadion. It's what keeps the realm functioning."

Eager to ingratiate himself, he replied, "Ah, the secret of your success, my lady."

"No, General. The secret of my success is brutality."

For the better part of two days, Stryke, Coilla, Haskeer, Jup and the grunts travelled uneventfully. They stopped as infrequently as possible and made the best time they could.

By the afternoon of the second day they were bone tired. But they could see a line of trees that marked the inlet, and far to the right, the edge of Drogan Forest.

As shadows were lengthening, the rear lookouts saw four horsemen coming at them from the east. There was no cover for miles and it seemed reasonable to assume they weren't part of a larger group.

"Trouble, you think?" Jup wondered.

"If it is I reckon we can handle four, don't you?" Stryke told him. He slowed the column to a trot.

A few minutes passed and Haskeer said, "They're orcs."

Stryke took a look for himself. "You're right."

"Doesn't mean to say they're friendly," Coilla reminded them.

"No. But like I said, they're only four."

In due course the quartet of riders arrived. The foremost threw up his arm in greeting. "Well met!"

"Well met," Stryke replied cautiously. "What's your business?"

The leading orc stared. "You're him, aren't you?"

"What?"

"Stryke. We've never met, Captain, but I've seen you once or twice." He scanned the others. "And these are Wolverines?"

"Yes, I'm Stryke. Who are you and what do you want?"

"Corporal Trispeer, sir." He nodded at his companions. "Troopers Pravod, Kaed and Rellep."

"You with a warband?"

"No. We were infantry in Queen Jennesta's horde."

"Were?" Jup picked up.

"We've . . . left."

"Nobody leaves Jennesta's service unless it's feet first," Coilla said. "Or has she started a retirement scheme?"

"We've gone AWOL, Corporal. Same as your band."

"Why?" Stryke wanted to know.

"I'm surprised at you asking, Captain. We've had enough of Jennesta, pure and simple. Her injustice, her cruelty. Orcs'll fight, you know that, and we'll do it without grumbling. But she's pushing us too far."

The trooper called Kaed added, "Lot of us don't feel comfortable fighting for humans neither, begging your pardon, sir."

"And we're not the only ones to vote with our feet," Trispeer went on. "Granted it's just a few so far, but we reckon it'll grow."

"You were looking for us?" Jup said.

"No, Sergeant. Well, not exactly. Once we deserted we had hoped to find you but didn't know where to look. Fact is we've just come from Hecklowe. Heard about the uproar there and figured it sounded like your band. Somebody told us you'd been seen riding west, so . . ."

"Why do you say you'd hoped to find us?" Stryke asked.

"Your band's been officially named renegades. There's a bounty on your heads. Big one."

"We know that."

"You're being slandered by everybody from Jennesta down. They say you're common outlaws, that you kill your own kind, and that you've stolen some kind of treasure belonging to the queen."

Stryke's face clouded. "I'm not surprised. What's your point?"

"Well, some of us reckon we're not being told the truth. You've always had a good reputation, Captain, and we know the way the queen and her lackeys lie about those who've fallen out of favour."

"For what it's worth," Coilla informed him, "they are lying about us."

"I knew it." He turned and nodded at his companions. They

nodded and smiled back. He went on, "So we reckoned you might be able to use us."

That puzzled Stryke. "What do you mean? Use you for what?"

"We figured that you've got to be mustering an army, a force of disenchanted orcs, like us. Maybe to fight Jennesta. Maybe to found a homeland. We want to join."

Stryke contemplated their hopeful faces for a moment. He sighed. "I'm not running a crusade, Corporal, and I'm certainly not looking for recruits. We didn't mean to set out on the path we're following and now we're having to make the best of it."

Trispeer's face fell. "But, Captain—"

"It's hard enough being responsible for the lives and fortunes of my band members. I don't want the burden of taking on more." Softening his tone, he added, "You'll have to find your own way."

The corporal looked disappointed. They all did. "You mean you're not making a stand? You don't want to strike a blow for all us orcs in bondage?"

"We're making a stand of sorts, but in our own way. It's going to take somebody else to strike that blow. You're looking in the wrong place. I'm sorry."

Trispeer decided to be philosophical. "Oh, well, perhaps I knew it was too good to be true. But you and your band's starting to be celebrated in the ranks. There'll be others thinking what we thought and wanting to join with you."

"I'll tell them what I've just told you."

"I guess we'll have to do something else, then."

Haskeer entered the conversation. "Like what?"

"Get ourselves to Black Rock Forest, maybe."

"To take up a life of banditry?" Coilla guessed.

"What else can we do?" Trispeer replied shamefacedly. "Apart from mercenary work, and none of us fancy that."

"That it should come to this for our kind," she brooded. "Fucking humans."

The corporal smiled. "It's them we'll concentrate on. An orc's got to eat."

"If that's what you decide, don't go too near Black Rock itself,"

Stryke advised. "There's kobolds there that aren't too fond of orcs after we had a recent run-in with them."

"We'll remember that. Anyway, maybe it won't be Black Rock, perhaps we'll just go freelance and fight humans for the hell of it. We'll see."

"Need anything?" Haskeer asked. "Not that we got much food or water, but—"

"No, thanks, Sergeant. We're fine for now."

"Maybe you could use a little of this," Stryke said. He dug out his pouch of pellucid. With his other hand he patted his jerkin, then drew the proclamation of the Wolverines' renegade status from a pocket. It was all he had that was suitable. Somehow it seemed apt. He folded it to make a rudimentary bag and poured in an ample quantity of the drug. This he handed to the corporal.

"Thanks, Captain, that's generous. Appreciate it." He beamed. "You know the old saying: 'Crystal gets you through times of no coin better than coin gets you through times of no crystal.'"

"Enjoy. Only use it wisely. It's been a mixed blessing for us."

Trispeer looked mystified by the comment but said nothing.

Stryke stretched out and offered the corporal a warrior's handshake. "We've got to be moving on to Drogan. Good luck."

"And to you. The gods be with you in whatever it is you're doing. Watch your backs."

He and his troopers saluted them, turned their horses and started galloping back more or less the way they had come.

As they watched them go, Coilla said, "They seemed like decent orcs."

"I thought so too," Jup agreed. "It's a pity we couldn't let them join us. You know, maybe we could use a few more swords."

Stryke firmly crushed that. "No. Like I said, I'm carrying enough of a load as it is."

"If what he said about you is true, Stryke," Coilla mused, "you could be a rallying point for—"

"I don't want to be no rallying point."

Jup grinned and announced melodramatically, "Stryke, messiah!" His commander just glared at him.

* * *

It was night when they arrived for the rendezvous.

Stryke wished he could have been more specific about where they were going to meet. He couldn't, because none of them knew the area well enough. So they had to ride along the treeline bordering the inlet, in the dark, looking for their comrades.

Haskeer, as of old, was the first to complain. "I think we're wasting our time. Why don't we wait 'til morning?"

This time Coilla was inclined to agree with him. "There might be something in that. We need light."

"We were late getting here," Stryke said. "Least we can do is try looking for them. We'll give it another hour. But I reckon we're best dismounting."

That gave Haskeer the opportunity for a bit more grumbling.

Leading their horses, they walked by the undergrowth that spread from the trees. They could hear the flow of water in the inlet, perhaps a hundred feet away.

"Maybe they didn't get here," Haskeer offered.

"What do you mean by that?" Jup asked.

"They were only half a band. Anything could have happened."

"*We're* only half a band," Stryke reminded him, "and we got here."

"Could be they went into Drogan to parley with the centaurs," Coilla suggested.

"We'll see. Now pipe down, all of you. There could be foes as well as friends about."

They'd trudged in silence for another ten minutes when there was a rustle in the undergrowth. Swords were quietly drawn. A pair of shadowy figures emerged from the bushes.

"Eldo! Noskaa!" Coilla exclaimed.

Greetings were exchanged, weapons resheathed. Then the grunts led them into the thicket and to their camp.

Alfray came forward, beaming, and clasped Coilla's arm. "Good to see you, Corporal! And Stryke, Jup!"

"I'm here too, you know," Haskeer rumbled.

Alfray frowned at him. "Yes, well, you've got some explaining to do."

"And it'll be done," Stryke promised. "Don't be too hard on him. How was your journey here? What's happening? Any developments?"

"Whoa!" Alfray grinned. "Journey more or less uneventful. Nothing much happening. No developments."

"Well, we've got a lot to tell *you*," Jup said.

"Come and eat, and rest. You look like you could use it."

The band reunited. Grunts hailed each other. There was back-slapping, warriors' grips, laughter and chatter. Food and drink were issued, and they allowed themselves a fire to temper the cold. Sitting round it, they bartered news.

At length they discussed the centaurs.

"We've seen nothing of them," Alfray reported. "Mind you, we haven't ventured far into the forest. Thought it best to stick to your advice and just observe."

"You did right," Stryke confirmed.

"So how best to handle it?"

"Peaceable approach. We've no argument with centaurs. Anyway, they're going to outnumber us and it's their home ground."

"Makes sense. Only don't forget that though they're slow to rouse, they can be unforgiving enemies."

"That's why we'll go in under a flag of truce and offer a trade."

"And if they won't treat, what then?" Haskeer said.

"Then we'll think about other ways. If that means hostile action, well, it's what we're trained for. But diplomacy first." He gave his sergeant a pointed look. "And I won't tolerate anybody in this band not toeing that line. We only fight if I say so, or if we're attacked out of hand."

With the exception of Haskeer, who said nothing, there was general agreement with that.

Alfray stretched his hands to the modest fire. Like everybody else's, his breath was visibly misting. "This damn cold isn't getting any less," he complained.

Stryke pulled closer his jerkin and nodded. "We could be better kitted out than this standard issue."

"We saw a small herd of lembarrs this morning. I was think-ing of bagging a few for furs. They're still quite plentiful in these parts, so we could cull a few without doing too much harm."

"Good idea. Fresh meat too. Going into the forest at this hour isn't wise; it could look like a raid. Let's rise early, do some hunt-ing, then get ourselves to Drogan."

They were up at first light.

Stryke decided to lead the hunting party himself. Jup and Haskeer volunteered to go along. They picked Zoda, Hystykk, Gleadeg, Vobe, Bhose and Orbon to join them. It was a good number; split into two stalking groups it wasn't too many to spook the prey, but enough to carry back the carcasses they'd need.

What they couldn't take were horses. Lembarrs had both an uncanny ability to detect their approach and an aversion to the animals. The best way to put a lembarr to flight was to go any-where near it on horseback. They had to be hunted on foot.

As they were about to set off, Alfray took Stryke aside. "I think you should leave the stars with me," he said.

Stryke was taken aback. "Why?"

"The more we get, the more precious they are. What if some-thing happens to you on the hunt and they're lost? Matter of fact, maybe we should do something similar to the crystal, like dividing them amongst the officers. Haskeer excepted, of course."

"Well . . ."

"You think I'm going to do the same as Haskeer and run off with them? With two-thirds of the band around me?"

"It's not that I don't trust you, old friend, you know that. But I've been thinking about what might have happened to Haskeer. Thinking about it a lot. Suppose it was an enchantment that made him act that way?"

"Cast by Jennesta, you mean?"

"She's the most likely suspect."

"Then what's to stop her doing the same to you? If it *was* one of her spells, that's an argument for leaving them here, isn't it? 'Cause the first thing I'd do is issue an order for the others to keep an eye on me, and if I started acting strange they'd hog-tie me. That or cut me down."

Stryke knew he meant it. "All right," he agreed reluctantly. He unclipped the pouch and gave it to him. "But we're going to have to give some thought to security for the future."

"Right. Trust me. Now go and get us some winter outfits."

18

In under an hour they were out on the plain and had sighted their first herd of lembarrs. They resembled small deer, and the males had antlers, but their build was much more robust. Their shaggy, abundant pelts, which were brown in colour and streaked with grey and white, were like bear fur, and almost as prized.

As the animals grazed unawares, the hunters split into two groups. Haskeer led four of the grunts. Their job was to act as beaters and drive the animals toward the second group for the kill. This group consisted of Stryke, Jup and the two remaining troopers.

The hunt started well. With the element of surprise on their side, they swiftly downed three lembarrs. After that, the quarry grew more wary and required some determined chasing. They were not exceptionally fleet beasts, and an orc could match their speed on the flat. It was when they got themselves into less certain terrain that the lembarrs' agility gave them an edge.

Stryke found himself working as a backstop, well to the rear of his group, as Haskeer's party stampeded half a dozen of the prey in their direction. Three took off at angles and were lost. Two bowled into Jup and the grunts, who proceeded to lay into them with spears and swords. The last slipped through and came Stryke's way, running fit to burst.

Raising his sword, he made ready to block the animal and finish it. The lembarr wasn't to be caught that easily. When only a couple of feet away it veered and shot past him. Stryke's blade cut air.

"*Mine!*" he yelled, and dashed after it.

He wasn't sure if the others heard him, absorbed as they were in slaughter.

The fleeing creature ran into a copse. He crashed in after it, ducking low and swatting branches away. A minute later they were out the other side and on level sward. Stryke began to gain. The lembarr swerved and headed for a series of hillocks. It climbed the first one like a goat, Stryke twenty paces behind. Then it was down into a dip and up the next incline.

It was hard work but Stryke was enjoying it.

He reached the next small plateau just a couple of feet behind his target. The creature went down the other, steeper side half running, half skidding, into a gully below. Stryke slid after it. The lembarr reached the bottom, spun to its right and flashed into some trees. Panting now, Stryke followed. He caught a glimpse of the white streaky fur a spear cast distant. Putting on a burst of speed, he dashed for it.

Then the world fell in on his head.

He went down, a searing pain hammering his temple, and rolled across the mushy leaf carpet. On his back, dizzy and hurting, he started to come out of the black maw that had nearly swallowed him.

Somebody was standing over him. He made that several somebodies as his vision cleared. One of them snatched away the sword he was still holding. They conversed with each other in a clipped, guttural and all too familiar tongue.

The goblins hauled him rudely to his feet. He groaned. They tore at his clothes, searching for other weapons. Satisfied he had none, they brandished maces at him, and one waved the club that had undoubtedly been used to bushwhack him. They had swords too, and their points jabbed and goaded him into motion. He lifted a hand to his head as he walked. One of the goblins roughly pulled it away and jabbered something he didn't understand. But the threatening tone was unmistakable.

They marched him to the end of the gully and up yet another hillock. His bones ached and he limped a little, yet they allowed no slowing of pace. At the top he looked down the far side and saw a sizeable longhouse. As they urged him to descend he thought that they couldn't have been too far from the rest of the hunting party. Trouble was, the chase had taken some unlikely twists and turns, and they might just as well have been half the land away. He couldn't count on help from that source.

Breathing heavily, he arrived at the building, surrounded by his posse of belligerent captors.

The longhouse could have been built by any one of a dozen races; it had the all-purpose look of a lot of Maras-Dantia's architecture. Simply but sturdily constructed from wood, with a thatched roof, it had a single door at one end. There had been a couple of windows at one time, which were now boarded over. The place had obviously been abandoned. It was decrepit. The thatch was badly weathered and wet rot had taken hold on some of the outer facing.

They bundled him through the door.

Razatt-Kheage was waiting for him.

The slaver grimaced hideously in what passed for a smile with goblins. His expression was redolent with triumph and vengeance. "Greetings, orc," he hissed.

"Greetings yourself." Stryke fought to regain his senses and rid his head of muddle. He defied the pain, pushing it away. "Couldn't wait to say goodbye properly, eh?"

"We trailed you."

"You don't say. Not to thank me, I'd guess."

"Oh, we want to . . . *thank* all of your band, personally. A plan that has the added advantage of money on your heads from Jennesta. And I've now seen a certain proclamation that indicates you have a relic of hers. I expect there'll be a reward for that too."

Stryke was glad he didn't have the stars on him. He looked to the six or seven goblins present. "You're going after my warband with this strength? Got a death wish or something?"

"I'm not doing it. I'll send word to Jennesta."

That sobered Stryke further. "And you think the band will stick around waiting for her army to get here?"

"As a matter of fact I was thinking of holding you hostage to make sure they do."

"They won't buy it, slaver. Not my band. You don't know much about orcs, do you?"

"Perhaps it would be amusing to learn something now," Razatt-Kheage replied mockingly. "Do feel free."

It suited Stryke to buy a little time and try to think of a strata-gem. "All orcs know that the cost of war is death. We grow up with the creed that you do your best to save a comrade in danger, but if that fails you don't go on risking everybody else's life for one individual. That's why using me as a hostage won't work. They'll walk away."

"Yet you did the exact opposite when you rescued your female comrade." He leered unpleasantly. "Perhaps some individuals are worth more than others. By which marker, the commander should be worth most of all. We shall see."

To keep him talking, Stryke changed the subject. "I don't see your human friends around."

"Business associates. They have gone their own way. It was a disagreeable parting. They seemed to blame me for being in some way responsible for you orcs escaping. I believe it might have come to *blows* if one of them hadn't been in need of a healer's assistance. Fortunately I was able to sell them a name."

"I bet they were grateful." He scanned the lengthy room. "So what now?"

"You'll be our guest while I draft a message for the Queen's agents." The slaver nodded at his henchlins.

They herded Stryke to the far end of the room. Like the rest of the hut there wasn't much there, save a brazier of glowing coals that took some of the chill out of the air. He was left near it while the guards conversed in their own tongue. Razatt-Kheage stayed near the door, standing at a rickety table. He had parchment and a quill.

Stryke glanced at the brazier. An insane idea formed. Something that would affect him as well as them, but he'd have the advantage of knowing it. Checking that nobody was watching, he slipped his hand into his belt pouch and scooped out a fistful of pellucid. He tossed it on to the fire. Then he dipped for some more and did it again. The massive quantity of pinkish crystals began discharging plumes of creamy white smoke.

No one noticed anything for a good half-minute as the smoke grew more copious. Stryke tried holding his breath. Then one of the goblins left his comrades and came over. He gawped at the smoking brazier. Stryke sneaked a quick look at the others. They hadn't realised anything was wrong yet. Time to act.

He didn't know very much about goblin biology. But he figured they shared one thing in common with most of the elder races. When he directed a sturdy kick at the goblin's crotch he found he was right. The henchlin emitted a keening squeak of pure agony and began to double up. So Stryke did it again.

The others were moving in. Stryke grasped the wheezing goblin's sword arm and brought it down hard on his upraised knee. The weapon was dislodged. Taking it and flipping his wrist, he drove the blade into the henchlin's back.

He made ready to face the others. They moved in warily, a semicircle of five heavily armed, determined assassins.

"You really do make a habit of this kind of thing, don't you?" Razatt-Kheage raged from behind them. "Every time you kill one of my servants you cost me coin! I think you'd be safer dead."

The henchlins levelled their weapons and kept coming. Stryke was still holding his breath.

More and more smoke billowed from the brazier. It began filling the enclosed longhouse. Milky tendrils started drifting across the floor. A thickening cloud formed in the rafters above.

One of the goblins moved in, hefting his mace.

Unable to hold his breath any longer, Stryke expelled it. By instinct he took another. He felt a familiar light-headedness and battled to hang on to his concentration.

Swinging his mace, the goblin charged.

Stryke side-stepped and slashed at him. *The rolling waves of an immense ocean.* He shook his head to clear it of the image. His swing had missed. He aimed another. That was avoided too. The henchlin sent in a blow of his own that came near to connecting with Stryke's shoulder. *A faultlessly blue sky.* Stryke backed off, desperately trying to focus on reality.

What worried him was that the goblin he was fighting didn't seem affected by the crystal. He couldn't tell if the others were or not.

Stryke went on the attack.

When he swung his blade it appeared to him to be many blades, each one birthing the next; a blade for every degree of space it passed through. So that at the end of its arc a shimmering multi-coloured fan hung in the air. The goblin's mace shattered it, imploding the chimera like a soap bubble.

That made Stryke mad. He powered forward, swiping at the henchlin, driving him back under a deluge of blows. As he did so, he thought he saw, through the kaleidoscopic pageant flashing in his mind's eye, that the goblin swayed unsteadily and wore a glassy expression.

Stryke took hold of his sword two-handed, as much to have something to hang on to as anything else, and dashed the mace from his opponent's hands. Then he lunged forward and skewered his chest.

It had never occurred to him before what a fetching colour blood was.

He snapped out of it, taking deep breaths to steady himself. Then realised that was a mistake.

A pair of goblins sleepwalked into view, moving in ponderous slow motion.

Crystalline droplets of rain on the petals of a yellow flower. He squared off with the nearest and engaged his sword. They fenced, though it felt more like wading through the depths of a peat bog. One of Stryke's passes opened his foe's arm, drawing fascinating, luminous crimson. He followed that with a gash to the goblin's stomach that exposed another palette of colours. As the dying henchlin fell for ever, Stryke spun, casually, to face his comrade.

The second goblin had a spear he could have better employed as a walking stick. His legs seemed fit to fold under him as he poked the weapon feebly in Stryke's direction. He struck out at the spear like *a searing bolt of lightning against a velvet blue sky* and succeeded in severing it. The goblin stood stupidly with half a spear in each hand, his pinprick eyes blinking at the wonder of it.

Stryke pierced his heart and revelled in the beautiful scarlet spray.

Riding on horseback through a forest of towering trees. No, that wasn't what he was doing. He focused blearily on the two remaining guards. They wanted to play a strange game with lives as wagers. He'd half forgotten the rules. All he could remember was that the object was to stop them moving. So he set about it.

The first of them, eyes dilated, was practically staggering. He had a sword in his hand and he swung it repeatedly. But mostly not in Stryke's direction. For his part, Stryke returned the swings, though he had to advance a step or two before their blades connected. *Moonlight on a river with trailing weeping willows.* That wasn't it either. He had to keep his mind on the game.

Something dazzling passed in front of his face. Turning, he realised it was the second guard's flailing sword. He thought that was unfriendly. To pay him back, he flashed his own sword towards the goblin's face. It struck deep and soft, inspiring a surprisingly musical wail that faded as the vanquished unhurriedly fell from sight.

That left one henchlin and Razatt-Kheage. The slaver still held back, his mouth twisted and working, disgorging silent words. *A ruined cliff-top fortress, white in the sun.* Stryke shook that one off and went for the guard. He took some finding in the pellucid fog.

Once located he bartered blows almost politely. For his part, Stryke stepped up the force and quantity of passes, doing his best to break the other's guard. Though in truth it was a guard that took little breaking. *A waterfall plunging down a granite precipice.* Pushing that back from him, he leapt forward, floating like a feather, and tried carving his initial on the henchlin's chest. Half an *S* and he was deprived of his canvas. *Verdant meadows, dotted with herds of grazing game.*

Stryke was finding it hard to stay on his feet. But he had to, the game wasn't over yet. There was one more player. He looked around for him. Razatt-Kheage was near the door but making no attempt to leave. Stryke swam toward him through a long, long tunnel filled with honey.

When he finally got there, the goblin hadn't moved. He couldn't, he was petrified. As Stryke faced him, the slaver went down on his knees, as though curtseying. The mouth was still working and Stryke still couldn't make out the words, or indeed hear a sound except a kind of faint sibilant whining. He supposed the goblin was pleading. That was something players did sometimes. *The sun blazing on an endless beach.* Only this creature wasn't playing. He was refusing to, and it had to be against the rules. Stryke didn't like that.

He drew back his sword. *Walking along an endless beach.* Razatt-Kheage, dirty little rule-breaker, carried on opening and closing his mouth. *Rolling green hills and exalted frosty clouds.*

Stryke's sword travelled home. The slaver's mouth stayed open, wide, in a silent scream. *The smiling face of the female orc of his dreams.*

The sword cleaved Razatt-Kheage's neck. His head leapt from his shoulders, flew upward and back. The body gushed and slumped. Stryke's gaze followed the spiralling head, a dumpy bird without wings, and fancied he saw it laugh.

Then it hit the floor a dozen feet away with a noise like a dropped ripe melon, bounced twice and was still.

Stryke leaned against the wall, exhausted. But elated too. He had done a *good* thing. He moved himself. Coughing and heaving, head full of sights and sounds and smells and music, he tottered to the door. A few seconds' fumbling with the bolts got it open.

He reeled out, wreathed in heady white smoke, and stumbled off into the dazzling landscape.

19

"Drink this," Alfray said, offering Stryke another cup of steaming green potion.

Head in hands, Stryke groaned, "Gods, not more."

"You took in a massive dose of crystal. If you want to clear your system of it, you need this, food, and plenty of water, to make you piss it out."

Stryke lifted his head and sighed. His eyes were puffy and red. "All right, give it here." He accepted the cup, downed the noisome brew in one draft and pulled a face.

"Good." Alfray took back the cup. Bending to the cauldron over the fire he scooped another ration. "This one you can sip until the food's ready." He pushed it into Stryke's hand. "I'm going to check on the preparations." He walked off to supervise the grunts loading their horses.

When he was sure Alfray wasn't looking, Stryke turned and poured the cup's contents into the grass.

It had been a couple of hours since he came out of the long-house. He'd wandered for a while, uncertain of his bearings, before running into the hunting party. They were dragging half a dozen dead lembarrs. Lurching erratically and mouthing gibberish, he had to be practically carried back to camp, where his faltering account of what had happened proved a jaw-dropper.

Now lembarr carcasses roasted on spits, giving off a delicious smell. Appetite sharpened by the pellucid, Stryke's mouth watered in anticipation.

Coilla arrived with two platters of meat and sat beside him. He wolfed his as if starving.

"I'm really grateful, you know," she said. "For killing Razatt-Kheage that is. Though I would have preferred doing it myself."

"My pleasure," he replied, mouth full.

She stared at him intently. "Are you *sure* he didn't say anything about where Lekmann and the others might have gone?"

Stryke was still coming down from the crystal. Right now, he didn't want to be nagged. "I've told you all I know. They've gone." He was a little testy.

Dissatisfied, Coilla frowned.

"I reckon you won't see them bounty hunters again," he added placatingly. "Cowards like that wouldn't tangle with a warband."

"They owe me a debt, Stryke," she said. "I'm going to collect it."

"I know, and we're going to help any way we can. But we can't go looking for them, not now. If our paths ever cross again—"

"Fuck that. It's time somebody hunted *them*."

"Don't you think this is getting to be a bit of an obsession?" He chewed as he talked.

"I *want* it to be an obsession! You'd feel the same way if you'd been humiliated and offered for sale like cattle."

"Yes, I would. Only there's nothing we can do about it at the moment. Let's talk about this later, shall we? My head, you know?"

She nodded, dropped her plate by the fire and walked off.

In the background, several grunts were stitching fur jerkins. There had been just enough pelts to go round.

Stryke was finishing his food when Alfray reported back.

"Well, we're ready for Drogan. Any time you are."

"I'm fine. Or I will be soon. I wouldn't say my head was exactly *clear*, but the ride will fix it."

Haskeer came over holding a pile of the fur jackets. Jup drifted after him.

"They ain't exactly refined," Haskeer opined as he sorted sizes.

"Wouldn't have thought that would have bothered you," the dwarf remarked.

Haskeer ignored him and started handing out the garments. "Let's see. Captain." He tossed a fur. "Alfray. And here's yours, Jup." He held it up for them to see. "Look at the size of that. Like a hatchling's. Wouldn't cover my arse!"

Jup snatched it. "You should use your head for that. It'd be an improvement."

Simmering, Haskeer strode off.

Stryke stood, ever so slightly unsteady on his feet, put on the fur jacket and wandered over to Alfray.

"How you feeling?" the corporal asked.

"Not too bad. Don't want to see any more crystal for a while, though."

Alfray smiled.

"You were right about the stars," Stryke went on. "If I'd had them on me—"

"I know. Lucky."

"I'll take them back now."

"Given any thought to dividing them?"

"I know it makes sense, but I reckon I'll hang on to them. If I'm going to be parted from the band again, I'll give them to you for safekeeping."

"You know best, Stryke." His tone indicated that he didn't agree, but perhaps he thought now wasn't the time to argue. He dug into a pocket and produced the three stars, but didn't return them immediately. He held them in his cupped palm and studied them. "You know, despite what I said about keeping these, I'm glad to be handing them back. Having them feels like an awesome responsibility."

Stryke accepted the stars and they were returned to his belt pouch. "I know what you mean."

"Strange, isn't it? We feel that way about them yet we still haven't got a clue what they're for. What we going to do, Stryke? I mean, whether we got another star from the centaurs or not?"

"It was always my idea to use them to barter a pardon from Jennesta. But the more I think about it, the more I reckon that's what we *shouldn't* do."

"Why not?"

"Well, for a start, can you see her honouring her end of any bargain? I can't. More important than that, though, is the power these things seem to have."

"But we don't know what kind of power it is. That's the point."

"No. But we've heard enough hints along the way. What Tannar had to say, for instance. And the fact that Jennesta, a sorceress, wants them."

"So what *do* we do with them?"

"I was thinking along the lines of finding somebody who could help us use them. But for good, not evil. To help orcs and the other elder races. Perhaps to strike a blow against humans, and our own despots."

"Where would we find somebody like that?"

"We found Mobbs, and he told us about the instrumentalities in the first place."

"Don't you sometimes wish he hadn't?"

"Things had to change. They *were* changing. Mobbs didn't make us do what we did. He just gave us a reason, albeit a pretty cloudy one. All I'm saying is that maybe we could find someone even more knowledgeable. A magician, an alchemist, whatever."

"So that's what you think we ought to do? Rather than trading them for our lives with Jennesta?"

"It's an idea, that's all. Think on this, Alfray. Even if we did get Jennesta to deal, and she stuck to it, what kind of a life would we have? Do you honestly think we could just go back to being what we were? Carrying on as if nothing's happened? No, that's over. Those days are gone. In any event, the whole land's going down in flames. Something bigger's needed." He slapped the pouch. "Maybe these things are the key to that."

"Maybe."

"Let's get to Drogan."

He gave the order to break camp.

The forest was only two or three hours away, and the route couldn't have been simpler. All they had to do was follow the inlet.

As he hoped, the ride, which they took steadily, helped clear Stryke's still-pounding head. But his mouth seemed permanently dry and he drank copious amounts of water on the way.

He offered the canteen to Coilla, riding next to him at the head of the column. She shook her head. "I've been talking to

Haskeer," she said, "or trying to, about what happened when he went off with the stars."

"And?"

"In most ways he seems like his old self again. Except when it comes to explaining what happened then."

"I believe him when he says he really doesn't know."

"I think I do too. Despite the whack over the head he gave me. But I'm not sure I can ever trust him again, Stryke. Even though he did help rescue me."

"Can't blame you for that. But I think what happened to him was somehow beyond his control. Hell, we have to believe that about a comrade, and whatever else you can say about Haskeer, he's no traitor."

"Just about the only thing he said was that the stars sang to him. Then he clammed up, embarrassed. That singing stuff sounds crazy."

"I don't think he's crazy."

"Neither do I. So, any idea what he means?"

"No. They're just dead objects far as I'm concerned."

"Still no idea what they're for?"

He grinned. "If I did, believe me, I'd have told you. Yelled it. I was talking to Alfray about this earlier. What I didn't say to him was that even if the stars are blind, useless pieces of wood or something, I'd still have us go after them."

Coilla gave him a quizzical look.

"No, I'm not crazy either," he told her, pushing his doubts about the dreams to arm's length. "I see it like this. If we need anything, we need a purpose. Without one, this band would fall apart quicker than you can spit. It's our military upbringing, I suppose. Even though we're not part of the horde any more we're still orcs and we're still part of the orc nation, scattered and reviled as that might be. I figure we hang together or get hanged apart."

"I understand. Maybe there's something in the orc nature that craves comradeship. I don't think we're really meant to be lone beings. Anyway, whatever happens, whatever we might or might not have thrown away, you've given us that purpose, Stryke. Even if it all goes murderously wrong any minute, we still had that. We tried."

Stryke smiled at her. "Yes, right. We tried."

They had reached the edge of the forest. It was mature, enormous, dark.

Stryke halted the column. He waved forward Alfray, Jup and Haskeer.

"What's the plan, chief?" Jup asked.

"Like I said before: simple and straightforward. We raise a flag of truce and try to make contact with Keppatawn's clan."

Alfray began preparing the flag, using the Wolverines' banner spar. "Suppose there's more than one clan in the forest, Stryke?" he said.

"We'll have to hope they're all friendly with each other and pass us on. Let's go."

With some apprehension they entered the trees. Alfray held aloft the flag. He was aware, as they all were, that it was universally recognised but not always universally respected.

The interior of the forest was cool and smelt earthy. It wasn't as dark inside as it appeared from without. The silence was near absolute, and that made all of them edgy.

After riding for ten minutes they entered a small clearing.

"Why do I feel I have to whisper?" Coilla whispered.

Alfray looked up at the forest's ceiling far above, where sunlight shafted. "This place seems almost holy, that's why."

Jup agreed. "I reckon the magic's strong here. The water from the inlet, the covering of trees; they both help hold it. This might be one of Maras-Dantia's few remaining untouched oases. Something like the way it once was."

Haskeer seemed oblivious to all that. "What do we do, just keep wandering about in here until we find a centaur?"

All around, scores of centaurs appeared from behind trees and crashed out of bushes. Some held long, slim spears. Most had short horn bows, notched and pointing the band's way.

"No," Coilla replied.

"Take it easy!" Stryke told the band. "Steady now."

A centaur came forward. He was young and proud. The hair on the lower, equine portion of his body was silken brown. He had a fine tail and sturdy hoofs. Above, where his body somewhat resembled that of a human, he had muscular arms and abundant chest hair. He was straight-backed. A curly beard adorned his face.

Several of the band's horses shied.

"You're in clan territory," the centaur announced. "What's your business here?"

"Peaceable business," Stryke assured him.

"Peaceable? You're orcs."

"And we have a reputation, yes. It tends to go before us. As does yours. But like you, we fight in just cause, and we don't betray a flag of truce."

"Well said. I am Gelorak."

"I'm Stryke. This is my warband, the Wolverines."

The centaur raised an eyebrow. "Your name's known here. Have you come on your own account or do you act for others?"

"We're here for ourselves."

The other centaurs still had their bows levelled at the band.

"You're gaining a reputation as an orc who brings trouble with him, Stryke. I ask again, what business have you here?"

"Nothing that brings you trouble. We seek a centaur called Keppatawn."

"Our chief? You require armaments?"

"No. We want to talk with him on another matter."

Gelorak studied them thoughtfully. "It's for him to decide whether he wishes to treat with you. I'll take you to him." He glanced at Stryke's sword. "I would not demean you by asking that you surrender your weapons during your stay here. That's not something one should lightly ask of an orc, I think. But you are on your honour not to draw them in anger."

"Thank you. We appreciate the consideration. Our weapons will not be drawn unless any draw theirs against us. You have my word."

"Very well. Come."

He waved a hand. The bows were lowered.

Gelorak led the band deeper into the great forest, the other centaurs close to hand. Eventually they came to a much larger clearing.

There were buildings that resembled stables, along with more conventional thatched, round huts. The largest structure by far looked like an open-fronted barn. It housed an enormous forge. In blasting heat and clouds of smoke, sweating centaurs hammered on anvils and worked bellows. Others used tongs to remove glowing pieces of metal from braziers. They plunged them, hissing and steaming, into barrels of water.

Fowl and pigs ran free. There was a distinct odour of dung in the air, and it wasn't all from the livestock.

Dozens of centaurs, young and old, were going about their chores. Most of them stopped and stared when the Wolverines arrived. Stryke took some comfort from the fact that their reaction seemed born more of curiosity than ill will.

"Wait here," Gelorak instructed. He cantered off towards the armoury.

"What do you think?" Coilla asked.

"They seem friendly enough," Stryke judged. "And they let us keep our weapons. That's a good sign."

Gelorak re-emerged accompanied by another centaur. He was of middle years and his beard was greying. The powerful, muscular physique that must have marked him out in youth was still in evidence, but it was tempered by a deformity. He was lame. Withered and spindly, his right foreleg dragged as he walked.

"Well met," Stryke greeted.

"Well met. I am Keppatawn. I'm also a centaur of direct impulses and busy. So you'll forgive me if I'm blunt. What do you want?"

"We have business to discuss with you. A trade that could prove to your advantage."

"That remains to be seen." He assessed them, eyes shrewd. His tone lightened. "But if it's business, that's always best discussed over a meal. Join us for food and drink."

"Thank you." Stryke dreaded the idea of anything else to eat, but knew protocol demanded acceptance.

The band was ushered to heavy oak tables placed near the clearing's centre. There were benches on just one side for the orcs' benefit; centaurs stood to eat.

Meat and fish were brought. There was freshly baked bread,

dishes of fruit, and baskets brimming with nuts, as befitted forest dwellers. Ale was provided too, along with jugs of heady red wine.

Once they were into the meal, which in Stryke's case meant eating just enough to avoid offence, he toasted their hosts. "A generous repast." He raised a flagon. "We thank you."

"I've often thought there are few disputes that can't be put right by a good meal and some fine wine," Keppatawn replied. He drained his own flagon, then belched. It was a demonstration of the centaurs' well-known liking for life's more sensual pleasures, which not uncommonly veered into excess. "Though I guess it's a little different with you orcs, eh?" he added. "We tend to ask questions first, preferably while feasting, then fight. It's the other way round with you, isn't it?"

"Not always, Keppatawn. We are capable of reason."

"Of course you are," he replied good-naturedly. "So what is it you want to be reasonable about today?"

"You have an item we'd like to trade for."

"If you're talking of weapons, you won't find better anywhere in Maras-Dantia."

"No, not weapons, though in truth yours are renowned." He lifted his cup and took a drink. "I'm talking about a relic. We call it a star. You may know it better as an instrumentality."

The remark silenced the table. Stryke hoped it hadn't put a permanent damper on things.

After a pause, Keppatawn smiled, signalling a resumption of chatter. Though it was at a lower level as all strained to hear. "We do have the artifact you refer to," he admitted. "And you're not the first to travel here hoping for it."

"There have been others?"

"Over the years, yes."

"Can I ask who?"

"Oh, a motley bunch. Scholars, soldiers of fortune, those claiming mastery of black sorcery and white, dreamers . . ."

"What was their fate?"

"We killed them."

The band stiffened a little at hearing that.

"But not us?" Stryke persisted.

"You've come asking, not trying to take. I'm talking about the ones who arrived with ill intent."

"There were those who didn't?"

"Some. We usually let them live, and of course they left disappointed."

"Why?"

"Because they couldn't, or wouldn't, meet my terms for bartering what you call the star."

"What might those terms be?"

"We'll get to that. I have somebody for you to meet." He turned to Gelorak, standing next to him. "Bring Hedgestus, and tell him to fetch the relic." Gelorak downed the last of his wine and trotted off. "Our shaman," Keppatawn explained to Stryke. "He's the instrumentality's keeper."

In due course, Gelorak came out of a small lodge on the fringe of the clearing with an ancient centaur of unsteady mien. Unlike any of the other clan members the band had seen, he wore several necklaces threaded with what looked like pebbles, or possibly nut shells. For his part, Gelorak carried a small wooden box. Both walked slowly.

After introductions, to which Hedgestus responded solemnly, Keppatawn ordered the star produced. The ornately carved box was placed on the table and opened.

It held a star that again differed from the others Stryke had. This one was grey, with just two spikes projecting from the central ball.

"Doesn't look like much, does it?" Keppatawn commented.

"No," Stryke agreed. "May I?"

The centaur chieftain nodded.

Stryke gently lifted the star from its box. It had occurred to him that it might be a fake. He tried applying some subtle pressure. The thing was absolutely solid, like the others.

Apparently Keppatawn realised what Stryke was doing, but didn't seem to mind. "It's more than tough, it's indestructible. I've never seen anything like it, and I've worked with every material there is. I tried it in the furnace once. Didn't even scorch it."

Stryke put the star back.

"Why do you want it?" Keppatawn said.

It was a question Stryke had hoped to avoid. He decided on an outdated answer, figuring that counted as partial truth. "We're out of Queen Jennesta's horde. We figured we might be able to use this to bargain our way back in." He added, "She has a passion for old religious artifacts."

"Given her reputation as a ruler, that seems a strange ambition."

"We're orcs and we need a horde. Hers is the only one we fit into."

Stryke had the distinct impression that Keppatawn didn't believe a word of it. And he feared he might have put a foot wrong by mentioning Jennesta. Everybody knew her character. The centaur could think she was an unsuitable custodian of the star.

So he was surprised when Keppatawn said, "I don't really care what you want it for. I'd be glad to get rid of the damn thing. It's brought us nothing but ill-luck." He nodded at the box. "What do you know of this and its rumoured fellows?"

Stryke latched on to the word *rumoured.* The centaurs didn't know for a fact that others existed. He made up his mind not to tell them he had any. "Very little, to be honest," he replied truth-fully.

"That's going to disappoint Hedgestus here. All we know is that they're supposed to have magical powers. But he's been trying to squeeze something out of this one for twenty seasons now without success. I think it's all lembarr shit."

Keppatawn wasn't offering information, he was asking for it. Stryke was relieved. A little knowledge could have complicated the situation. "You said you had some kind of terms laid down for trading the star," he reminded him, "and nobody's taken them up."

"Yes. None has even tried."

"Is it a question of trade? We can offer a large quantity of prime pellucid for—"

"No. What I require in exchange for the star is a deed, not riches. But I doubt you'll be willing to undertake it."

"What do you want done?"

"Bear with me while I explain. Have you not wondered *where* I got the star from?"

"It had crossed my mind."

"The star and my lameness I got from Adpar, Queen of the nyadd realm."

Stryke wasn't alone in being surprised by that. "We always thought her a myth."

"Perhaps you were encouraged in that belief by her sister, Jennesta. Adpar's no myth." His hand went to his spoilt leg. "She's all too real, as I discovered. She just doesn't leave her domain. And few who enter it uninvited come out again."

"Would you mind telling us what happened?" Coilla said.

"It's a simple story. Like your race, mine has certain rites of passage. When I was a youth I was vain. I wanted to achieve adulthood with a task no other centaur had dreamed of. So I took myself off to Adpar's palace in search of the star. By sheer blind luck I secured the thing, but I paid for it. I escaped with the star and my life, but barely. Adpar employed a spell that left me as you see me. Now instead of using weapons in the field I'm reduced to making them."

"I'm sorry for your trouble," Coilla told him. "But I for one don't understand what you want us to do."

"Restoring the full use of my body means more to me than any amount of gems or coin. Or even crystal. It's the only thing I would barter for the star."

"We're not healers," Jup reminded him. "How can we achieve that? Our comrade Alfray here has some curative powers, but—"

"Mending such an injury would be beyond my meagre abilities, I'm afraid," Alfray put in.

"You misread me," Keppatawn said. "I *know* how my condition can be righted."

Stryke swapped puzzled looks with his officers. "Then how can we be of help?"

"My hurt was magically inflicted. The only cure is itself magical."

"We aren't wizards either, Keppatawn."

"No, my friend; had it been that simple I would have engaged the services of a wizard long since. The only thing that will make me whole again is the application of one of Adpar's tears."

"What?"

There were general murmurs of disbelief from the orcs.

"You're taking the piss," Haskeer reckoned.

Stryke glared at him.

Fortunately, Keppatawn didn't take umbrage. "I wish I was, Sergeant. But I speak the truth. Adpar herself let it be known that such was the sole remedy."

The ensuing silence was broken by Coilla. "I suppose you've thought of offering her a trade? The star for the return of your health."

"Of course. Her treachery bars that. She would see it as a way of having both the star back and my life. I was only maimed in the first place because she couldn't kill me. Nyadds are a malicious and vengeful race. As we know too well from the raiding parties that occasionally swim up the inlet to the forest."

"Let's get this straight," Stryke said. "We get you one of Adpar's tears and you'll give us the star?"

"On my word."

"What would it involve, exactly?"

"A journey to her realm, which lies at the point where Scarrock Marsh blends into Mallowtor Islands. That's only a day's ride from here. But there's trouble there. Adpar makes war on her merz neighbours."

"They're peace loving, aren't they?" Haskeer asked. He used the word *peace* like a curse.

"With Adpar so close they've had to learn not to be. And there are disputes over food. The ocean is not immune from the disruption wrought on the supply of magic by humans. We have problems with nature's balance ourselves."

"Where does Adpar's palace lie, precisely?" Stryke wanted to know. "Can you show us on a map?"

"Yes. Though I fear getting there is by far the easiest part of the task. My father once mounted an expedition with the aim of seizing Adpar. He and all his companions were lost. It was a grievous blow to the clans in its time."

"No disrespect to your father's spirit, but we're used to fighting. We've handled determined opposition before."

"I don't doubt it. But that wasn't what I meant about the hardest part. I was wondering how you could induce a stony-hearted bitch like Adpar to produce a tear."

"The subject's a bit of a mystery to us," Coilla confessed.

"How so?"

"Orcs don't cry."

Keppatawn was taken aback. "I didn't know that. I'm sorry."

"Because our eyes don't leak?"

"We'll have to think on that aspect of it," Stryke interrupted. "But subject to talking this over with my band, we'll give it a go."

"You *will?*"

"I make no promises, Keppatawn. We'll spy out the land, and if it looks an impossible task we won't go on. Either way, we'd be back to tell you."

"Possibly," the centaur remarked in an undertone. "No slight intended, my friend."

"None taken. You've made the dangers clear."

"I suggest you rest here tonight and set out on the morrow. And I couldn't help but notice that your weapons are somewhat less than adequate. We'll re-equip you with the best we have."

"That's music to an orc's ears," Stryke replied.

"One more thing." Keppatawn slipped a hand into a pocket of his leather apron. He brought out a small ceramic phial and handed it to Stryke.

Alfray studied its exquisite decoration. "Do you mind if I ask where you got this?"

An expression came to Keppatawn's face that could almost be called bashful. "Another youthful prank," he admitted.

20

*Every time he ventured into what he persisted in thinking of as out
there, he paid a price. His powers diminished by a small but discernible
degree. The ability to properly co-ordinate his thoughts grew poorer.*

He hastened his own death.

*As he couldn't spend enough time here regenerating between visits,
the problem was likely to escalate. Indeed his actions were endangering
even here itself.*

*He dwelt on the very real likelihood that he made no difference by
going out. He might even have made things worse, for all that his inter-
ventions were light and as limited as he could manage.*

*On the last occasion he almost brought disaster down on their heads.
In trying to do the right thing he came near doing wrong again.*

*But there was no choice. Events were too advanced. And now even
the vessels of his own blood were turning on each other. Only unpredictable fate prevented catastrophe, and what little he might be able to do.
Weary as he felt, he had to prepare to go forth once more, in the guise.*

*He could have wished for death to remove the burden, but for the
guilt engendered by knowing he was responsible for so much suffering.
And for worse to come.*

The sombreness of the gathering was only outweighed by its
rising sense of panic.

Adpar lay in a dimly lit coral chamber. She had been placed
on a seaweed bed, whose healing properties were thought beneficial, through which water was allowed to ebb in the hope that
it too might prove rejuvenating. For good measure her body was
covered in plump leeches that gorged on her blood in the belief
it would thereby be purified.

She was in a delirium. Her lips trembled, and the silent words
she mouthed could be made sense of by nobody. When semi-

delirious she raged against the gods and, more vehemently, her sibling.

A select group was present, drawn from higher elders, the military's upper ranks and her personal healers.

The chief of all the elders took aside the Head Physician for a whispered conversation.

"Are you any nearer finding the cause of this malady?" he asked.

"No," the elderly physic admitted. "All the tests we have tried give no clue. She responds to none of our remedies." He moved closer, conspiratorially. "I suspect a magical influence. If it didn't go against all of Her Majesty's expressed wishes, when she was able to make them, I would have called in a sorcerer."

"Dare we disobey and do so anyway? Given that she seems beyond ken of what's happening?"

The healer drew an appraising breath through his scabrous nyadd teeth. "I know of no manipulator of the magic anywhere near competent enough to deal with this. Not least because she disposed of all the best ones herself. You know how much she dislikes the thought of rivalry."

"Then can we not summon one from outside the realm?"

"Even if you could find anyone willing to come, there's the question of time."

"Are you saying she might not survive?"

"I wouldn't care to pronounce on that, to be honest. But we have brought back patients with ailments as grave, though granted we knew what *they* were. I can only — "

"No procrastination, please, healer. The future of the realm is at stake. Will she live?"

He sighed, wetly. "At the moment she is more likely to pass than stay." Hurriedly he added, "Though we are of course making every possible effort to save her."

The elder looked at the queen's dreadfully pale, sweat-drenched face. "Can she hear us?"

"I'm not sure."

They moved back to the bedside. Lesser minions gave them room.

Stooping, the chief elder whispered gently, "Majesty?" There was no response. He repeated himself in a louder tone. This time she stirred slightly.

The physician delicately applied a damp sponge to her brow. Her colouring took on a paltry improvement.

"Your Majesty," the elder said again.

Her lips moved and her eyes flickered.

"Majesty," he repeated insistently. "Majesty, you must try to listen to me."

She managed a faint groan.

"There is no provision for the succession, Majesty. It is vital the issue be settled."

Adpar mumbled weakly.

"There are factions who will vie for the throne. That means chaos unless an heir is appointed." In truth he knew she had made sure there were no obvious contenders by the simple expedients of murder and exile. "You must speak, ma'am, and give a name."

She was definitely trying to speak now, but it didn't carry.

"A name, Majesty. Of who is to rule."

Her lips moved more tenaciously. He bowed and put his ear close to her face. Whatever she was saying was still unclear. He strained to understand.

Then it became clear. She was repeating a single word, over and over again.

". . . me . . . me . . . me . . . me . . ."

He knew it was hopeless then. Perhaps she wanted to leave chaos. Or perhaps she couldn't believe in her own mortality. Either way the result would be the same.

The elder looked to the others in the chamber. He knew they could see what was coming too.

This was the time when the inexorable process began. They would abandon confidence in the realm and start to think of themselves. As he had.

Stryke was aware that the centaurs didn't think the orcs would come back. He couldn't avoid knowing; they made no secret of it.

They had armed the band with excellent new weapons everybody approved of. Coilla was particularly happy with the set of perfectly balanced throwing knives they'd given her. Among other things, Jup had a handsome battleaxe, Alfray a fine sword. Stryke possessed the keenest blade he'd ever known.

Now the band was on its way and out of the centaurs' earshot, doubts had begun to surface.

Haskeer, not surprisingly, was the most forthright with criticisms. "What crazy scheme have you got us into now?" he grumbled.

"I've told you before, Sergeant, watch your mouth," Stryke warned. "If you want nothing to do with it, that's fine. You can head out somewhere else. But I thought you said something about wanting to prove you're worthy to be a member of this band."

"I meant it. But what good's that if the band's off on a suicide mission?"

"You're pitching it too high, as usual," Jup told him. "But what *are* we letting ourselves in for, Stryke?"

"A reconnaissance. And if we see anything we can't handle, we'll go back to Drogan and tell Keppatawn it isn't possible."

"Then what?" Alfray said.

"We'll try trading again. Maybe offer to undertake some other task. Like finding him a good healer."

"You know he ain't going to buy it, Captain," Haskeer reckoned, accurately. "If we want that damn star so badly we should go back and take it. We're going to end up fighting for it anyway, probably, so why not make use of the surprise element?"

"Because that's not honourable," Coilla informed him indignantly. "We said we'd try. That doesn't mean sneaking back and cutting their throats."

Alfray reinforced the sentiment. "We gave our word. I hope never to see the day when an orc goes back on an oath."

"All right, all right," Haskeer sighed.

They rode by a hill, its grass sickly and yellowing. An orc called out and pointed. They all turned and looked to its summit.

They caught a glimpse of a human on a white horse. He had a long blue cloak.

"Serapheim!" Stryke exclaimed.

"That's him?" Alfray asked.

"Shit, would you believe it?" Jup said.

Coilla was already spurring her horse. "I want a word with that human!"

They followed her headlong gallop up the hill. Meantime the human went down the other side and out of sight.

When the band got to the top there was no sign of him. Yet there was nowhere near by he could have concealed himself. The terrain was more or less even and they had good visibility in every direction.

"What in the name of the Square is going on?" Coilla wondered.

Haskeer twisted his head from side to side, a palm shading his eyes. "But how? Where? It's impossible."

"Can't be impossible, he did it," Jup told him.

"He's got to be down there somewhere," Coilla reasoned.

"Leave it," Stryke ordered. "I have a feeling we'd just be wasting our time."

"He's good at running, I'll say that for him," Haskeer remarked, getting in a last shot.

The start of Scarrock Marsh could be seen from their new vantage point. And beyond it, further west, the ocean with its broken necklace of brooding islands.

It had been too long since Jennesta rode at the head of an army and took personal control of a campaign.

Well, mission really, she conceded, and perhaps not even that, as she had no firm aim beyond a little pillaging and harassment of enemies. And maybe she harboured the hope that her travels might glean some clue as to the whereabouts of the hated Wolverines. Having acted at last in the matter of her too-ambitious sister, she had a little more zest for life and the taking of it.

But mostly it was just important to give herself an airing, and it was doing her a power of good.

No more than half a day out from Cairnbarrow, they had good fortune. Forward scouts reported a Uni settlement too new for the maps. It was unknown even to her spies. That was an oversight she would mete out punishments for when she got back. Meanwhile she led her army of orcs and dwarves, ten thousand strong, against the enclave.

If ever the cliché about using a battleaxe to crack a pixie's skull had any truth it was here. The settlement was a flimsy, poorly defended collection of half-built shacks and barns. Its inhabitants, numbering perhaps fifty, counting the children, hadn't even finished building the defensive wall.

She regarded the humans who chose to settle in that particular spot as fools, ignorant farmers and ranchers so lacking in sense that they knew no better than to encroach on her domain.

They compounded their error by trying to surrender. She wished all Unis were as easily defeated.

What followed made for a welcome addition to her magical resources — the hearts of near two score sacrifices, plucked from those she spared in the slaughter. She had only been able to consume a fraction of them, of course, but the abundance gave her the opportunity to test something she had found referred to in the writings of the ancients.

Before setting out on this adventure she had despatched agents to the north, deep into the Hojanger wastelands, to bring back wagonloads of ice and compacted snow. Suitably insulated in barrels swathed with hessian and furs, the cargo survived without melting. She had the organs packed into the barrels with the intention of thawing them as needed on the journey. Naturally there was no substitute for the fresh variety, but they would serve at a pinch.

If it worked, she was thinking of using it as a way of preserving food for her horde in its campaigns.

Jennesta came out of one of the huts, sated for now with torture and other indulgences, and dabbed her bloodied lips with a delicate lace handkerchief. She had surprised even herself with the energy she put into the scenes just enacted. Perhaps the open air had increased her already healthy appetites.

Mersadion didn't seem so content with the situation. He awaited her astride his mount, stiff and sour-faced.

"You look less than pleased, General," she said, wiping gore from her hands. "Is the victory not to your liking?"

"Of course it is, Majesty," he hurriedly replied, adopting a smile of patent falseness.

"Then what ails you?"

"My officers report more dissatisfaction in the ranks, ma'am. Not much, but enough to be of concern."

"I thought you were on top of that, Mersadion," she told him, her displeasure undisguised. "Did you not have troublemakers executed, as I ordered?"

"I did, ma'am, several from each regiment. It seems to have fomented further unrest."

"Then kill some more. What is the nature of today's complaints?"

"It seems some are questioning . . . well, questioning your order to raze this settlement, my lady."

"*What?*"

He blanched but carried on. "The feeling, among a very small minority, you understand, is that these buildings could be used to house the widows and orphans of orcs who have fallen in your service. Dependents who would otherwise be destitute, ma'am."

"I *want* them to be destitute! As a warning to the males. A warrior who knows his mate and hatchlings face such a fate should he fail is a better warrior."

"Yes, ma'am," Mersadion replied in a subdued tone.

"I'm starting to worry about your ability to keep order, General." He shrank in his saddle. "And I think the first thing we're going to have to do once back in Cairnbarrow is purge the ranks of these radicals once and for all."

"Ma'am."

"Now get me a brand."

"Ma'am?"

"A *brand*, for the gods' sake! Do I have to draw you a picture in the dirt?"

"No, Majesty. Right away." He dropped from his horse and ran towards the jumble of buildings.

As she waited impatiently for his return, she watched a squadron of her battle dragons soaring overhead, far up near the cloud cover.

Mersadion jogged back holding a wooden torch, its head wrapped in cloth and dipped with tar. He offered it to her.

"*Light* it," she intoned with dangerous deliberateness.

He fumbled with flints while she silently fumed. At last he got the brand alight.

"Give it here!" she barked, snatching it away. She stood near the door of the building she had so recently defiled. "This settlement is a hive of Uni pestilence. To do anything less than destroy it sends a weak message. And I'm not in the habit of displaying weakness, General." She tossed the brand into the hut. Flames immediately began to spread. Screams sounded inside from the few humans she had left alive.

She went to her horse and mounted. He did the same.

"Get the army moving," she ordered. "We'll look for the next nest."

As they came away she glanced at the settlement. The fire had a hold that wouldn't be broken.

"If you want something done properly, do it yourself," she informed the general cheerily. "As my esteemed mother Vermegram used to say."

21

Scarrock Marsh appeared to have its own weather.

It wasn't that the conditions were different from those on the plains the band had recently left, there just seemed to be *more* of it. The clouds were more lowering, the rain more incessant, the winds more biting. And it was colder. Perhaps that was because the squalls blowing down from the advancing ice sheet in the north were unimpeded. There were no mountains or forests to temper them, and once they arrived they combined with the frigid air generated by the great Norantellia Ocean.

Grateful for their recently acquired furs, the band stood on the edge of the marsh and took in its foreboding countenance.

What stretched before them was a vast, flat quagmire of black mud and sand. Ditches and even small lakes of dark gelatinous water littered the terrain. Here and there, dead, skeletal trees poked out of the barren landscape, indicating that the blight was spreading. The place stank of rotting fish and other, less wholesome things. There was no sign of life, not even a bird.

From their vantage point, on a slightly higher elevation than the marsh proper, they could see the beginnings of the ocean. It was sluggish and grey. The inky outlines of the Mallowtor Islands lay beyond, mist-shrouded and desolate. Somewhere out there, beneath the waves, the merz clung on to their precarious existence.

It was a forlorn scene, and one Stryke couldn't help but compare with the glorious seascape of his dreams.

"Right," Haskeer said, "we've seen it, I don't like it, let's go back."

"Hold your horses," Stryke told him. "We said we'd do a recce."

"I've seen all I need to know. It's a bloody wasteland."

"What did you expect?" Jup wondered. "Dancing maidens throwing rose petals?"

Coilla cut off their impending squabble by asking, "How are we going to go about this, Stryke?"

"According to Keppatawn, the nyadd realm lies on the far edge of the marsh, fringing the ocean. So a lot of it's submerged."

"Great," Haskeer muttered. "Now we're fish."

Stryke ignored him. "But Adpar's palace has access from both land and water sides, apparently. The way I see this mission is going in with the full strength, less whoever we leave with the horses."

"I hope you're not thinking of assigning me that detail," Alfray said. His manner was prickly.

It was the age thing again, Stryke guessed. He seemed to be getting more touchy about it. "Of course not. We need you with us. But like I said, we can't take the horses. Talag, Liffin, that's your job. Sorry, but it's important."

They nodded glumly. No orc liked being left on a routine duty when there was the prospect of combat.

Jup steered the conversation back to the matter at hand. "Straight in, you said. No scouting?"

"No. We'll cross the marsh and if conditions look right, we'll go for it. I don't want to spend any more time here than we have to."

"Now you've said something I agree with," Haskeer remarked.

"Remember, Keppatawn said there was trouble in Adpar's realm," Stryke went on. "That might help us, it might not. But if it looks too hot in there we're coming out without engaging. I figure the existence of this band is more important than a bit of local strife."

Jup nodded. "Suits me."

Stryke looked at the sky. "Let's go before we get some real rain." To Talag and Liffin he added, "Like I said, we don't intend hanging around in there. But to be safe give us until this time tomorrow. If we're not back by then consider yourself free of any obligation to the band. You can sell the horses. That should keep you for a while."

On that sobering note, they set off.

"Stick together, keep your eyes peeled," Stryke instructed. "If anything moves, drop it."

"Usual procedure, then," Jup commented.

"Remember, they'll be in their element," Stryke added. "They can live in air *and* water. We're strictly air. Got it, Haskeer?"

"Yeah." A thought hit him. "Why you telling *me?*"

They moved into the marsh. Like Drogan Forest, it was quiet. But it was a different kind of silence. That had been peaceful. This was uneasy, somehow malevolent. Where Drogan promised, this threatened. Again like Drogan, they felt the need to converse in whispers. Though they all knew it was unnecessary; there was nowhere for an enemy to hide.

The going shifted from spongy to oozing. Stryke looked around and saw that Haskeer was walking a little apart from the others. "Stay together," he called out. "Don't get separated. We don't know what this place holds in the way of surprises."

"Don't worry, chief," Haskeer replied dismissively, "I know what I'm doing."

There was a loud sucking noise. He instantly sank waist deep in a mire.

They rushed over to him. He was still sinking.

"Don't struggle, you'll only make it worse," Alfray advised.

"Get me out of here!" He went down some more. "Don't just stand there, *do* something!"

Stryke folded his arms. "I'm thinking about whether to let it get to your mouth. Might be the only thing to shut it."

"Come on, Captain!" his sergeant pleaded. "It's fucking *cold* in here!"

"All right, get him out."

With some difficulty they hauled him clear. He came out cursing. His kit was filthy. Black tenacious ooze clung to him.

"Phew, I stink!" Haskeer complained, creasing his face.

"Don't worry," Jup said, "nobody'll notice."

"Thank the Square you didn't fall in yourself, shortshanks! Two foot and it would have been over your head!"

Coilla lifted her hand to cover a grin.

"This time let's stick together, shall we?" Stryke suggested.

They resumed the trek with Haskeer grumbling under his breath and his boots squelching.

After an hour of careful footwork they saw a line of irregularly shaped rocks dead ahead. Stryke ordered the band to spread out and watch their step.

On arriving they found the rocks towered over them. Several had cave mouths. In one or two cases, large round holes bored straight through the rocks and the ocean could be seen.

Coilla frowned. "If this is the beginning of the nyadd realm, shouldn't there be guards?"

"You'd think so," Stryke agreed. "Maybe they're further on."

"So where to?" Alfray said.

"Keppatawn said at least one of these entrances leads where we want to go. Pity he couldn't remember which. Pick a cave."

Alfray thought about it and pointed. "That one."

They approached stealthily and went in. It was just a cave.

"Good thing you didn't have a wager on that, Alfray," Haskeer ribbed. "Now what, Stryke?"

"We keep picking them until we get in."

They had three more tries and drew three more blanks.

"I'm getting sick of caves," Haskeer told them. "I feel like a bat."

Then Coilla chose one that turned out more promising. It went back a long way, and the light from its entrance was barely enough to guide them. But at its end there was a natural archway. They crept to it. The arch opened on to a sloping tunnel, like a slide. There was a green glow at the bottom.

Weapons drawn, they went down fast, ready for trouble.

Instead of waiting nyadds, they found themselves in a grotto. It was damp and echoing. The emerald illumination came from hundreds of pieces of coral-like material that seemed to be growing out of the walls and ceiling.

Alfray studied the slithers of radiant green. "I don't know what this stuff is, but it's damn useful," he whispered.

"Right," Haskeer said. He snapped off a chunk resembling a stalactite and handed it to him.

"Take some more," Stryke ordered.

Several of the grunts set to dislodging pieces.

There was only one way to go—a narrow tunnel in the far wall. Unlike the grotto, it was unlit, so the makeshift torches came in handy. The band filed into it. Stryke leading.

It turned out to be quite short, and led into a round cave. This had high walls but its top was open to the air. Three more dark tunnels ran from it. Everywhere, water flowed freely, ankle deep.

"Time to play choose again," Coilla said.

"*Ssshh!*" Alfray had a finger to his lips.

The band froze. They heard a sloshing sound. Something was approaching along one of the tunnels. They couldn't tell which.

Stryke ushered them back into the shaft they came out of. The glowing brands were concealed. As they watched, two nyadds came out of the centre tunnel. They moved in their race's characteristic undulating fashion, impelled by immensely powerful lower muscles. These were creatures that may well have been more at home, and certainly more graceful, in water, but there was no doubt they had command of land too. On an evolutionary scale they were at equipoise, though whether they were heading for a future of exclusively air or of water dwelling was a moot point.

They were armed with their traditional jagged half-sword, half-spears, fashioned from hardened shale mined in the ocean's depths. Coral daggers were strapped to their shiny carapaces.

Alfray whispered, "Just the two?"

"I think so. Try to keep one alive. Jup, make sure our rear's guarded."

At his signal, Alfray, Haskeer and Coilla rushed out with him to engage the nyadds. Three or four grunts backed them.

Taken by surprise, overwhelmed by numbers, the creatures had no realistic chance. Alfray and Haskeer hacked one of them about the head and neck until it fell. Stryke and Coilla took the other, and inflicted wounds that downed it but weren't immediately fatal. It lay heaving like a crushed armoured slug, its blood mingling with the running water.

Stryke knelt. "The queen," he demanded. "Which way to the palace?"

The nyadd took shuddering, rapid breaths and made no reply.

"Where's the queen?" Stryke repeated, his tone more threatening. He used the tip of his sword to back his words.

With an effort, the nyadd lifted an arm and pointed a shaking
webbed hand. It indicated the right-hand tunnel.

"The palace?" Stryke persisted. "That way?"

The nyadd managed to weakly nod its massive head. Then it
slumped to a prone position.

"You better not be lying," Haskeer warned.

"Save it," Coilla said. "He's dead."

Jup and the rest of the band splashed out of their hiding place.
The bodies were left where they fell. Cautiously, the band
entered the indicated tunnel, producing the sticks that glowed
to light their way.

It proved a longer tunnel than the previous one. But eventually it took them to another area open to the sky. The difference
this time was that they were on a ledge. Sweeping down before
them was a series of uneven rocky tiers, like piled slabs, that led
to a jumble of further passageways and tunnels.

Ahead, and looming high above, was a huge contorted con-
fection of a structure. A bizarre fusion of nature and nyadd handiwork, it featured no straight line or untwisted tower. Rock and
shell and ocean weeds combined to give the whole a wetly glistening organic aspect.

"Well, we've found it," Stryke declared.

Jup tugged his sleeve and pointed downward. A dozen tiers
below, and far to the left, a commotion was spilling into view.
Two groups of nyadds were fighting each other. It was a vicious,
no-holds-barred blood match, and even as the band watched
several combatants went down.

"Keppatawn was right about there being trouble here," Coilla
said.

"If they've fallen into chaos it's the perfect cover," Jup added.
"Seems we timed our visit well."

"But if they've fallen into civil war," Stryke reasoned, "maybe
Adpar's already dead."

"If she governed wisely this shouldn't be happening," Coilla
reckoned. "What kind of a ruler is it who's selfish enough to let
her realm die with her?"

"The usual kind, from what I've seen," Jup told her. "And she's Jennesta's sister, remember. Maybe it runs in the family."

Stryke indicated a wide carved passageway, directly ahead and below, that seemed to approach the palace. "Right, let's go."

Keeping low, lest they be seen by the fighting parties, the band quickly moved down the rocky tiers to the passage. They got to it, and into it, without incident. Once inside it was a different story.

About twenty paces in, the tunnel took a sharp turn. Before they reached it, five nyadds came around the corner. Four were armed, and they seemed to be escorting the fifth, who bore no weapons. But he didn't look like a prisoner.

Mutual surprise was soon overcome. The nyadds levelled their weapons and moved in.

Coilla put one out of the picture instantly with a well-aimed knife lob. Conscious of the creatures' tough shells, she aimed for the head. Her blade penetrated its eye.

The rest were tackled at close quarters, and again the orcs' superiority of numbers swayed it.

Haskeer, hefting his sword two-handed, simply bludgeoned his hapless foe into oblivion. Alfray and Jup, working together, slashed at their opponent with determined efficiency. He went down with a multiplicity of wounds. Several grunts overwhelmed and killed the remaining warrior.

Coilla made sure she retrieved her knife. It was the best blade she'd ever owned.

That left just the unarmed nyadd. He cowered. "I'm an elder! Non-military! Spare me! *Spare me!*" he pleaded.

"Where's Adpar?" Stryke demanded.

"What?"

"You want to live, take us to her."

"I don't—"

Haskeer put a blade to his throat.

"All right, all right," the elder blurted. "I'll take you."

"No tricks," Jup warned him.

He took them through a maze of stony, lichen-covered passages. As they had everywhere else they'd seen in the nyadds' land, they waded through inches of water all the way.

At length they arrived at a broad corridor illuminated by slivers of the glowing rock. A pair of great doors stood at its end, guarded by two warriors. The band gave them little time to react, piling into them as a mob and cutting them to pieces. One ended the encounter with his head near completely severed.

Several grunts dragged the corpses out of sight. The terrified nyadd elder was brought forward.

"Is there anybody in there apart from her?" Stryke asked.

"I don't know. A healer, perhaps. Our realm is in confusion. Rival factions are at each other's throats. For all I know the queen may already be dead."

"Damn!" Jup exclaimed.

The elder looked puzzled. "You mean that you're not here to kill her?"

"What we're here for is too complicated to explain," Alfray told him. "But your queen still being alive is pretty important to it."

Stryke nodded and with caution they tried the doors. They weren't locked. Throwing them open, the band tumbled in.

There was no one in the private chamber except the queen herself, spread out on her bed of swaying green tendrils. Everybody splashed over to her.

"Gods," Coilla murmured on seeing the queen's face. "The resemblance to Jennesta's uncanny."

"Yes," Alfray agreed. "A bit sobering, eh?"

"And they left her alone at the end," Jup said.

"Says a lot about what they thought of her, doesn't it?" Coilla replied.

"The point is, is she still alive?" Stryke wanted to know.

Alfray checked. "Just."

The elder, forgotten, sneaked to the door. He got through it and sped along the corridor yelling, *"Guards! Guards!"*

"Shit," Stryke said.

"Leave it to me," Coilla snapped.

She flew to the doorway, plucking a knife. Back went her arm. The missile struck the fleeing elder in the back of the neck. He twisted and fell, displacing gouts of water.

"Said they were good blades," Coilla remarked.

Stryke assigned a couple of grunts to watch the door and they returned their attention to Adpar.

"We've been lucky so far," he told them. "It won't last. Do you reckon she can hear us, Alfray?"

"Difficult to say. She's pretty far gone."

Stryke leaned in to her. "Adpar. *Adpar!* Hear me. You are dying."

Her head moved slightly on its emerald pillow.

"Hear me, Adpar. You are dying, and your sister Jennesta is responsible."

The queen's lips began to move. She grew more agitated, albeit weakly.

"Hear me, nyadd queen. Your own sister did this to you. Jennesta was the one. *Jennesta.*"

There was some fluttering of eyelids and quivering of lips. Her gills pulsated a little. Otherwise there was no reaction.

"It's hopeless," Coilla sighed.

Haskeer weighed in with, "Yeah, face it, Stryke, it ain't going to work. There's no use just standing here repeating 'Jennesta, Jennesta, Jennesta.'"

Stryke was crestfallen. He began to turn away from the death-bed. "I just thought—"

"Wait!" Jup exclaimed. "Look!"

Adpar's eyelids were flickering, blinking almost.

"It started when Haskeer repeated Jennesta's name," Jup reported.

As they watched, the lashes of Adpar's eyes moistened. Then a single tear appeared and ran a little way down her cheek.

"Quickly!" Alfray urged. "The phial!"

Stryke got out the tiny container and tried laying it against Adpar's flesh. His hands were clumsy.

"Here," Coilla said, taking the phial. "This needs a female's touch."

Very carefully, she got the neck of the little bottle under the tear and gently compressed the cheek. The tear rolled and was caught. Coilla replaced the stopper and handed it to Stryke.

"Ironic, isn't it?" she said. "I'll bet she never shed a single tear in her whole life for the suffering she inflicted on others. It took self-pity to do it."

Stryke studied the phial. "You know, I never thought we'd do this."

"*Now* he tells us," Haskeer grumbled.

"And the gods were with us," Alfray announced, lowering Adpar's wrist. "She's dead."

"Fitting that her last act should be the healing of one of her victims," Stryke judged.

"All we have to do now is get out of here," Jup said.

22

Jennesta was in the middle of a strategy meeting with Mersadion when it happened.

Reality reconfigured itself, became pliant. Changed. She had something like a vision, only it wasn't precisely that. It was more an overwhelming impression of *knowing*, a certainty that an event of great importance had taken place. And parallel with the knowledge came another thing, a distinct and vivid message, for want of a better word, that she found equally exciting.

Jennesta had never before experienced anything like the sensation that possessed her. She supposed it resulted from the intimate telepathic link she involuntarily shared with her sibling. *Had* shared, she corrected herself. Adpar was dead. Jennesta knew that without a doubt. And it wasn't all she now knew.

She hadn't realised that her eyes were closed, nor that she had reached out for the back of a chair to steady herself. Her head began to clear. She straightened and took some deep breaths.

Mersadion was staring at her, a look of alarm on his face. "Are you . . . all right, Majesty?" he ventured.

She blinked at him, uncomprehending for a moment, then gathered herself. "All right? Yes, I'm all right. In fact I've rarely felt better. I've had some news."

He couldn't see how she could have. She had simply stopped mid flow and looked set to faint. No messenger had arrived, no notes had been passed into the tent. He snapped out of gaping at her and said, "Good news, I trust."

"Indeed. A cause for rejoicing. In more ways than one." Her somewhat dreamy, detached manner melted away. In a determined tone nearer the style he was used to, she snapped, "Bring me a map of the western region."

"Ma'am." He hurried to comply.

They laid the map on the table and she circled one of her bizarrely long fingernails around an area embracing Drogan and Scarrock Marsh. "There," she announced.

He was puzzled, again. "There . . . *what*, Majesty?"

"The Wolverines. They're to be found in this vicinity."

"Begging your pardon, ma'am, but how do you know that?"

She smiled. It was triumphant and cold. "You'll just have to take my word for it, General. But that's where they are. Or at least one of them—their leader, Stryke. We're moving as soon as you can organise the army. Which is to say in no more than two hours."

"Two hours is very tight, Majesty, for a force of this size."

"Don't *argue* with me, Mersadion," she seethed. "Timing is vital. This is the first solid lead we've had to that damned warband's whereabouts. I'm not throwing it away because of your sloth. Now get out there and set things in train!"

"Majesty!" He made for the tent flap.

"And send Glozellan in right away," she added.

The Dragon Dam appeared a few minutes later. Without preamble, Jennesta beckoned her to the map. "I have intelligence that the Wolverines are here somewhere. You'll take a squadron of dragons and go ahead of the army. Scan the area for them. But *don't* attack unless you absolutely have to. Corner them if you must, but I want them intact when we get there."

"Yes, Your Majesty."

"Well, don't just stand there! Move yourself!"

The haughty brownie gave a tiny bow and slipped from the tent.

Jennesta began gathering what she needed for the journey. For the first time in weeks she felt positive about the turn of events. And she was rid of Adpar, which came like a great weight lifted.

Then it seemed to her that the air in the tent grew somehow more . . . pliable. And the light was dimming, despite the lamps. She thought it must be the return of what she had undergone earlier, and wondered what else the cosmos might have to convey.

But she was wrong. In almost total and unaccountable

darkness now, she saw a pinprick of light wink into existence a couple of feet away. It was quickly joined by scores of others. They swirled and took on a more robust form. Jennesta made ready to defend herself against an attack of sorcery.

A blotch of pulsing light hovered in the air. It coalesced and became something she could recognise. A face.

"Sanara!" she exclaimed. "How the hell did you do that?"

"*It seems my abilities have grown stronger,*" her surviving sibling explained. "*But that isn't the point.*"

"What is?"

"*Your wickedness.*"

"Oh. You too, eh?"

"*How could you do it, Jennesta? How could you subject our sister to such a fate?*"

"You always thought her as . . ." she struggled for a word ". . . as *reprehensible* as me! Why change your tune now?"

"*I never thought her beyond redemption. I didn't wish her death.*"

"Of course, you're assuming I had anything to do with it."

"*Oh, come on, Jennesta.*"

"Well, what if I did?" she replied defensively. "She deserved it."

"*What you've done is not only evil, it adds complexity to a situation already fraught with uncertainty.*"

"What the hell does that mean?"

"*This game you're playing, with the relics. The bid for even greater destructive power. There are other players now, sister, and their abilities may well outstrip your own.*"

"Who? What are you talking about?"

"*Repent. While there is still time.*"

"Answer me, Sanara! Don't palm me off with platitudes! Who have I to fear?"

"*In the end, only yourself.*"

"Tell me!"

"*They say that when the barbarians are at the gate, civilisation is as good as dead. Don't be a barbarian, Jennesta. Make good your ways, redeem your life.*"

"You're so *bloody* strait-laced!" Jennesta raged. "Not to mention obscure! Explain yourself!"

"I think you know what I mean, in your heart. Don't think what you have done to Adpar will go unrecorded, or unpunished."

The likeness of her face faded and disappeared, despite Jennesta's ravings.

In another tent, not too far away in Maras-Dantian terms, a father and daughter conversed.

"You promised me, Daddy," Mercy Hobrow whined. "You said I'd have the benefit."

"And you will, poppet, you will. I said I'd get back the heritage for you and I meant it. We're working on where those savages might be right now."

She pouted grotesquely. "Will it be long?"

"No, not long now. And soon I'll make you a queen. You'll be a handmaiden of our Lord, and together we'll cleanse this land of the sub-humans." He stood. "Now dry your tears. I need to attend to this very business." He planted a kiss on her cheek and went out of the tent.

Kimball Hobrow walked a couple of yards to the fire and the group of custodians. The bodies of three orcs had been laid to one side. The fourth, still alive but only just, had now been finished with.

Hobrow nodded to the Inquisitor. "Well?"

"They're tough. But this one broke at the last, praise the Lord."

"And?"

"They've gone to Drogan."

The death rattle sounded in Corporal Trispeer's throat and he died.

The growing chaos aided the band in getting out of Adpar's palace. They took some wrong turns in the labyrinth of passages, and had a skirmish or two with warriors encountered, but generally the populace were too busy fighting their own battles.

But the exit they found was nowhere near the way they came in.

"Looks like we've come out further north," Stryke reckoned.

"What do we do, go back in and try again?" Jup said.

"No, it's too much of a risk." He pointed. "If we can cross that stretch of water yonder, then veer east, we should reach the marsh near where we left the horses."

Coilla frowned. "Hell of a diversion, isn't it?"

"I reckon going back into the palace is more chancy. One of those factions is going to come out on top any time soon. Then they'll notice interlopers."

"Let's get started, shall we?" Alfray suggested. "We're too exposed here."

They traversed a spread of jagged rocks at double time, reached a flat and faced the water. It was covered in green scum.

"Smells about as pleasant as everything else here," Haskeer observed. "How deep do you think it is, Stryke?"

"Only one way to find out." He eased himself in. It was cold, but his feet touched the bottom at waist-height. "Going's a bit soft, but it seems all right otherwise. Come on."

They followed him, weapons held high, and began wading.

"We should get extra pay for this," Haskeer moaned.

"*Extra?*" Jup said. "Hell, Sergeant, we don't get *any* at the moment."

"Yeah! I'd forgotten that!"

They carried on for another ten minutes. It looked as if they were going to make it. The marshy shore was in sight.

Then there was turbulence in the water a few yards ahead. Bubbles reached the surface and burst. The band stopped.

More mini whirlpools appeared in other places. More bubbles drifted up.

"Maybe this wasn't such a good idea after all," Jup muttered.

A plume of water erupted. Dead ahead, a nyadd appeared.

In short order more emerged from the fetid liquid clutching their saw-toothed weapons.

"Remember what you said about fighting them in their own element, Stryke?" Coilla reminded him.

"It's too late to turn back now, Corporal."

Splashes from behind had them turning. More nyadds were coming up. They began moving in, front and behind.

"Let's carve some flesh," Stryke growled.

The back half of the band took up a rearguard action, led by Jup and Haskeer. Stryke, Coilla and Alfray were in the vanguard of the coming fight. As it stood, the band outnumbered the nyadds they faced. But Stryke reckoned fighting in water at least evened the odds.

He augmented his swords with a knife and lashed out at the foremost creature. His sword struck the creature's crusty shell and did some damage. Blood trickled. But the wound wasn't sufficient to put the warrior out of the fight. Stryke gritted his teeth and went in again, this time aided by a couple of grunts harrying the nyadd from either side. They succeeded in battering it into a dive.

Coilla proceeded to toss throwing knives at the enemy's heads. But every shot meant a lost blade and her supply was limited. She spent two knives to no good effect, then her next shot connected with the side of her target's head. The nyadd bellowed and disappeared beneath the water, leaving a widening cloud of red.

A triumphant roar from behind marked their first confirmed kill.

"We're thinning their ranks," Stryke yelled, "but not fast enough. If more come—!"

He broke off as a nyadd propelled itself towards him waving its jagged spear. The warrior swiped at him. Stryke ducked, and in doing so took himself below the surface. The cold, foul water covered his head. He counted to three, hoping that meant the swing had passed, and resurfaced.

The nyadd was practically on top of him. Stryke rammed his sword into its belly with all his might. The carapace crunched and shattered. Blood flowed. Another great gout issued from the creature's mouth and it disappeared beneath the water. Stryke coughed up a lungful of the putrid stuff.

Haskeer and Jup were hacking at a foe from both sides. They'd already torn open one of its arms, and it was fighting to keep them off.

Wading in, Haskeer aimed a heavy blow at the creature's neck. The nyadd moved down, instinctively seeking the protection of water. It would have done better going in any other direction. The blade cleaved its head, spilling brains.

That left just four nyadds, and though they looked no less murderous, Stryke was confident they could be overcome. The whole band went for three of them.

Except Coilla, who splashed forward to engage the remaining one, which lurked apart. She didn't see another emerge from the water on her blind side, moving with remarkable speed. She spun at the last minute, two nyadds to deal with. One raised its sword.

Kestix had noticed. *"Look out, Corporal!"* he yelled, propelling himself in her direction.

He got between her and the second nyadd's swinging blade. If he hoped to deflect it with his own sword, he miscalculated.

The nyadd's wickedly sharp weapon cut into his chest as if into butter. There was an explosion of gore. Kestix cried out in agony.

"No!" Coilla screamed. Then she had to pay heed to the other raider, bringing up her own sword to block his.

Kestix, still alive but grievously wounded, had been grabbed by his assailant. He struggled feebly. His cries had been heard by the others. Several, including Stryke, answered the call.

They got there just in time to see him dragged under water by the submerging nyadd. Only a bloody stain was left behind.

A couple of grunts splashed around, ducking their heads under trying to save their comrade.

"Leave it!" Stryke ordered. "It's too late for him."

They turned their grief-driven fury on the remaining nyadds.

Near defeating them, they noticed fresh turbulence and bubbles breaking out all around.

"Shit, chief," Jup panted, "we can't take much more of this!"

The band braced themselves for a last stand.

More heads began appearing.

But they weren't nyadds. They were merz. Dozens of them, armed with trident spears and daggers.

"Gods!" Alfray exclaimed. "Are they out for us too?"

"I don't think so," Stryke replied.

His judgement proved true. The merz set about the few nyadds still present, tearing into them with savagery born of injustice.

One of the merz turned and raised a dripping hand to the orcs. It was a salute.

Stryke wasn't alone in returning it.

"We owe them one," he told his comrades. "Now let's get out of here."

They left the slaughter and made their way to the bank, mourning Kestix.

23

The journey back to Liffin and Talag was a sombre affair. Things were no less dismal on the return journey to Drogan, despite their victory.

"Is any of this worth one orc's life?" Alfray wondered. "Let alone one as valiant as Kestix?"

"Risking our lives is what we do," Stryke reminded him. "And orcs have died for less good causes."

"You're really sure this *is* a good cause? Gathering together a bunch of objects we don't know the purpose of for some end we can't see?"

"We have to believe that, Alfray. And I'm sure the day will come when we'll toast Kestix, and the others who have fallen, as heroes of a new order. But don't ask me what that might be. I just feel it has to be better." Stryke wished he entirely believed that himself. As it was he was trying not to show the crushing sense of responsibility he felt at their comrade's death.

For his part, Alfray fell silent and stared up at the band's war banner he was clutching. He seemed to draw some kind of comfort from it, perhaps musing on the unity it represented. Or that which it once did.

They were almost within sight of Drogan Forest when Jup called out, "Eyes west!"

A large party of riders was heading their way, and they weren't far off.

"I think they're Hobrow's men," the dwarf reported.

"Don't we ever get any peace?" Coilla complained.

"Not today, by the looks of it," Stryke replied. "Burn leather."

They broke into a gallop.

"They've seen us!" Haskeer yelled. "And they're putting on a hell of a spurt!"

A chase began in earnest. The band rode at breakneck speed for the sanctuary of the forest. But the custodians were determined and gaining.

Urging the Wolverines onward, Stryke found himself at the back of their onward rush. Then disaster struck. As the rest of the band rounded a bend and disappeared from sight, his horse caught its hoof in a rabbit hole and went down. Stryke was thrown clear. As he scrambled to his feet the horse rose and bolted.

The thunder of other hoofs had him spinning around.

A charging mob of custodians was bearing down on him. Stryke looked around desperately for cover. None presented itself. He drew his sword.

A great shadow covered him.

Just above, a dragon hovered, the beat of its mighty wings throwing up dust and leaves. The custodians, terrified, pulled up to a skidding halt. Several of them tumbled from their saddles at the violence of their halt.

For his part, Stryke was sure he was finished. It was one of Jennesta's war dragons, he was sure of that, and he expected nothing but incineration.

The dragon sank down between him and the human posse. When it was near level he saw that the handler was Glozellan herself.

She extended a hand. "Get on, Stryke," she urged. "Come on! What have you to lose?"

He climbed the beast's scaly hide and sat behind her.

"Hold tight!" she shouted, and they were away.

The climb was fast and dizzying. Stryke looked down. He saw silvery snaking rivers, green pastures, burgeoning forests. From up here it didn't look like a land raped.

He tried shouting questions at Glozellan over the wind's rush, but she either couldn't hear or ignored him. They flew north.

Perhaps an hour elapsed. They approached a mountain. Unerringly, the dragon made for its plateau. Minutes later they touched down.

"Get off," the brownie ordered.

He slid to the ground.

"What's happening, Glozellan?" he asked. "Am I a prisoner?"

"I can't explain now. You'll be safe here."

She stuck her heels into the dragon's flanks. It began rising again.

"Wait!" he cried. "Don't leave me here!"

"I'll be back!" she called. "Have courage."

He watched until the dragon became a dot, then disappeared altogether.

He sat for hours on his involuntary mountaintop retreat, brooding over events, regretting lives lost.

Having established that there was no possible way down, he took out the stars and contemplated them.

"Well met."

He leapt up at the sound of the voice.

Serapheim stood before him.

Stryke was confounded. "How did you get here? Were you another of Glozellan's passengers?"

"No, my friend. How I got here isn't important. But I wanted to apologise for leading you into that trap set by the goblin slavers. It was not my intention."

"It turned out right in the end. I have no hard feelings towards you."

"I'm glad."

Stryke sighed. "Not that any of it matters much. Things seem to be falling apart faster than I can cope with. And now I've lost my band."

"Not lost, merely mislaid." He smiled. "The important thing is that you do not despair. There is still much for you to do. Now is not the time to surrender to defeatism. Have you ever heard the story of the boy and the sabre leopards?"

Now it was Stryke's turn to smile, albeit a little cynically. "A story. Well, I suppose it's as good a way of passing the time as any."

"There was once a boy walking in the forest," Serapheim began, "when he came across a savage sabre leopard. The leopard saw the boy. The boy ran with the leopard in hot pursuit. Then the boy came to the edge of a cliff. There were vines trailing over the edge, so he lowered himself down them, leaving the beast growling impotently above. But then the boy looked down and saw another, equally hungry leopard below, waiting for him. He could neither go up nor go down. Next thing, the boy heard a scratching sound. He glanced up and saw two small mice, one white and one black, chewing through the vine he was holding on to. But he saw something else. Off to one side, almost out of reach, a wild strawberry was growing. Stretching as far as he could, the boy plucked the stawberry and popped it into his mouth. And do you know something, Stryke? It was the sweetest, most delicious thing he'd ever tasted."

"You know, I think I almost understand that. It reminds me of the sort of thing someone I know might have said . . . in a dream."

"Dreams are good. You should pay heed to them. You know, the magic energy flows a bit stronger in these parts. It could have some effect on those." He nodded at the stars in Stryke's hand.

"There's a connection?"

"Oh, yes." Serapheim paused. "Will you give them to me?"

Stryke was shocked. "Like hell I will."

"There was a time when I could have taken them from you, with ease. And when I would have been inclined to do so. But now it seems the gods want you to have them."

Stryke glanced down at them. When he looked up again the human had gone. Impossibly.

He would have wondered at it, but now something else had claimed his awe.

The stars were singing to him.

BOOK

3

WARRIORS OF THE TEMPEST

Dedicated with love and fond memories to
Eileen Costelloe (1951–2001)

1

They rode like harpies fresh out of hell.

Jup turned in his saddle and looked back at their pursuers. He reckoned there were maybe a hundred of them, outnumbering the Wolverines four or five to one. They wore black and were heavily armed, and the length of the chase had done nothing to cool their fire.

Now the leading humans were near enough to spit at.

He glanced at Coilla, riding abreast of him at the band's rear. She leaned forward, head low, teeth resolutely clenched, bunched hair flowing like rippled bay smoke. The angular, tattooed corporal's stripes patterning her cheeks stressed her stern features.

Ahead of Coilla, sergeant Haskeer and corporal Alfray galloped headlong, their foaming mounts' hooves pounding the frigid turf, kicking up clods of mud. The rest of the orcs were spread out on either side, grim-faced, bent into the lashing wind.

All eyes were on the distant shelter of Drogan Forest.

"They're gaining!" Jup bellowed.

If any but Coilla heard, they didn't show it. *"Then don't waste breath!"* she yelled, glaring at the dwarf. *"Keep moving!"*

Her mind was still on the spectacle they had witnessed earlier, of Stryke unhorsed, then carried off by a war dragon. They had to assume it was one of Jennesta's, and that he was lost.

Jup shouted again, puncturing her brief reverie. He had an arm thrust out, pointing toward her neglected left side. She swung her head. A custodian had drawn parallel with her. His sword was raised and his horse was about to barrel into hers.

"Shit!" Coilla snapped. She pulled hard on the reins, turning herself aside. It got her clear and bought enough time to unsheathe her own blade.

The human pressed in. He was waving the weapon and roaring, his words obliterated by the thunder of the chase. His first swing was wide, the blade tip hewing air just short of her calf. A rapid second stroke came closer and higher, and would have cleaved her waist if she hadn't tilted from him.

That made Coilla mad.

She whipped round and sent out a stroke of her own. The man ducked and it cut a whistling arc inches above his head. He returned a thrust meant for her chest, but Coilla blocked it, knocking aside his sword. He made another pass, and another. She deflected both, their blades connecting with a jarring, steely clatter.

Hunters and hunted sped on, pell-mell. They entered a small ravine perhaps a dozen horses wide. The terrain flashed by, a blur of green and brown. On the edge of her vision Coilla was aware of more humans crowding the band.

She stretched out and swiped at her antagonist again. The stroke missed, and overreaching she almost toppled. He countered. Their weapons clashed, edge to edge, metal ringing. Neither found an opening.

There was a fleeting respite as they realigned themselves and Coilla checked the way ahead. It was as well she did. The forward riders were splitting to either side of a dead tree square in their path, flowing around it like fast-running water against a huge ship's prow. She tugged the reins to the right, throwing her centre of balance in the same direction. The horse swerved and skimmed past the trunk. For an instant she had sight of the bark's scabrous grain. A skeletal branch raked her shoulder. Then she was clear.

Where Coilla passed to the tree's right, the human took a route to the left. But it was an obstacle for the rest of his kind. Their greater numbers clogged at the bottleneck, and for a moment he was alone. Set on being rid of him, Coilla steered his way. They recommenced their duel as the gully gave way to open plains.

Trading blows, she was aware of the decamping Wolverines, with Jup staring at her over his shoulder. At the same time the main body of custodians, coming up behind, was renewing speed. Coilla settled on a bold move. She let go of her reins, giving the horse its head, and clasped her sword two-handed. Inviting a fall was a risky ploy, but she took the gamble.

It paid off.

This time, putting all her strength and reach into the swing, the blade bit flesh. It made contact at the elbow joint of the custodian's sword arm, hacking deep. Blood jetted. Crying out, he dropped his weapon and clamped the wound. Coilla's follow-up struck his chest, shattering bone, freeing a copious ruby gush. He swayed, head rolling. She made to strike again.

There was no need. The bridle slipped from the wounded human's fist. For a second he bumped along insensibly, a mere passenger, carried like a rag doll by his racing horse. Then he fell. A confusion of askew limbs and tangled clothing, he hit the ground tumbling.

Before he came to rest, the custodian vanguard rode over him. Some went down in the collision and were trampled in their turn. A chaotic scrum of screaming men and horses formed.

Coilla snatched her flailing reins and spurred onward, several riderless mounts in her wake.

She reached the tail end of the fleeing band to find Jup hanging back for her. As they rode on together the enemy regrouped behind them.

"They're not gonna quit," Jup decided.

"Do they ever?" She surveyed the land ahead. It was turning boggy. "And this isn't running country," she added.

"We're not thinking."

"Eh?"

"We can't lead 'em to Drogan."

Coilla frowned. "No," she agreed, her gaze flicking to the tree line. "Bad way of repaying Keppatawn."

"Right."

"What, then?"

"Come *on*, Coilla."

"*Shit*."

"Got another plan?"

She eyed the mob of humans. They were closing. "No," she sighed. "Let's do it."

Urging her horse, she put on a burst. Jup followed. They

weaved through the ranks of grunts to the band's head, where Alfray and Haskeer were leading the charge. The marshy footing was checking progress, yet still the pace smarted Coilla's eyes.

"Not the forest!" she called across. *"Not to the forest!"*

Alfray understood. "A stand?" he shouted back, hefting the band's streaming war banner.

It was Jup who answered. "What else?" he bawled.

"Stand, yes!" Haskeer chimed in. "Orcs don't run! We *fight!"*

That was enough for Coilla. She curbed her mount. The others took her cue and reined in. At their hind the custodians were coming up rapidly.

Wheeling about, she boomed, *"Stand fast! We're meeting 'em!"*

It wasn't her place to command. As the highest-ranking officers, Jup or Haskeer should have given the order. But nobody was thinking of formalities.

"Spread out!" Jup barked. *"Make a line!"*

With the enemy almost on them, the troop swiftly obeyed. They produced slingshots, throwing knives, short spears and bows, though in spears and bows they were miserably equipped, having no more than four of each among them. Snub blades and shot were more plentiful.

The custodians were baying as they swept in. Individual faces could be made out, twisted with bloodlust. Their horses' steaming breath was visible. The earth rumbled.

"Steady!" Alfray cautioned.

Then they were a rock's lob from the orc line.

"Now!" Jup yelled.

The band loosed its meagre armoury. Arrows were fired, spears soared, clusters of stones flew.

There was a moment of chaos as the humans braked. Several were tossed from their horses by the sudden halt. Others were felled by arrows and stinging shot. Here and there, shields went up.

Retaliation was swift, if ragged. A few arrows winged back, several spears sailed over; but from their sparseness it seemed the custodians were as badly supplied as the Wolverines.

Where they had them, orcs raised their own shields. Projectiles rattled off them.

Soon the stockpiles were exhausted, and the sides fell to swapping jeers and taunts. Hands were filled with close-combat weapons.

"I give it another two minutes," Coilla predicted.

She was wrong. The stand-off was broken in half that time.

Emboldened by their greater numbers, the humans suddenly rushed forward, a black tide thick with steel.

"This is it," Jup muttered darkly, hiking a butterfly axe from its saddle scabbard.

Haskeer drew a broadsword. Scooping back a sleeve, Coilla plucked a throwing knife from her arm sheath.

Alfray levelled the spiked banner spar. *"Hold fast! And watch those flanks!"*

Any other advice was drowned by the onslaught.

The custodians' larger numbers and lesser discipline had them grouping together as they came in to confront the lesser force, hampering themselves. It didn't change the fact that each Wolverine faced towering odds, but it did buy a few seconds' grace.

Coilla used it to try picking off some of the enemy before they reached her. She flung her knife at the nearest human. It smacked home in his windpipe and he plunged from his mount. Quickly snatching another blade, she pitched it underarm at the next foe, spiking his eye. Her third throw was wide of its mark, and proved the last. Now they were too close for anything but hand-to-hand. Shrieking a battle cry, she brought her sword into play.

The first warrior to reach Jup paid for it dearly. A blow from the dwarf's weighty axe split his skull, showering blood and bone shards on all in range. Two more custodians waded in. Dodging their blades, Jup sent out a wide horizontal swing that severed the hand of one and stove in the other's chest. There was no pause. More opponents replaced the fallen. His weathered, bearded face straining with effort, Jup laid into them.

Haskeer's savage rain of blows downed both his initial attackers. But the second took the blade with him as he fell, leaving

Haskeer to face his next assailant bare-handed. The man had a pike. They wrestled for it, knuckles white, the barbed spear jerking back and forth. Plumbing all his strength, Haskeer drove the butt into the man's stomach, breaking his grip. With a dextrous flip, the weapon was delivered to its owner's innards. Prised free, it served again on another custodian. But this victim's writhing snapped it, leaving Haskeer with a useless length of shank.

Then two things happened at once. Another human moved in on him with flashing sword. And a lone arrow zipped from the scrum to pierce Haskeer's forearm.

Howling more with fury than pain, he wrenched out the gory shaft. Brandishing the arrow he lurched forward and employed it like a dagger, stabbing at the custodian's face. The distraction let Haskeer snatch away the wailing man's blade and gut him. His place was instantly taken. Haskeer fought on.

Favouring a hatchet over the spar for close combat, Alfray wielded it with deadly precision. But in truth it was all he could do to hold back the storm. Though he had an orc's lust for blood-letting, his years were beginning to tell. Yet despite his waning stamina he matched any in butchery. For now.

He scanned the mêlée and saw that he wasn't the only one overextended. The whole band was on the point of being over-whelmed, with fighting especially brutal at the wings, where the enemy was trying to outflank them. The Wolverines may have had little option other than a stand, but it was proving too bold a move. They were taking wounds, though so far none of them had gone down. That wouldn't last.

Though only a corporal, Alfray was on the point of ignoring protocol and shouting the order himself. Jup beat him to it, yelling words that stuck in an orc's throat.

"Fall back! Fall back!"

The instruction spread along the besieged line. Grunts hastily disentangled themselves and withdrew. The face-off became a rearguard action. But the custodians, suspicious of a feint, were wary of going after their quarry with any zeal. The band knew their reluctance was temporary.

Arms aching from the exertion of slaughter, Coilla retreated with the rest, reopening the gap between the lines. The Wolverines moved closer together.

She came to Jup. "What now? Run again?"

"No chance," the dwarf panted.

Coilla ran a palm over her cheek, wiping blood. "Thought so."

Their opponents were working themselves up for the final assault.

At Coilla's shoulder, Alfray said, "We got a good few."

"Not enough," Haskeer responded gruffly.

In undertones, some of the grunts were calling on orc deities to guide their blades. Or to make their deaths suitably heroic and swift. Coilla suspected the humans were appealing to their own god in similar vein.

The custodians began advancing.

There was a keening sound in the air. A fast-moving shadow passed over the Wolverines. They looked up and saw something like a swarm of elongated insects sweeping across the sky. The dark cloud had already reached its apex and was curving down towards the enemy.

It fell upon them wrathfully. The forefront of the custodian line was riddled with lethal bolts. They bored into upturned faces and chests, arms and thighs. Their velocity took them through the paltry defences of helmets and visors. Shields could have been made of paper for all the good they did. Peppered with numerous shafts, men and horses succumbed wholesale in a struggling, bloodied mass.

A large force was riding, hell-bent, from the direction of the forest, and even as the band spied them they unleashed another deadly cloud. The arrows' great arching path was well above the Wolverines, yet still they instinctively ducked. Once more death rained mercilessly on the heads of the humans, bringing further mayhem and chaos.

As their allies approached, the band began to make them out.

Squinting at the reinforcements, eyes shaded with a hand, Alfray exclaimed, "Keppatawn's clan!"

Jup nodded. "And well timed."

The small army of centaurs at least equalled the humans

in strength of numbers. And they would reach the fray in minutes.

"Who's at their head?" Alfray wondered.

Knowing him to be lame, the band didn't expect Keppatawn himself to be leading the offensive.

"Looks like Gelorak," Jup reported.

The young centaur's muscular physique and distinctive flowing chestnut mane were now plain to see.

Haskeer finished wrapping a piece of dirty cloth around his wound. "Why talk when there's killing undone?" he grumbled.

"Too right," Coilla agreed, breaking ranks. *"At the bastards!"*

They weren't slow in following her lead.

The custodians were in bedlam from the arrow blizzard, their dead and maimed littering the plain. Loose horses and walking wounded added to the anarchy, and those custodians still mounted milled in a directionless daze. They were easy pickings for a vengeful warband.

No sooner had the orcs waded in and commenced their slaughter than they were joined by the troop of centaurs. With clubs, spears, short bows and crooked blades they assured the rout. The rump of the custodian force soon turned and fled, chased off by a knot of fleet-footed centaurs.

Exhausted, battle-grimed, Coilla surveyed the aftermath. The auxiliary chief of the Drogan clan trotted to her side and sheathed his sword. He pawed the ground a couple of times.

"Thanks, Gelorak," she said.

"Our pleasure. We have no need of such unwanted guests." He gave a flick of his plaited tail. "Who were they?"

"Just a bunch of humans serving their god of love."

He smiled wryly, then asked, "How went your journey to Scarrock?"

"Well and . . . not so well."

Gelorak cast his eye over the warband. "I do not see Stryke."

"No," Coilla replied softly. "No, you don't."

She stared at the darkening sky and tried to hold back her despair.

2

He was in a narrow tunnel that stretched endlessly before and behind him.

His head almost touched the ceiling, and when he extended his arms he could lay his hands on either wall, which felt cold and slightly clammy. Ceiling, walls and floor were made of stone but the tunnel seemed to have been bored rather than constructed because there were no joints or sign of blocks having been fitted together. There was no illumination of any kind either, yet he could see quite clearly. The only sound was his own laboured breathing.

He didn't know where he was or how he came to be here.

For a while he stood quite still, trying to make sense of his surroundings and uncertain of what to do. Then a white light appeared far ahead. No such light showed in the other direction, so he assumed he was facing the tunnel's exit. He began walking towards it. Unlike the slippery smoothness of the walls and ceiling, the floor was rough in texture, giving him purchase.

It was hard to keep track of time but after about ten minutes, as best he could reckon, the light didn't look any nearer. The features of the tunnel remained absolutely uniform, and the silence was unbroken save for his footfalls. He pressed on, moving as fast as he could in the confined space.

His lack of a sense of time became timelessness. All notion of the passing of minutes and hours deserted him. There was only an endless now, and a universe consisting solely of his pursuit of a light he could never reach. His body became a trudging automaton.

At some indefinable point in his monotonous journey he was roused by a fancy that the light had grown brighter, though not necessarily larger. Soon he found it hard to look directly at it for more than a few seconds.

With each step he took, the pure white light grew stronger and *stronger, until walls, floor, ceiling, everything was obliterated. He closed his eyes and still saw it. Keeping on, he clamped his hands to his face to shut it out, but that made no difference.*

Now it pulsated, throbbing to a beat he could feel pounding at his chest, tearing at the very core of his being.

The light was pain.

He wanted to turn and run away. He couldn't. He was no longer walking but being sucked into its blinding, agonising, searingly cold heart.

He cried out.

The light died.

Slowly, he lowered his hands and opened his eyes.

Before him stretched a vast barren plain. There were no trees, no blades of greenery, nothing he could equate with any landscape he had ever seen before. It resembled a desert, though the sand was pewter-coloured and very fine, like volcanic ash. All that broke the desolate scene were numerous jagged, ebony-hued rocks, large and small, strewn across and partly buried by the sediment.

The atmosphere was tropical. Tendrils of yellowish-green mist crept sluggishly at ankle level, and there was an unpleasant odour in the air that reminded him of sulphur and rotting fish. Way off in the distance towered black mountains of impossible height.

But what shocked him most was the sky.

It was blood red and cloudless. There were no stars. But close to the horizon hung a moon, and it was vast. He could see every pockmarked, scarred detail of its glowing, tawny surface. So large and near was it that he half believed he could pierce the great globe with an arrow. He wondered why it didn't fall and crush this forsaken land.

Tearing his eyes away, he turned and looked behind him. The view was exactly the same. Silver-grey sand, craggy rocks, distant mountains, crimson sky. There was nothing that could have been a tunnel mouth.

Despite the moist warmth, an ominous thought chilled his spine. Could he have died and gone to Xentagia, the orcs' hell? This certainly looked like a place of eternal purgatory. Would Aik, Zeenoth, Neaphetar and Wystendel, his race's holy Tetrad, descend on fiery war chariots and condemn his spirit to everlasting punishment?

Then it occurred to him that if this was Xentagia it appeared sparsely

populated indeed. Was he the only orc in history to deserve being con-
signed here? Had he alone committed some crime against the gods, of
which he was unaware, that warranted damnation? And where were
the tormenting demons, the Sluagh, that some said inhabited the infer-
nal regions and whose single pleasure was making misery for errant
souls?

Something caught his eye. Across the blasted expanse there was
movement. He strained to make it out. At first he couldn't. Then he
realised he was watching a cloud of the yellow-green, all-pervasive
smog. Only this was thicker and travelling with purpose. His way.

Had he been right? Was he about to be judged? Denounced by the
gods? Horribly tortured?

His instinct was to put up a fight. On second thought, how futile a
plan that would be if he really was going to be confronted by the gods.
The idea of running seemed just as stupid. He determined to face what-
ever it was. Whether deity or demon he wasn't about to betray his creed
with an act of cowardice.

He squared his shoulders and readied himself as best he could.

There wasn't long to wait. The cloud, which billowed but somehow
remained compact, rolled directly to him. There was no question of it
being blown by the wind. It moved too precisely for that, and there was
no wind anyway.

The cloud settled in front of him, perhaps a spear's measure short.
It continued to spin, and he would have expected to feel the misplaced
air, but didn't. This close he could see there were uncountable numbers
of golden pinpoints woven into the swirling smoke. He was less sure of
what the cloud contained. But there was a shape of some kind.

Almost immediately the sphere's rotation slowed. The dense mist
began stripping off, layer by layer, and melted into the air. The darker
form it surrounded gradually started to reveal itself. It became obvious
that it was a figure.

He tensed.

The last wisps dissolved and a creature stood before him.

He had imagined many things, but not this.

The being was short and stocky. It had green-tinged, wrinkly skin
and a large round head with spiky, projecting ears. Its attenuated,
slightly protruding eyes had inky orbs with yellow-veined white sur-
rounds and pulpy lids. No hair covered the pate or face, but there were

bushy, reddish-brown sideburns, turning ashen. The nose was small and pinched, the mouth had the quality of hardened tree sap serrated with a file. Its clothing consisted of a modest robe of neutral colour, held with a cord.

The creature was very old.

"Mobbs?" Stryke whispered.

"Greetings, Captain of the orcs," the gremlin replied. He spoke softly, and a faint smile lightened his face.

Myriad questions filled Stryke's mind. He settled on, "What are you doing here?"

"I have no choice."

"And I do? Where am I, Mobbs? Is this some kind of hell?"

The gremlin shook his head. "No. At least not in the sense you mean."

"Where, then?"

"This is a . . . between land, neither of your world nor mine."

"What are you talking about? Aren't we both Maras-Dantians?"

"Such questions are less important than what I have to tell you." Mobbs indicated their surroundings with an absent sweep of his hand. "Accept this. See it as a forum that enables us to meet."

"More riddles than answers. You're ever the scholar, Mobbs."

"I thought I was. Since being here I've realised I knew nothing."

"But where—"

"Time is short." With hardly a pause he added, "Do you remember our first meeting?"

"Of course I do. It changed everything."

"Helped a change already under way, more like. An act of midwifery perhaps. Though neither of us knew the magnitude of what was to come once you chose your new path."

"I don't know about magnitude." Stryke pronounced it with the faltering respect due a word he'd never used before. "All it's brought me and my band is trouble."

"It will bring you more, and worse, before you triumph." The gremlin corrected himself: "If you triumph."

"We're holding together with spit and gumption, running around looking for pieces of a puzzle we don't understand. Why do we want more trouble when we don't even know what we're doing?"

"But you know why you're doing it. Freedom, truth, the unveiling of mystery. Big prizes, Stryke. And they have a price. In the end you may or may not think that price worth paying."

"I don't know that it's worth it now, Mobbs. I've lost comrades, watched order crumble, seen our lives torn apart . . ."

"You think it wasn't coming to that anyway? The whole of Maras-Dantia is on a downward track, the incomers have ensured that. You have a chance to make a difference, at least for some. If you stop now, you guarantee defeat. Carry on and you have a slim chance of victory. I won't pretend it's more than that."

"Then tell me what to do."

"You want to know where to find the last instrumentality and what to do with them all once you have?"

Stryke nodded.

"I can't tell you. I have no more knowledge than you in that respect. But have you considered the possibility that the objects of your search want to be found?"

"That's crazy. They're just . . . things."

"Perhaps."

"So you've nothing to offer me but warnings?"

"And encouragement. You're so close. You will be given the chance of completing your task, I don't doubt that. Though there will be more blood, more death, more heartache. Despite this you must keep on."

"You speak with such certainty. How do you know these things?"

"My present . . . state brings me a small insight into events yet to be. Not particulars, but a glimpse of the larger currents shaping future times." His face darkened. "And a fire is coming."

Stryke's backbone prickled again as realisation dawned. "You said you had no choice in being here," he mouthed, half aloud.

Mobbs didn't reply.

Stryke repeated his earlier question, this time with some force. "Where are we, Mobbs?"

The aged scholar sighed. "You might call it a repository. A realm of shades."

"How long have you been here?"

"Since just after we parted. Courtesy of another orc, a Captain Delorran."

The gremlin pulled aside the edges of his robe and revealed his chest. He bore a wound, dry of blood now, so deep and pernicious it could have had only one effect.

Confirmation of his suspicion had the colour draining from Stryke's face. "You're . . ."

"Dead. Undead. Between two worlds. And not likely to rest until things are resolved in yours."

"Mobbs, I . . . I'm sorry." It seemed such a weak thing to say.

"Don't be," the gremlin replied gently, closing his robe.

"Delorran was chasing me. If I hadn't involved you—"

"Forget that. I have no ill will for you, and Delorran himself has paid. But can't you see? Free yourself and you free me."

"But—"

"Whether you like it or not, Stryke, the game is afoot and you're a player." Mobbs stretched an arm to point over the orc's shoulder. "Heed!"

Mystified, Stryke spun around. And gaped at insanity.

The gigantic moon, just beginning to set behind the mountain range, had transformed into a face. It had the features of a female, and one he knew too well. Her hair was black, her eyes were unfathomable. She had skin that glinted with a faint emerald and silver lustre, as though flesh had commingled with fish scales.

Jennesta, hybrid queen, opened her overly broad, canine-toothed mouth and roared with silent laughter.

A hand rose from behind the range. It was of the same incredible scale as the face. Its unnaturally slender fingers, tipped with nails half as long again, clutched some vast object. With an almost casual flip, the hand pitched its load toward the plain.

Stryke stared, dumbfounded, as the thing tumbled end over end and hit the ground at an angle. A massive plume of dust went up. The earth shuddered. Then the object bounced, spun in the air, came down and bounced again.

When it had done that half a dozen times two things dawned on Stryke.

First, he recognised the object. It was what Mobbs called an instrumentality and the Wolverines had dubbed a star. It was the first one the band found, at Homefield, a Uni settlement. But whereas Stryke knew it as something he could easily fit into his palm, now it was of titanic *proportions. Its sandy-coloured central sphere would have taken a team of horses to move. The seven projecting spikes were as big as mature oaks.*

Second, he realised it was coming straight at him.

He turned to where Mobbs was standing. The gremlin had vanished.

Tumbling, rocking the ground like a small earthquake every time it touched down, the star bounded closer. It didn't seem to lose momentum.

Stryke started to run.

He pelted across the bizarre wasteland, zigzagging boulders, arms pumping. The star gained on him, beating the ash with bone-jarring blows, crushing rocks, throwing up clouds of dust, spiralling through the air with awesome splendour.

Stryke could hear it, feel it, at his back. Straining to outpace it, he sneaked a look over his shoulder. He saw two of the mighty spikes smash down like the legs of a giant, fall forward, rip out of the ash and fly off again. A wave of dust blinded him for a second, then another crash tossed the ground and the star was close enough to touch.

He threw himself aside using every ounce of muscle power the sprint had left him. As he rolled in the clinging ash his fear was that the star would turn and continue the chase. He came to rest and scrambled to his feet, ready to bolt.

The star kept to its path, flattening every obstacle, drumming a thunderous rhythm as it careered away. He watched as it sprang across the plain. When it was a distant speck he let out the breath he'd been holding.

His eyes were drawn back to what he hoped would be a restored moon. That hope was dashed. Jennesta's enormous form remained, floating in an ocean of blood, glaring down at him.

Once more, she raised her hand. It held more than before. She cast again, and this time a trio of stars cascaded, striking the ground in a ragged line. Triple puffs of ash erupted. The stars bounced and headed for Stryke.

He recognised these, too. The first was green with five spikes, the second dark blue with four spikes, the last grey with two spikes. They were the other stars the band had collected.

As they ranged in on him it seemed there was an intelligence at work, guiding them more cunningly than the first star. One came in an unerringly straight line. The ones on either side of it travelled in a more meandering fashion, bouncing far out and then back close. It was a classic pincer formation. And Stryke was sure they were moving at much greater speed than the initial star.

Again he ran. He took an erratic, unpredictable route to make it harder for them. But every time he looked back they were still on his trail, and they remained in the same relationship to each other, like a trawl net ready to scoop him. He put on all the speed he could muster. His limbs throbbed with pain. When he gulped for breath it felt like inhaling fire.

Then one of the tremendous stars bounced down on his right-hand side, erupting ash. He veered to the left. Another landed, blocking his way. The third was spinning above him. Stumbling, he fell awkwardly. He rolled onto his back. A shadow covered him. Helplessly he saw the airborne star plunge towards him, knowing that in an instant he'd be pulverised.

He was trapped like an insect, watching as a great boot descended to grind him to pulp.

And he thought he could hear a strange, lilting, faraway song.

He was yelling.

It took him a moment to realise he was awake. And alive. A few seconds more passed before he was sure of where he was. Sitting up, he used his sleeve to wipe at the sweat that covered his face despite the cold. He was panting, his breath clouding in the thin, chill air.

The dream wasn't like the others, but it was just as vivid, every bit as real. He tried to make sense of it, running through it in his mind. Then he thought of Mobbs.

More blood on his hands.

Stryke checked himself. It was stupid to feel guilty because of a dream. For all he knew, Mobbs was alive and well. But somehow he couldn't quite bring himself to believe that.

He was still muddled and had to get a grip. Climbing to his feet, he walked to the edge of his prison.

The mountaintop plateau he'd been deposited on by Glozellan, Jennesta's Dragon Dam, was quite small, perhaps a hundred paces long by sixty wide, with only a couple of rock outcrops to give some protection from the wind. He didn't know why Glozellan had brought him here. The probability was that he had been snatched at the behest of her mistress, and it was just a matter of time before he faced her wrath.

He surveyed the view, not really sure where he was, beyond it being some way north of Drogan. Maybe one of the peaks in Bandar Gizatt or Goff. The fact that he had a glimpse of ocean to the west, and could clearly see the looming ice field further north, seemed to confirm this. Not that it mattered.

The temperature was low and the keen wind stung. Stryke was glad of his fur jerkin, and pulled it tighter about himself as he pondered the last few hours' events. Glozellan had left without explanation. Shortly after, the mysterious human who called himself Serapheim had been here, though how he came and went from such an inaccessible place was beyond Stryke's understanding. Then there were the instrumentalities, the stars.

The stars.

He remembered them singing. Just before he slept they were making some kind of sound. But it wasn't out loud, it was in his head. It wasn't singing either, but that was the nearest he could come to describing it. Just like Haskeer.

That gave him pause.

Stryke slipped a freezing hand into his belt pouch and brought out the stars. He examined them. The one they got at Home-field, sandy-coloured with seven spikes of varying lengths; the Trinity star, green with five spikes; the dark blue one with four spikes, from Scratch. They weren't "singing" now.

He frowned. Nothing to do with these things made any sense.

Then he saw something approaching, several miles distant. A great black shape with lazily flapping saw-toothed wings. There was no mistaking it.

He stood ready, hand on sword.

3

The band was escorted into Drogan Forest.

Guards had been doubled in case the humans returned, and the centaurs were on a war footing.

Alfray took Haskeer away to dress his wound properly, and to tend to the injured grunts. The other Wolverines scattered through the settlement, looking for food and drink. Accompanied by Gelorak, Coilla and Jup made their way to the clan chief.

Keppatawn was found at the entrance to his weapons forge, barking orders and despatching messengers. He was once fit and muscular, but age had greyed his beard and lined his face. He was lame, his withered right foreleg dragging uselessly.

After greeting Gelorak, he turned to the pair of Wolverines. "Sergeant. Corporal. Welcome back."

Jup nodded.

"Sorry to bring you trouble, Keppatawn," Coilla told him.

"Don't be. A good fight now and again sharpens our mettle." The centaur grinned roguishly. "So, how went your mission?"

"We got what you wanted."

"You *did?*" Keppatawn beamed. "Wonderful news! Everything they say about you orcs—" He saw their faces. "What's wrong?"

Neither answered.

Keppatawn looked about the clearing. "Where's Stryke?"

"We don't know," Jup admitted glumly.

"Meaning?"

"His horse fell when we were trying to outrun the humans," Coilla explained. "Then a war dragon came out of nowhere and took him."

"You're saying he was captured?"

"We didn't see him being forced, if that's what you mean. Too busy running for that. But Jennesta's one of the few with command of dragons these days."

"I got a look at the handler," Jup said. "I'm pretty sure it was Glozellan."

Coilla sighed. "Jennesta's Dragon Dam. That settles it."

"Maybe not," the dwarf offered. "Can you imagine a *brownie* making Stryke do something he didn't want?"

"I . . . I just don't know, Jup. All I know is Stryke's gone, and the stars and the tear have gone with him." To Keppatawn she added, "Sorry. Should have said."

The chieftain betrayed no obvious disappointment, but they all noticed his hand absently rub against the thigh of his ravaged leg. "I can't miss what I've never had," he replied stoically. "As to your Captain, we'll scour the area."

"The band should be doing that," Jup said. "He's one of our own."

"You need rest, and we know the terrain." He addressed his second-in-command. "Muster search parties, Gelorak, and post lookouts on higher ground." The young centaur nodded and galloped off. Keppatawn returned his attention to Jup and Coilla. "There's nothing more we can do at the moment. Come."

He led them to an oak trestle-table. They slid wearily onto its bench seat. A centaur was passing, towing a small two-wheeled cart loaded with rations. Keppatawn reached out and yanked a narrow-necked stone jug from the creaking load.

"I think you could use ale," he ventured. Sinking his teeth into the jug's cork stopper he drew it out and spat it away, then slammed the jug on the table.

"What the hell," Jup responded. He raised the jug two-handed and drank. It was offered to Coilla. She shook her head.

Easily hoisting the jug with one hand, Keppatawn gulped a long draft. He wiped the back of his arm across his mouth. "Now tell me what happened."

Coilla took the lead. "Stryke wasn't the only band member we lost. On the way back one of our grunts, Kestix, was killed by nyadd warriors in Scarrock Marsh." She felt a stab of anguish. Kestix had died saving her.

"I'm truly sorry," Keppatawn said. "The more so as you undertook the task for me."

"We did it as much for ourselves. You're not to blame."

"Frankly, I'm surprised our casualties weren't heavier," Jup put in, "given the chaos down there."

"How so?" Keppatawn asked.

"Adpar's dead."

"*What?* Are you sure?"

"We were there when she died," Coilla told him. "And no, it wasn't us."

"You had an eventful journey indeed. How did she die?"

"It was Jennesta's doing."

"*She* was there?"

"Well . . . no."

"Then how do you know it was her?"

It was a good question. Coilla hadn't really had time to think it through. Now she realised there was a mystery. "Stryke said so," she replied distantly. "He seemed certain of it."

Apparently Jup hadn't given it much thought either. "Yes, but how?"

"Must have known something we didn't," Coilla decided, though she couldn't imagine how.

"Anyway, there was anarchy in the nyadd realm," she summed up tersely. "We only got out because the merz helped us."

Keppatawn looked reflective. He stroked his full-bearded chin with thumb and forefinger. "We'll have to be even more alert after this. Adpar's death changes the whole power structure in this region. And not necessarily for the better."

"But she was a tyrant."

"Yes. But at least we knew where we were with her. Now others will move to fill the void she leaves, and they're an unknown quantity. It can only bring more instability, and Maras-Dantia already has plenty of that."

They were interrupted by the arrival of a swaggering Haskeer. He had his arm in a sling and was wolfing a hunk of roast meat. His lips and cheeks shone with grease.

"Where's Alfray?" Coilla said.

"Bimbing whoons," Haskeer replied with a full mouth.

She nodded at his arm. "How's yours?"

He swallowed, tossed away the stripped bone and loudly belched. "All right." Without asking he snatched the jug and guzzled heartily, head back, ale dribbling down his face. He belched again.

"As ever, your courtly manners put us all to shame," Jup commented.

Haskeer looked dimly baffled. "You what?"

"Forget it."

There was a time when the dwarf's gibe would have had the two sergeants at each other's throats. Perhaps Haskeer was mellowing, or simply didn't understand he was the butt of sarcasm, but in the event he just shrugged and asked, "What do we do now?"

"Try to find Stryke. Apart from that, we don't know," Jup confessed.

Haskeer wiped his oily fingers on his fur jerkin. "Suppose we can't find him?"

"Don't even *think* that," Coilla rumbled ominously.

The truth was that she could think of nothing else herself.

Stryke watched as the behemoth sank through the air and touched down on the mountain plateau.

The dragon's sinewy wings crackled as they folded in on themselves. Its great head slowly turned to regard him, slitty yellow eyes unblinking, milky smoke curling from cavernous nostrils. The creature was panting, dog fashion, a glistening tongue the size of a horse blanket lolling from its massive jaws. It brought with it a smell of raw fish, halitosis and broken wind.

Stryke retreated a few steps.

The beast's handler disengaged herself and slid from its scaly back.

Almost everything she wore comprised shades of brown, from jerkin and trews to high boots and thin-brimmed hat. The hat's white and grey decorative feather, and simple gold strands at her wrists and neck, were the only departure.

It was an enigma that brownies, a hybrid race born of elves

and goblins, neither of which excelled in height, should be so lanky. She was even taller than the norm, and her height was more striking because she held herself totally erect. Her frame looked deceptively delicate and she was overly thin. As with all brownies her proud expression could be mistaken for conceit.

"*Glozellan!* What the *hell's* going on?" Stryke demanded.

She seemed unfazed. "I'm sorry to have left you so long. I couldn't avoid it."

"Am I a prisoner here?" He still clutched his sword.

She arched her almost non-existent brown eyebrows. Otherwise she stayed glacial. "No, you're not a prisoner; *I'm* hardly capable of holding you captive. And there are no dragon squadrons on their way, loaded with Jennesta's troops, if that's what you think." Her voice took on an even more caustic edge. "It looks like you've not fully understood that I was trying to help you. Perhaps I didn't make that clear."

"You didn't make *anything* clear."

"I thought rescuing you from those humans was clear enough."

"Yes . . . Yes, it should have been. Thank you for that."

She gave an almost imperceptible nod of acknowledgement, then said, "Now put that sword away." He lingered and she added in a mocking tone, "You're quite safe."

Contritely he sheathed his blade. "But you can't blame me, you being the Queen's Dragon Mistress and —"

"No longer." Her face was unreadable.

"Explain yourself."

"Too many slights, too many blows. I've had enough, Stryke. I've left her. As a member of a race that prides itself on its loyalty, it wasn't an easy decision. But Jennesta's cruelty and misrule have overridden that. So, I'm a deserter. Like you."

"These really are strange days."

"Two other dragon handlers and their beasts deserted with me. I left you here to go and aid them."

"That'll be a blow to Jennesta."

"Others are deserting too, Stryke. Not in hordes, but there's a steady bleed." She paused. "Many would rally to you."

"They don't *know* me, I'm no saviour. I didn't even *mean* to desert."

"But you're a leader. You've proved that commanding the Wolverines."

"Heading a warband isn't the same as running an army or a realm. Most who do are false, wicked. Jennesta, Adpar, Kimball Hobrow . . . I don't want to be like them."

"You wouldn't. You'd be helping to remove their kind."

"The elder races shouldn't be fighting amongst themselves. It's the humans we have to stand against. Or at least the Unis."

"Exactly. And to do that the races have to be united."

"Well, let somebody else do the uniting. I'm just a simple soldier." He looked to the advancing ice sheet and the unnatural glow suffusing the gloomy sky above it. As though on cue, a few flakes of snow began falling. The dragon gave a rumbling snort.

"Humans are mad, irrational, needlessly destructive. They eat the magic. But they aren't alone in destroying Maras-Dantia. Other races—"

"*I know.* You're not going to change me on this, Glozellan, so don't try."

"As you wish. Though it could be that you'll have no choice in the matter."

He let that go and changed the subject. "Talking of humans, do you know the name Serapheim?"

There was no hint of recognition. "I've known few humans, and certainly none called that."

"You didn't bring anybody else here last night, before or after me?"

"No. Why should I? You mean a human?"

Half suspecting the story-weaver's appearance had been some kind of delusion, he backed off. "I expect I . . . A dream. Forget it."

She stared at him curiously. The snow swirled thicker. After a moment she said, "The rumours are that you have something Jennesta wants."

He weighed his response before deciding she could be trusted.

After all, she'd likely saved his life. "It's more than one thing," he said, digging into his belt satchel.

The three stars filled his cupped palm. Glozellan gazed at the strange objects.

"I don't really know what they are or what they're for," he confessed, "except they're called instrumentalities. My band calls them stars."

"These are instrumentalities. *Really?*"

He nodded. It was the first time he'd seen her express anything approaching awe. No mean achievement with a brownie.

"You've heard of them?" he asked.

She gathered herself. "The legend of the instrumentalities is known to my folk."

"What can you tell me about them?"

"In truth, not much. I know there are supposed to be five, and that they're very old. There is one story connecting them with my race. We have a famous ancestor, Prillenda, though little is known about him either. He was . . . well, a kind of philosopher-seer, and it's said he was inspired to make prophecies by one of these things."

"Prophecies? About what?"

"If they were predictions, they were lost long ago. But they were supposed to have something to do with the End Days, the time when the gods roll up this world and play another game."

"We orcs have a similar myth."

"Anyway, how the instrumentality came to him or where it went isn't recorded. Some say it led to his death in some way. I always thought the whole thing was a tale told by pollen-crazed fairies, to be honest." She stared at the stars. "But now you have three of the things. Are you sure they're genuine?"

"I'm sure." He put them away.

"I have no better idea of what they're capable of doing than you, Stryke, but whoever possesses them commands power. The stories always made that plain if nothing else."

After his latest dream, if it was a dream, he reckoned that power was greater than either of them could guess. But he didn't mention that to her. Nor did he say anything about the stars "singing" to him.

"I can see why Jennesta thinks them such a prize," Glozellan said. "Even if they have no magic they have power as totems. They could restore her crumbling authority. If *you* were to use them to muster opposition—"

"Enough." His tone invited no further comment. "What are you going to do now?"

"I'm not sure. I'd like to return to my kith for a spell of contemplation. But we brownies are southerners, and as you know there are more humans in the south than anywhere else. My folk have scattered long since. So perhaps I'll go to a dragon fastness, stick to high-up places." She turned and gave her charge an affectionate pat. With drooping eyes the slumbering dragon accepted it passively. "Brownies and dragons have always had a kind of understanding. They're the only other race we really trust, and they seem to feel the same way about us. Perhaps we see each other as allies in adversity."

Stryke realised she was as much an outcast as the orcs had become, and felt a pang of sympathy for her.

"Will you keep on opposing the Queen?" Glozellan said.

"When I have to, and I'll fight humans and any other race that gets in my path. But I'm not going out of my way to do it. All I'm really trying to do is keep my band alive."

"The gods might have other ideas."

He laughed. It was a little sour. "Whatever. But first things first. I have to get back to the Wolverines."

"Then we should leave before the weather gets too bad. Come, I'll take you."

4

Now she rode a black chariot embellished with arcane symbols in silver and gold. It was pulled by a pair of sable horses, leather face masks smothered with pyramid barbs, iron studs peppering their leggings. Burnished scythes jutted from the chariot's wheels.

At Jennesta's back marched an army above ten thousand strong, comprising orcs, dwarves and a goodly smattering of humans dedicated to the Mani cause. The horde bristled with standards and spears. White-canvassed ox-drawn wagons swayed in the flow. Regiments of cavalry shepherded the flanks.

They had skirted Taklakameer, the vast inland sea, and crossed most of the upper Great Plains, keeping Drogan well to their south and Bevis to the north. Soon she would lead them to the shores of Norantellia and the Scarrock peninsula. In that marshy realm of the nyadds, so recently governed by Adpar, the sister she killed with sorcery, Jennesta would hunt the Wolverines and her prize.

She knew they were there, or at least had been. Adpar's dying psychic burst revealed it.

Jennesta's Dragon Dam, Glozellan, had been sent on ahead with three of her beasts to spy out the land. Reinforcements had been summoned and would swell Jennesta's army. Elite warbands were on their way from Cairnbarrow, her seat of power. All was in hand. Contingencies had been planned for. She was as near as she had ever been to revenge and advancement. The army she headed was testament to her authority.

Yet she was not content.

The butt of her displeasure rode alongside the chariot. General Mersadion, horde Commander, was in his prime but serving a mistress so demanding had made him careworn. More than the usual number of lines creased his forehead and he was hollow-eyed. If male orcs had hair, his would be greying.

Jennesta harassed him.

"Whenever it shows itself, crush it. Disloyalty's a canker that quickly festers if it isn't cut out."

"With respect, ma'am, I think you overestimate the problem," he dared to suggest, quickly appending, "The *majority* are loyal."

"So you keep saying. Yet still we have sedition and deserters. Make every hint of disobedience, every whisper of rebellion a capital offence. With no exceptions, whatever the rank."

"We're doing that, Majesty." He might have added that she well knew it, had he felt suicidal.

"Then you can't be applying the principle rigidly enough." *Withering* was too poor a word to describe the look she gave him. "A fish rots from the head, General."

She meant him, of course, but Mersadion saw the unintended irony. He kept his reply to a prudent, "Ma'am."

"Those who serve me well are rewarded. Bad servants pay the price."

It was news to him that there were rewards. He'd had none apart from an unasked-for promotion to an impossible job.

"Do I need remind you of your predecessor, Kysthan, and his protégé Captain Delorran?" she went on, and not for the first time.

"No, Majesty, you don't."

"Then ponder their fate."

He did. Often. It was part of living on the edge of a volcano. He was starting to think the deserters could hardly be blamed, and that her increasing harshness was worsening the situation. Swiftly he checked that line of thought. He knew it was irrational, but he had an abiding fear that she might be able to read his mind.

She spoke then, and he almost started. But it was more to herself than him. "When I get what I want, none of you will have a choice in the matter of loyalty or anything else," she muttered. In a clearer tone she ordered, "Get them moving! I want no more delay."

Her whip cracked on the back of the horses and the chariot surged ahead. Mersadion had to move smartly to avoid the scythes. As he spurred to catch up, he glanced at the display she'd arranged.

A line of fourteen "dissidents," all dead now, hanging in cages suspended by gibbets over large open fires.

The subdued army was being made to pass by them to appreciate their mistress's justice. Some looked away. Many held cloths to their noses and mouths against the fearful odour.

Ash fluttered in the wind. Clouds of orange sparks twisted skyward.

Orcs were meant for the ground.

Stryke had that confirmed for the second time as Glozellan took him to Drogan. The wind was brutal, and the beating of the dragon's wings added an updraft that made him wonder if he could hang on. His rear was numb from the beast's knobbly back, swirling snow made his eyes water and it was so cold he lost feeling in his hands. When he tried to talk to the Dragon Dam he couldn't make himself heard over the buffeting.

He concentrated on the view. The glacier in the north looked like a milk spill inching across the landscape, and he was startled by how great an area it covered. Then the dragon wheeled about and he was looking down at lesser mountain ranges with white-tipped peaks. They gave way to sheer cliffs falling to rugged ground dotted with scrub.

Lines of hills passed beneath, and valleys resembling long, ribbed leaves. Mirror-surfaced lakes swathed in cottony mist. Waving woods. At length they came to the rolling Great Plains. Later he spotted the silver thread of the Calyparr Inlet, the green cluster of Drogan Forest.

The dragon roared. It blasted his ears and shook his bones. Glozellan shouted something he couldn't make out.

They fell, it seemed to him, then dived, the rush of air stopping his breath. He felt the dragon realigning itself, levelling, and the dive became a glide. The ground sucked them closer, the tops of trees grew from raindrops to barrel lids. Screeching flocks of birds scattered.

Then the land was parallel, moving underneath faster than a charge. They were flying away from the forest, but in a banking arc that would eventually encircle it. He understood Glozellan was scouting for lingering custodians or other hostile forces, and lent his eyes to the cause.

Their girdling of Drogan took them briefly over a lip of ocean. He glimpsed waves hammering craggy rocks; pebbly beaches; an expanse of land; grass; trees. The slash of the inlet appeared, straight at this point, a god's burnished blade. Then the plains again, and the closing of their circle.

There was an exodus from the forest even before they touched down. Centaurs, and orcs on horseback and foot, raced to meet them.

The dragon landed with a gentle bump. Stiff-limbed, Stryke clambered down from behind Glozellan. She stayed perched on the rumbling giant.

He looked up at her. "Thank you, Glozellan. Whatever you do, good luck with it."

"And you, Captain. But I've something else to say that you must heed. Jennesta is heading for Scarrock, and she's leading an army. She's only a couple of days behind us, and could easily pick up your trail. You aren't safe here."

Before he could reply she whispered something in the dragon's capacious ear and urged it away. It lifted, sturdy wings working their rhythm, fleshy legs gathering in. The backwash had Stryke retreating a few paces and shading his eyes with a hand.

He watched the leviathan impossibly rise, and saw its bulk convert to grace. It climbed, swung, described a courtly circuit overhead. Glozellan's arm went up and out. He returned the farewell. Then she took an eastward bearing and soared away.

Stryke was still staring when the others arrived.

Alfray, Haskeer, Jup and several grunts had ridden. Coilla had too, on Gelorak's back. There were scores of other centaurs with them, and the first of the running orcs approached at speed. They gathered around him, everyone's relief palpable. A clamour went up.

He waved them quiet. "I'm fine! It's all right, I'm fine."

Coilla slid from the centaur's back. "What's been happening, Stryke? Where have you been?"

"Learning that an enemy turned out to be a friend."

"What—"

"I'll explain. But over food and drink."

He was given a horse and they headed for the forest.

The short journey allowed him a little time to think about Glozellan's news, and the fact that there seemed no rest.

Not far from the forest stood a crooked line of low hills topped with copses. On one, hidden in the trees, three figures stretched out, watching events below. They had their horses hobbled in the thicket behind, and were vigilant for patrols.

The watchers were human.

"Those *bastards*," one of them rumbled vehemently.

He had a look of depravity that matched his companions', but he was shorter and scrawnier, and had a wiry, nervous energy they lacked. His sickly yellow hair was as thin as his near-transparent goatee, and his teeth were ruins. What nature and self-neglect hadn't given him was provided by enemies; a black leather patch covered his right eye, most of his left ear had been torn off, the little finger of his right hand was grubbily bandaged.

"Makes me want to puke, looking at the things," he went on, staring at the retreating centaurs, and especially at the orcs. "Damned filthy, lousy—"

"Will you shut the *fuck* up, Greever?" hissed the man lying next to him. "I can't think for your never-ending whine."

The first human wouldn't normally take that kind of talk, but the group's self-appointed leader wasn't somebody to gainsay. He was beefy, if starting to run to seed through dissipation. A scar branded his pockmarked face, travelling from the centre of his cheek to the corner of his mouth. He had greasy black hair and an unkempt moustache. His eyes were dark and harsh.

"*You* ain't lost what *I* have, Micah," the other returned in a grating whisper. He indicated his eye, ear and finger. "All because of that orc *bitch*."

"Not your eye though, Greever," the third human reminded him.

"What?"

"Not your eye. She didn't do that."

"No, Jabeez, she didn't." The reply was delivered as though to a wilful and brainless child. "It . . . was . . . another . . . orc. *Same difference!*"

Forehead crimped, the third man took a few seconds to absorb that, then said, "Oh, yeah."

In appearance he was the most conspicuous of the trio. Had the other two been combined into one being he would still easily outweigh them. But his huge bulk was due to muscle, not fat. His head and face were completely hairless. His nose had been broken at least once and set badly. He had a banal mouth, like a knife slash in dough, and the eyes of a newborn hog.

"Mind you," he added, "as for the *new* wound—"

Big and dim as he was, the first human's expression stopped him.

Greever Aulay and Micah Lekmann returned their attention to the forest scene. The last of the orcs and centaurs were entering the forest. Jabeez Blaan fidgeted, impersonating a flesh molehill trying to flatten itself.

"So what do we do, Micah?" Aulay wanted to know. "Attack?"

"Attack? You got a death wish? Course we don't attack!"

"They're only fucking *orcs!*"

"*Only* orcs? You mean only the best fighters in Centrasia, after our kind? Only the ones that done for your good looks?" He sniggered unpleasantly. "Them the orcs you mean?"

Aulay took that but looked murderous. "We've killed enough of 'em in our time."

"Yeah, but not by going square against a band that size, and never in anything like a fair fight. You know that."

"So what do we do, Micah?" Blaan asked.

"Use our heads." He regarded the questioner. "Or some of them, anyway. Which is what Greever here ain't doing. He's all fired up, and that clouds his sense." Lekmann nodded at the forest. "What we gotta do with this bunch is the tried and tested. Bide our time, take 'em down singly or in small groups. Play our cards smart, we could still turn a coin or two on this."

"This ain't about coin no more," Aulay growled. "It's about getting even."

"You bet. And I want those freaks as much as you do. But maybe we can pick up some bounties too. And that relic thing they stole, that's gotta have value. Revenge tastes sweet and all that, but so do food, drink, the finer things. We need where-withal."

"Who's going to give us bounty or buy that relic except Jennesta? And I reckon we ain't her favourites since we double-dealed her."

"I prefer 'left her service,' " Lekmann corrected.

"Whatever you call it, I don't think it was too wise a move."

"Careful, Greever, you're straying into thinking and that's my territory. I can handle Jennesta."

His companions looked doubtful. Aulay replied, "Maybe you can, maybe you can't. I'm beyond that now. I just want that orc bitch, that Coilla."

"But if there's spoils too you'll take 'em, right?" His voice hardened. "Don't go fucking this. We work together or we're lost."

"Don't fret about me, Micah." He brought up his left hand. Or rather what had been. Now a cylindrical metal plug extended from his wrist. Attached to its end was a sharpened curve of steel, part billhook, part blade. Its polished surface caught and amplified the dismal light. "Just get us near enough to those freaks and I'll earn my keep."

5

As Stryke dug in his belt pouch he was afraid the phial might have broken. But the miniature ceramic bottle was intact and its tiny stopper was still in place.

He laid it in Keppatawn's outstretched palm. The centaur stared at it for a moment and seemed uncharacteristically lost for words. Then in an undertone he managed, "Thank you."

"We try to keep our word," Stryke told him.

"I never doubted that. But I regret you losing one of your band doing it."

"Kestix knew the score. All orcs do. And the mission suited our aim as much as yours."

Coilla nodded at the phial and asked, "What do you do with it?"

"Good question," Keppatawn replied. "I'll have to consult our shaman about that. In any event we need him to complete our bargain. Gelorak, fetch Hedgestus."

His second-in-command moved across the encampment toward the seer's coop.

Stryke was relieved that attention had shifted from him to some extent. He had been fed, watered and generally fussed over. Then, with a sizeable audience looking on, he explained what had happened. But he didn't say anything about Serapheim appearing on the mountaintop, or his strange dream. Nor did he mention the stars "singing," although the memory of it had him eyeing Haskeer with something like sympathy.

Most of the others had melted away to their chores, leaving just the Wolverine officers, Keppatawn and Gelorak. Stryke preferred a small group. He didn't know how the centaurs would take the news about Jennesta.

Gelorak re-emerged from the shelter with the ancient seer in tow. Hedgestus moved slowly and falteringly on uncertain legs. A small ornamented chest was tucked under one of Gelorak's arms; he used the other to steady his ward.

Hedgestus greeted the orcs as Keppatawn took the box. He opened it and showed them the star. It was as they remembered: a grey sphere with two spikes of irregular lengths, made from unidentifiable matter.

"We keep our word too," Keppatawn said, holding the box out to Stryke.

"We never doubted it," Stryke told him dryly.

"Before you take this," the centaur added, "are you sure you want to?"

"*What?*" Jup exclaimed. "Course we do! Why do you think we went through all that mud and shit?"

"Stryke knows what I mean."

"Do I?"

Keppatawn nodded. "I think so. This could be a poisoned chalice. More harm than good may come from it. That's the reputation of these things, and our experience."

"We already figured that out," Coilla said, hinting mild sarcasm.

"We've chosen our path," Alfray put in, "we can't stop now."

Unusually for him, Haskeer voiced no opinion. Stryke thought he knew why.

He reached out and took the star. "As my officers say, we didn't come this far to give up. Besides, we've no option, no other plan."

But then Haskeer offered, "We do. We could toss those things away. Ride out of trouble."

"Where would we ride to that isn't trouble for us?" Coilla asked. "Outside a dream, that is."

Stryke stiffened, then decided she meant nothing by it. "Coilla's right," he told Haskeer. "There's nowhere for us to go, not the way Maras-Dantia is now. And we'd never get Jennesta and the rest off our backs. The stars give us an edge."

"We hope," Jup murmured.

"The band agreed," Stryke continued pointedly, "*all* of us. We said we'd go after the stars."

"Never liked the idea," Haskeer grumbled.

"You've had plenty of chances to get out."

"It's not the band. It's those fucking things. There's something wrong about 'em."

"Something wrong about *you*," Jup mumbled.

Haskeer caught it. "What'd you say?"

"All you've ever done is whinge," Jup said.

"Not true," Haskeer fumed.

"Oh, come on! And then there was all that cracked stuff about the stars singing at you—"

"Who you calling cracked?"

Haskeer was showing a flash of his old volatile self. Stryke wasn't displeased with that, but could see the name-calling about to escalate. It was a complication he didn't need. "That's enough!" he snapped "We're visitors here."

He turned his attention to Keppatawn, Gelorak and Hedgestus, who looked slightly perplexed. "We're all a bit tense," he explained.

"I understand," Keppatawn assured him.

Freeing the cover on his belt pouch, Stryke put the star with its fellows. He was aware of the others watching him do it, and especially of Haskeer, who wore an expression resembling distaste.

As the pouch was secured, Keppatawn sighed, "Good riddance."

That had Jup raising an eyebrow and the orcs exchanging looks, but none commented.

"Here," the centaur chieftain said, handing the phial to Hedgestus, "a tear shed by Adpar."

The old seer accepted it gingerly. "I confess I thought it impossible. That she was capable of something as humane as crying, I mean."

"Self-pity," Coilla informed him crisply.

"Ah."

"But what am I supposed to *do* with it?" Keppatawn asked.

"There are precedents in lore to guide us. As with the blood of a warlock or the ground bones of a sorceress, we must assume this essence to be very powerful. It should be employed as a dilution, combined with ten thousand parts of purified water."

"Which I drink?"

"Not if you value your life."

"Or your bladder," Jup let slip.

Stryke fixed him with a stern gaze but Keppatawn took it in good humour and smiled.

Hedgestus cleared his throat. "The potion is to be applied to the afflicted limb," he went on. "Not all at once but over three days, and for the best effect during the hours of darkness."

"That's it?" Keppatawn said.

"Naturally there are also certain rituals to observe and incantations to be chanted which—"

"Which serve to do nought but fill the forest with caterwauling."

"They have an important function," Hedgestus objected indignantly, "and they—"

Grinning, Keppatawn waved him down. "Easy, easy. You know how I enjoy pulling your tail, old charger. If there's a chance of your concoction working you can wail for a month for all I care."

"Thank you," the seer responded doubtfully.

"So when do we start?"

"Preparing the solution should be a matter of . . . oh, four or five hours. You can have the first application tonight."

"Good!" Keppatawn gave the seer's shoulder a genial if weighty slap. Hedgestus tottered slightly and Gelorak lent his arm again. "Now we celebrate! Feast, drink, swap lies!" He scanned their faces and paused. "You seem less than keen, Stryke, from your look. I know you lost a trooper, but this isn't disrespect. It's just our way."

"No, it's not that."

"What's up, Stryke?" Coilla said.

"The tear isn't all we brought."

Haskeer gawped at him. "You what?"

Keppatawn was puzzled. "Really?"

"I should have told you earlier," Stryke admitted. "Jennesta's on her way to these parts, with an army."

"Shit," Jup whispered.

"How do you know this?" Alfray asked.

"Glozellan told me. She'd no reason to lie."

"How long before she arrives?" Keppatawn wanted to know.

"Two, three days. I'm sorry, Keppatawn. She's after us—" he patted his belt bag "—and these."

"She has no fight with us, nor we with her."

"That wouldn't stop her."

"We're used to defending ourselves, should it come to that. But if it's you she's after, why squander her followers' lives? Why divert herself?"

"In search of us. I reckon she's somehow found out we were in Scarrock. When she sees we're not there, she could end up at your door."

"Then we'll make it clear you aren't here either. And if Jennesta wants to argue the point she'll find it costly."

"We'll stand with you," Haskeer promised.

"Yes," Stryke agreed, "we should stay and fight. There are Hobrow's custodians too. They could return."

Keppatawn considered that for a moment. "It's good of you to offer, but . . . no. The stars are important, I see that. We can fight our own battles. You have to get away from here."

There was a brief silence, then Jup said, "Where to?"

Stryke sighed. "That's our next problem."

"But not one you need worry about now," Keppatawn told him. "Join us in food and ale, shrug off your cares for a few hours. Call it celebration or wake, it's your choice."

"With the enemy bearing down?"

"Is whether we feast or not going to stop Jennesta's coming? I don't think so. No more than supping on gruel would."

"It's a good way of looking at it, Stryke," Alfray opined. "And the band could do with unwinding."

Stryke addressed Keppatawn. "Celebrating a warrior's life or a victory isn't unknown to us orcs. Though it's possible to celebrate too well." He was thinking of Homefield and how that particular occasion had led to all their later troubles. Before the centaur chief could question his remark, Stryke added, "We'd be honoured to join you."

The passing hours brought mellower moods.

Fowl, game and fish bones littered the banqueting boards,

along with nut husks, discarded fruit and scraps of bread. Honeyed ale had been downed and spilt in quantity.

Now servers moved among the tables with tankards of mulled wine, and fires were banked against the creeping cold. At Alfray's suggestion Stryke had some of the band's cache of pellucid broken out. Smouldering cobs were handed round.

Off to one side a troupe of centaurs made low music with pipes and hand-harp. Others used muffled beaters to pound drums fashioned from hollowed tree trunks.

As repleteness, liquor and crystal subdued the revelry, Keppatawn hammered his table with a flagon. The babble and music died.

"Long-winded speeches don't suit us," he boomed. "So let's just toast our allies, the Wolverines." Tankards were raised, ragged cheers went up. He directed his gaze at Stryke. "And a salute to your fallen."

Stryke got unsteadily to his feet. "To lost comrades. Slettal, Wrelbyd, Meklun, Darig and Kestix."

"May they feast in the halls of the gods," Alfray responded.

A more sombre toast was drunk.

Another tankard was placed in front of Stryke. The server dropped in spice, then plunged a red-hot iron brand into the wine to mull it, releasing its aromatic tang in a little cloud of steam.

Stryke held up the brew. "To you, Keppatawn, and your clan. And to the memory of your revered father . . ."

"Mylcaster," Keppatawn whispered.

". . . Mylcaster."

The name was echoed reverently by a number of the centaurs before they drank.

"To our enemies!" Keppatawn declared, drawing perplexed glances from the orcs. "May the gods confound their senses, dull their blades and bung up their arseholes!" That brought ribald laughter, particularly from the grunts. "Now take your ease, and let tomorrow look after itself."

The music struck up again. Chatter resumed.

But a cloud darkened Keppatawn's face as he turned to Stryke. "My father," he sighed. "The gods alone know what he would have made of the changes we've seen. *His* father would barely recognise the land. The seasons ailing, war and strife, the dying of the magic—"

"The coming of the humans."

"Aye, all our ills stem from that infernal race."

"But you don't seem to be doing too badly here in the forest," Alfray observed.

"Better than many. The weald nourishes us, protects us; it's our cradle and our grave. But we don't live in isolation. We still have to deal with the outside world, and it's going to hell. The chaos can't be held at bay forever."

"None of us will be free of it until the humans are driven out," Alfray replied.

"And perhaps not even then, my friend. Things may have gone down too far."

"We meant it when we offered to stay and fight," Stryke reminded him. "Just say the word."

"No. You have to move on and finish what you've started."

Stryke didn't tell him he had no idea how to do that. "Then at least let us help you beef up your fortifications," he suggested, "in case Jennesta does attack. We've a few days in hand."

"That I will agree to. Your special skills would be welcome. But I don't want you lingering too long for our sakes."

"All right."

"And while that's going on we'll forge new weapons for you." Pointedly, but with good humour, he added, "Seeing as you've been so careless with the last batch we made you."

"We get through a lot of weapons," Jup informed him. "It's an overhead of our trade."

"Thanks, Keppatawn," Stryke said. "It's good for us to kick in something. We seem to have taken much from you and given so little in return."

The centaur waved that aside. "Weapons are nothing, we'll be making plenty in any case. As to giving, if you bring about the healing of this wretched limb—" he laid a hand on his blighted thigh "—you will have given more than I could ever hope for."

There was a stir at one of the paddocks. A small group of

chanting centaurs appeared. Hedgestus was at its head, supported by Gelorak, with four or five acolytes bringing up the rear. They began making their way across the clearing at a stately pace.

"Ah, the moment of truth," Keppatawn said, signalling the music to stop.

With everyone looking on, the procession arrived at his table, their chanting lowered to a murmur. Two of the aides were carrying between them a stout wooden tub with curved iron handles. The table was cleared and the tub carefully set down. It was two-thirds full of what appeared to be unremarkable plain water.

"Don't look like much, does it?" Haskeer remarked.

Stryke placed a finger to his lips and glared at him.

"Come on," Keppatawn urged the shaman, "let's get on with it."

A stool was brought and the chieftain lifted his leg onto it. Hedgestus held out his hand. One of the acolytes passed him a yellow sea sponge. He immersed it in the liquid, squeezed out the excess and with an effort bent to apply it. As he gently dabbed, the chanting swelled again.

If the onlookers expected an instant result they were disappointed.

After two or three swabbings Hedgestus noticed Keppatawn's quizzical expression. "We must be patient," he advised. "The enchantment will need a little time to effect itself."

Keppatawn tried to look stoical. The shaman continued with his ministration. Chanting droned on.

Eventually many of the bystanders started to melt away. Alfray sidled off with a clutch of grunts. Yawning cavernously, Haskeer went in search of more drink. Jup slouched, chin in hands, looking vacant.

Coilla, eyes as limpid as opals despite the alcohol and crystal, caught Stryke's attention. They quietly withdrew.

"I was getting worried about you," she confessed, "disappearing like that."

"To be honest, so was I." It was the first time he'd spoken to any of the band with nobody else around. He was glad to drop his defences a bit.

"I thought we'd really lost it this time," she said. "Not knowing if you'd gone willingly, and having the stars with you."

"Now we've got four." He fingered his belt pouch. "I never thought we'd get this far."

She smiled and indicated the others. "Don't tell them that."

His mood stayed doleful. "But we're no nearer knowing what they do."

"Or where we go next."

He nodded. After a moment he continued, "Something strange happened on that mountaintop. That human, Serapheim, was there."

"Glozellan took *him* there too?"

"That's the thing. She didn't. He just . . . appeared, somehow. Went the same way. And there was no getting off that peak without a dragon, believe me."

"You spoke to him?"

"Yes. But what he said wasn't plain. I sort of understood what he was getting at, but I . . ." He trailed off, lost for words. "He said I should carry on searching for the stars."

"Why would he do that? Who *is* he?"

Stryke shrugged.

Coilla studied his face. "You don't look too good," she decided. "What's wrong? Apart from all the shit we're going through, that is."

"I'm all right. Except . . ." He wanted to tell her about the dreams and how he feared for his sanity.

"Yes?" she coaxed.

"It's just that I'm—"

A grunt jogged up to them. "Sir! Corporal Alfray wants a rota for the work parties tomorrow."

"Very good, Orbon. Tell him I'll be right there."

"Chief." The trooper went off again.

"What were you going to say, Stryke?" Coilla asked.

The moment had passed. "Nothing." She was about to speak again. He stopped her. "It'll keep. Meantime, there's work to be done. Then we've got to get out of here. Jennesta's coming."

6

Kimball Hobrow looked on as the stragglers drifted into the bivouac.

He knew what had happened. Forward riders from his custodian regiment, bloodied and dispirited, had reported on the debacle at Drogan. The indignity of being bested by sub-humans cut deep with him and his rage had been towering. Then he fell to brooding on revenge and planning his next move.

At length he turned from the scene and trudged to the tent that served as temporary field command.

Weighed down by the mission he had taken upon himself and the sour taste of a defeat, he held his back a little less straight and his eyes lacked a mite of their usual steel. For all that, he couldn't help but be a striking figure. He was arrestingly tall and almost preternaturally thin. Black garb and a stovepipe hat added to his imposing appearance. His face was weathered and leathery, like a farmer's, though recent exertions had made it sallow. He had a slash of a mouth and a tapering chin adorned with silvering whiskers. It was a mien unwarmed by laughter or any of the gentler emotions.

But looks and dress were superficial in his case. Hobrow was the kind of man who, had he gone naked and wreathed in smiles, would still be marked out by the cold fervour in his heart.

"Father! *Father!*"

Sight of his daughter, standing at the tent's entrance, softened him to a small degree. He strode over and laid a hand on her shoulder.

"What's happening, Father?" she said. "Are the savages coming?"

"No," he assured her, "the heathens aren't coming. You have

nothing to be afraid of, Mercy. I'm here." He steered her back into the tent and sat her down.

Mercy Hobrow resembled more the mother they didn't talk about than him. There was nothing of the cadaverous about her. She had yet to fully cross the divide between childhood and adolescence, or shed her puppy fat. With honey blonde hair, a porcelain complexion and unclouded blue eyes, she appeared vaguely doll-like but that was offset by a certain malevolence in her face, and a mean mouth.

Compared with everyone else her father surrounded himself with, her clothing seemed almost flamboyant. Eschewing black, she wore restrained patterned fabrics, and even a hint of plain jewellery. It spoke of his indulgence towards her, in contrast to the way he dealt with the rest of the world.

"Did they beat us, Father?" she asked, wide-eyed. "Did the monsters beat us?"

"No, darling, they didn't. The Lord has punished us, not the sub-humans. He used them to send us a warning."

"Why is God warning us? Have we been bad?"

"Not bad, no. But not good enough. He has found us lacking in undertaking His work, I see that now. We must do more."

"How, Daddy?"

"He would have us grind the orcs and their like into the dust forever, along with the degenerate humans allied with them. I've sent for reinforcements from Trinity, and messengers have gone out to Hexton, Endurance, Ripple, Clipstone, Smokehouse and all the other decent, God-fearing settlements in Centrasia. When they heed the Lord's appeal we'll be more than an army, we'll be a crusade."

Mercy's face had clouded at the mention of orcs. "I *hate* them Wolverines," she hissed.

"You are right to, child. Those beasts have particularly incurred God's anger. They ruined my scheme to cleanse this land in the Lord's name, and they stole the relic."

"And that freak, that dwarf, he held a knife to my throat."

"I know." He gave her shoulder a squeeze. It was an action at once affectionate and distanced. "They have much to answer for."

"Make them die, Daddy." There was a pitiless edge to her voice.

"Their souls will burn," he promised.

"But we don't know where they are."

"We know where they were last; somewhere around Drogan, with that other band of ungodly brutes, those half-horse, half-man abominations. We'll look for their trail there."

"If God detests the inferior races so much, why did He create them?"

"As a test for us, maybe. Or it could be they aren't the Lord's work at all. Could be they're kith of the Horned, One." He dropped to a whisper. "Satan's issue, sent to plague the pure."

Mercy shuddered. "Lord preserve us," she breathed.

"That He will, and have us flourish too, providing we spread His Word. With blade and spear if need be. That's His command." Hobrow's eyes took on a different light. He fixed them on a point above. "Hear me, Lord? With Your guidance we'll bear the glorious burden of racial purity You have laid upon us. Arm me with Your sword of vengeance and Your shield of righteousness, and I will bring down the fire of Your wrath upon the savages!"

His daughter stared up at him with something like awe. "Amen," she whispered.

"Scurvy fat arse!"

"Shit breeches!"

Fists balled, Jup and Haskeer advanced on each other, eager to turn insults into action.

"*As you were!*" Stryke barked.

Glowering, the pair of sergeants lingered on the edge of mutiny. Stryke elbowed between them, palmed their chests and shoved them apart. "Are you *officers* in this band or what? Eh? You want to stay sergeants, act like it!"

They backed off, scowling.

"No way am I taking brawling from you two," Stryke told them. "If you've got a beef, save it for the opposition. And if you've got energy to spare, you can work it off. You're on fatigues." He flashed them a look that stifled their groans. "Haskeer, muck the horses." Jup smirked. Stryke turned to him. "See that tree, Sergeant?" He pointed at one of the tallest in sight. "Climb it. You're on lookout. Now *move!*"

They loped off, stony-faced.

"Their truce didn't last too long," Alfray said.

Coilla nodded. "Just like old times."

"I think they like being at odds," Stryke reckoned. "Gives 'em something to kick out at. And there's not a lot else going on right now."

"There's been a bit of unrest among the grunts too," Alfray reported. "Nothing serious. Squabbles, bitching, minor stuff."

"We've only been here thirty-six hours, for the gods' sake!" Stryke complained.

"It was a good thing we had work to do on the defences. They would have boiled over earlier without the vent. But now that's done—"

"I won't have indiscipline just because they have to cool their heels for a while."

"They're not *bored*, Stryke," Coilla corrected, "they're frustrated. About what we do next. Aren't you?"

He sighed. "Yes," he admitted. "I haven't a clue what we're going to do or how we go about finding the last star."

"Well, we can't stay here much longer while we figure it out. We've got to head somewhere. Unless you want to hang around for a parley with Jennesta."

"We're moving out today. Even if we have to toss a coin for where."

"And end up doing what?" Alfray wondered. "Pointless wandering? Spending the rest of our lives running from her and everybody else who wants what we've got?"

"You got a better idea, let's hear it," Stryke flared.

"Heads up," Coilla interrupted.

They looked the way she indicated. Keppatawn was approaching. Already his withered leg had improved noticeably. New, healthy skin was forming, and he walked with less of a limp. His whole demeanour seemed more robust.

When he reached them, Stryke commented on this.

"My affliction improves by the hour," the centaur replied,

"though it's not entirely healed yet. Hedgestus tells me tonight's final application will complete the process."

"That's good."

"It's thanks to you." He included Alfray and Coilla in his smiling approval. "All of you. I'm in your debt for this miracle."

"You owe us nothing."

"How go your preparations?" Keppatawn enquired. "Have you decided on your next move?" He added hastily, "Don't think we're being inhospitable."

"We don't. And in truth, no, we haven't settled on a destination. But we'll be going today, in any event. We know having us here would only make our enemies your enemies."

"I'm glad you understand. The weapons we're forging for you are ready, and—"

A shout stopped him. Jup ran to them, arms pumping.

Stryke glared at him. "I thought I told you—"

"Look what's coming," the dwarf panted.

Centaurs were escorting a group into the clearing. Four or five of the newcomers had the unmistakable physique and gait of pixies. They led strings of mules and horses, laden with saddle-bags, bolts of cloth, sacks and chests.

Grunts abandoned their chores and came to watch, followed by Haskeer. Stryke didn't reprimand them.

"See?" Jup nodded at a knot of figures, a dozen strong, marching at the caravan's rear.

They were orcs.

Alarm spread through the band. Weapons were drawn.

"Betrayal!" Haskeer growled.

Keppatawn reached out and grasped Stryke's sword hand. "No, my friend. You aren't in danger. These traders are regular visitors."

"And them?" He indicated the orcs.

"Not all of your kind are in hordes, you know that. Some manage an independent existence. These are freelance bodyguards. What better protection could the merchants buy? Trust me."

Stryke slowly resheathed his blade, then ordered the rest of the band to do the same. With some reluctance, particularly from Haskeer, they did as they were told.

The bodyguards were looking on, their bearing tense.

"It's a comedown for orcs," Alfray remarked, "reduced to hiring themselves out as chaperones for peddlers."

Pixies and centaurs began unpacking the wares. Silks and rugs were shaken out, boxes levered open, sacks upended. An orc moved away from the crowd and headed for the band.

"Please remember that they are guests too," Keppatawn said.

"Of course," Stryke replied. "We don't pick fights with our own kind."

"Unless they pick one with us," Coilla appended.

Keppatawn seemed a little pained at that, but held his tongue.

The orc arrived. He kept his hands well away from his weapons and looked as diffident as his nature allowed.

"Well met," he offered.

Stryke returned the greeting. The rest of the Wolverines contented themselves with wary nods.

"I'm Melox," the orc went on, "leader of our group. I was surprised to see you here."

"The feeling's mutual. I'm Stryke."

"Thought so. Wolverines, eh?"

"What of it?"

"We're out of Jennesta's horde too. Not in a band. Footsoldiers."

"How did you come to this?" Alfray wanted to know, a hint of disdain in his voice.

"Desert a horde and what's an orc to do? Still got to eat. Anyway, I could say the same about you. No disrespect."

"None taken," Stryke decided. "Nobody's judging you. These are hard times."

"Why did you leave Jennesta?" Coilla asked.

"Same reason you did, I reckon. Couldn't take no more."

"Wasn't quite like that with us. But it came out the same."

"Well, we think what you're doing's right. Should have happened long ago." He nodded the caravan's way. "This job, we'd drop it in a minute, all of us, if you'd take us on, Captain."

"We're not recruiting," Stryke told him. His tone was dismissive.

"But that's why you went AWOL, ain't it? To go against Jennesta? To get things back the way they were for us?"

"No."

"It's what everybody thinks."

"They think wrong."

A strained silence descended. Jup broke it. "You're being called."

The bodyguard's comrades were waving him back.

"Maybe we can talk later," Melox said.

"We're moving out today," Stryke replied.

"Oh. Right. Well, if you change your mind about letting us join . . ." He turned and walked away.

Coilla directed, "Good luck!" at his back. Then, "You were a bit hard on him, Stryke."

"I'm not leading a crusade, I've told you that."

"Looks like not everybody agrees."

"Another visitor," Haskeer rumbled.

One of the merchants was coming their way.

Keppatawn smiled. "This is somebody you should meet."

The individual who joined them was short and fairly robust, yet somehow gave an impression of fragility. His features inclined to the feminine, with lush lips, slightly tapering, dreamy eyes and smooth pale skin. His nose was pert and just a tad upturned. His ears were small and swept back to a point. A green felt cap didn't entirely confine his mop of black hair. His tunic and leggings were green too, but the effect was offset by a wide brown leather belt with a gleaming buckle, and by a black cape, lined in green. The ankle-length soft hide shoes he wore, whose necks curled outward petal-fashion, were known universally as "pixie boots."

It was impossible to tell his age because all his race had faces like infants'. The voice was no clue either. It could have been a child's, albeit a rather knowing one.

"Keppatawn!" the pixie gushed. "*Wonderful* to see you again, you old *knave* you!" His pitch rose to a near shriek. "And your *leg! Such* an improvement! How *delightful!*" He winked theatrically. "Suits you."

Laughing, Keppatawn accepted the pixie's delicate, outstretched hands in greeting. They were tiny compared to his. "Welcome back. It's good to see you." He wheeled his guest around. "Meet some friends, the Wolverines."

"I've *heard* of you," the pixie exclaimed. "Aren't you *outlaws?*"

"This is Stryke, band captain," Keppatawn explained. "Stryke, this is Katz, master merchant."

"Honoured, Captain." Katz thrust out a limp hand.

Bemused, Stryke took it, but didn't shake too vigorously for fear of fracture. "Er, me too."

The other officers were each introduced, and the grunts *en masse*. Katz simply nodded this time and didn't try offering his hand to any of them. Which in Haskeer's case was probably wise. He looked as though he might have bitten it off.

"You know, for a race with such a fearsome reputation, you orcs aren't at all bad," Katz prattled. "I've found that with my own retinue. Splendid fellows, every one of them. Always happy to oblige, nothing's too much trouble, and the best protection coin can buy, naturally. We pixies aren't warlike by nature, as I'm sure you know, and we—"

"Don't you ever shut up?" Haskeer grumbled.

"Of *course*, how thoughtless of me. Here I am engaging you in idle chit-chat when all you want is sight of my goods."

"Wha—?"

"I know what you're thinking. You're asking yourself how you can afford the amazing commodities I'm about to lay before you. Don't worry about it. My prices are so reasonable you'll think I'm robbing myself, which in truth I am, and if even the paltry cost is too much I'm open to trade."

"But I don't—"

"What's your need?" Katz ploughed on. "Cooking pots? New boots? A saddle? The finest handwoven horse blankets?" He prodded Haskeer's chest with a tiny finger. "How about a length of high quality cotton fabric with attractive flower patterns?"

"What would I want with *that?*"

"Hmmm, well, it might improve that dowdy uniform for a start."

A series of expressions crossed Haskeer's face as he tried to decide whether he'd been insulted. Shoulders heaving, Jup clamped a hand to his mouth. Coilla found her feet of great interest.

"How . . . how's business?" Alfray quickly put in.

Katz shrugged philosophically. "If you were selling hats they'd be born without heads."

"Sure as the sun rises," Keppatawn said, "merchants complain about trade."

"These are tough times," Katz protested. "The gods should give us honest tradesbeings a break." He sighed. "But it's preordained, I suppose."

Glad to shift the conversation away from Haskeer, who'd settled on fuming, Coilla took the bait. "You don't believe in free will?"

"Some. But I think most of what we do is set by the gods and the stars."

"Sol signs?" Haskeer sneered. "That's all . . . *pixieshit.*"

Katz ignored the slur. "Ah, there speaks a true Seagoat."

"Wrong," Haskeer grunted.

"A Viper, then."

"Nope."

"Er, an Archer?"

"No."

"Balladier, Grapnel, Scarab?"

"No, no and no."

Katz massaged his temple. "Don't tell me . . . uhm . . . Bear?"

"Wrong again."

"Eagle? Charioteer?"

Haskeer folded his arms and rocked on his heels.

"Basilisk? Longhorn? *Ah!* Yes! I see I hit the target there! Longhorn. Of course. I can always tell. It's a gift."

Haskeer mumbled something low and threatening.

"Anyway," Katz continued, "as a discerning Longhorn I know you'll appreciate the benefits of the exquisite fabrics I can offer you for only —"

Haskeer snapped. With a roar he lurched forward and seized Katz by his throat, hoisting him clear of the ground.

"*Sergeant, please!*" Keppatawn shouted. "Don't forget that pixies —"

There was a loud sound like ripping cloth and a spume of yellow flame shot from the merchant's hindquarters. Grunts standing three yards back scattered, then danced on the ignited grass.

"—have fire-starting abilities."

Haskeer dropped the pixie and swiftly retreated.

Katz grinned sheepishly. "Oops. Sorry. Nervous bowel condition."

Keppatawn stepped in. "I think it might be best if we got on with our business," he stated diplomatically, ushering Katz away.

The band and Haskeer, open-mouthed, watched as the pixie moved off with smouldering breeches and a slight hobble.

"They must have behinds like quartz," Jup remarked admiringly.

Gelorak placed a finger to his lips and quietly *shush*ed her.

At first Coilla couldn't make anything out as she squinted through the tangled undergrowth. Then there was movement and she saw their quarry.

There were two of them. They stood as tall as centaurs and looked muscular, particularly in the arms and legs, the latter completely covered in dark shaggy fur and ending in cloven feet. Their chests were bare and ordinarily hairy, again like a centaur's, or an hirsute human's. Both angular faces had pointed beards and upswept, bushy eyebrows. Their jet black, curly hair finished above their foreheads in widow's peaks. They had eyes that were penetrating, with a somewhat cunning attitude to them. One of the creatures clutched a set of wooden musical pipes.

"I've never seen one before," Coilla whispered.

"Satyrs are an extremely retiring race," Gelorak replied. "Even we rarely encounter them though we often hear their piping."

"Is there ever conflict between you?"

"No. They are forest dwellers too, and have as much right to be here as us. We leave each other alone."

She leaned forward for a better look and trod on a fallen branch. It gave a dry crack. The satyrs froze. Two pairs of yellow-green eyes, almost feline, briefly flashed in their direction. Then the creatures vanished with startling speed and remarkably little noise.

"*Damn*. Sorry."

"Don't worry, Coilla. We were fortunate to find them at all. You can count yourself as privileged." He looked up through the leafy canopy to patches of sky. "It's been over an hour. Your band will be readying to leave. Shall we go back?"

She nodded, smiling. "Thank you, Gelorak." Her mind was on whether Stryke had worked out where they were heading.

They battled their way through the scrub and came eventually to the clearing.

The Wolverines were packing up their gear. Most of the grunts clustered around the horses. Stryke, Alfray and Jup were talking with Katz. Haskeer stood off to one side, eyeing the pixie with suspicion.

Gelorak went off on a chore. Coilla joined the band.

Stryke was stuffing gear into his saddlebags.

"Decided where we're going yet?" she asked.

"I thought maybe north."

"Why?"

"Why not?"

"Fair enough." She wandered to Alfray and Jup.

Stryke crouched and emptied his belt pouch, placing the stars on the grass in front of him. Katz came over and watched, vocally restrained for once. After a moment he remarked casually, "I've seen one of those before. Couple of months ago."

Nobody really took that in, least of all Stryke, absorbed by sorting. "Hmmm?"

"One of these things. Here." He pointed with his toe. "Or similar anyway. In the hands of humans."

Stryke looked up. "What?"

"It was different to these. But near enough."

"These? The stars?"

"That what you call them? Yes, one of these." He saw Stryke's face, then straightened and looked at the others. "What's wrong?"

A small window opened on bedlam.

7

The band crowded round him, firing questions. Numbed by the onslaught, Katz gaped, wordless.

Haskeer pushed through and grabbed him by the scruff of the neck. *"Where? Who?"* he demanded, shaking the terrified pixie.

"Careful!" Alfray shouted.

"Don't point his arse at me!" Jup yelled.

"Steady, all of you!" Stryke ordered.

Haskeer checked himself and gingerly put the merchant down. The hubbub calmed.

"I'm sorry, Katz," Stryke said. He forced the others back, giving him air.

The pixie swallowed and took a breath. He rubbed his neck.

His bodyguards were running towards the band. Stryke held up his hands placatingly and called, *"It's all right! No problem!* Katz?"

"Yes," the pixie croaked, waving the bodyguards away. "Yes, I'm fine."

They stopped, and after a moment's hesitation reluctantly dispersed.

Stryke laid a hand on Katz's shoulder. He winced slightly. "We shouldn't have acted that way, but what you just said is very important to us. Can we go through it?"

Katz nodded.

"You say you've seen one of these before." He indicated the stars at his feet.

"Yes. Well, like them. Different colour and different number of bits sticking out. But the same sort of thing."

"You're sure?"

"It was a couple of months ago, but yes."

"Where?"

"Ruffetts View. Know it?"

"Mani township, down south."

"At the tip of the inlet, yes. There's a lot of building going on there, thought it might be a good place for trade."

"What kind of building?"

"You haven't heard?"

"Heard what?"

"They've got a breach. Earth energy escape. Big one. They were going to try capping it, store the magic somehow."

"Did they?"

"I don't know. When I left they weren't ready. They won't manage it, if you ask me. Nobody else has. Anyway, they were putting up some kind of holy place there, a temple, and that's where I saw the star. The Manis didn't like me seeing it, mind you. They had me out of there pretty quick." He stared at the stars. "So what are these things?"

"Some call them instrumentalities."

"Instru—*The* instrumentalities?"

"You've heard of them?"

"Who hasn't? But I thought they were a myth. They can't be genuine."

"We think they are."

"I've seen lots of so-called authentic relics all over Maras-Dantia. Not many of them turn out to be real."

"These are different."

A covetous light kindled in the pixie's eyes. "If these really are the genuine items they'd be worth a fortune to the right buyer. Now if you let me act as your agent—"

"No way," Stryke replied firmly. "They're not for sale."

Katz obviously found that a hard concept to come to terms with. "Why seek them if you don't want to realise their value?"

"There's different kinds of value," Coilla told him. "Theirs isn't reckoned in coin."

"But I've told you where there might be another one. Isn't that worth something?"

"Yeah," Haskeer drawled. "You get to live."

Keppatawn arrived, curtailing any unpleasantness. "What's happening?" he said.

"Looks like Katz here might have put us on to another star," Stryke explained.

"What? Where?"

"Ruffetts View."

"Have you heard about a magic escape there, Keppatawn?" Alfray wanted to know.

"Yes. It's been going on for some time."

"Why didn't you tell us about it?"

"Why should I? I had no reason to think it would interest you. Such fissures aren't as rare as they used to be, sadly, with humans interfering with the energy." He turned his attention to Katz. "You're certain about your information?"

"I saw something that looked like them." He pointed at the stars. "That's all I know."

"Why should he be any more right about this than about the sol signs?" Haskeer complained.

"Maybe he isn't," Stryke replied. "But it's the only lead we've got. We either roam without point or head for Ruffetts View. My money's on Ruffetts."

There was a murmur of agreement from the band. Stryke had nothing else to say.

"There's a purpose here," Keppatawn declared. "The instrumentalities emerging from obscurity. It's no coincidence."

"That's hard to believe," Alfray countered.

"You orcs have many admirable qualities. But if I may say so, you take too practical a view of life. We centaurs are down to earth too, but even we acknowledge that there is an unseen side to things. The hands of the gods may not be visible, yet they are behind much of our affairs."

"Can we stop flapping our jaws and decide?" Jup pleaded.

Stryke began scooping the stars back into his pouch. "We're going to Ruffetts View," he said.

A couple of hours later Drogan Forest was behind them.

The band had newly forged weapons, fresh horses and replenished rations. They also had a rekindled sense of purpose.

The route they followed was south-west, straight down the peninsula, with the Calyparr Inlet on their left. To their right,

modest cliffs marked the shingled coast of the darkly lapping
Norantellia Ocean. If they kept to a fair pace, Ruffetts View was
about two days' ride.

Stryke continued pondering whether to tell the others about
his dreams, and he hadn't mentioned to anybody that the stars
had sung to him. He had talked to Haskeer again about *his*
experience, although the Sergeant was no nearer making sense
of it and proved unusually tight-lipped. It seemed he wanted to
bury the incident. But Stryke drew some comfort from the fact
that it was unlikely both he and Haskeer should go insane in
exactly the same way. With that in mind, and somewhere to go,
he felt he had more of a grip. But not entirely. There were still
his dreams.

All of it lay heavily on him as they rode, and he was distracted
enough not to hear himself spoken to.

"Stryke? *Stryke!*"

"Huh?" He turned and saw Coilla staring at him. Riding on
her other side, Jup, Alfray and Haskeer looked on too.

"You were half the land away," she gently chided. "What's on
your mind?"

"Nothing."

He obviously wasn't inviting discussion on the subject. She
changed tack. "We were saying it was tough on Melox and the
others, having to take on that kind of work."

"You mean I should have let them join us."

"Well . . ."

"We're not a refuge for waifs and strays."

"They're hardly that, Stryke. You could at least have thought
about it."

"No, Coilla."

"I mean, what's going to become of them?"

"You could ask the same about us. Anyway, I'm not their
mother."

"They're our own kind."

"I know. But where would it end?"

"With you leading a serious revolt, maybe. Against Jennesta,
and the humans, and anybody else holding us down."

"Nice dream."

"Even if we lost, isn't it better to go down fighting, trying to make a difference?"

"Maybe. But in case you hadn't noticed, I'm just a captain, not a general. I'm not the one to do it."

"You really can't see how things are shaping up, can you?" she seethed. "You can't see the nose on your face sometimes!"

"I've enough to do leading this band. Somebody else can fight the world."

Infuriated by his obstinacy, she fell silent.

Alfray took on the argument. "If there's really a lot of disgruntled orcs deserting Jennesta, there's a chance to build an army here. The way things are going in this land there's something to be said for safety in numbers. Greater numbers, greater safety."

"And the more attention we'd draw," Stryke countered. "We're a warband. We've got mobility, we can hit and run. That suits me better than an army."

"Doesn't alter the fact that orcs always get the raw end of the deal. Could be a chance to change that."

"Yeah," Haskeer agreed, "we're everybody's punchbags. Even human kids are told we're monsters. They think we're built like brick shithouses with tusks."

"You want to fight for the whole orc race, go ahead," Stryke told him. "We'll concentrate on the last star, even if we die trying."

"So what's new?" Jup said.

A distant sound cut through their conversation, keening, doleful, uncanny. It prickled the back of their necks and goose-bumped their flesh. The horses shied.

"What the hell . . . ?" Coilla whispered.

Alfray had his head cocked, listening intently. To him it was unmistakable. "Banshee. Was a time when you could go your whole life and never hear one."

"First time I have," Jup admitted, suppressing a shudder. "I can see why they're supposed to foretell disaster."

"I heard it once before, years back. On the eve of one of the big battles with the humans, down Carascrag way. It earned its reputation then. Thousands slaughtered. You don't forget."

"They're not so rare anymore," Stryke added. "If you believe what's said, they're heard all over now."

After what seemed an impossibly long time the noise trailed off and died. It left them sobered.

Then it started to rain. Large drops the size of pearls came down, rust-coloured and rank-smelling.

"Shit," Jup complained. He turned up his collar and gathered in his jerkin.

"Something else to thank the fucking humans for," Haskeer said, following his example.

Several heads turned in the direction of the ice sheet to the north at their rear, out of sight but omnipresent. The band rode on miserably.

A sodden hour passed. When conversation eventually stirred again, somebody mentioned Adpar and the lot of tyrants. That jogged Coilla's memory. "There's something I've been meaning to ask you, Stryke. I completely forgot until now. When we were in Adpar's realm, at her deathbed, you told her she was dying because of Jennesta. How did you *know* that?"

"She's right," Alfray agreed. "We don't know what killed her."

Stryke was taken aback. He hadn't thought about it. "I . . . I just said it to get a reaction from her, I suppose."

"But it did the trick, didn't it? It goaded her back."

"Doesn't mean to say I was right. Maybe Jennesta's name was enough to rouse her."

"Maybe."

"Perhaps you're developing farsight, chief," Jup suggested, not entirely seriously. "Hope it works better than mine."

Stryke wasn't amused. "Orcs don't—"

An arrow zinged past his ear. His horse tried bolting and he struggled with the reins.

"To the rear!" Jup bellowed.

The band wheeled about, drawing weapons.

A group twice their size was galloping all out in their direction, mounted on dwarf yaks, shaggy-furred and malevolent-eyed. The riders were about a third shorter than orcs and chunkily built. Their spherical heads were disproportionately large, with jutting ears and attenuated, fleshy-lidded eyes. They were hairless, save for bushy sideburns, and their rugged hides had a green tint.

"Gremlins?" Haskeer exclaimed. "What the fuck we done to upset *them?*"

"Wanna go and ask?" Stryke retorted.

"They're coming in!" Alfray yelled.

Some in the gremlin first rank had miniature curved bows. They unleashed bolts as they rode. Several flew over the Wolverines' heads. One embedded itself in Haskeer's saddle. Another nicked a grunt's arm. A couple of Wolverines replied in kind.

"To hell with this," Stryke growled. *"Engage!"*

He spurred hard and took the lead, the band at his heels. Pounded by torrential rain, mud-splattered, they headed for the enemy ranks.

The two sides flowed into each other with cries and colliding steel. A mêlée of swinging swords, lunging spears and clashing shields broke out.

Stryke made short work of the first gremlin he met. Dodging the creature's misjudged stroke, he ribboned his chest and sent him flying. The next to jostle in laid his blade across Stryke's with startling fury. They chopped and hacked, steel beating steel in a primitive, shrill melody. Brute force got Stryke through his foe's guard. A further blow punctured the gremlin's lung. Without halt, another duel commenced.

Charging between two enemies, Alfray flipped his banner spar to the horizontal. It struck both of them, high enough and hard enough to unhorse the pair. A twist of the spar brought it to a defensive position in time to block a further opponent. Evading the raider's sword, Alfray rammed home the lance, turfing the eviscerated creature from its saddle.

An overhand lob delivered one of Coilla's knives to a gremlin's eye. He disappeared screeching in the rabble. Beading another target, she was about to throw again when a gremlin sideswiped her. His blade was already moving, and near lopped off her nose. She seized his sword wrist, her grip like a bear cub's jaw, then set about stabbing. A triad of strikes settled it, fast and deep. The corpse toppled.

One of the fallen's comrades moved in, shield up, scimitar gashing the air. She flattened back in her saddle and slammed her boot into the shield. Writhing to avoid his sword, grunting with effort, she pushed hard enough to tumble the gremlin from his mount. He fell to the mercies of pawing horses and yaks. No sooner was she up than another gremlin tried to make a name for himself. She ripped her sword free.

Haskeer's sword was buried in the guts of a previous victim and lost with him, several killings ago. His dagger had been spent in similar fashion. Now he ducked and weaved through the attackers seeking a weapon.

He saw his chance as he rode alongside a gremlin crossing swords with a grunt. The distracted creature was easy pickings for a blood frenzied orc. Haskeer reached out and hoisted him bodily from his mount. He swung the kicking foe over to his horse and brought the gremlin's back down onto the saddle's pommel, snapping his spine. Prising the sword from twitching fingers, he dumped the body.

An opponent rushed towards him with a levelled spear. Haskeer swerved and brought his sword down on the passing heft, slicing it in two. Turning quickly, he was in time to send a second blow to the back of his opponent's sinewy neck, dropping him. Then two more foes closed in. Bellowing a war cry, he powered into them.

In a fleeting lull, Stryke quickly scanned the scene. He reckoned they'd downed about half the enemy. The grunts were giving a good account of themselves and it looked like none of the band had taken serious wounds. One more push and they could end it. He bowled into the reeling scrum and commenced hacking.

Another ten minutes of furious combat decided the matter. The gremlins who were able began withdrawing, leaving the bodies of their comrades, and the odd dead yak, scattered across the muddy swath.

Coilla struck down a fleeing gremlin by pitching a knife between his shoulder-blades. Stryke galloped to her.

"Do we go after them?" she said.

He peered through the rain at the retreating raiders. "No. We haven't got time for games." He cupped his hands around his mouth and yelled, *"No pursuit! Hold back!"*

Several grunts who'd given chase quit and turned, spraying mud. The others took to checking the enemy corpses, wary for shamming.

Jup, Alfray and then Haskeer joined Stryke and Coilla.

"What the hell was that about?" Alfray wondered.

Stryke shook his head. "The gods know. Casualties?"

"Nothing serious, first look. I'll set to binding what we've got."

"I reckon it was bounty," Coilla volunteered.

"Or more of Jennesta's mercenaries," Jup suggested.

"You wouldn't hire gremlins for the job," Stryke said. "The bounty, maybe."

A grunt called to them.

"What is it, Hystykk?" Stryke bawled back.

"We've got a live one here, sir!"

They dismounted and sloshed over to see. Alfray was already there, kneeling in the slime next to a gremlin who could have been young, for all they knew. He had a bad chest wound, crusting his robe with gore. Rivulets of blood mixed with the drumming rain.

He was taking deep breaths. His eyes were open and he constantly licked his lips.

Jup got close and to the point. "What is it, the reward?" The gremlin focused, but didn't comprehend. "The bounty or what? Why the attack?"

Alfray started fussing at the wound. The gremlin coughed. A little scarlet trickle crept from the corner of his mouth. But he spoke.

"Retribution," he whispered.

Stryke was puzzled. "What do you mean?"

"Vendetta . . . revenge."

"For what? How have we wronged you?"

"Murder. A kinslin."

"You're saying we murdered your kin?"

"We killed any other gremlins lately?" Haskeer wondered out loud. Coilla shushed him.

"Who are we supposed to have murdered?" Stryke asked, his words deliberate.

"My clan . . . uncle," the gremlin stumbled, his breathing more laboured. "Just an . . . old, harmless . . . scholar. Didn't . . . deserve it."

An uncomfortable feeling grew from the pit of Stryke's stomach. "His name?"

The gremlin stared at him for a moment, then managed, "Mobbs."

Stryke flashed his dream and remembered thinking he'd visited the afterlife. His veins chilled.

"The bookworm?" Haskeer said.

Coilla bent to the gremlin. "You're wrong. We met Mobbs, that's all. He was fine when we left him." She wasn't sure if she was getting through.

Alfray's efforts with the wound were brisker. Blood still flowed. He dabbed his patient's face with a cloth to soak up some of the rain.

Stryke gathered himself. "I'm sorry about Mobbs' death. We all are. He wasn't our enemy. In a way, we have reason to be grateful to him."

Haskeer gave a small derisive snort.

"What makes you think it was us?" Stryke went on.

The gremlin's breathing was shallow now. "Our own kind . . . found him. Group of . . . orcs . . . in area. Black Rock." He achieved a look of contempt through the pain. "You know this."

"No!" Coilla exclaimed. "We *rescued* him, for the gods' sake!"

"And you've been tracking us all this time?" Stryke marvelled. "Your efforts were in vain, my friend."

"Delorran," Coilla said.

"Of course. Had to be." Stryke sighed. "And I'd wager Jennesta's not been slow in spreading this story to further blacken our names." He turned back to the gremlin. "It wasn't us. Believe that."

The creature seemed oblivious. "You have many . . . enemies. You'll . . . only last . . . so long."

"This has been a senseless waste of life," Stryke told him. "Isn't there enough killing without adding to it?"

"Rich talk . . . coming . . . from . . . an orc."

"We're not crazed animals. But attack orcs and you have to expect us to fight back. It's what we do. As for Mobbs, I'm telling you—"

Alfray laid a hand on his arm and slowly shook his head. Then he leaned forward and gently thumbed shut the gremlin's eyes.

Stryke got up. "Shit. All we do is bring death and suffering."

"And get blamed for everything," Jup added.

"Poor Mobbs," Coilla said.

"We *are* liable for his death," Stryke told her. "Not directly, but it's down to us."

"That's not so."

"Tell me how it isn't."

She didn't answer. None of them did.

For a split second, the thought occurred to Stryke that at least Delorran had paid. Then he realised he'd learnt that in a dream. Hadn't he?

It rained harder.

8

Rain drummed on the canvas tent.

Jennesta paced. Patience wasn't a virtue with her, and she had never seen the gain in cultivating it. Her creed was that the rabble waited while leaders took. Seizing what you wanted got things done. But what she wanted was just beyond her grasp.

She brooded too, on the depletion of the earth energies that made her sorcery erratic, and the lengths she had to go to in replenishing it.

Frustration and uncertainty made her more than usually dangerous. Which, in Jennesta's case, was saying a lot.

She was toying with the idea of issuing some capricious order. Something that would achieve nothing beyond the needless wasting of a few lives and her pleasure at the smell of blood. But then the flaps of the tent were parted and Mersadion deferentially entered.

He bowed and was about to speak.

"Are we ready to leave?" she demanded, eschewing formalities.

"Almost, Majesty."

"I hate this unnecessary waste of time."

"The army needed resting, ma'am, and the livestock had to be fed."

Jennesta knew the reasons well enough and waved aside his explanations. "If you didn't come to tell me you were ready, then what?"

His reply was hesitant. "News, ma'am."

"And from your face, not good."

"It concerns your Dragon Dam. Glozellan."

"I know her name, General. What about her?"

He tried to break it carefully. "She and . . . two other handlers, along with their charges, have . . . They've . . . left your service, Majesty."

As she took it in, tiny supernovas flared in her remarkable eyes. Darkly. *"Left my service."* She mouthed the sentence slowly and deliberately. "By which you mean they've deserted. Correct?"

She seemed to him for all the world like a coiled viper, ready to strike. Not trusting words, he nodded.

"You're sure of this?" She checked herself. "Of course you are. Else you wouldn't risk telling me."

Mersadion knew how true that was. "We have no reason to doubt the loyalty of the other handlers," he offered.

"As we had none concerning Glozellan." She was seething, building up to something.

He trod gingerly, hoping to placate her. "If you have misgivings, we can replace the handlers. And we still have sufficient dragons, ma'am, despite losing three. As to a new dam, there are several candidates for promotion who—"

"All the handlers are brownies. How can I trust *any* of them? There will be a purge in the dragon squadrons."

"Majesty."

"First the Wolverines, then the bounty hunters I sent after them; now the Mistress of Dragons has abandoned my cause." She fixed him with her wintry gaze. "And all the while a steady bleeding from my army. How do I come to be surrounded by so many cowards and traitors?

It was a question he would never dare answer. He thought to avoid it by shifting her view. "You could see it as the ranks purifying themselves, ma'am. Those left are bound to be the most loyal to Your Majesty."

She laughed. Head back, raven hair tumbling. A flash of sharp, white teeth. Her eyes glittering with mirth.

He adopted a nervous closed-mouth grin.

Jennesta gulped back her composure and, still smiling, said, "Don't think I see anything funny, Mersadion, this is pure derision."

His face resumed its wary slump.

"You have a politic way of putting things. You'd have me

believe the flagon's half full." She leaned in to him, her laughter already a fading memory. "But you're just an orc. When it comes to thinking, you punch above your weight. Let me tell *you* why treachery decays the ranks. It's because the officers aren't harsh enough in their discipline. And the line of command stops at your door."

Only when events went badly, Mersadion reflected.

Jennesta drew back. "I won't tolerate laxity. This is your last warning."

Whatever he expected her to say or do in no way prepared him for what happened next.

She spat at him.

The spray soaked his right cheek, below the eye and as far as the line of his ear. It was an action that shocked and bewildered him in equal parts, and he had no idea how to react.

Then he felt warmth on his flesh. Prickly heat spread all over the side of his face. He winced with discomfort and raised a hand, but touching the affected area made it worse. In seconds it grew hotter, like myriad fiery needles piercing his skin.

Jennesta stood and watched, rapt and faintly amused.

The sensation moved to scalding, as though vitriol had been splashed on him. He abandoned composure and cried out. His face blistered. He smelt the tissue burning. Pain became torment, then went beyond that. He screamed.

"Last warning," she repeated, weighting the words. "Ponder it." She discarded him with an indolent gesture.

Doubled in agony, effluvium rising from his ravaged features, he blundered his way out. Through the whipping flaps Jennesta caught a glimpse of him stumbling to a water butt. She heard him howl.

Her action was a scintilla of the rage she could have shown at his news. She'd had enough of reversals, and if he brought her more the price would be his life. But for now she was content to brand him a failure. Literally.

An unmeasured span of time passed as she reflected on events. It came to an end when several of her orc personal guard arrived, making an awkward show of subservience. They brought her a captive, bound with chains; an offering to revitalise her powers, if only temporarily. Despite her mood, the sight of the vessel stirred Jennesta's curiosity.

So many races, so large an appetite, so little time.

She had never had the chance to savour a nappee before. Nymphs of pastures and forests, they were a scarce, coy race, not often seen. This was a particularly fine example. The creature was tall for her kind at about three feet in height. She was slender, with sparkly, near luminous skin, and delicately beautiful.

Some said nappees had two hearts. Finding out would take Jennesta's mind off her travails for a while.

The rain had finally stopped.

Stryke allowed a short rest break, the band settling at a point where Norantellia's shore had partially eroded the inlet. Twilight thickened the sky, and the view was of frowning clouds over a black, wind-driven ocean.

After eating, Coilla and Stryke moved away from the others. Sitting on horse blankets, sharing a canteen of wine gifted by the centaurs, for a while they talked about the gremlin attack. But tiredness, the warmth of the alcohol and, above all, the desire to share his burden overtook Stryke. He steered the conversation to his bizarre dreams. Before long, Coilla knew all.

"Are you sure this place you dream about isn't somewhere you know?" she asked. "Somewhere in the . . . real world, I mean."

"No. The climate alone marks it out. When have we ever seen Maras-Dantia as it truly should be, as it was?"

"Then perhaps you've made it up for yourself," she ventured. "Your mind's somehow created what you *want* to be."

"Which sounds like another way of saying I'm mad."

"No! That's not what I meant. You aren't mad, Stryke. But with the world going to hell in a pisspot, it's natural to want—"

"I don't think it's that. Like I said, these dreams, or whatever they are, they're as real as being awake. Well, almost."

"And you always see this same female each time?"

"Yes. It's more than seeing her, too. I . . . *meet* her, talk with her, like I would with somebody when I'm awake. Except not everything she says makes sense."

Coilla frowned. "That's unusual for dreams. She's not some-body you've ever known?"

"I would have remembered, believe me."

"You say that like she's real. These are just dreams, Stryke."

"Are they? I only call them dreams because it's the nearest I can think of."

"They happen when you're asleep, don't they? What else does that make them except dreams?"

"It's the feeling I get, the . . ." He shook his head, frustrated with words. "I can't put it over. You'd have to go through it yourself."

"Let's get this clear," she stated matter-of-factly. "What are you saying's happening to you if they aren't dreams?"

"It's like . . . maybe when I sleep my guard's down, and that . . . lets something in."

"Listen to yourself. You're not making sense."

"I'm not, am I? But I know it's getting to where I don't want to sleep."

"You have these . . . dreams every time you sleep?"

"No, not every time. And that sort of makes it worse. It's like throwing dice whenever I need to sleep."

She weighed her next remark carefully. "If they aren't dreams, there's one possibility to think about. Could they be some sort of magical attack?"

"By Jennesta, you mean?"

Coilla nodded.

"I've thought of that, of course I have. Do you think it's some-thing she could do?"

"Who knows?"

"But why would she want to? I mean, what's the point?"

"To make you think you're insane. To sow the kind of doubts you're talking about and lay siege to your mind."

"That occurred to me, but somehow I don't believe it. As I said, in many ways the dreams are . . . pleasant. They've even strengthened my will once or twice. How would that serve Jen-nesta's plan?"

"I'm not saying it is her, just that it's a possibility. And who knows how her twisted reasoning works?"

"I grant you that. I still think she'd go for something more direct though." He studied Coilla's face, and what he saw there told him it was safe to lay everything out for her. "That isn't all."

"Uhm?"

"The dreams aren't the only strange thing. There's something else."

She looked puzzled, and apprehensive. "What do you mean?"

Stryke took a breath. "That business with Haskeer and the stars. Him saying they . . . sang to him."

"That was the fever."

"I had no fever."

It took a moment for that to soak in. Finally she said, "You too?" Her tone was incredulous.

"Me too."

"Gods, you've been bottling a lot up, haven't you?"

"Still think I'm sane?"

"If you're mad, Haskeer is too. Mind you . . ." They exchanged dry smiles. "What do you mean by *singing?*" she asked. "Can you put it better than he did?"

"Not really. It's like the dreams, hard to explain. But *singing's* as good a word as any." His hand went to the pouch at his belt. It had become an unconscious action, like the fingering of a fetish object. If asked, he would have said it was because he so feared losing them.

"I owe Haskeer an apology," she said. "I doubted him. We all did."

"It's changed the way I look at what he did," Stryke admitted. "But don't tell him. Don't tell anybody about any of this."

"Why not?"

"Wouldn't exactly inspire them, would it? Having a leader plagued by odd dreams and singing stars."

"But you've told me. Why?"

"I figured you'd hear me out. And I reckon that if you think I'm some kind of lunatic, you'd say so."

"As I said, I don't think you are. Something's happening to you, that's for sure, but it doesn't look like madness from where I'm standing."

"I hope you're right," he sighed. "So you'll keep this to yourself? For the sake of band discipline?"

"If that's what you want, yes. But I think they'd understand. The officers anyway. Even Haskeer. Hell, *especially* Haskeer. This isn't the kind of thing you can keep secret forever though."

"If it really starts getting in the way of commanding the Wolverines, I'll tell them."

"Then what?"

"We'll see."

She didn't press him on the point. "If you want to talk again," she offered, "you know I'm here."

"Thanks, Coilla." He felt better for unburdening himself, but also just a little shamed for confessing something he thought of as a weakness. Though it made some difference that she didn't seem to see it that way.

The rest of the band were packing away their gear and rolling up blankets. One or two were looking Stryke's way, expecting orders.

He passed the canteen to Coilla. "Warm yourself on this. We'll have to move again."

She took a swig and handed back the bottle. As they got to their feet, she asked, "What do you think our chances are at Ruffetts View?"

"Could be promising. That's what I feel anyway."

"Well, most of your hunches have paid off up to now. The longer the odds, you still come up. Maybe there's something in what Jup said about you getting farsight."

She meant it light-heartedly. They both knew orcs had never had magical powers. But it hinted at another layer of complexity, and mystery, neither found particularly amusing.

"Let's get out of here," Stryke said.

They rode on through the evening, alert for further trouble.

Coilla found herself at the back of the band, just forward of the rear lookouts, with Alfray at her side.

After some trivial exchanges he glanced ahead and behind, then confided, "I'm worried about Stryke."

She was taken aback, given her earlier conversation with Stryke, but didn't show it, and replied with a simple, "Why?"

"You must have noticed how he seems so buried in himself."

"He has been a bit distant at times," she conceded.

He looked at her sceptically. "More than that, I'd say."

"He's under great strain, you know that. Anyway, it's not as if he's leading us badly, is it?"

"There might be one or two in our ranks who disagree." He glanced her way. "You know I'm not one of them. I've seen a lot of leaders in my time," he added, "and served under quite a few. He's the best."

She nodded agreement, although her own experience was nothing against his. And in that second she realised how old Alfray was. At least, how old compared to the rest of them. It was something she always took for granted, and she was surprised at the impact the awareness had on her, at how unequal it was to the smallness of her observation. The danger they faced was drawing them all closer together, making them truly see each other for the first time.

"We've got to support him," Alfray said.

"Of course we will, we're a warband. The *finest* damned warband. Even those few dissenters you mentioned, they'll stand fast for Stryke." She didn't say it just because she thought that was what he wanted to hear.

He smiled approval, satisfied.

They rode on, preoccupied with their own thoughts and a mite drowsy from lack of sleep. Finally Coilla came out with, "That battle you mentioned, at Carascrag . . ."

"What about it?"

"It made me think how little history we know. It's being lost, like everything else. But you've seen so *much* . . ." She stopped, afraid he'd see that as a reference to his age, a subject he'd been touchy about lately. But his expression showed no affront.

"Yes, I have," he agreed. "I've seen Maras-Dantia in a better state, when I was a hatchling and a young orc. Not like it was in our forebears' times, but better than now. The humans weren't as numerous, and the magic had only just started to fail."

"But the elder races fought against the incomers."

"Eventually. The trouble is that what made this land great is also its biggest weakness. We're too diverse. The old suspicions and hostilities delayed the races uniting. Some didn't even see a threat until it was almost too late. Hell, maybe until it *was* too late."

"And things have gone downhill ever since."

"Which is why it's so important to keep the ancient customs alive." He slapped his palm against his heart. "Here, if nowhere else. The first place we respect the traditions is in each of us."

"That's becoming a bygone way of looking at it."

"Perhaps. But think of the comrades we've lost. Slettal, Wrelbyd, Meklun, Darig, and now Kestix. We couldn't give one of them a decent sending-off, and that cheapens their lives."

"We weren't able to. You know it's not always possible in combat."

"There was a time when it would have been. A time when the traditions were upheld."

She was surprised by his passion. "I didn't know you felt this strongly about it."

"Tradition is what's held us together, and we throw that away at our peril. It's one thing that keeps us different, keeps us . . . *us*. I mean, look at how the Square's disregarded these days, even scorned by some of the younger ones."

"I have to admit I sometimes wonder if religion's served us that well myself."

"Don't take this the wrong way, Coilla, but there was a time when no decent orc would say something like that."

"I honour the gods. But what have they done to shield us from our troubles lately? And what about the Unis and their single god? What has that brought but misery?"

"What do you expect of a false deity? As to our gods, perhaps they ignore us the more we ignore them."

She had no answer to that.

In any event their conversation was interrupted by cries from up and down the line. Grunts pointed to the west.

It was just possible to make out, far over the ocean, a blacker shape against the sable sky, travelling north. Its bulk obscured the stars as it moved, and its great saw-toothed wings could be seen flapping. A tiny burst of orange flame from the creature's head wiped away any doubts.

"Do you think we can be seen?" Alfray wondered.

"It's a long way off, and it's dark, so we'd be hard to spot. More to the point, is it one of Jennesta's or Glozellan's?"

"If it's hostile I reckon we'll know soon enough."

They watched until the dragon was swallowed by distance.

9

Blaan sat cross-legged, tongue curling from the corner of his mouth, as he scraped his shining pate with the edge of a knife.

Nearby, Lekmann used a branch to poke at the contents of a blackened pot hanging over a lively fire. Aulay was stretched out on a blanket, his head resting on his saddle, scowling one-eyed at the brightening sky.

Dew still whitened the grass. The inlet coursed sluggishly beside them, mist rising in the dawn chill. Drogan Forest was in sight, but far enough behind for them not to be spotted by centaur scouting parties.

"When the hell we moving?" Aulay grumbled, his breath visible in the frigid air. He was rubbing the spot where his wrist joined the plug that replaced his hand.

"When I'm good and ready," Lekmann told him. "We're close, I reckon, and we can't just go charging in. We got to be careful going against them orcs."

"I *know* that, Micah. I just want to know *when*."

"Soon. Now save your puff to cool your grub." He prodded at the concoction. It bubbled, releasing a disagreeable aroma.

"We eating now, Micah?" Blaan piped up, eyeing the pot.

"Watch out, pumpkin head's spotted fodder," Aulay muttered caustically.

Lekmann ignored him. "Yeah, Jabeez. Bring your bowl." He commenced dishing.

A platter was handed to Aulay. He sat with it on his knees, picking at the offering with his knife. "Slop," he complained, routinely.

Blaan noisily wolfed his down using his fingers, which he licked wetly between mouthfuls.

Aulay made a face. "Ugh."

"You're glad of him in a scrap," Lekmann reminded him.

"Don't mean I have to watch him eat." He turned his back and faced the forest.

Blaan finally realised they were talking about him. "Hey!" he protested, full-mouthed and greasy-chinned.

"*Company!*" Greever barked. He dumped his plate on the ground.

The others did the same. They quickly got to their feet, weapons ready.

A party of riders came along the trail from Drogan. They were humans and there were seven of them.

"Who'd you reckon they are?"

"They ain't them custodians, that's for sure, Greever. Unless their usual clothes are in the wash."

The riders were dressed not unlike the bounty hunters themselves. They favoured leather breeches, high boots and thick wool jerkins, uniformly shabby. Most wore skins against the cold. Their heads were topped with skull helmets and chainmail caps. They were lean, bearded, weather-bruised men toting a variety of arms.

"Could be reavers," Lekmann decided as they got nearer. "Hadn't heard there were any in these parts though."

Aulay spat. "All we need, fucking brigands."

"What do we do?" Blaan wanted to know.

"Play it peaceful," Lekmann replied. "Remember that we can get more by pouring honey than cutting throats. Besides, the odds are in their favour."

"You think so?" Aulay said.

"You stay calm, Greever, and let me do the talking. If it comes to force, follow my lead, and keep those blades out of sight. Got me?"

They agreed, Aulay reluctantly.

The riders had seen them by this time, and slowed. They were watchful but approached without guile.

When they reached the trio, Lekmann beamed and hailed them. "Well met!"

Two or three of the men nodded. A burly individual with a full beard and lengthy, unkempt hair was the only one to talk. "And you." He spoke gruffly and a little offhand.

"What do we owe this pleasure to?"

"Nothing in particular. Just going about our business."

"And what might that be?" Lekmann asked, the smile still plastered to his face.

"We're trailing renegades."

"Is that so?"

Aulay glowered but said nothing. Blaan looked on with his normal semi-vacant expression.

"Yeah," the leader said. "You?"

"Farmers. We're heading to buy some livestock up beyond Drogan."

The reaver looked them up and down, as did several of the others. Lekmann hoped they didn't know too much about farming.

"You ain't into that Mani or Uni crap, are you?" the leader said.

"Not us, friend. A plague on both. We just want a quiet life. On our farm," he added helpfully.

"Good." He stared Aulay and Blaan's way. "Your friends don't say much."

"They're just simple farm boys," Lekmann explained. He held his hand to one side of his face so Blaan couldn't see, winked conspiratorially, and added in a whisper, "The big one's simple-minded, but pay him no heed."

"He looks like he could knock down a door with his head."

"Nah, he's harmless." He cleared his throat. "So, you're renegade hunters. Don't suppose there's much the likes of us can do to help speed you."

"Only if you've seen any orcs in these parts."

Aulay and Blaan stiffened. Lekmann kept down his reaction. "Orcs? No. But if it's them murdering bastards you're after, you're all right by us." He made an expansive gesture towards the way of the camp fire. "You're welcome to share our food. We got fresh water and some wine too."

The reavers exchanged glances. Their leader made the decision, emboldened perhaps by their greater numbers. "That's neighbourly. We'll join you."

They dismounted. Lekmann offered canteens and told them to help themselves to food. They took him up on the former, were less eager about the latter once they looked in the pot. Aulay and Blaan stayed where they were. None of the reavers paid them much attention.

"Tell us more about these orcs you're tracking," Lekmann said, trying to sound casual.

"They're a desperate, bloodthirsty bunch by all accounts," the leader told him. He took a gulp from his canteen. "Warband. Call themselves the Wolverines."

Lekmann prayed that neither of his partners would blurt out anything. He was in luck. "You're going after a whole warband?"

"This is about half our force. The rest are searching over yonder." He nodded across the inlet. "I reckon we're more than a match for 'em."

"Them orcs got a fearsome reputation when it comes to fighting."

"Overrated, if you ask me."

"Had any sign of them?"

"Not yet. Thought we did last night. Turned out to be a pack of gremlins, riding like their arses were on fire."

"You seem sure those orcs are around here."

"They've been spotted, more than once."

"Big reward?"

"Pretty big." The reaver chief eyed him with what might have been a hint of suspicion. "Why? Thinking of trying for it yourselves?"

Lekmann managed a laugh. "What, us? You reckon we're the sort to tangle with orcs?"

The chief looked them over. "Now you come to mention it, no." Then he began laughing himself. "Not exactly bounty hunter types, eh, boys?"

His men found the idea so risible they joined in with the laughter. They pointed at the trio and rocked with crude, good-natured mockery. Lekmann laughed. Even Aulay made an effort, showing his rank teeth in the rictus of a patently false smile. Last in, Blaan started, great shoulders heaving, jowls aquiver, eyes watering.

Dawn broke on ten human males laughing in each other's faces.

Then something shook out of Blaan's jerkin, bounced and came to rest at the reaver chief's feet. Still laughing, he looked down at it.

The dark brown, shrivelled object was a shrunken orc's head. A sober cloud darkened the leader's face.

Lekmann swiftly drew his sword.

"What?" the leader said.

The blade slipped smoothly between his ribs. He gasped, the whites of his eyes showing. Then he went down, choking on blood. Some of his men hadn't finished laughing when realisation dawned.

Lekmann made straight for another reaver, slashing at him. Blaan lurched into the group, striking out with his fists. Aulay quickly snapped a blade attachment into his arm plug and filled his other hand with a dagger. The reavers struggled to defend themselves, in a confused scrabble for weapons.

Downing his second man, Lekmann moved in on the third. Now he met resistance. The target had his sword drawn, and intended butchery became a fight. They swapped blows, the reaver defending himself with fury, but it was immediately obvious that Lekmann was the superior fencer.

Having crushed his first victim's spine with a bear hug, Blaan discarded the corpse. Another reaver immediately charged and smashed his fist into the side of Blaan's head. It had as much effect as gentle rain on granite. The attacker staggered back, nursing his knuckles. Blaan moved in, enormous hands clasped together, and slammed them into his chest, audibly cracking bones. Face twisted in agony, the man collapsed like a puppet with slashed strings. Blaan began stomping him.

Riled by the commotion, the reavers' horses first milled in panic and then bolted, scattering across the inlet.

Aulay tugged his blade from his opponent's stomach and let him drop. The next reaver took his place, snarling with wrath and hefting an axe. It may have been a fearsome weapon but it gave Aulay the reach advantage. Ducking a swing, he lashed out and laid open the man's forearm. Bellowing, the reaver swung again. Aulay retreated fast, blundering into the cooking pot and sending it flying. Then he went straight in again, evaded the other's guard and spiked his heart.

Lekmann blocked the last feeble passes of the foe he'd already bettered. A second later he dashed the sword from the man's grasp and sliced his throat. The reaver sunk to his knees gushing blood, rocked and fell face downward.

Aulay and Lekmann coldly surveyed their work, the bodies sprawled in the kind of grotesque postures only death accorded. Then they looked to Blaan. He was on his knees with the head of the last living reaver in an armlock. A powerful jerk snapped the man's neck. Blaan got up and lumbered over to them.

Aulay eyed him murderously but said nothing.

"Did you *hear* that?" Lekmann seethed indignantly. "Did you hear what that son of a bitch said?" He scowled at the dead reaver chief. "What a nerve, going after the Wolverines. They're *our* orcs."

Aulay was wiping clean his blade. "Told you we should've moved sooner."

"Don't you start, Greever. Now let's get this sorted."

They set to plundering the corpses. Coins, baubles and weapons were filched. Blaan found a stale crust of bread in one of the dead men's pockets. He crammed chunks into his mouth as he ferreted through layers of clothing. Aulay discovered a pair of boots his size, and in better condition than his own, and tugged them roughly from their late owner.

Lekmann accompanied his scavengery with muttered complaints about the standard of modern morality.

"Look at this," Blaan exclaimed, spraying crumbs. He held up a rolled parchment.

"What's it say?" Then Lekmann remembered Blaan couldn't read. "Give it here," he said, snapping his fingers. He snatched the scroll and unfurled it. After a few seconds' lip moving and brow furrowing, he got the gist. "It's a copy of that proclamation of Jennesta's, saying how the Wolverines are outlaws and the big reward and all." He crushed the parchment into a ball and flung it away.

"Word's spreading, fuck it," Aulay grumbled.

"Yeah. Come on, they've got friends and we've got competition. We can't afford lingering here."

They began rolling the bodies into the river. The languid flow carried them slowly away in billowing red clouds.

What the trio didn't notice as they laboured was that they were being watched by a motionless figure, way back on the trail to Drogan. He was tall and straight, with lengthy auburn hair and a fluttering blue cloak. His horse was purest white.

But had they looked, he wouldn't have been there.

All she had found was chaos.

It was no more than Jennesta expected, having used her sorcery to slay her sister and throw her realm into confusion. But she had allowed herself to hope that the Wolverines might still be here, and it was becoming obvious they weren't.

She watched from her chariot on the edge of Scarrock Marsh as the last of her infantry trudged back after scouring the nyadd domain. A soupy haze clung to the marsh, and it stank of rotting vegetation. The more distant rugged peaks of the Mallowtor Islands were swathed in a greater fog and barely visible.

Jennesta didn't anticipate any differing reports from the returning troops to the ones she'd had earlier. All they had to tell was of skirmishes with the remainder of Adpar's warrior swarm and odd sightings of the elusive merz.

Unless she was brought some positive news soon she would let her anger have its head.

She turned to look at the scene behind her, where the bulk of the army was billeted. Between their massed ranks and her chariot a dragon had landed. Astride his horse, General Mersadion talked with the beast's handler. Eventually he broke off and galloped back to her.

On arrival he gave a brisk salute and reported. "We may have word on them, ma'am."

"Indeed?" She stared at him. The right side of his face was covered by a padded field dressing secured with ties. A hole had been cut in the bandages for his eye. Here and there, at the edges of the dressing, the beginnings of raw, scalded flesh could be seen. "Explain."

"A group fitting the Wolverines' description was seen past Drogan, going south along the inlet." There was an understandable frigidity in the tone he used with her, but also a greater deference.

"How reliable is this information?"

"It was a night sighting, Majesty, so there is some room for error. But the odds seem good, and it fits in with other reports from that area."

She glanced the way of the dragon. It was spreading its wings, ready to take off again. "Can we trust the handler?"

"After the threats I applied, I think so. Anyway, if rebellion was in their minds presumably they simply wouldn't have returned. You do have loyal followers, ma'am."

"How touching." There was unalloyed sarcasm in her reply. "But if it really was them," she mused, "where would they be going?"

"There are a few settlements down at the tip of the inlet, ma'am, mostly small. The biggest is Ruffetts View. All Mani, I believe. So your Majesty would be welcomed."

"I don't give a damn if they welcome me or not. They can ally themselves with me if they choose. If it turns out that anybody there harbours the band they're my enemies. Alliances are made to be broken, if it serves my interests."

"There are Manis in our own ranks, ma'am," he reminded her.

"Then it will be a testing time for them, won't it? Organise the rabble, General. We march to Ruffetts View."

Well back from the army's rump stood what was little more than a copse, although it was dignified by being named a wood. A clandestine party inhabited it, watchful for patrols whose sole job was rounding up deserters. They numbered about two dozen and they were all orcs.

The highest-ranking soldier present, as attested by the tattoos patterning his cheeks, was a corporal, and he had a plan.

"Even taking a loop round the army we can get to the inlet first, providing we travel light and fast. Then we stick to the coast most of the way to Ruffetts."

"Are we *sure* the Wolverines are there?" a troubled-looking grunt asked.

"So they reckon. One of the dragon handlers reported as much, a couple of hours ago. I was there, I heard it myself."

"Desertion, it's a big move," another waverer said. "Leaving Jennesta's downright dangerous."

"More dangerous than staying with her?" the corporal came back.

That got a broad murmur of agreement.

"Right!" somebody called out. "Look what she did to the General!"

Others took up the list of grievances.

"The executions!"

"Dumb orders and crazy suicide missions!"

"And the floggings!"

"All right, all right!" The corporal waved them silent. "We all know her crimes. Question is, what we going to do about it? Stay here and waste our lives for her cause or join Stryke?"

"What do we really know about this Stryke?" the first grunt shouted. "How do we know he'll be any better a leader?"

"Talk sense. Because he's one of our own, and he's been running circles round her lackeys. If you don't want to come, that's fine. The way I look at it, the life we got now ain't no life at all for an orc. Die here, die there, it's all the same." Most of them were nodding. "This way at least we get a chance to hit back!"

"At Jennesta *and* the humans!" an orc cried.

"That's right!" the corporal agreed. "And we won't be the last to rally to his banner. You know how many others are whispering about going over to him. Well, the time for talking's done!"

"Do you think it's true that the gods sent him to liberate us?" a voice piped up.

The corporal scanned their faces. "I don't know about that. But I reckon he's heaven-sent however he came to us. Let's stand with him!"

It was enough to tip the balance. They were decided.

"Follow Stryke!" the corporal yelled at them, and they yelled back.

"Follow Stryke!"

10

Total darkness. Nothing to hear, to touch, to smell. An utter void.

A pinprick of light. It grew rapidly. So rapidly it was like flying out of a well, and the rush gave him vertigo.

Sensation flooded in.

Brightness, a soft breeze against his skin, the scent of grass after rain, the sound of lapping water.

He realised he was clutching something. Looking down, he found he had a staff in his hands. And he saw that his feet were planted on robust timber planks. Uncomprehending, he lifted his head.

He was near the far end of a wooden jetty extending out into a vast tract of lucent water. Sunlight dappled its rippling surface, glinting intensely. The lake's farther shore was lined with trees in full leaf. Behind them rose gentle hills, then far-off blue mountains with their crests in downy clouds. Fragile birdsong attended the perfect day.

"Come back, dreamer."

He turned quickly.

She was there. Straight, proud, magnificent. Wearing a shimmering black feather headdress and clasping her own staff. Directing a steel smile at him.

He started to say something.

Instantly she snapped into a combat stance. She had the staff pointing at him, holding it shoulder-height like a spear, hands well apart. Her body was primed, ready.

The blow came so fast he hardly saw it.

Pure instinct brought up his stave, thrust out to take the tremendous crack she delivered.

He was shocked.

She drew back, flipped her staff so she held it level and attacked again. Once more he blocked her hit with the shank, feeling its impact soak into his taut arm muscles. Ducking, she tried a low stroke, aimed at his waist, but he was quick enough to deflect it.

"Wake up!" she scolded, dancing out of reach. She was grinning and her eyes shined.

Then it dawned on him that this was no unprovoked attack. The female was paying him the compliment, high in orc terms, of a mock duel. Although to any other race the idea that there might be anything complimentary or sham about it would ring hollow. It wasn't unusual for orc sparring to result in broken bones and even the occasional fatality.

"Stop resisting and start fighting!" she cried, confirming it. "It's no fun, you just parrying!"

In responding defensively he'd risked insulting her. Now he entered into the spirit.

He leapt forward and swept at her legs. Had he connected she would have toppled. But she jumped nimbly, clearing the shaft, and immediately returned a shot of her own. It missed more by luck than any design of his.

They circled each other, knees bent, stooping to offer less of a target.

She lashed out with a high swipe to his head. He countered it with one end of his staff, chancing it snapping, and her pole bounced off at the impact. His follow-up targeted her midriff, and would have knocked the air out of her if she hadn't batted it away.

Her comeback was a rain of heavy blows that had him swirling his staff like a juggler's club to avoid them. A second's let-up allowed him to seize the offensive again but hammering at her with a will only saw his blows fended off with swift dexterity.

They skipped apart.

He was enjoying it. The exhilaration of combat coursed through him, quickening his mind and springing his step. As to the female, she was a dazzling combatant, all an orc could hope for in a sparring partner.

They set to again. He swiped. She dodged and spun. Their staffs clacked with blow and counter blow. He weaved, attacked, withdrew. She melted from his sorties like liquid, then gave back as good as she got. Up and down the jetty they fought, rapping their woods, powering forward, being forced back.

Then she put out a downward stroke to his shoulder. He veered. Her staff smashed onto one of the jetty's timber uprights and snapped.

He caught her wrist and they laughed.

She cast her broken staff aside. It clattered on the boards. "Shall we call it a stand-off?"

He nodded, discarding his own weapon.

"You're a master in the profession of arms," she panted.

He returned the tribute. "And you're well versed in the way of the warrior."

They regarded each other with heightened respect. He found her glistening muscles, her moist sweatiness, particularly fetching.

The moment went by. She asked, "Have you yet achieved your goal? The task you spoke of, that means so much?"

"No. There are many blocks on my path. Too many, I think."

"You can get round them."

He didn't see it like that. "The orc way is to go through them."

"True. But sometimes a feather outweighs a sword."

His confusion was obvious.

There was a tiny splash close by. A fish, orange and gold with black whiskers, swam into view. It nosed at the reeds growing from under the jetty.

She nodded at it. "There's a creature that doesn't know the limits of its world, and in its ignorance has happiness of a sort." She knelt and skimmed her hand through the water. The fish darted away. "Be like a fish, and what stands in your way will be no more than water."

"I can't swim."

She laughed aloud, but there was no trace of derision in it. "I mean only this: think on how much better you are than a fish." While he pondered that, she stood and added, "Why is it that when we meet I feel there's something almost . . . ethereal about you?"

"What do you mean?"

"Other-worldly. As though you're here but not quite. I remember our encounters as being more like dreams than reality."

He wanted to know what she meant, and to tell her that's how it was for him, literally.

But he fell back into the void.

He came round with a start.

There were reins in his hands. He was riding with the band on the trail to Ruffetts View.

It was mid-morning. The day was overcast and drizzly.

He shook his head, then rubbed the bridge of his nose with forefinger and thumb.

"You all right, Stryke?"

Coilla rode beside him. She looked concerned.

"Yes. Just a bit—"

"Another dream?"

He nodded.

"But you only closed your eyes for half a minute."

He was confounded. "You're sure?"

"Maybe less than that. Just a few seconds."

"It seemed . . . so much longer."

"What was it about?" she asked tentatively.

"The female was . . . there." He was still muzzy-headed. "She told me things I sort of understood, but . . . not quite." He caught her eye. "Don't look at me like that."

She held up her hands to mollify him. "Just a little puzzled, that's all. What else?"

Stryke creased his brow, perplexed by the memory. "She said I seemed kind of . . . *unreal* to her."

For want of anything better to say, Coilla replied, "Well, why shouldn't a dream have dreams?"

That was too deep for him. "And we had a mock duel," he added.

She raised an eyebrow, aware that in certain circumstances a mock duel could be the orc equivalent of flirting.

"I know what you're thinking," he said. "But this is somebody in a dream!"

"Maybe," Coilla ventured cautiously, "you've created your perfect female. In your mind."

"Oh, that makes me sound really sane," he came back sarcastically.

"No, no, no, I didn't mean that. It's understandable, in a way. You've never mated. Few of us have, given the life we lead. But you can't deny your . . . natural urges forever. So it comes out in dreams."

"How can I think about having an alliance with somebody who doesn't exist? Unless I really am halfway to madness."

"You're not, trust me. I mean, perhaps this dream female is what you want, not what you can have."

"It doesn't feel like that. Then again . . ." He couldn't explain. "I'll tell you one thing that really pisses me off though. I never get to learn her damn *name*."

Several hours passed uneventfully.

By the afternoon Stryke had to order another halt to replenish their food and water before the final push to Ruffetts. Groups were sent off to hunt and fish. Others were assigned to gather wood, roots and berries.

Stryke left Coilla out of the foraging parties. He steered her well away from the others, and they settled by a thicket on the inlet's ocean side.

"What is it?" she asked, thinking that perhaps he wanted to talk about his troubling dreams again.

"Something I noticed earlier. I don't know what to make of it." He reached into his belt pouch and brought out the stars, then laid them next to each other on the grass between them. "I was looking at these and . . . Well, let's see if I can do it again."

She was puzzled, and not a little intrigued.

He selected the sandy-coloured seven-spiked star they got from Homefield, followed by the dark blue one with four spikes from Scratch. An intense look on his face, he brought the two artifacts together. A minute or two's fiddling ensued. "I don't know if . . ." There was a dull click. "Ah! There."

The stars had melded together, held fast by several of their spikes, although it was hard to see how they could.

"How did you *do* that?" she said.

"I'm not really sure, to be honest." He passed the coupled stars to her.

Even close up she couldn't quite grasp what the mechanism was that united the two objects. Yet they fitted together so perfectly they now looked like they were designed as a single piece. "This can't be right," she muttered, turning the thing over in her hands.

"I know. It's almost as though it shouldn't be possible, isn't it?"

She nodded abstractly, engrossed by the mystery. "I guess

whoever made them was very clever." That didn't convince even her. She had never come across a craftsbeing this smart. Tugging at them, she asked, "Do they come apart again as easily?"

"Takes a bit of jiggling and some force. But maybe that's because I'm not doing it quite right." He held out his hand and she gave them back. "Thing is, they look right, don't they? As though they were meant to do this. It's not just a fluke, is it?"

"No, I don't think it is." She couldn't take her eyes off them. "You found this out by chance?"

"Sort of. Like I said, I was looking at them, and suddenly I . . . *knew*. It seemed obvious somehow."

"You've hidden talents. It never would have occurred to me." Her gaze was still on the linked stars. There was something about their union that seemed to defy logic. "But what does it mean?"

He shrugged. "I don't know."

"Of course, you've realised that if two go together—"

"The others might as well, yes. There was no time to try it."

"There is now."

He reached for one of the other stars. Then checked himself. What stopped him was a rustling in the undergrowth beside them. They stood up.

Bushes parted and a figure stepped out, no more than two yards away.

"*You!*" Coilla exclaimed, hand flying to her sword.

"What the *hell?*" Stryke thundered.

"I promised we'd see each other again," Micah Lekmann reminded them.

"Good," Coilla seethed, regaining her poise. "Now I can finish the job properly."

The bounty hunter disregarded her threat and looked down at the stars. "Very considerate of you, having these ready for me."

"You want them, you come and take them," Stryke replied coldly.

"Hear that, Greever?" Lekmann called out.

A second human emerged from the thicket on Stryke and

Coilla's other side. His false hand had a saw-toothed blade projecting from it; his real hand held a knife.

"What is this," Coilla sneered, "an assembly of bastards?"

Aulay glared at her, radiating pure hatred.

"See, Greever?" Lekmann said. "Divide and conquer."

Pointing his sword attachment at Coilla, Aulay growled, "It's time for payback, bitch."

"Whenever you're ready, one-eye. Or should that be one-hand? Or ear?"

His face boiled with rage.

"Where's the stupid one?" Stryke wondered.

"The *other* stupid one," she corrected.

Another clump of scrub was breached and Blaan erupted in a shower of leaves. He carried a hefty club of seasoned wood, topped with sharpened studs.

There was no sign of any of the other Wolverines.

"All we want is your heads," Lekmann stated matter-of-factly, "and them." He indicated the scattered stars. "So let's not make too much of a fuss, eh?"

"In your wildest dreams, poxbag," Coilla told him.

Weapons slid from greased sheaths.

Stryke and Coilla moved back-to-back. She faced Aulay, by preference. He took Lekmann and Blaan.

The bounty hunters moved in.

Stryke hit out at Lekmann's probing sword. Once, twice, three times their blades met, briskly clattering. A small retreat by Lekmann gave Stryke the chance to turn swiftly and kick Blaan hard in the stomach. The big man half doubled and almost stopped coming. Stryke returned to beating metal with the leader.

On Coilla's side a four-bladed storm raged. To match her adversary she had armed herself with sword and knife. Now she engaged in a blurring round of strokes and counter-strokes. Swipes glided over heads and just short of guts. Jabs were sidestepped, chops deflected. Their blades locked and she booted his shin like a mule to part them. He hobbled back, fury bursting. His quick recovery almost had her throat, but she swatted aside his pass and repaid it with her own.

Blaan was crowding Stryke again. Dodging Lekmann's blade, Stryke spun and whipped his sword the big man's way. It was a close miss, but enough to repel him for a moment. Then it was back to hacking at the swordsman.

Aulay braved Coilla's flashing blades and got himself through. A backhand swipe of his dagger barely missed her face, and she was lucky to escape a thrust to her chest. Rallying, she sent out a combination of blows that forced him to retreat. While he was still off-balance she leapt forward and took a swing with her sword that by rights should have split his trunk. Instead it glanced off his artificial hand, striking blue sparks and adding to his frenzy.

Stryke had to make a choice. Both his opponents were near enough to cause real grief, and it was a question of who to deal with first. Blaan decided it. His club came down in an arc that would have crushed Stryke's skull if his footwork hadn't defied it. Stryke's blade whipped out like a viper and laid open Blaan's arm. The human roared, rage outweighing his pain.

Coilla and Aulay had fought to something like a stand-off. They fell into pure slog, each battering away to breach the other's guard, both possessed by stubborn bloodlust.

Taking advantage of Stryke's diversion with Blaan, Lekmann charged in, speed hazing his blade. Stryke stood his ground, repulsing every stroke. Then he went on the attack, powering into the human, driving him back pace by pace. The chance of a kill was good. Blaan spoilt it. Blood streaming from his wound, club swinging, he barged into the fray again. Stryke directed a side-sweep at him. It didn't strike home, but it did send him reeling back to crash against the bushes.

Blaan was about to rejoin the fight when a great shudder ran through him. He moved away from the bushes, walking stiffly, eyes glazed. A further step revealed his fate.

He had an axe buried in his back.

The spectacle stopped the duellists in their tracks. Coilla and Aulay, Stryke and Lekmann, backed off and gaped as Blaan shambled, the club still in his hand.

Haskeer exploding from the thicket broke the spell. Jup and two or three grunts were close behind.

Lekmann and Aulay turned and fled, plunging into the copse several yards distant. Jup and the grunts belted after them. Coilla joined the chase.

Stryke and Haskeer stayed where they were, mesmerised by Blaan. The axe head was sunk deep between his shoulder blades, with rivulets of blood running down his back, yet he kept on walking. His ire was aimed at Haskeer. Somehow he lifted his club. Lurching forward, he made to brain the orc with it.

Haskeer and Stryke acted simultaneously. One planted his sword in Blaan's chest, the other in his side. Tugging their blades free they watched the giant sway, then fall heavily, face first. The ground shook.

There was a commotion in the thicket. Mounted on horses, Aulay and Lekmann tore out, swiping at the orcs chasing them on foot. Stryke and Haskeer threw themselves aside and the riders thundered through. Coilla ran up and lobbed a knife. It whistled over Aulay's shoulder. The bounty hunters put on a burst and rode hell for leather along the inlet.

"Do we go after them?" Coilla said. She was panting.

"By the time we got to our horses there'd be no point," Stryke judged. "Let 'em go. There'll be another time."

"Bet on it," she replied.

Stryke gathered the stars, then turned to Haskeer. "Good work, Sergeant."

"My pleasure. Anyway, I owed him." He walked to Blaan's corpse, put his foot on its back and pulled out the axe. Stooping, he began to wipe its head with handfuls of grass.

Jup wandered over and stared down at the mountainous body. "Well, at least the carrion eaters are going to feed well today."

"This is getting to be one hell of a crowded inlet," Coilla complained.

"Yes," Stryke agreed, "we do seem to have a lot of unwanted suitors at the moment."

"Don't expect it to get any better," Jup told them.

11

It was early evening when the band arrived at Ruffetts View.

Their first sign of the settlement came when they spotted a hillside with an acutely angled slope. Chalk figures had been cut into the surface: a stylised dragon, an eagle with spread wings and a simple representation of a building fronted with pillars. The markings were fresh, their lines almost luminously bright in the gathering dusk.

The settlement was in a small valley close to the shore. A tributary snaked past it, and a wooden landing-stage had been built on the encampment-side bank. Several canoes and dugouts were tied up by it.

A vigilant approach took the band to a hill overlooking the colony. Stryke assigned a couple of grunts to tend the horses, then led the rest of the Wolverines to the hill's peak.

Ruffetts View had grown over the years to occupy a fair portion of the valley. It was a walled settlement. Tall timber uprights surrounded the whole sprawling community. Here and there, watchtowers poked above the walls, like modest cabins elevated beyond their status. There were several pairs of gates, and they were open.

"They don't seem to think they're under any threat," Coilla remarked, indicating the gates.

"But it's obviously designed to be defended," Stryke said. "They're not complete fools."

"That's one hell of a weird-looking place," Jup decided.

What they saw inside the perimeter bore out his opinion. A track of compacted shard ran just inside the walls, following their lines. On the other side of that was a jumble of shacks and humble lodges, mostly built of wood, though some were stone, slate and even wattle-walled. Others seemed to be dwellings, but on a finer scale than those in the outer rim.

The centre of the settlement held the most bizarre sights. It was made up of three enormous adjoining clearings. In the one on the left stood Ruffetts' second-highest structure, a stone pyramid taller than the outer walls. Rather than having a pointed tip, it was crowned with a plateau and low ramparts. Recent light rain had made its surfaces shine.

In the levelled space on the right stood a building still under construction. Through scaffolding, the upper part of its timber skeleton could be seen. The area below had been faced with what might have been grey and white marble. Pillars were being erected. It was obvious that the chalk etching they had seen earlier was a crude likeness of this structure. They took it to be the temple mentioned by Katz.

But what was in the centre clearing, by far the biggest, awed them most.

This area was surrounded by a circle of huge, blue-tinted standing stones. Most were in pairs, tall as houses, supporting a third, horizontal stone. The impression was of a series of high, narrow arches.

"The amount of work that must have taken," Alfray marvelled.

"Humans are mad," Haskeer stated. "What a *waste*."

Other lower stones, equally massive, were scattered within the circle in no obvious pattern.

Coilla gazed at what was in the circle's core. "That's amazing," she whispered.

"You've not seen one before?" Alfray asked.

She shook her head.

"Me neither," Jup added.

"I've seen one or two," Alfray said. "But never this big."

At the centre of the circle was a further set of the blue stones, ten of them, laid to form a pentangle.

From its heart erupted a geyser of magic.

It was silent and shimmering, like a vertical rainbow, but with a quality resembling steam that made it waver and dance. Its fluctuating edges were marked with a slightly darker, constantly changing palette of primary colours. The air around the energy spout was distorted, as though it was a hot day.

The peculiarity of it struck them dumb.

At length, Jup remarked, "The magic must be strong here, with so much escaping to soak the land."

"But it has to be constantly replenished," Alfray reminded him. "It belongs in the earth, *feeding* the land, not bleeding from it."

There were plenty of people about in the settlement, and they all seemed to be moving with purpose. They thronged the streets, leading horses, driving carts, running errands. More swarmed over the temple, working on stone and wood, the sound of their labours just audible.

Coilla turned to Stryke. "So what do we do?"

He was distracted by the incredible sight of the magic flow, but drew his eyes away. "Well, these are Manis. They should be more welcoming of elder races."

"You're talking about humans," Haskeer reminded him. "You can't rely on anything they do."

"Haskeer's right," Alfray agreed. "Suppose they decide to be hostile?"

"We've got two choices here," Stryke judged. "Either they're going to be friendly and maybe we can trade for the star. Else they're hostile and there's nothing we can do against that number. So we might as well be open and go in under a flag of truce."

Coilla nodded. "I agree. After all, we know Katz got in there. So they're welcoming of pixies at least."

"But remember what Katz said," Jup put in. "They're building that temple to house the star. If they'd go to that much trouble they're unlikely to part with it easily."

"Yes," Alfray said. "A few bags of crystal aren't going to sway them."

"Here's another thought," Coilla ventured. "If they prize their star so highly, how wise is it walking in there with four more of them?"

"We wouldn't exactly shout about it," Stryke assured her.

"No, but what's to stop them forcibly searching us?"

"You could leave the stars with a couple of the band out here, Stryke," Alfray suggested.

"I'm not happy with that. Not that I don't trust any member of the band. It's just, that would make whoever we left vulnerable to attack by a larger force. I'd prefer to hang on to them."

Coilla thought that wasn't the whole reason, and that he simply couldn't be parted from the things, but kept the opinion to herself. "You really want all or nothing at all, don't you?"

He didn't answer.

Haskeer spoke up. "This is just like what happened at Trinity, ain't it? Why can't we go about it a similar way?"

"No," Stryke replied, "it's different. There were dwarfs there that Jup could mingle with. Can anybody see any dwarfs down below?" They couldn't. "Right. No other fish to swim amongst."

If they thought that was an odd analogy they kept it to themselves.

"So what's the plan?"

"I reckon that, given the gates are open and there being no patrols, they're trying to live peaceably. I say we get down there. Spy out things. See what the humans are like."

"And try to steal their star," Jup finished for him.

"If we have to. If they won't trade for it, or listen to reason."

"We have *reason* on our side?" the dwarf came back sardonically.

"I want to think on this," Stryke told them. He looked at the sky. "We either go in right now, before it gets too dark, or wait for daybreak. I vote for daybreak."

The others could see his mind was set. They agreed.

Though Alfray cautioned, "You said yourself there's a lot of activity in these parts. It won't do to linger too long here. We might have unwanted company breathing down our necks."

"I know. We'll have double guards, and any sleep's going to be done with an eye open."

On another hill, not that far away, Kimball Hobrow was moved by the spirit and in full flow.

" . . . *marching under the banner of our Lord God Almighty!*" he bellowed.

The roar of many throats answered his words.

He stood next to Mercy, bathed in the eerie, flickering light of stands of torches burning on either side. Before them stretched a vast army, an ocean of human faces, holding aloft their own myriad brands. His custodians made up the front ranks, in pride of place.

"Our hour of deliverance is near!" he promised them. *"We need only the will, my brethren, to go forth and smash the heathens! To grind the bones of the dissenter Manis and the godless elder races! And I have that will!"*

Another avalanche of roars urged him on. Pikes and pennons jabbed the air.

"I have that will and I have the broad shoulders of the God of creation to back it!" As they cheered he scanned them, making a theatrical show of it. His was a ragtag horde, with custodians, Unis from farther afield who heeded the call, and a smattering of dwarf clans. But they had the Holy Spirit moving in them. Except for the dwarves, who were here for coin. *"We have many foes,"* he warned, *"for the black affliction of wickedness is everywhere! As I speak, one such is ahead of us in our crusade to Ruffetts! You know her! She is the Whore of the scriptures, the viper in God's earthly Kingdom! But together we shall rout her!"*

Approval rang out like thunder.

"We are many and we will be more! We march for the future of our races!" He had to include the wretched dwarf element, for now. *"For the children!"* Hobrow thrust a hand out to direct their gaze at Mercy's forlorn expression. *"For our immortal souls!"*

His army's clamour was fit to raise the dead.

Three to four hundred human corpses littered the killing field, along with an uncounted number of horses and beasts of burden. Overturned wagons and carts, some burning, formed islands in the slaughter.

Jennesta watched, uninterested, as her troopers moved through the fallen by torchlight, pillaging and killing the wounded.

Mersadion, his face swathed, invited her to celebrate the small victory.

She was in no mood to. "I *curse* it. Having those fools blunder into us means more delay. Nothing is as important as the band and the instrumentality."

Forgetting herself, she had used a word she had never used to him before. He had some small idea of its weight, but fought not to show it. "The dying words of one of the enemy, ma'am, were that this force was on its way to join a greater Uni army."

"Where?"

"That we couldn't discover, my lady. But we think not far."

"Then increase security, strengthen the guard. Do what you have to. Don't bother me with these matters." Her temper rose sharply. "Just get us to Ruffetts View!" She flicked her hand to dismiss him.

He went back into the night, nursing his growing canker of resentment.

There was a rivulet flowing nearby. She plucked a torch from its bracket, and went over to settle on the low bank and brood.

Her brand, thrust into the earth beside her, cast its flickering light on the dark waters. After a while she became aware that the reflection had taken on a more distinct tone. The pattern of its movement on the surface subtly changed, its brightness grew. Fire and water united and swirled.

More in weary resignation than surprise, Jennesta watched as the likeness of a face coalesced. A result of Adpar's death was that an elaborate medium was no longer necessary should Jennesta and her surviving sibling want to communicate. The trouble was it worked both ways.

"You're all I need, Sanara."

"You cannot hide from the consequences of your actions."

"What would you know about my actions, you . . . prodnose?"

"I know the wickedness you practised on our sister."

Jennesta thought that given the chance she'd happily do it again. And intended to. "You should be glad of what I did. It made for one less tyrant in the land. That's the sort of thing to please you, isn't it?"

"Your hypocrisy's breathtaking. Don't you realise that many consider you the greatest tyrant of all?"

Jennesta put on a flattered expression. "Oh, really?"

"You know full well that your despotism is blacker than most."

"Worse than the tyranny of the Unis' absurd sole deity? Harder than the followers of that unforgiving god?"

"You're likening yourself to a god now, are you?"

"You know what I mean. Anyway, where is the evidence that the accursed Uni god even exists?"

"You could say the same of the elder races' gods."

"Who's setting herself above the gods now?" Jennesta sneered. "Anyway, was this visitation only to berate me? Or do you have something useful to say? I am busy, you know."

"You drive away even those who try to help you. You drive everybody away."

"I'm still strong enough to achieve what I must."

"Perhaps. And I suppose I should be content that your support will in time bleed dry."

"I'll have what I want long before that, and then there'll be no need of corporeal followers."

"There are other, powerful players in this game. And perhaps they include someone you need fear."

"Who?" Jennesta snapped. "Who would dare? Unis, Manis, religious fanatics? Or those orcs I pursue? A band that runs and won't even stand to fight me? Those stupid savages?"

"You mock them but they've proved more successful than you in this enterprise."

"What do you mean?"

"I've said enough."

"They have more than one of the instrumentalities now, is that it?" She did little to disguise the eagerness in her voice.

Sanara didn't reply.

"Your silence is eloquent, sister. Well, I should thank you for that. Now I know that catching this band promises even more riches than I suspected. They've done the work for me."

"You're courting death and damnation."

"Is *that* all? I am the mistress of both, Sanara, and neither holds any fears for me."

"We shall see. But why cause so much grief? There's still time to mend your ways."

"Oh, fiddle me another air, you pathetic little whinger!"

"Don't say you weren't warned."

"You plucked the words from my mouth," Jennesta intoned menacingly, then slashed her hand through the water, breaking their connection.

She conceded to herself that dealing Sanara a similar fate to Adpar's wouldn't be as easy. Sanara's protection was so much stronger. But she resolved to put the task near the top of her list.

Stryke and the band were still on their hill when dawn broke.

Shafts from the rising sun glanced off the structures below. Birds were singing.

Those of the band on sleep rota started to wake. Stryke had hardly slept at all. Coilla hadn't much either.

"Are they never still?" she wondered, nodding at the settlement.

People moved around purposefully, even at this hour. Materials were being carted to the temple and hoisted up the scaffolding.

"They're a busy lot," Stryke replied. "They worked on the building all night."

There were humans outside the gates too. Some on foot, some riding along the front of the walls on horses.

Yawning, Jup said, "They do seem to have patrols then."

"They'd be fools not to," Haskeer muttered.

Alfray stretched. "Decided what we're going to do yet, Stryke?"

"Go in, I reckon, open and peaceable."

"If you say so."

"You seem doubtful."

"We all are, a bit," Coilla told him. "We'd be hostages to fortune if things go wrong."

"What else can we do? Like I said—" He looked over his shoulder, downhill, away from the settlement, an attentive expression on his face.

"What? What is it?" Coilla said.

Alfray joined in. "Stryke?"

"Something's coming," Stryke declared.

Haskeer stared at him. "Huh?"

Then they saw them. A group of riders on the trail into the valley.

"Gods!" Jup exclaimed. "They must be a couple of hundred strong."

Coilla shaded her eyes with a hand. "And they're orcs."

"By the Square, they *are*," Alfray confirmed. "What do you reckon this is, Stryke?"

"If our luck's out, it's another of Jennesta's hunting parties."

"They've seen us," Haskeer informed them.

Some of the mounted figures were waving shields and spears.

"They don't look hostile," Jup said.

"Unless it's a trap," Haskeer warned.

"I told you so, Stryke!" the dwarf blurted out. "Farsight!"

"What do you mean?" Stryke was uncomfortable.

"You knew they were coming before we saw them. They made no noise. So how?"

"Just a . . . hunch." He was aware of them looking at him strangely. "What's the matter, don't any of you ever trust to instinct?"

Alfray nodded towards the riders. "This isn't the time. What are we going to do about them?"

Stryke sighed. "I'm going down to them. You and Coilla come with me, along with four grunts."

He turned to Jup and Haskeer. "You two assume command until we get back."

If any of them thought this was a bad idea they didn't say it.

Stryke, Coilla and Alfray started down the hill, mustering Orbon, Prooq, Vobe and Finje on the way.

They arrived on the level at the same time as the mounted orcs. They looked peaceable. Many were smiling. Stryke thought that a couple of them were among Katz's bodyguard back in Drogan.

A corporal in the front rank seemed to be in charge. He hailed them. "I'm Krenad. Well met! You're Stryke, right?"

"What of it?"

"It's you we've come to join."

"I'm not recruiting."

Corporal Krenad's face lost some of its shine.

"Hear him out, Stryke," Coilla whispered.

When Stryke spoke again it was more placatingly. "Where you from?"

"All over, Captain. Most of us deserted Jennesta's horde. The rest we picked up on the way here. And there's others coming, no doubt of that."

"Why? Why do so many of you persist in following me?"

"I would have thought that was obvious, sir," the corporal responded in a baffled tone.

"How did you know where to find us?" Alfray interrupted.

"From Jennesta, in a way."

"What?" Coilla said.

"She's coming here, with an army. Big one. And not all the warriors she leads feel disloyalty the way we did. Far from it. Travelling light, we outpaced her. She's been trailing you for a while now, and one of her dragon handlers spotted you."

"Well, we knew she was heading for Drogan," Alfray conceded.

"Once you were spotted moving down the inlet she decided to skirt the forest," Krenad explained.

"At least the centaurs should be spared her attention," Coilla said.

"Oh, it's you she wants. Badly. But that ain't all."

She raised an eyebrow. "It gets worse?"

"There's another army ahead of her, coming this way too. Unis, we reckon. Both should be here in a day or so."

"Shit, it does," Coilla murmured. She turned to Stryke. "You can't send them away. Not with Jennesta and the gods know who else on our heels."

Stryke looked doubtful.

"We're on the end of a peninsula, if you hadn't noticed," Alfray put in. "If we have to fight our way out of this box some extra help's going to be useful."

Stryke considered that.

"Come on," Coilla urged. "Military logic alone tells you it makes sense."

"All right," Stryke relented. "For now. But until we get things sorted you're under my command, right, Corporal?"

"Yes, sir! That's just what we want."

Somebody in the ranks shouted, "When do we start fighting?"

"I've no plans for that!" he returned. Then he addressed the four Wolverine grunts. "Get these soldiers billeted." To the corporal he added, "You'll take your orders from these troopers as though they were mine. Understood?"

Krenad nodded.

Stryke turned and began trudging back up the hill, Coilla and Alfray in tow.

"*Damn,*" he breathed. "A force this large is going to make the Manis think we're here to attack."

Coilla shook her head. "Not necessarily. Not if we get in there now and explain things. An open-handed approach, as you said."

"Maybe it's providential that these orcs have come," Alfray pronounced.

Stryke glared at him.

Coilla smiled. "Looks like you're being cast as a leader whether you like it or not, Stryke."

He glanced back at the expectant warriors. "I don't want this."

"You've got it. Cope."

12

Holding aloft a flag of truce, and on foot, Stryke marched to the settlement's gates. Coilla, Alfray and Jup went with him. Haskeer had been left in charge of the forces outside.

A group of Mani guards, half a dozen strong, appeared at the gates as Stryke's party reached them. They were dressed uniformly in dark brown jerkins and black trews with high leather boots. All wore swords, and two or three had bows looped over their arms.

"Well met," Stryke said. "We come in peace."

One of the guards wore a green arm sash that seemed to indicate his seniority. "Approach in peace and we accept you in that spirit," he responded, apparently reciting a protocol. He departed from it to add, "*Why* have you come?"

"To speak with your leader."

"We have no one leader. There's a council made up of the people's elders, the military and the priesthood. Decisions are taken communally."

"Fine. Can we see somebody from the council then?"

"We don't refuse audiences unreasonably, but tell me the nature of your business."

"We simply seek the protection of your walls while we rest before moving on."

"You have a large force with you, and you're orcs. Is our protection necessary?"

"Even orcs need to sleep, and these are anxious times. And we're no threat, you have my word on that. We'd even be prepared to give up our weapons."

That seemed to tilt the balance.

"That's not an easy offer for an orc to make, I think," the officer said. "You can keep your weapons. But be warned that trickery will be met by force." He pointed up at one of the watch-towers, then another on the opposite side of the gates. Several archers stood in each, bows notched. "Your movements will be shadowed, and they have orders to cut you down at any sign of violence." He gave a light, almost apologetic smile. "You'll understand the need for our caution."

"Of course. Like I said, anxious times."

The officer nodded. Then he led them into the settlement.

"That's a promising start," Coilla whispered.

Before Stryke could answer, they were facing another wel-coming committee. It consisted of two humans they took to be elders, and a straight-backed military type whose triple green arm patches implied high rank.

One of the elders stepped forward. "I'm Councilman Tray-lor, this is Councilman Yandell. Greetings. And Commander Rellston here leads our armed forces."

The Commander didn't speak or even break a smile. He was in his prime, as far as the orcs could tell when it came to humans, with the beginnings of grey in his hair and full blond beard. His bearing, manner and weathered features spoke of a life as a soldier. He surveyed them with hard eyes.

Stryke remembered himself and responded. "Greetings. I'm Stryke. These are some of my officers. Thank you for making us welcome."

Rellston snorted. "You're the Wolverines, right?" It wasn't really a question.

There seemed no point denying it. "Yes."

"I've heard you've been causing trouble in various parts."

"We don't go looking for it, and any we've caused has been with Unis." That wasn't entirely true, but it wouldn't have done to be totally honest.

"Maybe so," Rellston replied sceptically. "Let me tell you that trouble isn't something we encourage here. We try to live peace-able, and regard our neighbours, but at the end of the day we just want to be left alone. Anybody bringing us strife, particu-larly if they're of another . . . race, gets dealt with."

Stryke was glad Haskeer wasn't with them. The gods knew how he'd react to the Commander's pomposity and attitude.

"We're here with no bad designs," he assured him. Thinking of the star he knew that to be at least half a lie.

"What do you want of us?"

"Nothing that will do you harm."

"To be specific?"

"We only need to rest in a safe place. We won't even ask for provisions or water."

"Nevertheless, this isn't a haven for charity cases."

"Remember we fight for the same cause."

"That's debatable."

Stryke didn't take the hook. In any event the Commander was more or less right.

Before anything else could be said they were joined by two more humans, an adult female and a boy child.

She was tall and slim, with long black hair, its glossy locks enfolded by a headband studded with discreet opalescent gems. Her complexion was peachy, her eyes cobalt blue. They matched her golden-corded robe and the patterning on her soft suede boots. Her face was open and seemed kindly. In so far as orcs and dwarfs could judge such things, she would be considered handsome by her kind.

Traylor said, "This is Krista Galby, our High Priestess."

Stryke named himself for her. She held out a hand. The gesture almost startled him, unused as he was to human customs. But he took it, careful not to squeeze her slender, elegant fingers too hard, and shook. The hand was soft and warm, and quite unlike the healthy, rough clamminess of an orc's touch. Diplomatically he hid his distaste.

"These are some of the famous Wolverines," Traylor informed her.

"Indeed?" the priestess responded. "You have bloodied a few noses in recent times."

"Only ones we found stuck in our business," Coilla said.

Krista laughed. It sounded genuine, unforced. "Well said! Although of course I do not approve of violent behaviour." She added, "Unless strictly justified."

Coilla, Alfray and Jup were introduced as Rellston looked on disapprovingly. Then Krista laid a tender hand on the boy's head, ruffling his ebony hair and drawing a shy smile from him. "This is my son, Aidan."

There was no mistaking that he was her offspring, even to orc eyes. He shared his mother's likeness and her comely features. Stryke reckoned him to be seven or eight seasons old.

He noticed also that Krista Galby obviously had authority here. The others, even the Commander in his surly way, acted deferentially to her.

"What is the purpose of your visit?" she asked.

Stryke didn't get the chance to explain as Councilman Yandell spoke then, for the first time. "Stryke and his company wish our protection." He glanced Rellston's way. "The Commander has some reservations on the matter."

"He is right to be prudent about our security," she replied tactfully, "and as ever we are all grateful for his vigilance."

Stryke suspected he was witnessing a play-off between the spiritual and temporal powers in this place. He thought she was handling it well.

"But I see no reason to doubt the good intentions of our guests," she went on, "and it is a principle of our community that we welcome all who come without malice."

The pair of elders nodded in agreement.

"You would have them stay without limit?" Rellston queried.

"I would have them benefit from the usual custom, Commander, and enjoy our hospitality for a day. I'll take responsibility for them. Is that acceptable to you, Captain?"

"It's all we need," Stryke confirmed.

The elders made their excuses, stating that there was much work to be overseen, and left.

Rellston lingered. "Do you require an escort, ma'am?" he asked pointedly.

"No, Commander, that won't be necessary."

With a parting glare he moved off.

"You must forgive him," she told the Wolverines. "Rellston is a good military man but he lacks . . . shall we say a rapport with other races. We aren't all like that."

Coilla changed the subject. "There seems to be so much activity here. Can we ask what's going on?"

The High Priestess pointed in the direction of the magic geyser, its upper plume visible above the rooftops. "All we do revolves around that."

"When did it start?" Alfray wanted to know.

"There was a small escape when the community was established some years ago, when I was no older than Aidan here. It's the reason the founders chose this place. Just lately the cleft has grown to what you see now."

"The escape of so much energy must be bad for the land," Jup remarked.

"Very bad. But we've never found a way to cap it. So we've turned to another solution."

"What might that be?"

She looked at them for a moment, seeming to weigh things in her mind. "I'll show you," she decided. To her son, she said, "Aidan, back to your studies." It was obvious he would have preferred to stay, but under her beaming gaze he obeyed. They watched as he ran into the settlement's jumble of streets.

Krista headed the Wolverines in a different direction.

As they walked, Jup, in an undertone, said, "Just a day . . ."

Stryke gave a small nod. He knew full well they needed to work fast to achieve their aim in that short a time.

The High Priestess led them toward the heart of the settlement. On the way they were the object of curiosity, but no overt hostility. Then they took a path that fetched up at the half-built temple.

It was an imposing structure, even unfinished. The material being used for facing was marble, as they'd suspected, and the pillars on either side of the entrance, six in all, were as tall as mature oaks. A flight of broad steps swept up to the great double-door entrance, which was guarded by troopers with pikes. The interior was lit by lamps and brands, and there was a hint of that most precious material, stained glass. Hundreds of men and women swarmed in and out of the building, and over the wooden scaffolding encasing it. Wagons lined up to deliver their loads.

"I'm sorry," Krista apologised, "but we aren't allowing anyone in unless engaged in the construction work. Visitors would only slow things down."

Stryke suspected that wasn't the main reason.

"It's an amazing achievement," Alfray marvelled, straining his neck to take in the uncompleted domed roof.

"We're very proud of it," she answered. "Do you know anything about our system here?"

Jup spoke for all of them. "Nothing beyond you being Manis and sharing our loyalty to the true gods, and a respect for Nature."

"Yes, that's right. But here in Ruffetts we've melded some of our own traditions to that. Our belief is that creation functions as a triad. On a secular level, that's how we govern ourselves, with major decisions made by a board of Citizenry, Military and Priesthood. The dictum of a trinity upholds our spiritual life too. We call them Harmony, Knowledge and Power." She nodded at the temple. "This is Knowledge. Come and see Harmony and Power."

Intrigued, they followed her, taking a southward avenue.

At length they came to the middle clearing and its circle of blue stones. Up close, their true enormity came home to them.

But the magic geyser at the circle's centre was much more impressive.

"The energy's strong here," Jup said. "Very strong. I can almost *taste* it."

Stryke thought he could too, like he'd been sucking a chunk of metal. He had goosebumps all over his flesh, and was aware of a faint ringing in his ears. But orcs weren't supposed to be susceptible to the magic, and neither Alfray nor Coilla commented on any effects, so he kept his counsel.

"This is Harmony," Krista explained. "These particular stones have a certain . . . property. I admit we don't really understand what it is. We do know they can attract and direct the earth energy." She indicated the pyramid. "Then it goes there, to Power, to be stored."

"And you've done this?" Jup asked.

A slightly downcast expression passed across the Priestess' face. "Not yet. But we think we're close. The earth energy is a mysterious force. We know so little about it."

"Perhaps that's all the more reason not to mess with it."

"I agree, and I know it was us incomers who have caused the problem. Or the Unis, rather, and their meddling with the power lines."

"I meant no offence."

"I take none. But believe me, here at least we are trying to heal the land and restore its power. We feel responsible for what humans generally have done."

"Then this is an enterprise to be supported," Alfray reckoned.

"We believe that all races can live together, and work harmoniously with Nature. I know this seems an absurd dream in the present climate."

"That it does, ma'am," the dwarf agreed.

"But it's no reason not to try," Coilla butted in. "We all have a dream to chase."

Krista picked up the implication in her words. "Well, I hope you catch whatever dreams you're after." Her tone was sincere.

For the Wolverines, a sympathetic human was a rare experience. None of them knew quite how to react.

"What's life without a dream?" Coilla said.

Krista smiled at her. "That's how we see it."

Outside, the rest of the Wolverines and the orc deserters were growing restive. It helped when some Mani guardsmen, along with a few citizens, came out to pass the time of day and distribute a little food and ale. But the troopers were still frustrated by having to kick their heels.

The end of their hiatus was at hand, had they known it.

One of several lookouts on top of the adjacent hill began shouting and frantically waving his arms. Then the others joined in. They were just a bit too far away, and the wind was just a bit too intrusive, for their words to be clear.

Haskeer turned to one of the grunts standing nearby. "What they saying, Eldo?"

He shrugged. "Dunno, sir."

Cupping an ear, Haskeer tried listening again. None the wiser, he started bellowing back. The lookouts gave up and began pelting down the hill.

The first to arrive was gasping for breath. *"Riders. Lots . . . of . . . riders. Coming . . . valley."*

"What are they?" Haskeer barked.

"Black . . . shirts. Hundreds."

"Shit! Hobrow's men! *Krenad!* Get over here!"

The corporal dashed to him.

"I thought you said they were behind Jennesta!"

"So they were, Sergeant!"

"You're saying Unis are coming?" a Mani guard caught on.

"Yes," Haskeer told him. "Custodians, out of Trinity."

"Hell. We have to get everybody inside and raise the alarm."

"Right! Eldo, Vobe, Orbon! Get everybody through those gates, on the double!"

As the grunts ran to spread the word, the Mani said, "We've got to go in on foot! If we ride in, we'll spread panic!"

"What?"

"My people will think you're attacking!" he explained impatiently.

"Got it." He put his hands to his mouth. *"Walk the horses! No riding in! Walk your horses!"*

There was a rush for the gates.

Stryke and Krista were discussing how best to bring in their waiting troopers when they were interrupted by a distant commotion. Then a bell began ringing. One by one, others took up the peal all over the settlement.

"The alarm!" she exclaimed. "We're under attack!"

"But who—?" Coilla began. The arrival of the Commander on horseback cut her short.

"What is it, Rellston?" Krista called out. "What's happening?"

"Unis! Approaching at speed!" He scowled at the band. "Looks like treachery to me!"

"No!" Stryke protested. "Why would we be plotting with Unis? This has nothing to do with us."

"So you say."

"Use your head, Commander!" Krista intervened. "If our guests were hostile they'd hardly present themselves as hostages."

"Are these humans black-clad?" Alfray asked.

"Yes," Rellston replied.

"Custodians. Kimball Hobrow's followers."

"Hobrow?" Krista mouthed.

"You know of him?" Coilla said.

"Of course. One of the more implacable of the Unis. And his followers are fanatical."

"Tell us about it," Jup contributed.

"Come on!" Stryke snapped. "To the gates!"

"Hold it!" Rellston bellowed. "*I'm* in charge of security here!"

"We're professional fighters. We can help!"

"There's no time to argue!" Krista reminded them. "Let the orcs help, Commander. I must be at the temple!" She ran off.

Looking disgusted, Rellston wheeled about his horse and galloped away.

The band ran for the gates.

Arriving minutes later, they found most of the orcs had got in, although a few stragglers were still on their way. A crowd of Manis had gathered, handing out weapons. Humans and orcs stood ready to close the gates. Haskeer was in the middle of the tide, mustering a defence.

Prooq came out of the mob and reported to Stryke. "Sir! Force of Hobrow's men. Four, maybe five hundred. Right behind us."

Orcs were still streaming through the gates, which had begun to shut.

Krenad arrived.

"Didn't you say Jennesta would arrive first?" Stryke shouted at him.

"She's either been held up or this is some breakaway group sent ahead by the Unis."

"Does it *matter?*" Coilla complained. "They're still attacking!"

Stryke took the point and started shouting orders. Between times he told Krenad how to deploy the deserter force.

Through the part-open gates they saw the remaining latecomers racing home. A large force of custodians was close behind. Once the orcs were safely through, many hands strained to close the doors.

Before they could, the first twenty or thirty custodians forced their way through. Defenders scattered. The Unis set about the crowd with swords and spears.

"Let's get 'em!" Stryke yelled.

They flowed into the scrum as the gates were finally closed on a mass of Unis trying to get in. The defenders, mostly on foot, had their work cut out dealing with those that had made it through.

Haskeer adopted a typically direct solution. He lifted a barrel and hurled it at the next passing rider. It struck the man squarely, crashing him to the ground. The barrel shattered in an explosion of broken wood and metal hasps. Red wine showered everybody in reach.

"What a waste," Jup sneered. He clamped a knife in his teeth and clambered to the top of the barrel's mate. A custodian came close. Jup leapt at him. They plunged to the ground together in a battling tangle. The dwarf finished it with his knife. Then he was up and looking for another mark.

Coilla grabbed the reins of a riderless horse and quickly gained its saddle. Drawing her blade, she made for a Uni busy hacking at a couple of men with pikes. He turned to engage her. They swapped three or four passes before she inflicted a wound. The custodian fell and the pikemen rushed in to deal with him. Coilla quickly snatched the vacant horse's bridle and held it until Stryke climbed on. Then they went hunting separately.

He made a first easy kill by chopping a Uni low to his back, freeing another horse. The next human put on a better fight. They hacked at each other as their mounts spun and reared. At last Stryke buried his sword in the enemy's chest. This time the steed bolted, carrying the dead weight into a knot of Manis who unceremoniously pulled off the corpse. One of their number vaulted aboard and went looking for prey.

Alfray found himself the quarry. A Uni bore down on him, jabbing with a spear. He batted it away, backing to the wall. Suddenly a pair of orcs appeared and threw themselves at the rider. They tugged at him, dodging his flailing spear. His balance was ruined. He came to grief on the compacted earth, a grunt's sword across his throat.

Jup downed a Uni with a lucky knife throw. Haskeer dragged one free of his horse and pummelled him senseless.

Greater numbers told, and in minutes the invaders were dead or dying.

Stryke and his officers gathered.

"That would have been just the opening salvo," he told them. "Opportunistic, probably. We have to make this place secure before the rest get themselves organised."

The bells took on a new urgency. They heard a distant roar.

A grunt they didn't know ran up to pass on the word. "There's trouble at the west gates! They couldn't shut 'em in time!"

"Krenad!" Stryke shouted. "Half your group with me! You stay with the rest and guard these gates!"

Manis were already running west. A greater uproar rose from that direction. More bells rang out.

"This is going to get out of hand if we don't act quickly!" Alfray bawled, climbing onto a commandeered horse.

Haskeer and Jup had rides too. The orc foot-soldiers moved to them *en masse*.

"All speed!" Stryke ordered, spurring hard.

He took his troops to the source of the turmoil.

13

The small army of orcs thundered through the streets, picking up citizenry as they went. Stryke and his officers rode. Bar a handful, the others ran.

Their passing added further confusion because many of Ruffetts View's inhabitants had no idea who this unknown force was. Every few yards they had to be vouched for by Manis jogging with them who knew the score.

When they got to the west gates they were wide open.

A huge fight was boiling around the entrance, with many more custodians inside than at the other gates. Most of the defenders were on foot, though some mounted Manis swam through the sea of bodies. Commander Rellston was one of them. They could see his sword working up and down above the crowd.

More of the enemy were spilling in. The humans trying to close the doors had a hopeless task. As things stood, with their numbers almost equalling the defenders in the area, the raiders were near having the upper hand.

"What's the plan, chief?" Jup asked.

"Take half the strength and engage the Unis in here. I'll lead the other half for command of those gates." Then he had the best orc riders brought to him, and told them, "Take our horses. What we need to do has to be on foot. Your targets are the Uni cavalry. Got that?"

The grunts mounted and stood ready.

"Coilla! Haskeer!" Stryke called out. "You're with me for the gates! Alfray, follow Jup! Now get those troops mustered!"

A custodian was laying about the humans trying to close one of the gates. An arrow flew across the top of the crowd and downed him. A tattered cheer went up from those who saw it.

With a much larger number of orcs, many unused to their

new commanders and band discipline, it took precious minutes to organise things. But Jup finally got his sixty or so grunts
divided into five groups. He would lead one, Alfray another.
Experienced grunts were given command of the remaining
three.

The dwarf confided to the old warrior that he was worried
about working with unknown soldiers.

"But they're orcs! You can rely on them."

"I never doubted that. But I don't *know* them. Suppose there's
a bunch of dwarf haters in their ranks?"

Alfray almost laughed. "Don't worry. They're new, anxious to
please. They'll jump the right way."

Stryke's sixty were formed into a battle wedge. All the while
he drummed into them that their only focus was the gates.

When everything was ready, Stryke yelled, "Hold until I give
the word!" He elbowed himself into the prow of the wedge,
sword and dagger drawn. Haskeer and Coilla stood beside
him.

He bawled the order and a two-stage operation began.

The first required Jup and Alfray to soften up the opposition.

Their five groups went in, entering the fray from as many different directions. From the start they found they were expend-
ing as much energy on clearing Manis from their paths as
engaging with their targets.

The squad Alfray fronted met little resistance at first. That was
mostly due to spending several minutes reaching the first knot
of wildly battling Unis. And once he got there, Alfray saw that
beyond them, at the gates proper, Uni footsoldiers were spilling
in. The enemy was dangerously near to establishing a foothold.
Alfray began the work of thwarting that.

A custodian's horse waded over and its rider picked Alfray
to shower with blows. He could do little more than deflect them
with his shield. While he looked for an opening to counter-
attack, another Uni joined in, battering at the raised swords of
the troopers beside him.

Determination and seasoned skill got Alfray through his opponent's guard. His blade raked the man's outstretched arm. It was
enough. Almost immediately another of Alfray's squad rushed in

to skewer the man on a pike, clearing him off his horse. The second rider was overcome by the sheer weight of half a dozen frenzied grunts.

Then there were no more horsemen ahead. But there were footmen aplenty. Alfray preferred that. It put things on a level.

He was about to pick a target from the plentiful supply when one chose him. A well-built and particularly mean-looking individual dashed in, howling, armed with a sword and hatchet.

Alfray blocked the first blow from the axe. He parried the sword and returned a swipe. All the while he was aware of the rest of his group engaging in vicious hand-to-hand combat. Over the racket he could hear Unis shouting praise and entreaties to their god.

There wasn't much finesse in his duel with the Uni. It was a battering contest, down to the basics of strength and stamina. But Alfray had equipped himself with a shield, and in those conditions that gave him leverage. They chopped and hacked, pummelling each other's blades, trying to do down the other by sheer slog.

Alfray felt his age, something he didn't welcome this early in a conflict. But no sooner did he have the thought than it energised him. He began hitting out with greater force and wider swipes. The Uni started backing. Alfray blocked a cross with his shield. Then he sent out a blow of his own and it connected, gashing the man's side. It wasn't a profound wound, but pain had its way of wrecking a fighter's concentration.

The Uni tried to rally, and did a reasonable job of fighting back, but it was downhill for him from there. Alfray found it easier to dodge the man's subsequent passes as he waited for an opening. His chance came when the human put out a swipe too wide and too high. Alfray darted in and clashed his shield against the hatchet, neutralising it.

Then his sword flashed into the custodian's heart.

Fights boiled all around. As Alfray withdrew from his kill, a grunt went down next to him with his skull shattered. He wasn't a Wolverine.

Alfray faced another incomer's blade.

A bird, or a watchtower lookout, might have discerned some

pattern in the anarchy below. They would have seen Alfray's group well into the mêlée, with Jup's almost parallel. The other three squads would show as having eaten through the fighting mob to a lesser extent. But all were inexorably working their way to the heart of infection.

Stryke held his contingent back, awaiting the opportune moment.

Jup's group was having no easier a time of it than any of the others. He saw comrades fall. Every step forward had to be paid for dearly, every kill was hard fought.

In unison with two of his squad, he managed to avoid the probing spear of a mounted Uni and help pull him from his saddle. The dwarf's companions killed the spilt custodian. Jup made a snatch for the horse's reins but the spooked animal bolted, trampling Manis and Unis alike. Confronted by a human looking for a mount, it reared and brought down his hooves on the unfortunate's chest. Then the beast was lost in the scrum.

There was no time to worry about the loss. Jup's detachment was embroiled in fights with more riders, and now Uni foot-soldiers had joined the quarrel.

Two black-uniformed, sword-toting fanatics closed in on him. His comrades were more than fully occupied; he would have to deal with the threat alone. He didn't wait for the first of his foes to arrive. Yelling a battle cry, he powered into the man, slashing maniacally. The custodian immediately went on the defensive. All the while his companion weaved on the periphery, looking for a way through Jup's fury.

He almost found it when the dwarf, swerving away from a thrust, stumbled and nearly fell. The second Uni rushed at him, sword levelled, with the intention of running him through. Jup deflected the blade and with swift instinct swiped his own across the man's throat.

The first custodian wasn't slow in trying to exact revenge. He took a chop at the dwarf's legs, intending to hamstring him. Jup skipped aside and narrowly escaped the injury. Then he forced himself back on the man, windmilling his sword, giving his blood-lust its head. The Uni stood his ground, Jup gave him that, but it might have gone better with him if he hadn't. A blur of muscle-aching swordplay turned the tide against him. At last, Jup laid his blade across the man's face, cutting deep. He howled and his head went down. He was seen off with a hefty downward chop to the nape of his neck.

There was barely time for Jup to take a breath before a new contender stepped in to bait him.

Stryke judged the moment right to take in the wedge. He bellowed an order. Shields were raised. With Haskeer to his right and Coilla on his left, he plunged them into the mob. They bulldozed and booted aside Mani allies when they obstructed their course. Any Unis in reach were butchered. The wedge had the hardest job of all. They had to get to the very heart of the enemy breach, clear it and master the gates. Stryke wondered if a sixty-strong force would be enough.

He headed for the goal like a blinkered horse, cutting down anybody in black who got in the way. Haskeer and Coilla worked alongside, hacking, slashing, stabbing. A prickly, unstoppable leviathan, the wedge cut a swathe through the barrier of flesh, depositing a toll of dead and maimed in its wake. Stryke couldn't say with honesty that its only casualties were from the enemy side.

They were about halfway, and the going was even harder, when something significant swam into view.

Commander Rellston.

He was on his horse but only just, stranded in the middle of a pack of Unis about to overwhelm him.

Stryke came to a swift decision that in truth he wouldn't have otherwise made. But he knew the value of a commander, even a bigoted one. His plan meant a slight change of direction, taking them more toward the centre of the gates. This he conveyed with a snapped order.

He was glad he had two trusted officers up front with him, and that he'd positioned other Wolverines at crucial points in the wedge. They could be relied on to carry out the change and make sure the others complied.

Like a great ship tossed on an ocean of blood and tormented flesh, the wedge slowly turned to a new course. It might already have been too late for Rellston. He was besieged by more invaders than he could sensibly engage, and only luck had stopped him succumbing.

The wedge ploughed on, barrelling aside friends and enemies. At last it arrived at the Commander and began chewing his antagonists. At that moment his horse went down, slain by a hatchet blow to its head. Rellston all but disappeared in the chaotic struggle. Stryke, Haskeer and Coilla began carving through the Unis, the others covering their backs.

Rellston was half crouching, doing no more than warding off his foes with a shield.

Quickly felling the would-be murderers, Stryke and Coilla made room for Haskeer. He reached down, grabbed the Commander by the scruff and hoisted him to his feet. Half dragging him, they pulled Rellston into the relative protection of the wedge. He was bloodied and pale, but nodded his gratitude as the wedge resumed its journey.

Within six torturous paces the second-worst thing that can happen to somebody in a flying wedge befell Coilla.

A second's inattention had her missing an incoming blade until it almost hit. She ducked, jabbed back and lost her footing. Reality whirled and she was separated from her comrades, alone in the scrum. The wedge, unstoppable, rolled on. It moved slowly, but still she couldn't get back to it.

Then three Unis closed in, fresh from a kill.

Coilla didn't fool with the first. She knocked his sword aside and riddled his breast with rapid cross-strokes. The other two came at her with murderous speed. She glanced away the blade of one, delivered a blow to the other's shield.

A frantic exchange of swordplay ended with one Uni down, coughing blood. The remaining custodian tried to pay her back. She spun to him, averting his blade with a ringing impact. Their next exchange wound up with his abdomen lacerated. He sank to his knees, clutching his flowing stomach.

Coilla looked around. The end of the wedge was moving out of reach. It was close, but separated from her by layers of people. And other Unis were coming her way. Too many of them.

She had a crazy idea, thought, *What the hell*, and went for it.

Running the few paces between her and the disembowelled

human, she used his drooping shoulder as a springboard. He cried out as she left him to his fate. The added height gave her enough clearance to get over the heads of the crowd. She landed on the wedge, miraculously missing up-thrust swords and spears, thumping heavily on a shield. Helping hands lowered her, and she worked her way to the nose, breathless.

"Glad you could drop in," Stryke remarked sardonically.

Shortly after, the prow of the wedge met Jup's squad battling in from their left. They melded, and together attacked the final, clotted knot of Unis fighting to get in the gates. Aid came from arrows directed from a nearby watchtower. But bolts were winging in from the outside too. The danger of their position was underlined when a grunt caught one in his head and collapsed, lifeless.

Stryke peeled off twenty troopers and assigned ten to each gate. Once they joined the Manis already struggling with them, the great doors began to inch shut. With a supreme effort, the last of the fresh invaders were forced back. The gap between the gates narrowed. Then they met with an echoing crash. A massive wooden crossbar was hurriedly passed through iron loops to secure it. Numerous fists and sword hilts could be heard pounding against the other side.

There were still invaders within the walls, but they were isolated and outnumbered now. It didn't take long to quell them.

Jup slumped against the gate, sweat pouring down his face. "That was too close," he panted.

An hour or two later, Stryke and Coilla climbed to a walkway at the top of Ruffetts' outer wall. There were other Manis on it, standing apart from them, gazing over the fortifications. The orcs stared too, trying to estimate the size of the army laying siege. It occupied a vast area. Hundreds of humans topped the surrounding hills too, including the one which just hours before the orcs had occupied. Stryke and Coilla agreed that they numbered fifteen to twenty thousand, which would match the settlement's population, if not actually outstrip it.

Down in the township some kind of Mani religious ceremony was going on. It centred around the geyser, which could just be seen through gaps in the buildings, and above them. Figures were outlined by the eerie glow, with hands linked and robes billowing. Beyond stood the temple, bathed in the soft radiance.

Stryke wasn't happy. "The defence of those gates was a shambles," he complained. "We lost seventeen. The gods know how many Manis went down. Plus injuries. It shouldn't have happened."

"These people aren't fighters," Coilla said. "The military contingent here's probably no more than ten per cent. They're not like us. Warfare doesn't come naturally to them. You can't blame them."

"I'm not. I'm just saying that you need the right tools for the job. You can't cut butter with a club."

"They've got their dream." She wondered if that was an appropriate word to use to him, all things considered. But he didn't react. "It seems to be all that matters to them."

"They should learn that dreams have to be defended." He looked out at the army again. "If it isn't already too late."

"So how do we get out of this mess?"

"We could just cut and run. We might make it."

"Without the star? And leaving these humans to fight alone?"

"Is that really our problem?"

"They offered us hospitality, Stryke."

He sighed. "The other option is to throw in our lot with them and help get a proper defence sorted."

"Post orcs throughout the settlement," she speculated. "Maybe divide our force into five or six units and command one each."

He nodded.

"You'll have Rellston to convince," she told him.

"He may be pig-headed but I hope he's not a fool. If he's got any military blood at all, he'll see the necessity."

"And saving him should count for something."

"Maybe. But he's a human, isn't he?"

"I kind of like Krista," she admitted. "And that isn't something you'll hear me say about a human very often. We've come across worse specimens of their race. Take a look outside."

"What a mess. Getting stuck in a siege wasn't part of the plan."

"We had a *plan*? Look, we have to make our alliances where we can. At least we're locked in with the star."

"How do we know that? We haven't seen it." He did his instinctive thing of absently reaching for the belt pouch.

"I believe Katz. And they're building that temple to house something."

"They might have moved the star somewhere else since he was here."

"We'll never know unless we take the trouble to find out."

"How? Walk into the temple and ask?"

"I want your permission to try getting into that place to check."

"It's risky."

"I know that. But when did risk figure too highly in what we've done lately?"

"All right," he replied warily. "But only when the time's right, and only a look. Now's obviously not the time to steal it."

"Obviously," she returned dryly. She allowed herself a little petulance at what she considered an unnecessary comment and fell silent.

They returned to staring at the army.

Outside Ruffetts, in the broadest part of the valley, Kimball Hobrow walked through the massed ranks of his army with Mercy at his side. Men called out good wishes to them, and godly supplications.

"The failure of the first onslaught is a disappointment," he confessed to his daughter, "but at least it did the heathens some damage. Generally God has been good. He got us here before the Whore."

"And the Wolverines are inside. He delivered them to our justice, Daddy."

"*His* justice, Mercy. As it's *His* will that we expunge this nest of vermin from His good earth. When we burn this place it'll be the first beacon, letting the whole land know that the righteous are on the move. Then let the sub-humans beware."

She gave an excited little clap of her hands, taking an almost childlike delight at the prospect.

"If need be we'll build siege engines to get us in there."

They came to a crowd of custodians, gathered around a punishment detail. The men parted at sight of them. A man was spread and tied, face forward, on a whipping frame. His bare back was bloody and lined with red weals.

"What's this man's crime?" Hobrow asked of the custodian with the whip.

"Cowardice, Master. He ran from the fight at the settlement."

"Then he is fortunate to keep his life." He raised his voice for the benefit of them all. "Heed this well! The same fate awaits any who defy the Lord's will! Proceed with the punishment."

The whip-man resumed his lashing.

Mercy wanted to linger and watch. Her father didn't like to deny her.

14

The more Stryke saw of the settlement's defences, the more he realised how tenuously protected the place was.

He was walking the streets of Ruffetts View with Commander Rellston. The human's surly nature had hardly improved, but at least he was now amenable to the orcs helping with the defences. And Stryke admitted to himself that he had some admiration for the man, as far as he could have for any human. They saw eye to eye on military matters.

What shocked Stryke was that Coilla's estimate of ten per cent under arms was probably optimistic. Seasoned warriors were in a definite minority here.

They came to a group of citizens, twenty or thirty strong, practising in pairs with staffs. A soldier was drilling them. It took no more than a minute to realise they were at best raw, at worst useless.

"You see what I have to work with?" Rellston complained.

"It's been obvious since we got here, with the exception of your crew. How did the settlement come to this?"

"It's never really been any different. A legacy of the founders. This colony was established on the principle of harmony, and even those of us who chose the martial life agree with that. But times have changed. It's always been hard, but in recent years it's become a lot more dangerous. Our military force hasn't grown to match the threat. And so much goes into the new temple: manpower, coin. Now I fear we're paying for it."

It was the longest speech Stryke had heard him make. "The land grows more perilous daily," he agreed. "But right now we have to see what we can do to shorten our odds on getting through this. I wanted to suggest that I break down my force into five or six more manageable groups. That way we spread their expertise around."

"It would give the citizens a bit of backbone, yes. Hmm. All right. Let me know what I can do to help."

"There's something you can help me with now."

"What's that?"

"Tell me where to find the High Priestess."

"It's no secret. Go to the back of the temple. You'll find just two houses in the roadway directly opposite. She occupies the first."

Stryke thanked him and they parted.

He followed the directions and found the house easily. It was large and built well of durable materials, but he guessed that reflected her rank. He had no need to approach the door. The building had a small, low-walled garden to one side, and Krista Galby was working in it. Her child played nearby.

She saw Stryke coming and greeted him.

"Well met," he returned. "Am I troubling you?"

"No." She dusted her hands. "I tend the plants as much for spiritual reasons as anything else. It's good to have contact with the earth at a time like this. Is there news?"

"Not really. The Unis are getting themselves organised out there. Just biding their time for the attack, I reckon."

"There's no chance they'll go away?"

"Unlikely."

"Are they here because of you?"

The question took him by surprise. "I . . . If they are, I'm sorry. It wasn't our plan, I promise you that."

"I believe you. I'm not blaming you for anything, Captain. It's just . . ." Her gaze went to the boy. "It's just that I hate warfare. Oh, I know it's necessary sometimes. I'm not so naive as to think we shouldn't defend ourselves. But war is usually stupid, wanton and pointless. I hope you'll forgive me for insulting your trade."

"Some call it an art." He smiled thinly. "I take no offence. We orcs are born to war, but we take no pride in suffering or injustice. Though most won't believe it."

"I do. You know, you're the first member of your race I've actually spoken to. Orcs follow the Tetrad, don't they? The Square?"

"Many do."

"Excuse my curiosity. But I am after all a High Priestess of the Followers of the Manifold Path. Naturally the topic interests me. Do you follow the Square?"

It was another question that threw him. "I . . . suppose I do. It's the way I was brought up. All of us were. I haven't given these things much thought lately."

"Perhaps you should. The gods can comfort us in troubled times."

"Mine have done precious little of that for a while." There was an edge of bitterness in his voice that startled even him. He tried changing the subject. "What happened to Aidan's father?"

"Should something have?"

"I don't see him here."

"He's dead. In one of the endless conflicts with the Unis. Over something so trivial it would be amusing if it weren't . . ." She gave up on the memory.

"I'm sorry if I caused you pain."

"That's all right. It was a while ago. I should be over it by now."

He thought of why he was there and felt a pang of guilt. "Loss is always with us," he said. Then despite himself he shivered.

She noticed. "You're cold?"

"No. Just . . ."

"Like somebody walked over your grave, to coin a phrase?"

"Sort of."

"Has this happened to you before, while you've been here in Ruffetts?"

"Why the questions? I just shivered."

"I do it too, quite often. It's the escaping earth energy. I feel it like goosebumps, or liquid trickling on my skin."

That was a fair description of what he'd just felt.

"But it doesn't happen to everybody," she went on, "just the attuned. The energy flows through me, I'm aware of it all the time. For most people, most of the elder races too, I think, it isn't like that."

"You're saying that I'm . . . *attuned?*"

"It can't be. Orcs don't have any affinity with the magic, do they? No magical skills. Which we believe comes from you not absorbing the energy somehow, the way many of the other elder races do. Unless . . ."

"Unless what?"

"Do you ever have sudden flashes of perception? Farsight, perhaps? Or prophetic dreams?"

She was sharply intuitive and it troubled him.

"You do, don't you?" Krista gently insisted. "Your face betrays you, for all its inscrutable qualities."

He wrinkled his craggy brow. "What are you getting at?"

"You could be a sport, like me. There are many different kinds. In my case, quaintness, as my people sometimes call it, means I can feel the flow. Of magic."

"I don't understand."

"From time to time all races seem to throw up a very small number of special individuals. They have a sort of . . . *twist,* compared to everybody else. Usually their twist has something to do with the earth energies. Sometimes it's a completely wild talent. These special types are known as sports. Many wise beings have pondered their mystery. Some think they're rare deviations from the racial norm. Mutations."

"Doesn't that mean a freak?"

"Only to the ignorant who want conformity. Like the Unis, Hobrow's brand in particular, who would see it as some kind of abomination to be persecuted."

"You've made a lot out of a shiver."

She smiled. "There are other signs. Sports are said to be characterised by a higher than normal intelligence, for instance. Not always—there have been idiot savant sports—but usually."

"What cause have I given you to think that of me?"

"Your actions."

"I'm just a simple soldier."

"I think you could be much more than that, Captain. You already have a reputation, you know. Even we've heard of it, and how there are many who would follow you. Sports are often leaders. Or messiahs."

"I'm neither. I want no followers."

"It seems to me you've already attracted some. Either that or warbands have grown considerably bigger."

"That wasn't of my choosing. I didn't ask them to dog me."

"Perhaps the gods desire it. You should learn to bend to their will, Stryke."

"What of *my* will? Do I have no say in it?"

"Our will is as important as the gods', because we use it to carry out their design." Krista thought for a moment. "These strange experiences you've been having . . ." She saw the attempted denial in his face. ". . . that you imply haven't happened, did they begin recently?"

"There might have been one or two . . . odd dreams." Stryke was amazed hearing himself admit it to her. "But I think you're wrong about all this," he added hurriedly. "As I said, I'm a soldier, not a mystic."

"If it *has* started recently," she ploughed on, ignoring him, "and you had no hint of sport before, something must have triggered it. Or rather, boosted what was already there, what was innate." Smiling, she added, "Of course, I could be wrong."

"I have to go," he told her.

"Not for anything I've said, I hope. Because, even if I'm right, it shouldn't be seen as a bad thing. It can be a very rocky road or a blessing; it's up to you."

"It's nothing you've said," he assured her. "I have to help with the defences."

"We should speak about this again." When he made no reply to that, she asked, "Why did you come?"

"No reason. Just passing."

Stryke left suffering another twinge of guilt. But at least he should have given Coilla enough time to check the temple without the High Priestess being there.

Coilla should have been in and out by now. She hadn't even got in. The guards had seen to that.

Stryke had agreed that this was the best opportunity. For the first time, work had been suspended on the temple due to the siege and there were no workers smothering the place. He had gone off to distract Krista Galby, to prevent her turning up unexpectedly. It might be Coilla's only chance. But for those damned guards.

There were four of them and they took turns patrolling. One pair stayed at the gates while the other did the rounds, then it was turnabout and off again. She'd crouched miserably in a clump of bushes opposite for nearly an hour, watching the guards and keeping an eye on passing citizenry. If she didn't see a way in soon she'd have to abandon the mission.

No sooner had the thought occurred than her break came. Four relief guards arrived. They mustered at the bottom of the temple's steps, and the old guards walked down to greet them. The doors were unprotected. If Coilla moved very fast, hugging the shadows, she might just get herself up the side of the steps and in. But it would take only one of the gossiping soldiers to turn and see her for the game to be up. A big risk, that had to be taken now or never.

She took it. Stooping low, running fast, she rushed from her hiding place and got across the avenue. She scaled the steps two or three at a time. Then she was at the doors, which were conveniently in a pool of gloom. There was a moment's anxiety when she thought the place might be locked. But obviously no one saw the necessity with guards about. The round iron handle, big as her hand, turned freely. Pushing the door just enough to sidle in, she carefully closed it behind her.

Standing absolutely still and silent, she listened, just in case there was somebody inside. Detecting nothing, she looked around. There were no lamps or candles burning. But light came in from the open roof, lofty windows and a high section of uncompleted wall. It was dull but enough to see by.

There were some internal furnishings, including rows of benches and the beginnings of an altar. Several pillars had been erected, taller and slimmer than the ones outside, presumably as roof supports. A single, shorter pillar, the circumference of a wagon wheel, stood beside the altar, near to a boarded window. She went over and saw that something was sitting on its flat top, arranged so that people on the benches could gaze up at it. Not being able to make out what it was, she climbed on to the altar to see better.

It looked as though she had found the star. Details were hard to make out, but she reckoned it was red, and it certainly had more spikes than the others.

That was all Coilla needed to know for now. She clambered down and padded back to the door. Very carefully and quietly she eased it open a crack. Then froze. Two sentries stood a couple of feet away, their backs to her. Worse, at the bottom of the steps the other guards were talking with the High Priestess and Commander Rellston. Praying she wouldn't be seen, she gently closed the door and retreated.

It was time to think fast. She scanned the massive building. Only one possibility presented itself, and it didn't look easy.

Creeping back to the altar, she scaled it again. Even standing on the edge, the stout pillar was just beyond reach. But she thought she might be able to jump to it if she took a short run. Her hands would have to connect with the flat top, and the pillar's fluting would have to be pronounced enough to give her feet purchase. Two big ifs.

She moved to the far side of the altar, beaded the target, took a breath and ran. As she leapt, it occurred to her that the pillar might be free-standing and go down when she hit it. In which case every guard in the settlement would be in here.

Luck was with her. Her hands came down on the pillar's top, painfully, and she held on. Her boots gripped on the fluting. The whole thing didn't collapse, as she'd feared. Then it was a case of scrabbling her way up until she was able to perch unsteadily on the plateau, crowding the star. And it was the star, she saw that clearly now. As she thought, it was red, and she counted no less than nine projecting spikes.

For a second she was tempted to take it. Good sense prevailed.

She hadn't finished yet. The next step was to get from the pillar to the boarded window, which fortunately had a deep sill. It was as long a jump as the one she'd just taken, and of course she couldn't have a run at it. There was no point delaying. Tensing her muscles, she launched herself. She made it to the sill, but only just. For a dizzying second she thought she was going to fall. Clamping her palms on the sides of the window's alcove saved her.

Drawing a knife, she set to work on the nails holding one of the boards. It was fortunate that they'd been hammered in from her side. What seemed an eternity went by as Coilla prised them loose. She expected the guards to burst in at any moment, or the Priestess to enter. At last she got the board off, and was relieved to see scaffolding outside. The plank she passed out through the gap. Next she began squeezing through herself. That proved tense too; the space was only just wide enough.

She kept low on the scaffolding, trusting she wouldn't be seen. Then the board had to be wedged back in place behind her, lest it be thought someone had broken in. Finally she scanned the street, saw no one, and swiftly descended to ground level.

Sighing with relief as she melted into the shadows, Coilla promised herself she'd never take up burglary as a profession.

Jennesta tossed scraps of raw meat to the flock as she rode.

The dozen or so scavengers swooped and screeched, catching the titbits in the air and gulping them whole.

"Aren't they delightful?" she enthused.

Mersadion grunted a platitude and gazed at the harpies. He found their black leathery skin, bat-like crinkly wings and razor-toothed maws far from adorable. But it never did to gainsay his mistress.

His bandages were off now, and he was depressingly self-conscious about the wound. Angry blisters pockmarked the whole of the right side of his face, leaving his cheek a ruin. He looked like a partially melted candle.

For her part, Jennesta took pride in her handiwork, and had insisted that he ride on the left side of her chariot in order to admire it.

"You know," she mused, "I was a little piqued about that run-in earlier, letting Hobrow and the Unis beat us to Ruffetts View."

He could have laughed at her choice of words to describe the wrath she'd displayed at the time. Had he not valued his life.

"But I'm beginning to see the positive side of it," she finished.

"Ma'am?"

"Ever heard the expression 'rats in a trap,' General? Having the main forces of our enemy trapped at the end of that peninsula does hold certain advantages for us."

"And by rights, the Manis in Ruffetts View should ally with us against them."

"Only if it suits me. I'm in no mood to put up with nonsense from any source."

He wondered when she ever was.

"Another bonus," she continued, "is you telling me that deserters from my ranks may be there. We will shortly lop the head from more than one serpent, Mersadion. How does our strength compare with what we will meet?"

"Bigger than the Unis, Majesty. Should you require us to engage the Manis too, we might be able to match their combined forces." He hoped to the gods it didn't come to that.

She fell silent, contemplating a gratifying slaughter. Maybe even the final battle that would confirm her mastery. Most of all, she relished the thought of catching up with the Wolverines.

The last of her scraps had gone. Putting up a greater racket, the harpies clamoured for more.

"They're boring me," she decided. "Call for archers."

Coilla met up with Stryke in one of the rows of shacks Rellston had allotted the orcs as billets. Jup, Alfray and Haskeer were there too. Stryke wanted to tell her what Krista had said to him, but not with an audience, so it would have to wait.

She wasted no time reporting. "You were right, it's there. I had a hell of a time finding out though."

"Tell me about that later. What does it look like?"

"Red, with nine spikes."

"Easy to get out?" Alfray asked.

"Well, once you're inside the temple, yes. It's just sitting on top of a pillar. But the place is guarded. And as to getting it out of the settlement—"

"What we gonna do about that, Stryke?" Haskeer interrupted.

"I don't know. We need to think this through."

"I reckon the humans here won't hold off the Unis for too long. I say we grab the star and fight our way out with it."

"Taking on both the whole of Ruffetts *and* the army outside? Talk sense."

"Besides," Coilla said, "the humans in this place deserve better than that. They've done nothing against us."

Haskeer gave her a dirty look, but said no more.

"For now, our survival depends on riding out the siege," Stryke judged, "and we're going to have to help with that. If and when we can get our hands on the star, we will."

"That seems right," Alfray agreed.

"Is there anything else, chief?" Jup wondered. "We're going to be missed if we're much longer."

"There's one thing," Stryke replied. His face wore a curious expression, part apprehensive, part something that might have been excitement. They were intrigued.

He dug out the stars one by one and placed them on the table. Finally, he brought out the two he'd somehow fused together and put them down too.

"What the hell?" the dwarf said. He reached out and hefted the united pair.

They gathered round and examined them. There was universal bafflement.

"Coilla already knew about this," Stryke admitted. "I was waiting for the right time to show the rest of you."

"How did you manage to do it?" Alfray wanted to know.

"That's not easy to explain. But watch this."

He took the coupled stars back, then selected the grey, two-spiked instrumentality they got at Drogan. Concentrating hard, he began fiddling with them.

"What's he doing?" Haskeer muttered.

"*Ssshhh!*" Coilla hissed.

They watched him wrestling with the things in uncomprehending silence for over a minute.

"There," he declared at last, holding up the result.

All three stars were joined, looking like one seamless artifact. They passed it round.

"I don't get this," Jup confessed. "I can't see how they connect, yet . . ."

Stryke nodded. "Strange, isn't it?"

"How *do* you do it?" Alfray repeated.

"Just playing around with them at first. Then I kind of . . . *saw* how they went together. Any of you probably would too, if you worked on it long enough."

Alfray stared at the newly constructed object. "I'm not so sure about that. I certainly can't make out the trick."

"It's not a trick. They must have been designed to do this."

"Why?" Haskeer asked, eyeing the stars suspiciously.

"Your guess is as good as mine."

"It stands to reason that they'll all fit like this," Jup surmised. "Have you tried, Stryke?"

"Yes, when I've had the time. I can't do it beyond those three. The other one just won't go. Maybe we need the last star to make it work."

"But what does it mean? Once it's together, what's it *for*?"

If Stryke had an opinion, they were destined not to hear it.

The alarm bells rang out.

"Shit," the dwarf cursed. "They're back."

15

The township was full of running people and galloping horses. Wagons careened around corners, platoons of defenders jogged to defensive positions, civilians doled out weapons from handcarts.

Stryke and his officers, along with several score grunts, raced to their mustering point in the shadow of the pyramid. The rest of the orcs were already there, or close to arriving. Bellowing over the commotion, Stryke ordered them into their six designated squads of approximately forty troopers each. He, Alfray, Coilla, Haskeer and Jup headed groups one to five. Corporal Krenad had been given command of group six.

With Rellston's agreement, the squads had been designated areas to fortify, alongside the Mani defenders but independent of them. But they also had a roving brief. They could go where needed to help strengthen the defences.

"Keep an eye on the watchtowers!" Stryke reminded them. "They'll signal where you might be needed! The alarm bells are a signal too, remember!" It was a far-from-perfect system, but the best they could do. "You don't move from your positions unless your leaders say so!" he added.

One by one, the commanders raised an arm to indicate they were ready.

"To your places!" Stryke roared.

Coilla's squad passed his on its way out. "Good luck," she mouthed.

The six groups set off for their scattered posts. Stryke's was on the south wall. That pleased him. He'd be facing the main bulk of the attacking army.

He got there in minutes, and immediately started urging the grunts up the many ladders to the walkway. Then he scaled a ladder himself, and spent a moment ordering his squad into position. There were hundreds of Mani militia on the gangway already. Stryke was careful to mix his force in with them.

He spotted a young Mani officer. "What's happening?"

"You can see for yourself. They've been grouping themselves for a couple of hours. Now this." He nodded at the landscape.

What Stryke saw was not one army but at least four. The Unis had divided into segments, thousands strong, and each was moving towards the settlement. There were covered wagons at the rear of each segment. The divisions on the flanks were going off at tangents, Stryke guessed in order to surround Ruffetts.

"They're going to hit us on several sides at once," he told the officer.

"And they've held back reserves." The human pointed.

Thousands more troopers had stayed in the enemy camp's staging area at the far end of the valley.

"It's the smart thing to do," Stryke said. He looked up and down the battlements. "Do we have water wagons nearby?"

"I'm not sure."

"I think you should. Fire's one of the biggest hazards in this kind of situation."

The officer went off to sort it out.

Down below, the miniature armies approached. Each consisted of about two-thirds infantry and the balance cavalry. The foot-soldiers dictated the pace of advance, which was consequently slow. But there was something about their ponderous movement that made them seem the more inexorable and threatening.

Stryke walked the gangway, checking that his command was in order. He came to a pair of Wolverine grunts, and felt glad they were there.

"Noskaa. Finje."

They returned the greeting.

"What do you reckon they'll try, sir?" Finje asked.

"If you don't count that little skirmish last night, this is the first really determined assault. I reckon they'll stick by the book. Strong contingents to the gates and ladders for the walls."

"But they're religious fanatics, sir," Noskaa remarked. "There's no telling what they'll do."

"It does you credit to realise it, trooper. Always expect the unexpected. But in a siege both sides' options are limited. We're in here, they're out there. Our job's to keep it that way."

"Yes, sir," they chorused.

"Keep an eye on the watchtowers," he reminded them, "and help out the Manis wherever you can. Providing that doesn't contravene any order of mine," he added.

They nodded.

Stryke resumed his inspection. That done, like thousands of others all he could do was watch the attackers nearing.

As the next hour or two stretched out, the four divisions of the Uni army moved into position, facing the settlement from each point of the compass. That meant Stryke and his comrades were looking down on a mass of troops. Those on the battlements and those on the ground jeered at each other and slung insults.

Stryke paced the walkway, dealing out encouraging back-slaps and cheering words. "Steady, lads . . . hold your fire . . . stand solid . . . watch each other's backs . . ."

Then it went very quiet.

A series of high-pitched piping notes rose from the besieging armies, made by reed whistles.

"That's their signal!" Stryke barked. "Prepare to repel!"

A deafening roar went up from the attackers and they flooded in on all sides. The defenders sent up their own answering cries and the siege proper commenced.

The first priority was to stop the attackers reaching the walls. Mani archers took the brunt of that, loosing arrows by the hundred down on the charging infantry. Shields went up below and bolts rattled off them. But many found their fleshy targets. Soldiers fell with pierced eyes, throats, chests. Some unfortunates in the front ranks were peppered by numerous arrows and went down to be trampled by the troops behind. Horses fell, spilling their riders, and they too succumbed to the rain of spikes.

A party of enemy archers, hundreds strong, tilted their bows skyward and loosed their own swarm over the walls.

"Incoming!" Stryke bellowed.

Everybody who could, took cover. Scores of arrows showered on the walkway, killing and wounding, but most overshot and fell into the settlement itself. Reservists and civilian auxiliaries caught the storm. Men, women and pack animals collapsed under the downrush. People ran for cover, some screaming. Field-surgeon teams began dashing to the wounded.

Stryke heard the blasted bells ringing everywhere. He looked up to the nearest watchtower, but none of the lookouts was trying to signal. Then again they had their own problems, with dozens of enemy archers trying to pick them off. He stayed put.

He realised he was crouching next to the young Mani officer. He looked scared.

"First siege?" Stryke asked.

The white-faced officer nodded, too nervous to speak.

"They're just as frightened as we are, if it's any help," Stryke told him. "And remember that your men's lives depend on you."

The young man nodded again, with more resolve, Stryke thought.

"We're likely to see nothing more than an arrow exchange for some minutes yet," he explained. "They're trying to keep us pinned down so they can get close enough to start scaling."

The Mani archers knew that. They were popping up at random to fire their arrows, then ducking to reload.

"Can we hold them off?" the officer said.

"No. Not unless both sides have an endless supply of arrows. Even if they did, their officers are going to be urging them to the walls soon."

Stryke looked down into the settlement and saw a water wagon drawing up, pulled by oxen. It was essentially a huge barrel on wheels, with rows of wooden buckets swinging on its sides. Arrows clattered on and around it. A couple pierced the oxen's backs and they lowed pitifully.

A shout went up from the battlements, not just Stryke's but all around.

"They're bringing in the ladders!" somebody yelled.

Stryke braved the fusillade and peeked over the wall. Hundreds of ladder carriers, working in pairs, were racing towards the fortifications. As he watched, at least three of them went down. But their numbers, and the covering fire, meant a goodly portion would get through.

He turned to the officer and held his gaze. "Our best chance is to make sure as few of them as possible get over. Just a handful can cause mayhem if they're determined enough." He heard the blood-chilling war cries of the besiegers. "And this lot are determined if nothing else."

The tops of ladders showed above the battlements, swaying as the men holding them below struggled to get them against the walls. The Mani archers, and spear-throwers too now, began targeting the holders. They were particularly vulnerable and succumbed in droves.

But inevitably more than half the ladders slapped against the walls, their tops visible above the screen. Defenders moved to dislodge them.

One crashed into place next to the officer and Stryke.

"Come on!" he said.

They scrambled to it and grasped its uprights. With a mighty heave they pushed it away. There was nobody on it. They watched it fall back and the soldiers below scattering.

Other ladders were being climbed. Lines of Unis swarmed up them with swords drawn and raised shields. Stryke and the officer rushed to help topple them. The first one they reached had three or four of the enemy more than halfway up. With a couple of grunts aiding, they managed to push the ladder clear of the wall. It swayed for a second in an upright position, then went over with its screaming load.

There was no respite. Numerous ladders were clamping themselves to the wall now and the defenders who weren't hurling projectiles or firing arrows dashed from one to the other. Stryke knew this was happening all around the settlement. He just hoped there was no weak point that would allow a major breach.

As he had the thought, the first Uni got to the top of the wall and began scrambling over. Stryke bounded over to him and slashed his face to ribbons. The howling man fell, striking his fellows on the lower rungs, and they all plunged together.

Now another Uni head appeared, and another, and several

more. In the space of a few seconds a couple of dozen made the top and many got on to the walkway. They had to be dealt with. Stryke barrelled into one, blocked his cross and gutted him. The man fell into the settlement. A sword swished over Stryke's head. He turned and felled the attacker, kicking his corpse over the side. The young officer was engaged in a fight himself, and giving a good account. He despatched his opponent and turned to face another. Stryke got involved with his own duel.

There were brawls all along the walkway, and bodies of Unis, Manis and orcs plunged screaming from the height. A ladder poked up at an unattended stretch of wall. A Mani defender, not much more than a boy, threw himself at the man who jumped over from it. He was outmatched. The officer saw what was happening and ran to help. A furious exchange with the invader showed that he was no match for him either. Three or four passes into the duel, the Uni buried his sword in the officer's chest. The Mani went down. The interloper returned his attention to the boy.

Stryke raced over and commenced battering at the invader. It took him half a minute to break through his defences and see him off. Kneeling by the fallen officer, Stryke immediately realised he was dead. "Shit!" he hissed. The boy was looking at them. "Do your duty!" Stryke yelled. The boy rejoined the fray. A grunt caught Stryke's eye and nodded. He went to shadow the youngster.

Stryke took up his sword again and cleaved the next head to show.

Coilla was on the other side of the settlement, helping defend the opposite wall.

The position was similar to Stryke's. Ladders were slamming against the battlements. Grappling hooks flew over. Perhaps ten Unis had made the walkway and they were being engaged with vigour.

Coilla ended combat with a foe by hewing deep into his neck. Then she went straight on to the next, hacking at his shield like a mad thing. That was finished for her when a grunt cut down her opponent from the rear.

As she backed off, a clay pot sailed over the wall and shattered on the gangway. The oil it contained immediately ignited, sending a sheet of flame over the boards. Another pot landed on the gangway behind her.

"Hell's teeth!" she exclaimed. *"Get some water up here!"*

Fights boiled on despite the flames. Some Manis and orcs tried beating out the flames with blankets while they dodged arrows. Then the colony's fire-fighters arrived and got a chain going. Slopping buckets of water were passed up the interior ladders to be emptied and thrown back.

Coilla left them to it and skirted the fires to engage a fresh batch of Unis. She downed one instantly as he straddled the wall. The next got over and put up a fight. He couldn't match her speed or fury and took a stroke to the heart. A third was sent howling back to the ground with her dagger in his chest.

She didn't know how much longer they could hold them off.

Over at the west gates, scene of the incursion the day before, Haskeer was in the eye of the storm. There was conflict all around on the walls, and he could hear the sound of battle at other gates, but nothing was happening here. The only sign of hostility was a pounding on the doors he guarded. Even that sounded more like individual hatchets and fists rather than a war engine.

He kept one eye on the watchtowers, hoping for a signal that would take him to the action. As yet, none had come.

"Just my luck to get stuck with the third tit, Liffin," he grumbled.

"Yeah, it's not fair, Sarge," the grunt agreed.

"What's the matter with those Uni bastards? Can't they knock down one pair of gates for a good fight?"

"Inconsiderate," Liffin sniffed.

An object sailed high over the wall and fell towards them. They could see it was one of the enemy's fire canisters, its fuse smouldering.

Haskeer brightened. "That's more like it!"

They followed the clay bottle's trajectory as the crowd scattered. It fell about five yards in front of them and didn't go off.

"Bull's bollocks," Haskeer groaned.

"Better luck next time, eh, Sarge?" Liffin commiserated.

The bell in the watchtower above rang out. The lookouts were signalling.

"At *last*," Haskeer sighed. "Hive off half the strength, Liffin, and take command here. I'm needed at a hot spot."

"Yes, Sarge," Liffin replied glumly.

Alfray was on another wall. Apart from that, his experience was the same as Stryke's and Coilla's. Raiders flowed over the ramparts and they did their best to kill them.

The object of Alfray's attention was a whiskered bully trying to part his head from his shoulders. He was using a two-handed axe to realise the ambition, but the orc had other ideas. He also had a nimbler weapon. His sword flashed beneath the axeman's guard not once but twice. The Uni staggered and went down. One of the grunts snatched up his axe and turned it on another interloper.

Alfray's limbs ached and he already felt exhausted. But he pushed that back and bowled into a new knot of custodians. Working in unison with a pair of grunts, he drove them back to the screen. One went over it. The other two were felled where they stood.

He turned, running the back of a hand over his brow, and saw black smoke rising from the direction of Coilla's wall.

Jup had been called to firefight on the seaward side.

There was a small gate there, falling within Krenad's remit, but things had got out of hand. The Unis had rammed it with a burning wagon. The gate was part open, part on fire, and the enemy were filing in through a gap.

The narrowness of the entrance helped. It meant the attackers couldn't establish a bridgehead of any size as long as the defenders kept striking them down on arrival. Heaps of dead, mostly Unis, surrounded the gate. But the flood of invaders was so strong it was hard to tackle them all.

Jup and half his squad upped the odds on re-sealing the fissure. He went about it by sending a wedge of thirty shielded troopers to the cleft with the aim of stopping the inflow. Thirty more were assigned to shove out the wagon and get the doors closed. The remainder of Jup's and Krenad's squads were busied with dousing the fire and going after the loose Unis already inside.

It was touch and go for a while, but they staunched the flow.

He would have liked a breather. He didn't get it. The local watchtower's bell sounded and the guards frantically signalled his next destination.

Stryke had answered a call for help too.

In the event, the incident he had rushed to, on the north side, proved relatively easy to cope with. He was grumpy about being sent on a wild-goose chase, but glad he took only ten troopers with him. More than that he didn't dare spare from the wall.

Now he was returning at all speed, with the grunt Talag at his side, the others close behind. As they turned at a group of buildings and entered the stretch running to their post, they saw a commotion ahead.

A lone Uni on horseback was tearing towards them. An angry mob snapped at his heels. The man must have got in one of the breached gates and somehow evaded the welcoming committees. He was travelling all out, whipping the horse's flanks with his reins.

About halfway between the rider and Stryke's squad, somebody tried to run across the avenue. It was a child.

Stryke recognised him as Aidan Galby.

The orcs shouted at him, and the crowd did the same. For his part, the rider kept coming and didn't alter course.

He hit the boy, bowling him aside like a rag puppet. Aidan tumbled across the path and came to rest face down in front of a building.

The impact slowed the Uni, although it didn't deter his flight. As he was spurring again, half Stryke's squad rushed at him. Talag was one of the first to get there. He and two others snatched the horse's reins. But it was Talag who tasted the Uni's wrath. The man struck him down with his sword, cleaving his neck with a savage blow.

Stryke rushed forward and took hold of the rider's trailing greatcoat, pulling him from the mount. Then he ran him through with his blade, piercing his heart. Letting the body drop, he turned to Talag. One look was enough.

He ran on and reached the boy. There was no doubt he was badly hurt. He was unconscious and breathing feebly. Stryke knew it was unwise to move anyone who was injured, but he needed to get the hatchling to a proper healer. Gently, he lifted the child's prone form.

Noskaa appeared on the gangway above and called down.

"You're in charge until I get back!" Stryke shouted at him.

He ran with the boy in his arms.

16

Stryke ran through the chaos, clutching the injured child. Sounds of the siege still raged on every side. Bodies continued to plunge from the ramparts. Fires blackened the sky. He turned away from the outer rim and headed to the settlement's core, weaving through narrow streets, side-stepping or barging aside the bustling humans.

Finally he came to Krista's house. It was being used as a makeshift field hospital. Stretcher-bearers queued to carry in the injured and walking wounded jammed the entrance. But when they saw his burden they moved aside.

He crashed into the building and found it overflowing with the stricken. Scores of makeshift beds filled every room and lined the corridors. Less seriously damaged individuals sat and leaned as their hurts were tended. The nursing was undertaken by female acolytes of the Mani order.

"The High Priestess!" he demanded forcefully. "Where is she?"

Shocked novices pointed to a room packed with occupied beds. He rushed into it. Krista stood at the far end, ministering to a wounded soldier. She looked up and saw him. Her face contorted with shock and dread, her eyes widened.

"What's happened?" she cried, rushing to take the child.

Stryke hastily explained.

She gently laid the boy on a vacant straw mattress and called to him. "Aidan. *Aidan!*" She turned to Stryke. The colour was draining from her features. "He was supposed to be here. I don't understand. He—"

"I reckon he got caught up in the chaos and was hurrying back to you when it happened. How bad is he?"

"I'm not skilled enough to know. But it doesn't look good."

Physicians arrived, homing in on the commotion. They were Mani healers with incense swingers and poultices. Clustering around the patient they commenced prodding and conferring. They didn't look hopeful. Or to Stryke's eyes, very competent. But he didn't voice that opinion.

He glanced at Krista. She was beginning to be swallowed by quiet despair.

Unnoticed, he slipped away. Once out of the house and through the press at its door he started running.

He went to the wall Alfray was helping defend. Sections of it were smouldering from recent fires, and there was still a measure of chaos. But there seemed to be fewer attackers coming over. Stryke thought the onslaught might be abating. Pushing through the mob of defenders, he eventually found his corporal at one end of the walkway, wiping blood from his sword. His clothes were spattered with it too. So were Stryke's, now he came to notice.

"Stryke?" Alfray said. "What is it?"

"Krista Galby's child. Aidan. He's been hurt."

"How so?"

"Hit by a horse. A runaway Uni in the settlement. He's in a bad way, I reckon."

"What are his injuries?"

"He was out cold when I just saw him. I think he took the blow to his chest and side mostly."

"Any bleeding? Wounds? Broken skin?"

"I'm pretty sure not. There was no sign of blood anyway. He was having a hard time breathing."

"Hmm. What treatment's he getting?"

"I don't know. Well, a bunch of Mani healers were around him when I left. You know the sort. Chanting and incense."

"They must be doing more than *that* for him."

"Whether they are or not they didn't fill me with confidence," Stryke confided. "You've dealt with injuries like that before, haven't you?"

"Plenty of times. From falls and combat. Maybe half who get 'em pull through. Of course, I can't say how bad it might be without seeing him."

"I'm thinking they need a decent combat physician over there."

"Surely he'll get the best of care, being the High Priestess' son?"

"Maybe he will. But in this chaos? I'm doubtful. Will you come now and look at him?"

"How are they going to feel about an outsider, and an orc at that, sticking his nose in?"

"I should think Krista would be glad of any help. And I reckon you've had more experience of real healing than most here. The treatment many of the wounded are getting seems very basic; you must have noticed that."

Alfray mulled things over for a minute. "This has nothing to do with the star, does it?"

"What do you mean?"

"Could you be thinking, perhaps, that if we can help her son, the High Priestess might be grateful enough to . . . I can see that wasn't on your mind. I'm sorry. It was unworthy of me."

"It really isn't that. He's just a hatchling. This war wasn't of his making. Like the orc hatchlings and the innocent young of the other races who've suffered."

"Many of them at the hands of humans," Alfray replied cynically.

"Not these humans. Will you come?"

"Yes." He surveyed the scene along the wall. "Things are quietening a bit here. I think they can spare me."

He handed over control to a capable orc trooper. Then they commandeered a couple of horses for the return journey.

Krista's house was just as congested. If anything, more wounded were being delivered. The pair of orcs elbowed through, ignoring protests of the kind Stryke didn't get when he took in the human child earlier. They made their way to the far room, stepping over the injured, standing aside as sheet-wrapped bodies were carried out.

The assembly of Mani healers and holy men around Aidan's bed had grown to four. They were muttering charms and burning herbs. Krista herself was kneeling on the floor next to the boy, head slumped in her hands, obviously desperate. The arrival of the orcs had them all turning to look. Their blood-stained clothes and grimy faces were the object of scrutiny.

Stryke and Alfray strode to the bed.

"How is he?" Stryke asked.

"No change," Krista reported.

"You know my corporal here, Alfray. He's had a lot of experience with these kinds of injuries, in the field. Would you mind him asking some questions?"

Her eyes were glistening. "No. No, of course not."

The healers seemed less than pleased, but they didn't contradict their High Priestess.

"What's your judgement?" Alfray wanted to know.

The physicians exchanged meaningful glances. For a moment it looked as though nobody was going to reply. Then one, the oldest and most whiskery, spoke for them all. "The boy is injured inside. His innards are crushed." It came out like he was talking to a backward infant.

"What's your treatment?"

The ageing healer looked affronted at being asked. "The application of compresses, the burning of certain herbs so that he may inhale their goodness," he replied with slight indignation. "And entreaties to the gods, naturally."

"Herbs and prayers? That's all right as far as it goes. But something more practical might be better."

"Are you a healer? Have you studied the art?"

"Yes. On the battlefield. If you mean from books and sitting at an old man's feet, no."

The old man puffed himself up. "Age brings wisdom."

"With respect," Alfray responded, although it was obvious to Stryke at least that he felt little, "it can also bring a rigid way of looking at things. I speak from some knowledge of the subject. In orc terms I am not in the first flush of youth. Like you."

The healer looked affronted. His colleagues were evidently scandalised. Seeking higher authority, the elderly one appealed to Krista. "*Really*, ma'am, this is too much. How do you expect us—"

"Let Alfray look at the boy, High Priestess," Stryke interrupted. "What have you to lose?"

The old healer persisted. "But, ma'am—"

She overruled him. "This is my son we're talking about. If what Corporal Alfray has to say can help, I want to hear it. If not, you can continue with your ministrations. Please stand aside."

With resentful glances at the orcs and some under-the-breath comments, the four healers stepped away. They went off to the end of the room and conversed darkly in undertones.

"I need to examine him first," Alfray said.

The priestess nodded consent.

He bent to the boy and pulled back the blanket covering him. He was still wearing his shirt. Alfray drew a knife.

Krista gave a sharp intake of breath, a hand to her mouth.

Alfray gave her a reassuring smile. "It's just to expose the afflicted area. Don't be concerned. It's something I would expect to have been done already," he added, directing a pointed glance at the huddled physicians.

He used the blade to cut away Aidan's shirt and reveal his torso. The knife returned to its sheath, he gently probed the lad's chest and side with his hands. He indicated black-and-blue patches that were starting to colour the skin. "There's some bruising coming up. A good sign. There are no open wounds or blood flows. That can also be to the good." He felt around the area of the ribs. "There might be a break here. His breathing's shallow but regular. The pulse is regular too, though faint." He lifted the child's lids. "The eyes tell us much about the body's humours," he explained.

"What do my son's tell you?"

"That his injury is bad. But perhaps not so bad that he need pay for it with his life."

"Can you help?"

"With your permission I can try."

"You have it. What will you do?"

"The proper binding of his hurt is the first priority, to put right the shock his system took in the impact. But before that the affected area should be washed, lest any infections creep in. The gentle application of some balms I carry should also help."

"I can do that."

"It would be fitting. When he's able I'd also like him to take an infusion of herbs. The ones I use for *practical* purposes." It was another dig at the disgruntled healers. "That and rest are what I advise."

His manner impressed her. "I welcome your advice. Let's get started."

"Anything I can do?" Stryke said.

Alfray waved a distracted hand at him. "Leave us."

Peremptorily dismissed, Stryke crept out. He got back into the street and took a deep breath to clear his head of the odour of death and suffering.

People were running by, spreading word that the latest attack was dying down.

"The enemy are pulling back!" a passing youth shouted at him. *For now*, Stryke thought.

There were no more offensives in the following hours. By early evening the defenders had fallen into a kind of tense apathy, overlaid with exhaustion. Outside, the army was regrouping. Nobody thought they wouldn't try another assault.

Stryke, Alfray, Coilla, Jup and Haskeer were on a wall together, watching, just like thousands of others.

Haskeer was in the middle of a familiar diatribe. "I mean, it's not as though it's our fight anyway, is it?" He jerked a thumb at the settlement below. "When all's said and done, these are still humans, ain't they? What have they done for us, apart from losing us Talag?"

Regret at the loss of their fallen comrade was something they could all share.

"One of the band's longest-serving members," Alfray reminded them.

"We're lucky not to have lost more," Haskeer said.

"They've done plenty for us," Coilla responded. "I do wish you wouldn't see other races the way so many of them see us."

"You've changed your tune," he came back. "You didn't care for humans more than I did last time you spoke about it."

"That's not altogether true and you know it. Anyway, I'm coming to see life's more complicated than that. Maybe it's just down to good beings versus bad beings, and to hell with races."

"To an extent," Alfray cautioned. "But let's not lose our identities. They're too important."

"There are some races who don't seem to mind handing over their identities to others," Haskeer remarked, looking at Jup. It was a naked reference to dwarfs and their artifice.

"Gods, not that again!" Jup complained. "Will you stop blaming me for everything my race does? As though *I* was personally responsible."

"Yes, leave it, Haskeer," Stryke warned. "We've enough of a fight on our hands without you starting more."

"We won't be able to fight off another attack like the last one, I know that much," Haskeer grumbled. "Not with the humans here."

"They have spirit," Coilla reckoned. "That stands for a lot."

"Fighting spirit stands for more."

"You're too hard on them."

"Like I said, they're humans."

The exchange halted when someone appeared at the top of the ladder leading from the settlement. It was Krista Galby. She stepped onto the walkway holding the hem of her gown up slightly to avoid it snagging.

They greeted her, though Haskeer's welcome was subdued. She seemed in better spirits.

"I've come to tell you that Aidan's improved," she told them. "He's conscious and seems to recognise me. His breathing's better too." She moved to Alfray and took his coarse hands in hers. "I have you to thank for this. I don't know how I can ever repay you."

"You have no need. I'm glad to hear the boy's mending. But he still needs doctoring, and will for a week or two yet. I'll come by and see him again later."

"Thank you." She was smiling. "The gods have favoured my son, and you."

"Perhaps Alfray deserves the lion's share of gratitude on this occasion," Stryke said dryly.

"Don't mock the gods," Alfray cautioned. "It's unwise. My efforts would have come to nought without their approval."

Stryke nodded at the besieging army. "I wonder if they're thanking or cursing *their* deity?"

"You're a sceptic, Captain?" Krista asked.

"I don't know what I am these days, to be honest. Events tend to turn an orc's head."

None of them knew how to respond to that.

"I said I could never repay you," Krista repeated. "But if it's in my power to grant you something you desire, just tell me."

"What about the star?" Haskeer blurted.

The others gave him murderous looks.

"Star?" At first, she was mystified. Then her intuitive streak kicked in. "Do you mean the instrumentality?"

"The . . . what?" Jup replied innocently.

"Instrumentality. It's a religious relic. I suppose it does rather look like a simple star. Is that what you meant?"

They could hardly deny it.

Coilla quickly stepped in. "He meant, can we *see* it?"

"How did you know we had an instrumentality? We make no secret of it, but we don't boast of the fact either."

"A merchant we met on the road told us about it. Katz. A pixie."

"Ah, yes. I remember him."

"He made it sound so interesting," Coilla went on, hoping she wasn't digging an even bigger hole. "We promised ourselves that if we were ever in Ruffetts we'd try to take a look," she ended lamely.

"As I recall, Katz expressed a little interest in it. In fact, he abused our hospitality by entering the temple when forbidden. We had to ask him to leave."

"We didn't know that."

"The instrumentality is very important to us. It means much to my people, and to the gods. But I'd be glad to show it to you whenever you want. Though with respect I wouldn't have thought a religious relic would be of interest to a warband."

"Oh, it's not all fighting and mayhem with us," Jup told her. "We appreciate culture too. I mean, you really should hear Haskeer's poetry sometime."

"Is that so? Well, you obviously have hidden depths. I'd rather like to."

Haskeer gaped at her. "What?"

For an awful moment they thought she meant now.

"So, the instrumentality and poetry," she went on. "That's something we can look forward to."

"Yes. It would be . . . pleasant," Stryke replied unconvincingly.

"There's much to be attended to," the High Priestess said. "I have to go. Thank you again, Alfray. All of you."

They watched as she descended and moved off through the streets.

"You *idiot*, Haskeer!" Coilla stormed.

"Well, if you don't ask you don't get."

Jup put in his oar too. "You really are a prize fuckhead, Haskeer."

"Go and suck a rock. And why did you have to tell her I write poetry, you little snot?"

"Oh, shut up."

"Well, at least we know what she thinks about parting with the star," Alfray said.

"Yes," Coilla agreed. "But thanks to gnat brain here—" she indicated Haskeer "—we might have shown our hand."

"That bloody Katz could have told us he was kicked out," Jup complained. "Now what do we do?"

"Sleep, if you've got any sense," Stryke advised. "I'm going to. You should all do the same while you can."

"And make the most of it," Jup added sourly. "It might be the last time."

17

He was aware of her standing by his side. Together, they gazed out at the ocean.

A playful wind lightly whipped their clothes and faces. The sun was high and the day hot. Flocks of pure white birds winged above the distant islands. They gathered, too, at the tip of the peninsula to the south.

He felt no need to speak, and she seemed to feel the same. They simply let the vast, calm body of shining water cleanse and pacify their spirits.

At length, although their appetite for the scene had not been sated, and probably never could be, they turned away. Leaving behind their vantage point on the chalky cliffs, they began the gentle descent into rolling pastures. Soon, the grass was ankle-deep, its vivid emerald splashed here and there with clusters of flowers like golden nuggets.

"Is this not a fine place?" the female said.

"It outdoes any I've known," he replied, "and I've travelled far."

"Then you must have seen many regions to match its charm. Our land is hardly bereft of nature's wonders."

"Not where I come from."

"You've said that before. I confess myself puzzled as to where that might be."

"At times like this," he admitted, "so am I."

"Ever the riddler," she teased, her eyes flashing, amusement lighting her strong face.

"I don't mean to be."

"No, I truly think you don't. But you have the power to remove yourself from the mystery that seems to dog you."

"How?"

"Come and make a life here."

As with the first time she mooted the notion, he felt a shiver of excite-

ment and longing. It was partly the richness of the land, partly her and the implied role she would play in a new life. "I'm sore tempted."

"What's stopping you?"

"The two things that always stand in my way."

"And they are?"

"The task I would leave undone in my . . . own land."

"The other?"

"Perhaps the hardest to overcome. I have no understanding of how I come and go from this place. Nor control of it."

"Accomplish the first and you will conquer the second. You have the power. Your will can triumph, if you just let it."

"I can't see how."

"But not for want of looking, I'll wager. Be minded of the ocean back there. Were you to fill your palm with water from it and dwell upon that, would it mean the rest of the ocean had ceased to exist? Sometimes we cannot see because we look too closely."

"As ever, your words touch something in me, yet I can't quite grasp its shape."

"You will. Honour your obligations, as a good orc should, and a way will open from your land to mine. Trust me."

"I do." He laughed. "I don't know why, but you have my trust."

She joined in the laughter. "Is that so bad a thing?"

"No. Far from it."

They fell silent again.

Now the pastures were on a keener slope, and he saw that they were making their way down into a valley, surrounded by gentle hills, although one fell at a more acute angle.

Nestled in the middle of the lush depths was a small encampment. It consisted of perhaps a dozen thatched round dwellings and half again that number of longhouses, along with stockpens. There were no defensive fortifications, fire ditches or any other protective barriers. Orcs could be seen, and horses and livestock.

He couldn't remember ever seeing the camp before, but somehow it stirred a recollection that wouldn't quite be brought to mind.

As they approached, he asked, "Did this place ever have an outer wall?"

She seemed almost amused by the question. "No. There has never been the need. Why do you ask?"

"I just felt . . . I don't know. Is it named?"

"Yes. They call it Galletons Outlook."

"You're sure? Has it ever been called something else?"

"Of course I'm sure! What else could it be called?"

"I can't remember."

The mention of names diverted his thoughts from the enigma for a moment. *"There's something I'm determined to know this time,"* he told her resolutely.

"And what might that be?"

"Your name. You know mine. I've never discovered yours."

"How did we allow that to happen?" She smiled. *"I am Thirzarr."*

He repeated it several times under his breath, then declared, *"I like it. It has strength, and attends your character well."*

"As does your own, Stryke. I'm glad you approve."

That felt like some kind of victory to him, despite its seeming smallness, and for a moment he relished the feat. But when he glanced again at the valley floor and its settlement, something was once more roused in the recesses of his mind. He still couldn't bring it into focus.

They were on the level now and nearing the encampment. The feeling he couldn't name grew stronger. Before long they were entering the modest township. Nobody paid heed, except for one or two orcs who waved greetings at his female companion. At Thirzarr, he corrected himself.

Without let, they passed through the clearing, skirting huts and pens. Then, near the camp's southern end, Thirzarr stopped and pointed. He looked and saw she was indicating a pool, near perfectly round and filled with sparkling water. She went to it, and he followed.

They sat side by side on its rim. She ran her hand through the water, delighting in the liquid's sensuous caress. He was occupied with whatever it was that wouldn't yield to his recall.

"This pool . . . ," he said.

"Isn't it lovely. It was why they founded this settlement."

"There's something familiar about it. About all this."

"You could make it more familiar still if you were to come here and settle. If you were to come to me."

It should have been a moment of delight. Yet it was soured. For the first time in her company, he was troubled. Each element he had seen, could see now, tumbled through his mind. The ocean and peninsula.

*The valley with its hills. This pool. The steep bank yonder that should
have been decorated with chalk figures.*

Realisation hit him like a storm.

He leapt to his feet and cried, "I know this place!"

He sat upright, instantly awake.

A few seconds passed before he adjusted to his surroundings.
Slowly it dawned that he was in a shack in Ruffetts View, alone,
waiting for a besieging army's next assault.

Half a dozen deep breaths were needed to shake off the dream
and bring him back to reality.

What he couldn't free himself of was knowing where he had
just visited, if *visited* was the right word.

It was here.

The sun crept wearily above the horizon but there was no birdsong to greet it.

Pale, chill light threw long shadows from the eastern hills
but nothing could hide Hobrow's vast encampment. From tents
and picket-lines rose the murmur of purposeful activity. Sur-
geons were still labouring over yesterday's wounded but the
Unis were readying themselves for another assault, spurred on
by the black-garbed custodians. They were everywhere, urging
riders and foot-soldiers into formation. Never mind that many
bore blood-soaked bandages and half of them had found no
chance to eat.

Hobrow himself had no desire for food. He stood on a lightly
wooded slope, well beyond bowshot of the heathens in Ruffetts.
Though the breeze wafted delicious scents from the cook-fires,
the only hunger he had was for the Lord's work.

Beside him, Mercy knelt, fervently whispering, "Amen!"

Hobrow reached the end of his prayer and laid one hand on
her shoulder. "You see, my dear? See how fragile their defences
are? How thinly their defenders are stretched? Today the Lord
will give them into our grasp and they shall fall before our
blades like wheat before a scythe."

For a moment they stood side by side, ignoring the bustle
of his thousands of soldiers. From here the Mani settlement

seemed no more than a toy, the houses mere blocky shapes with threads of smoke from their chimneys drawing charcoal lines against the azure light of morning.

"They must know they're doomed, Father," Mercy said. "How can they possibly hold out against us?"

"They are blinded by their wickedness. See how that cesspool of evil throws its hideous vapours into the air?"

She could hardly avoid seeing. In the centre of the settlement the half-built dome of the temple glinted beneath its scaffolding, but she scarcely noticed the structure. Beside it, fountaining high above the little colony, the vent of earth power shimmered brightly with every colour Mercy could imagine.

Greatly daring, she answered, "How fair the face of evil seems. I could almost believe that such beauty can only come from the Lord."

"The Lord of Lies, perhaps. Do not be taken in, child. The Manis are a corruption before God and man. And today God will send them to the Hell they deserve."

In the settlement they were scarcely holding chaos at bay.

The last flames were almost out now, though the stink of burning was heavy and soot stained the exhausted firefighters. They'd worked all night to keep dozens of blazes under control as time and again the Unis had rained fire canisters down on the town. The pool in the square by the northern gate had shrunk under the assault of the bucket brigade. Now it was slowly filling again, its surface mirroring the dying fires in crimson and black. Manic hammering rang out from the stockade where new timbers were filling gaps. The clang of the blacksmiths answered as weapons were mended at the forge. Children were dashing about, their arms full of arrows for the watchmen on the walkway.

Still preoccupied with what he thought of as the revelation in his dream, Stryke trudged tiredly across a square to meet Rellston. He saw a family of humans standing, holding hands around a funeral pyre. The tiniest infant was bawling at the pain of her burnt and blistered face and the eldest lad, who couldn't have been more than ten seasons old, had his mouth set in a grim line though the effect was somewhat spoiled by the tracks of tears cutting through the dirt on his face. An old woman beside the widow couldn't stop coughing as the smoke eddied around the square.

Stryke saw Rellston, as weary as himself, jump aside as a cart rumbled around a corner. It was heaped high with more bodies for the pyre. He stopped for a word with a man who had a bloodied rag tied around his shoulder, then came straight towards the Wolverines' leader. "Join me for a drink, Stryke?" he asked, in an unusual show of openness. He didn't wait for an answer.

Stryke fell in beside him. "Where are we going?"

"The seaward wall. I want to see how the repairs are going." The human strode on, pushing his way through the crowded streets. He kept glancing at the orc then looking away as if he wasn't sure what to say.

Stryke wasn't about to help him.

Finally the man said awkwardly, "You made the difference, you know. You and the rest of your band. We're just not used to warfare on this scale. If it hadn't been for you we wouldn't have made it this far. Thank you."

Stryke nodded acknowledgement. "But you're still wondering if the Unis would have attacked at all if we hadn't been here."

"By the look of them they'd have come against us anyway sooner or later. That Hobrow's a fanatic."

The sun was a finger's breadth above the horizon now, a malevolent orange orb. Rellston squinted at it through the drifts of smoke. "How soon before they attack, d'you reckon?"

"Soon as they finish praying, I suppose. What plans have you got?"

They had reached the seaward wall now. The Mani commander ducked under a blanket hung across a blackened doorway. The door itself was a heap of ashes that squelched underfoot. He shrugged. "Keep doing what we're doing. And pray ourselves."

"That's all well and good," Stryke said thoughtfully, "but we have to do more than that. In the long run besiegers always have the advantage over the besieged."

Rellston stepped over three or four of his command, who were sleeping on the floor, and helped himself to a bottle from a cupboard. Not bothering to look for glasses, he took a swig of the fiery liquor and passed the bottle to the orc.

"We have our own wells here. So long as we can keep from being overrun we'll make it."

"Except you can't possibly have enough food to last forever." The orc slumped on a chair and nodded at the wall of the stockade, just visible through a window. "They do."

The Uni commander couldn't hide his desperation. "The gods know we can't keep taking losses like yesterday's! And they have enough men to come at us every night. What can we do?"

"I don't know yet. But something has to give. In the meantime, mind if I make a suggestion?"

"Help yourself. I don't have to follow your advice."

"Have you got bucket brigades sorted for the next attack?"

"Of course."

"Then get a team collecting cooking oil, axle grease, anything that'll burn. Put it in a pot with a rag for a wick and we can get our own back."

Rellston grinned, his teeth white in the sooty stubble of his face. "Fight fire with fire, you mean?"

"Exactly. After what they did to your township last night I don't think your people will have any moral objection. When they come again we can lob firepots of our own at the bastards."

"Trouble is," Rellston said, not grinning anymore, "their fighters still outnumber ours. They don't have women and children eating their supplies either." The commander hauled himself to his feet. "Better get in position. They'll be here again soon enough."

Stryke climbed the wall facing Hobrow's main encampment. He could see the Unis on their knees. Hobrow himself could be made out standing on a knoll, his arms upraised. But the light, salty breeze carried the man's words away and Stryke couldn't make out what he said. He knew it meant nothing good for orcs or Manis though.

From his vantage point, the Wolverine leader spotted his officers in a fierce conversation. Haskeer gestured and Coilla made damping motions, but when they spotted Stryke they surged towards him. Even now, some Manis gave them a wide berth.

He descended and met them. They all started speaking at once.

"Shut up!" he snapped. "The last thing I need is you lot arguing." He glanced at a tumbledown shack. "In there. We need to talk."

With Alfray keeping watch through a crack in the door, the rest of the Wolverine command squatted in the cobwebbed shadows.

"First off," Stryke said quietly, "it's pretty obvious this town won't make it. Half of them can't fight and Hobrow's got his followers stoked up. Any ideas?"

The Wolverines looked at each other. "We fight," said Coilla. "What else?"

"Exactly. 'What else?'" Stryke's words hung in the grimy air.

Jup asked slowly, "What do you mean?"

"I mean we *could* just leave them to it. With the humans fighting each other, they'll be too busy to come after us."

"You mean we just find a way out of here while they're occupied?" Haskeer said. "Sounds good to me."

Coilla hissed, "You can't mean that! We'd have had no chance against Hobrow's men if it wasn't for them. We can't desert them now."

"Think about it," Stryke urged. "I know the Manis are our allies now, sort of. But what do you think will happen if the last star falls into Hobrow's hands?"

Jup jumped to his feet. "Who cares about the star?" he said angrily. "We've got four of them, haven't we? Isn't that enough for you? Or do we have to throw our lives away too?"

Stryke glared at the dwarf. "Sit down and shut your mouth. Isn't it obvious to you that the star's got power? It's something to do with the magic of the land. If Hobrow gets his hands on it, that power will be his."

"Either that," Alfray said from his post by the door, "or he'll destroy it. But us getting killed is more likely out in the open against the whole Uni army. And I never was much for betraying people I've fought alongside."

"Look," Haskeer said as the dwarf sullenly resumed his place in the circle, "they're only humans, ain't they? All right, they've been welcoming to us, given us food and shelter, but they need us more than we need them. If it was the other way round, they'd take from us and think nothing of it. You know they would. That's human nature."

Coilla had been thinking about the implications behind Stryke's words. "You mean you've decided we're going for the star and done with it?"

Stryke nodded. "I say for the meantime we stay here and fight. Then, when we get a chance, we take the star and get out under cover of darkness."

One by one they agreed, some with more reluctance than others. Alfray was the least happy, but even he could see that Ruffetts View didn't stand much chance of surviving.

Swallowing down his own guilt, Stryke said, "Coilla? You've been in the temple. Do you think you could steal the star for us?"

"If I have to. It shouldn't be too difficult. After all, they haven't got time to guard the temple when there's a fucking siege going on, have they?"

"Look," Alfray said, abandoning his post and coming to stare down at Stryke with a spark of anger in his eyes, "if we're sneaking out of here, what are you planning on doing with the enlistees? You're not going to leave them behind just like that, are you? Because I'd find that hard to believe of the Stryke I know."

"No, Alfray, I'm not. I'm an orc and we look after our own. We'll let them know, don't worry."

"I'm not worried," the old corporal said. "I'm just not abandoning anybody, that's all."

"Neither am I, Alfray. Neither am I. So what I—"

Alarm bells began to sound. From the wall of the stockade men were shouting.

The orcs sprang to their feet, heading for the door. At that moment a fire canister burst on the thatched roof above them. Burning pieces of straw and wood showered down, filling the hut with smoke.

Stryke jumped forward, pulling Coilla out of the way of a falling timber. "Let's get out of here!"

The rain of fire continued, kept in check only by the archers Rellston had posted on the walls, and by the bucket brigades within. Sheltering under overhanging eaves where they could, the Wolverines pounded off to their respective posts. Dodging and ducking, they were just about to split up when a lookout called, "They've stopped! They're pulling back!"

"Must be so they don't hit their own troops," Stryke said. Then he shivered as something coursed through him.

Coilla hadn't noticed. "See that?" she said.

In the middle of the tension, with battle about to be joined, the High Priestess was chanting around the geyser of magic. Still in her blue robes, though they were somewhat stained now, she was slowly circling the fountain of rainbow light, hand in hand with a chain of her followers. Around her, tattered and worn, a group of women of all ages was watching. Red, green and yellow gleamed on their faces as they took up the eerie chant.

"What are they doing?" Jup said.

"Trying to turn the magic on the Unis," Stryke answered without thinking. Then wondered how he knew.

"Well, we need all the help we can get," the dwarf muttered.

Stryke tried to pull out of the strange feelings that rippled around him. "I'm all for calling on the gods," he said with an attempt at his former cynicism, "but there are times when a good sword is your best guide."

Coilla put a hand on his arm. "Why don't we tell them we have the other stars?"

He looked puzzled. "Why would we do that?"

She shrugged, seeming almost embarrassed now, if that were possible. "If they're as powerful as they're supposed to be, maybe the stars could help."

"Do you think anybody around here would know what to do with them?"

Jup grimaced. "We don't know what to do with them either."

Stryke fought to control himself. The waves of vibration inside him made it hard to think. The others looked at him expectantly while Krista and her handmaidens continued to sing their invocation to the Trinity. He found himself wishing that he'd had the time to tell Coilla what the Priestess had said about the possibility of his being a sport.

Consciously anchoring himself in reality by straightening his shoulders, he took a deep breath and said, "I still think the stars are better with us."

"But why?" Coilla's words burst out louder than she'd meant. Some of the singers turned to glare at her. "They've brought us nothing but trouble this far," she ended more quietly.

"I just don't want to risk them falling into the Unis' hands," Stryke said.

Coilla looked at him strangely. "Are you sure you just don't want to share them? You're getting mighty possessive about the damn things if you ask me."

"Yeah!" Haskeer said. "You won't even let me touch them any more."

Jup smirked. "Not since you went crazy."

"Shut up about that, will you? It was just the humans and their fucking plague, all right?"

Before anyone else could speak, Krista's chant reached such a high pitch that it was on the limits of hearing. The sound seemed to knife through Stryke. The Priestess and her acolytes were swaying backwards and forwards now, their faces alight with rapture.

"How can they stand that shrieking?" Jup whispered.

Alfray spoke, dispelling Stryke's mood. The old orc indicated Krista's unearthly hymn. "Think it'll work?"

"I bloody hope so," Jup said. "A battle's a battle, and all that, but I'm sick to death of everybody being after us."

For a moment an unusual sense of optimism held the band.

Then alarm bells sounded again and somebody shouted, "There's another army out there!"

"Oh, *fuck!*"

In the sudden silence that filled the holy place, Jup's words rang out somewhat louder than he intended.

18

Dashing to the walls, the orcs swarmed up to the walkway. As far as the eye could see there were soldiers marching, horses trampling, banners rippling. But with the smoke from the fires still burning in Ruffetts, and perhaps five hundred bonfires on the enemy side, nobody could see clearly for more than a few feet. But they didn't have to be able to see clearly to realise that the army of the besiegers had more than doubled in size.

Squinting, cloths tied around their faces to keep out the choking fumes, the Wolverines watched the endless tide of men and horses rolling black across the crests of the hills. By the time the newcomers' vanguard had reached the Uni camp there was no sign of the rearguard. Just an endless swarm that covered the landscape from one side of the horizon to the other.

Stryke closed his eyes in despair.

Haskeer was the first to find his voice. "Now the shit hits the windmill."

But suddenly the Uni camp was filled with shrieks. Coughing, Coilla said, "Doesn't sound much like a joyous reunion to me."

Jup leapt up and down in uncharacteristic glee. "They're *Manis!* Look, there are orcs up there, hundreds of 'em! The Manis have come to lift the siege!"

"You're right!" Coilla said. "They're attacking the Unis from the rear."

"There's dwarves!" Jup pointed excitedly at the first group of his own people he had seen in a while. "A whole mass of 'em!"

Haskeer sneered, "So what? They won't make a difference unless they're being paid well."

Jup grabbed him by the throat. "Says *who*, goat breath?"

Before Haskeer could reply Stryke pulled them apart. "We don't have time for this. Can anybody see whose army it is?"

Batting windblown sparks out of the smoky air, the Wolverines peered through the shimmering waves of heat.

"Don't know," Coilla decided. "Don't care. There's more of them than there is of the Unis and that's good enough for me."

Stryke rested his hands on the palisade. "This is gods-sent. We've got to get out there and help."

Inside Ruffetts View a frenzy of activity burst out, with Rellston snapping commands left, right and centre. Runners took his orders and within a short time forces were mustering. Footsoldiers forced their way through the crowds to line the streets near the northern gate. Meanwhile, riders were saddling up and pushing their way from the stables so they could form up around the small pool in the square.

The Ruffetts commander had his work cut out, sending citizens to the walls while the townswomen were left to battle the fires still raging in the poorer quarters, where houses were built mostly of wood.

Stryke pushed his way through the throng, wishing he hadn't told the enlistees to also assemble by the landmark pool. The noise was appalling. He dodged as a horse shied at the din, and shouldered his way through to the edge of the muddy water.

He wasn't surprised to see that even in the crowded square the humans had left a space around Corporal Krenad. Two hundred orc warriors were enough to give most beings a sense of respect.

"Ready for the charge, Corporal?"

The deserter's face split in a grin. "Much better than skulking around inside these poxy walls, sir. If you want a good sally, I'm your orc."

They had to shout to make themselves heard. Now a strange quiet fell on the muster.

Climbing into the saddle of a horse Krenad had brought him, Stryke found out why. High Priestess Krista Galby was walking through the square. Despite it being so packed, the inhabitants of Ruffetts still found space to make way for her.

Serene, Krista had a brief word with Commander Rellston, then headed for the Wolverines. Stryke heeled his horse forward to meet her.

She rested a hand on his leg and looked up into his eyes. "Once someone has felt the power of the land, it will grow in them," she whispered. "Sooner or later, the land won't be denied."

Suddenly she wasn't serious at all. With a gleam of exaltation in her eye, she straightened. Though she hardly raised her voice, her next words rang through the square. "Let each of you know that you fight for the land. So the land will strengthen you, bring the power of the earth into your hearts. Open yourselves to the power of the earth. Know that the wind is the earth's breath, and that we fight for the land's well-being. For the land will not be denied. Too long has it shed tears for its despoilers. Now, as the power of the earth soars above your heads—" from the geyser a plume of coruscating pseudo-flame leaped higher, by chance or by design "—your spirits will be renewed, in this life or the next, and the blessings of the Manifold Path will be above you and before you. They will be behind you and on either hand, to guard and guide and shield you as the land's own." Her hands rose in a graceful gesture of benediction. Then she vanished into the crowd.

Rellston's command burst into the silence. "Open the gates! At the trot!"

Flanked by Coilla, Jup, Alfray and Haskeer, Stryke held his restless horse in place by sheer muscular power.

Once more the square was filled with noise. Under its cover, Coilla said, "If anything happens to you all the stars will be lost at once. Split them up between us, Stryke."

"No chance." His automatic refusal brought her chin up stubbornly. He added persuasively, "They belong together, Coilla. I don't know why, they just do."

Already the first columns of trotting men were at the gates.

"Either that or you're just too possessive to let them out of your grasp," she said.

Secure in the centre of her army, Jennesta stared down from her chariot on the hilltop.

A seething battle was under way in front of the squalid, smoking settlement. Trapped by the steep sides of the valley, pinned down by her loyalists and those pathetic human and orcish renegades, Hobrow's Unis were grimly digging in.

She laughed. "Pitiful, aren't they, Mersadion?"

"Yes, my lady." Unconsciously, the general's hand lifted to touch his scarred and blistered cheek. "But there are still twenty thousand of them."

The queen's eyes glittered. "Your point?"

"That . . . that it will be a great victory for you, my lady."

"I like a great victory. And so should you, General. Because if I don't get one, you don't get to live. Do I make myself clear?"

Mersadion bowed to hide the hatred he could feel inside him. "Indeed you do, my lady."

"Good. Then arrange for a three-pronged attack. I want our humans ready for a frontal charge. Yes? Were you about to question my orders?"

"No, my lady. Never."

"That's right. We mustn't let ourselves get carried away, must we? I want the orcs on that ridge over there, ready to attack from the cover of the trees. The dwarves can take that hilltop on the left. When my humans feint with a charge, those stupid Unis won't be able to spread out sideways to encircle the charge. But some will be lured forward and *that's* when our flanks will attack theirs. Simple, you see?"

He did indeed. "It's brilliant, my lady."

"Of course it is." She smiled down on the sea of glittering pikes and swords below her. "And while we're at it, Mersadion, I want the harpies ready to fly once that Uni rabble has committed itself to a charge."

What's left of them, the general thought, turning away to pass on his orders. Why the queen had chosen to pleasure herself by setting the harpies on each other the night before, he could not fathom. Although insanity couldn't be ruled out.

Fortunately Jennesta was happy. Excited. Girlish even, at the thought of the bloodletting to come. She flicked her reins and began trundling her scythe-wheeled chariot to the front ranks of her vanguard. Once she was in position, she had Mersadion give the signal for the charge.

Step by step the horses flung themselves forward, gaining momentum. Knowing she looked magnificent, all aglitter in the sun, Jennesta thundered down on her enemy, sweeping her army out around her like a jewelled cloak.

This was going to be easy.

Kimball Hobrow could scarcely believe it. Just moments ago, he had been in charge of a besieging force that outnumbered the heathen scum in that wretched little dump below. He couldn't lose. He could even pity the stupidity of those Manis, laid out before him like ninepins, waiting for the will of God to bowl them aside as a testament to His power.

And now he was facing not one but *two* armies. Armies that made his own forces look like a temple picnic.

"What'll we do, sir?" said the sweat-streaked custodian before him.

"The Lord's will," Hobrow said, outwardly calm despite the first stirrings of panic in his breast.

"Is it a test, Father?" Mercy asked, turning her innocent-looking face up to his.

"It is, daughter." He raked the trembling custodian with a glance as the ground began to shake beneath Jennesta's chariot charge. "Why? Do you think the Lord has abandoned us? Is our faith so weak?"

"N . . . no, sir."

"Indeed not. We shall slay these unbelievers. The Lord's name will ring down glorified through the ages. If He is with us, how can we lose?"

The custodian could not find words. He shook his head as Hobrow made a blessing in the hot, dusty air.

"Get back to your place, man! Do the Lord's will!" Hobrow had already dismissed him from his thoughts. He beckoned to two of his inner circle. They trotted obediently to him. "I have bad news for you," he told them. "I know you long to take part in the glorious slaughter but the Lord has other plans for you."

Both of them actually looked regretful. "Tell us, master," they chorused.

"Guard my daughter with your lives, for did not the Lord command us to protect the innocent?"

They nodded, awestruck at the responsibility.

"Then take her to safety." Hobrow stooped, his angular body looking like some strange bird as he bent to kiss Mercy's brow. She bent her head in submission to his authority, but he had already gone.

One glance was enough to show him that the tatterdemalion force from Ruffetts View was no more than a few hundred beings. Already he could see the Whore, riding down on him in a glitter of gold and steel. Her front rank crashed into the Unis' pikemen with a shock that transmitted itself through the ground. For a moment he could even see the Queen, screaming in rage as one of her horses impaled itself on one of the deadly weapons.

Smiling to himself, Hobrow swung up into the saddle and galloped into the fray. How could she be so stupid? When had a cavalry charge ever broken through a solid line of pikemen? The Lord was with him indeed.

This was going to be easy.

As the dark mass of Jennesta's army shocked into the foremost rank of the Unis, Stryke spearheaded his orcish cavalry unit at their rear.

Although they were going uphill, not the best of tactics for a charge, their opponents were in confusion. Hobrow's soldiers had fired a single scant volley of arrows, most of which had fallen short. Firing downhill made it hard to judge distance.

"I guess the best of Hobrow's archers are up at the sharp end," Coilla said, crouching low over the neck of her racing mount.

"I ain't complaining," Haskeer replied.

The Wolverines thundered on. The smoke was thinner the further from Ruffetts they went, but the battle above was raising so much dust it might as well have been fog. The grass was grey with it, and even the sun was no more than a faint ball hanging halfway up the sky. It didn't stop the sounds of battle, though, and the very ground was trembling beneath the pounding hooves.

Stryke looked to his right. As agreed, Rellston's cavalry was sweeping down on Hobrow's flank from a gentle slope. The

Unis' own horsemen were somewhere up ahead, out of sight behind the shifting mass of the fighting. The Wolverine already knew the enemy would keep their horses at the major battle-front against the unexpected Mani army.

To either side, having set off some minutes earlier, Rellston's foot-soldiers were beginning to form into lines. The front row wielded short stabbing swords while their comrades levelled long lances. From behind them whistled flight upon flight of javelins. They plunged into the Unis' flanks. Some clattered off shields, but others found their mark and a ragged chorus of shrieks had Stryke and Coilla grinning with maniacal pleasure.

Only fifty yards before the orcish cavalry punched through the Uni lines. Twenty . . . Ten . . .

From straight overhead came unholy screams of laughter. Confused, the Wolverines looked upwards and recoiled.

A dozen winged creatures came out of the dust cloud, stooping down on the dumbstruck Unis. Hobrow's archers never knew what hit them. From behind the harpies swooped on them, dragging struggling bodies up into the air then hurling them down upon their comrades. A grisly rain of blood spattered on men and earth alike.

Only a handful of bowmen realised what was happening. Caught completely off guard, they sent a few arrows upwards but for the most part the shots fell back down, doing more harm to the Unis' own troops than to the harpies, who hid cackling behind the cloud.

Too late to stop his headlong dash, Stryke found himself riding down a boy whose mouth was an O of astonishment. The boy fell beneath the plunging hooves, his scream abruptly cut off. Then it was hack and slash, duck and parry.

Now that the orcs had torn a hole in the Unis' defence, Rellston's troops were through. Hobrow's forces gathered in tight knots, fighting for their lives. And every now and then a harpy would dive down to seize another victim, scattering his ripped limbs onto his terrified comrades.

The outcome was inevitable.

"Like spearing fish in a barrel!" Haskeer cried, his blade a whirling circle of crimson.

"Yeah," Jup panted, his own share of victims marking his path. "It's almost a crime."

At the battlefront above the narrowest part of the valley, Jennesta was incensed. True, her personal bodyguard had thrown themselves at the pikemen, their sheer ferocity driving back the Unis. But that still left her with an overturned chariot and a dead horse in the traces.

"Do something!" she screamed at Mersadion as she dragged herself to her feet.

"Yes, my lady." Cursing, the General ran after another chariot.

As soon as the driver slowed to hear his commander's orders, Mersadion leaped aboard and hurled the man out onto the trampled grass. Another team was right behind. With not so much as a backward glance Mersadion left the fallen charioteer to the mercy of spinning hub scythes.

He knew Jennesta in her turn would do the same to him. She bounced away across the rutted ground, whipping her horses to a headlong gallop.

The scent of blood was in her nostrils, singing through her whole being, filling her with a deep hunger. She drove straight at the gap where the pikemen had died and plunged into the battle. The remnants of her personal guard hurried to catch up with her.

Abruptly she slowed. It wouldn't do to get too far ahead of her men. And slowing the chariot to a stop, she opened her eyes wide in surprise.

A stray breeze had, for an instant, swept the dust aside. Clear as day, she saw that at the foot of the valley a force from the settlement had cleaved into the Unis' rear.

A force that included *orcs*.

It might mean nothing. After all, she had orcs of her own, and there were plenty of them scattered about Maras-Dantia.

But then again, it might mean something. It might mean she'd caught up with those thieving turncoats after all.

Jennesta's faint scaling gleamed as the sun lit up her flashing smile.

*   *   *

In the mêlée outside the north gate of Ruffetts View, the groups of Unis struggled on, unwilling to die without taking as many Manis with them as they could. There couldn't have been more than two or three thousand of them left at the bottom of the valley but they were selling themselves dear.

Weary beyond belief, Stryke stopped for a breather. It was bloody work, hot and sweaty despite the unnatural chill in the air. Happily, the harpies had gone now, either shot down by bowmen or fled back to wherever they had come from. Their appearance had bothered him. As far as Stryke knew, they hadn't touched one of the troops from Ruffetts View. How had they known to attack the Unis? Come to that, he had no idea why the other Mani army had turned up without warning.

Telling himself he was just reacting to Hobrow's fanaticism, Stryke reached for his water-flask. Then cursed as he realised it had been cut loose in the battle. Fortunately the stars were secure.

Coilla reined in beside him. "Gods! I'd kill for a drink of ale," she said, wiping blood and perspiration from her brow.

"You may have to," he answered. "There's bound to be some up there in their camp. Let's hope we get to it before these gods-botherers do."

He spurred his mount forward, his head rocking back with the impetus. Coilla looked after him and joined in his wild charge.

Then they caught a glimpse of Krenad. He was hanging upside down, one foot caught in his stirrup as his horse rocketed away in fright, dancing between the broken ranks of fighters.

Stryke took Krenad's attacker with a swipe from the side while Coilla dashed after the enlistee. She managed to cut in front of his steed and haul it to a standstill. Helping him free his foot, she was glad to see that he could still smile shakily in thanks.

Then a shout from Rellston drew them like a magnet. A pocket of several hundred Unis had taken refuge in a hollow. It was defended by a thicket, and they were making sorties out of it then rushing back to take shelter in the thorny trees.

Krenad pulled himself back onto his horse and passed round a flask of some spirit Stryke didn't recognise. It tasted foul but it put new heart in him. He looked about him and saw Alfray coming towards them out of the murk.

Suddenly the old warrior stopped as though he'd seen someone in his path. Not an enemy but someone he had no beef with. Stryke could see the puzzlement on his corporal's face. Following Alfray's gaze, for an instant Stryke thought he saw a glimpse of white. A white stallion, with a wiry, auburn-headed man on its back.

Serapheim?

The vision was obscured by the mêlée.

"Right," Stryke said, not quite managing to mask his superstitious shiver. "I want a real drink. Let's see what those sodding Unis have down there."

The sun was low now, and Hobrow's surviving troops had been forced to retreat.

Some fool had fired the thicket hours ago, driving out the pocket of Unis but threatening to scorch anybody who wanted to get past. Smouldering leaves drifted in the breeze, setting odd little fires in unexpected places. At times the smoke was so thick it would have choked a dragon. All day the battle had raged, a losing one as far as the Unis were concerned, but fierce nonetheless.

Now the Wolverines and Krenad's enlistees were side by side, many of them on foot, all of them smeared with blood. For the lucky ones it was somebody else's.

As evening drew on, a wind sprang up, whistling down the valley on its way to the sea. It tore apart the pall of smoke just long enough for the orcs to see who it was who had so fortuitously come to their aid.

Jennesta.

"My gods!" exclaimed Haskeer at the same time as Stryke cried her name.

The irony of it was not lost on them. Nor, apparently, on Jennesta. From the platform of her distant chariot she glared at them.

Far away as she was, they knew she would be raging with naked hatred. A tiny figure way up on the hillside, she raised her hand as though to cast an invisible spear.

Stryke and his Wolverines scattered. They had seen enough of her magic to know she had balls of dazzling energy at her command.

They needn't have worried. With another unpredictable shift the breeze dropped the curtain of smoke between them.

"Don't worry," Coilla said contemptuously. "She won't risk her precious self down in the real battle. Now let's find that murdering Uni chief and then get the hell out of here."

19

Kimball Hobrow had been behind his men all day, striding from place to place, urging them onward with increasingly desperate prayers. He'd shadowed them every step of the way, every hard-fought pace of the retreat. Now he was hiding out of sight behind an overturned wagon, still hoarsely shouting encouragement.

All at once he found himself with no one left to exhort. The last of his custodians sank to the ground with a tired sigh. Like a child falling asleep, the man gave up the ghost and died as the sun tucked itself behind the ridge.

The camp was off to one side of the valley. It should have been safe enough, hidden in a little dip lined with trees, a peaceful place for a man to make camp with his daughter. But he hadn't seen his daughter for hours. God alone knew where she was.

For the first time Hobrow wondered if God cared.

The Uni leader crouched lower, hardly aware of the splinters from the wagon board sticking into the flesh of his hand. His sword had long since vanished, dropped when a mob of howling savages came towards his gallant band. Now he had nothing with which to defend himself.

He spotted a couple of subhumans sneaking through the wreckage of his camp. They were wearing the uniform of the Great Whore. Jackknifing up and down again, he snagged a torn blanket from the heap caught on the wheel and pulled it over his head. Perhaps if he squatted and kept really still, they might miss him.

Trying to hold his breath, Hobrow heard his heart as loud as hoofbeats in his ears. Surely they must hear it too? For it was obvious now that he had grievously offended the Lord, and the Lord had deserted him. Hadn't he been doing God's will? Hadn't he been zealous enough?

Apparently not.

Suddenly the two creatures pounced. Tearing the blanket off, they grabbed him as he blinked in the last of the daylight.

"Oh Lord, smite these unbelievers who dare to profane your instru—" One of the orcs clouted him casually over the head.

Hobrow lay stunned for a breath or two. When reality crowded back in on him, he heard the fat one say, "Wonder if he's got anything worth looting?"

The tall one ferreted around in the pile of stuff that had fallen from the wagon. He tossed a holy book across the clearing, wiping his fingers afterwards on his jerkin. "Nah. Just a pile of old crap."

Hobrow forced himself up to one elbow. "You can't say that!" he exclaimed, aghast.

The fat one backhanded him, splitting Hobrow's lip. "Just did, lame-brain. You talk too much."

"Let's cut out his tongue! I could do with a laugh."

Hobrow scuttled backwards, his legs pedalling furiously. Before they could work out what he was doing he had crawled right under the smashed woodwork of the wagon bed.

The tall one vaulted over the broken traces and reached for him. Hobrow huddled in on himself beneath the broken planks, shrinking out of the orc's reach.

It made no difference. Casually, the fat one whacked the flat of his axe against Hobrow's knee. "Quit playing hide and seek, scumpouch."

Hobrow howled. "Let me go! I'm the Lord's servant. You can't hurt me." His tone tightened to a whine of self pity. "Please don't hurt me!"

The fat one fastened his fingers in Hobrow's once-tidy hair and hauled him out. He dragged the cringing Uni upright, shaking him like a rag doll. "Look," he said to his companion as a stain spread steamily across Hobrow's pants. "He's pissed himself."

Hobrow closed his eyes, feeling the final indignity start to cool and stick clammily on his thighs. His captor shoved him aside. Hobrow fell hard against the wagon wheel.

"Reckon it's worth taking him back to Her Majesty, Hrackash?" his captor said.

The tall one stared at the Lord's servant with contempt.

"Nah. He can't be anyone important. He's got less spine than a jellyfish."

Sunk in shame, Kimball Hobrow didn't even feel the knife that plunged into his heart.

As darkness came, Jennesta's troops fell back to their encampment. But unnatural howls floated across the shadowy battlefield. Furtive movements betrayed the fact that some of the Unis were making their escape over the ridge. Stryke wasn't aware that Mercy Hobrow was among them. But then, he had other things on his mind.

"We'd better get the last star and clear out," he decided. "That's Jennesta up there. I don't want to be anywhere near her come morning."

"Why's she helping us?" Jup wondered.

"She's not helping us. She's just getting the Unis out of the way. It's us she's after. Coilla? Are you in on this?"

"Of course I am!" She hesitated as Alfray bound up a cut on her shoulder. "It's just that . . . Well, you know, it doesn't seem right taking things from allies. It's not as though we've got that many friends, is it?"

"They owe us," Haskeer stated baldly. "Think of it as a reward."

"Oh, charming," Coilla said. "So now I get to rob our allies' temple."

A mass of tired riders shambled past them, heading for the town gates.

"Look," Stryke said. "These people don't stand a chance. When Jennesta comes through here in the morning, do you want her getting her hands on what might be a source of power?"

That clinched it.

The band made their way down to Ruffetts View, some of them limping, all of them weary.

Alfray grabbed Stryke's sleeve. "Did you . . . did you see that human, Serapheim, in the battle?"

Stryke hesitated. "I'm not sure. I thought I did, but—"

"But you're talking a load of bollocks," Haskeer finished. "Why would some wordsmith be farting around in a battle? Now let's get down there and find out how grateful these people *really* are."

*   *   *

Inside the gates, the cheering rose up at them like a wall. Someone pressed tankards into their hands. Others passed them chunks of bread and meat. People were capering about, singing, carousing or praying as the mood took them.

Standing in a circle of torchlight by the pool, Krista Galby shone as clean and bright as a candle flame. Beside her, one arm thrust through his green sash as a sling, Commander Rellston leaned exhausted against the low wall. As the orcs put on a bit of swagger, the two Mani leaders called out to them.

"Once again, Stryke, you have my gratitude," Krista said. "We couldn't have defeated them without you."

Rellston inclined his head stiffly. "Let me add my thanks. I don't suppose you saw that swine Hobrow, did you?"

"No."

Stryke made to carry on, but Rellston, determined to make up for his earlier mistrust, was summoning more flagons of ale. It was the first time the Wolverines had felt like turning down a drink.

As soon as they could decently get away, they headed towards the fiery column of light on the hill. Krenad's band watched them go, cracking remarks about orcs who couldn't take the pace. Haskeer wasn't the only one who wanted to wipe the smirks off their faces.

With all the celebrations going on in the town, the area around the temple was practically deserted. The Wolverines made no pretence at finesse. As they strolled towards the temple door, they suddenly swung into an attack. It was the last thing the guards expected. They fell without a fight.

"Tie 'em up," Stryke snapped, feeling a little guilty. But not enough to stop him storming inside.

On the threshold they halted. A votary lamp shone on the star on the column. It sat there, glinting steadily at them.

Coilla sighed and prepared to repeat her athletics of the day before.

"Fuck that," Haskeer growled. Hurling himself at the massive plinth, he toppled it.

It crashed to the earthen floor with a thud that echoed around the temple. With everyone down at the celebrations there was nobody to hear it but the Wolverines.

Stryke watched the many-spiked star rolling across the floor, bouncing a little like the ones in his dream. If it had been a dream. Quickly he caught it up, thrusting it into his belt pouch with the others.

"Right," he said. "Let's get the hell out of here."

They were in the stables before Coilla said, "Aren't you going to tell Krenad and the enlistees?"

Stryke tossed a saddle onto his horse's back a little harder than necessary. The beast sidled in protest. "They took their destiny into their own hands, just like us. They wanted freedom. They've got it. What they do with it is up to them." He jerked the cinch tight.

"Not if Jennesta comes down here in the morning it's not," Alfray reminded him. "She'll skin them alive."

"What do you want me to do? Try and hide with a whole army of orcs? Look, I don't like this any more than you do, but it's not as if we've got a lot of choice."

Alfray said, "We ought at least to warn them."

Jup backed him.

Coilla was more forthright. "Still scared you might start attracting a following?"

"What if I am?" Stryke whirled to glare at her. "I never said I wanted to take on Jennesta! Or anybody else for that matter. All I want is to get out of this in one piece. Let some other bastard wave the flag."

Alfray was disgusted. "So you're just going to leave Krenad to Jennesta's tender mercies? You're not the orc I thought you were."

Stryke stuck his face right in Alfray's. "Wrong. That's exactly my point. I'm a leader of a warband and that's all that I am. You're the one who's trying to make me into something else. Coilla, go and find Krenad. No, wait. I'll do it myself. The gods know what sort of hash you lot would make of it."

He found the enlistees' chief singing rude songs in a tavern.

"Come here." Stryke said brusquely.

Krenad was too happy, and too drunk, to get off the barrel he was sitting astride. "Wossamatter?" he mumbled.

Stryke hauled him outside and stuffed his head in a rainbutt until the deserter's eyes focused.

"Right. That's better. Now listen, Krenad. In case you didn't notice, the leader of the other army out there today was Jennesta."

"Nah. Couldn't have been. Was a silly human in a skinny hat."

Stryke held him under again until his sputtering grew frantic.

"Not him, you idiot! The other, *Mani* army. The one on the hill. With the harpies. Remember?"

Suddenly Krenad was completely sober. "Yes, sir. What time are we pulling out, sir?"

"*We're* pulling out now. You can pull out whenever you like."

"You mean we're going to split up and rendezvous later?"

"No. Look, Corporal, don't think we haven't appreciated you being around for the battle. But let me make it clear to you one last time. I'm not recruiting. I never have been recruiting. And tomorrow, when we're far away from that murdering bitch, I still won't be recruiting. It's every orc for himself. Got that?"

Later that same night, far across the hills as the stars wheeled towards dawn, the look Krenad had given him still haunted Stryke.

As the sun tiptoed above the eastern wall of the stockade, Krista Galby stood aghast in the temple.

One of the guards, nursing a sore head, was saying, ". . . and couldn't do a thing about it."

For a long minute the Priestess kept silent, staring at the toppled pillar. At last she sighed and said, "I don't imagine anybody saw them leave during the celebrations, but I suppose we at least have to ask."

She paused, schooling her face to calm. Almost dreamily she said, more to herself than to the men with her, "We have to find it and take it back. We built the temple to house it. It's been the centre of my life, and my mother's before me, and all the Priestesses' right back to the time Ruffett first settled here. In fact, if it hadn't been for his finding the star in the pool in the first place, he never *would* have settled here."

Unnerved by her preternatural tranquillity, the sore-headed guard mouthed into the silence, "Shall I ask the Commander to get a troop together?"

Krista gazed at him. "No. We don't want Stryke's band punished. Not after he saved Aidan's life." Her voice trailed away, to come back stronger as she added, "Round up all the temple guards who can still sit a horse. And saddle my mare for me."

The man was horrified. "You can't go, Priestess! Without the star we need you here more than ever."

"Who else can explain why we need it? Don't you see? I *have* to go."

In less than half an hour Krista was in the square before the northern gate. Sure enough, one of yesterday's widows had been mourning by her window. Long after the revelry had died away, she had seen a band of some thirty orcs riding out, with their horses' hooves muffled in rags. The gate-guard himself had no recollection of it. All he remembered was somebody coming over to offer him a drink and then clouting him on the back of the head.

Tenderly Krista hugged her son. Although he still couldn't walk far, his old nurse had asked one of the temple builders to carry him out to his mother. "Be good, Aidan, and do what Merrilis tells you. We want you to get strong again, don't we?"

The boy clung to her arm. "Don't go, Mother. Stay with me. There's bad things out there."

"There are good things too. And I have these fine guards to keep me safe. Don't worry, my love. I'll be back before you know it."

Krista looked at the old woman and the burly carpenter. "Take care of him for me. And Aidan, pet, you can stay here and see the Queen ride in. Won't that be nice?"

The chief of the temple guard came up and handed her the reins of a fine bay mare. Krista Galby blew her son a kiss.

Then she rode out with her followers as though a tidal wave was at her back.

*　　*　　*

Jennesta's chariot was decked with flowers.

She'd had the whirling knives removed. It wouldn't do to upset potential subjects by cutting their legs off. Now she nodded and smiled regally at the commoners lining the road to the gates of the squalid little town. What was it called again? Ah yes. Ruffetts View, or some such romantic notion. Though what was romantic about a collection of filthy hovels so far from her capital, she couldn't imagine. Behind her rode a fraction of her army, just to remind them who was who.

Men were cheering, girls were throwing late blooms, their bronze and crimson petals soon trampled into the muck. Jennesta glanced sidelong at Mersadion, sitting stiff in his saddle beside her, with his scars coming along nicely. At least he could see these unwashed peasants knew how to honour a queen.

Then a sunbeam lanced down, kissing the plume of magic with deeper fire. Her eyes were drawn upwards. The sight of such power brought a sly gleam to her eye. In her hands the reins fell slack and the horses slowed to a walk.

Their snorting brought her back to herself. Almost at the gates, a band of riders dared to cross her path. Without a word they pelted by at full gallop, hardly stopping to acknowledge her station.

But from within the gates came a roar as the townspeople saw her approach. Jennesta forced a smile to her lips and entered amid all the pomp she could muster.

In the very centre of the square was a muddy pool, rimmed with a low wall. Before it a man sat on a tall horse whose coat had been brushed until it shone. Despite the rapturous cheering, he seemed, of all things, to be glowering.

Rellston came back to himself with a start and bowed from the waist. His smile, Jennesta realised, was no more sincere than her own. But then, Rellston knew her reputation.

"Welcome," he said unenthusiastically. "And thank you for your timely aid."

Mersadion tipped his head a fraction towards the Queen.

Rellston took the hint. "Your Majesty," he added.

"Think nothing of it," Jennesta said, her voice like poisoned honey. "Do you happen to have a band of orcs in here? I'd like to . . . *thank* them personally."

"We did have. Your Majesty. But they've gone now."

"How disappointing," the Queen hissed. "Did they happen to say where?"

"No, Your Majesty. They left sometime in the night."

Mersadion edged his horse away, waiting for Jennesta's volcanic explosion of wrath.

It didn't come. With monumental effort the Queen said between gritted teeth, "And where is your High Priestess? Why is she not here to greet me?"

Rellston stiffened his back still further. "She charged me with messages of gratitude, Your Majesty. But I'm afraid she has . . . left on an errand. An *urgent* errand."

The Queen stared about her vindictively. Suddenly, out of the crowd, came a beefy man carrying a boy pickaback. Not in the least afraid, unlike the other cretins who stood gawping at her, the boy was a handsome black-haired charmer. He looked too cocksure to be the child of someone unimportant.

"And who is the urchin on that big human's shoulders?" she enquired acidly.

Reluctantly Rellston said, "It's the High Priestess's son, your Majesty."

"Is it? Is it indeed?"

He didn't like the way Jennesta eyed the boy with sudden sultry interest. It made his stomach turn to see her smile at Aidan with all the lasciviousness of a hired courtesan.

In the shelter of the copse at the head of the valley sat a tall, wiry human on a horse.

To either side of him bands of Unis were creeping away through the trees, but they didn't seem to see him. Nor did the few desultory scouts Mersadion had sent out on mopping-up operations.

The man's auburn hair gleamed in a dancing beam of sunshine. Thoughtfully, he observed the populace acclaiming Jennesta's triumphal entry into Ruffetts View.

Then he turned his stark white stallion and vanished into the woods.

20

Sickened, Rellston watched Jennesta all but drooling over the boy.

The Commander had felt obliged to offer her hospitality in the least damaged hostelry on the square. But the conversation wasn't exactly flowing, and she hadn't touched the goblet of mead the landlord had brought her. Aidan, however, was excited to be the centre of her Majesty's attention. But as the afternoon wore on, the young convalescent began to yawn.

Jennesta turned to him and said coldly, "I bore you, do I?"

"*No*, Your Majesty! I think you're beautiful."

She preened.

Aidan yawned again.

Forestalling the Queen's wrath, Rellston intervened. "Forgive him, your Majesty. He's not yet recovered from a wound he took two days ago. He was so badly hurt that for some time we didn't even expect him to live."

She flicked her fingers in contemptuous dismissal, not even deigning to ask how he had made so astonishing a recovery. Indeed, the Commander realised, she lost all interest as soon as he himself had stopped glowering at her.

Chagrined at being made game of, he remarked, "Your soldiers don't appear to have had much luck in searching for the objects you spoke of, ma'am. Perhaps you would care to join us in our meagre supper?"

Jennesta looked at him as though he'd crawled out from a latrine. "I don't think so," she announced imperiously, then stood up so abruptly her chair skidded across the floor of the inn. "I shall return to my army. A good commander sees to her forces."

Rellston bowed ironically but she missed it. She had already swept out.

As soon as her chariot was out of sight, he allowed his impatience and frustration free rein. He'd sneak out of Ruffetts if he had to. He'd do whatever he had to. But he couldn't leave the High Priestess out there with only a handful of men to protect her.

Late that afternoon, a ragged band of some thirty riders slowed to a walk. Before them lay a shallow incline but the horses were too exhausted to take it any faster.

Stryke looked at the slow, pewter waters of the Calyparr Inlet on his right. A brackish breeze rose to his nostrils. Not half a mile away lay the edge of the Norantellia Ocean but it was out of sight, behind a low, scrub-covered mound. That meant it was still several hours to Drogan Forest. He cursed and dismounted to give his horse a rest, leaning into the cold, sullen downpour as he plodded uphill.

"What's that?" Coilla whispered, pointing at a series of fast-moving shapes ahead of them.

"Unis, I think," Haskeer replied. "Fucking weather! Can't see a thing."

"They don't seem to have horses," Jup volunteered.

"Good!" Haskeer said. "Serves the bastards right, having to walk in the rain they've brought down on us. I'd kill every one of 'em if I had my way."

"We don't have time for that," Stryke wearily informed him.

At last they breasted the ridge and climbed back into the saddle. At a trot they rounded a rocky outcrop.

Stryke pulled up sharply. Straggling across the road were some twenty of Hobrow's routed troops, but they had no heart to fight. Swords drawn, they backed out of sight into the dripping shrubs. The band galloped on.

With enemies everywhere, the Wolverines made the best time they could. The further they went, the more frequently they passed dispirited custodians. A time or two Jup, riding scout, urged them under cover as bands of orcs rode past, but whether they were enlistees or loyal to Jennesta there was no way of knowing.

Eventually, as the day died into a sad grey twilight, Stryke reined. They seemed to have outdistanced all pursuit. Dark along the northern horizon lay the line of Drogan Forest. A watery moon peeped coyly through the clouds.

Not risking a fire, let alone being able to find anything that might burn, the Wolverines lay down to rest until full dark. Soon snores were sawing across the darkness. Every now and then came a slap as a sleeper flailed at a whining insect, but there were no larger beings within the sentries' sight.

Unable to nod off, Stryke wandered down to the Inlet. For a while he sat on the bank, throwing pebbles into the water. With the rush of the flow he didn't hear Coilla coming up behind him. The first he knew she was there was when she plumped down beside him, arms around her knees. "So what now, Stryke?" she asked. "Do we push on to Drogan and seek Keppatawn's hospitality again?"

"Perhaps. I don't know."

"Don't see where else we can go with Jennesta plaguing this end of the inlet."

"Then again," Stryke suggested, "that might be the first place she'd come looking for us. Gods! I haven't a clue what we do now."

Coilla threw a pebble of her own. It splashed into the Inlet. "What's most important to you?"

"Just staying alive, I think."

"What about the stars? Don't they matter any more?"

"Who knows? I wish we'd never started this." He leaned back on a mossy boulder.

Twin pebbles splashed into the water. After a time Coilla turned to him. "So what were you and Krista saying to each other back there while I was in the temple?"

"Nothing."

"You stood there talking for half an hour without actually saying anything? I don't believe it."

"The Priestess told me I might be a sport," he admitted reluctantly.

"A *what?*"

"In my case it's an orc who can feel magic." He took the stars out of his belt and flipped them between his hands as Coilla stared at him.

"That's not natural. Sorry, forget I said that. Did you tell her about the dreams?"

"I didn't have to. She seemed to think that was one of the . . . symptoms, whatever."

"Have you ever considered that pellucid might be responsible for them?"

"The crystal? Course I have. For a while I kind of half believed it was. Now I'm sure it isn't."

She changed tack. "What are we going to do?" she repeated.

"Beats me."

Stryke fussed with the stars, three in one fused piece and two still independent. Then he wearied of it and pushed them morosely across the grass.

For a time the two orcs peered through the moonlight at the puzzle. Neither of them could see how the instrumentalities were joined. The spikes melded them seamlessly together in a way that seemed to defy the laws of nature. There was something strange about the spidery mass, something that seemed to disappear into infinity.

Stryke took to fiddling with them again. Almost immediately the Ruffetts View star joined to the others with a dull click.

Coilla was impressed. "How did you do that?"

"I've no idea." He tried the last, the green, five-spiked one they'd lifted from Hobrow's settlement at Trinity.

"Here, give me that," Coilla finally said, and snatched it from him. She had no more luck than he did.

At last Stryke gave it up. He put the stars back into his pouch. "I guess we'd better be getting back. The others will be worried about us."

They hadn't taken a dozen steps when two figures stepped out from their hiding place and blocked their path.

Micah Lekmann and Greever Aulay.

"You're starting to make a habit of this," Coilla told them.

"Very nice," Lekmann said, his sword already naked in his hand. "Couple of lovers on a secret tryst."

"Shut up, Micah," Aulay snapped. "Why talk when we can kill?" He had his blade up too, its tip circling, as the orcs drew their swords.

*   *   *

On the banks of the Calyparr Inlet, two duels began.

Lekmann feinted at Stryke and slammed in a low hit. But the orc jumped his blade and spun to kick the bounty hunter in the knee. Lekmann swayed aside, almost overbalancing. Stryke's backhand stroke scored along his curving back, but Lekmann brought up his blade. It slithered along the edge of the orc's weapon, knocking it aside in a shower of sparks.

Meantime Coilla sprang back as Aulay drew something from under his coat. Then she watched, almost bemused, as he twisted his stump-cup free and plugged in a wicked knife. She leaped in at him but Aulay caught her blade on the long dagger he suddenly whipped out of his other sleeve.

"Gonna kill you, bitch."

"Is that with or without your other eye?" she returned, the tip of her sword just missing his cheek.

With a snarl of fury he lunged. His foot landed badly on the uneven turf and as he fell, his blade caught against a buried rock. It snapped off near the hilt.

Coilla slashed down at his overextended arm. Blood gushed out. Not even the cloth of his coat could stem the flow.

Again he roared. Scrambling to his feet and backing off, he pulled the knife-blade out of his stump and snapped a vicious, two-sided hook in its place. It looked like something a butcher would use to hang a carcass.

"This is for Blaan!" he yelled, slicing the hook towards her.

She let it swing past then jumped in to seize his forearm. Taken by surprise, Aulay couldn't resist as she turned the hook in on his guts and disembowelled him. She gave the hook another twist. "And this is for you, scumpouch."

His face was a picture of stunned disbelief as his lifeblood trickled away.

All this time Stryke had been trying to drive Lekmann down towards the river. The rough ground was proving more of a hindrance than a help, and the orc was too tired for dancing. Once on a better surface, Stryke let rip. His blade a blur of icy moonlight, he cut the stocky man's defence to shreds.

Lekmann disengaged, gasping for breath. But Stryke had had

enough. He sprang forward, his free hand slapping his thigh. The sound distracted his opponent for a brief second but it was enough. Stryke's sword plunged between Lekmann's ribs.

The orc put his foot on the bounty hunter's chest and pushed. Stryke's blade slid free of flesh and Lekmann hit the water with a splash. His greasy black hair fanned out around him as he lay face down in the wavelets.

The last Stryke saw of him, Lekmann was drifting along with the current, a deeper darkness spreading from his body.

Arms around each other's shoulders, the two orcs staggered back to their companions.

"I've had enough of quiet moments," Coilla muttered.

They were about to approach the cold, dark camp when Stryke suddenly pulled Coilla into the bushes. With the rising wind she couldn't hear a thing. But she was beginning to trust Stryke's hunches.

Moments later, a band of riders thundered to a halt on every side of the half-asleep orcs. There wasn't a thing the sentries could do about it. Stryke thought his band was getting sloppy, but that was hardly the point now.

From their hiding place Stryke and Coilla watched as Krista Galby stared down at the Wolverines. "Where is it?" she demanded bluntly.

"Where's what?" Haskeer blustered.

"Don't give us that!" the leader of Krista's temple guard said. He dismounted, never taking his sword's point from a line with Haskeer's throat.

"Jarno," the High Priestess warned. "These orcs were our allies. They fought alongside us. That old man there saved my son's life." She held her hands out to her sides, then dropped them in a weary gesture. "I don't want to hurt you. But you took something that belongs to us. It's important to us, a cornerstone of our faith."

Nobody said anything. The wind blew its uncanny chill across the clearing. In the bushes Coilla and Stryke felt their own brand of guilt.

"We *need* it," Krista added.

The uncomfortable silence stretched out.

Rellston's patience snapped. He had caught up with his Priestess's band several hours ago, and now a hundred men stirred restlessly around the Wolverines. The tension in the air was palpable. He dismounted and strode forward to stand over Jup and Haskeer.

Behind the screen of frost-browned leaves, Stryke whispered, "I knew we shouldn't have stopped."

Coilla nodded at the scene before them. "So why isn't your girlfriend keeping Rellston on a tight rein?"

"Maybe that's as tight as it gets. Come on," he said. "If they'd wanted to kill anybody they would have started by now. Let's go and talk to her before Rellston gets out of control."

They pushed their way out of the tangled leaves.

When Krista saw them, she said coldly, "You've done me two favours. Now I'll do you one. Give me the instrumentality and the Commander here won't exact a penalty for its theft."

"What if I need them?" Stryke said, and instantly could have cut his own tongue out.

"*Them?*" Krista returned. "You have more than one?"

"That's why we needed yours, don't you see?" He looked up at her, trying to read her face in the misty moonlight.

"No, I don't see." It wasn't Krista who spoke but Rellston. He stepped in close, staring down into Stryke's eyes. "If you've got another, you don't need ours. Give it back now." The tip of his sword came up to rest against Stryke's windpipe. "I knew I should never have trusted you. Orc trash."

"Calm down!" Krista insisted. She reached over and gently pulled Rellston's sword point clear of Stryke's flesh. "I'm sure we can solve this amicably."

"I'm not," Rellston growled, his anger barely in check.

All around them the Wolverines heard the restless sounds of men unsheathing weapons and climbing down from their horses. The orcs found themselves ringed by hostile townsmen. They began easing out their own weapons.

"Don't be more stupid than you have to be, Stryke," the Commander said. "You can't win. You're outnumbered. Just hand the thing over. That or I'll make you."

"Yeah?" snapped Haskeer. "You and whose army?"

"*This* one, lamebrain," a man called out from behind him.

One of the grunts suddenly cried out as someone shoved into him. The grunt shoved back. All around the camp scuffles were beginning to break out.

"Stop it!" Krista shouted. "*Stop it!*"

"Calm down!" Stryke yelled, trying to cool the situation. A swift clash of blades almost drowned his words. Louder he said, "You know us! We've fought alongside you. Do you really think a bunch like you can take us all?"

Rellston cursed, earning himself a hurt look from his Priestess. Then he said, "At ease, lads. Let them go for now."

"Wolverines, fall back," Stryke ordered. His blade hung loosely in his grasp, ready to attack at any moment as he covered his band's withdrawal.

Almost all of them had faded back into the night when one of Rellston's men suddenly called, "We can't let 'em get away! After 'em!"

Instantly, all was chaos.

"Don't kill anybody you don't have to!" Stryke shouted.

Their band's horses were out of reach, beyond the Mani force. Stryke yelled, "Let's get out of here!"

He plunged into the bushes at his back once more, ducking overhanging branches and trying not to step on any rotten twigs. It helped that the ground was so waterlogged; the thick layer of mud deadened any sound. Straining his senses to the utmost, he tracked his warband by intuition.

It scared him. But it worked. Soon he'd passed through the thin screen of trees.

He found himself facing an open meadow and, in the faint light that came before the dawn, he saw the darker lines of footsteps painted on the rain-silvered grass. Sprinting along in their wake, he crested a slight rise and saw yet another thicket, with the last of the Wolverines just disappearing into its protection.

He raced up the shallow slope and into the trees. "Should be safe here for a while," he panted.

"Oh yeah?" Haskeer grumbled from the dappled shadows not an arm's length away. "Take a look at that, then."

That was the far side of the copse. And beyond it lay Calyparr Inlet, dull grey beneath the cloudy morning.

Stryke spun around. On every side but one the waters rushed past the little headland on which they stood. And the Manis were streaming up across the meadow at them, Rellston in the lead.

"What we supposed to do now?" Haskeer shouted in frustration. "Swim?"

Jup snarled, "Just open your big mouth and drink it."

Oblivious of the Ruffetts View contingent bearing down on them, dwarf and orc glared at each other.

Coilla's temper snapped. "This is you and your bloody stars!" she yelled at Stryke, slashing her knife through the pouch at his belt.

The pouch fell apart. Almost in slow motion Stryke watched the single, five-spiked instrumentality spinning through the air. One hand belatedly trying to hold the pouch shut, he threw himself forward. But it was too late. The four joined pieces also tumbled out. His fingertips just touched it, sending it cartwheeling across a narrow clearing beneath the trees.

As the Manis burst into the woodland, Stryke saw the single green piece seem to leap upwards as it bounced off the stony turf.

Neither he nor the other orcs were aware of a sodden figure crawling out of the water and into the fringes of the wood.

As Stryke's scrabbling hands reached out to scoop up the single star, he knocked it flying straight at the rolling meshed pieces. Pouncing on his hoard, he scooped them up against his chest.

He felt more than heard them click together. The puzzle was complete.

Then reality took a step to the left.

21

Blackness.

There was a feeling of intense cold and Stryke's stomach clenched as though he were falling. His ears were ringing too much for him to hear anything. He reached out to save himself but there was nothing to grasp.

Nothing beneath his feet.

Nothing at all.

Then abruptly he landed.

He tumbled forward, his hands plunging into something icy and dazzling. The shock brought him to himself.

Snow.

Snow, under a blanket of cloud so light it was almost as pale as the whiteness beneath him. Where it had been night just heartbeats before, now it was broad daylight. Low on the southern horizon hung a bleached disc that must have been the sun.

Panic threatened to overwhelm him.

He called out but he couldn't hear himself shout. For a moment he was terrified he'd gone deaf. Then sound came roaring back. An arctic wind was shrieking around him, tearing at his clothing. Squinting, he could just make out the huddled dark shapes that were the other Wolverines.

Tottering to his feet, he felt the gale pushing at him. He scooped up the precious stars, which had again fallen from his grasp. Then he fought his way to Jup and Coilla, who were just making their first dizzy attempts at standing. Holding on to each other, they all began speaking at once. *"Where are we?"* and *"Where are the others?"* were the main questions.

Soon the other warband members staggered into view. They gathered in a slight depression nearby and it kept off the worst of the blast. Drifting snow blew in skeins over their heads and they had to bellow to make themselves heard.

"What the *fuck's* happening?" Haskeer yelled.

"I figure we're in the ice cap." Stryke's teeth were rattling with the cold.

"*What?* How?"

Coilla, arms folded across her body in a futile attempt to keep warm, said, "Never mind the philosophical debate. The real question is, how do we keep from freezing to death?"

Several of the warband had managed to snatch up packs or bedrolls as they fled from the Manis. Some, however, like Stryke and Coilla, had been too busy fending off the humans' attack. Even sharing their blankets and spare clothes there wasn't enough to go round.

"Jup," Stryke managed to say, through lips that were rapidly numbing with cold, "are you up to trying to find a high point? To get some idea of where we are?"

"Right, Chief!" The dwarf stumbled off into the teeth of the wind.

Huddling together for warmth, the rest of the orcs tried to work out what had happened.

"It's those bloody stars," Coilla muttered.

"If it was, they saved us from being cut to pieces," Alfray pointed out.

"Yeah, so we can freeze to death out here," Haskeer put in bitterly. "Wherever *here* is."

Stryke said, "It's got to be the northern glacier field. The sun was almost due south of us, but I don't know whether it's morning or evening now."

With stiff blue fingers he fumbled at his pouch, then remembered that Coilla had slashed it. Instead, he stuffed the stars inside his jerkin, just hoping he didn't fall on them if he tripped. At least he found his gloves tucked under his belt.

"We'll find out soon enough," said Alfray. "If we live that long." A gloomy thought struck him. "What if this is Jennesta getting her own back? It's just the sort of trick she'd play."

"No." Coilla's firm tone was marred by her shudders of cold.

"If she could do this, why didn't she just bring us all back to her camp so she could get her hands on us? And the stars?"

"This is pointless," Stryke decided. "We don't have enough to go on." He pulled his fur jerkin tighter around him. It seemed utterly inadequate in this place. "What provisions do we have?"

A short rummage amongst their salvaged possessions brought a few strips of dried meat to light, along with some crumbling trail bread and a couple of flasks of liquor. Not much to go around twenty-four hungry beings.

Trying to hide his disappointment, Stryke pointed to one of the grunts with a blanket. "Go up and see if you can make out what's happened to Jup, Calthmon."

Reluctantly the grunt waded up through the snowdrifts. He was almost knocked flying by the wind when he got above the rim of the depression. It wasn't that much longer before he returned with Jup following in his footsteps.

The dwarf hunkered down, rubbing his arms, then sticking his numb hands under his armpits.

"There's lots of crevasses," he managed through chattering teeth. "Some of them have got bridges of snow across them that won't bear an orc's weight. But I think I can see a way down over yonder." He nodded towards what Stryke thought was the southeast. "We're quite high up too." As he spoke, his misty breath crystallised on his beard.

"Anything else out there?" Stryke asked.

"Not that I can see. No smoke. No signs of any houses. I did think I saw something moving. But whatever it was, it kept well away."

"The sight of you would frighten anything with brains," Haskeer told him.

Jup didn't bother responding to the jibe. That in itself told Stryke how badly the devastating cold was affecting them.

"Right," he said. "First order of business is to get the hell off this damned ice sheet and find shelter."

In twos and threes they set off, with Jup trailblazing.

Within a short time the utter glaring whiteness had them seeing spots before their eyes. Limping, plunging through frozen crusts into snowdrifts as deep as an orc, they made their way east by south. It seemed like hours before they reached a bluff from which they could see quite a way around them.

Behind, to the north, towered the glacier, menacing in its vast solidity. It stretched from one side of the horizon to the other, a monument to the humans' stupidity in killing the magic of Maras-Dantia. Even at this distance it seemed to loom above them, threatening to crush them at any moment. As they watched, a segment of it fell away with a sound like thunder. Clouds of snow swirled into the air, and some of the heavier blocks must have bounced for half a mile.

Hastily they began to clamber down the southern face of the bluff. Not all of it was compacted snow. A huge granite boulder seemed to have been trapped in the ice. That made for solid footing, but the rock was slick with hoar-frost. Slithering and sliding, they cursed their way down to a plateau that couldn't have been more than a hundred and fifty feet above the frozen tundra.

They stopped to catch their breath. Here the rock kept the biting north wind off them. It also hid the intimidating bulk of the ice wall from view. That in itself was a blessing.

Below, in a curve between two thrusting glaciers, the land was flatter, pressed down, it seemed, by the weight of the advancing ice. It was grey with lichen and cut here and there by dark nets of streams that seemed threadlike at this range. Black against the horizon, there was a thin line that might or might not have been a forest. It was hard to tell with the sunlight glaring in their eyes.

"If we can make it down there," Stryke said, slapping his gloved hands to bring back the circulation, "we might find shelter. Fuel. Whatever."

"*If*'s the right word," grumbled Haskeer. "I'm an orc, not a fucking mountain goat."

But the trail down from the bluff wasn't as easy as it looked. Time and again they came up against a dead end, a drop so sheer they'd never make it.

"Is it me," said Coilla as they stared at yet another barrier, "or have you got that feeling there's somebody following us?"

"Yeah." Jup rubbed the back of his neck.

Stryke, when consulted, said he felt it too.

"Maybe it's one of those abominable snowmen," Coilla said, trying for levity.

"They're just myths," Alfray stated flatly. "What you've got to watch out for is snow leopards. Teeth the size of daggers."

"Thanks. I really needed to know that."

They trudged along in silence for a while.

"I see Jup's scouting is up to its usual standard," Haskeer muttered as they backtracked yet again.

The way was narrow, crowded with orcs changing direction. Even so, Jup managed to press himself back against the cliff, letting the others pass until Haskeer reached him. Jup's hand shot out to grasp the orc by the neck. "Think you can do any better, scumpouch?"

Haskeer shrugged Jup off. "A blind man on a lame horse could do better," he growled.

"Be my guest."

Haskeer leading, they set off again. It still seemed to take forever to get down to the barren plain. A grunt slipped, only his mate's grip on his jerkin saving him from certain death. After that they stumbled along holding on to each other's clothing.

The sun rolled low along the skyline, rather than falling from its zenith. Whether they had been travelling all day or only half of it was moot. What was certain was that night was now falling, and with it came a bank of cloud. It blotted out the sun, dimming the long twilight as it raced overhead. A fine, stinging snow began to fall.

"That's all we need," Jup muttered.

At last they were off the bluff. Haskeer jumped the final few feet and landed hard, grunting at the impact. Soon they were all milling on the level, staying in the lee of the glacier in the forlorn hope it might keep the rising wind off them.

"Did you see that?" Jup said. "That light over there?" He pointed south towards the edge of the ice tongue.

"Nothing there now," Haskeer said. "Maybe you imagined it."

The dwarf squared up to him. "I didn't *imagine* it. It was there!"

Before a fight could develop Stryke stepped between them. "Just a reflection, maybe? But it wouldn't hurt to find out. I'm not too keen on the idea of camping out if we don't have to. We'll give it half an hour. I want us to be settled before nightfall."

Without warning, the glacier gave a mighty crack. A block of ice the size of a house began to fall away at their heels. The orcs fled out across the tundra, slipping and staggering. At last, safely out of range, they puffed to a halt. Alfray, almost exhausted, was some way behind the rest.

"We're safe," Haskeer panted.

"No, we're not," Alfray contradicted. "Look!"

They followed his pointing finger. Racing towards them came a pack of creatures the size of lions. With their white coats they were almost invisible in the twilight.

"Form up!" Stryke yelled and pelted off towards Alfray.

Seeing Stryke dashing towards him, Alfray turned. The sight was enough to make anybody quail. With fangs like ivory sabres, five beasts were almost upon him.

Stryke cried out and whirled his sword. The lead snow leopard, startled, missed his spring. He rolled head over heels, his claws giving him purchase as he sprang to his feet.

Not taking his eyes off the monster, Stryke shouted, "This way!"

He had no time for more, because two of the leopards were now prowling around him, looking for an opening. The rest had swung round to herd the warband.

Stryke and Alfray backed away but one of the creatures bounded swiftly behind them. The smaller one feinted. At the same moment the dominant male leaped again. Distracted, Stryke almost fell to the raking claws but he got his sword up just in time. Blood sprayed from the beast's foreleg and with a savage scream the animal retreated.

For the moment the snow leopards circled just out of range of the orcs' blades.

In the meantime, Coilla was urging the rest of the orcs to shuffle closer in a body. Three of the leopard pack oozed sinuously around the defensive ring. The beasts faced a bristling wall of metal, but they blocked any attempt at rescuing Stryke and Alfray.

Again the pack leader came in at Alfray. Its claws spiked into his sleeve, knocking the old orc from his feet. But Stryke was there, his sword slashing out. The tip of his blade scored the beast's flank. A line of crimson darkened the creamy fur and the snow leopard bounded out of reach.

Stryke risked a glance. The rest of the warband were too far away to do him and Alfray any good. "You all right, old-timer?" he panted.

"Yeah. But enough of the *old-timer!* Keep 'em off a moment, will you?"

Stryke didn't have time to argue. Again and again the snow leopards darted in, playing a deadly game. One after the other, they feigned attack. He knew he couldn't hold them off forever, but dared not look away to discover what Alfray was doing.

Cursing his cold, stiff fingers, Alfray fumbled with the buckles on his healer's bag. At last, desperate, he managed to find a large stone bottle. Splashing the contents onto the wet snow, he pulled back just in time. Turquoise flames *whoomp*ed up, singeing his eyebrows. The cats sprang back, dazzled and disorientated.

"What's that?" Stryke gasped.

Alfray didn't reply. Instead he hacked through a roll of bandages, spearing the cloth on his sword then dipping it into the pungent blaze. He flicked his wrist and the fireball whisked through the air, landing on the younger leopard's back. Gouts of fire sizzled through its pelt to the fatty layer beneath.

Then the whole creature went up in flames. It gave an unearthly scream and hurtled out of sight across the darkling plain. Meantime the strange blue fire dwindled until it went out in a pool of slush at Alfray's knees.

Warily the other cat circled then sprang at the squatting corporal. Stryke dropped, holding his blade upright. As the beast passed over him he stabbed upwards with all his might. The razor-sharp metal sliced right through the leopard's belly. Stinking guts spilled out on the orc below. Hastily wiping his eyes on his sleeve, Stryke saw the pack leader collapse just beyond him in a heap of tangled limbs.

He drew a deep breath and coughed as the stench hit his lungs.

Alfray got upwind of him and managed to gasp, "Thanks, Stryke."

"Can you do that again?"

Alfray shook the bottle. Liquid sloshed in it. "Once or twice, maybe."

"Then let's go."

With no idea that salvation was trotting towards the warband, Coilla snapped, "Give me that!" and grabbed a grunt's sword.

She stepped free of the sheltering mass of bodies and pitched it at the nearest leopard. The blade ripped through its spine, leaving the beast running on its front legs for a moment before it realised its hind legs were paralysed. Coilla came up on it from the rear and thrust her sword through the back of its neck. Blood pumped out onto the snow.

Two to go. With Stryke covering Alfray, the healer mixed his fire-brew again. They took out one of the leopards but the last drops of potion weren't enough to ignite.

The remaining beast panicked. It leaped away from the blazing body of its companion and found itself almost on top of Stryke. It had no time to lower its bony skull. Head up, it left its throat exposed.

It ran straight onto his blade, its momentum driving its body almost up to the hilt. The monstrous teeth were just a hair's breadth from Stryke's face. With a look of surprise in its green eyes it keeled over, bloody froth bubbling from its neck.

Its fall twisted Stryke's sword from his grasp. Swearing, he drew back, groping for his knife, but all the leopards were dead. He sat on the flank of the one who'd taken his blade and said tiredly, "Butcher the damn things and take the fur. We might need it."

The long northern twilight lingered. The snow shower blew itself out, leaving stars shining in the north above the ice sheet. As the moon rose, the band headed back for the lee of the glacier, finding enough light reflected from it to guide their steps.

Jup, in the lead, suddenly stopped. "See?" he crowed. "Told you I saw a light!"

Ahead of them stood a gigantic ice palace.

*　　*　　*

As they got closer they slowed in awe.

The palace was immense, its slender spires gleaming in the moonlight, its whiteness making the glacier behind it seem dirty. Flying buttresses cradled the central face in elegant curves. Statues stood in dark niches, impossible to make out beneath their coating of crusted snow.

It might have been a spectral vision of beauty if it had not been for the lights twinkling in the turret windows. Hardly distinguishable from the stars, the yellow glow of candles gleamed fitfully behind arched casements.

"If we'd come here in daylight we'd never have seen it at all," breathed Coilla, gazing raptly upwards.

"Now that we have, let's get inside," Jup suggested. "This wind's freezing my bollocks off."

The Wolverines walked towards it. Jup zigzagged towards it but it didn't seem as though anybody was guarding the place. The huge gates stood open. Dwarfed by them, the orcs crept into the courtyard.

In its centre was a frozen fountain. White mounds proved to be trees snapped off by the killing cold.

"This place must have been wonderful before the ice sheet struck," Coilla said softly.

Haskeer wandered by. "Yeah. Before the humans fucked everything up. Anybody found a way in?"

They hadn't. Jup and the others scouted around, sticking close to the walls, but they couldn't find an entrance.

Haskeer suddenly bellowed, "Hello? Is anybody there?" His voice echoed back and a small avalanche slithered from a roof. But nothing answered.

Then a sharp wind slashed snow into their faces. Everything disappeared under a smothering blanket of white.

They were trapped outside in a blizzard.

Jennesta cursed and pushed back from the barrel of congealing blood. It didn't seem to be working. Her thoughts circled like a treadmill, ruining her concentration.

She suspected that the High Priestess of Ruffetts View had gone tearing off to track down the Wolverines, but she had no idea why. It was just that there was no other reason Krista Galby could have had for absenting herself from the royal audience.

What did it matter? Let the human wear herself out in sweaty pursuit. But first she needed information.

If only this vat of gore didn't keep scabbing over so quickly. All she kept seeing was white.

She snapped her fingers and a cowering flunkey handed her a goblet of spring water. Then, sighing, the Queen went back to her labours.

At first she thought it still wasn't functioning. Then she heard something. Someone. It was a woman's voice, pitched high, droning monotonously.

Sanara was talking to herself again.

Bending closer, Jennesta saw the vision expanding.

Sanara stood up, partially blocking a window. Now Jennesta realised what had happened. Her focus had been a little too high. All she had seen was the icy waste beyond. She realised she'd been seeing snow all along. Something—a distortion in the aether, perhaps—had been pulling her out of alignment. Now she shifted her viewpoint lower to see her sister's face.

On the point of speaking, Jennesta stopped. Ignoring Sanara completely, she stared past her and out into the night. Something was moving out there, something that exerted a strange pull on her.

Through the swirling flakes she saw the Wolverines huddled in the corner of a frozen courtyard. Some of them seemed to be covered in blood. Just the sight of it made her mouth water but she controlled her appetite. It wouldn't do to lose her concentration now.

Jennesta sent her essence floating among the spinning whiteness. "How the hell did they get there?" she asked herself. "It must be—"

She broke off. It didn't matter. The important thing was that she knew where they were.

Not a mile from the silken tent where Jennesta plied her necromancy with the blood of the Uni slain, Krista Galby and her weary troops rode in through the gates of Ruffetts View.

Night was falling and the flickering torches were haloed by the rain.

The High Priestess cast a glance up at the pearly geyser of magic, feeling a pang of guilt, but there would be time enough to renew the invocations in the morning. Right now she just wanted to see Aidan, have a hot bath and go to bed.

She bade goodnight to Rellston and made her way home. Jarno, the leader of the temple guard, accompanied her, but peeled off at her gate for his own house. She stepped inside her walled garden.

Then she paused, a sick feeling hollowing her stomach. At this time of evening there should have been lights inside, smoke from the chimney and cooking smells as Merrilis made dinner. She should have been able to hear Aidan's piping voice, perhaps raised in song or arguing with his motherly nurse.

She could hear nothing. And the house was dark.

"When I catch up with Merrilis I'll give her a piece of my mind," she told herself. "What does she mean by letting the fire go out?"

Forcing herself to face the worst, Krista Galby walked up to the door of her home. She didn't feel at all like the High Priestess now, more like a frightened mother.

The door swung open at her touch. The house seemed very empty now that its function as a hospital had ended, the patients moved elsewhere or dead.

She moved from room to room, searching the place, calling, "Aidan? Merrilis?"

But only echoes answered her. The hearth was cold and her home was deserted.

What could have happened? Surely if Merrilis had stepped out for a minute, Aidan should still be there? But what if something had happened to him? If his illness had come back? If he was . . . dead? Instantly the picture formed in her mind of his lifeless body laid out in the old wooden temple that was still used. There'd be candles around his waxen corpse, their yellow light burnishing his ebony hair.

Past rational thought she ran out into the street, pounding on her neighbour's door. The house was empty.

Tears burning hot tracks down her cheeks, Krista drove herself onwards, asking every passerby, "Have you seen my son? Have you seen Aidan?"

But nobody had.

22

The orcs huddled together under a heap of blankets and bloody snow leopard skins.

In the corner of the courtyard, the wind found it harder to get at them. To either side deep drifts were beginning to form against the walls and snow whirled down around them. It was difficult to see more than a couple of feet.

There came a lull in the blizzard. Cautiously Stryke poked his nose up. A rift in the clouds showed a dark scatter of stars.

"Jup," he said. "Take a couple of grunts and find us a way in. If we have to stay here all night, we'll freeze to death."

Haskeer grinned blearily. "Yeah, earn your keep."

"For that, Haskeer, you get to go with him. Now shut up and get a move on before it really starts snowing again."

Picking two of the taller grunts, Jup and Haskeer set off through the thigh-deep whiteness. The rest of the Wolverines burrowed down again, their breath mingling under the furs. All things considered, it was a pretty chastened band who speculated idly on who, or what, had built this vast castle in the middle of nowhere. Coilla concluded that anybody who could design such breathtaking beauty must possess a gentle soul. The males were derisive of that.

Eventually they heard muttered curses above the hiss of windblown snow. Taking another peek, Stryke said, "Good. They're back." He called, "Did you find anything?"

Haskeer answered. "Yeah! There's a doorway round the back. We'd never have found it if there hadn't been a light inside. I've left the grunts trying to get it open. If nothing else, it's more sheltered than this."

In a welter of elbows and trampling feet, the warband hauled themselves upright, the lucky ones slinging the furs and blankets around their shoulders. The strange, muffled procession set off, retracing the footprints in the deep snow. All around them eerie silence held sway.

Keeping to the flat part above the steep bank of the palace's moat, they came to where the towering glacier gripped the structure. But Jup turned the angle of the wall and there was a deep crack in the ice. It was lit from within by a soft golden glow.

"You sure this is safe?" Alfray said, remembering his terror as he tried to outrun the avalanche.

"Safe as houses," Haskeer replied gruffly. "You think you can do any better, help yourself."

Going deeper into the cleft, they heard hammering and swearing. Sure enough, as they clambered round a bend, there were Gant and Liffin, using their swords to hack at the ice sheathing an arched doorway. Soon a dozen orcs were at it. In the confined space the noise was appalling. Icicles and chunks of compacted snow began to patter down on them.

"Stop!" Stryke cried as a dagger of ice narrowly missed his head. "This is stupid. We're going to kill ourselves before we get in." He summoned Alfray through the crowd. "Have you got enough of that potion to set fire to something?"

"Maybe." He dug in his medicine bag. "It's just liniment that Keppatawn's healer gave me. He warned me against it mixing with water."

"Now we know why. Everybody! Get out anything you've got that's dry and might burn."

The Wolverines began pillaging their knapsacks. Stryke set a couple of them to shredding ancient shirts and some of Alfray's precious bandages. Combined with the tinder from everyone's tinder boxes, it soon turned into a heap that stretched across the centre of the massive doors.

Alfray upended his flask of liniment and Stryke melted some snow in his hands. As it dripped down onto the makeshift kindling, peacock flames flew up. Soon a blaze was going, billowing thick smoke. Those at the front fell back to keep from choking. The grunts at the rear rushed forward to soak up some of the priceless heat. A chaos of pushing and shoving ensued.

All at once a massive slab of ice began to lean out over them. The Wolverines fled back past the corner of the crevasse.

With a great grinding roar the ice fell away, smashing onto the floor of the archway and filling the air with frozen missiles. At last the noise died. The orcs crept forward.

And stopped.

The great upswept leaves of the doors were exquisite. Made of some substance like frosted glass, they were inlaid with golden vines. The warm yellow light shone brightly through them. They were so cunningly wrought that the fruit and flowers seemed to stand out, though when Stryke dared to touch them they were smooth and flat.

As his fingers caressed the silken surface the doors opened on noiseless hinges. Almost reverently the orcs stepped over the sodden ashes and crossed the threshold.

In a hushed group they looked about them wonderingly. They were inside a vast hall whose vaulted ceiling rose so high it dwindled in the distance. Darkened doorways opened off it, and curving staircases of pure white marble. Every inch of the place was carved, but thick shadows stopped them making sense of the shapes. The air held a sad scent of autumn.

Jup moved forward cautiously. Even his soft footfalls were enough to set off echoes that came back to them, weirdly distorted.

"I don't like this place," Coilla whispered.

Her words reverberated startlingly.

Stryke whipped around, feeling as though some unseen presence was creeping towards him. But there was nothing there. As he turned back to lead them deeper into the hall, he saw something halfway up the sweeping stairs.

It was a white-robed woman.

Poised tensely on a landing, her black hair flowing around her like a cloak, she seemed dwarfed by the chamber's immensity.

"Who—" He cleared his throat. "Who are you?"

She didn't answer him directly. In a thin, pure voice she said, "Leave this place. *Quickly*."

"Into the storm? We wouldn't stand a chance out there."

"Believe me," she implored, "the danger is worse in here. Go while you still can." Suddenly she gasped, cowering against the banister. Sheer terror twisted her beautiful face as she cast a glance behind her. "Go! Go *now!*"

"What's the matter?" Stryke said, moving to the foot of the staircase.

She didn't answer. He began climbing the steps, taking them two and three at a time.

When he reached her, he offered, "We'll protect you."

The woman gave a despairing laugh. "Too late."

Out of the doorway behind her came a pack of hideous creatures.

They looked like everybody's idea of demons, the tormenting spirits said to rule the halls of Xentagia with whips of fire.

Down in the hallway more of them poured out to surround the orcs.

No two of the creatures were entirely alike. Slithering, sidling, striding on spider-claws, their bodies subtly changed shape, moment by moment. Even their faces melted and reformed, now with one eye, now with tusks and snapping beaks. Some had wings like a bat, but without exception they all had fearsome claws. Their grey skin rippled continuously. They were so hideous Stryke couldn't look at them without courting nausea.

They must have numbered fifty or more.

Every member of the band viewed them with superstitious dread.

"Throw down your weapons!" the woman urged.

"We don't do that!" Haskeer responded.

"But it's your only chance! How can you fight them? The Sluagh won't kill you if you don't attack."

Stryke backed away from her and slowly retreated down the steps to his band. If he was to die, he didn't want it to be alone. Two of the beings undulated down the stairs behind him, snapping their fangs at his heels. As he reached the other Wolverines, the Sluagh reared above him, mouths agape.

"Do it!" Stryke snapped, throwing down his sword. It rang like a bell on the stone. His Sluagh guard drew back a little, coiling and uncoiling.

Outnumbered, the orcs reluctantly laid down their arms. The

creatures stayed close until every last weapon rested on the floor at their feet.

"I thought the Sluagh were just fireside tales," Coilla whispered.

"I thought they were creatures from hell," Alfray said.

Looking at them, it was easy to believe that they were.

Fear surrounded them like a miasma. Out of their dark aura thoughts slicked into Stryke's mind. He whirled around but could not locate which creature had spoken.

"Give us the instrumentalities," it said.

From their startled reactions, it was obvious that the whole band heard it, if *heard* was the word.

Stryke said aloud, "I don't have them."

This time the voices seemed to come from behind. *"You lie! We can feel their power."*

"They reach out to us."

"They call to us."

"Give us the instrumentalities and we may let you live."

Dizzy, the Wolverine leader fumbled beneath his tunic. His hands were clammy, slipping over the spiky mass. Nevertheless, he managed to break one of the stars from the meld. The rest were stuck as solidly as if they'd been soldered together. He touched the single one. It was the five-spiked green object he had first rescued from Hobrow in Trinity. It seemed an age ago. Gingerly, he held out the group of four.

A snaking tentacle plucked it from his grasp.

Something like a sigh whispered echoing to the ceiling.

"And the other? Where is the other?*"*

Stryke swallowed. "We haven't got it."

"Then you will suffer for all eternity."

Agony gripped Stryke's head. He felt like a firebrand had been thrust inside his skull. Clutching his temples, he fell writhing to the floor. Around him, the other Wolverines were equally in pain.

"Wait!" Stryke managed to say. "I meant we haven't got it *here*. But we can get it."

The anguish lessened. *"When? When can you get it?"*

"It's with the rest of our band," he lied. White heat jolted through his brain. "They're coming, they're coming," he gasped.

"How soon?" the hissing voices demanded.

"I don't know. We got separated in the blizzard. But they'll be here. Tomorrow, if the storms hold off."

"Then we can kill you now."

"You do that and you'll never get it!"

"If they are coming here they will not be able to stop us taking it."

"If we don't give them the signal, they won't enter this place." He directed a cold gaze at the nearest Sluagh. "I'm the only one who knows what it is," he bluffed. "And I'll die before you get it out of me."

On the fringes of his mind Stryke heard them conversing but he couldn't make out what they said.

At last a pug-faced demon said, *"Very well. We will let you live until tomorrow."*

"At dusk," another one said. *"If we do not have the instrumentality by then, you will never leave this place alive."*

"And you will loathe every heartbeat that you live."

The Sluagh herded them up the stairs. As they passed the white-robed human, she started as though coming awake. Silently she fell into step between Stryke and Coilla.

It was a long way up. The woman was visibly shaking with exhaustion by the time they reached the top. No doubt they were in the top of one of the turrets that had reared so high above the plain. If anything, the air was even chillier up here than it had been down in the hall.

As the first Sluagh reached the tiny landing a door swung open without a touch. Stryke saw that it had no handle, no latch. He stored the information for later, gazing into the circular chamber beyond. Again it was filled with golden light though he couldn't see where it came from, unless the air itself was glowing. Once more the walls were covered with carvings, hideous gargoyles this time that looked like Sluagh captured in stone. Long yellow curtains hung at random from the arched ceiling.

Now the demons crawled aside. Taking a deep breath Stryke led the band through the gilded door, the woman collapsing immediately with her back against one of the drapes.

Once they were all inside, the door slammed shut. Abruptly

the pain left them. Jup ran back to where the door had been. Before he even touched it a wall of light threw him halfway across the crowded room.

Alfray came to kneel beside him. "I think he's just stunned. At least I hope so. His heart's still beating."

They fanned out, looking behind draperies for another exit. There was nothing but endless carvings. For all their probing they couldn't find a key, a knob, anything that would let them out.

Eventually they gave up and slumped down to rest. The woman hadn't moved.

Shivering in the unnatural cold, Stryke wrenched a curtain loose and wrapped it around him like a shawl. Some of the grunts did likewise.

"You knew there was no way out, didn't you?" Stryke said, coming to sit beside the woman.

"But I still hoped you'd find one." Her voice was high, ethereal. "And now you want to know who I am."

Coilla came to squat at her side. "You bet we do." Her tone was harsh.

"Can't you see I'm just as much a prisoner as you are?"

"You still haven't told us your name," Stryke said.

"Sanara."

Realisation took a few seconds to soak in. "Jennesta's *sister* Sanara?"

"Yes. But don't judge me by her, I beg you. I'm not like her."

Coilla snorted. "Says you!"

"How can I convince you?"

"You can't." Coilla stood and walked away.

"You are not like her," Sanara told Stryke. "I sense the power of the land flowing around you, like the orcs of olden days. But that child has none of it."

"I wouldn't call Coilla a child to her face," he replied shortly.

She shrugged miserably. "What does it matter? At sundown tomorrow she'll be dying just the same. You didn't really think the Sluagh would let you go, did you?"

"I'd hoped they might."

"Dream on, orc. They thrive on the pain and suffering of

others. They'll spin your life out in endless agony until you're begging to die, but still they'll feast on your terror."

"My name's Stryke. If we're going to die together, we ought at least to be on first name terms."

In answer she waved a languid hand.

"So, Queen Sanara," he said at length, wishing he could pierce her shroud of indifference to find some answers that might get them out of here. "Am I supposed to call you Your Highness or something?"

As she shook her head a faint perfume of roses wafted from her hair. "No. I haven't been called that in a long time. Not since the humans ate the magic of my land."

"*Your* land?"

"My land. My realm." She smiled sadly. "Jennesta had the southlands, Adpar the nyadd domain. This is what my mother willed to me. But you see what it has become: a desert of snow and death. Whole cities lie imprisoned beneath the glaciers. Once this land was rich and good, a place of forests and meadows. Every single one of my subjects fled or perished when the ice swept down. It started when I first came to the throne, coming closer day by day. How could they not think it was my fault? Do you know what it's like, to be blamed for the death of the land? Can you imagine how sad it is seeing your friends, your lovers, turn away from you and die one by one?" Her eyes misted. "I tried to counter it but I have very little power now. All that remains of my capital, Illex, is this fortress."

"Why didn't Jennesta help you?"

She made an all too human sound of derision. "If you know my sister you know she doesn't help anybody but herself. That was why Mother sent her away. She hasn't been back to my realm for generations of your kind."

"Your mother?"

"Vermegram."

"The sorceress? *The* legendary Vermegram of old?"

Sanara sighed and nodded.

"Then you're not as human as you seem."

"Indeed not, no more than my brood sisters. But Vermegram

died many winters ago. And I was watching when you saw Adpar die by Jennesta's power."

"How did you know I was there?"

She gazed at him mysteriously. "I've had my eye on you for a long time, Stryke." But when he pressed her, she wouldn't say why.

Not liking where the conversation might be heading, Stryke fell silent for a time. At last he said against a background of orcish snores, "How come you let the Sluagh in?"

"What a strange question! How could I keep them out?"

Stryke conceded the point with a grimace. "Where did they come from? And why are they here?"

The former Queen sighed again and lay down, pillowing her head on her arm. She looked up at him with limpid green eyes that reminded him a little of Jennesta's. There was no scaling on her face though, just soft, milky skin. "They're an ancient race from the dawn of time. What they are is evil incarnate. You think Jennesta's bad? Compared to them, she's just an amateur. And they're here because they knew that sooner or later Jennesta would find out about the instrumentalities. They've held me prisoner here for longer than you've been alive. And I'll still be here when the Sluagh are chewing on your bones. They thought that she would seek them out—"

Trying not to dwell on the image of his demise, Stryke said, "She tried."

"And then the Sluagh would bargain me for them."

"Why do they want them?" he asked. "What do you know of the stars? The instrumentalities?"

Sanara seemed to look through him to some place that only she could see. Lost in her reverie, she hardly noticed Jup and Coilla drifting back to Stryke's side.

"They want to use them, of course," the pale Queen said dreamily.

"What for? What do they do?"

"All together they exist throughout the planes."

Jup thought he grasped some of that. "Is that what they do then? Move about from place to place? Is that how we got here?"

Sanara brushed her hair back from her face. "They don't

move. I told you, once they're joined they exist throughout the planes."

The Wolverines looked at her, baffled.

"Throughout space," she said. "Throughout time."

"And they brought us here?" Coilla asked, casting a bitter glance at Stryke.

"I presume so, if you did not walk."

"And is that time thing why it was night when we left and day a heartbeat later when we arrived here?"

The Queen nodded.

"Is that what they're for, then?" Jup wondered before Coilla could get another word in.

Sanara shook her head. "No. That's just . . . a side effect. It's not their main function."

"What *is* their main function?" the dwarf said.

"It is beyond the mind of mere mortals." She didn't seem to have taken to the dwarf.

Before any of them could respond, the perspective on the far wall shifted. It seemed to retreat into blue distances before snapping back into place.

Then a figure stood where before there had been nothing. He was swathed in shadows that obscured his face but could do nothing to disguise his height.

"On your feet!" Stryke cried. "Intruder!"

The orcs had no weapons. But there were almost thirty of them and only one opponent.

Besides, they were ready for a good fight.

23

The figure stepped out of its cloak of shadows, hands held up in a gesture of peace.

As it approached, the room's buttery light showed its face, revealing a human. The silver embroidery on his jerkin glinted and his belt held no scabbard.

It was Serapheim.

One or two of the warband shuffled back, casting sideways glances at each other and reaching for their swords, only to remember their sheaths were empty.

But their surprise was nothing compared to Sanara's. She turned even paler, if that were possible, and one hand went to her throat. Green eyes wide with shock, she sagged into Stryke's arms.

Serapheim moved forward to take her weight, folding his arms tightly around her. Her hands encircled his waist and she rested her head briefly against his shoulder. Almost at once she recovered her poise, drawing herself up as if to maintain some long-forgotten protocol. "I thought you were dead," she told him.

"You know this human?" Stryke said.

Serapheim and Sanara exchanged a look, laden with a meaning the Wolverines couldn't read. Then she acknowledged the question with a nod.

"How did you get in here?" Coilla asked, blazing suspicion.

"That's not important now," Serapheim replied. "We have more significant issues to deal with. But what I can tell you, I will. You must trust me."

"Yeah," Haskeer sneered cynically.

"I might be your only hope," the human said, "and you have nothing to lose by hearing me out."

"We do if you're going to spout nonsense again," Jup replied. "We've no time for your fairy tales."

"It's true I have a story. But it's no yarn spun by wordsmiths."

Serapheim took in their expectant faces. "All right. How about, you've stolen a world?"

While the rest puzzled over that, Coilla exclaimed, "What? *Us?* That's rich coming from your kind."

"Nevertheless, it's true."

"This does sound like another of your tales," Stryke judged. "You'd better explain yourself, Serapheim, or our patience gets revoked."

"There is much *to* explain, and you'd do well to attend. That or face death at the hands of the Sluagh."

"All right," Stryke relented. "Long as you keep it quick and clear. What's this about stealing worlds?"

"What would you say if I told you Maras-Dantia wasn't your land?"

One or two of the grunts laughed derisively.

"I'd say you humans haven't got it all yet."

"That isn't what I meant."

Stryke was beginning to show his frustration. "What *do* you mean? And no more riddles, Serapheim."

"Let me put it this way. Do the Sluagh seem to you as being of this world?"

"They're *here*, aren't they?" Jup countered.

"Yes, but have you ever seen anything like them before? Up to now, did you believe that they existed? Or were they the stuff of legend to you?"

"Take a look around Maras-Dantia," the dwarf advised. "You'll see one hell of a lot of very different races. Apart from being plug ugly, what's special about the Sluagh?"

"In a way, that's my point. How do you think this land came to be shared by so many different races? Why do you think Maras-Dantia's so rich in the kinds of life it holds? Or should I say Centrasia?"

"Only if you want your throat cut!" a grunt called out. "This is *our* land!"

Stryke shut him up. Turning back to the human, he said, "What kind of a question is that?"

"Probably the most important one ever put to you." He held

up a hand to still their response. "Bear with me, please. You'd understand me best if you concede for a moment that all the elder races came here from elsewhere."

"The way the humans came here, you mean, from outside?" Alfray asked.

"In a sense. Although we mean different things when we say . . . *outside*."

"Go on," Stryke said, intrigued despite himself.

"The elder races came here from other places. Believe that. And the artifacts you call stars are part of how they came here."

"This is making my head hurt," Haskeer complained. "If they, us, don't come from here, then where?"

"I'll try to put it in a way that can be grasped. Imagine that there are places where only gremlins dwell. Or pixies, nyadds and goblins. Or orcs."

Stryke frowned. "You mean lands where only these races live? No mixing? No humans?"

"Exactly. And were it not for the instrumentalities, none of you would be here at all."

"Including humans?"

"No. We have always been here."

An uproar ensued. Stryke had to use his best parade-ground roar to stifle it. "A story like that's all the better for proof, Serapheim. Where's yours?"

"If my plan succeeds, you'll have it. But we can't afford much more delay. Will you let me finish?"

Stryke nodded.

"I understand your disbelief," Serapheim told them all. "This place is all you've ever known, and your parents before you. But I assure you, much though you believe we humans are the invaders, we are not. The truth of what I'm saying lies here, in Illex, and if we help each other it can be confirmed. Perhaps used to your advantage."

"Put some flesh on the bones," Coilla said, "and maybe we'll see it differently."

"I'll try." He took counsel with himself, then continued, "That truth has to do with the abundance of magical energy here in what you call Maras-Dantia." Many present resented his choice of words, but they held their tongues. "Or at least the richness of energy there once was. Generations ago, as you know, humans began crossing the Scilantiun Desert in search of new land, and settled here, leaving their homes on the other side of the world. They came on foot and on horseback, trekking across the burning sands, leaving their dead behind them with their graves to mark the way. Only the strongest came, the most determined. With this lush continent providing everything they could possibly want, they had no need to breed cautiously. If this patch of earth was exhausted, why not move on to another? After all, who else was using it? Nobody who *settled*. Nobody who put down roots in one spot, or mined its riches. So they built, and they dug, and they burnt the forests for their crops. Most of them having no sensitivity for the earth energies, for the magic, they had no idea of the havoc they were causing. To them magic was just some sleight of hand, a little conjuring, a firework or two. Only a very few, who took the trouble to acquaint themselves with the elder races, knew this not to be so. That was the origin of the Manis."

"And you are one such," Alfray divined.

"I'm not a Mani, or a Uni either, come to that. But yes, a practitioner of the art. One of the few my race has produced."

"Why are you telling us this? Why involve yourself with our troubles when you could just stay clear?"

"I'm trying to rectify wrongs. But this isn't the time to say much more. Soon the Sluagh will wake from their slumbers in the ice. We have to act."

"Can you get us out of here?"

"I think so. But simply trying to escape isn't my plan. And where would you go in this icy waste?"

"What *is* your plan?" Stryke wanted to know.

"To retrieve the stars and have them effect your leaving this place."

Sanara spoke up then, reminding them all of her presence. "The portal?"

"Yes," Serapheim responded.

Stryke frowned. "And what's *that*?"

"Part of the mystery I seek to open to you. But first you must lend your sword arms." He looked around at them. "Let me guide you," he appealed. "If you see no benefit in what we're doing, what have you lost? You can abandon me and go your own way, brave Illex's fury and try to reach warmer climes."

"When you put it that way," Stryke reasoned, "I'm inclined to go along with you." He allowed his tone to become menacing. "But only so far. Any hint of treachery, or if we don't like the way things are heading, we will go it alone. And you'll be paying with your life."

"I expect no less. Thank you. Our first task is to get to the palace cellars."

"Why?"

"Because there lies the portal, and your salvation."

"Believe him," Sanara added. "This is the only way."

"We'll go along with it for now," Stryke agreed. "But talk of cellars is all very well when we can't even get out of this room."

"I can take myself out, the same way I came in, but nobody else," Serapheim said. "The dying of the magic has depleted my powers as much as everyone else's. And no, I can't open the door from the outside. Only the Sluagh can do that. I'm sure I can find how in their minds, but I don't want to get that close to them. My idea is to find and lure one in here. But once I have, it'll be your task to overcome it."

"They can be killed then?"

"Oh yes. They are not invulnerable or immortal, although they are incredibly tough and long-living."

"What about their pain weapon?"

"That's where Sanara and I come in. We'll assault it mentally while you attack it with whatever comes to hand. Though of course you have no weapons."

"We're good at improvising," Jup assured him.

"Good. Because you must not underestimate the Sluagh's powers. You must attack without let and in numbers."

"Count on it," the dwarf said.

"Then ready yourselves. It begins."

Serapheim moved back into the shadows.

He kept to them once he was outside the room.

His boots made no sound in the thick dust of the corridors.

He opened door after door, ready to flee at an instant's notice, but as he suspected the Sluagh had not yet risen from their icy cradles.

At last, as the sky began to lighten the south-east, he felt the rumble in his mind that meant Sluagh were talking nearby. Flattening himself against a wall's marble slabs, he peered around a corner.

There were four of them, their grey shapes shifting from one ugly conformation to another.

Cautiously, Serapheim withdrew.

He had hoped for fewer, but there wasn't time to search anymore. Steadying his resolve, he stepped boldly out in front of them, touching fingers to brow in a mocking salute.

Instantly pain whipped out at him. But he'd been expecting it and took to his heels.

They came after him. Two had fearsome insect limbs that propelled them swiftly along the passage. A third threw out scaly wings that creaked as they slapped the air, but the passage was too narrow for it to extend them fully. Instead it barely rose, floating ponderously above the last one, a slug-like being that left a shining, rancid trail.

Serapheim outpaced them. Pelting along past open doors, he headed through a long, dusky gallery. At the end of it he leaned panting against the wall.

Now he had reached the spiral staircase. It was like a nightmare, running throughout eternity up a neverending flight of steps, and with each stride he was slower. His pursuers were catching up to him. Serapheim was beginning to think he'd never make it.

He gasped and forced himself to greater speed, lungs burning, legs as heavy as logs. It was all he could do to put one foot in front of another. He grasped the banister and used that to haul himself higher. A glimpse over his shoulder showed him clawed tentacles reaching towards him. Terrified, he put on another spurt. Around and around the spiral stairway he staggered, thinking he'd never make it close enough to the room to transport himself inside. The Sluagh were almost at his back.

Pain lashed through his mind. His shields were weakening.

*   *   *

Inside the room at the top of the tower, Stryke looked around. They'd tossed their furs and their packs against the walls, clearing a space to fight in. There was nothing resembling furniture and all their weapons had been taken from them.

"We can always throw Jup at 'em," Haskeer suggested. Coilla swatted his head.

Stryke had an idea. "You and you!" he snapped at a couple of grunts. "Climb up those gargoyles and bring down the curtain poles. And the curtains as well, come to think of it. Then stand ready."

Time seemed to pass too slowly. The Wolverines were beginning to eye Sanara suspiciously, wondering if she was in on some plot with the human.

At last Serapheim wavered back into view, like a mirage turning to solid flesh. He took a couple of tottering steps and dropped to his knees on a pool of yellow cloth between Coilla and Haskeer.

"They're coming," he panted. "Four of them."

A heartbeat later the door burst open and slammed back against the wall. The entrance wasn't wide enough to accommodate more than one of the beings at a time. Stryke saw the others out on the landing, one hovering in mid-air on its rippling grey wings.

"Now!" he yelled.

The two orcs hurled their poles like javelins. They were flung hard enough to penetrate even the Sluagh's unnatural skin. Sticky black ichor began to flow from the nearest one's chest. It swayed in the doorway, blocking its companions as it changed from a six-limbed wolf to a snake that dropped in coils to the floor.

A gang of grunts rushed in and commenced stomping it enthusiastically. Their boots began to steam, but that didn't stop other orcs from joining in. One and all, they took out their frustrations on the slithering serpent. Little by little its strivings ceased, though its beady eyes continued staring at them implacably.

Flickers of pain rippled through the warband's minds. Then

the winged Sluagh arrowed down at them with its pinions folded behind it like a stooping hawk. Coilla and Haskeer sprang into action, holding the curtain up between them. The monster flew straight into it. Quickly they wrapped it then Haskeer dropped onto the bundle with all his weight. Another orc thwacked the netted Sluagh with his rod of iron. Foul stains began to seep through the yellow cloth.

All that time Serapheim hadn't moved from his place beside the door. Now he stepped forward, Sanara at his shoulder. Fingers intertwined, they raised their hands in a gesture that was far from peaceful. There were no flashes, no puffs of coloured smoke. In fact, nothing seemed to happen at all.

And that, Stryke realised, was the point. Though the two dead Sluagh were still in the room, the others hadn't entered.

"Cover us," commanded Serapheim.

Stryke and the others moved forward despite the fierce aches that rolled and retreated through their skulls.

Jup took a peek and bobbed back inside. "They're having a powwow about half a dozen steps down. No others about."

"Any advice?" Stryke asked the humans.

Serapheim shook his head. "No. Now that we've pushed them that far back, it's up to you."

Wielding his metal rod like a club, Stryke led the band out in a wild charge.

Orcs catapulted off the banisters and into a headlong dash down the stairs, or whipped round on the inside of the stairs with one hand around the newel. The Sluagh fled, the slug undulating obscenely and his insect-like fellow stilting away at high speed.

Down and down the band went, spiralling endlessly inside the shaft of white stone. Stryke raced down the middle of the stairs, flailing his curtain rod in hissing arcs that would have broken the neck of a dragon. But the Sluagh moved surprisingly fast. They kept well out of range in what seemed like heedless flight.

Nevertheless, when the demons reached a landing, they whipped round. Agony flared through the orcs' heads. Most of them fell to their knees, or rolled down the stairs in a whirl of limbs. Now, half the warband were helpless on the level space, unable to back up without trampling their companions.

Coilla's head smacked into the piers of the banister, her helmet tumbling down into the void. Sick, racked with pain, she lost hold of her weapon and it too clanged downwards from step to step until it wedged itself in an angle far below.

Now the Sluagh began to advance. "Use your magic, can't you?" Stryke grated.

"We are!" Serapheim yelled back. "That's why they're coming so slowly."

"Call that *slow?*" Squinting through the whorls of light that tormented his sight, he swung his weapon once more and hurled it with all his might.

It tangled in the insect-Sluagh's segmented legs. The monster tripped and stumbled, not even its six limbs enough to steady it until it bowled off the landing and down a half spiral. It landed on its back, rocking and waving its legs in the air, unable to turn itself in the tight space. An enraged fire roared in Stryke's ears.

Then the last monster reared to an awesome height. It seemed to draw itself up and out until it almost filled the width of the stairs. Before their horrified gaze it changed from a slug-like thing. Its lower part forked, forming claws on its massive hind feet, while a tooth-filled mouth gaped in a soundless roar. Tentacles sprouted from its torso once more, wreathing around it. The taloned paws clicked on the stone, then it built up speed and charged.

Haskeer threw himself flat on the floor, face upwards, the curtain rail pointing straight at the charging beast just as Stryke had done with the snow leopard. The Sluagh extended its legs and strode over him untouched. It used its tentacles to hurl other warriors aside, not even bothering to watch where they fell. Intent on reaching the humans, it trampled on the unconscious orcs in its headlong rush.

That was its undoing. The beast's talons caught in a Wolverine's jerkin. Just for a second, but that was long enough to unbalance the monster. Crashing to lie dazed on the stairs, it couldn't even shapeshift. A groaning trooper rolled over, yellow cloth draped over his arms. Another came to help him and just as the demonic creature jackknifed upright, the curtain billowed over his head.

At once it too began to transform into a snake but, by now, enough of the orcs had recovered to give it a pounding. The stink of its black blood rose thickly into the air. Steaming faintly through the fabric, it died.

With that, the dazzling pain was lifted from the band's minds. Most of them were able to stand, or at least to hang on to a less injured comrade. This time it was Jup who led the way, advancing one step at a time on the overturned insect that obstructed the stairs beneath them. He brought down his weapon on its neck but the metal clanged off its jointed scales. Acid filled the Wolverines' minds again, its keenness quickly dampening as Serapheim and Sanara came down as close as they dared.

"You dare to challenge me?" the Sluagh shrieked into their minds, so fiery it darkened their vision. It renewed its frantic scrabbling but still couldn't right itself.

"Damn right, I dare," Jup snapped, hammering at it blindly.

His blow tipped it over a fraction. Before the dwarf could blink it was spidering straight up the wall above his head. A scorpion tail slashed down at him.

That was its undoing. The extra weight made it bottom heavy. It skidded downwards and landed on Haskeer's rail. Its own weight drove the makeshift spear through its body. The top burst through the dome where its skull should have been. A pulpy mess fountained out, raining down in sticky black globs.

Stryke sank down onto a step, leaning his back against the balustrade. "Good work, everybody."

The orcs were rejoicing, slapping each other's backs or just grinning as they tottered to their feet.

Serapheim spoiled it. "Don't celebrate too soon. It's almost dawn and we still have to make it down to the cellars."

24

Trying not to get any of the disgusting ichor on them, orcs and humans clambered down over the Sluagh's body. It wasn't easy on the spiral stairs, but they managed it, eventually reaching the floor of the great hall where they were captured the day before.

Crouching behind the railing, Stryke watched a dozen Sluagh going about their business. In ones and twos they were heading sluggishly in different directions. All would be lost if just one decided to come their way, but miraculously none did. Then the last group had crossed into one of the shadowy arches and none of the hideous creatures was in sight.

Serapheim hissed, "Quick! This way!" and they set off at a lope across the vast hall. They made for another staircase on the far side and began running up it.

"Hold on," Stryke said. "I thought we were heading for the cellars. Why are we climbing stairs?"

"A small diversion for weapons." He motioned for the orcs to be still as they reached a wide gallery overlooking the hall. "See that corridor about halfway along? It leads to the armoury. Stay alert. There are other Sluagh about."

Indeed there were. Once more, grey-skinned horrors were going about their daily activities below. Crouching, the Wolverines kept in the shadows as they tiptoed along the gallery.

Typically, the way to the armoury was a maze of stairs and passages. But at least this part of the palace seemed to be deserted. The yellow light was patchy here, the dust deep underfoot, muffling their footsteps.

Serapheim and Sanara drew to a halt by yet another bend. The man made a gesture to Stryke, who peered round at what lay ahead.

"Two of them, either side of a door," he reported in a whisper. Using the band's hand signals, he split his forces. Jup, Coilla and

Haskeer were to take the further creature. He and Alfray would lead half the grunts against the gryphon-headed monster nearest them.

This time the fight was brief. It was much easier to attack when all the warband could come at the Sluagh at once. The creatures themselves were pinned against the wall with no place to retreat. Despite the lancing headaches it didn't take long before the monsters were no more than an oozing mush.

Stryke gestured to Serapheim to go first. The humans opened the door onto an armoury like no other. More than half the weapons weren't even things the orcs recognised. They headed straight for the ranks of spears and pikes clipped to the wall. As they went further, daylight from an iced-up window reflected off a heap of metal on the floor.

"My axe!" Jup exclaimed joyfully, sweeping up the butterfly-headed weapon. Soon, each of them had back the arms the Sluagh had taken the day before. In the more exotic part of the armoury Sanara and Serapheim helped themselves to bulbous tubes of what looked like glass.

Pillaging done, Serapheim guided them down a different way. Stryke got the feeling that this had once been the servants' area, for the stairs were of rough granite and the walls were plain.

The air, already cold, began to grow damp. There was a smell of decay, and mould began to appear in corners. It was beaded with frost. The square windows no longer showed daylight but the strange blue of the glacier outside. Then there were no more windows and they realised they were underground. Eventually they found themselves in the palace's cavernous cellars. Creeping through a labyrinthine series of tunnels, they had to watch their footing, for ice slicked the stone. Ahead there was more of the yellow glow. The band stopped while Jup scouted cautiously. "There's eight Sluagh in front of the weirdest doors you've ever seen," he reported.

Again Stryke detailed the band to separate targets. With swords, pikes and axes the Wolverines felt much happier about attacking a large force. Even so it was a bloody struggle. The Sluagh came at them with claws and webs of agony. Serapheim and Sanara edged round the walls, trying to get behind the monsters. When they did, their glass tubes began to glow eerily. Bolts of light shot from them. There was a deafening explosion and suddenly it was raining Sluagh blood. Then it was all over.

"Useful weapon," Coilla remarked admiringly.

Jup had been right. The doors formed a circle set deep into the rock. Once again, there was no obvious handle but ten little dimples were set into the frosty metal. It was Sanara who matched her fingertips to the depressions and pushed.

The doors swung back. Ducking, Serapheim led them inside. They found themselves in a doorway that must have burrowed ten feet through the rock.

Inside was the portal.

It stood, a platform canopied in granite, within a ring of standing stones. Here and there jewels winked in spiral patterns on the floor of the dais. Others glimmered from all the stones but one, which looked somehow dead. Some of the gems were the size of a pigeon's egg.

Haskeer bent down to caress a huge sapphire but recoiled, a look of confusion on his features as coloured lights swirled up into the musty air.

There was no hint of what the portal might do, but Stryke shivered all the same.

Coilla stopped. "What the hell is *that?*"

Serapheim said absently, "Something that's stood here for a long time."

The last of the warband crowded into the room. "Secure these doors," Stryke ordered.

It took five grunts to do it. When the doors slammed shut a hollow boom shook the ground. Now the only light was the rainbow flicker from the jewels.

When it was done, Stryke turned to the man, who stood with his arm around the Queen's shoulders. "All right, Serapheim. It's time you explained things."

Serapheim nodded. He and Sanara sat on the edge of the jewel-encrusted platform. "Think of this world as being just one of many others," he began. "An infinite number. Many of them would be more or less like this one. Many more would be unimaginably different. Now picture all these worlds existing side by side, stretching out forever. As though they had been laid out on an endless plain." He checked the faces of his audience to see if they were following. "Long ago, something fractured this plain. It left a gap, if you like, a corridor that beings could use, like mice between the walls of a house. This portal is one entrance to that corridor."

"So it was made by mice then?" Haskeer piped up.

The brighter ones took a moment to explain it to him in a more basic way. Finally he seemed to understand.

"Who found the portal, I don't know," Serapheim continued. "Nor who might have adorned it in this way. That was long ago, too. But the sorceress Vermegram, mother of Sanara here, and Jennesta and Adpar, rediscovered it in more recent times. She also discovered that with the aid of her magic she could actually see some of the other plains, as Stryke unwittingly has."

"What do you mean?" Stryke said.

"Your dreams."

"How did you know I've been having dreams?"

"Let's just say that I am attuned to the energies of the earth, and knew you had made that connection."

Stryke was speechless.

"The point is that they were not dreams. They were glimpses of another place. A place of orcs."

"I had another dream recently," Stryke confessed. "It wasn't about the . . . orc world. I was in a tunnel at the start, then I broke out of that into a strange landscape. Mobbs was there." By way of explanation he added, "A gremlin scholar we met."

All this was news to the Wolverines, and Stryke could see he'd have some explaining to do later.

"That dream would have been inspired by the instrumentalities' power too," Serapheim ventured. "The tunnel represents death and rebirth."

Stryke didn't know about that. He only hoped Mobbs would find peace.

"But the point is that this portal has been here since before the ice came," Serapheim went on. "The Sluagh's numbers have been dwindling since the climate changed. They have tried in vain to activate the portal in order to return to their world."

"And you want to *stop* them getting away?" Coilla said.

"I want to stop them having control of the portal. It would enable them to send conquering hordes into untold other worlds. That's unthinkable."

"This is a load of horse-shit," Haskeer sneered. "You said you'd *show* us something."

"That's why I brought you to the portal," Serapheim replied. "Without the stars, I can't activate it. But the vortex within can be made to give a view of the parallel worlds." He moved to it and did something at one of the stones. They couldn't see what.

Stryke's jaw dropped. There were gasps and exclamations.

A picture that moved, like a window on to a landscape, had appeared in the air. The scene it showed was unmistakably the world of Stryke's dreams. The verdant hills and valleys, mighty full-leafed forests and sparkling blue seas. There were hundreds of orcs battling in the sort of raid that blooded young warriors. Then views of orcs in rough-gamed carousing before roaring fires.

Stryke's strongest thought was that he wasn't insane. What he had been seeing was a vision of . . . home.

The picture dissolved in a glitter of golden motes and was gone.

"Now do you see?" Serapheim said. "*All* the elder races have their own worlds." He stared straight into Jup's eyes. "And that includes dwarfs."

Now the scene showed orc hatchlings laughing as they practised with their first wooden swords, their birth-mothers looking on proudly from the doors of longhouses.

"In the beginning the portal was just a kind of window that let Vermegram see as you are seeing. But as she observed the orc world, she conceived the idea of using your naturally militaristic race for her own ends. At last she . . . found a way to bring a number of your race through the portal, activating it with magic. She wanted to establish an army of super warriors she could control by sorcery." He paused. "The next part you might not favour. Something went wrong and the orcs she transported were altered in the process. They remained just as warlike but their intelligence was diminished, a defect that continued through subsequent generations."

Haskeer thrust his jaw out belligerently. "You saying we're stupid?"

"No, no. You're . . . as you should be. The one who is a throwback is you, Stryke. A sport. You're the closest to the orcs on your race's home world."

"If orcs were . . . changed going through that thing in the first place," Alfray pointed out, "what's to stop it happening again? Is it safe?"

"Quite safe. The accident, shall we call it, happened because of Vermegram's inexperience with the portal. The instrumentalities prevent it occurring again."

Suddenly they heard a heavy pounding on the door.

"It will take time for even them to get through that," he judged. "Let me finish quickly. Vermegram meant only to bring orcs into this world. But activating the portal meant that beings in other worlds who had access to their own portals could also come here. I suspect that for most it was an accident. In its natural state, an invisible cleft in space and time, a portal, is often impossible to detect. It would be easy to be swept into one unawares."

"Just a minute," Coilla interrupted. "Vermegram was a nyadd, wasn't she? So how could she be here before the—"

"No, she wasn't a nyadd. She was human."

"But everybody says . . ." She cast an eye at Sanara. "Her offspring. They're symbiotes, aren't they? Where did they get their nyadd blood?"

"When they were in her womb. A nyadd colony had been established here by then."

"I don't understand."

"She found a way to insert nyadd seed into the forming child she was carrying."

"Why would she do such a thing?"

"What interested her was the fact that nyadds always give birth to triplets. She wanted that too, and thought she had isolated the tiny particle of nyadd matter that caused it. Shortly after, the sole child she carried mutated into a triple birth. This was done as much in a spirit of curiosity as out of a desire for three offspring." He gave Sanara a sympathetic smile.

"She sounds a charmer," Jup said.

"What did she want orc warriors for?" Stryke asked.

"To help her defeat a warlock called Tentarr Arngrim. He had watched power corrupt her, make her cruel and meddlesome. When he tried to stop her, she turned on him. The irony was that Vermegram and Tentarr Arngrim had once been lovers. They even had a child together before she became evil." He pulled Sanara into an embrace. "*This* child. My daughter."

There was general uproar.

"This is too fucking much," Haskeer complained.

"You're asking us to swallow a lot, Serapheim," Alfray told him.

Serapheim held up his hands for silence, and got it. "I am Tentarr Arngrim, once a mighty sorcerer, now much reduced." The sheer force of his words held them. "It was I who made the instrumentalities, who fashioned them from alchemy and tempered them with magic when the power was full in me."

"Why?"

"To make it possible for the elder races to return to their home worlds, should they so choose. For that I needed control, and in essence the instrumentalities were a key. I brought them here. But Vermegram had her warriors steal them and hide them away. That led to war between us. She died with only a fraction of her powers, but I was depleted too. By the time my body had recovered from its wounds, the instrumentalities were scattered, the magic all but lost. The stars became stuff of myth, and I was never able to make any more. I have waited aeons for them all to be found. But I knew they would be. I knew when the right beings came they would hear the music of the stars."

There was a renewed clamour at the door. They hardly noticed.

"I told you they were singing to me!" Haskeer exclaimed.

"If they were," Serapheim told him, "then you must have a brain . . . *something* like your captain's. There's a bit of sport in you too, Sergeant."

Haskeer grinned, full of himself.

"That could be the most amazing thing you've told us," Coilla remarked dryly.

"I don't say your comrade has as highly sharpened a mind as Stryke—"

"No," Jup said, "he's a dolt."

Haskeer gave him a lemon-suck look.

"*Unpolished diamond* might be a better description," the wizard concluded diplomatically.

Again the Sluagh assaulted the door. Thick as it was, a tiny crack appeared between its two halves. "Now we must move for the other stars and activate the portal." He could see that doubts still lingered. "What is there for you here? You must accept that this world belongs to my kind, whatever their faults or virtues."

"And leave humans to wallow in their own shit after all the destruction they've wrought?" Coilla remarked.

"Perhaps it won't be that way forever. Things just might improve."

"You'll understand we find that hard to believe."

Thin, worm-like tentacles began to creep through the gap in the doors. Sanara aimed her weapon at them. The bulb of the tube filled with light, then shot out in a beam of golden power. A shriek echoed through the warband's minds. The worms had turned to smoking shreds.

"Some of you will need to stay and guard the portal," Serapheim suggested, "while the rest go after the instrumentalities."

Haskeer liked the sound of that. "Now you're talking. All this jaw-wagging's doing my head in."

Stryke picked the grunts to stay with the portal, along with Sanara and Serapheim, and added, "You'll be here too, Alfray."

"Leaving the oldest out of the action again, is that it?"

Stryke drew him aside. "That's why I want you here. We daren't lose the portal. It's too important. I need somebody experienced to steady this crew. You can see how jumpy some of them are."

Alfray seemed to accept that.

Sanara joined them. "Hear me on this, Stryke. I know you won't like the idea, but you should leave the one star you have with me." She headed off his protest. "It will help me draw power from the portal to keep your men safe. Besides, now you're attuned to the song of the stars the Sluagh will not be able to hide them from you. But they could if your mind was filled with this one's presence."

She was right, he didn't like it, but it made sense. He took the star from his jerkin and handed it to her.

As the raiding party formed up, Coilla and Serapheim found themselves standing apart from the others. Something was troubling her. "You talked about redeeming yourself. But from what you've said, this whole mess was Vermegram's fault."

"Not all of it. You see . . . Well . . . you were loyal to Jennesta at the time and . . ."

"Spit it out."

"I commissioned the kobolds to snatch the first instrumentality from you," he confessed.

"You devious *bastard*," she hissed.

"As I said, you were loyal to my daughter then. Or at least I thought you were. I'd just made the decision to try re-gathering the stars and—"

"And using the kobolds seemed a good idea. But they double-crossed you, right?"

He nodded.

"So you got us into this in the first place. Well, you and our own lack of discipline after the raid on Homefield." She glanced at the band. "I can imagine their reaction to *that* piece of news. But I won't tell them until we're through this. If we *do* get through. We've got enough on our plates."

He quietly thanked her.

At that moment, the door gave. Serapheim hurried towards it. Sanara joined him. They levelled their glass weapons at the mass of Sluagh trying to get in. Blasts of searing yellow light sliced into the creatures. There were hideous shrieks. A stink of burning flesh filled the air.

"That's the last of these," Serapheim announced, throwing his glass tube aside, "they're drained. You're on your own now, Wolverines."

"If we get separated, meet back here," Stryke instructed them. "Now *move!*"

The band set out, wading through the mass of pulpy bodies.

Stryke wasn't aware of the strange mental tug that called him back to the star he'd left below until it faded. By that time they were on their way out of the cellar's labyrinth.

But as they ran up yet another flight of steps, he was aware of the first notes of a celestial song somewhere above. Seconds later, they reached another dimly lit corridor, with a large open chamber in front of them.

It was filled with demons.

Something like a triumphal chord crashed into his mind as Stryke led the charge.

The Sluagh never knew what hit them. They seemed deaf and blind to all but the joined stars, sitting on a table in their midst. Spears sliced the air, lancing through demons hanging down from the ceiling. Jup's axe bit deep into a shaggy grey back while Coilla decapitated another Sluagh with a frenzy of hacking.

Now the monsters began to fight back. Perhaps a dozen of them turned, their limbs flowing into new and deadly shapes. One, a serpent, instantly formed a dragonlike maw and whipped round, its hideous jaws salivating. Once again the Sluagh began to pour their foul acid pain into the orcs' minds. Some of the grunts toppled, hands battened to their ears, but the rest fought grimly on.

At last the remaining Sluagh gave way before the Wolverines' onslaught. Most of the demons were bleeding darkly on the floor. Scattered limbs were still twitching. The last two monsters had been pushed back towards the far wall. In one last desperate welter of claws and fangs they tried to get back to the stars, but half the Wolverines were between them and their goal. Defeated, dripping ichor from a score of wounds, they turned and fled, undulating rapidly down through an open stairwell.

As they disappeared, so did their gift of pain. The Wolverines pulled themselves together, astonished to find themselves alive. Haskeer turned to scoop the stars from the table.

They weren't there. Neither was Stryke.

*   *   *

In the mêlée, he had seen a Sluagh snatch the stars and scurry to an open balcony with them. Dextrously, the creature began climbing the outside of the palace. Now Stryke was bounding up a staircase, a spear in his hand, hoping to catch up with it.

Above him the stairs split, leading off in two different directions. And there was the Sluagh, spidering downwards on the farther side, not twenty paces from him. With all his strength he hurled the spear. The creature dropped like a stone.

It was wounded, not dead. Pushing out a claw to the stars it had dropped, it tried to pull them closer. Stryke dashed forward and sliced its limb clean through. But the Sluagh wasn't finished. It shot out a blade-like appendage and gashed his shoulder. Stryke quickly retreated, clutching the wound, and watched the thing die. Then he grabbed the stars and ran.

As he reached the point where the stairs branched he heard sounds of combat. He threw himself into the shadows. A pack of Sluagh slithered into sight, and they were retreating from a greater force. He blinked through the gloom, trying to make out who. Then he saw them.

Humans and orcs.

Manis.

Stryke was almost shockproof after recent revelations, but this new twist took some beating. The only comfort he could take was that, although he had no idea what they were doing here, the Manis would put more pressure on the Sluagh. Allies, but not necessarily friends. In a moment they would reach the joining of the stairways and block his downward flight. Tucking the stars into his jerkin, he took the only course open to him and went up.

Closing his mind to the pain of his wound, which was troublesome but far from the worst he'd taken, he paused to listen at the next landing. The echoing clash of weapons was fading away. Presumably the Sluagh and Manis had gone down, the way he'd intended travelling. Moving quietly, sword at the ready, he continued climbing upwards, looking for a way to outflank the strangers and get back down to the portal.

He thought he must be somewhere near the palace's broad

front. By a window, he stopped to knot a tourniquet round his upper arm. Then movement outside caught his eye. He peered through a broken pane, past the fringe of icicles on the casement.

A seething army sprawled across the wintry plain. Columns of soldiers were heading towards the palace. Others clustered around the entrance below.

The sound of halting footsteps drew him from the sight. He turned, his blade up and ready.

Somebody limped out of the gloom.

Stryke couldn't believe it. Nor did he exactly need it at a time like this.

"What does it take to kill you?" he said. Though in truth, the one he addressed looked half dead anyway.

"It ain't that easy," Micah Lekmann replied. Insanity blazed in his eyes. "I don't know how I got here, or you neither, but I can't believe I've been given another chance to kill you. Maybe there are gods after all."

The man was clearly deranged. Stryke thought of him tracking them through snow and ice in his skimpy clothes. His eyes were red-rimmed, the fingers of his left hand blackened with frostbite.

"This is crazy, Lekmann," he said. "Give it up."

"No way!" His sword lashed out, low and dangerous. Stryke jumped out of its path. The bounty hunter, a crazed grin plastered on his face, kept coming, thrusting again and again with the fury of a madman.

Stryke parried and fought back. His counter-blows seemed feeble for all the effect they had. Lekmann drank them up and kept coming. They battered it out, up and down the corridor, Stryke desperate to find an opening and end another distraction he didn't need. It wasn't proving easy. The human seemed to have dispensed with fear and caution. He fought like a ravening beast.

Suddenly Stryke was blinded by an intense flare of light. Bewildered, he pulled back out of range, straining to recover his vision. When it returned there were motes in his eyes, as though he'd been staring at the sun. But that didn't obscure what he was looking at.

Lekmann stood in front of him, quite still, his sword at his feet.

He had a gaping hole in his chest. Broken ribs showed white in the spilling gore. The edge of the wound was charred and smoking. Through it, Stryke caught a glimpse of the wall beyond.

Almost casually, Lekmann lowered his head and stared at the damage. He didn't look as if he was in agony, though he must have been. The expression he wore was one of dazed affrontedness. Then he disgorged a mouthful of blood, swayed like a drunk and went down, face first. Smouldering.

As Stryke gaped, trying to make sense of what had happened, another figure moved from more distant shadows.

Jennesta's mouth twisted in an ugly grimace as she saw him. The scream she let out, equal parts rage and triumph, cut through him like a blade. Her hands came up, presumably to deal him a similar fate.

He was already moving. Even so, he barely managed to avoid the dazzling gout of lightning she flung at him. It struck a carved pillar a hairsbreadth away, pulverising the marble and sending shards flying.

Stumbling, in pain, he vaulted down the next staircase. Another bolt hit, over his head, bringing down a plaster shower. He half jumped, half fell, down the broad flight of steps. In a corridor off the landing below, Mani troopers were battling more Sluagh. He dodged past them and pounded down the next flight, letting the song of the stars guide him back to the portal.

The odds were against him making it.

25

"Do you sense something?" Serapheim asked, without looking round.

His back to the gemmed portal, he stared about the chamber. Nothing moved, though faint vapours were rising from the downed Sluagh at the entrance.

"Yes," Sanara answered. "They're close."

"Who are?" Alfray said.

As if in reply, one of the grunts near the door signalled urgently. Seconds later, the hunting party ran in.

Alfray scanned their ranks. "Where's Stryke?"

"We were hoping he was here," Coilla told him. She explained what had happened.

"For what it's worth, I have felt no disturbance in the life web indicating he might be dead," Serapheim declared.

Haskeer said, "What?"

"A question of sensitivity. There's no time to explain now. The stars?"

"I don't know," Coilla admitted. "Maybe Stryke has them. They went missing the same time he did. But listen! There's a whole army of Manis storming the place. They're engaging the Sluagh."

"You confirm what my daughter and I already suspected," Serapheim revealed. "Jennesta's here."

"Gods!"

"We have to find Stryke," he continued. "And do what we can to sow discord in the ranks of her forces. Jennesta mustn't get the upper hand."

"I'll take a group to search for him," Jup offered.

"Sanara will go with you. From this end I should be able to

channel power through to her." He turned to his daughter. "Are you willing, Sanara?"

"Of course."

"How's she going to help us find Stryke?"

"She's not. But if your troops can get her to a safe place as near the interlopers as possible, we might be able to do something about Jennesta. Trust me."

"But what about *Stryke?*" Coilla demanded.

"Perhaps you'll find him while you're escorting Sanara."

"That's not good enough! We can't abandon one of our own."

"Then I suggest you split into two groups. But you must hurry!"

"Reafdaw!" she shouted. The grunt came over to her, blood trickling from a cut above his ear. "You stay here with Alfray. Haskeer, we'll go after Stryke, all right? The rest of you, follow Jup."

The Wolverines readied themselves. Some shared their last dregs of water, others patched their wounds.

Then Haskeer, as officer in charge, barked the order and the two groups set off again.

Trying to reach the cellars drew on all of Stryke's reserves of skill and stamina.

With Manis and Sluagh battling at every turn, there was chaos in the palace. He tried to stay clear of conflict, sidestepping fights and skirting any challenging him.

His luck ran out when he rounded a corner and found himself confronted by a pair of orcs. For a second he dared hope they might think he was part of Jennesta's horde. But they obviously knew his face.

"That's Stryke!" one of them yelled.

They advanced, weapons raised.

He tried diplomacy. "Whoa! Just hold it." He lifted his hands to mollify them. "There's no need for this."

"There is," the first grunt told him. "You're top of our mistress's wanted list."

"She was my mistress too. You must know she's no friend of orcs."

"She fills our bellies, gives us shelter. Some of us have stayed loyal."

"And how loyal do you think she'd be to you, when it comes to it?"

Stryke thought the one who hadn't named him seemed to waver.

"She'll reward us for your head," the first trooper said. "That's more than you'd do, if we let you keep it."

"We shouldn't be fighting each other. Not us, not orcs."

"The brotherhood of orcs, eh? Sorry, not this time." He began moving forward, adding, "It's nothing personal, Captain. Just doing my job."

The second trooper called out, "Careful, Freendo, that's Stryke you're up against! You know his reputation!"

"He's just an orc, ain't he? Like us."

He charged in, slashing with his sword. Stryke tensed, ready to meet him. But even now he wanted to incapacitate, not kill. If that was possible. From the corner of his eye he saw that the other grunt was holding back.

Their blades clashed, the sound ringing through the dusty corridor. Stryke battered at the other's sword, trying to dislodge it. His opponent's intentions were obviously more lethal. He was doing his best to reach flesh.

They sparred for a moment, Stryke on the defensive, but he was growing restive. He had no time to waste on a couple of boneheads. If he had to put them down, so be it, they'd had their chance. Powering in, he went for a kill. His foe, the lesser swordsman for all that he was an orc, started backing, a look of alarm filling his face.

Then Stryke saw his chance. The grunt had tried a low sweep. It left his upper body unprotected. Stryke sent in a sideswipe with the flat of his blade striking the orc across the mouth. He heard the crunch of broken teeth. The orc bounded backwards, almost falling, spitting blood. His sword was lost. Stryke advanced, kicking the fallen sword to one side. The grunt, his face whitening, waited for the killing blow.

"Now fuck off," Stryke told him. He sent a menacing sneer the way of the waverer too.

They stared at him for a second, then turned and fled.

Stryke sighed and resumed his journey, reflecting on the irony of fighting fellow orcs, and humans he was until so recently allied with.

Jup's group, surrounding Sanara to protect her, fought their way to the top of a tower.

They found an empty stone chamber there with an open balcony. While some guarded the stairs, she stepped out on to it, Jup beside her.

Jennesta's army was spread out across the icy wilderness below. There was a scrum at the palace's gates as details rushed to get in. Then someone cried out and they looked up to see dragons in the sky.

"Shit, that's all we need," the dwarf proclaimed gloomily.

But then the dragons dived and began spitting gouts of flame at Jennesta's troops. A ragged cheer broke out in the tower.

"That's got to be Glozellan," Jup guessed. "Good for her!"

He turned, beaming, to Sanara. Her eyes were closed, and as he watched she slowly began to raise her arms.

The band stared at her, mystified.

In the cellars, Alfray and Reafdaw looked on as Serapheim seemed to go into some kind of trance. His eyes were glazed and his arms were raised, and for all the notice he took of the orcs they might have not been there.

Then a hum, strange and low, issued from the area of the portal. Gingerly, Alfray approached it. He held out a cautious hand and felt a warm, tingling sensation caressing his palm.

He stepped back and exchanged baffled expressions with the grunt.

Stryke was passing a stove-in window when something extraordinary caught his eye.

He looked out and saw Jennesta's army, their vast number covering the ice to the middle distance. But it wasn't that which held him.

There was something in the sky.

The best he could liken it to was a canvas. But its picture moved, and changed to other views as he watched. He realised it was like the vision Serapheim had conjured at the portal, only writ enormously across the leaden heavens. It showed similar scenes of orc tranquillity and verdant splendour.

There were roars below. But they were not the battle cries of stoked-up warriors. They were shouts of wonder, followed by discontent.

He saw the magician's plan. What better way to sow discord in the ranks than by showing them the lie of their existence? That, plus filling them with dread at this supernatural manifestation. It would likely baffle them as much as turn their loyalties, but that could be enough to buy the time they needed.

The sound of running feet came to him. He readied for another clash. But it was Coilla and Haskeer's group that dashed along an adjacent corridor.

"Thank the gods!" she cried. "We thought we'd lost you!"

"Jennesta's here!"

"We noticed," she replied dryly.

"Then let's get to the cellars!"

They crashed down to them, broaching all opposition, cutting down any in their way. They sliced through the turmoil like knives through chickens' necks.

Eventually, breathing hard and sweating despite the cold, they arrived at the portal chamber and rushed in.

Serapheim held his trance-like pose, with Alfray and Reafdaw looking on. A small version of the picture glowing in the sky outside hovered in the portal's circle.

Almost at once the magician snapped out of his reverie. The picture flickered and died. "We can do no more," he panted, looking like a man who had engaged in hard physical toil.

"It was a smart trick," Stryke complimented him. "Now what?"

Before Serapheim could answer, Jup's group returned, still marvelling aloud at the display. They were bloodied, breathless, but whole. Sanara ran to her father's arms.

"Give me the instrumentalities," Serapheim said.

Stryke handed over the four that were fused and got the single loose artifact back from Sanara. With nimble fingers Serapheim swiftly united them.

"There is one thing I haven't mentioned," he confessed.

"What's that?" Coilla asked warily.

"Activating the portal will liberate a vast amount of energy. It will likely destroy the palace."

"*Now* you tell us." She glared at him.

"Had I said so earlier, it might have influenced your decision."

"Will it stop us using the thing?" Stryke said.

"No, if you go through swiftly."

Most of the band had doubt in their faces. Serapheim indicated the increasing sound of discord above. "Your choice has narrowed. Use the portal or face anarchy up there."

Stryke nodded assent.

Serapheim went forward and picked out one of the larger bejewelled stones. He laid the five-part star on its surface.

"Is that it?" Haskeer said.

"Wait," the human replied.

The space above the portal's dais suddenly transformed into something wondrous. It was like an inverted waterfall of millions of tiny golden stars, whirling, flowing, never still. And there was a throb of energy they could feel through the soles of their boots.

All present were transfixed by the fantastic sight. The myriad stars threw off a glow that reflected on their faces, their clothes, the walls around them.

"I need to attune it to your destination," Serapheim explained, approaching the circle.

"It's beautiful," Coilla whispered.

"Awesome," Jup reckoned.

"*And mine!*"

Everyone turned.

Jennesta stood at the door. General Mersadion, his face ravaged, was beside her.

Serapheim was the first to recover. "You're too late," he told her.

"It's nice to see you too, Father dear," she replied sarcastically. "I have a contingent of my Royal Guard at my heels. Surrender or die, it's all the same to me."

"I think not," Sanara said. "I can't see you passing on the opportunity to slay those you think have wronged you."

"You know me so well, sister. And how pleasant to see you in the flesh again. I look forward to despoiling it."

"If you think we're giving up without a fight," Stryke declared, "you're wrong. We've nothing to lose."

"Ah, Captain Stryke." She cast a disdainful eye over the warband. "And the Wolverines. I've relished the thought of meeting you again in particular." Her voice became granite. "Now throw down your weapons."

There was a sudden flurry of movement. Alfray rushed towards her, a sword in his hand.

Mersadion leapt in to counter it. His blade flashed. Then it was buried in the corporal's chest. The general tugged it free. Alfray still stood, looking down at the blood on his hands.

He swayed and fell.

There was a moment of shock that rooted them all to the spot.

The spell shattered. Haskeer, Jup, Coilla and Stryke all rushed at Mersadion and unleashed their frenzy. Every grunt in the room would have done the same but for the crush.

Mersadion didn't even have time to cry out. He was cut to pieces in seconds.

The band turned from his mangled corpse and moved Jennesta's way, ready to further sate their fury. She was weaving a contorted pattern in the air with her hands.

"No!" Serapheim shouted.

An orange fireball like a miniature sun ignited between her hands. She flung it. The band scattered. With blurring speed the firebrand sailed over their heads and exploded against a wall with a shattering report. Jennesta began forming another.

But Serapheim and Sanara had found each other, and together they faced her. Their hands lifted and a sheet of ethereal flame appeared like a shield in front of them, masking the room and its occupants. Jennesta hurled the new fireball at it, but saw its intense energy absorbed by the blazing barrier.

The portal's display of splendour continued unabated. But its destructive bent was becoming apparent. A deep rumbling had started to shake the castle's foundations. Unheeding, the band gathered around Alfray.

Coilla and Stryke went down on their knees beside him. They saw how severe his wound was. Coilla took his wrist, then looked into her Captain's eyes. "He's bad, Stryke."

"Alfray," Stryke said. *"Alfray,* can you hear me?"

The old orc managed to open his eyes. He seemed comforted by the sight of his comrades. *"So . . . this is how . . . it ends."*

"No," Coilla said. "We can tend your wound. We—"

"You have . . . no need to . . . lie . . . to me. Not now. Let me . . . at least have the . . . dignity of . . . truth."

"Hell, Alfray," Stryke whispered, his voice choking. "I got you into this. I'm so sorry."

Alfray smiled weakly. *"We got into . . . this . . . together. It was a . . . good mission, eh, Stryke?"*

"Yes. A good mission. And you were the best comrade an orc could have, old friend."

"I take . . . that as a . . . compliment to . . . be proud . . . of." Now his lips were working but no sound came. Stryke leaned close and put his ear close to Alfray's mouth. Faintly he heard, *"Sword . . ."*

Stryke took his blade and pressed its grip into Alfray's trembling palm. He closed the fingers around it. Alfray gripped feebly and looked content. *"Remember the . . . old ways,"* he rasped. *"Honour . . . the . . . traditions."*

"We will," Stryke promised. "And your memory. Always."

The ground gave another bass rumble. Showers of plaster fell from the ceiling. Off to one side of the vast chamber Jennesta and her kin battled on in a blaze of supernatural radiance and flashing lights.

Alfray's breath was thin and laboured. *"I will . . . drink . . . a toast to you . . . all . . . in the . . . halls of . . . Vartania."*

Then his eyes closed for the last time.

"No," Coilla said. "No, Alfray." She started shaking him. "We need you. Don't go, the band needs you. Alfray?"

Stryke took her by the shoulders and forced her to look at him. "He's . . . gone, Coilla. He's gone."

She stared at him, not seeming to comprehend.

Orcs weren't supposed to be able to cry. It was something humans did. The mist filling her eyes belied that.

Jup had his face in his hands. Haskeer's head was bowed. The grunts were struck dumb with the shock of grief.

Stryke gently took back his sword. Then he looked up at the magical duel and rage began to return. They all felt it. But they felt impotence too. There was no way they dared intervene in the exchange of sorcery, nor could they pass it.

No more than a minute later their quandary was resolved.

Jennesta cried out. Her fiery magical shield flickered and died. She staggered, her head down, looking exhausted. Damp locks of ebony hair were plastered to her face.

The enchanted, flaming buffer protecting Serapheim and Sanara vanished too, snuffed out like a candle. He darted the few steps separating them from Jennesta and seized her wrist. Drained by the efforts of their duel, she put up little resistance as he began dragging her toward the portal.

Leaping to their feet, the band made to charge and vent their wrath on her.

"No!" Serapheim bellowed. "She's my daughter! I have a responsibility for all she's done! I'll deal with this myself!"

Such was the force of his outburst that it stopped them in their tracks.

They watched as Serapheim pulled her the last few feet to the portal's edge. As they arrived, she came to herself a little and realised where they were. Her eyes moved from the dancing grandeur of the portal's vortex to her father's face. She seemed to divine his intention, but she showed no fear.

"You wouldn't dare," she sneered.

"Once, perhaps," he returned, "before the full horror of your wickedness was brought home to me. Not now." Still holding her wrist in an iron grip, he thrust her hand near to the portal's cascading brilliance, the tips of her fingers almost in the flow. "I brought you into this world. Now I'm taking you out of it. You should appreciate the symmetry of the act."

"You're a fool," she hissed, "you always were. And a coward. I have an army here. If anything happens to me, you'll die a death beyond your wildest imagination." She flicked her gaze to Sanara. "You both will."

"I don't care," he told her.

"Nor I," Sanara backed him.

"Some prices are worth paying to rid the world of evil," Serapheim said, pushing her hand nearer the sparkling flux.

She gazed into his eyes and knew he meant it. Her cocksure expression weakened somewhat then, and she began to struggle.

"At least face your end with dignity," he told her. "Or is that too much to ask?"

"*Never.*"

He forced her hand into the vortex, then let go and retreated a pace.

She squirmed and fought to pull her hand free but the gushing fountain of energy held it as sure as a vice. Then a change came upon the trapped flesh. Very slowly, it began to dissolve away, releasing itself as thousands of particles that flew into the swarm of stars and spiralled with them. The process increased apace, the vortex gobbling up her wrist. Rapidly she was drawn in to the depth of her arm, which likewise disintegrated and scattered.

The band was rooted, their expressions a mixture of horror and macabre fascination.

Her leg had been sucked in now, and it was melting before their eyes. Strands of her hair followed, as though inhaled by an invisible giant. Jennesta's disintegration speeded up, her matter eaten into by the surging vortex at a faster and faster rate.

When it began to consume her face she finally screamed. The sound was almost instantly cut off as the energy took the rest of her in several gulps. The last of her matter gyrated for a moment in the spinning energy field before it became nothingness.

Serapheim looked as though he was going to faint. Sanara went to him and they embraced.

Coilla punctured the awed silence. "What happened to her?"

Serapheim gathered himself. "She made contact with the portal before it was set for a destination. She's either been torn apart by the titanic forces it contains or flung into another dimension. Either way, she's gone. Finished."

Stryke wasn't the only one who felt a pang of pity for him, despite their hatred of Jennesta. "Is that how *we'll* go?" he asked.

There was another rumble beneath their feet, deeper, longer than any before.

"No, my friend. I will set the location. Your transition will be profound, but not like that. It will feel just like walking through a door." He disengaged himself from Sanara. "Come, there's no time to waste."

He made his way to one of the stones surrounding the portal and fiddled with the instrumentalities.

"What about you?" Coilla said.

"I will remain here in Maras-Dantia. Where else would I go? Here I can witness either the end of things or try to do some good if the land recovers from its blight."

All present knew that his real choice was death.

"I will remain here also," Sanara said. "This is my world. For better or worse." Tears stained her cheeks.

The earth grumbled more persistently.

"Come, Jup," Serapheim urged. "We'll send you to the domain of dwarfs first."

"No," he said.

"What?" Haskeer exclaimed.

"This is the only world I know too. I've had no visions of a dwarf world. It sounds tempting, but who would I know there? I'd really be a stranger in a strange land."

"You won't change your mind?" Stryke asked.

"No, Chief. I've given it a lot of thought. I'll stay here and take my chances."

Haskeer stepped forward. "You sure, Jup?"

"What's the matter, miss somebody to argue with?"

"I'll always find somebody to do that with." He regarded the dwarf for a moment. "But it won't be the same."

They exchanged the warrior's clasp.

"Then please take Sanara with you," Serapheim said. "Protect her for me,"

Jup nodded. Then with a last look at the band he escorted Sanara from the chamber.

"Now we must move with all speed," Serapheim announced. "Into the portal."

Everybody looked sheepish.

"I promise you that no harm will befall any of you."

"On the double!" Stryke barked.

Gleadeg stepped forward.

"In you go," Stryke told him. He added more softly, "Have no fear, trooper."

The grunt took a breath and moved into the portal. Instantly he vanished.

"Come on! Come on!" Stryke shouted.

One by one, the remainder of the grunts passed through.

Then it was Haskeer's turn. He leapt in, a battle cry on his lips.

Coilla, taking a last look at Serapheim, and then turning her eyes to Stryke, went next.

Stryke and Serapheim stood alone in the trembling chamber. "Thank you," the orc said.

"It was the least I could do. Here." He pushed the stars into his hand. "Take these."

"But—"

"I have no further need of them. You do with them as you will. But don't argue now!"

Stryke accepted them.

"Fare thee well, Stryke of the Wolverines."

"And you, Sorcerer."

He stepped to the lip of the vortex. The palace began to fall. Serapheim made no move to escape. Stryke hadn't thought he would. He lifted an arm and gave the human a clipped salute.

There was a moment of chaos and transition. Somehow, perhaps via the dreadful power of the stars and their portal, he had a brief flashing vision of many wondrous things.

He saw Aidan Galby, walking hand in hand with Jup and Sanara across a pastoral scene. He glimpsed Mercy Hobrow astride a unicorn. He knew again the allure of his orc homeland.

His last thought was that the humans could have their world, and welcome to it.

Then he turned and stepped into the light.

Acknowledgments

If it wasn't for our human support system, writers' lives would be intolerably isolated. So thanks are due to Steve Jackson and Heather Matuozzo, for friendship and laughter; Harry and Helen Knibb, for their matchless Internet expertise and kindness; Sandy Auden, for chocolate wisdom and Carrying On; Simon Spanton, for keeping a firm hand on the editorial tiller; and Nicola Sinclair, for publicity expertise above and beyond.

extras

orbit

meet the author

Peter Coleborn

STAN NICHOLLS is the author of more than two dozen books, most of them in the fantasy and science fiction genres, for both children and adults. His books have been published in over twenty countries. Before taking up writing full-time in 1981, he co-owned and managed the West London bookstore Bookends and managed specialist SF bookshop Dark They Were and Golden Eyed. He was also Forbidden Planet's first manager and helped establish and run the New York branch. A journalist for national and specialist publications and the Internet, he was the science fiction and fantasy book reviewer for London listings magazine *Time Out* for six years and subsequently reviewed popular science titles for the magazine. He received the Le Fantastique Lifetime Achievement Award for Contributions to Literature in April 2007.

interview

Over the course of your career you have written many science fiction and fantasy novels. How did you get your start in the genre?

I suppose you could say I got started as a child, when I first became interested in these subjects. I've likened a passion for science fiction and fantasy to malaria; if you're bitten young the fever tends to rage life-long. But from a fairly early age I didn't just want to consume fantastical stories, I wanted to tell them myself. The first manifestation of that was probably in the playground, where I inadvertently discovered the *Thousand and One Nights* principle. In the school I attended, a glib tongue proved a useful alternative to fight or flight when you weren't very competent at those activities. Making yourself a sort of entertainment asset was a good way of keeping your teeth.

I was a cuckoo in the nest of the poor, not particularly bookish family I grew up in. Despite being the last boy in my year at school who learned to read, once I knew how, I took to it. There wasn't much money for luxuries like reading material in our house, but I managed to get my hands on a steady stream of novels, magazines, and comic books. When I was nine or ten years old I wrote what I inaccurately, and hilariously, referred to as a novel. I wrote it in colored felt-tip in a cheap reporter's notebook. I knew that novels were divided into things called chapters, but I didn't know how long they were supposed to be.

So I made every page a chapter. This "novel" was about a bunch of feisty kids who start off seeing a flying saucer and end up foiling an alien invasion. It was, not surprisingly, dire.

When I left school I worked in a book-exporting company that incorporated the London office of the Library of Congress, which was fascinating. Then I managed a series of specialist bookshops, including Dark They Were and Golden Eyed and Forbidden Planet. But this was all a diversion; I really wanted to write, and only got into bookselling to be near books and authors, hoping perhaps that I'd absorb the skill through some kind of osmosis. I was writing whenever I could find the time, and in my teens I'd joined with friends to publish fanzines devoted to sf, fantasy, and horror, but I became increasingly aware that to make a life as a writer I'd have to focus on it exclusively. When I finally took the plunge it was as a journalist. Fiction writing being an unpredictable way to earn a living, my thought was that journalism would pay the bills while I worked at the craft of storytelling. I concentrated as much as possible on the genres that interested me, but you can't really prosper as a journalist if you write only about science fiction. So I became a jobbing hack, taking commissions on almost any subject from practically any publication that would pay me. I'd recommend journalism to anyone interested in a writing career, even a career in fiction. It teaches you positive attributes, like a respect for deadlines, an ability to get the job done, and brevity of expression. During this period I also worked as a first reader — or slush pile reader, as we rather unkindly call it in the UK — for a number of publishers and literary agents. That taught me a lot too, though sadly most of the lessons were about how *not* to do it.

One day I got a call from an agent who had seen my work and wanted to know if I was interested in writing a book. That led to a series of commissions writing movie novelizations and TV tie-ins. People trying to break into the profession can be a bit disdainful of this kind of work, but again I'd recommend it. In this business your only collateral is your track record, and any kind of book helps build a profile, as well as giving you the chance to master the skills needed for novel writing. Having proved myself to some extent with these projects, I eventually graduated to pitching my own ideas.

Who/what would you consider to be your influences?

I've had the privilege of reading very widely in the sf, fantasy, and supernatural fields, and took inspiration from all these genres. I'm not someone who sees the various branches of speculative fiction as being dissimilar in quality or interest. For me, the science fiction, fantasy, and horror genres simply occupy different points on a spectrum, and I've enjoyed reading, and to some extent writing, in each of them. I could list numerous authors who influenced me, but that makes for dull reading, and I'd be bound to overlook some important names. So I'll just say that it was the totality of these genres that motivated me.

One thing I'll add is that although prose, the printed word, is what's always captivated me most, other mediums have had an effect too. When I was younger I had a passion for science fiction and horror movies, and an enthusiasm for comic books. All of this feeds into your work on some level, even if you aren't always aware of it.

Are you mainly a science fiction and fantasy reader, or are there other genres that you're partial to?

If it was possible to count up everything I've ever read, no doubt sf and fantasy would form by far the greatest part. But

I've long felt that reading exclusively in these genres isn't necessarily a positive thing. If you read only science fiction, all you have to compare it with is other books in the same category. You lose perspective. So I've kept up a little with other fields, and to some extent mainstream literature, though my tastes usually run to genre, like crime and thrillers.

But in common with a lot of authors, I tend to read less and less fiction the more I write it myself. And I rarely read any when I'm actually working on a book. I suppose that's because when you're trying to think your way through the ramifications of your own plot, world, and characters, you don't want to be distracted by somebody else's. There's probably also an element of anxiety about unconscious plagiarism, which is something we all dread. I still read — I couldn't imagine not doing that — but these days it's more likely to be nonfiction, in the shape of a book on history or a biography.

How do you fill your time when you aren't writing?

I recently made a pact with my wife, Anne — who's a writer herself and understands the process — that I'd try to achieve a better work-life balance. You know, take a few days off occasionally and interact with real people rather than ones I've made up, that sort of thing. Writing has a tendency to be all-consuming, and when it's flowing well there's a reluctance to notice the clock. You could argue that being totally immersed is a necessary prerequisite for a writer, which it is, but there's also a case for equilibrium. I'm mindful of the old adage that says being able to write is only half the story; you have to have something to write *about*. Keeping one foot in the real world is what feeds that, even for a writer of fantasy.

When I do escape my workroom I enjoy walking, particularly

in the English countryside, or when I travel abroad, which is another interest. Recently I've been trying to learn how to record these excursions via photography. I hope to reach competent one of these years. I like history and can usually be tempted into a museum or historic monument; and art intrigues me, possibly because it's a talent I'm completely devoid of and envy in others, so galleries are a prime destination. Of course I people-watch, as writers will, and I savor conversation — I share the delight many writers have in talking, which is why there are so many donkeys around here with missing hind legs.

The intriguing conceit of Orcs *is that you have turned traditional fantasy conventions upside down. What made you decide that it was time for the orcs to tell their story?*

That's precisely it — their story had never been told. Orcs were always depicted as a mindless horde fit only to dash themselves against the heroes' blades. I got to pondering about how winners write the history books, and thought, "Suppose orcs just had a bad press?" What if they were supreme warriors, and certainly capable of ruthlessness, but not actually evil? Suppose they had some kind of code of honor, albeit crude, and, dare I say it, even a certain nobility? Why shouldn't they have a history, a culture, hopes, fears, dreams, and beliefs, just like other fantasy races?

Of course, most people associate orcs with Tolkien. But while he undoubtedly brought them into the general consciousness, he didn't create them. I'm fond of saying that Tolkien didn't invent orcs any more than Bram Stoker invented vampires or Anne McCaffrey invented dragons. Needing agents of evil — arrow fodder, to put it bluntly — he took creatures from European myth and fashioned them to his purpose. Not that this is in any way a criticism of Tolkien. *The Lord of the Rings* is a wonderful, unique creation that I have enormous respect for. No one will ever equal it on its own terms, and anybody who tries is wasting their time. I'm not trying to add anything to it, or take anything away, which would be impossible. I'm just offering my own take on a species, as you might call them, in the same way others have explored elves, trolls, gnomes, dwarfs, fairies, and all the rest. I wanted to look at them in a different way, and give them their due.

Do you have a favorite character? If so, why?

For some reason my favorite characters in any of my books are usually female. I'm not sure why. Perhaps it's because I was raised in an almost completely matriarchal environment. It might have something to do with the fact that I'm the sort of man who generally gets along better with women than with my own gender — at any given time my female friends usually outnumber the males. Maybe it's because I've long regarded myself as profeminist and enjoy writing strong female characters. Though some critics have questioned my intentions in this respect because of Jennesta, the villain in the *Orcs* trilogy, who gets up to some pretty vile things. But it seems to me that saying you shouldn't have a bad character who's female, and by extension that women should only be cast as "good," implies a patronizing and outmoded mind-set. And it ignores the heroic female characters who more than balance her. So to answer your question, my favorite character in the *Orcs* series is Coilla. I'm very fond of her, and find her the easiest character to write. If I was forced to pick a second favorite, I'll contradict what I've just said slightly and go for Haskeer. He's a dolt, and you wouldn't want to run into him under any circumstances, but I can't help feeling a certain affection for the character.

extras

In terms of cover art, have you found it interesting to see how different countries have published Orcs*?*

The books are published worldwide now, and it's been fascinating to see all the different interpretations. To refer back to *The Lord of the Rings* for a moment, if you read what Tolkien says about orcs you'll find that he's very light on describing them. And just an aside here: when I started writing the series I deliberately didn't reread Tolkien, except for some of the passages about orcs. As this was going to be my exploration of the race, I didn't want to be influenced in any way. But I decided to do as he had and keep my description of orcs fairly basic. I did this because of what you might call the Charlie Brown Syndrome. When the animated versions of the *Peanuts* strip started appearing, a common criticism was "They've got the voices wrong! They don't sound like *that!*" What people meant was that they didn't sound like that *in their heads*. Everybody had their own idea of how the characters should sound. It's a bit like that with orcs. Given that they've never been fully described before — with the possible exception of some interpretations in the gaming world, of which I'm largely ignorant — everybody has a picture of orcs in their mind. And the movie versions of *Lord of the Rings* and its view of orcs didn't come into this because I started writing the books well before the films were released. The point is that I didn't want to fall victim to the Charlie Brown Syndrome by describing them in too much detail. I wanted to leave enough room in my depiction of these creatures for people to fill in the gaps themselves. In fact, that's not a bad rule as far as many aspects of fantasy fiction are concerned — leave some space for the reader to dream in.

So it's been really interesting seeing how different countries handle the covers, and I often wonder whether the artwork conveys

extras

some kind of national characteristic. Some countries, for example Holland, go for abstract covers implying martial artifacts like shields. The German editions started that way, with the stark image of an ax, but lately the illustrations have turned into something almost demonic. In the Czech Republic they see orcs as quite monstrous, while the French go for a slightly cartoonish but definitely epic quality. The Chinese orcs have something of Eastern mythology about them and the style of the covers has a faint echo of *manga*. My Italian editions are very hard-edged and feature scary armored helmets. The Russians . . . well, one of the Russian editions had me in stitches. Their orc looks just like Alfred E. Neuman!

What's next for Stryke and his warband?

It was always my hope and intention to continue the story of Stryke and the Wolverines, and at this moment I'm halfway through writing the second trilogy, *Orcs: Bad Blood.* The first volume's called *Weapons of Magical Destruction* and the second has the working title *Army of Shadows.* These books carry on the story begun in the original trilogy — we find out what became of the Wolverines after they entered the portal in search of their home world, and what happened next. All the characters from the first trilogy are featured — or at least the ones who survived — and we discover Jennesta's true fate. There are quite a few new characters too, including some unlikely companions for an orc warband. And the plot opens out a lot more, in that it isn't restricted to a single world. What I certainly didn't want to do was serve up a rehash of the first trilogy — you owe readers better than that — and I'm working hard to give this continuation some fresh twists. The fact that I worked out a story arc that included the events in this new trilogy before I started writing the very first book has helped with that.

Finally, if you were walking down a dark alley, who would you be more scared to come across, Jup or Coilla?

Well, as I created them, I'd like to think they'd grasp my wrist warrior-style and invite me to join them for a tankard of ale. But let's assume that didn't happen. Jup would be a formidable opponent and tough as old leather, so you wouldn't want to get on his wrong side. But in terms of savagery, fighting skill, and a propensity for bloodletting, Coilla would have to be the one to steer clear of. She's an orc.

short story

It was always my intention to write a series of short stories centering on the characters featured in the Orcs *series. "The Taking" is the first of these. Set before the events depicted in* Orcs, *it takes place on the day Coilla joined the Wolverines. I'm proud of the fact that "The Taking" was short-listed for the 2001 British Fantasy Award.*

—Stan Nicholls, February 8, 2008

THE TAKING

Humans were eating the magic.

The ice was encroaching and autumn had arrived in early summer. There was war on all sides and the rape of Maras-Dantia continued unchecked.

But today none of that seemed to matter.

It didn't matter to Stryke. His only concern was the arcing blade threatening to cleave his skull. He ducked and let it rip vacant air. Bringing up his shield, he blocked the follow-through, taking the jolts as his opponent beat the steel like a forge. Once that spent itself Stryke was back on the offensive. He sent out two rapid passes. The first was parried, metal ringing. The next breached his rival's guard, forcing him into a staggering retreat.

They circled, breathing heavily, looking for an opening.

Stryke advanced, shield levelled, sword prowling. Another flurry ensued, the combatants toe to toe, neither giving. The onlookers roared and catcalled.

Raining blows, Stryke powered forward, delivering a mix of thrusts and slashes that ribboned the other's defences. There was a brief rally, a further exchange of swipes and counter swipes. But Stryke's greater skill paid off. A jarring hit dashed away his foe's sword. More pounding dislodged the shield, sending it bouncing across the yellowed grass. Then Stryke was looming over his downed opponent with raised blade. The watchers bayed.

He plunged his sword into the earth and tossed aside his shield. Offering the fallen his hand, he hoisted him to his feet. "Not bad, Kestix. But watch that guard."

The grunt managed a broken-toothed grin. "Right, chief," he panted.

Somebody yelled, *"Heads up!"*

As they all turned to look, Stryke snapped, " 'ten-*shun!*"

The figure striding toward them was a good forty seasons in age. His ramrod bearing and war weathered face told of status, never mind the rank tattoos marking his cheeks. He regarded the assembled band, two dozen or so grunts and four officers, through rheumy eyes.

"General Kysthan, *sir!*" Stryke greeted, saluting with fist to chest.

"At ease, Captain, and the rest of you."

The troop relaxed, most of them eyeing the second figure, who stayed mounted a spear's lob distant.

"Sorry to spoil your pleasure," the general told them, "especially today."

"No problem, sir," Stryke assured him. "What do you need?"

"Just for you to take delivery of that corporal you're lacking. I've brought a replacement."

More curious glances went the way of whoever was on the horse.

"Thank you, sir. And this replacement's joining us now?"

"Yes, captain."

"On *Braetagg's Day?*" a hulking sergeant blurted. In a humbler tone he added, "Begging your pardon, General, sir."

Stryke shot him a homicidal look.

The general appeared more benevolent. "That's all right, Sergeant—"

"Haskeer, General."

"Sergeant Haskeer. These are troubled times. Even Braetagg's Day isn't exempt from military needs. I want this corporal inducted and you back up to strength."

Haskeer nodded sagely, as though imagining he conferred with an equal. Stryke suspected he only got away with it because of what day it was. He made a note to have him lightly flogged later.

Kysthan waved the rider to approach. "Good kill tally in the horde," he explained as they waited. "Meets the band's standard, and a gift for strategy."

The steed came at pace, reining in by them, spattering clods of soil. Its passenger slid from the saddle like mercury down slingshot.

"Corporal Coilla," the general announced.

The new arrival gave them a smile with real flint in it.

Stryke regarded her. They were probably of an age, a score of seasons or thereabouts, and not far off in height. Her craggy, slightly mottled hide looked healthy enough and she was pleasingly muscular. She had obvious pride, and a hard certainty in her eyes. A fitting demeanour. There was no denying she was a handsome orc.

She returned his gaze. What she saw was what she'd expected: a battle-tempered, robust warrior stamped with command. But there might have been a hint of something more, a small quirk of manner that betrayed deeper concerns than even the martial. Perhaps because of that, there was no denying he was a handsome orc.

"Well met," she said, extending her hand.

He took it warrior-style, forearm clasping forearm, and thought how nicely humid her touch was. "Well met. Welcome to the Wolverines."

Coilla scanned the others, lingering on each face for a fraction of a second yet scrutinising them all. She dwelt just a little longer on the only dwarf present, whose facial tattoos indicated he was a sergeant. Then her eyes flicked back to Stryke. She said nothing.

"You know what a hardy outfit this is," General Kysthan told her. "I'm relying on you to fit in. Your record says you can. But put a foot wrong in a warband like the Wolverines and you're liable to end up dead."

"Yes, sir."

Kysthan was already moving towards his ride. The band stiffened to attention again. "Good luck, Corporal." He tugged a pair of black leather gloves from his belt. "Stryke, keep me informed on her progress." The gloves flicked out in a parting gesture, as though he were swatting at a fly. "Enjoy the day!"

They watched him mount, wheel the horse and gallop across the parade ground through swelling crowds. His route led to the sugar white edifice of Cairnbarrow's royal palace, its walls shining from dawn rain, its lofty towers piercing leaden clouds.

Coilla and the band eyed each other.

"What happened to the corporal I'm replacing?" she asked abruptly.

"What do you think?" Stryke replied. "Warbands take casualties. If that's a problem —"

"No, no problem. It's what I'd expect. So when do we start getting me invested?"

extras

"I dunno why we have to do it at all on Braetagg's Day," Haskeer grumbled again.

"It's as good as any other day," responded an orc who looked the oldest, and who, like Coilla, bore the markings of a corporal. He turned to Stryke. "Maybe we should introduce her to the band before we do anything else, Chief," he suggested.

Stryke indicated he should do it.

"I'm Alfray," the ageing corporal told her. "Haskeer you've already heard from. He's —"

"A moron," the dwarf rumbled.

The sergeants exchanged murderous glances.

"And this is Jup," Alfray said.

The dwarf winked at her, a bit roguishly she thought. A flash of white teeth lit his bearded face.

Coilla spoke impetuously. "I was expecting . . ."

"Somebody taller?"

"Somebody a little less . . . dwarfish," she replied dryly. "I mean, I didn't think there were that many in warbands."

"You orcs aren't the only ones skilled in combat."

"In your dreams," Haskeer muttered.

"More like a nightmare with your mug," Jup returned.

"*Shut up,*" Stryke growled menacingly, "the pair of you."

They retreated into morose silence.

Alfray cleared his throat. "The troopers," he continued, commencing to point them out. "That's Kestix. There's Finje and Zoda. Hystykk, Bhose, Slettal, Darig. Let's see. Vobe, Liffin, Noskaa . . . er . . . Calthmon, Wrelbyd, Prooq. That's Meklun . . . Reafdaw, Gant, Jad . . . Gleadeg, Toche, Breggin." He blinked at the farthest faces. "Talag and . . . Seafe. Oh, and Nep, Orbon and Eldo, at the back there."

Some of the grunts acknowledged Coilla; others kept a wary reserve.

"Right," Stryke announced, glad that was over. "You'll be billeting here, Corporal." He jabbed a thumb at the wooden longhouses behind them, bedecked with clan shields. "But there's not much we'll be doing this day. Let's see how things are going with the celebrations."

There were murmurs of approval from the band.

Coilla shrugged. "Fine by me."

They strolled in the direction of the main square, Coilla walking beside the other officers. The grunts stuck together in their own group, indulging in a certain amount of horseplay she imagined Stryke wouldn't normally allow.

Crowds were gathering for the festivities. They were mostly orcs, as would be expected on such a day, but with a smattering of other races, including a few humans of the Mani creed. A knot of gremlin emissaries passed by, solemn in grey robes. Daintily framed elf servants bustled on errands. Brownie dragon handlers, proud and aloof, weaved through the mass. Far overhead, a squadron of their charges circled on leathery, serrated wings.

Chill gusts came in from both the eastern ocean and the advancing ice sheet in the north. More rain threatened.

Wrapping his jerkin tighter, Alfray broke the silence. "It gets a little worse every year. In my time, Braetagg's Day was a summer festival. Look at it now."

"*Humans,*" Haskeer spat. "Fucking up the magic."

"Unis anyway," Alfray corrected. "Them and their wretched single god."

"Manis, Unis; not much to choose between them if you ask me."

"Don't be too loose in spreading that thought, Haskeer," Stryke cautioned. "You wouldn't want it getting back to our mistress."

"The Queen's a chancer," Alfray said, "we all know that. She'll back the Manis only as long as it suits her."

"That's enough careless talk," Stryke decreed, glancing around for flapping ears.

"I don't know a lot about Braetagg's Day," Jup confessed. "I've never actually been in Cairnbarrow for it before. Tell me about it."

"Admitting you're ignorant, eh?" Haskeer gibed.

"Ignorance I leave to you. You're so much better equipped for it."

"Braetagg was a great orc chieftain," Alfray quickly put in. "You must know that much."

"Course," Jup said. "The rest of it's a bit vague though."

"To be honest, it's not all that clear to us either. We don't know where he came from or exactly when he lived, except it was about a century ago. What we do know is that he led our race in some famous victories. That was when the United Orc Clans was a *real* power. Before things started going down. He struck off the yoke at a time when some of the other elder races looked to enslave us. So, above all, we honour him as a liberator."

"Pity it didn't stick," Coilla remarked sourly.

From his expression it was obvious Stryke thought that was dangerous talk too. But he kept his peace.

As they continued their trek, Coilla found herself slightly apart from the others, with only Jup to hand.

"Take a tip?" he asked in an undertone.

She nodded.

"Watch your tongue. You're not in the horde any longer. Things get noticed more in a smaller group like this." He let that soak in, then added, "Not that I'm saying we don't agree with you."

"All right. Question?"

"Sure."

"What's the beef between you and Haskeer?"

"I haven't got one. Well, maybe a bit," he relented. "It comes down to this thing about dwarfs. Lots of beings feel the way he does."

"You mean the way dwarfs . . . blow with the wind?"

"We both know what we're talking about, Coilla. My race has a reputation for siding with whoever has the most coin, even if they happen to be Unis. Some see it as treachery. I reckon we're just . . . practical."

"So how practical is it being in one of Jennesta's warbands? You could be doing something less dangerous, and probably better paid."

"I can't answer for all my kind, much as Haskeer keeps trying to hold me to account. It might seem strange to you, what with you orcs having been bartered into the Queen's service and all, but some of us think there's a cause worth fighting for here. Somebody's got to stop the humans tearing the guts out of Maras-Dantia. The bad ones, anyway."

"Indentured or not, most of us think that too. Look, Sergeant, I don't give a fuck about the politics. All I care about is whether my comrades are good at their job and are gonna cover my back."

"That's the way I see it. And that's the thing about Haskeer. He's a bastard, but he's a good fighter, and he's enough of a team player to be there when you want him. It's one of the things I like about orcs." He smiled. "By the way, forget the rank. Call me Jup."

"Is he the only one giving you a hard time?"

"He is now, more or less. I had to do a lot to prove myself when I first joined this band. It'll be the same with you for a while."

"Only dwarf and only female, eh?"

"Right. But at least you have the advantage of being an orc."

They entered the square. Strands of bunting had been hung and pennants billowed in the wind. Numerous clan shields were racked in columns. Mountainous bone-fires stood ready for kindling by tarred arrows at the height of the celebrations.

Skirting roped-off areas set aside for tourneys later in the day, the band moved into the shadow of the palace. A grand tent had been pitched, cloth flapping, regal ensigns basted on either side of its entrance. Two orc sentinels guarded it, spears crossed. Recognising Stryke, they stepped aside, allowing the band to file into the cavernous interior.

Burning brands and watery sunlight dappled by the marquise's fabric gave the place an eerie illumination.

As one they stopped, regarding with awe what was housed there.

Alfray laid a hand on Coilla's arm. "First time you've seen him?"

A nod was all she could manage.

Most of the grunts stared with something near reverence, and not a little superstitious dread.

At length, Jup decided, "I think it's unnatural, and probably unsanitary."

"Watch what you're insulting, short-arse," Haskeer rumbled ominously.

Stryke gave them a stern look and mouthed, *"Show respect."*

A throne of some splendour had been placed in the centre of the tent. It was embellished with beaten gold inlays and silver tracings. Its backrest was fashioned into the likeness of a phoenix rising from artfully carved flames. Rubies served as the beast's eyes, and burned crimson. If not quite managing the grandeur of any of Jennesta's thrones, it was still fit for a warlord.

Braetagg sat in it.

More accurately, he was propped, one hand resting on the hilt of a jutting broadsword. The empty scabbard lay across his lap, and he wore a simple gold crown. His mail shone, his leather trews were unsullied and his boots had been polished.

His skin was stretched, clearly showing the outlines of bones beneath, and it had the colour of yellowing parchment. Once stitched, his mouth now had a rictus that displayed several teeth of similar hue. The eyes were hollow sockets. There was a faint tint about the corpse's parched flesh that spoke of the unguents and herbs employed by the embalmers.

"He looks like he could stand up and talk to us," Haskeer declared wonderingly.

"I fucking hope not," Jup said.

Horns of ale and canteens of rugged wine were snapped from belt clips. Handing them round, the band took turns toasting their forebear. In solidarity, even Jup had his share. When it came to Coilla, they all watched approvingly as she downed hers without blanching. She noticed Haskeer draining his flask in a single draft.

They lingered for a while, then Stryke ordered them out.

Blinking in the stronger light, they took a second to realise the crowd was facing the palace, heads craning. They followed their gazes to a high balcony and the figure standing there.

Queen Jennesta was dressed in white, her cascade of ebony hair flowing free in the keen breeze. From where they were standing her features couldn't really be made out. But they were familiar enough with her half-human, half-nyadd ancestry, and the abnormal geometry of her dark beauty.

The Wolverines had come late to her address, or quite possibly harangue. In any event, distance and the wind made it hard to catch more than odd words. They were trying to interpret what they could hear when she raised her arms and began negotiating a complex series of hand gestures.

There was a blinding flash of orangey-green light. Something like a fireball streaked down from her lofty perch, leaving a vivid red trace-line in its wake. It struck one of the steeped bonfires with a thunderous roar and the pile instantly erupted in flames. The crowd cheered and hooted.

"Bread and circuses," Alfray sniffed, seemingly unimpressed.

"Come *on*," Jup told him, "Braetagg's Day existed long before she came along."

"And purloined it."

They watched the pyre consume itself, their enthusiasm a little dampened.

The Wolverines were lounging on the decking of one of their long-house billets when Reafdaw came back from his errand.

"Get it?" Stryke said.

"Yes, Chief." Smiling, the grunt took a small pouch from his belt satchel and handed it over.

The others gathered to watch Stryke open it. Inside was a quantity of tiny crystals, translucent but with a faint purple-pinkish hue.

"Seems choice," Alfray judged.

Coilla leaned over to look. "Hmmm, pellucid. That should brighten the day."

"You can't beat a good charge of crystal lightning," Jup agreed.

"Don't think we're going to make a habit of this," Stryke warned them. "See it as Braetagg's treat. Do the honours, will you, Alfray?"

The corporal rummaged in his field medical bag for a mortar and pestle, then set to grinding the crystals into a fine powder. Reafdaw helped him pack it into cobs.

Soon a distinctive aroma perfumed the air as the first pipes were passed round.

Expelling a long plume of chalky smoke, Jup wheezed, "I think I'm warming to this Braetagg."

"That better dot be nisrespectful," Haskeer said. "Er . . . Bhat tetter . . . Uhm . . . Just don't *take the piss,* right?"

"Yuck fou," the dwarf returned jovially.

Haskeer's glazed eyes took on a puzzled cast.

Ribald jokes were told, triggering helpless laughter. Grunts took turns at the peculiarly orcish art of boasting, embellishing their deeds to points beyond absurdity. There was a lot of giggling.

Stryke leaned against the wall, the back of his head cradled in linked hands. "Another hour of this and the festivities proper should be getting under way."

"If we can still walk to it," Alfray slurred.

Jup was adrift in a convoluted and largely incoherent anecdote when Coilla interrupted with, "Who's that?"

Bloodshot eyes lazily turned the way she indicated. Three mounted orcs galloped towards them. One had a fluttering purple cloak.

"Shit," Stryke cursed, scrambling unsteadily to his feet. "Crelim."

Coilla squinted at him. "Who?"

"Crelim. The General's aide-de-camp. *Up!* All of you, *up!*"

There was an unsteady rising, aided by the tip of Stryke's boot. Swaying orcs brushed dirt from their breeches and watched the party arrive.

Perfunctory salutes exchanged, Crelim lost no more time on formalities. "Direct orders from General Kysthan. Special assignment. You're to come with me. Now."

"Today, Major?" Stryke protested. "Is it really nec —"

"Our enemies are no respecters of days, Captain, and I'm not here for a debate." He took in their appearance and reckoned their state. "Get your heads into a water butt first if you have to, only *move your arses!*"

Accompanying themselves with wholesale low-key grumbling, they did as they were told.

The crowds were bigger and growing. Crelim and his outriders, wordless, led them back to the square, and across it to the tent. A mass of orcs were outside, marshalled by a strong contingent of sentries.

"Jennesta's own Imperial Guard, no less," Alfray whispered.

Stryke nodded, still trying to clear out the fug.

When they dismounted, Crelim ordered the grunts to stay outside. He went in with Stryke, Haskeer, Alfray, Jup and Coilla.

There were more guards inside, living and dead. The detail assigned to protect Braetagg was sprawled on the ground, throats cut or backs knifed. Blood had splashed the tent walls.

More shocking was the absence of Braetagg himself.

Jup regarded the empty throne and said, "Maybe you were right, Haskeer. He got up and walked away."

"That's more than you'll be doing if you don't shut that mouth."

Stryke silenced them with a chopping motion and a venomous face.

Crelim pointed to a wide slash in the back of the tent. "That's how they got him out."

"Why would anybody want to take him?" Coilla wondered. "I mean, what *for?*"

The Major shrugged. "All I know is that if the festivities start and there's no Braetagg there could be disorder."

"To put it mildly," Alfray said.

"We can't afford this getting out," Crelim went on, "which is why we've brought in a special-operations band. You're to act in secret. Your orders are to retrieve Braetagg's remains and get them back here pronto."

"And if we don't?" Stryke asked.

"The Queen herself wants this resolved."

"Don't bother coming back, in other words."

"You said it, Captain."

Eyes closed, Stryke massaged the bridge of his nose with thumb and forefinger. He sighed. "Any idea who might have done this?"

"No. But there's one possibility. Some pyros have been seen in the area over the last couple of days. One of the dragon patrols sighted a party of them just yesterday afternoon, down towards Hecklowe."

"And that's all there is to go on?"

Crelim nodded. "We're relying on you. Don't tarry."

He turned and left, retinue in tow.

"On fucking Braetagg's—"

"*Don't say it, Haskeer,*" Stryke cautioned in even, icy tones.

"Pyros?" Coilla said.

"A human cult. Fire worshippers or some such."

"What, Manis? Unis?"

"Don't think they're either."

"They're a magical sect," Alfray explained.

Coilla was disdainful. "*What?* Since when did humans have magic any more than orcs do? They're only good at bleeding it."

"Maybe they're seekers of magic rather than actually possessing it," Jup suggested. "They probably want some mastery of the earth energies, like most of the other elder races."

"Sounds crazy to me," Haskeer opined.

"And your point is? We're talking about *humans,* bonehead."

"Who you calling a bonehead, you little scumpouch?"

"*Enough!*" Stryke growled. "Who knows what good Braetagg's corpse is to these pyros, *if* they took it. What's important is getting it back, else the day ends in bloodshed."

Jup was examining the area around the empty throne. "Perhaps magic's the key," he told them. "My mild magic, farsight. Though it's much depleted, thanks to those fucking interfering humans." He knelt and plucked something from the seat of the throne. They saw it was a minute scrap of cloth. "This isn't Braetagg's. It's a coarse weave, not like anything he was wearing."

"Could be anybody's."

"True. But it doesn't match any of the guards' uniforms either."
He looked up at Stryke. "Most of all, it's the only clue we have."

"Is it enough?" Alfray wondered. "For the farsight?"

"I don't know," the dwarf replied. "Could be. What do you
reckon, Stryke?"

"You're supposed to be a trailblazer. Blaze."

They were around ten miles west of Cairnbarrow. The palace's
spires could still be seen, but so too could the bulwark of the glacier, a thin white line dominating the northern horizon. Light rain
had begun to fall. It was sallow, with a vaguely unpleasant odour
reminding them of sulphur and decaying things.

The mounted band looked on as Jup crouched with his hands
immersed in mud, eyes closed, sampling the earth energies. Eventually he stood and started wiping the muck away. "The strength's
irregular. Bastard humans."

"But?" Stryke said.

"But I think they're heading for Taklakameer."

"It's kind of a big area to cover, isn't it?" Coilla ventured. "For
just thirty of us?"

"Yes," Stryke agreed. "So the sooner we get on, the better."

They continued westward. Every so often, Jup used his erratic
farsight and insisted their quarry was still moving towards the
inland sea.

Eventually the band arrived at a bluff overlooking the wind-
rippled waters. The vastness of the sea, and the curling mists
clinging to its surface, meant the far shores couldn't be seen. But
the water lapping the nearest bank was scummy and defiled.

"Now what?" Alfray wanted to know.

"Can your farsight narrow the search, Jup?" Stryke asked.

"Not much more than this. You know water can smother it."

"How so?" Coilla said.

"Water holds the magic, in the same way forest glades and remote valleys do. Maybe because those are harder places for humans to plough up, mine and graze."

"If there's more magic, doesn't that increase your farsight?"

"That's the problem. It heightens the power but also everything I pick up. It's hard to explain. You could say it's a bit like being blinded by the light."

Stryke had a plan. "We'll split into two groups and scour the shore north and south. I'll lead one, along with you, Alfray, and you, Coilla. We'll take half the grunts and head south. Haskeer and Jup, you'll take the other half. If either group comes across anything they can't handle, send a runner."

They set off.

Stryke's group hugged the shoreline, and they could see Jup and Haskeer's doing the same. Soon they were out of sight of each other.

After riding in silence for a few minutes, Coilla ventured, "Is it safe leaving those two together, Captain?"

"Who?"

"Jup and Haskeer, of course."

"It's true there's not a lot of love lost between them, but when the cards are down, they're Wolverines first. Anyway, they're not hatchlings. If they behave like they are, on a mission, they're out and they know it."

"Have you run into these pyros before?"

"Not really. Some of the other bands have."

"They're not numerous but they are fanatical," Alfray added, "and that's often more dangerous."

"What's the plan if we find them?" Coilla said.

Stryke looked as though he found the question odd. "We kill them. What else?"

*   *   *

"Keep your eyes peeled."

"That's a fucking stupid thing to say," Haskeer flared. "What else do you think I'd be doing?"

"I don't know," the dwarf said. "Playing with your fertilising sac?"

"Get off that horse and I'll ram your head up its arse."

"It'd be an improvement over looking at your face."

"You want yours rearranged, just say."

"Yeah, in the middle of a mission. That'd be really smart."

"*Sergeants!*" one of the grunts hissed.

"What?" they chorused irritably.

"Over there." He pointed.

Off to their right, inland from the shore, stood a brace of low dumpy hills with a copse between. The light of a fire could be seen through the trees.

Haskeer and Jup brought the column to a halt.

"What do you reckon?" Haskeer said.

"Let's do a recce."

"All of us?"

"Nah, we can handle this by ourselves."

The grunts were ordered to stay with the horses. Jup and Haskeer went off.

They approached the copse stealthily, keeping low, cutting a zigzag path. Then they were on their bellies, crawling in the undergrowth, until they stopped at the fringe of a clearing.

A large fire had been built at its centre. Twenty or thirty figures clustered around it, their shadows elongated and grotesque in the gathering dusk. The figures had oddly shaped heads.

Haskeer gawped at them. "What the hell race are they?"

"*Humans*, dolt," Jup whispered. "They're wearing wolves' heads." Something else caught his eye. "Look over there."

761

At the edge of the firelight, Braetagg's body lay stretched out on a flat rock. One of the wolf-headed humans stood close by. The arcane movements of his hands, accompanied by a low chant from many of the others present, implied a ritual of some kind.

"We need the full strength for this," Jup reckoned. "Let's get out of here."

Haskeer nodded. "Right."

"*Wrong.*"

They didn't even get a chance to turn and see who'd spoken. Seized by rough hands, they were hauled to their feet. Half a dozen humans, sporting wolves' heads like macabre cowls, surrounded them. Blades against their throats, the Wolverines were disarmed and their wrists bound.

Haskeer shot Jup a venomous look. "'*We can handle this by ourselves,*'" he mocked.

"*Hold your noise!*" one of the humans ordered. "Least until the Master gets started on you." He smirked at his comrades. They broke into unpleasant laughter.

The captives were frog-marched into the clearing, their appearance putting a stop to the dirge. Led through the staring ranks, they were taken to the man standing next to Braetagg's corpse. From his arrogant bearing, and the deferential way the others addressed him, he was obviously the sect's leader.

Eyes as dead as those on the wolf headgear he wore, the human regarded Jup and Haskeer contemptuously. "So. Intruders. And sub-humans at that."

"We ain't sub anything to do with *your* kind," the dwarf retorted.

For his trouble he took a sharp crack across his face with a gauntlet. Trickles of blood snaked from his nose and the side of his mouth.

"What you doing with Braetagg?" Haskeer demanded. He strained against his bonds, uselessly.

"Seeking magic," the Master told him, his voice intense. "Tapping the energy the same way you so-called elder races do."

"Mine doesn't."

Haskeer's reward was a blow to the stomach that doubled him.

"How can a corpse have anything to do with the magic?" Jup raged. "You crazy bastards!"

"Crazy?" the Master repeated, looking genuinely affronted.

He turned to the corpse and seemed to study it for a moment. Then he grasped the smallest finger of Braetagg's right hand and snapped it off with an audible crack. A tiny puff of grey dust attended the break.

Haskeer's hollered protest was stifled by fresh blows. For good measure, the pyros gave Jup's kidneys a pummelling too. Ignoring their struggles, the leader held the finger up at eye level, examining it. That done, he tossed it into the fire.

The flames instantly blazed more brightly, liberating a myriad of swirling, multicoloured sparks. By turns, the pyre burned emerald, scarlet, gold and turquoise, each with an intensity so dazzling it was hard to look at. It beggared belief that a scrap of arid flesh could make such tumult. Haskeer and Jup were confounded by the sight of it.

"A taste of Braetagg's potency," the Master declared as the effect abated. "With proper ritual and a thorough grinding of the cadaver, the resultant essence will grant me the power of sorcery."

"You're fucking mad," Jup growled.

"So you said." The leader's bushy eyebrows arched. "But you won't be here to see me disprove that. Like most rituals, this one is all the better for a little blood sacrifice." He signalled to his minions. "Make them ready!"

"This is getting us nowhere," Alfray complained.

"You've a better idea?" Stryke said.

"Maybe we could split into smaller groups and speed the search."

"No, we're split enough as it is."

They rode on in silence.

At length, Coilla exclaimed, "Over there!" They looked the way she pointed. The light of a fire glinted faintly on the opposite bank. "Ours?" she wondered.

"Even those two wouldn't be so stupid as to light a fire," Stryke assured her.

"So?" Alfray said.

"So it's all we've got." He barked an order and the half-band wheeled about.

They travelled at a clip, ducking branches, following the shore's camber as tight as they dared.

An arrow's flight further and a bunch of grunts waved them down. There were swift explanations of the sergeants' absence.

"Perfect," Stryke fumed, "now we've got a corpse *and* two idiots to rescue."

"How do we do it?" Coilla asked.

"Three groups, and you're leading one of them. Calthmon, Darig, you'll stay here with the horses. That leaves . . . twenty-six. My group and Alfray's will take eight grunts each. You get ten, Coilla."

"Thanks for trusting me."

"It's a case of needs must, Corporal. Fuck this up and you're out."

"What's the plan?" Alfray said.

"Nothing fancy. We go into that copse from three sides. Priority is getting Haskeer and Jup out in one piece, then Braetagg if we can manage it. Questions?"

They had none. Quickly mustered into their three groups, they set out, left, right and straight ahead.

Coilla's detail took the right-hand course, and was soon creeping through foliage to the clearing. No guards were encountered. They saw the fire and Braetagg's body stretched out on its rock slab, Jup and Haskeer captive beside it. Two humans had hold of the sergeants; another seemed to be performing a ritual. The rest of the wolf-headed pyros stood further back, droning a rhythmic chant.

Coilla turned to the nearest grunt. "It's . . . Slettal, isn't it?" she whispered.

"Ma'am."

"How many good archers have we got with us?"

He frowned. "How good?"

"They'd have one chance to hit those two holding the sergeants."

"Sorry, Corporal. We're all handy with a bow, but a shot like that . . ."

"I should have guessed," she sighed. "All right, I'll try it myself." He went to hand her a bow. She waved it aside and raked back one of her baggy shirtsleeves, revealing an arm scabbard of throwing knives. "I prefer these," she explained, plucking out a pair of snub blades.

Slettal looked from her to her distant targets and back again. "You can do that?"

"I can try. If I manage it, all of you be ready to go in fast and tackle the main body. If I don't, we make for the two I missed and that priest type. At least we can avenge the sergeants. Got that? Good. Now stand ready."

She knew the other Wolverines were likely to attack at any second, risking Jup and Haskeer's lives. There was no time to spare. She took a bead on the hardest mark first, the human almost completely shielded by Haskeer. The second, restraining Jup, offered a softer target. Though in truth neither was easy. The third human, the one she took to be the leader, was growing more animated as the ritual climaxed.

Centring herself, breath held, Coilla pitched a knife. It was still in the air as she lobbed the second.

The human grasping Haskeer caught his blade in an eye, reeled and dropped. His comrade stopped the next throw with his chest and went down shrieking.

"*Move!*" Coilla yelled.

They burst into the clearing. Simultaneously, Stryke's and Alfray's groups attacked. Coilla made for the sergeants. The rest of her crew obeyed orders and piled into the greater knot of humans at her rear. A chaotic mêlée of shouting, screaming, and ringing steel broke out.

As she dashed forward, Coilla noticed that the fire was behaving strangely. It blazed with an unusual ferocity, the flames permeated with brilliant primary colours. But she had no time to ponder it. The pyro leader, face twisted with fury, had drawn a sword. She accelerated and veered past him, narrowly avoiding the slicing blade. Then she was with the sergeants and slashing their bonds.

"*Incoming!*" Jup shouted.

Several armed pyros were running their way. Coilla passed one of her blades to the dwarf. Haskeer scooped his own from a fallen guard. Bellowing war cries, they rushed to engage them.

Coilla was left to confront the leader. He came at her in a frenzied state, roaring incoherently, splitting the air with his broadsword. She set to fending his wild blows, answering each with a foray of her own.

"Meddling ingrates!" he raged. "*Savages!*"

"That's rich from somebody wearing a dead animal," she retorted coolly, needling him further.

Another ferocious outburst ensued. Coilla ducked and dodged, blocking his thrusts and repaying them.

"*The ritual!*" the leader stormed. "You broke the ritual! *Fools!*"

Then his expression froze. He pulled back, forgetting his guard, and stared beyond her, eyes wide. Assuming a feint, but not entirely sure, she rapidly moved to one side and turned her head. What she saw made her jaw drop.

Braetagg's corpse was moving.

It sat up. Stiffly, it seemed to stretch, dry old bones creaking. It slowly swung its legs and placed its feet on the ground. At once it rose, and for a second swayed. Then it began to walk, ponderous at first, its limbs working sluggishly.

Coilla tore her gaze away and looked at the human. He stood immobile, face ashen. All the others in the clearing were at a distance, occupied by the mêlée, and seemed unaware of Braetagg's tramping husk.

The corpse continued to trudge with grim, deliberate purpose, leaving a faint trail of whitish dust. Coilla tensed as it lurched past, heedless of her, and she fancied there was some kind of subtle light in its hollow eyes.

Shaking off his inertia, though still in the grip of terror, the sect's leader took up his sword to shield himself. It was a fainthearted effort. With shocking speed, the cadaver closed in and dashed the blade aside with ease. The living and the dead melded.

Coilla looked on, her view obscured by the intense glare of the fire and the thick cloud rolling from it. She could make out the pair grappling, but little more. Then a scream came. Hideous, drawn-out, despairing. Human.

Several figures came at her through the swirl. She dropped her defensive stance when she saw it was Stryke and the others, wiping gore from their swords and hatchets.

extras

"You did well," Stryke said.

The fire was dying. A puff of wind diluted the smoke. It let her see the leader, sprawled on the earth, limbs at crazy angles. Death had stamped a frightful expression on his face. She looked to the stone slab. Braetagg's body lay on it, his pose unchanged.

Stryke stared at her. "What's the matter?"

She blinked at him, shook her head. Decided. "Nothing. It . . . it's the crystal. Still muzzing my brain."

They rode hell for leather, Braetagg's remains swathed in blankets and draped over a spare horse.

Making Cairnbarrow in record time, the band took the streets at a clip, ploughing the crowds of revellers. The main square held three times its earlier mass and slowed progress. Struggling through, they came to restless lines of orcs barred from the tent by Imperial guards.

Major Crelim appeared. A path was opened. The Wolverines' five officers were ushered in, along with a brace of grunts hauling their shrouded burden. They placed it on the floor and peeled back the blankets.

"I didn't think you'd do it," Crelim confessed. "Quickly, get him onto the throne. And be *careful*."

Gentle hands hoisted the corpse. Braetagg was positioned, his crown replaced, his parched hand laid upon the sword hilt. Coilla followed the proceedings with especial interest.

"He's missing a finger!" the Major exclaimed.

"Er, yes," Stryke admitted. "Not bad, considering what he might have lost. You could cover it with . . . his sleeve or something."

"I don't know," Crelim mused doubtfully.

Haskeer swaggered to the throne. "The Captain's right, sir. Nobody's going to notice that small a bit's not there. Braetagg's a tough old charger." He moved nearer the corpse, ignoring the others' frantic signals for restraint. "Nothing to worry about there. Tough as dragon hide soaked in piss for a month." He brought back his balled hand in a gesture of bonhomie.

"*No!*" they all cried.

Too late to stay Haskeer's fist. The comradely punch impacted Braetagg's shoulder with a dull thud, raising as much dust as a beaten carpet. Haskeer gagged. Braetagg's arm came away, hung momentarily by a dried sinew, then fell. It hit the floor with a sound like a dropped roll of ancient parchment.

"You *slugbrain!*" Jup yelled.

"*Sergeant Haskeer!*" Crelim bellowed, face cerulean with fury.

All present vied to blacken Haskeer's parentage, and eyes.

Stryke edged away from the furore and sidled up to Coilla.

"Before you ask," she said, "I don't darn."

He shrugged his shoulders and let out a long, weary breath. "Oh, well. Happy Braetagg's Day."

THE ORCS RETURN IN:

ORCS: BAD BLOOD

VOLUME 1

Stan Nicholls

When the orcs discovered a world filled with their own kind,
they thought they would live there till the end of their days. But
the appearance of an unlikely ally will change everything.

This ally — a human — tells of the atrocities being
visited upon orcs back in the other world. He implores
Stryke and his companions to come back so that they
may save their kind from extinction and wreak vengeance
upon the humans who've wronged them.

But can this human be trusted? Is he a rare friend to
the orc — or is he there to lure them back for their own
personal annihilation?

Coming in 2009

Available wherever good books are sold